To the women—living and dead—
of my family, all of them
ladies and *guerreiras*

And to James, who always believed

The Seamstress

FRANCES DE PONTES PEEBLES was born in Pernambuco, Brazil. A graduate of the University of Texas at Austin and the Iowa Writers' Workshop, she has received several awards and her short stories have appeared in *Zeotrope: All-Story*, the *Indiana Review*, the *Missouri Review* and the *O. Henry Prize Story Collection 2005*. *The Seamstress* is her first novel.

The Seamstress

Frances de Pontes Peebles

BLOOMSBURY

LONDON · BERLIN · NEW YORK

First published in Great Britain 2009
This paperback edition published 2009

Copyright © 2008 by Frances de Pontes Peebles

The moral right of the author has been asserted

Bloomsbury Publishing Plc
36 Soho Square
London W1D 3QY

www.bloomsbury.com/francesdepontespeebles

Bloomsbury Publishing, London, New York and Berlin

A CIP catalogue record for this book
is available from the British Library

ISBN 978 0 7475 9619 6
10 9 8 7 6 5 4 3 2

Printed in Great Britain by Clays Ltd, St Ives plc

FSC
Mixed Sources
Product group from well-managed
forests and other controlled sources
Cert no. SGS-COC-2061
www.fsc.org
© 1996 Forest Stewardship Council

The paper this book is printed on is certified independently in accordance with the rules of the FSC.
It is ancient-forest friendly. The printer holds chain of custody.

. . . rising toward a saint
still honored in these parts,
the paper chambers flush and fill with light
that comes and goes, like hearts . . .

receding, dwindling, solemnly
and steadily forsaking us,
or, in the downdraft from a peak,
suddenly turning dangerous . . .

—Elizabeth Bishop, "The Armadillo"

The Seamstress

Northeast Brazil

During the Old Republic

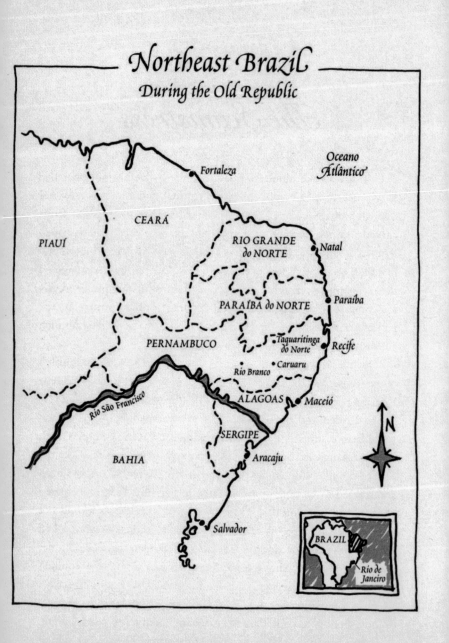

Oceano Atlântico

Fortaleza

CEARÁ

PIAUÍ

RIO GRANDE do NORTE

Natal

PARAÍBA do NORTE

Paraíba

PERNAMBUCO

Taquaritinga do Norte

Recife

Rio Branco · Caruaru

ALAGOAS · Maceió

Rio São Francisco

SERGIPE

BAHIA

Aracaju

Salvador

N

BRAZIL

Rio de Janeiro

PROLOGUE

Recife, Brazil
January 14, 1935

/ / / / / / / / /

*E*mília awoke alone. She lay in the massive antique that had once been her mother-in-law's bridal bed and was now her own. It was the color of burnt sugar with clusters of cashew fruits carved into its giant head- and footboard. The meaty, bell-shaped fruits that emerged from the jacarandá wood looked so smooth and real that, on her first few evenings in this bed, Emília had imagined them ripening overnight—their wooden skins turning pink and yellow, their solid meat becoming soft and fragrant by morning. By the end of her first year in the Coelho house, Emília had given up such childish imaginings.

Outside, it was dark. The street was quiet. The Coelho family's white house was the largest of all of the newly built estates on Rua Real da Torre, a recently paved road that stretched from the old Capunga Bridge and out into unclaimed swampland. Emília always woke before sunrise, before peddlers invaded Recife's streets with their creaking carts and their voices that rose to her window like the calls of strange birds. In her old home in the countryside, she'd been accustomed to waking up to roosters, to her aunt Sofia's whispered prayers, and most of all, to her sister Luzia's breath, even and hot against her shoulder. As a girl, Emília had disliked sharing a bed with her sister. Luzia was too tall; she kicked open the mosquito net with her long legs. She stole the covers. Their aunt Sofia couldn't afford to buy them separate beds and insisted it was good to have a sleeping companion—it would teach the girls to occupy little space, to move gently, to sleep silently, preparing them to be good wives.

In the first days of her marriage, Emília had kept to her side of the bed, afraid to move. Degas complained that her skin was too warm, her breathing too loud, her feet too cold. After a week, he'd moved across the hall, back to the snug sheets and narrow mattress of his childhood bed. Emília quickly learned to sleep alone, to sprawl, to take up space. Only one male shared her room and he slept in the corner, in a crib that was quickly becoming too small to hold his growing body. At three years of age, Expedito's hands and feet nearly touched the crib's wooden bars. One day, Emília hoped, he would have a real bed in his own room, but not here. Not while they lived in the Coelhos' house.

The sun rose and the sky lightened. Emília heard shouting in the streets. Six years before, on her first morning in the Coelho house, Emília had trembled and held the bedsheet to her chest until she realized the voices outside the gates were not intruders. They were not calling her name, but the names of fruits and vegetables, baskets and brooms. Each Carnaval, the peddlers' voices were replaced by the thunderous beating of maracatu drums and the drunken shouts of revelers. Five years earlier, during the first week of October, the peddlers had disappeared completely. Throughout Brazil there were gunshots and calls for a new president. By the next year, things had calmed. The government had changed hands. The peddlers returned.

Emília now found comfort in their voices. The men and women sang the names of their wares: "Oranges! Brooms! Alpercata sandals! Belts! Brushes! Needles!" Their voices were strong and cheerful, a relief from the whispers Emília had endured all week. A long, black ribbon hung from the bell attached to the Coelhos' iron gate. The ribbon warned neighbors, the milkman, the ice wagon, and all delivery boys dropping off flowers and black-bordered condolence cards that this was a house in mourning. The family inside was nurturing its grief, and should not be disturbed by loud noises or unnecessary visits. Those who rang the bell did so tentatively. Some clapped to announce their presence, afraid to touch the black ribbon. The peddlers ignored it. They shouted over the fence, their voices carrying past the massive metal gate, through the Coelho house's drawn curtains, and into its dark hallways. "Soap! String! Flour! Thread!" The peddlers didn't concern themselves with death; even grieving people needed the things the peddlers sold, the small necessities of life.

Emília rose from bed.

She slipped a dress over her head but didn't zip it; the noise might wake Expedito. He lay diagonally across his crib, safely beneath mosquito netting. His forehead shone with sweat. His mouth was set in a tight line. Even in sleep he was a serious child. He'd been that way as an infant, when Emília had discovered him. He'd been skinny and covered in dust. "A foundling," the maids called him. "A child of the backlands." He was born there during the infamous drought of 1932. It was impossible that he would remember his real mother, or those first hard months of his life, but sometimes, when Expedito stared at Emília with his dark, deep-set eyes, he had the stern and knowing look of an old man. Since the funeral he'd often looked at Emília in this way, as if reminding her that they should not linger in the Coelho house. They should travel back to the countryside, for his sake as well as hers. They should deliver a warning. They should fulfill their promise.

Emília felt a pinch in her chest. All week she'd felt as if there was a rope within her, stretched from her feet to her head and knotted at her heart. The longer she remained in the Coelho house, the more the knot tightened.

She left the room and zipped up her dress. The fabric gave off a sharp, metallic smell. It had been soaked in a vat of black dye and then dipped in vinegar, to set the new color. The dress had been light blue. It was cut in a modern style with soft, fluttering sleeves and a slim skirt. Emília had been a trendsetter. Now all of her solid-colored dresses were dyed black and her patterned ones packed away until her year of mourning was officially over. Emília had hidden three dresses and three bolero jackets in a suitcase under her bed. The jackets were heavy; each had a thick wad of bills sewn into its satin lining. Emília had also packed a tiny valise with Expedito's clothing, shoes, and toys. When they escaped from the Coelho house, she'd have to carry the bags herself. Knowing this, she'd packed only necessities. Before her marriage, Emília had placed too much stock in luxuries. She'd believed that fine possessions had the power to transform; that owning a stylish dress, a gas stove, a tiled kitchen, or an automobile would erase her origins. Such possessions, Emília had thought, would make people look past the calluses on her hands or her rough country manners, and see a lady. After her marriage and her arrival in Recife, Emília discovered this wasn't true.

Halfway downstairs, she smelled funeral wreaths. The round floral arrangements cluttered the foyer and front hallway. Some were as small as plates, others so large they sat on wooden easels. All were tightly packed with white and purple flowers—gardenias, violets, lilies, roses—and had dark ribbons pinned across their empty centers. Scrawled across the ribbons, painted in gold ink, were the senders' names and consoling phrases: "Our Deepest Sympathies," "Our Prayers Are with You." The older wreaths were limp, their gardenias yellowed, their lilies shriveled. They gave off a tangy, putrid smell. The air was thick with it.

Emília held the staircase banister. Four weeks ago her husband, Degas, had sat with her on those marble steps. He'd tried to warn her, but she hadn't listened; Degas had tricked her too many times before. Since his death, Emília spent her days and nights wondering if Degas' warning hadn't been a trick at all, but a final attempt at redemption.

Emília walked into the front hall. There was a new wreath, its lilies rigid and thick, their stamens heavy with orange pollen. Emília pitied those lilies. They had no roots, no soil, no way of sustaining themselves, and yet they bloomed. They acted as if they were still fecund and strong when really they were already dead—they just didn't know it. Emília felt the knot in her chest tighten. Her instincts said Degas had been right, his warning a valid one. And she was like those condolence wreaths, giving him the recognition he so desperately wanted in life but only received in death.

The funeral wreath was a rite unique to Recife. In the country-side it was often too dry to grow flowers. People who died during the rainy months were both blessed and cursed: their bodies decayed faster, and mourners had to pinch their noses during wakes, but there were dahlias, rooster's crest, and Beneditas bunched into thick bouquets and placed inside the deceased's funeral hammock before it was carried to town. Emília had attended many funerals. Among them was her mother's, which she could barely remember. Her father's funeral occurred later, when Emília was fourteen and Luzia twelve. They lived with their aunt Sofia after that, and though Emília loved her aunt, she couldn't wait to run away, to live in the capital. As a girl, Emília had always believed that she would leave Sofia and Luzia. Instead, they'd left her.

Emília slipped a black-bordered card from the newest wreath. It was addressed to her father-in-law, Dr. Duarte Coelho.

"Grief cannot be measured," the card said. "Neither can our esteem for you. Come back to work soon! From: Your colleagues at the Criminology Institute." The wreaths and cards weren't meant for Degas. The gifts that arrived at the Coelho house were sent to curry favor with the living. Most of the floral arrangements were from politicians, or from Green Party compatriots, or from underlings in Dr. Duarte's Criminology Institute. A few of the wreaths were from society women hoping to be in Emília's good graces. The women had been customers in Emília's dress shop. They hoped her mourning wouldn't stifle her dressmaking hobby. Respectable women didn't have careers, so Emília's thriving dress shop was considered a diversion, like crochet or charity work. Emília and her sister had been seamstresses. In the countryside, their profession was highly regarded, but in Recife this tier of respectability didn't exist—a seamstress was the same as a maid or a washerwoman. And to the Coelhos' dismay, their son had taken up with one. According to the Coelhos, Emília had two saving graces: she was pretty and she had no family. There wouldn't be parents or siblings clapping at the front gate and asking for handouts. Dr. Duarte and his wife, Dona Dulce, knew Emília had a sister but believed that she—like Emília's parents and her aunt Sofia—had died. Emília didn't contradict this belief. As seamstresses, both she and Luzia knew how to cut, how to mend, and how to conceal.

"A great seamstress must be brave." This was what Aunt Sofia used to say. For a long time, Emília disagreed. She believed that bravery involved risk. With sewing, everything was measured, traced, tried on, and revised. The only risk was error.

A good seamstress took exact measurements and then, using a sharp pencil, transferred those measurements onto paper. She traced the paper pattern onto cheap muslin, cut out the pieces, and sewed them into a sample garment that her client tried on and which she—the seamstress—pinned and remeasured to correct the flaws in her pattern. The muslin always looked bland and unappealing. At this point, the seamstress had to be enthusiastic, envisioning the garment in a beautiful fabric and convincing the client of her vision. From the pins and markings on the muslin, she revised the paper pattern and traced it onto good fabric: silk, fine-woven linen, or sturdy cotton. Next, she cut. Finally, she sewed those pieces together, ironing after each step in order to have crisp lines and straight seams. There was no bravery in this. There was only patience and meticulousness.

Luzia never made muslins or patterns. She traced her measurements directly onto the final fabric and cut. In Emília's eyes this wasn't bravery either—it was skill. Luzia was good at measuring people. She knew exactly where to wind a tape around arms and waists in order to get the most accurate dimensions. But her skill wasn't dependent on accuracy; Luzia saw beyond numbers. She knew that numbers could lie. Aunt Sofia had taught them that the human body had no straight lines. The measuring tape could miscalculate the curve of a slumped back, the arc of a shoulder, the dip of a waist, the bend of an elbow. Luzia and Emília were taught to be wary of measuring tapes. "Don't trust a strange tape!" their aunt Sofia often yelled at them. "Trust your own eyes!" So Emília and Luzia learned to see where a garment had to be taken in, let out, lengthened or shortened before they'd even unrolled their measuring tapes. Sewing was a language, their aunt said. It was the language of shapes. A good seamstress could envision a garment encircling a body and see the same garment laid flat on a cutting table, broken into its individual pieces. One rarely resembled the other. When laid flat, the pieces of a garment were odd shapes broken into two halves. Every piece had its opposite, its mirror image.

Unlike Luzia, Emília preferred making paper patterns. She wasn't as confident at measurement and felt nervous each time she took up her scissors and sliced the final cloth. Cutting was unforgiving. If the pieces of a garment were cut incorrectly, it meant hours of work at the sewing machine. Often these hours were futile—there were some mistakes sewing could never fix.

Emília replaced the condolence card. She walked past the funeral wreaths. At the end of the entrance hall was an easel without flowers propped upon it. Instead, there was a portrait. The Coelhos had commissioned an oil painting for their son's wake. The Capibaribe River was deep and its currents strong, but police had managed to find Degas' body. It had been too bloated to have an open casket during the wake, so Dr. Duarte had a portrait of his son made instead. In the portrait, Emília's husband was smiling, thin, and confident—all of the things he'd never been in life. The only aspect the painter had gotten right was Degas' hands. They had tapered fingers and buffed, immaculate nails. Degas had been stout, with a thick neck and wide fleshy arms, but his hands were slender, almost womanly. Emília wished she'd noticed this the minute she'd met him.

Police deemed Degas' death an accident. The officers were loyal to Dr. Duarte because he'd founded the state's first Criminology Institute. Recife, however, was a city that prized scandal. Accidents were dull, blame interesting. During the wake, Emília had heard mourners whispering. They tried to root out the responsible parties: the car, the rainstorm, the slick bridge, the rough waters of the river, or Degas himself, alone at the wheel of his Chrysler Imperial. Dona Dulce—Emília's mother-in-law—insisted on the police's version of events. She knew that her son had lied, saying he was going to his office to pick up papers related to an upcoming business trip, the first such trip Degas had ever taken. He never went to his office. Instead he drove aimlessly around the city. Dona Dulce did not blame Emília for Degas' death; she blamed her daughter-in-law for the aimlessness that had caused it. A proper wife—a well-bred city girl—would have cured Degas' weaknesses and given him a child. Dr. Duarte was more sympathetic toward Emília. Her father-in-law had arranged Degas' so-called business trip. Without Dona Dulce's knowledge, Dr. Duarte had reserved a spot for their son at the prestigious Pinel Sanitorium in São Paulo. Dr. Duarte had believed that the clinic's electric baths would accomplish what marriage and self-discipline had not.

Emília stepped closer to the portrait, as if proximity would make its subject more familiar. She was twenty-five years old and already a widow, mourning a husband she hadn't understood. At times, she'd hated him. Other times, she'd felt an unexpected kinship with Degas. Emília knew how it felt to love what was prohibited, and to deny that love, to betray it. That kind of emotion was a burden—a weight so heavy it could drag a person to the bottom of the Capibaribe River and keep him there.

She'd been sloppy with her life. She'd been so eager to leave the countryside that she'd chosen Degas without studying him, without measuring him. In the years since her escape, she'd tried to fix the mistakes inherent in her hasty beginning. But some things weren't worth fixing. When she realized this, Emília finally understood what Aunt Sofia had meant about bravery. Any seamstress could be meticulous. Novice and expert alike could fuss over measurements and pattern drawings, but precision didn't guarantee success. An unskilled seamstress delivered poorly sewn clothes without trying to hide the mistakes. Good seamstresses felt an attachment to their projects and spent days trying to fix them. Great ones didn't do this. They were brave enough to start over. To admit they'd been wrong, throw away their doomed attempts, and begin again.

Emília stepped away from Degas' funeral portrait. In bare feet, she padded out of the hall and into the Coelho house's courtyard. At the center of the fern-lined patio stood a fountain. A mythical creature—half horse, half fish—spat water from its copper mouth. Across the courtyard, the glass-paneled dining room doors were propped open. The curtains across the entrance were closed, shifting with the breeze. Behind them, Emília heard Dona Dulce. Her mother-in-law spoke sternly to a maid, telling her to set the table correctly. Dr. Duarte complained that his newspaper was late. Like Emília, he was always anxious for the newspaper.

On the right end of the courtyard were doors that led to Dr. Duarte's study. Emília walked quickly toward them, careful not to trip over the jabotis. The turtles always scuttled in the courtyard. They were family heirlooms, each fifty years old and purchased by her husband's grandfather. The turtles were the only animals allowed in the Coelho house and they were content with bumping up against the glazed tile walls of the courtyard, hiding among the ferns and eating scraps of fruit the maids brought them. Emília and Expedito liked to pick them up when no one was looking. They were heavy things; she had to use both hands. The turtles' wrinkled limbs flapped wildly each time Emília held them, and when she tried to stroke their faces they snapped at her fingers. The only parts of them she could touch were their shells, which were thick and unfeeling, like the turtles themselves.

In the countryside she'd been surrounded by animals. There were lizards in the dry summer months and toads in the winter. There were hummingbirds and centipedes and stray cats that begged for milk at the back door. Aunt Sofia raised chickens and goats, but those were destined for the dinner table, so Emília never got friendly with them. But Emília used to have three singing birds in wooden cages. Every morning after she fed them, she would put her finger through the cage's bars and allow the birds to pick under her fingernails. "Those birds were tricked," her sister Luzia said every time she saw Emília feeding them. "You should let them go." Luzia disliked the way they'd been caught. Local boys would put a bit of melon or pumpkin in cages and lay in wait, latching the cage's doors as soon as a bird hopped inside. Then the boys sold those red-beaked finches and tiny canaries at the weekly market. When the wild birds got wise to the boys' trick and avoided the food inside the empty cages, the bird catchers used another strategy—one that never failed. They tied a tame bird inside the cage to make the wild ones believe it was safe. One bird unknowingly lured the other.

In his study, Emília's father-in law had an orange-winged corrupião that he'd trained to sing the first strophe of the national anthem. There was always a great racket in the Coelhos' kitchen where Emília's mother-in-law commanded her legion of maids in making jams and cheeses and sweetmeats. But sometimes, under the noise, Emília could hear the corrupião singing the somber notes of the anthem, like a ghost calling from within the walls.

The bird chirped when Emília eased the study doors open. The corrupião sat in a brass cage in the middle of Dr. Duarte's office, among his phrenological charts, his collection of pickled and colorless organs floating in glass jars, and his row of porcelain skulls with their brains categorized and numbered. Emília's underarms were wet. She smelled something sour, and was unsure if the scent came from her dyed dress or from her own sweat. Dr. Duarte didn't allow people in his study uninvited—not even maids. If caught, Emília would say she was checking on the corrupião. She ignored the bird and went to Dr. Duarte's desk. On it were stacks of unanswered condolence cards. There were papers listing the cranial measurements of all detainees at the Downtown Detention Center. There was the handwritten draft of a speech Dr. Duarte would give at the end of the month. Words were crossed out. The speech's conclusion was blank; Dr. Duarte hadn't yet obtained his prize specimen, the female criminal whose cranial measurements would confirm his theories and conclude his lecture. Emília flipped though piles of papers. There was nothing resembling a bill of sale. There were no customs forms, no train logs, no dated evidence of an unusual shipment to Brazil. She looked for words written in a foreign tongue, knowing she would recognize one in particular: *Bergmann*. The name was the same in German as in Portuguese.

Emília found only newspaper clippings. She had a similar collection, locked in her jewelry box so the Coelho maids couldn't find them. Some articles were yellowed by years of exposure to Recife's humidity. Some still smelled of ink. All centered on the brutal cangaceiro Antônio Teixeira—nicknamed the Hawk because of his penchant for plucking out the eyes of his victims—and his wife, called the Seamstress. They were not fugitives because they had never been caught. They were not outlaws because the countryside had no laws, not until recently, when President Gomes had tried to implement his own. The definition of a cangaceiro depended on who was asked. To tenant farmers, they were heroes and protectors. To vaqueiros and merchants, they were thieves. To farm girls, they were fine dancers and romantic heroes. To the mothers of those girls, cangaceiros were defilers and devils. Schoolchildren, who often played cangaceiros versus police, fought for the roles of cangaceiros even though their teachers scolded them for it. Finally, to the colonels—the largest landowners in the countryside—cangaceiros were an inevitable nuisance, like the droughts that killed cotton crops, or the deadly brucellosis that infected cattle. Cangaceiros were blights that the colonels and their fathers, grandfathers, and great-grandfathers before them had had to withstand. Cangaceiros lived like nomads in the scrubland's thorny wilderness, stealing cattle and goats, raiding towns, exacting revenge on enemies. They were men who could not be frightened into obedience or whipped into submission.

The Hawk and the Seamstress were a new breed of cangaceiro. They knew how to read and write. They dispatched telegrams to the *Diário de Pernambuco* newspaper offices and even sent personal notes to the governor and the president, which newspapers photographed and reprinted. The notes were written on fine linen paper, with the outlaw's seal—a large letter *H*—embossed on the top. In them, the Hawk condemned the government's roadway project, the Trans-Nordestino Highway, and vowed to attack all construction sites in the scrub. The Hawk insisted he was no lowly goat thief; he was a leader. He offered to divide the state of Pernambuco, leaving the coast to the republic and the countryside to the cangaceiros. Emília studied the Hawk's penmanship. It was feminine in its curling script, much like the cursive that Padre Otto, the German immigrant priest who ran her old grade school, had taught her and Luzia as children.

Reports said that the Hawk's group numbered between twenty and fifty well-armed men and women. The leading female, the Seamstress, was famous for her brutality, for her talent with a gun, and for her looks. She was not attractive, but was so tall that she stood above most of the men. And she had a crippled arm, bent permanently at the elbow. No one knew where the name the Seamstress had come from. Some said it was because of her precise aim; the Seamstress could fill a man with holes, just like a sewing machine poked cloth with its needle. Others said she really knew how to sew and that she was responsible for the cangaceiros' elaborate uniforms. The *Diário* had printed the only photo of the group; Emília kept a copy of it in her jewelry box. The cangaceiros wore well-tailored jackets and pants. Their hats had the brims cracked and upturned, resembling half-moons. Everything the cangaceiros carried—from their thick-strapped bornal bags to their cartridge belts—was elaborately decorated with stars, circles, and other indecipherable symbols. Their clothes were heavily embroidered. Their leather rifle straps were tooled and studded. To Emília, the cangaceiros looked both splendid and ridiculous.

The final theory about the Seamstress's name was the only one Emília believed. They called that tall, crippled woman the Seamstress because she held her cangaceiro group together. Despite the drought of 1932, despite President Gomes's efforts to exterminate the group, despite the Criminology Institute's cash rewards in exchange for the bandits' heads, the cangaceiros had survived. They even accepted women into their ranks. Many attributed this success to the Seamstress. There were theories—unproven but persistent—that the Hawk had died. The Seamstress had planned all of the roadway attacks. She had written the letters addressed to the president. She had sent telegrams bearing the Hawk's name. Most politicians, police, and even President Gomes himself deemed this theory impossible. The Seamstress was tall, callous, and perverse but she was still a woman.

Emília searched the final stack of papers on her father-in-law's desk. Newspaper clippings stuck to her sweaty palms. She shook them off. She'd never understood the Seamstress's behavior, but Emília admired the cangaceira's boldness, her strength. In the days after Degas' death, she'd prayed for those attributes.

Within the Coelho house, a bell chimed. Breakfast was served. Emília's mother-in-law kept a brass bell beside her chair in the dining room. She used it to call servants and to indicate mealtimes. The bell rang a second time; Dona Dulce disliked stragglers. Emília straightened the papers on her father-in-law's desk and left.

She sat in her designated place at the far end of the dining table, removed from its other occupants. Her father-in-law sat at the head, sipping coffee from his porcelain cup and unwrapping his newspaper. Emília's mother-in-law sat beside him, pale and rigid in her mourning dress. Between them was an empty chair, its back covered in a black cloth, where Emília's husband had sat. Degas' place was neatly set with the Coelhos' blue-and-white china, as if Dona Dulce expected her son to return. Emília stared at her own place setting. There were too many utensils to navigate. There was a medium-size spoon to mix her coffee, a larger spoon for her cornmeal, a tiny spoon for jam, and an array of forks for eggs and fried bananas. Years ago, during her first weeks with the Coelhos, Emília hadn't known which utensil was which. She didn't dare guess, either, with her mother-in-law scrutinizing her from across the table. There was no need for such complications, such finery in the morning, and in her first months at the Coelho table Emília believed her mother-in-law set the elaborate table just to confuse her.

Emília ignored the plate of eggs and the steaming mound of cornmeal at the center of the table. She sipped coffee. Near her, Dr. Duarte held up his newspaper and smiled. His teeth were wide and yellow.

"Look!" he shouted, shaking the *Diário de Pernambuco*'s pages. The paper's headline fluttered before Emília's eyes.

Raid on Cangaceiros Successful! Seamstress &
Hawk Believed Dead! Heads Transported to Recife.

Emília stood. She walked to the head of the table.

The article said that the president of the republic would not tolerate anarchy. That troops were sent into the backlands equipped with their new weapon, the Bergmann machine gun. The gun was a modern marvel, spitting out five hundred rounds per minute. It had been imported from Germany by Coelho & Son, Ltd., the import-export firm owned by renowned criminologist Dr. Duarte Coelho and his recently deceased son, Degas. The shipment of Bergmanns had arrived in secret, earlier than anyone had expected.

The article reported that, before the ambush, the cangaceiros had looted and burned a highway construction site. They had raided a town. Eyewitnesses—tenant farmers and the local accordion player—said that the outlaws had rightfully purchased a case of Fleur d'Amour toilet water and had thrown gold coins to children in the streets. They said that the cangaceiros had attended mass and had even gone to confession. Then the Seamstress and the Hawk took their cangaceiros to the São Francisco River, to lodge on a doctor's ranch. Once a trusted friend of the cangaceiros, the doctor had secretly sided with the state and telegrammed nearby troops to inform them of the Hawk's presence. *The bird is home,* the doctor wrote in his message.

The cangaceiros were camped in a dry gulley when government troops invaded. It was dark, which made it hard to aim. But with their new Bergmann guns, the troops didn't have to. They easily hit their marks. The next morning a vaqueiro, who was releasing his herd at dawn, said he'd witnessed a few cangaceiros escaping from their battle with the troops. He claimed he saw a small group of individuals—all wearing the cangacieros' distinctive leather hats, their brims flipped up in the shape of a half-moon—limping across the state border. But police officials proclaimed that the outlaws were all dead, shot down and decapitated, even the Seamstress.

Emília read the article's last line and did not feel the porcelain coffee cup slip from her hands and break into bits against the slate floor. She did not feel the burning liquid splash onto her ankles, did not hear her mother-in-law gasp and exclaim that she had no manners, did not see the maid crawl beneath the veined marble table to pick up the mess.

Emília rushed up the tiled staircase to her bedroom—the last room at the end of the carpeted and musty hallway. Expedito was there. He sat on Emília's bed while the nanny combed his wet hair. Emília dismissed the woman. She lifted her boy from the bed.

When he squirmed in her tight embrace, Emília released him. She pulled a polished wooden box from beneath the bed. Emília unclasped the gold chain around her neck and used the small brass key that dangled from it to open the box's lock. Inside was a velvet-lined tray, empty except for a ring and a pearl necklace. Degas had bought her the largest jewelry box he could find, promising to fill it. Emília lifted the tray. In the deep space beneath it—a place meant to hold pendants, or tiaras, or thick bracelets—was Emília's collection of newspaper articles, bound with a blue ribbon. Beneath those was a small framed photograph. Two girls stood side by side. Both wore white dresses. Both held Bibles. One girl smiled widely. Her eyes, however, did not match her mouth's rigid happiness. They looked anxious, expectant. The other girl had moved when the picture was taken, and so she was blurred. Unless one looked closely, unless one knew her, you could not tell exactly who she was.

Emília had cradled this communion portrait in her arms as she rode on horseback out of her hometown of Taquaritinga. She'd held it in her lap during the bumping train ride to Recife. In the Coelho house, she'd placed it in her jewelry box, the only place the Coelho maids were prohibited from probing.

Emília knelt beside the portrait. Her boy copied her, clasping his hands firmly to his chest as Emília had taught him. He stared at her. In the morning sunlight, his eyes were not as dark as they sometimes seemed—within the brown were specks of green. Emília bowed her head.

She prayed to Santa Luzia, the patron saint of the eyes, her sister's namesake and protector. She prayed to the Virgin, the great guardian of women. And she prayed most fervently to Saint Expedito, the answerer of all impossible requests.

Emília had given up many of her old, foolish beliefs in this house—a place where her husband had not been her husband but some stranger she did not care to know, where maids were not maids but spies for her mother-in-law, where fruits were not fruits but wood, polished and dead. But Emília still believed in the saints. She believed in their powers. Expedito had brought her sister back from death once. He could do it again.

Chapter 1

EMÍLIA

Taquaritinga do Norte, Pernambuco
March 1928

1

///////

*B*eneath her bed, Aunt Sofia kept a wooden box that held her husband's bones. Each morning Emília heard the rustle of starched bedsheets, the pop of Aunt Sofia's knees as she knelt and tugged the box from its resting place. "My falecido," her aunt whispered, because the dead were not allowed names. Aunt Sofia called him this on her better days. If she woke irritated—her arthritis bothering her, or her mind plagued with worries over Emília and Luzia— she addressed the box sternly as "my husband." If she had stayed up late the night before, rocking in her chair and squinting up at the family portraits, the next day Aunt Sofia addressed the box in a low, sweet whisper as "my departed." And if the drought worsened, or there was too little sewing work, or Emília had once again disobeyed her, Aunt Sofia sighed and said, "Oh my corpse, my burden."

This was how Emília guessed her aunt's moods. She knew when to ask for new dress fabric and when to stay quiet. She knew when she could get away with wearing a dab of perfume and rouge, and when to keep her face clean.

Their rooms were divided by a whitewashed wall that rose three meters from the floor and then stopped, giving way to wooden posts that supported the roof beams and rows of orange tiles. Aunt Sofia's whispered prayers rose over the low bedroom wall. Emília shared a bed with her sister. A dusty beam of light shone through a crack in the roof tiles. It entered their yellowed mosquito netting. Emília squinted. She heard the click of rosary beads rubbed between her aunt's palms. There was a grunt, then the hollow rattle of Uncle Tirço's bones as Aunt Sofia pushed him back beneath the bed. The daily dragging of the box had worn away a path in the floor—two indentations lighter than the oiled brick that paved each room of their house except for the kitchen.

Their kitchen floor was made of packed earth; it was orange and always damp. Emília swore its moisture seeped through the soles of her leather sandals. Aunt Sofia and Luzia walked barefoot on that floor, but Emília insisted on wearing shoes. As a child, she'd roamed the house barefoot and the bottoms of her feet had become orange, like her aunt's and her sister's. Emília scrubbed her soles with boiled water and a loofah in order to make them white, the way a lady's feet should look. But the stains remained and Emília blamed the floor.

That year, the winter rains had been sparse and the January rains had not come at all. Their neighbors' coffee trees had not flowered. The purple blossoms of the bean plants Aunt Sofia tended in their backyard had shriveled and they'd lost half of their yearly crop. Even the kitchen floor had become dry and cracked. Emília had to sweep it three times a day to keep the orange dust from filming up the pots, settling in the water jugs, and staining the hems of their dresses. She was saving to install a proper floor—sewing extra nightshirts and handkerchiefs for their employers, Colonel Pereira and his wife, Dona Conceição. When she had enough money, Emília would purchase half a sack of cement powder and the packed dirt would disappear under a thick coating of concrete.

Luzia's side of the bed was empty. Her sister was praying, no doubt, as she did every morning in front of her saints' altar in the kitchen pantry. Emília slipped under the mosquito netting and climbed out of bed; she had her own altar. On their dressing trunk was a small image of Santo Antônio, clipped from the latest issue of *Fon Fon*—her favorite periodical, which featured sewing patterns, romance serials, and the occasional prayer guide. Dona Conceição gave Emília backdated copies of *Fon Fon* and Emília's other cherished magazine, *O Capricho*. She kept them in three neat stacks under her bed even though Aunt Sofia insisted this would attract mice.

Emília knelt before the old black trunk. *Fon Fon* instructed you to place the image of Santo Antônio—the matchmaker saint—in front of a mirror with a white rose next to him. "Find your love match!" the magazine said. "A prayer to ensure you find the right beau." *Fon Fon* assured readers that three Our Fathers and three Ave Marias to Santo Antônio each morning would do the trick.

Emília had placed the saint's image next to her foggy mirror—it was a bit of glass the size of her palm that she had purchased with her savings. It was nothing compared to the full-length mirror in Dona Conceição's fitting room, but Emília could prop her little mirror on the dressing trunk and get a good look at her face and hair. There were no white roses in her town, though. There were no flowers at all. The hearty Beneditas that grew along the roadsides had lost all of their pink and yellow petals and had dropped their seeds onto the hard, dry ground. Aunt Sofia's dahlias hung their heavy heads and disappeared into their bulbs beneath the earth, hiding from the heat. Even the rows of cashew trees and coffee plants looked sickly, their leaves yellowed from constant sun. So Emília had sewn a rose from stray scraps of fabric; Santo Antônio would have to understand. She wrapped her hands together and prayed.

She was nineteen and already an old maid. The town gossips had predicted that she and Luzia would become spinsters, but for different reasons. Luzia's fate had been sealed with the accident she'd suffered as a child: at eleven, she'd fallen from a tall tree and nearly died. The misfortune had deformed her arm and left Luzia—the gossips proclaimed—slightly addled. No man would want a crippled wife, they said, much less one with Luzia's temper. Emília had no physical deformities, thank the good Lord. She'd had many suitors; they had turned up at the house like stray dogs. Aunt Sofia offered them coffee and macaxeira cake while Emília hid in her room and pleaded with Luzia to shoo them away.

If they insisted on staying, Emília stood beside the door frame and peeked into the kitchen. Her suitors were young farmers who looked older than their years. They wore misshapen hats, sat with their legs wide apart, and cracked their enormous, calloused knuckles. During courtship they were all awkwardness and smiles. But Emília had seen them negotiating at the weekly market, shouting and swaggering, taking up roosters by the wings and swiftly cracking the birds' necks. After she'd rejected a suitor, Emília often saw him parading a new wife around the Saturday market, pulling his shy bride this way and that as if the girl were some skittish animal that would escape from her husband's grip.

Emília read the romances in *Fon Fon*. Outside of Taquaritinga there existed another breed of man. Gentlemen were perfumed and suave. Their mustaches were combed, their hair oiled, their beards trimmed, their clothing ironed. It had nothing to do with wealth, but with bearing. She was not a snob, as the town gossips said. She craved refinement, not wealth. Mystery, not money. At night, after prayers, Emília imagined herself as one of those smartly dressed *Fon Fon* heroines, in love with a captain whose boat was lost at sea. She pictured herself on a dune, shouting his name over the water. Or as his nurse, treating him when he returned. He'd gone mute and she became his voice, watching his dark eyebrows move up and down, communicating in a language only she understood. This mystery, this sad longing that ran through all of the *Fon Fon* stories, seemed to be the source of love. Emília prayed it would come to her. She slept without a pillow, swore off sweets, pricked her finger thirty times with her sewing needle as an offering to the saints for their help. Nothing had worked. The white rose and her *Fon Fon* prayers were her last hope.

Emília placed the newspaper clipping of Santo Antônio in her hands and squeezed.

"Professor Célio," she said between prayers.

Célio, her sewing instructor, was not mysterious or tragic. He was a skinny man with doe eyes and long fingers. But he was different from the Taquaritinga boys. He wore freshly pressed suits and shined shoes. And he came from São Paulo, the great metropolis of Brazil, and would return there when the sewing course was over.

"Please, Santo Antônio," Emília whispered, "let me go with him."

"You shouldn't ask the saints for trivial things," Luzia said. She stood in their bedroom doorway. Her head nearly touched the top of the whitewashed frame. When she entered a room she seemed to fill it, making the space feel smaller than it actually was. Her shoulders were wide and the muscles of her right arm—her good arm—were round and hard, conditioned from years of turning the crank of Aunt Sofia's sewing machine. Her eyes were her best, most feminine feature. Emília envied them. They were heavy lidded, like a cat's, and green. Beneath Luzia's thick brows and black lashes, their color was startling, like the shoots of Aunt Sofia's dahlias emerging from dark soil. Luzia cradled her left arm—her crippled arm—in her right. The arm's elbow was forever locked in a sharp right angle. Luzia's fingers and shoulder worked perfectly, but the elbow had never healed correctly. Aunt Sofia blamed the encanadeira for her poor work in setting the broken bones.

"Love isn't trivial," Emília said. She closed her eyes to resume her prayers.

"Santo Antônio isn't even the one to ask," Luzia said. "He'll make the wrong match. You ask for a stallion and he'll give you a donkey."

"Well, Fon Fon says otherwise."

"You should pray to São Pedro."

"You say your prayers and I'll say mine," Emília said, pressing the picture of Santo Antônio harder between her palms.

"You should light a candle to get his attention," Luzia continued. "Flowers won't work. That's not even a real flower."

"Be quiet!" Emília snapped.

Luzia shrugged and left. Emília tried to concentrate on her prayers but could not. She tucked her hair behind her ears, kissed her picture of Santo Antônio, and followed her sister out of their room.

2

Aunt Sofia's house was small but sturdy, with brick on the outside and finished walls on the inside, plastered and painted with whitewash. When people visited, they held their hands to the walls' powdery surface, amazed by this extravagance. Aunt Sofia had also installed an outhouse in the back, complete with a wooden door and a clay-lined cavity in the dirt floor. People said that she was playing at being rich, that she spoiled her young nieces with such luxuries. Their aunt was the town's best seamstress. There were other women who sewed but, according to Aunt Sofia, they were not professionals; they had clumsy stitching and they didn't reinforce the seams of pants or know how to tailor a gentleman's dress shirt. Aunt Sofia's sewing machine—a hand-operated Singer with a round crank and a wooden base—was ancient. The machine's hand crank had rusted and grown hard to turn, the needle had dulled, and the lever that popped the foot of the sewing needle up and down often stuck. But Aunt Sofia insisted that it was not the sewing machine that made a seamstress. A good seamstress had to pay attention to detail, to recognize the shape of people's bodies and understand how different fabrics would fall or cling to that shape, to be efficient with these fabrics, never cutting too much or too little, and finally, once a cloth was cut and set under her machine's needle, she could not waver, she could not hesitate. A good seamstress had to be decisive.

When they were very young, Aunt Sofia made them cut out doll's clothes from butcher paper and then trace the patterns onto scraps of real cloth. She taught them how to stitch by hand first, which had been easier for Luzia, and then showed them how to operate the sewing machine. The hand-cranked machine had been a challenge for Emília's sister. Luzia's good arm ran the crank while her petrified arm moved the cloth through the needle. Because her arm would not bend, Luzia had to move her whole upper body in order to keep the cloth from slipping and to keep the stitches straight. Most people hired Aunt Sofia, Emília, and Luzia to sew their children's First Communion gowns, their daughters' wedding dresses, their fathers' death suits, but these were rare and solemn occasions. Their main clients were the colonel and his wife, Dona Conceição.

Emília adored sewing at the colonel's house. She loved eating the sugared guava cakes that the maid brought into the sewing room as a snack. She loved the strong smell of floor wax, the sounds of Dona Conceição's heels clicking on the black-and-white tiles, the grandfather clock's deep chiming in the front hall. The colonel's ceiling was covered with plaster and paint, which hid the orange roof tiles from view. It was smooth and white, like the frosted top of a cake.

Dona Conceição had recently purchased a state-of-the-art machine: a pedal-operated Singer. The machine was set on top of a heavy wooden base with iron legs. It had floral designs engraved on its shining, silver face. It had taken both of the colonel's pack mules to carry the Singer up the winding mountain trail into town. Its operation was much more complicated than Aunt Sofia's ancient, hand-operated machine. Because of this, the Singer Company shipped instructors across Brazil and offered seven free lessons with each purchase. Dona Conceição insisted Emília and Luzia take them. Luzia didn't appreciate the lessons, but Emília did. They'd introduced her to Professor Célio, who, she hoped, would introduce her to the world.

On lesson days, Emília shortened her prayers to Santo Antônio so that she could wash her hair. It had to be completely dry before Aunt Sofia allowed her out of the house. Her aunt believed in the perils of wet hair—it caused fevers, terrible illness, even deformity. When they were children, Aunt Sofia often repeated the story of a rebellious little girl who went outdoors with wet hair. The wind hit her and made her crooked for the rest of her life, her whole body twisted up and useless.

Emília made her way to the kitchen. Kindling glowed and jutted out from the sooty mouth of the cookstove. Aunt Sofia poked the fire with her long kitchen stick, then flicked a woven fan back and forth before a small hole in the brick stove, below the flames. Her aunt's legs were as thick as fence posts, her ankles indistinct from her calves. Blue veins bulged beneath the skin of her ankles and behind her knees from years of sitting at a sewing machine. A long, white braid hung down Aunt Sofia's back.

"Bless me, Tia," Emília yawned.

Her aunt stopped fanning the stove. She kissed Emília's forehead.

"You're blessed." Aunt Sofia frowned. She tugged at Emília's hair. "You look like a man with this—like one of those cangaceiros."

The models in the newest *Fon Fon*—pencil-sketched women with long bodies and rouged lips—had dark, shining bobs that looked like fine-cut silk framing their faces at sharp angles. A week before, Emília had taken the large sewing scissors and copied their haircut. Aunt Sofia nearly fainted when she saw it. "Dear Lord!" her aunt had screamed. She took Emília by the arm and led her into the saints' closet to pray for forgiveness. Since then, Aunt Sofia made her tie a scarf over her head each time she left the house. Emília had expected such a reaction from her aunt—it had been years since Uncle Tirço had passed away, yet Aunt Sofia wore only black dresses with two camisoles underneath. Wearing any less, Aunt Sofia declared, was the equivalent of walking about naked. She never allowed Luzia or Emília to wear the color red, or encarnado, as Aunt Sofia called it, because it was the color of sin. And when Emília wore her first califom, Aunt Sofia had tied the strings of the brassiere so tightly that Emília almost fainted.

"Tia, do I have to wear a scarf today?" Emília asked.

"Of course," Aunt Sofia replied. "You'll wear it until your hair grows back."

"But everyone in the capital wears their hair like this."

"We aren't in the capital."

"Please, Tia, just today. Just for the sewing lesson?"

"No." Aunt Sofia fanned the fire faster. The kindling glowed orange.

"But I look like a coffee picker."

"Better to look like a coffee picker than an easy woman!" Aunt Sofia shouted. "There's no shame in being a coffee picker. Your mother picked coffee when she was a girl."

Emília let out a long sigh. She didn't like to imagine her mother that way.

"Don't sulk," Aunt Sofia said, pointing the black-tipped fire stick at Emília's head. "You should have thought before you did . . . that."

"Yes, ma'am," Emília replied. She removed the cloth covering from the clay jug beside the stove and scooped a cupful of water into their metal washbasin. In the far kitchen corner, Aunt Sofia had rigged a makeshift curtain so that they could bathe in private. Emília took her bar of perfumed soap from its hiding place on the windowsill. It was a gift from Dona Conceição. Emília preferred it to the cheap black soap Aunt Sofia purchased, which made everything smell like ashes. She crouched beside the washbasin and scooped water over her head. She rolled the small, perfumed nub in her hands.

"Bless me, Tia," Luzia said. She entered barefoot through the back door, an empty bowl in her large hands. She'd been throwing corn to the guinea hens. Emília disliked those speckled chickens— whenever she fed them, they pecked at her toes and fluttered near her face. With Luzia the guineas were deferential. They moved from her path and let out their unusually high-pitched call, which sounded like a tribe of old women repeating the words, "I'm weak, I'm weak, I'm weak."

"Washing your hair again?" Luzia asked. When Emília ignored her, she rested her hands on her hips. "You're wasting water. What if it doesn't rain for another four months?"

"I'm not an animal," Emília replied, shaking her head. Sprinkles darkened the dirt floor. "I refuse to smell like one."

Aunt Sofia grabbed a tangled chunk of Luzia's hair and held it to her face. She crinkled her nose. "You smell like a tacaca! Stop chiding your sister and wash up, too. I won't have you go to your sewing lesson dirty."

"I hate those lessons," Luzia said, pulling away from her aunt's grip.

"Hush up!" Aunt Sofia said. "Be grateful."

Luzia flopped onto a wooden kitchen stool. She cradled her bent arm in her good one, a habit that made them both look normal, as if Luzia was exasperated and was simply crossing her arms across her chest.

"I am grateful," she mumbled. "I only have to watch Emília fawn over our professor once a month."

"I do not fawn!" Emília said. She felt her face flush. "I'm respectful. He's our teacher."

Aunt Sofia would never approve of the perfumed letters, the secret smiles. Their aunt believed that holding hands in public was shameful, that a kiss in a public square meant marriage.

"You're jealous," Emília said. "I can work the Singer and you can't."

Luzia eyed her. "I'm not jealous of you," she said. "Balaio butt."

Emília stopped drying her hair. The children at the priest's school had called her that name when her body changed and she began to fill out her dresses. Emília couldn't even look at the massive, round balaio baskets on sale at the market without feeling a pang in her heart.

"Victrola!" Emília yelled.

For an instant, Luzia's eyes widened, her pupils like holes cut into those bright green circles. Then they narrowed. Luzia grabbed the nub of perfumed soap and flung it out the window. Emília rose, nearly knocking over the washbasin. She undid the bolts on the kitchen door. Her lavender soap lay near the outhouse, in a scattering of dried corn. The guinea hens pecked at it. Emília rushed outside, kicking them away.

"Two donkeys!" Aunt Sofia shouted. She followed Emília and flung a towel over her wet curls. "I've raised two donkeys!"

Back inside, Aunt Sofia crossed herself and spoke to the ceiling, as if Emília and Luzia weren't present. "Dear Lord, full of mercy and grace," she said. "Let these girls realize that they are flesh and blood. That all they have in this world is each other!"

Luzia left the kitchen. Emília wiped bits of corn from her soap. She tried to ignore her aunt's voice; she'd heard this prayer a dozen times and each time she wished it wasn't true.

3

Only Aunt Sofia and Emília used Luzia's given name. Everyone else called her Victrola.

The name had originated in Padre Otto's schoolyard. Emília had been the first girl in their church class to develop—her hips and breasts filling out so quickly that Aunt Sofia had to rip her dresses in half and sew in new panels. When she was thirteen, a boy grabbed her during recess. He pressed his lips roughly to her neck. Emília squealed. She squirmed from his grip. The boy tugged her back.

Luzia looked on, her dark eyebrows knitting together. She strode toward them. She was only eleven but already taller than most boys in their class. That winter she'd grown as thin and gangly as a papaya tree. Aunt Sofia had stopped letting out the hems of her dresses and instead, began adding mismatched strips of fabric around the bottoms.

"Let go of my sister," Luzia said, her voice low and husky. She smelled of sour milk. Her locked elbow was swaddled in cloth and slathered with butter and lard. Aunt Sofia and the encanadeira still believed they could grease the joint loose.

The boy smirked. "Victrola!" he yelled. "Victrola arm!"

Only two citizens in Taquaritinga owned the fancy, wind-up record players. Once a year, during the São João festival, they brought the Victrolas into the town square. The machines' brass speakers looked like giant trumpet flowers. They blasted forró music, and when a song ended, their owners carefully moved the machine's bent brass arm onto a new wax record.

"Victrola! Victrola!" the other children laughed and shouted. Luzia's head fell into her chest. Emília believed she was crying. Suddenly, Luzia reared up. On their way to school she and Emília often passed goats grazing on weeds. When the animals fought, they rammed their enemies with their foreheads, then flicked their faces upward to pierce an eye or a belly with their horns. Luzia rammed the boy headfirst. She would have stepped back and done it a second time if their teacher, Padre Otto, had not stopped her. He led the weeping boy, his mouth and shirt bloody, inside the church. After the incident, people began calling Luzia Victrola. They did it secretly at first, but the name caught on quickly and everyone, even Padre Otto, used it. Before long, Luzia disappeared and Victrola took her place.

Before her accident, Luzia had been boisterous, playful. People called her the yolk and Emília the white, a nickname that had irritated Emília because it implied that her little sister was more concentrated, powerful. After the fall, Luzia was replaced by Victrola, who was quiet and brooding. She liked sitting alone and embroidering scraps of fabric that sat in piles in their home. On those throwaway cloths she stitched armadillos with chicken heads, panthers with wings, hawks and owls with human faces, goats with frog legs. At school, Victrola was uninterested in their lessons. There were no desks in the schoolroom, only long tables with wooden benches that hurt Emília's backside by midmorning. Jesus hung on the front wall, above Padre Otto's desk. The paint on Christ's feet was chipped, revealing a gray gesso. He stared at them with pitying eyes as they did their lessons. Victrola stared back. She scratched her stiff arm, as if trying to make the bones come alive again, and squinted up at the Jesus. Padre Otto knew Victrola wasn't paying attention during lessons but, believing she was consumed by Christ's suffering, he didn't chastise her as he would Emília or the other children in class. But when Emília saw her sister's green eyes glaze over she knew Luzia was looking past the Jesus, lost in her own imagination. Her sister often went into this state at home. She burned rice or spilled water or sewed in a crooked line until Emília shook her and told her to wake up.

Although Luzia had come out of her accident alive, she'd left some vital part of herself behind, in another realm where no one could reach it. She'd left Emília to deal with the town's vicious gossips, their aunt's superstitions, and her own changing body, which grew suddenly ample and soft. Emília no longer wanted to squat in the dirt and poke at ant holes or crack clay wasps' nests with farm girls her own age. Their games seemed dull and uncultured. Luzia, too, wanted no part in the games but for different reasons. The girls made fun of her arm, her size, and Luzia inevitably fought them, tugging their hair and bloodying their noses. Emília was the only one who could calm her sister. So they were left alone, isolated in Aunt Sofia's sturdy house, with only their sewing and their family's portraits to comfort them.

Three framed portraits hung in the front room of Aunt Sofia's house. As a girl, Emília liked to climb onto the wooden sewing table where Aunt Sofia measured and cut cloth. She would place her hands on either side of the framed pictures. The whitewashed wall felt cool and powdery under her palms.

The first photograph was a black-and-white wedding portrait of her parents. The edges were warped from rainwater that had trickled between the roof tiles and seeped into the frame. They sat side by side, her father's hand blurred over her mother's. They looked frightened. His hair was oiled slick and parted in the middle. His skin was a pale gray while her mother's skin, obscured slightly by her chin-length veil, was dark, the color of ashes or stone. She bit her lip in the picture, making it look as if she was trembling. Their mother had bled to death immediately after giving birth to Luzia, and after the funeral Aunt Sofia removed the bedsheets and the soiled capim grass mattress and burned them both in the yard, near the outhouse.

Their father was Aunt Sofia's youngest brother. He was a tall man and made his living as a beekeeper, caring for several hives on the rocky side of the mountain and selling honey, pollen, and propolis. Emília had foggy memories of playing with propolis—rolling the tacky substance in her palms before her father took the gray lump and placed it in a tin boiler. She recalled her father's makeshift bee suit: brown leather gloves, thick canvas jacket, and a leather hat with mosquito netting stretched tightly from the brim and tied around his neck. There were some beekeepers who could put their bare hands in hives without so much as a sting. Her father was not one of those men.

When Emília was five and Luzia only three, he left them at Aunt Sofia's house and never picked them up again. He preferred to sit at the tin shacks along the roadside and consume shots of cane liquor. He grew into a raspy-voiced and unkempt drunk who liked leaning on tree stumps or sitting on street corners, talking to himself and to passersby. On his good days, he visited Aunt Sofia's house smelling of vomit and cheap cologne. His startlingly green eyes shone from between the wrinkled folds of his face, which had grown as brown and coarse as the leather seat of a saddle.

Each time Emília asked her aunt about their father's affliction, Sofia gave the same response. "He has nervous tendencies," she said. Then she cranked the handle of her sewing machine harder, or stirred a pot of beans on the stove faster to indicate that the conversation was over.

On his bad days, their father saw his small daughters walking to Padre Otto's school and confused Emília with his dead wife. *Maria!* he called to her, tears falling from his glassy eyes. His toenails were cracked and rimmed with blood from tripping on things. He had a penchant for losing his shoes, and once a month Aunt Sofia bought him cheap rope sandals. *Maria!* he called out, slurring the last letters of her mother's name, and Emília looked down at her sandals and kept walking, afraid of her father's gaze.

When Emília was fourteen and Luzia twelve, he returned to his hives. The mountain path was overgrown with vines. The lids of the hive boxes were thick with propolis. The bees had grown angry and wild. Two farmers had to dress from head to toe in leather vaqueiro uniforms in order to bring their father back down. They carried his bloated body—which looked, to Emília, like a sack of skin filled with water—down the main trail and into town. Emília and Luzia sewed his death suit.

Each Sunday, she and Luzia put flowers on their parents' crypt. She placed proper flowers—bunches of dahlias mixed with long stalks of blood red rooster's crest—next to the wilted and oddly sized bunches of weeds Luzia liked to pick. Once a year, on the Finados holiday, Emília and Luzia brought a pail and brushes to the cemetery and whitewashed the crypt. Each time she passed the chalky liquid over her parents' grave Emília felt nervous, believing that all of the inert bodies in that yard were watching and yearning for a fresh coat over their own resting places. There were rows of tiny crypts—the size of Emília's sewing box—for "angels," as their distraught mothers called them, born too weak to survive. There were larger graves decorated with rosaries and photographs of the dead, men mostly, their leather knife holsters placed beside their portraits. Taquaritinga was like any other town in the countryside; owning a knife was more common than owning shoes. Peixeiras, they called them, their short blades sharpened across flat rocks to a perfect, shining edge. They sliced through rope; hacked cornstalks; cut melons from their vines; pierced the necks of goats and steers, then skinned and gutted them. If there was an argument, knives settled it. Taquaritinga had no sheriff—only a Military Police sergeant who appeared twice a year and dined with the colonel. Padre Otto encouraged men to settle their differences with words, and Emília felt sorry for him during these sermons. Before he arrived, there was no school. Words were elusive, awkward, difficult to grasp. A knife was much easier. People found bodies stabbed and abandoned on isolated paths. Almost always the dead man had insulted another man's wife, or had stolen from someone, or had compromised someone's honor, so he had to be dealt with. Sometimes the fights became feuds and families lost their men, one by one, leaving the women to bury them. Women, too, had their perils. Births were often accompanied by funerals, and one of Emília's childhood acquaintances from church school—a quiet girl with buckteeth—had fallen prey to her husband's temper. So death, with all of its rites and rituals, its incense and prayers, its long masses and white burial hammocks, was common, while life was rare. Life was frightening. Even Emília, who disliked superstition as much as she disliked sloppy dressing, ended her sentences, her plans, her prayers with "God willing." Nothing, it seemed, was certain. Anyone, at any moment, could be touched—an arm caught in a manioc press, a swift donkey kick, or an accident similar to that of Uncle Tirço's.

The second portrait on Aunt Sofia's wall was a painting of Emília's uncle. The man in the painting was young—his mouth turned down and his chin lifted in a serious pose. He had a thick mustache and wore a short-brimmed leather hat that strapped beneath his chin. The painting was commissioned by the very first Colonel Pereira, who'd died in 1915 and left his only son—the second and current Colonel Pereira—one thousand head of cattle, eight hundred hectares of land, and his title. Many whispered that the first Colonel Pereira had purchased the title by bribing a politician in Recife. Colonels were not military officials, although they had small cadres of men who were loyal to them. In the backlands, colonels were the major landholders. Because of this, they made their own laws and enforced them. Many colonels employed networks of capangas and cabras—silent, loyal men trained to make examples of thieves and dissidents and political rivals by cutting off a hand, or branding a face, or making them disappear completely, sending a message to local citizens that their colonel could be magnanimous or he could be cruel, depending on their level of obedience.

Emília knew that there were two types of colonels: those who had inherited or purchased their titles, like the current Colonel Pereira, and those who had earned them through sheer force—building indomitable reputations, hiring small armies of loyal men, and then forging a bloody path acquiring land, then money, and later, influence. Both types of colonels were extremely wealthy, but one was more dangerous than the other. Colonel Chico Heráclio of Limoeiro was so rich, it was rumored that he had a mouth filled with gold teeth. Colonel Clóvis Lucena shot a man for getting dust on his shoes. And Colonel Guilherme de Pontes, who ran Caruaru, was said to be the most powerful of all, owning so much of the state it was rumored that he had private meetings with the governor.

Uncle Tirço had worked as a vaqueiro, herding cattle for the late Colonel Pereira during the great drought of 1908. According to Aunt Sofia, people and animals alike were subsisting on cactus. The old colonel's cows were collapsing. "Losing a cow or horse was more tragic than losing a man," Aunt Sofia often explained to Emília and Luzia. She told Uncle Tirço's story in the evenings, while massaging their fingers and the pads of their hands before bed. Aunt Sofia's massage invariably became halfhearted, her touch lighter and less concentrated as she became lost in her memories. Her falecido liked black coffee. Her falecido combed his mustache before church. Her falecido protected the colonel's cattle as if they were his own. And one day, he did not come back with the herd. No one knew what had happened to him: if cangaceiros caught him, if he was bitten by a scorpion or a snake, or if he had simply died of exposure.

The colonel sent two other vaqueiros to find him. They walked through the caatinga scrub below the mountain. They called his name. They scanned the horizon for vultures. Three days later they found him deep in the arid pasture, his body picked clean. The first colonel commissioned a portrait and a wooden box for the bones. Padre Otto blessed the box, agreeing that as long as Uncle Tirço was buried eventually, it would not hurt to keep him near his loved ones. Luzia found the box of bones romantic, but Luzia knew nothing of romance. Pinning your lover's handkerchief to the inside of your blouse was romantic. Exchanging perfumed notecards was romantic. Living with the flame of unreturned love in your heart, as the women in the *Fon Fon* serials did, was romantic. Keeping bones, Emília thought, was something dogs did.

The third and final portrait nailed to the front wall was a photograph of her and Luzia. It was a portrait of their First Communion. Padre Otto stood between them, resting a white hand on each of their shoulders. Aunt Sofia said that Padre Otto had been a spectacle when he first came into town, riding up the mountain on an oxcart filled with books and trunks and rolled-up maps of the world. He smiled and sweated, his face bright pink above his priest's collar. Aunt Sofia had never seen a man that color—like the insides of a guava. He didn't come out pink in the photograph though; in the portrait he was as white as their Communion dresses.

Padre Otto had come from Germany during the first Great War. Each morning he rang Taquaritinga's church bells and waited for his school's few students to file inside. Padre Otto's was the only school in town, but its seats were never full. Colonel Pereira hired private tutors for his children, and many other residents of Taquaritinga believed schooling was a waste. Boys would inevitably become what their fathers had been: farmers or vaqueiros or the next colonel's capangas. They did not need to read or write. And for farm girls, literacy was a barrier rather than an asset. Wives who could read would put on airs, trick their illiterate husbands, and worst of all, be able to write love letters. There were a few residents, however—merchants, carpenters, and other tradespeople—who valued Padre Otto's school. Even though she didn't know how to read or write, Aunt Sofia was one of these. Printed dress patterns were becoming more and more popular, and most sewing machines came with thick, detailed instruction manuals. Aunt Sofia wanted Emília and Luzia to keep up with the times.

Geography was Emília's favorite subject. Below Jesus was a map of the world with countries painted in pastel colors and their names written in calligraphic script. Padre Otto quizzed the class daily, and all of them, except Luzia, recited the countries' names in unison. When they shouted *Germany!* Emília always pictured it as a place filled with Padre Ottos—short, stout men and women with pink faces, blue eyes, and hair that was so thin and blond it looked as white as manioc flour.

There was a large map of Brazil, too. Padre Otto pointed out their state of Pernambuco many times during each lesson. It was near the top of the republic, longer than it was wide. Emília thought it looked like an outstretched arm reaching toward the coast. At the shoulder was the caatinga scrubland—often called the sertão—where water was scarce and only cactus grew. Padre Otto said that runaway slaves and Dutch soldiers and Indians retreating from the coast had all settled there, protected by the harsh desert climate. Emília pictured these dark and light tribes of men living together, spearing snakes and hawks for their dinners. At the elbow of the state was her town of Taquaritinga, set on a small mountain range that was the gateway to the scrubland. At the wrist were the plantations, the stretches of Atlantic forest that had been slashed and burned to grow sugarcane. At the knuckles was the capital—Recife—with its cobblestone streets, its rows of tightly stacked houses, and its immense port that Emília pictured filled with warships and smoking cannons because of the paintings depicting the Dutch invasion she'd seen in one of Padre Otto's history books. And at the fingertips of her state was the ocean. Emília dreamed of visiting that ocean, of putting her toe in its saltwater. She pictured it as green, dark green, even though the oceans on the map were all painted a powder blue.

Taquaritinga was a week's journey from the coast, on a mountaintop near the state border with Paraíba. The first thing people saw as they hiked up the curved mountain trail was the church steeple; but in the rainy winter season they could see only a mist of clouds. The town square around the church had been dirt until the colonel commissioned it to be cobbled, and for months there were piles of rocks and the sounds of workmen heaving sledgehammers, pounding stone against earth. Emília often asked Padre Otto what real cities were like. *Crowded,* he said, and Emília imagined him in his dark priest's cloak, making his way through masses of women and children who all wore bright clothing and hats decorated with ostrich feathers. *Crowded and not half as beautiful as Taquaritinga,* Padre Otto assured her. Emília did not believe this.

On their First Communion, Padre Otto had given Emília and Luzia two white, palm-size Bibles specially ordered from Recife. They'd held the books to their chests when they posed for their Communion portrait. Aunt Sofia had saved for three months in order to pay the photographer. The skinny man would take only one shot. Emília wanted the portrait to be perfect. She stood for what seemed like an eternity, waiting for the shutter to click. The corners of her mouth shook. She tried to keep perfectly still so that the rosary dangling from her hands would not sway. Luzia did not keep still. Perhaps she was ashamed of her bent arm, which the photographer had concealed by draping a scrap of lace over it. Perhaps she disliked the mousy man hidden beneath the camera's black cloth. Or perhaps it was because Luzia didn't realize, as Emília did, that they had only one chance to get it right, that with one click they would be framed forever.

Just as the flashbulbs popped, Luzia shifted. Her rosary swayed, her Communion veil went crooked, and the lace drape slid off her locked arm and onto the floor. When the portrait came back from the photographer's laboratory, Emília was bitterly disappointed. In it, her sister was blurred. It looked as if there was a ghost moving behind Luzia, as if there were three little girls in the portrait instead of two.

4

The sun rose slowly over the church's yellow bell tower. Luzia walked fast. She hooked her sewing bag on her bent arm. She had found subtle ways to make her Victrola arm useful, as if she preferred it that way. Emília tried to keep up with Luzia's long strides, but her feet ached. She wore a pair of black patent pumps that had once belonged to Dona Conceição. The shoes' straps and narrow sides cut into Emília's feet. She stepped gingerly along the dirt path.

Their sewing lessons were in Vertentes—a real town. It had a narrow dirt trail connecting it to Surubim and beyond. It had the first official doctor in the region and the first lawyer—both with diplomas from the Federal University in Recife. Emília knew that Vertentes people judged you by your shoes. Respectable people wore alpercata sandals with leather straps and rubber soles. Common farmers wore rope flip-flops. Pé-rapados wore no shoes at all; they had to scrape the mud-crusted soles of their feet with the dull edges of knives before entering stores or attending church. Gentlemen wore wingtips, and ladies—real ladies—wore heeled pumps. Aunt

Sofia did not approve of heeled shoes, so Emília hid the pumps in her sewing bag and put them on after she left the house.

Luzia slowed her stride. She looked disapprovingly at Emília's shoes but said nothing. Emília was thankful for her sister's silence; she didn't want another quarrel that morning. Two women swept their front steps. Plumes of dust rose around their feet. They leaned upon their brooms as Emília and Luzia passed.

"Good day," Luzia said, nodding.

"Victrola," the older woman replied.

"Emília," the younger woman said, then covered her mouth to suppress her laughter. The older woman smiled and shook her head. Emília gripped the scarf that covered her shorn hair.

"It looks fine," Luzia whispered. She flashed the giggling women a stern look, then shouted, "If you want a laugh, buy a mirror and take a look at yourselves!"

Emília smiled. She squeezed her sister's hand. Months before, Emília had seen a hat in *Fon Fon*—a beautiful feathered creation that clipped to the hair like a small skullcap. Emília admired the little hat so much she sewed one of her own. She couldn't find smooth black feathers like the ones on the model's hat, so when Aunt Sofia killed a rooster, Emília saved the prettiest feathers: red, orange, and some black speckled with white. Despite Aunt Sofia's objections, Emília wore her feathered skullcap to the market. She felt quite elegant, but as they moved through the market stalls people laughed and called her a strange chicken. Emília wanted to rip the hat from her head in embarrassment, but Luzia whispered: *Don't take it off.* She held out her crooked arm and Emília took it. As they moved past the vegetable stalls and around the butchers' pens, Luzia stared ahead, her body straight and tall, her face ferociously still. Luzia did not have the pale, petite looks of a *Fon Fon* model, but she had somehow mastered their elegance, their look of confident disdain. Afterward, Emília had tried to copy that look in her little mirror. She never could.

"You know, Lu, you're quite good on the new machine," Emília whispered.

Luzia shrugged. "You're better. I'm sorry about your soap."

Emília nodded. It could have been worse. At least Luzia had not revealed anything about the notecards. Emília had purchased a set of sky blue correspondence cards from the papelaria in Vertentes. Each month she addressed one to Professor Célio. She sharpened their thick sewing pencil to a perfect point (they did not have an ink pen; Emília longed for one) and composed her messages on scraps of butcher paper before carefully transferring the words to the correspondence card. The messages were tentative at first:

> *I would like to compliment you on your teaching abilities.*
> *Sincerely,*
> *Maria Emília dos Santos*

Professor Célio wrote back—*It is because I have talented pupils*—and Emília's messages grew bolder:

> *Dear Professor, my heart beats quickly each time you stand near my machine.*
> *Yours Sincerely,*
> *Maria Emília dos Santos*

And he responded in kind, in her favorite note yet—

> *Dearest Emília,*
> *I have watched the way you guide cloth through the machine.*
> *You have lovely, nimble fingers.*
> *Atenciosamente,*
> *Professor Célio Ribeiro da Silva*

Emília patted her sewing bag. The envelope inside had two wet circles where Emília had spritzed her perfume—jasmine toilet water she'd purchased with a chunk of her savings. This card was the boldest yet, suggesting a meeting outside class. Emília felt a nervous shiver run though her. She held her bag tighter.

Colonel Pereira's house stood in the distance, beyond the bustle of the market. It was a large white mansion at the top of the hill, behind the church. Red and orange bougainvillea fell over the sides of his fence. Both of the colonel's capangas stood on either side of his front gate, feet apart, hats tilted, hands resting on their holsters. Beside them, the colonel's white-haired farmhand tightened the saddles on two mules.

At first, Dona Conceição had offered the sewing lessons to Aunt Sofia. She'd refused, claiming she already knew how to sew. "But I will be the girls' chaperone," Aunt Sofia had insisted. It wasn't safe for young ladies to travel alone. There was no real road into Taquaritinga, just a steep mountain path. The trip to Vertentes took three hours down the mountain and four hours back. Emília spent a sleepless night fretting over Aunt Sofia's presence in class. Their aunt would not sit quietly; she would interrupt the instructor, telling him how to sew this stitch and that one, embarrassing Emília. Before the classes began, Emília spoke confidentially with Dona Conceição, who convinced Aunt Sofia that her elderly farmhand was a reliable, vigilant man. The old man lived up to his reputation. If it rained during the ride, he stopped the mules and produced umbrellas from his satchel. In Vertentes, he would not allow Emília and Luzia to walk to class—it was unseemly for young women to wander alone—and guided their mules to the classroom's front door. Emília hated arriving on the back of a mule. She and Luzia rode the animals sidesaddle, like proper ladies, squeezed between the saddle horn that bumped their hips and the mule's large cargo baskets that chafed their legs. Emília had to constantly adjust the skirt of her dress, which hiked up during the bumpy ride.

Emília wished they could ride to class on the colonel's horses, two purebred manga-largas whose trots were smooth enough to suit Dona Conceição. Or in an automobile! The colonel stored his motorcar in Vertentes. It was a black Ford with an engine crank in the front grille. The colonel hauled it up to Taquaritinga only once, on an oxcart. When it arrived, Aunt Sofia was wary. She insisted there was an animal or spirit working within the machine. How would a metal contraption move on its own? The colonel insisted on turning the engine crank himself. His Ford was one of five automobiles outside of the capital, and he would not risk his hired men breaking it. He took off his suit coat. Sweat ran into his eyes. It beaded on his gray mustache. The crank rattled around and around until suddenly, from the belly of the car came a sputter, then a growl. The colonel climbed into the driver's seat. He steered the Ford around the square. Old men, children, even Emília herself ran behind the car, hoping to touch it. The colonel honked the horn. It sounded like a hoarse moan, calling out to Emília above the din of the crowd. She would never forget the sound of it.

5

Women congregated at the door to the sewing class. Emília pressed to the front of the crowd. Luzia pulled her back. Their chaperone had disappeared into Vertentes' dusty streets, off to run errands for the colonel.

"Let's skip today," Luzia said. "Let's explore. He'll never notice."

Emília shook her head. "I won't miss a lesson."

"What do you care about the lessons?" Luzia said, releasing her arm. "You only want to see your professor. I can't believe you're fond of him."

Luzia kicked a stone with the toe of her sandal. Her feet were long and thin—thin enough to fit into Dona Conceição's pumps without squeezing.

"He's cultured," Emília said.

"He's a sissy," Luzia replied. "And his hands!" She squirmed dramatically. "They're like the skin of a jia!"

"They're a gentleman's hands," Emília said. "You can marry some brute with sandpaper fingers, but I won't."

Luzia pointed to the Singer building. "If he gets fresh with you I'll poke him with my sewing needle."

"Do it," Emília said, her cheeks hot, "and I'll throw your saints in the outhouse."

She walked away from her sister and entered the crowd at the classroom door. Emília had always admired Professor Célio's hands. She did not think they were clammy and cold like a frog's skin. They weren't marked with scars or rough from calluses, and she'd often imagined what it would feel like to have those soft things press against her face, her neck. Emília calmed herself and smoothed her dress. It was her best one, copied from a pattern in *Fon Fon*. It had a low waist and tubular skirt meant to fall midcalf, but Aunt Sofia would never have allowed it. Emília cut the skirt to fall at her ankle. She and Luzia each had three dresses: one housedress made of coarse bramante and two outside dresses made of sturdy gingham and cotton. Emília begged Aunt Sofia for a ream of low-grade crepe or linen, but she wouldn't allow it. When Aunt Sofia was Emília's age, she and her older sister could never go into town together. One of them had to stay locked in the house with their baby brother because they had only one dress and one set of shoes to split between the two of them. "And that dress was made out of sewing scraps," Aunt Sofia chuckled, but Emília never thought the story funny.

When the doors opened, Emília walked into the hot classroom and sat in her usual station—machine 16. Luzia sat facing her, at 17. Professor Célio did not greet them. He examined each station thoroughly, ripping away loose threads and straightening chairs. A piece of his hair fell into his eyes. He removed a metal comb from his breast pocket and brushed it back. When he reached Emília's station, he dusted her Singer and smiled. Emília's face grew hot. A giggle rose within her and she covered her mouth to stifle it. Beside her, Luzia sighed loudly and riffled through her sewing bag.

Professor Célio knew how to take apart the sewing machines and put them back together. He knew how to read and write, and spoke with a São Paulo accent that bore no resemblance to their Northeastern twang. He did not cut off the ends of words—he let his *o*'s and *s*'s, linger on his tongue, savoring them, before releasing them into the world. During classes, he sat behind his desk and read while the women sewed. He was unfazed by the clatter of the machines. Periodically he walked around and helped the women with their work, teaching them how to adjust the pedals, how to pull sheer linens through the falling needle without ripping them, how to prevent the thread from clumping as it made its way down into the machine's base. He helped all of the women, especially Luzia, who crossed her arms and slid her chair away from the machine while Professor Célio gave advice.

The room was hot. Emília's leg grew stiff from pumping the machine's pedal. Luzia fumbled with the bobbins on the base of her machine. She leaned across the Singer at odd angles, using her Victrola arm to keep her cloth taut and her good one to slowly push it through the needle. Her foot tapped the iron pedal. Her knees bumped against the underside of the sewing table. Emília liked to watch Luzia when she thought no one was looking. She didn't like to see her sister struggle; she liked the moments when the struggle ceased, when Luzia found a clever way to prop her arm or move her body in order to accomplish her task. Luzia's face changed when this happened. It softened, revealing a hint of womanliness, a break in her fierce pride. Once, Emília had caught her dancing alone in their room. Luzia had positioned her arms before her, the Victrola arm permanently bent on her imaginary partner's shoulder, the straight one holding his hand. Her good arm had flopped and her hips had moved so awkwardly that Emília couldn't help but giggle. Luzia had stopped and stormed from their room. Emília hadn't laughed out of meanness, but out of joy. She'd always wished for a normal sister— one who liked fine dresses and magazines, makeup and dancing. One who wanted to leave Taquaritinga as much as Emília did. Seeing Luzia dancing awkwardly before the mirror confirmed what Emília had always hoped—that beneath the crooked arm and the serious face, Luzia was a normal girl after all.

Emília stopped pedaling and removed a bundle of cloth from her sewing bag. The perfumed card was neatly tucked into its folds. Professor Célio bent over her shoulder and arranged her new cloth in the machine. They were learning to sew scalloped edges, and the correct placement of the cloth dictated the success of the assignment. Emília began to pedal. Professor Célio helped her guide the cloth back and forth beneath the needle. For a brief moment, their hands met. Emília grasped his cold fingers and slipped him the card. Then Professor Célio stepped away from her machine, coughed, and placed the note in his suit pocket.

Emília's heart pumped wildly. She slowed her pedaling and pressed her hands against her cheeks to cool them. When she looked up, Luzia was watching her. Her sister's eyes were fierce. Her mouth was a thin, white line. Emília stared back. She would not look away. She would not cower. Any time she triumphed, any time she snatched a bit of lace as a keepsake from Dona Conceição's sewing closet, or purchased a bottle of perfume, or wore her heeled shoes, or wrote her correspondence cards, she was met with this look. Ever since they were children, ever since Luzia had fallen from that tree and crippled her arm, she had felt she had the right to pass judgment upon Emília, to ruin her happiness before it even began.

6

It happened on a Sunday, after church.

Each Sunday when they were children, Aunt Sofia woke them before sunrise and pulled their church dresses over their heads. The dresses were coarse cotton ironed with goma starch, which hardened them into a stiff, canvaslike mold. Luzia was only ten but she was already taller than Emília, her dress exposing her skinned knees.

During mass, Padre Otto held firmly to the pulpit with his stubby fingers and delivered his homily. His prayers rose up above the shuffling sounds and sneezes in the congregation. He pronounced his r's roughly, as if he had a coin on the roof of his mouth and was trying to hold it in place with his tongue. There was a painting of Santo Amaro on the church ceiling. It was huge and sooty from candle smoke and Emília liked to stare up at the bald saint; the candle he held glowed so brightly it attracted the angels. After mass, Emília, Luzia, and Aunt Sofia left church and walked to comadre Zefinha's house.

Josefa da Silva had an affinity for cabidela chicken, and on the last Sunday of each month she skipped church and sliced open her fattest rooster's neck, mixing its fresh blood with vinegar and onions. Zefinha was their aunt Sofia's childhood friend. The two women had grown up in Taquaritinga, had performed their First Communions together, and had stayed best friends despite the fact that after they were married, Sofia stayed near town while Zefinha moved to a farm farther up the mountain. Zefinha was plump and kind and every Sunday after church she fried cheese with cornmeal and let Luzia and Emília eat it straight from the pan, scraping out the last bits of cheese with their forks.

After lunch they sat on Zefinha's porch. To ward away the blood-sucking gnats that flew under their skirts and around their faces, they rubbed a concoction of lemongrass and lard over their legs and arms and faces, making them shine like glass dolls. The two women sat in wooden chairs. Emília lolled in a hammock with Luzia. Her sister swung them impatiently back and forth with the tip of her toe. Emília leaned her chin off the side of the hammock and watched Zefinha's youngest son straightening the shed near the side of the house. He rolled a worn bit of rope to make a perfect coil. His tan forearms bulged with each turn.

"Can we play?" Luzia asked. Emília sat up.

"Let them go," Zefinha said. A large mosquito, its back legs long and curled up like whiskers, floated around her gray head.

Their aunt thought a minute. "Stay near the house. Don't get your dresses dirty. Emília, watch your sister."

Emília nodded, then chased after Luzia into the grove of banana trees behind Zefinha's house. Their sandals crunched and sank into the dried palm fronds that littered the ground. The banana palms bobbed in the breeze, which, over time, had ripped their green fronds into ribbonlike slivers. Emília heard a donkey bay.

"Look!" Luzia said. In the distance was a mango tree, its branches heavy with fruit. A sagging wire fence separated Zefinha's property from her neighbor's. Luzia crawled under the fence, then held up the rusted wire for Emília. The neighbor's land was crowded with spindly coffee trees. Luzia pulled leaves from their branches as she ran toward the mango tree.

Emília followed her sister's example. She grasped a low branch and hoisted herself into the tree. Her sandals slipped on the trunk. Emília held tightly to a nearby branch and scrambled up. The bark scraped her palms. Across from her, Luzia balanced on a high limb. She reached into the boughs above her and ripped down two ripe mangoes. Cradling the fruits in the skirt of her dress, Luzia carefully sat. She produced a small knife from her pocket. It had been a present from their father, who, during one of his strange visits had shown up at Sofia's house with bloodshot eyes and breath smelling of sugarcane liquor. Emília had paid him little attention. He'd patted his pockets for something to give them and pulled out his penknife. In his days as a beekeeper, he'd used the knife to slice wax and to scrape propolis, so it had a stubby and sharp blade. On its handle he'd carved the image of a bee. Luzia kept the knife, hiding it from her aunt and carrying it always in her dress pocket or school satchel.

Luzia cut holes into the mangoes' tops. She handed one to Emília. They sucked out the fruits' insides, smashing the soft mounds between their fingers like bread dough. When they finished, Luzia threw down her flaccid fruit. She lifted her skirt. Slowly, she untied the drawstring of her knee-length knickers and shifted from side to side on the tree branch, pushing her underpants around her ankles. Then, Luzia gripped the branch above her. She leaned her body back. Emília saw a neat streak of liquid fall from between her sister's legs and onto the ground below. It bubbled into the orange earth.

"Do it, Mília," Luzia said. "I dare you."

Emília could not bring herself to do such a thing. She could not take her underpants off in front of her little sister, embarrassed by the curling black hairs that had begun to grow on that part of her body. She heard a rustling in the coffee trees—saw the leaves ripple in waves.

"Someone's coming!" Emília hissed.

Luzia rushed to pull up her knickers. She took both arms from the branch above her. In an instant, Emília saw her sister's face change from a look of surprise to one of dread—her eyebrows furrowing and teeth clenching as if prepared for the impact. Luzia tipped backward.

"Luzia!" Emília shouted. She grabbed for her sister. Their fingers touched, sticky and wet from mango juice, then moved apart.

Luzia's head thudded against two thick branches. She flopped onto the earth, exhaling a small sigh before closing her eyes. Her left arm was twisted at a horrendous angle beneath her body. She looked like one of their rag dolls—her limbs splayed and limp. Emília wrapped her arms around the tree's trunk and scrambled down, scraping her knees and the pads of her hands. Zefinha's neighbor appeared from the coffee trees, ready to yell at the girls for stealing his fruit. His scowl disappeared when he saw Luzia.

Emília knelt and quickly pulled up Luzia's underpants. "Pick her up!" she ordered the old farmer, her voice sounding unfamiliar to her, too high pitched and insistent.

Aunt Sofia covered her mouth when she saw them emerge from the trees: Emília shouting orders, Zefinha's neighbor wide-eyed and frantic, Luzia limp in his arms. They laid her on the kitchen table. Blood leaked from a wound on the back of her head.

"I found her like this," the neighbor said, holding his dark and calloused hands together as if in prayer. "They were in my tree."

"We'll put her hands in cold water," Zefinha said, then ran and filled two clay bowls. Luzia's hands hung limply inside them. Her left arm was twisted elbow side up, as if it had been sewn on backward. Aunt Sofia stroked Luzia's hair away from her forehead. She did not wake. They poured water over her face, wafted a bottle of strong vinegar under her nose, pinched her cheeks and pulled her hair, but Luzia did not move.

"Her breath," Aunt Sofia whispered, "is so shallow." She looked intently at Luzia's chest. "I can barely see it rise."

Zefinha lifted Luzia's head gingerly and slipped a towel beneath it to soak up the blood. She faced her son. "Ride to town," she ordered. "Get the midwife."

Dona Augusta, the local midwife, was the closest thing Taquaritinga had to a trained doctor. Aunt Sofia fell to her knees. Everyone followed. The dirt floor felt cold against Emília's knees. The neighbor shifted next to her, curling the brim of his hat in his hands. He smelled of onions and dirt. Emília felt dizzy. She shuffled away from him and clasped her hands together.

Aunt Sofia recited a series of prayers to the Virgin. They opened their eyes after each one, hoping to see Luzia stir. When she did not, they quickly lowered their heads again.

"My Santo Expedito," Aunt Sofia called out, her voice shaking and grave, "guardian of all just and urgent causes, help us in this moment of affliction and despair. You, the warrior saint. You, the saint of all afflictions. You, the saint of all impossible causes. Protect my niece. Help her; give her strength. Don't let her go to that dark place. My Santo Expedito, she will be eternally grateful and will carry your name for the rest of her life." Aunt Sofia stood. She put her head to Luzia's chest. "I can barely hear the beating," she said.

"We should get a candle," the neighbor said.

Aunt Sofia gripped her rosary tighter. The deep, V-shaped creases that ran across her forehead twitched. "No," she said. "She's still alive."

Zefinha placed her hand on her friend's arm. "Sofia," she whispered, "her breath is so faint. What if she doesn't wake? She'll need that light."

Emília clasped her hands tighter. There was a metallic taste in her mouth. Her spit felt viscous and thick. She remembered when Cosmo Ferreira, a local farmer, was bucked by his donkey one Saturday during the market. Aunt Sofia had tried to cover Emília's eyes but she squirmed and saw everything. His face had been smashed and he lay twisted and bloody near the donkey corral. A storekeeper put a lit banana frond in the farmer's limp hands so that the light could guide his departing soul into heaven and guard against the darkness that surrounds death.

"Let me get a candle," Aunt Sofia wept. "Just in case."

Emília held her hands together so tightly her fingers tingled. She prayed to all of the saints she could remember; prayed to Jesus and the Holy Ghost and to the soul of her mother. Over and over she prayed, until the words of her prayers sounded foreign and meaningless, like the nonsense songs she and Luzia had sung when they were very small.

Zefinha produced a thick white candle. She lit it with a piece of kindling from the cook fire. Aunt Sofia arranged Luzia's limp right hand onto her chest and wrapped the candle in her small fingers. Then, their aunt moved the twisted left arm. Luzia's eyes fluttered open. She scanned the room as if lost, then looked down at her arm. Her mouth twisted in pain.

"Ave Maria!" Aunt Sofia cried. "Thank God!"

Luzia sat up. The candle fell to floor. Zefinha quickly stamped it out.

"It hurts," Luzia croaked, her voice hoarse, the back of her hair matted with blood. She slid from the table. "It hurts," she said, louder this time, glaring at Emília.

Emília felt trapped by her sister's stare. There was pain, confusion, a wild anger in Luzia's eyes. Emília saw blame there, too. She looked at her clasped hands and pretended to pray. Luzia cried. She ran about the kitchen, finally dunking her broken arm into a water jug beside Zefinha's stove.

Her son returned minutes later. His horse's velvety nostrils were large and circular, opening and closing with its deep breaths. The midwife was nowhere to be found, so he'd brought Padre Otto. The priest sat precariously behind Zefinha's boy, his bald head shining with sweat, his black pants hiked up, revealing white ankles. He crossed himself when he saw Luzia, who stood with her arm in the water jug. Her face was dangerously pale. Zefinha's son raced back to town to find the bonesetter.

"What happened here?" Padre Otto asked.

"She was almost gone," Aunt Sofia whispered to the priest. "It's a miracle, isn't it, Father? She came back to us. A miracle."

Aunt Sofia explained the accident and Padre Otto nodded solemnly. He did not take his eyes from Luzia's. When Aunt Sofia finished, the room grew quiet. Padre Otto took Luzia's chin between his thick forefinger and thumb.

"Miracles are rare, young lady," he said. "They are gifts. Don't fall from any more trees."

Emília knelt, forgotten in the corner of the whitewashed kitchen, like a stranger bearing witness to a private family event. She felt a cold certainty prick her, as steely and sharp as Aunt Sofia's sewing needles: this was what her life would be like, living with a sister who had come back from the brink of death.

7

Emília knotted the scarf more tightly over her hair. The arid country below the mountain was hot and dusty. They crossed paths with a caravan of donkeys. The animals carried kerosene tins and crates of soaps, hair tonics, and other packaged goods from Limoeiro. Barefoot children ran beside the trail. They kicked up dust. Emília closed her eyes.

Professor Célio had not written her a note. In the past, he'd scribbled a response on a slip of newspaper print torn from his Singer manual. After their lesson, Emília had lingered at her machine, straightening her chair and brushing away loose threads while Luzia waited impatiently by the door. Professor Célio stayed behind his desk, answering the other students' questions. It was the scarf, Emília concluded. Before copying the Fon Fon models, she'd had curling black hair that she tied back with a ribbon. Now she looked like a farmer's wife. Next time she would disobey her aunt. She'd set her curls with goma water to keep them from flattening beneath the scarf, and she'd take it off as soon as she entered the Singer building.

"Look," Luzia said.

Emília kept her eyes closed. During their trips home, Luzia pointed out the same boulders—rocks so weathered by rain and time that they looked soft and almost porous. People had recently white-washed them with political slogans: *Vote # 25, Celestino Gomes!* Luzia hated the signs. Emília did not know who the man was—politicians were strange, phantom figures whose crackling voices occasionally appeared in radio broadcasts or whose names were painted onto rocks or fences and endorsed by local colonels. Only literate men could vote. The few who fit this profile in Taquaritinga rarely saw a ballot; Colonel Pereira filled them out as he saw fit. Luzia swore that if she were a man, she'd never support the candidate who ruined boulders with his slogans. Emília ignored her; she liked the painted rocks. They added freshness to the brown barrenness of the countryside. To Emília, they were a sign of civilization among the cracked mud houses and tightly bound goat fences, whose constant repetition made her clutch her scarf and then her stomach, where she felt a fluttering, an awful tightening of her insides that she could only identify as disgust.

"Look," Luzia insisted.

Her sister's elbow jabbed her ribs. Emília opened her eyes. They'd already passed the painted boulders. Four figures blocked the road.

"Whoa!" their elderly chaperone yelled. He held the mules' reins in one hand and felt beneath the bottom of his shirt with the other, revealing a shabby knife holster. There were thefts along the roadways—groups of cangaceiros or even lone outlaws sometimes took merchandise and money. Some people in town lived in fear of cangaceiros, even though Taquaritinga hadn't been attacked in Emília's short lifetime. Dona Ester, the barber's wife, insisted that the cangaceiros were not heroes, as some claimed, but hoodlums and killers of the worst kind. Repentista singers, who passed through town wearing threadbare suits and carrying polished violas, sang of the cangacieros' cruelty: how they burned down entire towns, killed whole families, slaughtered livestock. Then, immediately afterward, the same men sang of the cangacieros' mercy and generosity; how the outlaws threw gold pieces and left treasure chests behind for kind hosts.

Dona Teresa, an elderly woman who sold chickens and cinnamon sticks at the Saturday market, believed that the cangaceiros were simply poor farmhands who got fed up with the colonels' petty territory wars. The old woman's nephew—a sweet boy, she insisted— had become a cangaceiro to avenge the death of his sweetheart at the hands of an enemy colonel. This was a common story. There were three kinds of cangaceiros: those who entered for revenge, those who entered to escape revenge, and those who were simply thieves. Emília believed that the first two eventually had to become the third kind; they could not live by scavenging in the scrub like animals. Still, in the backlands, revenge was sacred. It was a duty, an honor. Even those who feared the cangaceiros as thieves respected them as men. "Cangaceiros don't bow their heads to the colonels," Zé Muela, a shopkeeper, often whispered when he was sure Colonel Pereira was far from his store. "They handle things. They don't cross their legs like women."

Some of the girls Emília had gone to school with believed cangaceiros were romantic, even handsome. Emília disagreed. Whatever their motivations, cangaceiros were those very farm boys she disliked, except worse—they were made bolder by guns and prestige. They were, Emília thought, like the band of feral dogs that prowled Taquaritinga each evening. Once docile, they'd grown wild and rabid—pilfering chickens, snapping the necks of baby goats, roaming gloomily through town with their bloodied coats and awful stench. They were unpredictable, ungrateful mutts that would turn on each other if given the chance. Some of her neighbors felt pity and fed the dogs. Emília preferred to keep her distance.

As the mules slowed, the men drew closer. They wore flat-brimmed leather hats and green uniforms. There was so much brown below the mountain that the uniforms looked vibrant, alive. Their chaperone moved his hand away from his holster.

"Checkpoint," he murmured. "Monkeys."

Emília had seen a soldier only once before, during a visit to Caruaru, where she and Luzia observed a group of them drinking beer and catcalling women. Caruaru was the largest metropolis in the interior of the state, but even there real officials of the law were rare. Colonel Pereira complained about their current governor who, he said, had bribed poor city boys, given them ancient weapons, and proclaimed them soldiers before sending them to posts in the countryside. There, the soldiers made more trouble than good. They were boisterous one moment and vicious the next, as unruly and cruel as a band of cangaceiros. People in the interior had nicknamed them monkeys.

The donkeys slowed. Luzia straightened. Emília tightened her scarf. The soldier held a thick-barreled rifle across his body, ready to aim. The gun was scratched, its wooden butt cracked. The other soldiers did not have weapons, but stood with their feet spread apart, blocking the mules' path. The armed soldier surveyed Emília and Luzia.

"Your business?" he asked.

"Sewing lessons," Luzia responded.

The soldier nodded. "No chaperone?"

"I'm their chaperone," the old man said, removing his hat. "I work for Colonel Carlos Pereira."

The soldier shook his head. "And where is this colonel from? There are so many around here it's hard for me to keep track." The other soldiers laughed.

The old man looked shocked. "He runs the land from that mountain"—he pointed before them, to the blue shadow in the distance—"and beyond. Taquaritinga and Frei Miguelinho. He runs it all."

"He may own it," the soldier said, suddenly stern, "but the law runs it. The state of Pernambuco runs it."

Their chaperone looked down and nodded. Emília felt a surge of annoyance. If they had ridden in the colonel's Ford, would they have been chastised like this? If she had Professor Célio beside her instead of an old farmhand, would they have been bothered?

"All right," the soldier said, motioning with his rifle, pointing it up the road. "Be on your way. But be alert. The Hawk's in the area."

Their chaperone froze for an instant, his hat curled tightly in his hands, then thanked the soldier. He grabbed the mules' reins and shouted for the animals to move. Emília felt a shiver. She held tightly to her saddle horn.

Everyone knew his story. At eighteen, the Hawk had become a cangaceiro when he killed the famous Colonel Bartolomeu of Serra Negra in his own study, bypassing the colonel's capangas and gutting him with his own letter opener. Citizens from Rio Branco later dubbed him "the Hawk" after a raid on their town, where he'd cut out his victims' eyes with the point of his knife. There was a bird in the arid countryside below Taquaritinga—the caracará—a type of hawk that swooped down and ate the eyes and tongues of baby goats and calves. Aunt Sofia, like many other mothers in town, used the hawk as a way to keep Emília and Luzia from roaming too far from home.

Caracará, Aunt Sofia used to sing in her deep, scratchy voice, *looks for children who aren't wise. When he catches them alone, he plucks out their eyes!*

It was said that the Hawk wore a collection of his victims' dried eyeballs around his neck. It was said that he was enormous, with blond hair and blue eyes, like some ancient Dutch soldier. Some said he was thick, squat, and dark, like an Indian. Some said he was the devil himself. Padre Otto tried to dispel this particular myth. The devil, he warned, would not have such an obvious guise. "Satan is no outlaw," the priest said. "He is a trickster, a charmer. He doesn't bear weapons but gifts, making us mistake shadows for substance, the kingdom of heaven for the pleasures of earth."

Emília twisted in her saddle and stared back at the soldiers, feeling sorry for them suddenly, with their bright uniforms and old gun. Easy prey. She looked at Luzia, sitting tall on the mule beside her. Her sister lifted her Victrola arm. The locked elbow jutted at an awkward angle. She cupped her hand over her dark brows and stared at the horizon.

8

When they reached Taquaritinga, the air became cooler, lighter. The summer's last cicadas buzzed weakly. Birds twittered. In the market, the last vendors took apart their stalls. People stared at the darkening horizon, hoping for rain.

Their chaperone stopped the mules in front of the colonel's white mansion. The old man had tried to speed up the animals, hoping to shorten their trip up the mountain. But the mules plodded stubbornly up the trail, hastening only at the sound of the crop, then slowing again. The mules did not care if the Hawk was hiding among the rocks or behind the brush. Their old chaperone, however, held fast to his knife holster. Emília and Luzia flicked their heads toward every scuttling lizard, every low-flying bird. When they finally arrived, Emília's head ached. The saddle horn had chafed her hip. Her good dress was covered in dust. Only a note from Professor Célio would cheer her mood; she'd have to wait another month before he slipped a reply into her hands.

She and Luzia thanked their chaperone and left him and the mules at the colonel's gate. They walked through the town square, which was empty except for a few engaged couples strolling hand in hand. Their chaperones—old women thumbing rosaries—shuffled closely behind the couples. Emília limped beside her sister, her feet swelling against the leather straps of her hand-me-down shoes. Still, she would not take them off.

"I saw you," Luzia whispered, staring upward, as if speaking to the sky. "I saw you pass him a note."

"Who?"

"Please, Mília. My machine is across from yours."

Emília shifted her sewing bag from one shoulder to the other. "He's going to take me away," she said. "We're going to São Paulo."

Luzia stopped walking. Her breath was quick, her eyes wide. Emília felt a surge of giddiness in knowing that she could disconcert her sister.

"Has he told you that?" Luzia asked.

"He's discreet. Cultured men never boldly state their intentions."

"What if his intentions are bad?" Luzia said, her stance wide, her arms cocked on her hips, her chest puffed out like a rooster ready for a fight. She spoke loudly. Emília hushed her.

"You sound just like Tia," Emília whispered. "Professor Célio is a gentleman. He doesn't have to tell me. I can feel it."

"If he's a gentleman, why doesn't he visit the house? Why doesn't he ask Tia's permission to court you?"

"It's a long trip to Taquaritinga," Emília said. Her face felt hot. She'd thought of the possibility, but felt a rush of shame each time she pictured Professor Célio walking on the dirt floor of their kitchen, watching Aunt Sofia fry manioc pancakes and enduring Luzia's bullying stare. Emília shuddered. Then she lied. "He offered to visit," she said. "I told him not to take the trouble."

"Why?" Luzia asked.

Emília forced a laugh. "In São Paulo they have ten-story buildings, Luzia! They have parks and apartment houses and trolley cars. What would he think of this?" She spread her hands wide, as if trying to fit the entire town in her reach.

"What does it matter?" Luzia asked.

"It matters to a cultured person."

"How would you know?" Luzia said.

Emília's throat tightened. Heat prickled her cheeks. Luzia regarded her with a pitying stare, as if she sensed things Emília could not. Emília was sick of that stare. Luzia's long body and crooked arm set her apart, giving her a freedom Emília would never know. Victrola had no marriage hopes. No reputation to preserve. Victrola was an oddity, free from gossip or judgment. Free to act as she pleased, to say what she pleased, without consequences. Emília had no such luxuries. Ever since she was a child, Aunt Sofia and others had warned her time and again—"Remember your beginnings." They said it kindly, as if doling out sacred advice. They said it to save her embarrassment and hurt. *Remember your beginnings,* they said, and Emília knew what was behind those words: remember the orange stains on your feet, the sewing calluses on your fingertips, the ugly cloth of your dresses. Remember that you are the daughter of a coffee picker and the town drunk. Remember that you can have your *Fon Fon*s and entertain your dreams and ideas, but in the end they will do more harm than good. You may forget your beginnings, but no one else will.

"I hate you," Emília said.

She turned away from Luzia and walked fast, hoping to elude her sister's long strides. Her feet throbbed. Her eyes stung. It didn't matter if her shoes hurt, or if her hair was strange. She had Professor Célio. And someday he would take her to a real city, with streetlights and trolley cars and restaurants. She had never been to a restaurant. He would take her to a city where people knew how to read and write, where they signed their names with real ink pens instead of pressing their fingers on a blotter and stamping documents with an illiterate's thumbprint. A city where there were no droughts in the summer or floods in the winter; where water tamely flowed through pipes and sewers. She imagined her house—a place with tile floors and a gas stove. She imagined her revenge—how she would leave Luzia there, among the goats and gossips and toothless men. And one day, Emília would return to find Luzia old and lonely. She would take her sister out of Taquaritinga and back to her tiled home, to a place where no one would call her Victrola ever again. And Luzia would finally see that all of Emília's magazines and perfumes, her notecards, her homemade hats and ill-fitting shoes were not silly things at all, but small steps, necessary steps, on her way to a better place.

Chapter 2
LUZIA

Taquaritinga do Norte, Pernambuco
May 1928

1

----

*I*t was still dark. Birds clustered in the wooden rafters. Luzia lit a candle and entered the small closet beside the pantry. There, she lit several candles using the one in her hand. The little room glowed orange with light. The painted eyes of saints stared at her from their altar. Hardened wax, like petrified tears, dripped down the lace doilies that lined the shelves. Candle smoke swirled upward and exited through two small holes in the roof tiles, all of them black with soot.

Luzia knelt. Her knees fell comfortably into the indentations in the dirt floor, left there from years of prayers. She had come to the saints' closet every morning since she was eleven. Aunt Sofia believed that the saints had mustered their powers to revive Luzia after her fall from the mango tree. Luzia hadn't asked for the saints' help, but was required to show gratitude. Especially to Saint Expedito, who, Aunt Sofia and Padre Otto agreed, had lived up to his fame as the patron of just and urgent causes. In return for bringing her back from near death, Luzia owed Expedito an offering on her eighteenth birthday. When a saint demanded a sign of thanks from a woman, she could not give food or money or anything material. She had to give something of great personal value; to most women, this meant their hair. Luzia had not cut hers since falling from the mango tree.

Her hair hung thick and brown, nearly hitting her waist. When she turned eighteen, she would have to sever her braid and take it to church, placing it on Expedito's altar. After that, perhaps she could style her hair in a daring bob, like her sister. Luzia rolled the rosary beads in her hands. She shook her head; she would look ridiculous. Still, the offering had to be made.

She wasn't sure if she believed in the powers of the saints, and often thought them vain for requiring so much attention. But she liked the fact that they had once been people—they'd believed, suffered, and been rewarded. If the reward was granted for their suffering or for their faith, Luzia could never be sure. As a child, she'd asked Padre Otto. In response, he'd handed her a leather-bound book on the saints' lives and deaths. Early on he'd believed, like some others in town, that although her locked arm restricted her from marriage, it made her a candidate for a higher vocation; there were fine convents in Garanhuns and Recife. Luzia did not want to become a nun, but she liked reading the priest's musty books while the rest of her classmates went to recess. Page by page she'd sifted through the saints' lives and learned that they were not the painted figurines that sat meekly on her wax-covered altar, but real people. Santa Inês was just a girl when she was sold to a brothel and burned at the stake. Santa Rita de Cássia had been quartered, her flesh cut off bit by bit—first the fingers, then the wrists, then the arms. Santa Dorothea the Beautiful's naked body was branded with hot irons. Santa Luzia's eyes had been plucked from her head by the point of a pagan's knife. Throughout their suffering, the book said, the saints had prayed for their souls and not for their poor bodies. Luzia admired their resolve, but she didn't believe it.

She recalled her own accident—not the fall itself, but the dreadful feeling of tipping backward, of losing her balance and realizing that there was no invisible hand, no guardian angel to catch her. There were only tree limbs, and then darkness. When she awoke she saw Aunt Sofia's face and felt a pain so great she believed she was floating away. It grew worse when the encanadeira arrived and snapped her flopping arm right side up. Luzia heard a terrible ringing in her ears.

Then she fainted. They forced her arm between paletas: two long wooden sticks on either side of her forearm tied together with cloth and held in place by a sling around her neck. The broken joint ached. It burned, pinched, shot waves of heat and stinging jolts up her arm. Luzia sweated. She shuddered. Many nights she could not sleep. She knelt in the saints' closet and sent up long and fervent pleas, made childish bargains and countless offerings, all for her arm. But beneath the paletas the joint slowly hardened. When they took off the wooden sticks, Luzia's elbow was locked, the bone petrified into place.

The encanadeira said there was still hope. She used a special tape and measured every inch of Luzia's body, as if fitting her for her burial gown. After she made her measurements, the encanadeira knelt and prayed for Jesus to stretch the arm straight. She gave them a concoction of herbs and butter, ordering Luzia to rub it into her elbow three times a day, to grease the bone, as if it were a cog in a machine. By then the pain had dulled to a constant, prickling presence, like needles lodged beneath her skin. So when Padre Otto's large leather book said that the saints forgot their pain and disregarded their bodies, Luzia had slapped it shut. She no longer wanted to read during recess. She no longer wanted to attend the church school, where the children had renamed her Victrola. She felt something hard and bitter, like the pit of a pitomba fruit, lodge in her chest. Every so often this pit cracked open, releasing a terrible heat that bubbled and rose, overflowing like milk in a pan. Luzia stomped on bean plants. She kicked her schoolmates' shins. She ripped Aunt Sofia's dahlias from their thin stems. She pinched Emília's lovely brown arms until they were dotted with blue. She did not feel anger but despair, and she wanted the world to feel it, too. Soon, Padre Otto stopped lending her books. He stopped describing the lovely convent courtyards lined with roses and herbs. Victrola, it seemed, was not meant for the religious life.

With time, her temper calmed, but its fame remained. Her arm did not grow straight but her body did. As she got taller and taller, Aunt Sofia insisted that the encanadeira had miscalculated, that her prayers had stretched the bones in Luzia's legs instead of her arms. The women in town whispered—it was a shame that she and Emília had no brother to look after them. A house filled with females was a pitiful thing. As they grew older, Aunt Sofia became strict with Emília, keeping her indoors and away from trouble. Girls were only worth their ability to stay untouched. This wasn't a concern for Luzia; she was already spoiled. Who, the townswomen asked, laughing, would be desperate enough to touch Victrola? So Luzia could roam where she pleased. After her morning prayers in the saints' closet, she took long walks. Before the sun rose, Luzia wandered the dark town and the mountainside farms. She liked the quiet and the cool morning air. She liked feeling as if she was the only person alive.

Luzia rolled the rosary in her palms. The candles' heat warmed her face. She stared at the figurines before her. There was São Francisco, with two birds in his outstretched hands. There was São Bento in a purple cape; São Brás, with a red ribbon tied around his neck; and São Benedito, his face so black that his eyes looked round and startled. There was Santo Expedito, his shield upheld, his soldier's armor crookedly painted on his body, his lips red and full. The saints' faces seemed too womanly to her, too childlike and soft. She knew Emília thought them beautiful in their delicateness, like Professor Célio.

Luzia didn't like the sewing instructor. Not because of his trimmed beard or his bleached shirts. Luzia respected his cleanliness; she knew it took effort. It was impossible to find a barber and difficult to scrub away the stubborn dust that found its way into every piece of clothing's fibers, making even the whitest shirts dingy and yellow. It was brave really, in their world of farmers and vaqueiros, for a common man to dress like a colonel. What Luzia disliked was the way the sewing teacher flicked loose threads from his desk, as if disgusted by them. He had a terrible habit of tapping his foot and sighing when a pupil couldn't replace the metal bobbin in her machine. He feared staining his trousers with oil, so if a machine creaked he gave the oil tin one quick squirt and backed away, letting his pupil wipe up any mess. He thought himself above teaching stitches—he was a technician and not a tailor, he often emphasized—so he opened the Singer manual and showed them pictures of ponto à jour and picot borders, then went to his desk and let them figure it out for themselves. But when it came to the machines he was long-winded and attentive, clicking latches up and down, winding and unwinding the thread bobbins, making the students step back as he worked, as if the machine were a dangerous mystery and not just metal and wood.

On the first day of class, he had stared at Luzia's arm and in a booming, gallant voice asked if she would like assistance. Luzia declined, then turned to her sister. "He must be a terrible teacher if they sent him here and not to a real city," she said loudly, making Emília blush. After that, the instructor let her be. That was how Luzia wanted it.

Perhaps she should have let him help her. Perhaps she should have acted clumsy and helpless, occupying his time so that he couldn't pay attention to Emília. Still, Emília would have caught his eye, even if it meant forcing herself into his field of vision.

Emília knew how to move her face, how to control her expressions to get what she wanted. Luzia had seen her practicing in her little mirror, opening and narrowing her large brown eyes. Each time Professor Célio slipped her a note, Emília palmed it and kept her eyes on her work, looking concentrated and serious, giving the professor only a shy hint of a smile. With the cloth vendors at the market, Emília pouted and furrowed her brow until they gave her a good price. With Dona Conceição she was reverent and wide-eyed. With her former suitors—the scared farm boys who sat nervously in Aunt Sofia's kitchen—Emília curled her thick upper lip into a sneer. It was only before sleep, when Luzia and Emília whispered to each other, telling stories and secrets, that Emília's expressions were not studied. In the candlelight, Emília looked like the photograph of their mother, but her stare was not frightened or unsure. It was keen. Stubborn. "God help the man who marries you," Aunt Sofia often joked during Emília's tirades. "He'll think he's getting sugar, but he's really getting rapadura!" They bought the brown blocks once a month, shaving slivers into their coffee and cornmeal. The rapadura smelled of molasses and attracted bees. But for all of its sweetness, the block was as hard as stone, known to break teeth and bend knives. Emília's will was just as firm. One day, she would move to Recife or even São Paulo.

Luzia felt a pang of jealousy. She wrapped her rosary tightly between her fingers. The beads pinched her palms.

She did not want her sister's beauty. It would be tiresome to style her hair and worry over dresses. But Luzia envied the opportunity that beauty offered. Emília talked of becoming a typist or a salesgirl in the city. Luzia would have liked to apply for such jobs, but there was little chance for her to get outside work. Sometimes, when they whispered in bed and Emília confided her plans, Luzia wanted to say, *Take me with you.* She never did. She did not really want to live in a city. Luzia loved Aunt Sofia's house. She loved feeding the cranky guinea hens, tending the dahlias, and taking her long morning walks before the sun rose. Still, she felt a thrilling jolt at the thought of escaping, of becoming anyone but Victrola.

The smoke in the saints' closet made Luzia's eyes sting. A drop of candle wax fell on her forearm. She pulled back and rubbed the red circle it made on her skin. Luzia closed her eyes. She prayed for Aunt Sofia's health. She prayed for Emília's happiness, but not with the sewing instructor. When it came time to pray for herself, Luzia wasn't sure what to ask for. Her life seemed foggy and uneventful, like a childhood she would never leave behind.

She stared at the center of the saints' altar. There was the Virgin Mother, her hands outstretched and her face rubbed clean of soot. Her head was bowed. Her eyes were lifted, not demurely, but knowingly, as if saying, *My love is great but do not try my patience.*

Luzia quickly finished her prayers. She blew out the saints' candles and left the closet. In the pantry, she felt along the shelves until she found a slab of sun-dried beef. She sliced off a small chunk and dropped it in her dress pocket. Then she unlatched the kitchen door and made her way into the dark garden.

2

/ / / / / / / /

Aunt Sofia called the hours before twelve "the mouth of the night."
Decent people went to bed after sunset—only drunks and dogs wandered in night's mouth. Anyone else silly enough to do so risked
being consumed; by what, Luzia was never sure. Perhaps by spirits or
drink or thieves. Or by the night itself. Before midnight there was a
chorus of sounds: the buzz of crickets, the soft hoots of frogs, the
howls of mutts. After midnight was the first owl's cry, then the second. And after that, there was silence.

Luzia took her walks during this early morning quiet. Frogs
went back into their holes. Dogs returned from their adventures and
dozed on stoops. There was only the soft rustle of banana palms and
the sound of her steps. Whitewashed houses, like hers, glowed blue
in the moonlight. Clay houses were dark gray. Window shutters
were closed. Doors were bolted. Birdcages hung from the houses'
eaves, where rats could not reach them. Some cages were covered in
cloth, shielding the birds from the night air. Other, less careful owners left their cages uncovered and the birds inside puffed their feathers and stuck their heads beneath their wings. There were large
brown sabiás cramped into their cages and fed malagueta peppers to
improve their singing. There were wild finches with red-tipped
wings. There were fighting canaries, trained to peck out each other's
eyes.

Recently, the caged birds had been disappearing. There was a
thief. Some believed it was a sprite—the copper-skinned caipora
said to be born with backward feet so you could never track him.
Others blamed the boys who had originally caught and sold the
birds, believing they were releasing them and reselling them in the
market. There had been a fight recently when a farmer saw his sabiá
for sale. Some owners had resolved to put their birds indoors, but the
animals made noise, hopping about and pecking at the houses' clay
walls. Others had tied their dogs beneath the birds' cages and wired
the reed doors shut.

Some people suspected Luzia. But just as she had been disqualified from marriage and, in turn, from any chance of a productive life, Victrola was quickly discounted. Thievery—much like being a wife and bearing children—required a certain amount of bravery and skill. How could Victrola silence dogs and unwire cage doors? Also, she kept birds at home. Or Emília did. Their father had given her three azulões, whose feathers molted from black to iridescent blue once a year. Like the other birds in town, they had once been wild, and had been tricked into a too small cage. Still, Emília loved them. Each day, she gave the birds eggshells and cornmeal. Each night she placed them beneath their parents' portrait and gave Luzia a stern look. Emília, unlike everyone else in town, did not underestimate Victrola's capabilities.

A low-lying mist covered the top of the mountain. The air was humid. The trail was slick. Luzia moved up the hill faster. Her leg muscles burned. When she exerted herself, a deep calm overcame her. She felt none of her childhood bitterness. Each September, when manioc was harvested and everyone in town congregated at the mill to pound and press the tubers into flour, Luzia was the one who stayed the longest. She scraped and grated until her good arm burned. On regular days she washed clothes, sewed, and hoisted water jugs to and from the spring. Most days she gladly took on Emília's chores. The work soothed her. She loved the slap of wet laundry against rocks. Loved wringing the clothes so tightly that when they unwound, they squirmed and writhed in her hands, as if alive. She loved pressing the water jugs' cool clay against her arms. Loved the metallic smell of her hands after cranking Aunt Sofia's rusted sewing machine.

When she sewed, no one interrupted Luzia's work. No one corrected her. Even Aunt Sofia looked on silently, nodding her head in approval as Luzia attached lace to the skirts of Communion gowns, made the angled lapels of death suits, or embroidered rows of somber black and purple flowers onto Padre Otto's Lenten robe. When Emília turned the robe inside out and saw that the embroidered stitches were so small and even, the knots so well hidden that the back of the robe was almost as perfectly wrought as the front, she kissed Luzia's cheek and asked for help on her own projects. Emília was a skilled seamstress, but she was more interested in drawing dress designs inspired from her *Fon Fon*s than embroidering dish towels or sewing death suits. When she sewed, Emília did it quickly, impatient to see the final product. Emília liked the results of her work. Luzia liked the work itself. She enjoyed the exactness of taking measurements, the challenge of translating those measurements onto cloth, the precision of cutting that cloth into individual pieces, and the satisfaction of joining those pieces together into a whole.

During her morning walks, Luzia took the steepest trails to the mountain ridge where, before sunrise, she looked over the edge and saw the scrubland below. In the past week it had turned from gray to brown, a sign that the recent rains had trickled down the mountain. The summer drought had stretched into March, then April. Streams had vanished. Dams had emptied. The spring where she and Emília fetched drinking water grew so dry that they had to lie on its edge and scoop out the silty water with tin cups. People were forced to sell their best goats and heifers because they could not sustain them. And Taquaritinga still had water, which was more than most places. On their rides to sewing class, she and Emília passed animal carcasses alongside the road. Farmhouses below the mountain—houses where laundry used to swing from ropes between the spindly juazeiro trees and where children once played in the dusty front yards—were slowly abandoned. People flocked up the mountain to Taquaritinga, where they could get water. They set up tents along the mule trail. Once, these tents were burned in the night. Drunks were blamed, but Luzia heard whispers that it had been locals hoping to protect their water. Everyone was thirsty, including the Hawk. His group had been sighted along the mountain range. They'd attacked Triunfo, a twelve-day trip from Taquaritinga. There were rumors that the Military Police had been dispatched to the area. People in town were nervous, hiding valuables from the police and the cangaceiros. Their sewing professor panicked and spoke of canceling class. He fretted at his desk and did not pass Emília any notes. Emília blamed his disinterest on her short haircut, but Luzia knew better. It was the lack of rain. Everyone was haunted by the prospect of a drought, especially strangers. Those with means had left. The colonel sent his wife, Dona Conceição, to Campina Grande. She made no dress orders. Luzia, Emília, and Aunt Sofia sewed kitchen towels, handkerchiefs, and an occasional shirt for the colonel, but it was barely enough to sustain them.

The colonel gave them goat's milk to make up for the lack of sewing duties. They had grown beans on the tiny strip of land behind their house, and manioc flour was affordable. But they had eaten all of their guineas during the dry months and fresh meat had become a luxury. They could only afford strips of dried, salted beef and Luzia was sick of it—sick of eating cornmeal for breakfast and beans, manioc, and that tough carne-de-sol each afternoon for supper. She craved a bit of steamed pumpkin or a flank of goat, the meat so tender it fell off the bone.

And then it rained. One afternoon, clouds—dark and looming—hung over the mountain. Luzia ignored them. She'd seen many clouds over the dry months, clouds that had darkened the sky and brought the hope of rain, only to sweep past and disappoint her. But Luzia's stiff elbow began to ache, and then the frogs emerged from their dirt tunnels and called out, answering one another's soft croaks. When the rains hit, the ground sizzled. Dust rose, and with it came a scent. Luzia loved the smell of winter rains. It was as if all of the withering plants—the wilted coffee trees, the brown banana palms, the tufts of manioc and stalks of stunted corn—let out a perfume to celebrate. She and Emília abandoned their sewing and ran outside. They dragged the empty clay water jugs outdoors one by one and watched the rain fill them. They laughed and turned their mouths toward the sky. Emília grabbed her special bar of soap and they stood, their dresses wet and clinging, under the dented aluminum drainpipe and washed their hair as they used to do, when they were girls. Even Aunt Sofia laughed and clapped in the open doorway, thanking Jesus and São Pedro. It had been a wonderful afternoon.

Luzia shivered. Her breath was quick. She patted the dried meat in her pocket. Before her stood a clay house. Young plants grew from the muddy ground around it. The roof tiles were slick with moss. Near the house's front window hung a covered cage, its white sheet hovering over the ground like a ghost. Luzia heard no growling, saw no dog post or chain. She edged closer and lifted her good arm. She did not have to strain to reach the cage. Beneath the sheet were tightly woven reeds, their pattern broken by two rope hinges and a latch. Luzia's fingers twisted the wire latch loose. Inside, the bird shuddered. Wire nicked Luzia's finger but she twisted harder. The sheet draped over the cage suddenly slid off. Uncovered, the bird chirped. Luzia tugged the reed door open and ran.

The trail was slick from rain. Her smooth-soled alpercata sandals slid, making Luzia fumble for balance. She fell. Clay covered her hands. Last winter, in that same spot, she'd come across a brick pit. Several men from town had crouched beside the pit, shaping mounds of clay into blocks and setting them to dry. The ground was soft from the rains. The men within the pit had dug past the soil's rocky layer to reach clay. They heaved up large, orange shovelfuls. Their hair had disappeared, slicked back beneath a thick layer of clay. They wore no shirts; their arms and chests were coated in orange earth. Their pants clung, heavy and wet, to their legs. Their feet disappeared into the pit's soft bottom. The diggers had no features, no hair, no scars, no brows or lids. The clay had covered them and erased everything except the clean lines of their bodies. Only their eyes appeared, glistening and dark, standing out against their orange skins. Luzia had not thought that those common farmers—boys she had known in school and men she had often ignored—could be so lovely.

Luzia blushed at the memory. Heat rose in the pit of her stomach. She wiped her hands across her skirt and moved on. The sky was changing; soon, the sun would break over the horizon. Luzia quickened her pace. She had one more house to visit.

Away from the main trail, near the ridge, lived a widower who loved catching sofreus. They were scrubland birds, trapped below the mountain and brought to live in Taquaritinga. They were lovely, with red-crested heads and black wings. But they weren't hardy like sabiás or aggressive like canaries. Their name came from the fact that they suffered in cages, and if caught, they almost always died. Still, the widower on the hill continued to snare them, hoping to prove the legend wrong. Each time Luzia saw him at the weekly market she had the urge to twist his neck.

His house was similar to the first: simple, clay, with closed shutters and surrounded by banana palms and coffee trees. But he had a dog. It was a skinny gray mutt roped to the front porch, beneath the birdcage. When Luzia arrived, the dog stood stiffly at attention. Luzia cut a bit of dried beef with her penknife. She threw the meat to the dog. It sniffed the beef and then the air, as if it did not know which deserved its attention. Luzia smelled it, too. She tried to define the scent around the house but could not. It was musty, like wet chicken feathers, but with a rank sweetness like rotten melon. And something else, something heady and lingering, like billy goats at the market.

The dog took the beef and chewed gingerly, its old teeth rotted. Luzia cut away another piece of meat and stepped toward the house. The sofreu hung on the side eave. There was no cloth over its cage and the bird looked limp, its crest bald and discolored. Luzia moved forward. The dog sniffed the air and circled nervously. She threw it more beef. The mutt snatched it up, then cocked its ears and dropped the meat. The smell grew stronger. The dog let out a low bark. Luzia turned around.

Three men had emerged from the banana palms. The center man wore a large-brimmed leather hat, like a rancher, but with a gold chain around the brim instead of a cloth hatband. His hair settled around his shoulders. He held a thick-barreled pistol. The men on either side of him—one tall, one short—wore leather hats with the brims cracked backward to form half-moons. Only cangaceiros wore such hats. Rifles sat stiffly in their hands. The sun slowly rose behind the men; Luzia could not see their faces. But she could smell them. The animal strength of their scent surprised her. She raised her hand to cover her nose.

"So," the man in the middle said, "you're the bird thief?"

Luzia shuddered at the sound of his voice. It was deep and thick, as if his throat was coated in molasses. He moved closer. There were gold rings on all of his brown fingers. Luzia wondered how he could grip the gun with so many jewels loaded onto his hands. Their clothing was ragged and soiled, but thick cartridge belts circled their waists, each strung with brass-tipped bullets that glimmered in the morning light. Stuffed prominently between their leather belts and the waistbands of their pants were silver knives. The handles had circular knobs that tapered into narrow throats, where the men's hands could grip them. The tall man was a dark-skinned mulatto with finely carved features. The shorter man had kinky hair. And while most men wore beards, these had shaved faces, like priests.

"Are you mute?" the deep-voiced man asked.

His kinky-haired friend giggled and Luzia realized he was not a short man, but a boy.

"No," Luzia said. Her voice trembled and she cleared her throat to remedy it. "I don't steal them. I just open the doors. It's the bird's choice to stay or go."

The central man laughed. His head tipped backward. The shadow cast by his hat brim vanished, revealing his face. Luzia took a breath. On his right cheek was a scar, two fingers thick, which roped from the corner of his thick lips and disappeared beneath his ear. The scar's flesh was lighter than his skin, like a crack in the top of a cake when the batter rises and splits the browned crust. The left side of his mouth opened in a smile, but the scarred side remained serious, paralyzed. He pushed his hat farther back. His fingers were short and thick, like a cluster of bananas.

"This farmer," he said, pointing to the house, "is a friend. He lets us camp here. Gives us water. I do favors for my friends. He has a bird problem. I promised him I'd solve it. I told him I'd shoot the thief, and I'm a man of my word."

Luzia's hands felt cold. Her underarms were wet. Ever since she was a girl, ever since the children poked and prodded her bent arm in the church schoolyard, Luzia had learned what to do when tears threatened. She pressed her lips together, hard, until they grew white and bloodless. Then she released them and the blood rushed back, warm and tingling. She did this over and over, focusing on the pain and the release, and not on her dry throat and stinging eyes.

"You may be lucky," the scarred man continued, "I'm a great respecter of ladies. I don't shoot them. But not all women are ladies. So what are you?"

Luzia's heart drummed against her chest. She was not a lady, not a dona or a senhora. But she certainly wasn't the other kind of woman—the kind Aunt Sofia warned her against. She was Victrola. Useless. Purposeless. She had never called herself by that name, had never said it aloud. Luzia lengthened her neck, pulled back her shoulders, and stepped into the sun.

"I am a seamstress," she said, and the man put down his pistol.

3

As she started down the trail, it began to rain. It fell softly at first, then thickened into large, slapping drops. Luzia would not run. She kept her pace steady, allowing herself to look back only twice. Her heart felt as if it wanted to push through her skin.

Both times she'd turned around, the path was clear. She didn't expect the scarred man to be there. Yet she felt he was everywhere. Hidden. Invisible. Watching her as she made her way home. His smell lingered in her nose. She wanted to sprint, to slide down the slick trail and lock herself in the saints' closet. But she would not give him that satisfaction. He had released her and she had thanked him, but she would not run. Not for his sake.

The rings, rifles, and half-moon hats had instantly given them away as cangaceiros. The Hawk's group was rumored to be in the area; Luzia had heard stories of that cangaceiro leader. He was supposed to be tall, muscular, handsome. The scarred man was none of those things.

At the house, she slipped through the front door. Luzia heard Aunt Sofia shuffling in the kitchen. There was the clang of a pan, the sizzle of butter, the soft crackle of manioc flour poured into the hot skillet. Above her, Luzia heard sharp clinks, like a thousand pins falling onto the roof tiles. She shivered. Her dress was soaked. Her hair hung, heavy and wet, down her back.

In the narrow hall, Emília emerged from their bedroom. Her hair was curled. Her dress was ironed. She caught sight of her sister. Luzia pressed her finger to her mouth. Their aunt would ask a dozen questions that she did not want to answer. Emília rushed to her side.

"You're late for breakfast," Emília hissed. "Tia was worried. Have you caused trouble?" Emília looked toward her azulões. The birds hopped from rung to rung of the cage. She sighed, then looked back at Luzia. Her voice softened. "Your skirt is covered in mud."

"I fell," Luzia choked out.

Emília moved toward her. Her arms were warm, her hair perfumed. Luzia felt the moisture of her dress soaking into her sister's clean frock. She tried to back away from the embrace but Emília held her firmly.

"Come," Emília whispered. "Let's get you changed before Tia has an attack."

In the kitchen, Aunt Sofia padded around the stove. Her feet were as flat and wide as the metal base of the enxada they used to dig in the garden. She lifted manioc hotcakes gingerly from the griddle, folding them into white half-moons and wiping them with butter. The cakes were warm and dry in Luzia's mouth. She left most of them on her plate; it took too much effort to chew. Outside, the rain subsided. The dahlias bowed their heads with the weight of their own petals.

They spent the day in a flurry of chores. Aunt Sofia swept beneath the beds. Emília and Luzia shook out their capim grass mattresses and laid them in the sun. They beat dust from the esteiras that lay across the bed boards, protecting their mattresses from snagging on the rough wood. They swept the brick floor, scrubbed the kitchen table and stone counter with a solution of oranges and vinegar, aired the bed linens, and wrapped cloths around their noses before pouring lye into the clay-lined hole in the outhouse. Luzia lagged behind. Emília prodded her, joked, sang. Luzia smiled at her sister's efforts, but could not push away her thoughts. The men on the ridge were cangaceiros. Should she have warned the colonel? Should she have told Padre Otto? She wanted to take Emília aside and tell her. But what would she say? Luzia rehearsed the words in her mind: *Today I met a man with half a face. He wore a dozen rings. He stuffed a round-handled knife into his belt. There was a boy on one side of him and a man on the other. He threatened me and then he let me go.*

It sounded like a dream. A lie. She'd been relieved when he released her. "Go," he'd said, flicking his hand in the air as if shooing away a bug or a bad thought. But in her relief there was also disappointment. When she'd emerged from that porch, the men had lowered their guns, widened their eyes, and lifted their heads to face her. They had not seen Victrola, but someone else. For an instant Luzia felt a power she could not name. Then, with the flick of his hand, it had disappeared.

It was late afternoon by the time they began to clean the kitchen. Luzia placed the rapadura too close to the cook fire and it melted into a sticky mess. She tripped on a stool. She dropped a dish.

"You're sick," Aunt Sofia proclaimed, pressing her chapped hand to Luzia's forehead. "No more morning walks. No more wandering about. You think I don't know your habits, but I do."

Luzia was about to protest when a knock rattled the back door.

"Who is it?" Aunt Sofia said.

"Sofia!" a shrill voice yelled. "Let me in! Before the hooligans catch me!"

It was Dona Chaves. Aunt Sofia disliked their neighbor because she wore heeled shoes. *Who does she think she is?* Sofia snorted each time Dona Maria Chaves wrung out laundry or fed her chickens in her heeled sandals. According to Aunt Sofia, heeled shoes were reserved for church, and even then, only a discreet heel was appropriate. Day-to-day use of heeled shoes, Sofia often lectured, was something for Dona Conceição, and not for people like Dona Chaves, a saddle-maker's wife. Luzia undid the bolts on the door and lifted away the wooden crossbar.

Dona Chaves scurried inside. She opened her mouth but no words came. The loose flap of skin under her chin trembled and swayed with each deep breath. Finally, her hand fluttered over her chest and she gasped, "Cangaceiros!"

Emília led her to the kitchen table. Luzia grabbed a tin mug and dunked it into one of the water jugs. She held the mug to their neighbor's lips and Dona Chaves gulped so fast that a small line of water ran from the side of her wrinkled mouth and down her chin.

"They killed both of the colonel's capangas," she sputtered after handing the mug back to Luzia. "They caught one capanga on the road. Such a young man! Gutted." She breathed in again. "Slashed open, from here"—Dona Chaves pointed a wrinkled finger to her neck—"to here." She crisscrossed the finger down her chest to the bottom of her stomach, then shook her head. "And his eyes were missing, cut out of his head!"

Luzia's grip loosened on the tin mug. It tipped, dribbling water along her wrist. Luzia took a breath and set the mug down. "Did you see it?" she asked.

Dona Chaves looked up, startled. "God help me if I did!"

"Then how do you know it's true?" Luzia asked. Emília hushed her.

"They kidnapped Mr. Chaves, Victrola," Dona Chaves replied, her voice cracking.

"I'm sorry," Luzia said, sitting beside their neighbor. On her upper lip Dona Chaves had a large mole that looked like a black bean. When she spoke, the mole bobbed up and down and Luzia had the urge to take a napkin and brush it off, as if Dona Chaves were a small child, a messy eater.

"They found him hiding under his stand," their neighbor continued. "They sequestered him to fix their hats and sandals!"

Mr. Chaves worked with leather. He spent most of his time curing hides and crafting saddles commissioned by the colonel.

Mr. Chaves spent weeks burning designs into the leather, adding rivets and decorative buckles, extra cushioning on the seat, and tiny braided sections on the bit and bridle. Only the colonel could afford such things. Most days, Mr. Chaves stood at a small stand at the edge of the outdoor market and repaired people's worn alpercata sandals—nailing new straps onto the hard leather bases and adding fat strips of rubber to the soles.

"They told me he was trembling when they led him away!" Dona Chaves held a handkerchief to her eyes even though she was not crying. Aunt Sofia stood beside her.

"My kitchen is a mess." Dona Chaves gulped. "I hid all the chickens inside."

Aunt Sofia patted Dona Chaves's back.

"Did they take anyone else?" Emília asked. Their neighbor nodded and held on to the edge of the table, a gesture Luzia recognized from Dona Chaves's weekly visits. She performed this dramatic pause each time she delivered some bit of gossip—the butcher's broken love affair, how Dona Ester's prize pumpkin was stolen right off the vine, how Severino Santos stole manure from his neighbor, scooping it right out from under their shared fence, and how his neighbor responded by killing Severino's dog with a ball of poison wrapped in goat meat. Dona Chaves informed them that she had crept from house to house that afternoon; that was how she'd heard of her husband's abduction. "There were two visiting soldiers. They're killed, strung up in the square," Dona Chaves informed them. "*He* won't allow anyone to touch them. *He* will kill anyone who tries to bury them."

"Who?" Emília asked.

"The Hawk!" Dona Chaves whispered, as if the dreaded cangaceiro was in the other room. Aunt Sofia crossed herself. The soldiers, Dona Chaves informed them, had been part of a group sent from Caruaru to patrol smaller towns in the region. The rumor was that they were set to reunite with their battalion the next day. "What will happen when they don't show up?" Dona Chaves asked. "I'll tell you what: the monkeys will track them here. They'll invade."

Luzia's mouth felt dry. She could not look at her sister or her aunt. Their town hadn't been invaded by troops or cangaceiros in Luzia's lifetime. They didn't owe this safety to the current Colonel Pereira, who was a businessman and not a fighter. They'd had such a long stint of peace because Taquaritinga was a mountain town, making it hard to reach. Thieves wanted merchandise or money, soldiers wanted entertainment, and cangaceiros wanted all of those things. Taquaritinga had no lucrative ranches, no large shops or dance halls; for many, the long hike up its precarious mountain trail was not worth the effort. Unless they wanted water. During the dry months, water and food were the town's most precious commodities, but these things were readily available in the farms along the mountainside. Often, travelers went unnoticed in the hills. This made the town forget about outside threats and focus on its own petty rivalries, its family fights, its small scandals. Only the colonel's two capangas carried pistols; everyone else was content with their sharp peixeiras and a few rusted hunting rifles that shot small chumbo pellets. They would be no match for a group of cangaceiros.

Shame settled, heavy and sour, in Luzia's belly. It tightened the tendons in her neck. It made her ears burn. If she had spoken earlier, Padre Otto could have rung the church bells in alarm. People could have prepared. Luzia hadn't thought of the consequences of her silence. She'd wanted to keep her encounter with the cangaceiros to herself. She'd wanted to hoard it and later, to turn it over in her mind, the same way Emília stashed *Fon Fon* magazines beneath their bed and read them at night with a lantern. Luzia had watched her many times; Emília stared at those pale models, those perfect cityscapes, those ads for rice powder and egg-oil hair creams. Emília turned the pages carefully. Her plucked brows furrowed, her eyes shone. Luzia had never felt such concentrated wanting, such avarice. *I can't help myself,* Emília said once when Aunt Sofia chided her. Luzia had not understood her sister then. Anything could be helped; anything could be pushed out of a person's mind if they tried hard enough. She knew better now.

"There're twenty cangaceiros," Dona Chaves continued. "He's got them posted along the trail to Vertentes. No one can leave." She went on to tell the rest of the afternoon's news: the Hawk had sacked the town's two stores. Xavier had locked the doors to his shop and the cangaceiros had broken in. They turned over tubs of manioc flour and beans; they knifed open massive jute bags of coffee beans and held them over their shoulders like bodies, pouring their contents onto the floor. They stomped on Xavier's stock of salted meats and codfish with their dirty sandals. But Zé Muela had left the doors to his shop open, and the outlaws strode in like patrons. Zé Muela stood behind his counter, dutifully packaging all of the items the cangaceiros picked out: five kilos of coffee, three kilos of rapadura to sweeten the coffee, five kilos of salted beef, manioc flour and beans, and ten cans of brilliantine hair paste. The Hawk set three pure gold coins on the counter. "One from 1786!" Dona Chaves said and slapped the table.

He took all of the ammunition from Xavier's back room. He called on Padre Otto, who gave Holy Communion to the whole lot of them, then asked the Hawk to show mercy on the town and its residents. "He's taken over the colonel's house," Dona Chaves said, then requested more water.

Aunt Sofia ignored Dona Chaves's thirst. She shoved past their neighbor and closed the window shutters. She slid the metal bolts into their holes along the sides of the kitchen door. Then she shoved a wooden beam diagonally across the top part of the door. The room was dark.

They huddled in the kitchen for the rest of the afternoon. Aunt Sofia prayed, alternating between oaths to São Dimas, the protector against thieves, and the Virgin. She dozed off occasionally. Luzia heard her aunt's prayers grow softer, saw her head bob and her chin slowly rest on her chest. She jolted awake each time shots were fired outside. They left their chairs when they heard the gunshots—loud pops coming from the direction of the town square and followed by a succession of hoots and whistles—and peeked through the broken slats in the window shutters. There was nothing to see.

Emília lit a candle and split three oranges for their dinner. They put out the fire in the cookstove, dousing the kindling so that smoke would not emerge from the roof tiles.

"You shouldn't sleep alone tonight," Aunt Sofia said, patting Dona Chaves's hand. "It isn't safe."

"I won't be any trouble," Dona Chaves said. "I assure you."

Dona Chaves's poor back prohibited her from sleeping in a hammock, and Emília and Luzia's bed was much too soft for her old bones. After much cajoling, Dona Chaves agreed to take Aunt Sofia's bed. Luzia strung up their old cloth hammock across the front room. Emília brought her a blanket and lingered there, picking at the tangled fringe that dangled along the hammock's sides. As little girls, they had twisted the white strings into tight braids, ripping them out and starting over again, until the fringe became uneven and snarled.

"I don't want to sleep with Tia," Emília pouted. "She kicks."

"Then sleep with Dona Chaves," Luzia whispered.

"No! She smells like chickens!"

They burst into giggles. Emília almost dropped her candle. Luzia covered her mouth.

"Girls!" Aunt Sofia shouted from their room.

"Good night," Emília said. She kissed Luzia's cheek and walked away, taking the candlelight with her.

As a child, Luzia had slept comfortably in that hammock, pretending she was a seed in a pod. But she had grown since then. Her feet popped out of one side, and when she tried to adjust them, her head popped from the other. Luzia could not sleep. She closed her eyes and recalled the men from that morning. The boy was no more than thirteen. The mulatto was older—in his twenties perhaps. The scarred man seemed both old and young at the same time. Was he the Hawk? Had he done the things Dona Chaves spoke of?

The way to tell a fine piece of embroidery was to look at the back. Aunt Sofia had taught her this. Luzia always turned over any embroidered nightgown or wedding dress or handkerchief and inspected the stitching. By looking at the back stitching, she could see how many times the thread was knotted and how small the knots were. If a seamstress was sloppy, they were large and few. If she was lazy, there were diagonal marks running across the back of the design because she had not bothered to cut and knot and then rethread her needle. The stitching told her everything. But people were not as easy to decipher.

The night was quiet. There were no more gunshots, no more hoots or hollers. Mosquitoes buzzed in Luzia's ears, fed on her feet. She rubbed one foot with the other. She did not know how long she lay there, falling in and out of sleep, before she heard music in the distance—long, sad notes squeezed from an accordion. She shifted and almost whispered, "Do you hear that?" but realized that Emília was not there. She was awake as well, Luzia was sure of it, and she wanted to call out to her, wanted to tiptoe into their room and crawl into their bed, pressing her face to her sister's back, as she had since they were children, settling into Emília's warmth.

She slept fitfully in the hammock, slapping away mosquitoes and shivering in the early morning cold. When she finally nodded off, she slept well past her prayer time. She awoke to loud knocking. For an instant, she believed it was the saints in their closet, angry because she had forgotten them. Luzia nearly fell from the hammock.

"Mary Mother of God!" Dona Chaves cried from the far room.

The knock came once more, louder this time. "Come out!" a man yelled.

Aunt Sofia entered the front room. She wore a shawl over her nightgown. Dona Chaves clutched her arm.

"They've discovered my chickens!" their neighbor hissed.

Aunt Sofia shooed Luzia away from the front door, then unbolted it. Emília and Dona Chaves crowded at the window, competing to catch a glimpse of who stood outside. Luzia peeked over their heads. It was the boy from the ridge. His kinky hair had been washed and slicked back. His jacket was threadbare but clean. Four leather knife sheaths dangled from his belt, two on each side, within close reach of his hands. Each sheath held a different-size knife: one long and thin, another the length of a hand, one very thick, and one slightly curved. He was accompanied by an older cangaceiro Luzia did not recognize. His ears were so large and round that they bent beneath the leather rim of his hat. His lips were pinched, like the drawstrings of Luzia's sewing purse. He had a rifle slung over his shoulder.

"You work for the colonel?" He addressed Aunt Sofia.

Their aunt hesitated. Her lips moved and Luzia knew she murmured a prayer under her breath. The boy cangaceiro stepped closer to the house. He looked into the window and spotted them. Dona Chaves gasped. Emília quickly closed the shutter.

"Yes," Aunt Sofia replied. "I do. I sew for him."

The boy whispered to the big-eared man, then motioned to the house.

"You're the only one," the man asked, "who sews?"

"No." Aunt Sofia hesitated, glancing toward the window. "My nieces help me. But they're just girls. They have no talent."

"Doesn't matter," the cangaceiro said. "Get dressed and get outside—you and whoever helps you."

"For what?" Aunt Sofia said.

"To work," the big-eared cangaceiro replied. "The captain wants a seamstress."

4

They were a strange procession: a cangaceiro boy carting Aunt Sofia's ancient sewing machine on his shoulder; three women holding hands, heads bowed, lips moving in prayer; and the big-eared man walking behind them all, his hand on his gun, his eyes darting in all directions. The town's streets were empty, but Luzia saw faces peeking from behind window shutters and between the cracks of doors.

At the square Luzia heard buzzing, as if a swarm of bees was circling. Slumped against the flamboyant trees' crooked trunks were two uniformed soldiers and the colonel's capangas, stripped of their black boots and leather hats. Without their boots, their feet looked soft and white, like infants'. They were tied back-to-back against the trees and their heads lolled sideways, as if whispering to each other. Flies filled their open mouths, their eyes, their bellies. The insects moved in a great, iridescent mass, making the bodies seem to twitch with life. Beneath the men, sliding down their pale feet, were dark puddles.

"Look away," Aunt Sofia ordered. Emília obeyed, shielding her eyes. Luzia did not.

She had seen blood before—she had killed turkeys and chickens. All her life she had witnessed the Saturday-morning slaughter near the market in town. The cattle strung up onto two wooden posts, their hindquarters facing the air, their necks bent beneath the weight of their own bodies. The butcher's sons skinned them from tail to head, slicing the hide away with their knives, and stray dogs sniffed and licked the blood, which ran from the cattle's open mouths and mixed with the dirt. She had also once seen the rigid body of a criminal in the town square, his face and chest white from the quicklime that the colonel had ordered poured on the corpse in order to preserve it. But Luzia had never seen a man's blood flowing from him. For an instant, she had the urge to touch the soldiers' blood, to see if it was still warm. Then a terrible queasiness overtook her. Luzia covered her mouth and held Emília's hand.

Colonel Pereira looked weary. He stood at the gate, relieved to see them. His capangas had been replaced by two cangaceiros who propped their sandaled feet against the colonel's white wall, smearing it with dirt. The men were freshly washed, their foul smell muted, their wet hair soaking the backs of their tunics and staining the leather canteen straps that crisscrossed their chests. The cangaceiros stared at Emília, who crossed her arms over her bosom. Luzia moved closer to her sister. One of the men placed his brown fingers in his mouth. He let out a whistle so shrill and loud it made Luzia jump. Two more cangaceiros appeared at the gate. The men took possession of the sewing machine and each of their sewing bags before walking toward the house.

"They've promised to be respectful, Sofia," the colonel whispered. "They want new clothing. Nothing more."

Aunt Sofia nodded. She did not take her eyes from the colonel's. "My nieces aren't women, Colonel," she said. "They're still moças. I won't have them leave here any different."

"I don't control these men, Sofia," the colonel said, shaking his head. "But I have their word."

"Do you trust a cangaceiro's word?" Aunt Sofia asked, her voice stern. "I don't."

The colonel straightened. He took Aunt Sofia's hand. "Then trust mine. Whatever happens inside these gates, outside them your girls will still have their honor."

Luzia placed her hand on Emília's back, steadying her. Her sister breathed quickly, her face turning sallow and dull, like a dead banana leaf. Luzia guessed Emília's fears because they were her own: a moça became a woman on the first night with her husband, never before. Or, in Luzia's case, if marriage was not an option, she had to live and die a moça, with her honor always intact. Girls who gave themselves without marriage were considered lost. Ruined, like a stained dress or a burnt cake. Luzia held Emília's wet palm, unsure if the sweat was her sister's or her own. If the cangaceiros didn't keep their word, the colonel would protect only their reputations. Luzia suddenly hated the colonel. Hated his trimmed mustache and his slicked gray hair. Hated his calm.

"Our honor's not below our stomachs," Luzia said, her voice shaking.

Emília coughed. The colonel reddened, then stared at Aunt Sofia as if waiting for her to reproach Luzia. When their aunt stayed silent, the colonel turned and led them from the gate.

The colonel's yard was filled with men, camped wherever there was shade. Three of them swung back and forth on the porch hammock, its cloth spread taut from their weight. Six men sprawled in the grass beneath the colonel's avocado tree and smoked thickly rolled cigarettes, giddy from the tobacco. Two men buffed their alpercata sandals on the porch steps. Chicken bones were scattered around them, picked clean and shining with grease and saliva. They looked to Luzia like a swarm of strange white insects—albino cicadas ready to take flight.

Aunt Sofia gasped. Two young cangaceiros, soapy and naked, ran from the service area behind the house, splashing each other with water from metal pails. Their bodies were the color of coffee and milk, but their hands and faces were as dark as cured leather. It looked as if they wore masks and gloves.

"Dear Lord!" Aunt Sofia cried. She tried to cover Luzia's eyes but could not reach. She cupped her big-knuckled hands over Emília's instead.

"I apologize," the colonel said. "They refuse to bathe in the house. They insist on bathing near the laundry tank. They've ordered my maids to wash their filthy underclothes in the kitchen sink, in the bathing basin."

"Pigs," Aunt Sofia hissed.

"I don't know what I'll tell my wife when she returns," the colonel said. He rubbed his eyes. "Thank goodness Felipe isn't here."

The colonel's only son, Felipe, studied law at the Federal University in Recife. The colonel had allowed him to move to the capital on the condition that he would come back eventually and run the ranch. Behind the colonel's back, most people doubted Felipe would ever return. He was a freckled, handsome young man ten years older than Luzia. He slicked his hair and carried a cane instead of a peixeira knife. Unlike the sons of other colonels, Felipe had never disgraced a local girl. His father did not have to pay families a monthly allowance in order to bring up bastard children. Luzia had overheard the colonel declare wistfully that, in his youth, his own father had had to give away two goats each year as compensation for his son's dalliances. But Felipe was no pai-de-chiqueiro, the colonel sighed, as if his son had forsaken his birthright. People in town also took offense at Felipe's disinterest in their daughters. They secretly called the colonel's boy "Pig Eyes" because of his pale lashes and hazel irises. Felipe was an avid horseman, and on the rare occasions when he visited Taquaritinga he spent his days riding his prize mare, or lolling in the porch hammock for hours, watching the street but never setting foot in it. Long before he'd left for law school, Emília had tried to attract Felipe's attention. Each time they'd delivered their sewing to the colonel's house Emília had attempted to engage him in conversation, but he rolled his eyes and looked away. Luzia thought him a terrible snot. She was disappointed Pig Eyes wasn't present for the cangaceiros' visit.

From the colonel's porch there came another whistle, higher and more melodic.

"He's calling us," the colonel said, guiding them up the steps.

The scarred man sat before a small mahogany table, his face partially covered in shaving foam. His long hair was dark and wet, tied behind his neck with a bit of twine. The tall mulatto, who Luzia recognized from the ridge, now held a mirror before the scarred man's face. A porcelain basin and water jug sat on the table alongside a tattered leather pouch. Arranged in a line on the pouch were a gold razor, gold clippers, and small gold scissors. The man swished his golden straight razor in the water basin and scraped the blade against his cheek. Luzia could see the path of his scar better now, with his hair tied back. It ran from his mouth all the way behind his ear, where it turned paler, thinner.

The colonel cleared his throat. "Here are the seamstresses. This is Dona Sofia and these are her nieces, Emília and Victrola."

The man continued to shave. He wore a dirty cotton tunic untucked over his pants. His feet were bare and thickly calloused. His toes budded from them like the growths of old potatoes stored too long in the pantry. He stared into his shaving mirror, looking not at his reflection but at the guests behind him. He scanned Luzia quickly. She felt relief, but beneath it, prickling like a splinter, was disappointment. She couldn't tell if he'd actually forgotten her or was simply pretending, and she wasn't sure which option bothered her most. He tapped his razor against the porcelain basin, as if calling his visitors to attention.

"My men need some new undershirts," he said. "New jackets and pants."

He went on to explain that there were bolts of fabric in the house and plenty of thread, but Luzia barely listened. He shaved as he spoke, and she watched him move the blade gingerly around his thick scar, as if it still pained him. *My men,* he'd said, and as his face emerged from underneath the shaving foam, Luzia understood that he was the leader. He was the Hawk.

"We'll need everyone's clothes," Aunt Sofia announced. "To trace."

"All right," the Hawk said. "Then my men will be naked this afternoon."

"Dear Lord!" Aunt Sofia said, holding tightly to her rosary. "We don't need the clothes. We'll measure everyone."

"Of course," the Hawk chuckled, extending his chin and shaving the underside of his brown neck. "That's why I sent for you."

5

Without their half-moon hats, their cartridge belts, their rifles and silver-handled knives, they were long-haired boys. Their clothing was shabby. Their feet were bare. Their hair fell to their shoulders or curled in kinky masses at their ears. The Hawk walked up and down the line like a father examining his sons, telling them to stand up straight, slapping them on the shoulders, ruffling their freshly washed hair. They took turns—some stood in the measuring line, while others put on their hats and belts and stood guard at the gate.

If pants were requested, Aunt Sofia insisted on performing the measurements herself. Luzia was only permitted to measure above the waist. Emília followed them with a writing tablet and a thick pencil, nervously jotting down the men's measurements alongside their names. They were not proper names but childish and odd designations. Some were named for trees and birds, others for places.

Some had names that fit their looks: Jacaré had a mouth full of large white teeth; Caju's nose was as hooked and brown as a massive cashew nut; and Branco was the lightest skinned of the bunch, with a sunburned face and dozens of freckles. Some names were their opposites: the big-eared cangaceiro called himself Little Ear; a stocky young man with drooping eyes and slurred speech introduced himself as Inteligente. Then there were names that made no sense, except to the cangaceiros themselves. There was Canjica, a sharp-eyed man with a limp and graying hair who seemed to be the oldest of the bunch. The kinky-haired boy called himself Ponta Fina. He was the youngest of the group. His teeth reminded Luzia of sugar cubes— very white and square, but with brown, bumpy edges, as if they were slowly dissolving in his mouth. There was a young man who called himself Chico Coffin, and another with a milky eye the color of curdled cream who called himself Half-Moon. There was Safety Pin, Jurema, and Sabiá. The tall mulatto was Baiano. The man with skin as dark and shining as a beetle husk was named Sweet Talker. And the Hawk was never called Hawk, but Captain.

"You," he said to Luzia before she could measure her first man. "You measure me."

The scarless side of his face moved too much—twisting and rising as if pulled by invisible strings. It was boyish and animated. But the slack side of his face was placid, serious. It looked sensible, as if it did not approve of the other side's behavior. Despite the scar, the right half of his mouth moved slightly, the lips barely opening and closing as he spoke. His right eye blinked slowly, languidly, as if winking. The eye had a teary glaze. He dabbed it with a handkerchief and then walked into the yard, far removed from the line of men.

Luzia looked to her aunt and her sister. Aunt Sofia crossed herself, then motioned for Luzia to go. Emília looked confused.

Luzia stood before the Hawk and held out the measuring tape, stretching her good arm as long as it would go. Her fingers pressed against the metal rivets at the ends of the cloth tape and she studied it intently, searching the hand-drawn numbers—the ticks of centimeters and meters—as if the tape would reveal some great mystery, or at least tell her how she should comport herself.

"What would you like?" she asked, her eyes focused on the strip of tape. When she looked at him, the skin of Luzia's scalp and along the back of her neck seemed to shrink.

"What can you make?"

"Anything." Her hands felt rubbery and useless and she disliked him for making her feel so clumsy.

"Then measure me for anything," he said.

Luzia sighed. She never enjoyed measuring the living. The living squirmed, asked questions, looked curiously at her arm as she bent and stretched her body to compensate for its limited range. When weeping families knocked on their door requesting a death suit, it was always Luzia who took the deceased's measurements. The colonel already had his death suit prepared and hanging in his closet—a fancy double-breasted affair made of the thinnest, softest linen Luzia had ever touched. But other families, modest families, had to order death suits and gowns after the fact. Emília hated it; she felt squeamish at the thought of a body. But Luzia preferred the silence, the solemnity, the importance that came with measuring the dead. Some bodies, depending on the cause of death, were in better shape than others. But most were laid flat on beds or tables, and Luzia had to circle them, careful not to overturn the bowls of water filled with lemon and orange slices laid out around the corpse to take away the smell. She slipped the tape around their wrists and across their chests. She always estimated the back and shoulder and waist measurements, so the family would not be forced to move the body. They would sew the suit as quickly as possible for the wake and funeral—among the three of them, they could make a simple suit or burial gown in a few hours—and Luzia always felt warmly satisfied when the suits and gowns fit perfectly, when her secret estimates proved correct.

"I'll measure you for a jacket and shirt, then," Luzia said, forcing herself to face him.

His nose was long, its bridge mashed. His tunic was stained yellow at the neck and under the arms. Beneath the scent of shaving soap and the colonel's sandalwood aftershave was the heady, animal scent from the other morning. Luzia pointed to the green silk bandanna tied around his neck.

"You'll have to take that off," she said. She would measure him as she measured the dead—quickly and quietly, estimating as much as she could.

He obliged. His hands were dark and ridged with veins. The rings he wore—one on each thick finger—clinked against each other as he unknotted the bandanna and bunched it in his hand. He loosened the top two buttons of his tunic as well, and beneath the scarf and shirt was a tangle of gold chains and red string. She was surprised to see a small golden cross dangling from one of the chains; the other necklaces held a collection of saints' medallions. Luzia almost reached out to touch them, to ask him which saints he worshipped, which ones he asked for help and guidance. Instead, she slid the measuring tape around his neck and pinched it closed with her fingers. He was shorter than she was—Emília's height—and she had to lean in to read the tape. There was a nick in his neck, from shaving no doubt, and a spot of blood bubbled from his tan skin. Luzia wondered about his body—was he pale like the bathing boys? Or was he dark all over? Her face grew hot.

"Thirty-seven centimeters," she said, and held the tape in place. Luzia looked back at the row of men, at Emília with her pad and pencil. "I have nowhere to write it."

"I'll remember it," he said. His breath smelled spicy. His mouth felt too close to her face and she backed away, moving to measure the back of his body.

Luzia held the tape along his back, from shoulder to shoulder, pressing the edges firmly with her fingers. "Fifty-one centimeters," she said.

"How tall are you?" he asked.

"One meter ninety."

He whistled. "You're taller than my man Baiano."

Luzia turned and spotted the hulking mulatto who'd held the mirror earlier. Aunt Sofia stood on her tiptoes beside him, trying to reach his neck. "Yes. I suppose so."

Luzia held the tape from the base of his neck to his shoulder, and in the middle of this measured space, where a dip should be, there was a large lump. She slid her fingers along the tape and felt the mound.

"It's a callous," he said. His voice startled her.

"I was only making certain it didn't alter the measurement."

"We all have them," he continued. "Bullets and water are heavy." He twisted his neck to look at her.

"It must be a relief to put those things down," Luzia said, avoiding his gaze.

He laughed. "We're like oxen with their cangas. They get so used to those wood collars that they can't live without them. I need my things to weigh me down or else I don't feel right. I feel too light."

Luzia nodded. "Lift your arms."

She measured from shoulder to wrist. Fifty-eight centimeters.

"Pardon me," he said, lowering his arms. "What is your name? Your given name."

"Luzia."

"And that"—he pointed to her arm—"is why they call you Victrola?"

"Yes," she said. She felt embarrassed and strangely giddy. "It wasn't always this way. It was an accident."

She had finished all of the measurements required for a simple jacket. She could walk away. She could call Aunt Sofia to measure his pants. But she continued to press the tape to him, as if fitting him for a fancy dress shirt. Luzia tried to wrap the tape around his waist but tucked into his belt was the silver-handled knife. Two gold rings were molded onto its bulbous top.

The Hawk shifted it within his belt. "Measure around it. Please."

Luzia slid the tape under the knife handle and around his waist.

Seventy-eight centimeters. He was thinner than she had imagined— the hat and bullet harnesses he'd worn earlier had made him look larger. But the tape showed her that he was a small man, a lean man. "No fat, no flavor," Aunt Sophia always said before selecting a chicken from their backyard brood. Luzia measured from his collarbone to his upper thigh. "Sixty-six centimeters," she said.

"That bird from yesterday," he interrupted. "The sofreu. It's dead."

"Oh?" Luzia said, startled. He remembered her after all.

"It got sick," the Hawk continued. The brow on the good side of his face rose. "Did you curse it?"

"No," Luzia said, keeping her voice low. "Curses don't exist. It was already weak. Sofreus aren't pets."

"That's a foolish bird, don't you think?"

"Why?"

The Hawk shrugged. "It's hardheaded. All it had to do was make its owner happy. All it had to do was sing for him, and it would've had shade and fresh water. An easy life."

"It sings for itself," Luzia mumbled. "Maybe it didn't want an easy life."

"Then what did it want?"

Luzia faced him. "I wouldn't know," she said. "I'm not a bird."

"No," he said, the left side of his mouth rising in a smile. "You're a thief."

The words stung, like a hundred prickling ant bites. Heat filled Luzia's chest. It rushed through her arms, making her fingers feel thick. The measuring tape fell from her hand. Luzia crouched to retrieve it. The Hawk followed her.

"I was playing," he said. "Pardon me."

"I'm not a thief," Luzia said.

"I know."

He handed her the tape. There was a stain around his right cuff—a reddish brown splattering—a color Luzia had seen countless time before, when they cut their chickens' throats and let the blood flow into a bowl with vinegar, or in the middle of each month when she felt a heaviness in the bottom of her stomach and would go to the outhouse and see that her knickers were stained. Luzia took the tape from his hand. She began to roll it tightly, focusing all of her energy into making it into a perfect, rigidly wound ball. She stared at his cuff. The blood, she reasoned, could be anyone's. It could be his own.

"I'm finished here," she said.

The Hawk nodded, then held out his hand. "I didn't properly introduce myself. I'm Antônio."

Those hands, Luzia thought, had done terrible things. Those hands had sinned. But they looked no different from any working-man's hands—the tops tanned, the knuckles dry, the palms rough like uncured leather. The only difference was the jewelry. Some of the gold rings on his fingers were dented and misshapen, their stones foggy, but they fit each of his fingers so snugly that they looked as if they had been welded on at birth.

His hand was warm, the grip firm. His rings pinched the skin of her palm. Her eyes focused again on the stained cuff and when he saw her staring at it, he retracted his arm and stepped away.

6

They worked in the colonel's sitting room. The sewing room could not hold three seamstresses and two Singers, so the cangaceiros carried Dona Conceição's new machine and Aunt Sofia's old one into the largest room in the house. Emília ran the pedal-operated Singer. Aunt Sofia used her sewing machine with the help of Ponta Fina, who turned the stiff, circular handle. Luzia had hoped to talk to her sister when they were alone, but the young cangaceiro's presence made them wary and tense. They all worked quietly except for Aunt Sofia.

"Faster," she grunted as she slid precut jacket and pants panels through the machine's needle. Ponta Fina turned the handle quickly. "No! Slower, slower," Aunt Sofia said, careful not to yell at the boy.

Luzia cut the cloth. The cangaceiros had stolen three bolts of strong bramante fabric. The Hawk had purchased another bolt—a finer bramante, thinner and less canvaslike—for himself. Luzia read Emília's notes and marked each man's measurements on the tan fabric with a charcoal pencil. She used her bent arm to steady the cloth and with her mobile arm she held her sewing scissors and sliced though the bramante in long sweeps.

When she was a girl—just when she was beginning to learn how to sew—Luzia had her accident and suddenly her arm became a burden. She didn't know how to maneuver herself. She dropped eggs and plates. Anything that required two hands took a tortuous amount of time: making up the bed, bathing, dipping a chicken in hot water and plucking off its steaming feathers without burning her fingers, running the hand-cranked sewing machine. Aunt Sofia refused to help her. "I won't raise an incompetent in my house," she declared each time Luzia stormed off into the banana grove, sick of fumbling with her rigid arm.

When Luzia was thirteen, Dona Conceição ordered an expensive piece of Portuguese silk for slips and undergarments. Aunt Sofia made Luzia cut it. Luzia stood before the silk, knowing that they had to be frugal with the material, that if she made a crooked cut, much of it would be wasted and Dona Conceição would be livid. Aunt Sofia stood beside her. Luzia placed the slippery silk on a table and switched the scissors back and forth between her hands. "You must do this now or you will never do it," Aunt Sofia said. There was a pinching feeling at the tip of Luzia's nose, as if someone were twisting it. Her eyes grew warm and wet. "Don't waste your tears," Aunt Sofia said, as she always did when she found Luzia or Emília crying, as if tears were precious things, as if you were born with a limited supply and had to preserve them for truly important moments. Luzia grew up believing this. But Emília got angry each time Aunt Sofia chided her for crying over silly or inexplicable things. *I want to waste them! They're my tears to waste!* Emília would roar. Luzia stared at that costly silk and wanted to weep as her sister did—not suppressing her tears or locking herself in the saints' closet—but crying loudly and breathlessly, for everyone to hear. Aunt Sofia took her hand and held it under her own. "If you want to be a seamstress, you can never be afraid. You must cut. Cut straight and cut fast." And together they sliced through the silk so quickly that Luzia didn't have time to make a mistake. Just like that, she lost her fear.

Luzia placed the bramante cutouts according to size around the room. The front and back panels of cangaceiro jackets hung over Dona Conceição's wicker-backed settee. The loose legs of slacks were draped across her chairs. The tubes of sleeves lay in neat piles on her glass-paneled liquor cabinets. The only measurements Luzia had not written down were the Hawk's. *Antônio*, Luzia thought, then chided herself. Each time a cangaceiro appeared at the sitting room door, Emília and Aunt Sofia stopped pedaling. Luzia did not look up from her work. Instead, she kept her eyes on the fabric, afraid of making a crooked cut. To their surprise, the cangaceiros did not bother or threaten them. Instead, they delivered cups of water and, later, plates of rice and chicken for lunch. It had been so long since Luzia had tasted chicken that she ate each piece slowly, stripping every bit of meat from the fragile bones and tendons. Ponta Fina gulped down his lunch at the far end of the sitting room.

"Luzia," Emília whispered, her eyes on the young cangaceiro. "You need to cut more slowly."

"I'm going as slow as I can," Luzia hissed.

They had heard of cangaceiros sacrificing their helpers once their work was done. That way, there would be no witnesses to describe them. As long as there was still sewing to do, they were safe. They'd worked straight through the morning and had only finished eight trousers and seven jackets. But there were only twenty uniforms to make and their pattern was simple; the cangaceiros would expect experienced seamstresses to finish quickly.

"The colonel will protect us," Aunt Sofia said. "I'm sure of it."

After lunch, as Luzia measured and cut her last jacket, she heard voices rise and fall through the open windows. She heard the colonel's and then Antônio's voice, unmistakable in its tone and depth. But the sewing machines clattered so loudly that she could not determine what, exactly, they were saying. Luzia kept cutting, but when the voices rose to yells she looked nervously at Emília. Her sister slowed her pedaling. They heard a clatter—a cup or dish falling and breaking, and then a gunshot. It echoed through the house. Luzia's cut went crooked. The sewing machines stopped.

The colonel appeared at the door, pale and sweating. He held a handkerchief—one that Luzia herself had sewn—to his white hairline.

"Nothing to worry over, ladies," he said. "It was a misfire." His eyes flitted around the room, falling on the chairs and tables draped with finished and unfinished uniforms. "Keep at it," the colonel said, nodding, then backed out of the room.

Minutes later, the Hawk stood at the edge of her cutting table. Luzia did not look up. He recited his measurements one by one. Luzia jotted them on the writing tablet.

"My man Baiano—the tall one—will have two suits," the Hawk said. "Make him two suits."

Luzia nodded.

When the colonel's grandfather clock let out six long clangs, they had only four jackets to go. Luzia took over for Aunt Sofia, who rested on the settee. Kerosene lanterns sat beside the sewing machines. The lanterns hissed and sputtered, heating the air around them. Luzia wiped sweat from her neck. She kept her perfectly wound measuring tape close by, to check any odd swatches. Emília stopped every half hour to stretch her legs. She had been switching feet to pump the pedals, but by dusk, she complained that her toes were numb. One by one, the cangaceiros had picked up their pants and jackets. Some had thanked them, others had simply taken their clothes without a word. A bonfire crackled outside, and as the sky grew dark, the firelight made shadows in the sitting room. The men threw their old uniforms into the fire. They hooted and sang as the rotten cloth burned.

At six fifteen, Little Ear entered the sitting room. He wore his new uniform. Without his hat, his long hair masked his ears.

"The captain wants you outside," he said.

"Who?" Aunt Sofia asked, rising from the settee.

"All of you."

"But we still have work to do," Emília said nervously.

"Now," Little Ear said. "Don't dawdle."

The men stood in a semicircle in the yard. The bonfire burned alongside them. The Hawk stood in the middle of this half circle and the colonel knelt before him, his head bowed.

"Kneel," the Hawk ordered.

He motioned for them to take places beside the colonel. The firelight bloomed and faded along the slack side of his face. Luzia helped Aunt Sofia to the ground. Emília knelt on the other side of their aunt. Luzia held her measuring tape, wound into a tight ball, between her hands. She squeezed it. Luzia wanted to speak, to tell him that they were not finished, that they had more to sew. Perhaps he would let them finish the jackets. Perhaps they could take their time, go stitch by stitch without the machines, in order to plan some kind of escape.

The Hawk moved from the center of the semicircle. He stood directly in front of her. Luzia closed her eyes. There was a long silence, then a collective shifting and a great thump. When she opened her eyes, he knelt before her. All of his men knelt in their places in the semicircle. Their heads were bowed. The Hawk held a rock in his open palm—a white pebble, no different from any of the other quartz scattered along the arid pastures below the mountain. He began to speak.

"My crystal rock that was found in the ocean between the chalice and the sacred host. The earth trembles but not our father Jesus Christ. At the altar also tremble the hearts of my enemies when they see me. With the love of the Virgin Mary, I am covered with the blood of my father Jesus Christ. I am bound. Whosoever should want to shoot me cannot do so. If they shoot at me, water will run from the barrels of their guns. If they try to stab me, their knives will fall from their hands. And if they lock me up, the doors will open. Delivered I was, delivered I am, and delivered I shall be with the key to the tabernacle. I seal myself."

The cangaceiros repeated the prayer, their voices rising and falling like an off-key choir. At the end, they were quiet. Then, one by one, each man spoke.

"I seal myself."

"I seal myself."

"I seal myself."

After the last man, the Hawk looked at Luzia. "Say it," he whispered.

The colonel kept his head bowed. Luzia looked to Aunt Sofia and then to Emília. They stared back, bewildered. What would happen if she did not speak? Would her obedience save them all?

"Don't be afraid," the Hawk said, louder this time, making the words into a warning rather than a comfort. "Say it."

Luzia stared at his crooked face, at his dark, lively eyes. One teared, the other remained dry. She could not look away. His face had snared her. It made her curious and repulsed her. It made her forget the measuring tape—that perfectly wound, impossibly tight skein of ink and numbers—between her palms. Luzia's grip relaxed. The tape unraveled in her hands.

"I seal myself," she said and the left side of the Hawk's face rose in a smile.

Chapter 3

EMÍLIA

Taquaritinga do Norte, Pernambuco
June–November 1928

1

mília had one night to sew Aunt Sofia's death dress. It was made of the softest black linen the colonel could find. Dona Conceição gave her four mother-of-pearl buttons and a meter of black lace. Emília sewed the dress on the pedal-operated Singer in the colonel's house, leaving Aunt Sofia lying stiffly in her bed under the care of Dona Chaves and comadre Zefinha who wept and bickered as they lit candles, muttered Ave Marias, and placed lemon wedges in boiling water to mask the smell. Emília already knew her aunt's measurements. She was smart with the lace, applying it to the dress's collar and using the four precious buttons on the bodice, where mourners could see them. When the dress was finished, she soaked it in goma water. Then, despite her fatigue, her numb legs and swollen eyes, Emília lifted the dress from the goma water and prepared the iron. Coals clinked against its metal casing. Emília waved the iron back and forth, as if preparing to fling it across the room. Embers flew. Smoke puffed from its metal nose. When its flat face met the dress, it sizzled. Emília worked fast so that the dress would not dry and the wrinkles set. Sweat stung her eyes. Emília pressed on. Pressed hard. As if each wrinkle, each wet fold was a dark crease within her that needed to be warmed, smoothed, and erased.

She and Uncle Tirço were the only ones present during Aunt Sofia's last hours. Emília placed the box of bones beside her aunt. She had refused help of any kind. She alone boiled mastruz with milk and spooned it into Aunt Sofia's mouth to ease her cough. She alone placed steaming towels with hortelã mint on Aunt Sofia's chest to aid her breathing. She alone scrubbed the soiled bedsheets, held handkerchiefs to her aunt's nose, and smoothed Aunt Sofia's chapped lips with coconut oil. In her worst moments, when the cough relented and the fever took over, Aunt Sofia had spoken.

"Tirço!" she screamed at the wooden box. "Those goddamn vultures!" Emília patted her aunt's forehead with a cool towel. Aunt Sofia grabbed her wrist. "Maria," she said, confusing Emília with her mother. "You take care of that child in your belly. People will see you, so pretty and pregnant, and they'll put the evil eye on you. They'll put it on your girls."

When Aunt Sofia spoke of her mother, Emília wanted to know more but inevitably her aunt's eyes closed and she faded into a feverish sleep. There were times when Aunt Sofia was lucid. She smiled weakly at Emília and prayed for the Lord to watch over her girls after she had left the world. Emília shushed her. She assured Aunt Sofia that she would not leave their world, not yet. But one evening Aunt Sofia could not stop coughing. She gulped for air. Her chest shuddered. Then she looked up at the ceiling intently, as if she had caught sight of something in the roof tiles. Aunt Sofia released a long, wheezing breath and grew quiet.

"Tia?" Emília whispered. "Tia?"

In her final fit of coughing, Aunt Sofia had thrown aside the covers. Emília saw a gray stain bloom on the mattress. She felt the sheet; it was wet and warm. Emília rejoiced—if Aunt Sofia had relieved herself, then she was still alive and sleeping. But after an hour, then two, Aunt Sofia remained frozen despite Emília's calls for her to wake. The spot on the mattress grew cold. Emília lit a candle and wrapped it in her aunt's hands.

2

The dress was ready in time for the velório. Aunt Sofia lay on the floor, arranged on top of the white funeral hammock Emília had spread beneath her. It was on loan from the colonel and meant to be used at his own funeral when the time came. The canvas was soft and sturdy, bordered with an intricately woven varanda that swished along the ground when the hammock was lifted. According to custom, Aunt Sofia's feet were bare and they faced the door, so that her soul would leave the house easily. Emília had placed heaps of dahlias around her aunt, and Dona Chaves had sprinkled her body with an entire vial of potent Dirce eau de toilette. Despite the two tufts of cotton stuffed into her nostrils, Aunt Sofia's face had frozen into a tight-lipped and stern look, as if she did not approve of the perfume she'd been doused with.

The death dress looked elegant. Emília was proud of her work. "Doesn't she look fine?" the mourners whispered as they knelt beside the body. No one called her "Sofia," because if the dead heard their names, they would haunt the living world, believing they were still needed.

The next morning, a group of men would lift the hammock with Aunt Sofia cloaked within it and carry her to Padre Otto's church service and later to the cemetery. Until then, Emília had to greet mourners. It was the eve of São João—an inopportune time for a wake. People wanted to celebrate: to set off firecrackers, light bonfires with their families, and watch their children dance in the local quadrilha. Aunt Sofia had always enjoyed the rowdy holiday. Each year, she and Luzia and Emília had spent a whole week building a fire balloon out of dry sticks and colored scraps of paper. On the eve of São João, they lit the tiny kerosene tin within the balloon and released it into the wind to pay homage to Saint John. They stood side by side and watched the balloon slowly rise into the night sky. First the paper caught fire and then the wood, until the entire contraption erupted in flames and descended, like a comet falling back to earth. That year there would be no fire balloon. There would only be a funeral.

The house was thick with smoke. Candles cluttered the sewing table and the windowsills. The colonel had placed four brass candleholders—as tall as Emília herself—around Aunt Sofia. He had spared no expense. It was his fault, after all. Emília knew that there were others to blame: the cangaceiros who had taken her sister, the cold night air and rain. But the colonel could have prevented it. He could have called upon his farmhands and vaqueiros to go after her sister. He could have found a proper doctor for her aunt. Each time Emília saw his hunched frame or his eyes that would not meet her own, she sensed the colonel's remorse and blamed him even more.

Mourners entered the house one by one, greeting Emília and then crowding around Aunt Sofia. Xavier, the shopkeeper, lifted Emília's hand from Uncle Tirço's box in her lap and pressed it between his own.

"If there is anything you need," he said, "do not hesitate to order it. I'll put it on credit."

His eyes scanned the house. He would find nothing, Emília thought. None of them would. Her home had become a curiosity—the place where cangaceiros had invaded, taking poor Victrola—and nosy mourners looked for signs of struggle. There were none. Even before Aunt Sofia died, people insisted on mourning Luzia, advising Emília and her aunt to schedule a mass and to drape the old Communion portrait—the only photograph of Luzia—in black cloth. Now that Aunt Sofia was gone, they hinted even more strongly. Emília refused to listen. She'd left the Communion portrait on the wall. She'd used the dressing trunk to barricade the door to her bedroom so that the curious could not wander inside. She had blocked the entrance to Luzia's saints' closet with a kitchen chair.

The front room was hot with bodies. A group of women recited Ave Marias over and over again, until Emília felt lulled by their voices. Outside, the whinny of horses broke through the chants. Dona Conceição and the colonel had arrived.

When Aunt Sofia fell ill, Dona Conceição sent a box of soaps to express her sympathy. They were round, perfumed balls individually wrapped in pastel tissue. Emília had not used them. Instead, she placed them around Aunt Sofia, between her dahlias and bowls of lemon water. Dona Conceição held a handkerchief in her gloved hands and wore a hat with a black lace veil. Weeks before, Emília would have thought her patroness the height of elegance, but now her stylishness seemed silly, almost callous. Dona Conceição lifted her veil.

"My dear," she said, taking Emília's face in her gloved hands, "how can I help?"

The mourners were quiet. The Ave Marias became whispers. Emília was expected to thank her patroness. To beg Dona Conceição for her continued support.

"There is one more sewing class," Emília replied. Dona Conceição's eyes widened. "It is the final class," Emília said. "I cannot miss it."

Dona Conceição retracted, removing her hands from Emília's face. She lowered her veil. "Yes," she said. "Of course. I will give you an escort."

Emília had missed the May and June installments of her lessons since Luzia had been stolen and her aunt had fallen ill. She'd asked their old chaperone to send word to Professor Célio of her family difficulties, and to tell him that she would not miss their last class. The lesson was in one week and Emília was prepared. When she'd finished Aunt Sofia's death dress, Emília had stopped by Xavier's shop and put all of her savings—fifty mil-réis, a small fortune—on his counter. She'd pointed to a cloth-covered valise. It was green, with a horn handle and metal corners. She'd walked home with the death dress in one hand and the valise in the other. There were whispers, of course, but Emília endured them. She refused to run away with Professor Célio with a jute bag slung across her back like some matuta. She, Emília dos Santos, was no coarse country girl.

She'd given her old valise—a scratched, cracked leather bag—to Luzia on the night her sister left with the cangaceiros. Afterward,

Emília could not think of buying a new valise; just the thought of packing upset her stomach. In the days following the cangaceiros' departure, Padre Otto headed a search party. Everyone had expected him to return with a body, but when he found nothing, even the colonel was confused. Cangaceiros were rumored to be fickle: sometimes they stole goods, other times they purchased them; some people they killed, others they simply punished; some women they disgraced, others they left alone. No one had heard of them taking a woman and keeping her.

The town hoped that the news of Luzia's abduction and the two soldiers' deaths would spread. The colonel telegraphed the coast. The bodies stayed in the square, covered in quicklime powder, as evidence. But the capital did not respond. No regiment appeared. Taquaritinga was too small and far away for such consideration. They would have to fend for themselves.

They buried the bodies. Padre Otto held massive prayer circles for Luzia, performing novenas that lasted nine days and nine nights and then began again. If Emília wobbled with sleep, if her eyes closed or her neck tilted sideways during the prayer circles, Aunt Sofia nudged her and they continued. Emília's knees bruised. Her neck stiffened. By the time Aunt Sofia's fever worsened, she could barely kneel.

Emília's nights were often restless. She slept in a chair beside Aunt Sofia's bed to soothe her aunt's coughing fits. She preferred it to her own bed, where she woke confused and startled by the empty space beside her. Had Luzia gone to the outhouse, or to get a cup of water? Then Emília's mind cleared and within her chest she felt an ache—painful and raw—like a burn moving from the inside out. Luzia was gone. Her body told her this, but her mind would not accept it. Each time Emília cooked or swept, she saw something move in the edge of her vision and expected it to be Luzia turning a corner in the house, or emerging from her saints' closet, or returning from her morning walk. Emília was always disappointed when she realized that the movement was actually her own shadow, or a moth, or a clear-bellied lizard scuttling after a mosquito. Even after the month of May had passed, after the prayer circles dwindled, after Aunt Sofia's health worsened and Emília slipped the box of bones from beneath her aunt's bed, Emília still believed that her sister would return. She dusted Luzia's saints' altar. She put her sister's unfinished embroidery in the sun each week to protect it from mildew and moths.

When Dona Conceição left, the mourners remained quiet. They stared at Emília over their clasped hands and beaded rosaries. Widows could live alone, protected by the memory of their lost husbands. And orphaned men could do whatever they pleased. But an unmarried young woman, an attractive young woman, with no family or income to speak of, was a rare and dangerous thing, ripe for gossip. Emília didn't broadcast her intentions. She didn't share her plans with anyone in town, so the mourners watched her, staring from behind their black mantillas and beneath their leather caps, hoping to see a clue. Emília kept her face frozen, composed. She stood, placed Uncle Tirço beneath her arm, and left the room.

People talked about the wooden box. They said it was proof that Emília was unwell. She carried it each time she left the house. She took it to the kitchen when she cooked her meals. To Emília, the wooden box was proof that she was not alone. She still had her uncle Tirço, and his presence soothed her.

Most of the mourners congregated in the front room, but some needed a cup of water or a slice of sticky macaxeira cake to endure the entire velório. Those quickly found their way to the kitchen. They stood beside the extinguished cookstove and around the kitchen table. They tried to keep their voices hushed, but Emília heard them from the hallway. She stood beside the kitchen door, keeping her body angled away from the entrance and her breath quiet, as she'd done a dozen times before when she'd spied on her former suitors.

"Poor thing," a woman whispered.

"She needs to toughen up," Dona Chaves interrupted; Emília recognized her nasal voice. "That girl was born with too many knots in her back—always so snooty—and Sofia encouraged it. Now she'll have to marry a Taquaritinga boy whether she likes it or not."

"I meant her sister."

"Oh," Dona Chaves sighed. "Of course. That poor Victrola! Well, God only knows what they've done to her."

"He should be ashamed of himself," Mr. Chaves joined in. "Colonel Pontes would never have allowed it in Caruaru."

"That's because Colonel Pontes didn't have everything handed to him on a platter," another, older man said. Emília could not identify his raspy voice. "When he was a boy, he didn't even have a stick to beat a dog with. He knows what it means to fight for things."

"If Colonel Pereira had a backbone, they wouldn't have come here in the first place."

"Yes, but if she was his daughter, they would have found her body by now. She would be properly buried."

The old man grunted. "If it were my daughter, I would have shot her, right in front of those bastards. I'd rather have a daughter of mine dead than carried away by a horde of men."

Emília entered the kitchen. The mourners fell silent. She placed Uncle Tirço's box in the center of the table. Dona Chaves and the rest of them did not look at Emília; they kept their eyes on the box. One by one, slowly, they left the kitchen. Emília sat. She poured herself a cup of water and cut a slice of cake. She heard voices from the front room. It was not the monotonous drone of prayers, but hasty, overlapping chatter. Emília ignored it.

Later, when the sky grew dark and Aunt Sofia's mourners left to light their São João bonfires and eat their cobs of grilled corn, only Emília and Uncle Tirço remained. While she sat, slumped in a chair beside her aunt's body, and the firecrackers outside startled her from sleep, reminding her to rise and light more candles, her Uncle Tirço was there, steadfast in the box beside her feet.

3

//////////

Emília had feared the cangaceiros would harm her, not Luzia. When she walked up and down the row of men in the colonel's yard, jotting down their measurements, Emília had stayed close to Aunt Sofia. She'd hunched her shoulders and held her writing tablet high, to hide her chest. She did not meet their eyes. And when the Hawk called out, "You!" Emília had turned around. She'd steadied herself, then looked up from her writing tablet. When she realized that he was looking at Luzia and not at her, Emília felt both startled and relieved.

The man unnerved her. It was not his looks—he would have been handsome if it weren't for his poor hygiene and scarred face. It was his manner that bothered her. Emília was accustomed to loud men: farmers who screamed at each other across fields, butchers and shopkeepers who greeted each other at the weekly market with booming voices and violent thwacks on the back. Only men of higher station, like Professor Célio, were subdued. But the Hawk commanded attention silently—moving the good side of his face, tilting his head, or pointing his thick finger. His men constantly looked down the measuring line at him for these quiet cues. He fooled most into believing he was discreet and subdued, but not Emília. His voice betrayed him. He rarely spoke, but when he did, his voice thundered out of him and startled everyone to attention. He was just as uncouth as any poor farmer. Worse, in Emília's eyes, because he tried to mask it.

She'd watched her sister measure him. She'd looked up from her writing tablet and seen Luzia drop her tape. It was unlike her. Ever since her accident, Luzia had lost all sense of nervousness or shame. If a person displeased her, Luzia loomed over them, taking them in from her great height, like a bird, as if they were not a part of her world but something lower, lesser. The Hawk, too, acted strangely. When Luzia stepped behind him to measure his back, she ran the tape across his shoulder blades and smoothed it out with the palm of her good arm. As she ran her hand along his back, the Hawk closed his eyes. Emília saw him. He looked as if he was savoring a bite of food. And when her sister stepped back around, he opened his eyes and stared down the row of men, pretending he was not interested in her measurements at all. He was unhinged, Emília decided. Absolutely unhinged.

She said this later, to Luzia, as they walked home. It was well past ten at night. Emília walked between Aunt Sofia and Luzia, holding their arms. Their dresses smelled of sweat and smoke from the bonfire. Emília's eyes burned. Her legs ached. Luzia was very quiet, until Emília whispered about the Hawk.

"He's not well," she said. Aunt Sofia grunted in agreement.

"You didn't even talk to him," Luzia mumbled.

"I didn't have to," Emília said. "He frightened us to death, making us kneel in the garden. And for what? For a prayer about a rock, of all things."

"At least they're God-fearing," Aunt Sofia said, then hushed them, worried someone would overhear.

Emília did not have the energy to argue with her sister. When they arrived home, she and Luzia helped each other out of their dresses and fell into bed wearing only their camisoles and knickers. Emília slept deeply. So deeply that, hours later, she did not hear twenty-one pairs of sandaled feet march down the muddy road. She did not see the glow of kerosene lanterns surround the front of their house. And when she heard the voice—a man's voice, smooth and stern—she thought it was in her dreams. Emília shifted and smiled, believing the voice belonged to Professor Célio and that he'd traveled all the way up the mountain to wake her.

Luzia.

Emília sat up.

Luzia.

Luzia lay with her eyes open and the quilt pulled down to her waist, as if she'd been expecting this strange visitor.

Luzia, the voice called again. *Come outside.*

Aunt Sofia reached the door first. Emília and Luzia huddled behind her. A fine rain blew through the slats of the window shutters. It was the kind of winter rain that Emília hated—deceptively light, but so persistent that it soaked through hair and clothes and soil, making everything a muddy mess. Emília pulled a shawl over her shoulders. Luzia had tugged the quilt from their bed, upsetting the mosquito netting.

"What kind of interruption is this?" Aunt Sofia muttered. "At this hour!"

Emília peered through the window slats. Outside, the colonel stood, shivering, beside the group of cangaceiros.

"Sir?" Aunt Sofia asked. She opened the front door. "What's the matter? Are the uniforms all right?"

The colonel nodded. Emília saw only the front row of cangaceiros, the ones who held lanterns. The rest were shadows; she saw the silhouettes of their half-moon hat brims. The men seemed larger, bulkier. They wore their new uniforms, but with a padding of blankets sloppily wrapped in oilcloth and tied around their torsos. Over this, each man had two canvas packs slung across his body, so that the straps crisscrossed his chest. The straps were thick—at least a palm wide—and decorated with metal rivets that shone in the lantern light. Their rifle straps, too, had metal rivets that glittered on their shoulders. Their pants appeared cropped at the knees, but when Emília looked more closely, she saw that the men wore leather shin guards, strapped with crisscrossed cords, around the bottoms of their legs. Thick cartridge belts, wet and shining from the rain, surrounded their waists. And shoved at an angle into their belts were long, gleaming knives. The Hawk's was the longest.

"Dona," the Hawk said, addressing Aunt Sofia, "I came to speak to Miss Luzia."

Beside her, Emília felt her sister tense at the sound of her name. The Hawk carried a bundle beneath his arm. He wore a plain rancher's hat and the shadow cast by the brim hid his eyes.

"What do they want with my child?" Aunt Sofia asked the colonel. He lowered his head.

"We won't hurt her," the Hawk said. "I assure you."

Emília held her sister's locked arm. Aunt Sofia held the other. They stepped outside together. The front yard was muddy and pocked with puddles. The ground felt cold beneath Emília's feet. The Hawk motioned for Luzia to step forward. When Emília and Aunt Sofia moved with her, he raised his palm, telling them to stay back.

"It's fine," Luzia whispered.

She gathered the quilt around her body and pulled her shoulders back, straightening to her full height. The quilt trailed behind her like a cape. Rain glittered in her hair. The Hawk lifted the brim of his hat and raised his head to face Luzia; he seemed no match for her. Emília felt relief. She could not see her sister's face, only her long, dark braid. The Hawk whispered something. His lips moved crookedly. He handed her the bundle beneath his arm. Luzia stayed rigid. The Hawk's mouth moved once more. Luzia took the bundle and turned around. She walked toward the house, past Emília and Aunt Sofia, her stare focused on some faraway point. Her lips were pinched tightly together. Emília recognized this face—Luzia had made it years before, when they took her arm from the paletas and told her it would never again straighten. She'd made it when their father's bloated body was carried down the mountain and into town. She'd made it before each school-yard fight, when her classmates' teasing threatened to disturb her rigid composure.

"You," the Hawk said, disrupting Emília's thoughts. "Come here. Please."

Emília stepped forward. The shawl around her shoulders was heavy with rain.

"Go inside and pack her things," he said slowly, as if coaxing a small child. "Not too much. Just what she can carry."

Baiano, the tall mulatto, accompanied Emília into the house and stood guard at their bedroom doorway. When Emília entered the house, their room was empty, as was Aunt Sofia's. No noise came from the kitchen. Emília quietly rejoiced—her sister had hidden, or escaped through the back door! Emília would move slowly, to give Luzia more time. Her hands shook. She carefully pushed aside the mosquito netting and placed their old valise—its latch rusted and loose—on their bed. Emília sifted through their dressing trunk, plucking out Luzia's oldest slip, her rattiest knickers. If Luzia had escaped, she would not need those things. Still, Emília folded each item carefully before placing it in the valise, wary of the cangaceiro's gaze. She packed her sister's faded cotton dress, a broken barrette, a ripped nightgown, some odd-colored spools of embroidery thread, an old needle cushion.

"What are you doing?"

Emília froze; Luzia stood in the doorway. Her camisole was bunched at the waist, sloppily tucked into tan trousers. The pants cuffs were too short, exposing Luzia's ankles and her long, sandaled feet. Unbuttoned over the camisole was a tan jacket. Emília recognized the cloth—it was the thick bramante she'd slid through the Singer's needle that afternoon. The jacket's canvas sleeves exposed Luzia's wrists. The cloth was creased and tight at her bent elbow.

"Why are you here?" Emília asked. "Where were you?"

"In the saints' closet," Luzia replied. "Praying."

Emília steadied herself against their dressing trunk. Her chest felt tight, her breath too short.

"He told me to pack your things," she said.

Luzia nodded. In the candlelight, her thick brows glistened with rainwater. Her eyes shone. Emília could focus on nothing else. When they were children, they used to lock arms and spin, turning round and round in the front yard. They moved so quickly that Emília felt powerless and frightened. The world went out of focus and the only thing she saw clearly was Luzia's face before her, her green eyes reflecting Emília's dread. There was comfort reflected there, too, because if they fell, they would do it together. And there was wonder—a strange, anxious delight—at the knowledge that they had set something in motion that they could not stop.

Outside, there was a whistle.

"Time to go," Baiano ordered.

"Wait," Emília said, focusing again on the room, the bed, the open valise filled with rags. Luzia's penknife sat where she always placed it before bed—on the dressing trunk between her measuring tape and Emília's stack of hairpins. In one fluid motion, Emília scooped up the knife along with the pins. She dropped them into the valise and quickly shut the lid.

When Aunt Sofia saw Luzia in the cangaceiro uniform, she placed her hand to her chest. The rain had thickened. Aunt Sofia's white hair looked translucent against her scalp. Emília saw flickers of candlelight behind the shutter slats of houses across the road. The town was watching.

"Stop this craziness," Aunt Sofia said to the colonel, who stayed very still except for his chattering teeth. "Get your men!" she yelled. "Call your vaqueiros, or your other capangas!" When he did not respond, Aunt Sofia raised her arm and pointed two shaking fingers at the Hawk. "I curse you," she said, then mustered the energy and stepped forward. "I curse you!"

The Hawk walked toward her. Emília tried to push her aunt's hand down.

"You're old," he said, his face nearly touching the tip of her outstretched fingers. "Get out of this rain."

Two cangaceiros flanked Luzia, holding her arms. She did not struggle or shout. She stood rigid and erect, as if posing for a photograph. Luzia was taller than all of the men who surrounded her, and for the first time Emília wondered what it must be like to have such a view—to see the scalps of men, to know that people must lift their faces to speak to you, making everyone look childlike and worshipful. And how far away everything must seem: the muddy ground, the men's wet sandals, the pistols and knives harnessed around their waists. As they walked away, Emília knew that she should speak. She should stand in Luzia's place. Emília was the oldest, with two good arms and legs. But she did not want to go with those men, and was afraid that if she offered herself in trade, they would take her without hesitation.

"Luzia!" Emília yelled suddenly, surprised by the sound of her voice. The men's marching slowed. Luzia craned her head around.

Wisps of wet hair clung to her face. Luzia had always been good with words, unlike Emília, who grew tongue-tied and ineffectual during any conflict. She'd called her sister's name without knowing why, or what to say next.

"I'm sorry," Emília sputtered, straining to see her sister's face. "I packed all the wrong things."

4

For the last sewing lesson, Emília had to wear a mourning dress. She'd sewn two after Aunt Sofia's funeral—one black, one gray— both made from a dull, itchy fabric Dona Conceição had given her. Emília had tried to make them stylish, capping the sleeves and lowering the waistline into a long, tubular skirt like the fashionable dresses she'd seen in *Fon Fon,* but there were limits to her talents. The fabric did not fall well, and tradition dictated that mourning dresses were supposed to be practical, not stylish. Her official luto for Aunt Sofia was required to last a year. A year of itchy dresses. A year in a darkened house, the shutters drawn and any mirrors covered with cloth. A year of regimented piety that Emília could not stomach. She missed Aunt Sofia terribly, but luto would not bring her back. The dark dresses and somber house only served as reminders to others to extend their smug condolences to Emília, who did not need reminding of her losses. She did not need peoples' sharp-tongued advice, telling her to stop living alone and to get married, or else she would become a ruined woman. Emília ignored them; she refused to be trapped in the countryside and wouldn't follow its petty rules. She would leave Taquaritinga, and every whisper, every stern look, every shaking head hardened her resolve.

Before the last sewing class, Emília put on an embroidered slip and a new pair of knickers beneath her mourning dress. She'd rubbed handfuls of jasmine water on her neck, behind her ears, along the insides of her arms, and on the backs of her knees. She had never worn so much perfume and each time the colonel's mule shuddered and sneezed beneath her, she believed that the animal was chastising her for her extravagance.

Emília stared out across the mountain ridge, unable to look at the mule beside her. Its back was empty except for cargo baskets. Emília's green valise—so small it fit only a few undergarments, a nightgown, her blue dress, and her sewing bag—was tucked into her mule's basket. The old chaperone had looked at her strangely when she handed him the valise. "My new sewing bag," Emília had explained, and he'd believed her. People would comment on the valise, Emília knew, but only to say that she was back to her old, extravagant ways. Better to carry a valise than her uncle's bones, they'd say.

The night before, Emília had stayed up late, hidden in her windowless bedroom so that people would not see the candlelight and speculate. She'd packed her valise, polished Dona Conceição's donated shoes, and wrapped her hair between scraps of cloth to make it perfectly wavy. That morning, early, she'd taken her azulões into the backyard and opened their cage door. She'd closed her eyes so as not to see them go. Then she'd composed a note for Luzia, in case her sister came back. It was simple: she was going to São Paulo, but would return one day. Before leaving, Emília pried their Communion portrait off its nail and stuffed it into her valise.

During Aunt Sofia's burial, Emília had placed Uncle Tirço in the crypt with her aunt. Afterward, alone in her house without even Uncle Tirço to comfort her, Emília thought of Professor Célio. She'd reread his notes, looked through each page of her Singer student manual, knelt at her altar to Santo Antônio and imagined a new life for herself. A quiet life, interrupted only by the rattle of a sewing machine, the shrieks and laughter of children, and the whistle of a kettle upon a gas range. Professor Célio had not visited or written, but gentlemen were considerate, Emília convinced herself. Perhaps he'd heard of her misfortune and did not want to trouble her. Emília imagined her empty sewing machine during class. She imagined Professor Célio feeling her absence as much as she felt his. And if he hadn't missed her, Emília would make him realize, upon seeing her again, that he secretly had. He just hadn't known it.

People in Taquaritinga would think the worst of her absence. They would say that Emília had become the kind of woman Aunt Sofia had always warned her about—a woman who led an easy life. Most of Emília's old schoolmates had gone on to fill decent positions in town. They became maids at the colonel's house or they married farmers and helped work their husband's land. But there were other girls—girls who had never gone to school—who wore too much rouge and lip paint and lingered near the drunks at the wooden barracas. Sometimes, in the early mornings on her way to sewing class, Emília caught sight of these girls teetering home with no shoes on their feet and their hair a matted mess. Emília would never become like those women. She was running away, yes, but she would marry. She would become a respectable wife, a *dona de casa*. "Dona Emília," people would call her, and she would nod and extend her hand.

Emília closed her eyes. She combed her fingers through the mule's rough mane. The ride to Vertentes seemed interminable. Her stomach churned. Luzia's old warnings lingered in her memory: *Did she truly think that Célio would marry her, a matuta? Did she believe that his intentions were honest?* Emília shook her head, shooing away Luzia's voice. Emília knew that she valued the sewing instructor more than he valued her. She sensed she might startle him with her requests. But she also knew that Professor Célio was a gentleman. He'd written her letters. He'd praised her. A gentleman didn't correspond with a girl unless his intentions were serious. Emília had read this in *Fon Fon* and she'd memorized it. She'd willed herself to believe it, despite her own doubts and her sister's warnings. Luzia was gone and didn't know what it was like to lose Aunt Sofia. Luzia didn't know how ashamed Emília felt, receiving charity from the colonel and Dona Conceição. Suddenly they called upon Emília to sew new curtains and sheets and tablecloths. Dona Conceição no longer insisted she economize on cloth. She didn't stand over Emília's machine to check on her progress. And when Emília delivered the finished items, Dona Conceição simply cast them aside or stuffed them into a closet without even inspecting the quality of the stitching, as she'd always done in the past. Luzia had no business invading Emília's mind with baseless warnings. Luzia did not know how lonely Emília's life had become.

Emília quickly chided herself. She stared at the empty mule beside her. She didn't know which was worse—resigning herself to Luzia's death, or continuing to believe she was alive. If her sister lived, she'd probably suffered more than Emília could imagine. Still, Emília couldn't help wishing for Luzia's existence. She missed her sister's strength, her common sense. Emília had so many doubts and questions. To be a real dona, Emília knew what was required of her. Or, at least, she had a notion. The romance serials in *Fon Fon* spoke of passionate embraces. Emília could picture these. She could picture Professor Célio—his hands soft and white, his thin frame hunched beneath his linen vest—embracing her, even kissing her, but she was confused as to what, exactly, would happen next. She and Luzia had speculated many times, before sleep.

"What do you think it's like?" Emília had whispered once, cupping her hands to her sister's ear so Aunt Sofia wouldn't hear. "It must be terribly romantic."

"It's just like animals," Luzia replied. "That's what Ana Maria said."

"No!" Emília hissed. She disliked the shopkeeper's daughter. "Ana Maria is vulgar."

Emília had seen the guinea hens cluck and scurry each time Dona Chaves's rooster puffed his feathers and chased after them. She'd seen female pigs and goats go into heat, banging against the walls of their pens with their heads or hooves until they were placed with a male. Once, on their way to school, Emília and Luzia had witnessed two horses "in the sacred act," as Aunt Sofia called it. Two men pulled a mare by a rope bridle and placed her in a small, fenced area with a stallion. The stallion flitted from side to side, releasing short, heaving puffs from his nostrils. The mare whinnied and ran in circles, kicking up clouds of dust. When she calmed, the stallion sprang forward. His hind legs seemed too thin to support his great weight. His belly was rounded, his front legs curled beneath him, his private parts dark and dangling nearly to the ground. He fell upon the mare's back. She seemed to buckle beneath him, but sustained his weight. Emília refused to believe that it was the same between men and women. Perhaps the brutes from Taquaritinga were like animals in pens, but cultured men were different.

The mule beside her bayed. The old chaperone slapped its hindquarters with a stick. Emília closed her eyes. She imagined that with Professor Célio, she would feel only softness—a great softness that consumed her until she fell into a peaceful sleep beside him. Yes, Emília assured herself, that was the way it would be.

5

Emília trembled behind the sewing machine. Her foot caught on the pedal. She'd taken off her head scarf before class, stuffing it into her valise and revealing her bobbed hair. But the sewing room's heat and her own sweat sabotaged her carefully made curls, making them flat and droopy. Machine number 17—Luzia's place—sat empty before her. Their last lesson was embroidery. Professor Célio was kind and attentive, assuring Emília that she would catch up. The other women in class ran their tablecloths back and forth under the machine's thick needles until the stitches became bulky, solid designs of flowers and curling vines. Emília could not focus. Her flowers did not look like flowers but like awful red blobs. She was grateful and frightened when the clock above Professor Célio's desk finally chimed and class was over.

The older matrons crowded around Professor Célio and asked him their final, desperate questions. They tugged at his suit sleeves, vying for his attention.

"Professor, what if my needle breaks?"

"Professor, what if the pedal on my machine sticks?"

"Professor, why do my stitches always come out crooked?"

Emília took her time cleaning her workspace. She folded and refolded her practice cloth. She wound all of her thread tightly onto its wooden spindles. She clicked her valise lid shut. The young mother from machine 12 lingered near Emília's chair. She stared at Emília's dark dress and asked, "Where is your sister, dear?"

Emília tugged at the thread in the base of her machine.

"I'm sad to hear the other Miss dos Santos is ill," Professor Célio interjected, taking his place beside Emília's machine. "I hope you'll teach her what you've learned today."

Emília nodded. She felt flushed with love for him. Around her, the women began to list recommendations for Luzia's fictional illness—copaíba oil for headaches, arruda tea for pain. Emília nodded absently. She watched Professor Célio run the metal comb through his hair. Quickly, gracefully, he dusted the machines and straightened the chairs. When the last of the women had left, Emília hung back.

"Today's class was very good," she said. "I'm sorry I had to miss the others." Sweat dribbled down her side. Emília lowered her voice. "Do you know why I was absent?"

Professor Célio raised his pale hands, motioning for her to stop. "Your chaperone stopped in and informed me," he said. "It is a matter of great discretion."

"Yes," Emília sighed, relieved. *A matter of great discretion,* she repeated to herself. How lovely. She peered out of the classroom window; her chaperone was late. Time was precious. Her hands felt slippery against the horn handle of her valise. She had prepared her speech carefully, her mind cluttered with words for days prior to the class as she fine-tuned each phrase and practiced each pause, rehearsing her plea in the hopes of sounding more dignified than desperate. She cleared her throat.

"When will you meet your chaperone?" Professor Célio asked.

"I'm not meeting him."

"Oh?" Professor Célio paused, inspecting her valise. "Will you stay here, in Vertentes? Do you have family in these parts?"

"I have no family."

"Forgive me," Professor Célio said gravely. He shook his head, then took Emília's hand in his. His fingers were as delicate and clammy as a child's. He pressed his lips to her hand. Emília's throat felt very dry and she gulped down saliva so as not to cough and spoil the moment. Professor Célio raised his eyes, keeping her hand near his mouth.

"Forgive my boldness," he said. "I will be leaving for São Paulo in a few days. A new Singer representative will take over here. I was hoping to spend time with you. Perhaps—" he reddened, then continued—"perhaps without your chaperone."

"Célio," Emília began, the words imprinted in her memory like the blue tick marks of a sewing pattern, showing her what to attach and what to cut away. "As you know, I am in a desperate situation—"

"Of course," Célio interrupted. "I understand, I just—"

"I know . . . ," Emília continued, the pattern clear in her mind, "I am rushing our courtship."

"Courtship?"

"Yes," she sighed, annoyed by his interruptions. Célio had dropped her hand. Emília reached down and clasped his. It had not been this hard to focus when she was alone at home, uttering this speech while she scoured pots or peered into the dark rafters before bed. "I know I am rushing our courtship. I would never want to burden you. But I know we are compatible—"

"Courtship?"

Emília squeezed his hand harder, exasperated by his repetition of such a tiny point. Flustered, she skipped ahead.

"I'm a fine seamstress. I can help you with any expenses. I am prepared to pay for my own train ticket." Emília took a breath. This was a fib—she did not have enough for train fare—but she hoped that Célio would insist on paying for her. If he couldn't, she would ask the colonel. Célio tugged his hand from hers.

"I'm not quite sure what you're implying, Miss dos Santos."

"I am asking you to hasten things. To take me with you, to São Paulo."

"I'm very confused, Miss dos Santos. I will be traveling to São Paulo alone."

"Oh," Emília said. She'd worried he might say this, but had put the thought out of her mind. "Does that mean you'd like to extend our courtship?"

"We don't have a courtship!" Professor Célio sputtered.

"But your letters? *Our* letters—"

"Those were notes. Notes are *not* letters, Miss dos Santos."

Emília felt dizzy. She focused on a loose string of thread curled on Célio's gray lapel. She had expected him to call her by her given name, not *Miss dos Santos,* which sounded prim and stodgy, as if she was a spinster. She tried to concentrate once more on her speech, but the words in her mind were jumbled and useless.

"I'm in a desperate situation," Emília whispered. "I'm a fine seamstress." Finally, she took a deep breath and faced him; his eyes were wide and panicked. Emília pressed on. "If you give me this chance, I promise you, you will never lack for care or affection. I know how to manage a house. I know how to iron a shirt. I will always be presentable." She held his hand. "Please."

Professor Célio slumped into machine number 15's chair. He pursed his lips and released a long, slow breath.

"Miss dos Santos, I'm sorry. I believed this was an innocent flirtation." He shook his head. "I should have known better."

"Known what?" Emília demanded. Her eyes felt warm.

"It isn't your fault, Miss dos Santos. It is mine. I didn't take into account where I was." He wafted the air with his hands. "You seemed very fun loving. Very modern." He shook his head again. His foot tapped the machine's iron leg. "I've been away from São Paulo too long."

Emília coughed. She cupped her hands to her face.

"Please, Miss dos Santos, don't blame yourself. It's perfectly understandable that you formed an attachment to me."

Emília hiccupped into her hands. She wished she could be composed, like her sister. She wished she could gulp her tears down, somewhere deep inside herself, as Luzia did.

"You'd better go," Célio said. He cupped her elbow in his clammy hand and led her to the classroom's glass-paneled doors. "Miss dos Santos, please accept my deepest apologies," he said, handing her the green valise. "You are a very attractive young woman and you have wonderful penmanship. But it was irresponsible of me to begin a flirtation with you. I overestimated your sophistication. I am truly sorry for whatever hurt I have caused you."

Before she could speak, he'd herded her out of the door and into the sunlit road. Vendors carting wheelbarrows filled with cilantro and other winter vegetables scooted past her. The colonel's donkeys stood across the road, unattended, their bridles hitched to a spindly tree, her chaperone gone to fetch some forgotten bit of merchandise. The green valise looked small and pathetic at her feet. Emília heard the door's lock click behind her.

6

The heels of Dona Conceição's hand-me-down shoes wobbled in the dirt. Their thin leather straps rubbed the bridges of Emília's feet raw. At the first bend in the steep trail to Taquaritinga, she tugged the shoes off. She held them in one hand and her green valise in the other. Emília wanted to be alone; she couldn't imagine riding back to Taquaritinga with the colonel's old chaperone, on the backs of those godforsaken donkeys. Halfway up the mountain, she regretted her decision. It had begun to rain. The rain was light and scattered at first, and Emília walked in a crooked pattern, trying to dodge the drops. A cover of gray clouds settled along the steep serra to Taquaritinga, until Emília could no longer see the town of Vertentes below. Soon, the rain became fine and more consistent.

Her mourning dress grew heavy. Its wet fabric slapped against Emília's legs. The rain felt soothing on her face, however. Back in Vertentes, Emília had rubbed away her tears so ferociously that the

skin around her eyes felt plump and tender. She couldn't cry anymore, and this irritated her. Why did she have to blubber in front of
Professor Célio and finally grow composed when she was alone? A
green raindrop fell on her foot. Emília stopped. She lifted her valise.
The case's canvas sides were soft, buckling inward from the rain.
The fabric was streaked and uneven; the green dye bled onto the
ground below.

"I'm sick of you!" Emília sputtered, shaking the bag.

She had the urge to throw the valise over the side of the serra.
She walked fast. Her feet slapped the wet ground. She cursed Célio.
Wished his silver comb would rust. Wished all of his precious hair
would fall out. She cursed Santo Antônio and resolved to break
apart her altar, to throw the white cloth rose into the outhouse. She
would not ask the saints for any further help. She would sew until
her fingers hurt. Until her legs ached. She would save her money.
She would leave on her own.

A caramel-colored mare blocked Emília's path. It chewed on the
tall winter grasses that sprouted along the edges of the trail. A man
sat upon the horse. He kicked its sides.

"Go on! Go on!" he yelled.

He wore a straw fedora. His suit jacket was bunched before him,
stuffed between his body and the saddle horn. His blue dress shirt
clung to his skin, and beneath its wet folds Emília saw his frame—
rotund and ample, like a jackfruit. He wore linen suit pants. One
cuff had stuck to the stirrup strap, bunching at the calf. Unlike his
torso, his leg was tapered and thin. A band circled his brown calf and
his sock was attached to it, held in place by a silver clip. The sock
clip was round and etched, like a medallion. Emília thought it was a
shame to hide such a lovely thing beneath pants.

The man swatted the mare's hindquarters awkwardly with his
crop. The horse swished his tail. The man tried to hit the horse
harder but stopped, startled to see Emília. He was not handsome, but
his teeth were exceptionally small and white and his smile so wide
that she could see both lines of his gums.

"I can't quite get this besta to move," he said.

It had always irritated Emília when people—men especially—called their mares idiots. Now it made her livid.

"She's no besta," Emília said. "It looks like she's smarter than you."

The man flicked the brim of his straw fedora. Water dribbled onto his shoulders. "That's true," he said, his eyes widening, as if seeing Emília for the first time. "You're right."

Emília had prepared herself for an insult in response to her own. Instead, she felt flattered by his belief in her. Emília put down her valise. "Are you going up the mountain or down?"

"Up," the man said. He released the reins and stared at his horse. "I hate animals."

He wiggled his feet in the stirrups. The soles of his ankle-high boots were smooth, unscratched. The leather had no creases. Emília put down her shoes. She walked up to the mare and held the bottom half of the reins. Emília clucked and tugged it away from the road-side weeds. The animal puffed air from its nostrils. Emília kept hold of the reins while she knelt, picking up her valise and shoes with her free hand.

"Wait," the man said. "This won't do. I can't have a lady leading my horse."

He lifted a wet leg up and off the horse's back. The mare shifted forward. The man's other foot stuck in the stirrup and he hopped to get it out. When both of his feet were firmly on the ground, he grabbed his crumpled suit jacket and put it on.

"Why don't I lead and you ride," he said.

Emília shook her head. She felt tired and cold. "It knows it doesn't have to obey you. It won't let you lead."

The man's brow creased. He pressed his fingers to his small, trimmed mustache and shook his head, as if pondering greater questions.

"Well," he finally sighed, "then the three of us will walk."

He insisted on carrying Emília's things while she led the horse. Emília was embarrassed handing him the shabby shoes and the buckling valise. She touched her hair and inspected her mourning dress; she looked a fright. But so did he. They walked in silence. As they made their way up the trail, the man panted. He stopped many times, pretending to admire the cloudy vista when Emília knew he was, in fact, catching his breath.

"I'm not used to trekking," he said. "I didn't realize it was so remote. They informed me in Vertentes that the only way to make it up the mountain was by horse or by foot. Are you visiting this town—Taquaritinga?"

"No," she said. The pain of her encounter with Célio came back and made her voice break. "I live here, but I wish I didn't."

A large toad, camouflaged in the dirt road, suddenly hopped toward them. The man staggered back, losing his hat. Emília giggled. The man's face reddened, but he quickly laughed and picked up his fedora.

"We don't have frogs that size in Recife," he said, wiping mud from his hat's brim.

"You're from Recife?" Emília asked. "What on earth are you doing here?"

"I'm making a visit. A law school friend of mine lives here."

Emília stared at him. He looked too old to be a student. He looked older than Professor Célio, in his thirties or perhaps even his forties. "Is your friend the colonel's son?" she asked. "Felipe?"

"Yes," he replied. "How did you guess?"

"He's the only person who attends university."

The man nodded. "It's our winter holiday at the law school. I plan on spending the rest of July here. My father believes the country environment will do me good." He rolled his eyes and kicked at a stone with his new boots. It was an odd gesture, one that reminded Emília more of a sullen boy than a grown man.

"You look more mature than Felipe," Emília ventured.

"I became interested in the law late in life," the man said curtly. "I tried my hand at medicine and business, but both are better suited to my father." He stopped himself, as if he had revealed too much. He inspected Emília. His eyes lingered on her hair, then trailed down to her bare feet. "The girls in Recife are wearing their hair that way. I mistook you for a city girl at first."

Emília realized the significance of his last words—*at first*. Meaning, he had made the mistake of believing she was a city girl when really, she was nothing but a matuta. Behind her, the horse flicked its head and tugged the reins. Emília tugged back.

"I'm moving to the city," she said. "Perhaps I will see you there." She held out a hand. "Emília dos Santos."

The man smiled widely, exposing his small teeth and dark gums. He put down her valise and took off his straw fedora with a flourish.

"Where are my manners?" he said, gripping her hand tightly. "Degas van der Ley Feijó Coelho. Please, call me Degas, like the painter."

Emília nodded, though she didn't know what painter he referred to. His first name was odd, but she was startled by his long string of last names. They sounded important, as if the three families he'd listed represented a long, noble line he could trace back to the beginning of time. They made her name seem meager, simplistic.

"Look!" Degas gasped and pointed behind her. Emília turned. The clouds around the mountain had parted. The scrubland was green. White squares of houses dotted the landscape and the yellow church steeple of Vertentes looked small and unimposing in the midst of so much land.

"What a marvelous vista!" Degas sighed.

He walked to the rocky edge and held his hat to his heart. Wind ruffled his white suit, making the damp lapels flap against his chest. The thin gold chain of his pocket watch dangled from his jacket and swayed against his stomach like a charmed snake. Emília stared at his profile—his café-au-lait-colored skin; his prominent nose that arched downward, the flesh at its tip rounded like a teardrop. He looked powerful and Arabic, like one of the sheiks in her romances. The mare nudged Emília's arm with its soft snout again and again, as if trying to shake her from such daydreams.

7

When she returned to Taquaritinga, Emília welcomed the colonel's charity. She sewed more dresses and table linens and kitchen towels for Dona Conceição than she ever had before. At the end of each week, she hid her payment—a wad of crumpled mil-réis notes—under her bed, next to her forgotten *Fon Fon*s. She grated her own cornmeal and purchased the lowest grade of sun-dried beef, soaking the strips for a full day in order to make them edible. She used the hardest, blackest soap to wash her clothes and her body. She could do without small luxuries if her sacrifice helped her to buy a train ticket. It was only a matter of patience.

Her work kept her from feeling the emptiness of the house. It kept her from thinking of Luzia. And it distracted Emília from the gossip aimed at her. Only "women of the life" lived alone. Or hermits. So, Emília was either indecent or unwell, or both. Her neighbor, Dona Chaves, made impromptu visits to spy on her condition. Word of Emília's poor housekeeping—dust caked the windowsill and scraps of fabric littered the house's floors—soon spread. Padre Otto counseled her to move in with Dona Chaves, or take a position as a maid with Dona Conceição. Emília paid him no heed. It was as if they were speaking of another girl, another Emília, and she was a passive observer of a life that had nothing to do with her own. Her life had become the monotonous pumping of the Singer's pedal, the clicking of its needle, the feel of cloth beneath her calloused fingertips. Soon, she could identify fabrics by touch: the ridged *crepe da china*, the crosshatched linen, the rough *brim*, the filmy *algodãozinho*. The only things that broke the monotony of her life were the growing stack of mil-réis beneath her bed and the presence of Degas Coelho.

They had not spoken since that day on the ridge. When they'd reached the colonel's gate, Degas spotted Felipe—pale eyed and freckled—resting in the porch hammock, waiting. Degas hastily thanked Emília and rushed inside the gates, forgetting his mare.

Emília tied its reins to a tree and went home. The next morning, she saw three mules shuffle past her window, driven in the direction of the colonel's house. There were three leather suitcases strapped to their backs, along with two wooden rackets and a round hatbox. Each day afterward, when Emília sewed on Dona Conceição's pedal-operated Singer, she heard Degas Coelho's voice. It carried across the colonel's checkered tile floor and into the sewing room. Emília slowed her pedaling to better hear him. He complimented the cook and instructed the maids on how to starch his shirts. He huffed and groaned while playing badminton with Felipe in the side yard. He thanked the houseboy each time the child ran to retrieve their over-shot birdie. During meals, Degas gossiped with Dona Conceição about Recife society. He peppered his Portuguese with foreign phrases. The words were garbled and strange.

"What the devil did he say?" the colonel often shouted, asking Felipe instead of Degas, as if their guest was not present.

The colonel was the only one Degas could not charm. While Dona Conceição tried on her new dresses behind the sewing room's screen, the colonel paced the small room and whispered complaints to his wife. Emília kept quiet at her machine. Their guest could not ride a horse and was not interested in visiting the colonel's ranch below the mountain. He did not care for cattle or goats. Worst of all, he kept Recife hours. He and Felipe played chess or read poetry late into the night, only waking in time for lunch. Each morning, the colonel insisted that Emília leave the sewing room door wide open. Adding to the Singer's clatter, the colonel spoke loudly, dragged chairs and slammed doors until his son and his guest arose, bleary-eyed and grumpy, at a decent hour.

"You are a man, not a bat, Felipe," the colonel often chastised his son.

This continued well past July. The law professors at the Federal University had called a strike and Degas stayed long after his winter recess had ended. For the first months of his stay, Degas did not notice Emília's presence. The sewing room, near the laundry area and the water tank, was in a part of the house where Degas rarely ventured.

But the sewing room's window looked out onto the colonel's side porch, where, one afternoon, Degas paced back and forth. Rings of sweat darkened the underarms of his shirt. It was the end of September and the sun was stiflingly hot, a sign that the summer drought would start early. Degas held a telegram in his hands. He read it, then pouted and paced again. Emília had never seen a person receive so many telegrams. Every other week a messenger delivered an envelope with a message dispatched from Recife. Emília stopped pedaling. She stood to catch a glimpse of the telegram's thin, yellow paper. One day, she mused, she would receive telegrams.

Degas stopped pacing. He lifted his head. Whether he'd finished reading the message or grown accustomed to the clatter of the sewing machine and was stunned by the sudden silence, Emília did not know. He looked into the sewing room window. The shutters were open; the thin cotton curtain drawn back. Emília was in plain view. Degas walked to the windowsill.

"Ahh," he sighed. "My savior. My horsewoman."

Emília sat. She leaned into the machine and went back to work, feverishly pumping the iron pedal. When she looked up, Degas was gone. Emília kept sewing for fear he would notice the silence and come back. Her fingers felt hot. Her throat constricted. His savior. His horsewoman. She had never been claimed before, not by a farmer or a gentleman. It was brazen, audacious. Something a spoiled child would say. It angered her—she was no horsewoman—and yet she felt comfort in the claim. To be claimed meant to exist outside of the sewing room, outside of her dark, empty house, and to have a place in the mind of a man she did not know.

The next day, Degas propped his thick forearms on the windowsill and watched her work. The next week, he leaned against the sewing room's door frame. Emília began to listen for his steps on the tile. She waited for Degas to clear his throat and announce his presence before she looked up and saw his gummy smile. Eventually, Degas made his way into the sewing room. He sat in a chair opposite the Singer. He spoke little at first, complaining of his boredom, his wish to return to Recife. Emília slowed her pedaling and listened. Perhaps it was Emília's eager silence, or the heat, or the dull monotony of his days, or the constant hypnotizing clatter of the Singer, that loosened Degas' tongue. Or perhaps, Emília thought afterward, he simply liked to talk about himself.

He was thirty-six. He had no siblings. His father had been trained as a doctor but came from a long line of moneylenders and merchants who sold imported machines to sugar plantations. His mother's family, the van der Leys, had owned one of those plantations. When the price of sugar fell, they could not pay for their machines. They engaged their daughter, Dulce, to the young merchant and their debts were forgiven. As a boy, Degas had gone to boarding school in England. Emília recalled the island on Padre Otto's map. He traveled by steamship. At the boarding dock in the port of Recife, his parents had pinned his name to his jacket, but during the long trip, the pin had come undone and Degas was petrified he would be lost forever.

When Degas spoke of his travels, Emília wanted to stop pedaling altogether, but she was afraid of startling Degas from his stories. Degas described snow, and how the extreme cold could feel just like extreme heat—a tingling, painful sensation against your skin. He described the watery oats he ate each morning in the boarding school's dining hall. He recalled how the British boys had tormented him, calling him a "dirty gypsy" because of his nose and his complexion.

"Why?" Emília interrupted. "Is everyone there pink? Like Padre Otto?"

Degas leaned his head back and laughed. Emília tugged a loose thread from the Singer's needle. She chided herself for asking such a question. She arranged her feet on the pedal, but before she could begin, Degas reached toward the machine. He placed his hand over hers.

"You're quite lovely," he said.

Unlike Professor Célio's fingers, Degas' were thin and brown. His hand was moist with sweat. Cupped over hers, it felt hot. Emília tried to slip her hand away, hoping he would continue his story.

With her first, slight tug, Degas' smile faded. His face had a way of suddenly darkening, his good humor disappearing so abruptly that it seemed as if it had never truly existed, that the real Degas was not a charming, worldly man but the grim, dejected figure who lay underneath. He shifted in his chair, as if uncomfortable in his starched suit. There was a childlike earnestness, a flicker of desperation in his eyes that stilled Emília. She wanted, suddenly, to put him at ease. She kept her hand beneath his.

"The women in Recife are tigresses," he continued. "They've got nothing in their heads but gossip and secrets. They are cunning. But you"—he squeezed her hand tightly—"you are sweet, like a child. A beautiful child."

From that evening forward, Degas waited for her beside the kitchen door, among the dripping laundry and slumped sacks of cornmeal, and escorted her home. During their walks, he held her sewing bag in one hand and a lit cigarette in the other. He smoked quickly, taking a few long puffs and then throwing the half-finished stub a few paces from their feet. As they negotiated the road's crooked cobblestones, Emília admired Degas' two-toned leather shoes. As the evenings grew warmer and the summer began, dust settled on his shoes and their patent-leather tips grew dull, like the shells of beetles.

She did not feel giddy or nervous around Degas, as she had with Professor Célio. She never had the urge to take Degas' hand or brush back his hair. She never felt warmth rise in her stomach when he came near. Apart from the instance in the sewing room, he, too, never tried to take her hand. He never walked too close. Never stared at her when he believed she wasn't looking. At night, when Emília could not sleep because her bed felt too empty and the house too quiet, she tried to conjure up romantic daydreams about Degas, but his full frame and gummy smile intruded upon her musings, making her recall other images: Degas pressing a water glass to his broad forehead; Degas discreetly plucking a stray thread from the shoulder of her dress; Degas removing a poorly folded handkerchief from Felipe's jacket pocket, refolding it, and gently tucking it back into place.

As summer began, the banana palms lost most of their fronds, making Taquaritinga's serra look brown and barren. Some evenings, during their walks, Emília saw farmhouses, white and smaller than fingernails, perched upon the mountainside. On these summer evenings, when the sun set slowly and their shadows fell long and distorted before them, Emília wanted to interrupt their quiet walks and tell Degas: "My sister had a bent arm. People called her Victrola."

She never told him this. When Degas finally asked about her family, Emília told him they were dead. Being a gentleman, he didn't ask for details. She assumed Degas had heard about Luzia's abduction, but she wasn't sure. The colonel didn't like to broadcast his failings, especially to a guest he did not like. Felipe had been in the capital when the cangaceiros invaded. Most likely the colonel's son knew about the abduction, but with his cool disdain for Taquaritinga it was possible Felipe didn't recall Victrola or associate her with being Emília's sister. And the town itself avoided mentioning Luzia, as if speaking her name would call forth a ghost that would haunt them all. It was as if her sister had never existed, had never walked those streets beside Emília, had never broken a boy's teeth with her skull, had never fallen from that mango tree. Emília only spoke of Luzia to Padre Otto. Each week, she sat within the cramped confessional and stared at the priest's profile through the latticed wood. She confided that she slept in Aunt Sofia's bedroom. That she had pinned a curtain across her old bedroom's doorway because she felt sick with shame each time she looked inside and saw Luzia's things: undergarments made of sturdy fabric, a pair of thick stockings, a shawl that could have kept her sister warm, if only Emília had packed it. Although they plagued her, Emília never shared these thoughts with Degas. One evening, however, she spoke of the pile of mil-réis beneath her bed.

"People don't believe it," she said to Degas, "but one day, I will go to the city. I will have a seamstress of my own."

She slowed her stride and lowered her voice to a whisper. One day, Emília confided, she would have a tiled kitchen. She would eat fresh beef. She would own a cloche hat. She would honk a car's horn.

Degas stared at her. The corners of his mouth twitched. He covered it with his hand but could not stifle his laughter. Emília stepped away from him. It was easy for Degas to laugh at such things. He had a dress shirt for each day of the week; Emília had seen them, perfumed and immaculate, lined up in the laundry area like a row of Padre Otto's altar boys in their stiff white robes. Degas would never have to scrub sweat stains from his clothing each night. Degas had the luxury of leaving food on his plate, which Dona Conceição's maids later ate, when their patroness wasn't looking. Emília used to be unwilling to eat scraps, but after Aunt Sofia's death hunger overcame her pride and she, too, picked up the half-eaten slices of cake and the fatty rinds of picanha steak. There were things that, Emília knew, Degas never took into account: the leather laces on his shoes, the soft fabrics of his clothing, the silk tags sewn into each of his hats with the address of a milliner on Rua do Sol. What seemed trivial things to Degas were, to Emília, vital clues to another world, a world to which she wanted admittance. But each month, train fares rose. Each month Emília had to recalculate the time and effort it would take for her to raise the money for her ticket. By October, the train ticket was becoming just like Dona Conceição's silk dresses, her intricate laces, her silver utensils: things so near Emília, but always beyond her reach.

Degas' laughter faded. He dabbed his eyes with a handkerchief. Emília grabbed her sewing bag from his hands.

"No," Degas said, his smile suddenly disappearing. "I'm sorry. I didn't mean to laugh." He fumbled with his hands, then continued. "It's your innocence that strikes me, Emília. Your simplicity. It refreshes me. It makes me see everything with new eyes."

Emília nodded and allowed Degas to escort her home.

By late October, there was vicious gossip about their unchaperoned walks. "You're earning a reputation," comadre Zefinha said angrily. "What would your aunt say?" Emília ignored her. There was no harm in their walks. Everyone saw Degas leave her at her door and then return to the colonel's house. But still they asked, what would a city man, a university student, possibly want with a pretty orphan? The women at the market thought they knew, and they gossiped loudly each time Emília passed their booths: "That girl won't be able to show her sheets on her wedding night." If Luzia were present, she would have confronted the women and said something clever. Emília simply walked away, her hands shaking, her face flushed. Comadre Zefinha was right—the evening walks were risking her already troubled reputation—but Emília didn't care. She didn't try to guess Degas' intentions; after the incident with Professor Célio, Emília wouldn't allow herself to have romantic expectations or to make physical advances. Only men, it seemed, had those rights. Still, Emília harbored intentions of her own. One day she would go to the capital, and she had to know what awaited her there. The walks with Degas allowed Emília to hear his stories, to soak in his perceptions of city life, to create a mental portrait of Recife and beyond.

In response to the gossip, the colonel wanted to put an end to their evening strolls but Dona Conceição calmed him. She suggested that they provide a chaperone for Emília's walks, and when the colonel assented, she winked at Emília. With that wink, Emília understood that her walks with Degas were more than walks. Dona Conceição was her senior and her patroness, but she was also a woman who understood both the risks and the possibilities that those walks represented. Dona Conceição was willing to gamble on possibility. From then on, Felipe accompanied the couple, sulking behind them, kicking at rocks, huffing each time Degas laughed. With a chaperone present, their walks turned into something official. Neither Emília nor Degas spoke of the change.

On the first day of November, Degas stopped halfway through their evening walk. They stood in the town square. He took off his hat. The hair beneath it was wispy and thin, like a baby's.

"I've received a telegram from my father," Degas said. "The university strike is over. I must go back."

Degas waited for a reaction. Emília tried to muster feelings, but there was only calm. It startled her, how little she would miss him.

Degas looked nervously behind them, at Felipe. He was busy lighting a cigarette. The match in his hand flared. The day's last rays of sun illuminated his face. Felipe's freckles had darkened that summer, after many horse rides and badminton games with Degas. It looked as if cinnamon had been sprinkled across his face, fanning across his forehead, clotting densely on his cheeks and nose. Felipe squinted in the sunlight, then turned his back. Quickly, Degas took Emília's hand. She'd allowed him to hold it once before, in the sewing room, but that was a private place and not the public square. Emília recalled the women at the market, gossiping about her sheets. She tugged her hand away.

Degas shrugged, as if he had tried his hand at romance but could not fathom it.

"Emília," he sighed, "I lost the ability to make castles out of air long ago. You and I, we both have necessities. You need to leave here, and I need . . ."

His voice lowered. He gripped her hand again, tighter this time. He breathed heavily and it smelled of tobacco. Emília felt dizzy.

"I will return to the capital," Degas said. "And if you accept, you will come with me. It will be more than a visit. You will go as my wife."

The sun had nearly disappeared over the horizon. Emília heard birds fly from the square, their flapping wings like the sound of good, stiff fabric snapping on a laundry line. Behind Degas, she saw the shadow of Felipe's face. The lit end of his cigarette glowed. She heard him exhale and smoke swirled around them.

"You will go as my wife," Degas repeated, louder this time.

Emília nodded.

Later that week, after the entire town had heard the news of their engagement and Degas had sent and received a dozen telegrams to and from his parents in Recife, Emília went to see Padre Otto. She had her confession to make and a ceremony to schedule. She and Degas would travel as man and wife. The rumor in Taquaritinga was that Degas had ruined her, and in order to keep the town's honor—they couldn't have city boys visiting and seducing their daughters—

the colonel had forced his guest to marry immediately. Degas did not dispel the rumor. Neither did Emília; her reputation was not as important as her escape. She admitted this during her confession to Padre Otto.

"After all," Emília said, staring at the handkerchief in her hands and not at the priest's profile through the latticed wood, "most Taquaritinga girls marry out of necessity and not love."

Aunt Sofia had told her this time and again when trying to coax Emília to be kind to her suitors. Love was not like a bee sting, her aunt had said. It didn't strike quickly and painfully when you weren't paying attention. It was earned over years of companionship and struggle, so that a couple could look at each other after decades of marriage and say, proudly, that they had eaten much salt together. It would be that way with Degas, Emília reasoned, but not so bitter. She was resourceful by nature: she'd turned chicken feathers into a stylish hat, had made lovely creations out of poor cloth. Degas was finer stuff than Emília had ever worked with before. He had praised her innocence, her sweetness, her childlike nature—things Emília never knew she had until Degas insisted upon them. With time and imagination, she could create a husband out of such a man. She could shape him. And with his refinement and his worldly knowledge, Degas could guide her hand.

The priest was solemn and kind. Only at the end of her confession did he speak.

"Remember, sin calls softly," he said. "It speaks kindly. It does not yell; it whispers. It beckons you with sweetness and possibility."

Afterward, as Emília walked to the colonel's house, the priest's words grated against her mind. Who wouldn't want sweetness? Who wouldn't want a whisper rather than a shout? Who wanted only toil and austerity? To her, the monotony of goodness seemed as sterile and empty as Dona Conceição's sewing room—all white walls and work. She had lost her aunt and her sister. She had done away with her shrine to Santo Antônio. She had stopped reading the romance serials in *Fon Fon*. There was only Degas.

I lost the ability to make castles out of air.

Once, not long ago, Emília would have been chilled by those words. But when Degas said them, she hadn't been disappointed. She didn't want anything made of air. She wanted tile and concrete. She wanted running water. She wanted a fine dress, an elegant hat, and a first-class train ticket that she could present proudly to the conductor, who would take her gloved hand and help her aboard.

Chapter 4
LUZIA

Caatinga scrubland, interior of Pernambuco
May–September 1928

1

In the beginning, she was one of many things acquired on their raids. She was like the red-lacquered accordion with eight baixos; like the gold rings they tugged off the fingers of disobedient colonels; like the crucifixes and mother-of-pearl-faced pocket watches they scooped out of jewelry boxes. The Hawk carried a golden shaving set, a silver flask, a pair of brass binoculars in a velvet-lined case. He and his men carved their initials into each of the things they acquired, adorning them with metal rivets and leather straps, carrying them through the toughest stretches of drought-stricken scrubland. When they finally entered a town, priests and children, farmers and colonels alike gawked at the cangaceiros' amazing wealth, and the treasures became worth their terrible weight. During her first long weeks with the group, Luzia felt like one of those possessions—she was a useless treasure, an extra burden acquired in a moment of weakness and fascination. And like those binoculars and cigarette cases and countless golden crucifixes that became stained by the cangaceiros' own sweat, corroded by winter rains, scratched and bullet ridden after raids, Luzia feared that she, too, would be irrevocably transformed.

When he spoke to her outside Aunt Sofia's house, he did not shout. He did not threaten. He gave her no comforts or guarantees.

He simply handed her the extra uniform she'd sewn for Baiano and said, "I have never seen a woman like you." Yet he regarded her without pity or fascination. He didn't even glance at her bent arm.

"Let's see if you have a preference," he said.

It was a challenge, not a question. *Let's see.* Luzia took the uniform and walked into the house, into her saints' closet. She would ask them for guidance, for direction. What made up her mind were not the saints but the floor. Those hollow indentations made by her knees, by years of prayer and deliberation. Luzia ran her fingers along the dents as if tracing a map of her life. They would grow deeper and deeper with her daily prayers. There would be drought and rain. There would be weddings and funerals. Each July, Luzia would pull the bean vines from the ground and store them in piles inside the living room. Each August, she would put them outside to dry. In January came the cashews, in April the cajá fruits. Eventually, Emília would leave. Aunt Sofia would pass on, a candle placed in her stiff hands to light her way to heaven. And Luzia would stay behind, kneeling in the saints' closet and praying for her aunt's soul and her sister's happiness. Waiting. For what, she did not know. Not death—that would already have come to her, slowly and stealthily, killing her little by little each day of her lonely existence—but some kind of salvation. Some bit of grace that the dented floor and those fickle saints could never give her, because no matter how hard she prayed or how many candles she lit, she would always be Victrola—crooked, sullen Victrola—and never anything more.

Luzia pulled her hand away from the indentations and cradled her bent arm. Something bitter had welled up within her, as if she'd eaten sour manioc flour. She moved her hand across the floor and found the canvas cangaceiro suit. Carefully, she stepped into the trousers. It felt strange to have her legs divided one from the other. She walked back and forth in the dark kitchen. In trousers, she could take longer strides. She didn't have to worry about a fluttering skirt or a dragging hem. She felt enclosed by the pants, protected and yet free. Was this how men felt?

She'd almost told Emília about this feeling, this freedom. Her sister had wanted to make ladies' trousers for herself ever since she'd seen a pair in her magazines, but that night Emília's eyes were glazed and distracted, her movements frantic. She'd been ordered to pack Luzia's things.

To pack for her! He hadn't even waited for her decision! Luzia felt a rush of anger, then fear. But it was too late. She was dressed, her things packed, and the tall mulatto led her out the door with a firm grip on her arm. As Aunt Sofia often said, there could be no mending. The cloth was already cut.

2

The men did not touch her. They did not stare or speak. They did not joke or sing as they had at the colonel's house. They walked. Each day they moved in a silent line through the scrub, ducking and rising, bending and leaning to avoid barbed vines and tangled branches. They kept up a rhythmic pace, each man placing his foot in the steps of the one before him, so that it looked like one man and not twenty were crossing the caatinga. One man and one woman, because Luzia could not keep up.

Blisters bubbled across her toes, beneath the heel straps of her alpercatas, and in tender crescents on the soles of her feet. When they burst, her sandals became slick with water and then blood. Monk's-head cacti littered the ground, their bulbous tops emerging from the earth like men buried neck high in the dirt. Their thorns stabbed Luzia's ankles, the tips breaking and lodging beneath her skin. Her ankles swelled. Her feet grew heavy and numb. Ponta Fina carried a medicine bag with mercurochrome and gauze. On the Hawk's orders, they stopped while Ponta unbuckled her alpercatas and poured the red liquid across her feet. When the burning began, Luzia clenched her teeth and closed her eyes. She tried to go deep within herself, to that silent space in her mind where she had retreated so many times before: when the encanadeira snapped her broken arm together, or when Padre Otto made her kneel on the church's stone floor and repeat a hundred Our Fathers in forgiveness for something she had done. But Luzia could no longer gain access to that place.

The entire group had halted, and many of the men—the big-eared one especially—stared at her, irritated.

"My feet hurt, too, at first," Ponta Fina whispered as he wrapped her feet in gauze. Stiff curls of hair were beginning to sprout from the boy's pimpled chin. "You'll get used to it," he said.

Luzia nodded. She forced herself to move forward, to take one step, then another. As long as they kept walking, the men paid attention to their destination and not to her. Movement kept her safe, but not invisible. The men glanced at her while they walked, studying her when they believed she wasn't aware. Luzia cradled her crooked arm. The freedom she'd felt when she'd first stepped into her new trousers was gone. In the saints' closet, she'd only imagined the thrill of leaving. She hadn't thought of what would come afterward. In Taquaritinga, Luzia was immune from Aunt Sofia's concerns about the dangers a girl faced. She'd never felt the risk of losing her virtue. But that safety came from being Victrola, which she wasn't anymore. There, in that strange scrubland, she was a woman—the lone woman in a pack of men. Luzia kept walking.

In the evenings, when it grew dark and they could no longer move easily about the scrub, the men made camp. They looked for jurema trees, whose roots were poison to the plants around them, making the soil beneath their spindly branches free of undergrowth. The ground was sandy but not smooth. They laid blankets on it; the Hawk did not allow hammocks. Men slept too deeply in hammocks, he insisted. The ground was rocky and uncomfortable, which made them keep one eye open. Luzia slept on her own blanket. During the first few nights, she couldn't rest. She held her penknife close to her chest, ready to swipe at any man who came near. None of them did. In later days, as her feet grew more blistered and raw, Luzia looked forward to evening and the possibility of rest, but when it finally came, she still could not sleep. A chilling desperation moved through her, starting at the pit of her stomach and surging into her chest. She bunched a damp corner of blanket into her mouth. The cloth dried her tongue, and the sand that stuck to the cover's fibers gritted between her teeth. Still, the blanket muffled her sobs. Her life and her virtue depended on those men's mercy. It was a thought Luzia could not stomach. Mercy, after all, was divine. Those men were not. They were unwashed and crude. They lived lives based on instinct and desire. Mercy was beyond such impulses; it required restraint, deliberation. So far, the cangaceiros had not touched her, but that was no guarantee. Luzia bit down on the blanket. She sensed the men listening in the darkness, eavesdropping from their own sandy beds. In the mornings, after a night of fitful sleep, some of the cangaceiros smirked at her. Most ignored her. None commented on her crying.

In the beginning, rains did not touch the caatinga scrub. The trees were gray and stunted, as if they'd been torched by fire. Orange-backed lizards were the only animals that appeared, rushing from tree to tree, the dry underbrush crackling beneath their clawed feet. But rain would come; Luzia felt a constant ache in her locked elbow. Dark clouds hung on the horizon, like a gray lid placed over the land, leaving Luzia and the cangaceiros to stew in the muggy air.

When the rain came, it fell in quick, torrential bursts. It washed away the sand, exposed the knotted roots of trees, made the smallest of gullies into great channels. In response, the caatinga bristled with life. Shoots as tall and straight as spears emerged from the spiky clumps of agave. Leaves appeared between the black thorns of ju-rema bushes. Vines emerged from the dirt. Some were threadlike and sticky, others waxy and barbed. They snaked along the ground and wrapped themselves around bushes and tree trunks. They festooned the massive, many-limbed facheiro cacti. They moved across the scrub and turned the gray forest green.

The rain soothed her feet but soaked her leather shin guards, making them heavy and black with mold. Her canvas suit was never dry. Beneath it, Luzia felt her skin grow puckered and slack. She imagined it loosening bit by bit, like the peel of an overripe fruit. And she felt as if the rain had entered her mind as well, seeping inside like it did with the kitchen door in Aunt Sofia's house, making it warped and thick and unable to close out the world around her. Luzia heard every droning mosquito. She heard the jangle of the men's cartridge belts, the clinking of their tin mugs against the barrels of their rifles. She heard the hollow tapping of their water gourds against the silver handles of their knives. Often the sounds merged, becoming a long, deep ringing in her ears. She stumbled. The Hawk forced a sweet chunk of rapadura into her mouth. Luzia shook her head roughly. Her saliva was as thick as paste. She tried to speak but no sound came.

Each night the men sliced the squat xique-xique cactus into rounds, plucked out its thorns, and pressed down upon the slices with the flat faces of their knives. A yellow juice squirted out. They filled Luzia's gourd with this juice and nothing else. It was an old sertanejo trick—a desperate trick—that kept animals and people hydrated during the worst droughts. The xique-xique's juice saved lives, but it burned throats. Luzia recalled the rumors she'd heard as a child: tales of entire families subsisting on xique-xique, of farmers forcing the juice into the mouths of their cattle and goats, who, after a week of drinking the bitter fluid, would open their mouths in hoarse, voiceless bays. All new members of the Hawk's group were required to drink the juice.

"It teaches us silence," the Hawk said as he poured the first, frothy yellow batch into her gourd. "A quiet man listens. Out here, a man who doesn't listen isn't a man. He's a corpse."

Perhaps the xique-xique worked; the men had keen ears. They could distinguish between the baying of a lost goat and that of an injured one. They grew suspicious if they heard a cock crowing at the wrong hour or when they sensed the smell of sweat that was not their own. They'd spent so much time in those backlands that, like the scrub foxes or the wild caititu pigs or even the fabled spotted panthers, they sensed any foreign element.

Luzia had learned this when she tried to escape. During the first days of their journey, when Taquaritinga's mountainside still loomed in the distance, Luzia said she needed to relieve herself. The men stopped. She walked far into the scrub, wary of the cangaceiros watching her. Her mind felt numb from lack of food. Her thoughts were plodding and trivial, until she looked up and saw, beyond the scrub trees, Taquaritinga's mountain. It was blue-gray, like a shadow, and it seemed so close. Only when she started running toward the mountain did Luzia realize that the men were waiting, that they might punish her or even kill her for tricking them. Her heart thumped wildly. Her blistered feet burned. She ran harder. The underbrush crackled loudly beneath her feet. Dry tree limbs lashed her arms and then her face; the scrub trees grew taller the farther she ran. Before long, they blocked the view of the mountain. Luzia's direction faltered. She turned, weaving back between bushes and trees. It wasn't long before she heard footsteps and the men quietly surrounded her.

That night it rained, and the cangaceiros made their toldas—stringing up oilcloth tarps and digging small moats around them with the tips of their machetes—while Ponta Fina guarded her. The men were quiet and wary around her, as if she were a wild thing the Hawk had lured into camp and did not want to frighten away.

With each day that passed, Luzia felt wildness creeping into her. Each morning, the Hawk handed her a sliver of sun-dried beef. A downy coating of mold grew on the meat, and during her first days, Luzia ate around it. But later, she snatched the slivers from the Hawk's hand and ate them whole. On the rare occasions when the men caught and cooked a stray goat, Luzia sucked on the bones long after she had devoured her small share of meat. Most evenings, the men killed rolinha doves with slingshots or trapped and gutted massive, black teú lizards. For days afterward, Luzia craved the lizards' tough white meat and crackling tails. She searched the ground as she walked, desperate to catch one with her own shaking hands. Sometimes, before a dizzy spell, she thought she heard Aunt Sofia's voice. It rose above the season's last screeching cicadas. Above the sad, incessant whoops of the cururu frogs.

I caught your mother eating dirt, Aunt Sofia had said. *When she had you in her belly.*

It was something her aunt had told her long ago, when Luzia was small. As a child, Luzia could not imagine her mother—that pretty woman from the wedding portrait—eating earth. But after weeks with the cangaceiros, she understood. At night, Luzia crouched at the edge of her damp blankets and dug into the wet ground, past the thin topsoil, until she reached clay. She took quick, forceful bites. She did not like the clay's metallic taste or the thick, pasty residue it left in her mouth. But something murky and insistent had risen within her, something she could not control.

Perhaps the Hawk heard her clawing at the ground. Perhaps he saw her orange fingertips or noticed how she choked down the juice in her gourd. He began to cook her entire rolinha doves. He gave her long sips of water from his canteen. Luzia felt surges of gratitude, then disgust. She clenched her teeth, refusing his gifts. The Hawk calmly pried her mouth open with his thick fingers. He held her jaw and forced her to chew. Each night, after prayers, he ordered Ponta Fina to hold Luzia's arms while he unbuckled her alpercatas. He placed her feet in a warm pot of quixabeira bark tea and then unwound their wet bandages. He moved his thumbs in hard circles around her heel, her arch, her ankle. Luzia felt a tingle through the numbness. The Hawk pressed harder. There was a burning pain, as if she'd been stung by a hundred red wasps. Luzia squirmed along the ground, trying to break free of his grip. Ponta Fina held her arms. The Hawk clamped her foot in his hands.

"Shhh," he whispered. "Shhh."

She let out a long, choked breath. She wanted to tug her feet away, but her body rebelled. Her leg muscles were rubbery and weak. The Hawk repeated his long, slow hiss. *Shhhh. Shhhh.* Like a hushed whistle. Luzia closed her eyes.

As a girl, she'd visited Colonel Pereira's ranch. She'd watched their hired man break mules. He'd tied ropes to their bridles and held tight as the animals kicked and bucked, their ribs protruding beneath their coats, their mouths frothy. With quiet persistence, the man held those ropes until the animals collapsed from exhaustion and hunger. Then he spoke to them in a soft voice, stroking their muzzles and feeding them from his hands until they stood and followed him. She and Emília had left the ranch troubled and angry. Her sister hated the man, while Luzia hated the mules, not for their final collapse but for their short memories.

By the time the first full moon rose, as round and white as one of Padre Otto's Communion wafers, Luzia, too, had forgotten. She could not recall Aunt Sofia's smell or Emília's capable hands. Her mind became as cloudy and thick as the cactus juice in her gourd. There were no hours or minutes. No today or tomorrow. There were only her labored steps and her heavy feet, as red and raw as hunks of meat. There was only her cramping stomach, her burning throat, her pungent and amber-colored urine. She felt no fear, no regret.

3

An empty jar is easily filled. That was what Aunt Sofia used to say. This was why Luzia's aunt obsessively kept each of her clay water jugs full—if one was left empty it soon became home to spiders, lizards, or the shiny-backed cockroaches that came from the banana palms. Looking back upon her first weeks with the cangaceiros, Luzia felt as though her mind had been turned over and emptied out like one of Aunt Sofia's clay jugs. But slowly, her dizzy spells decreased. Her feet grew a thick, yellow skin. Her hands darkened in the sun, becoming the color of burnt sugar. The skin on her face and neck burned and peeled so many times that it felt taut and rough when she touched it. As her body healed, her mind sharpened.

She began to see the difference between the gnarled trunks of the canela-de-velho trees (which made her recall Aunt Sofia's arthritic fingers) and the smooth yellow bark of the inaé. She learned to dodge the pincushion-shaped bulbs of monk's-head cacti that littered her path. She learned to distinguish between the hoarse call of the cancão bird and the musical twitter of the leather jacket. Luzia began to study the men, too. Soon, like the scrub's trees and birds, each cangaceiro became distinct and familiar. As they walked, she could define them by their heights and by the hair that sprang from beneath their leather hats. A few, like the Hawk, had fine and tangled hair, honey colored at the tips, from the sun. The others—Ponta Fina, Sweet Talker, Baiano, Little Ear—had hair that ranged from tightly wound curls to springy muffs. When the cangaceiros weren't walking, they were busy setting up camp, building fires, and catching food. It was only during prayers that the men stayed still enough for Luzia to study them.

Each day, before dawn, the men prayed. They rose from their blankets and pulled their thick-strapped bornal bags over their heads. They slipped off their leather water pouches, their hollowed gourds, and the heavy ribbons of bullets that they wore even during sleep. They knelt before the Hawk and unbuttoned their jackets. Pinned to their tunics were pieces of their past: a sister's faded photograph, a lock of hair, an unraveling red ribbon, a damp slip of paper. They placed their hands over these objects and bent their heads.

They prayed not for their souls but for their bodies, repeating the prayer of corpo fechado to close their bodies off from illness, injury, and death. When they finished, each man removed an item from his bornal and placed it on the ground before him. Baiano put down a dented pocket watch. Ponta Fina put down his array of knives. Sabiá, the group's best singer, placed the red-lacquered accordion before him. The balding Chico Coffin put down an initialed cigarette case; the hook-nosed Caju, a bag of gold teeth. Sweet Talker put down a riding crop with silver studs on its handle. Little Ear placed a book before him, though he didn't know how to read. One by one, all but the Hawk laid objects before them. Luzia bowed her head but did not pray. She watched the men instead.

She saw that Ponta Fina bit his fingernails. Baiano, the tall mulatto, was the Hawk's second in command. He kept a necklace of red seeds wrapped around his wrist to ward off snakes. Caju wouldn't tolerate jokes about his large nose. Jacaré chewed juá bark incessantly to keep his teeth white. Chico Coffin had a habit of patting the bald patch on his head, as if making sure it was not spreading. One morning, Luzia overheard the men's conversation and learned that Half-Moon's eye had been damaged when he was a boy, during a game of cangaceiros versus colonels. A cactus thorn had lodged in it, turning it the dull beige of a boiled egg. The charcoal-skinned Sweet Talker had earned his nickname for the line of tick marks on his knife sheath, one for each lady he'd seduced. *Raparigas don't count,* he said. Branco, the freckled one, stammered when he spoke. Safety Pin had a vast collection of paper saints pinned to his tunic, hidden under his jacket. Jurema had long, skinny arms that flapped wildly each time he played Sabiá's accordion. Coral had a fear of choking, which made him chew his food a dozen times before swallowing. Tatu had an oversize belly. Furão had long, deft fingers. Surubim was the only cangaceiro who knew how to swim. Inteligente became tangled in his bornal straps each morning and Canjica, the group's old cook, patiently helped untangle them. Vanity had small, piggish eyes and many missing teeth, but each evening he meticulously cleaned his uniform, polishing the coins sewn onto his hat brim and shining his alpercatas. And Little Ear fell into a petulant silence each time the Hawk requested Baiano's counsel instead of his.

The Hawk always knelt in the center of their prayer circle. He stared intently at the ground and spoke the prayers slowly, pronouncing the longer words syllable by syllable, as if he had memorized them but did not fully know their meaning.

"Beloved sir," the Hawk began, his voice deep and steady. "Who was sent from God's breast to absolve our sins, give us your grace and mercy. Take away the fury of our enemies and hold us, your children, in your gracious arms."

He clasped his hands tightly together. His fingernails were short and white tipped. Each morning he scrubbed them clean with a hard-bristled brush. In the evenings he often sat alone, away from the cook fire, and stared into the scrub's darkness. He lifted his nose and took deep, concentrated breaths, as if sniffing out a scent. Some evenings he spoke with Baiano. Luzia could not hear their conversations. She could only see a meticulously rolled palha cigarette bobbing between his thick, crooked lips. When the cigarette was finished, he rubbed his face roughly, as though trying to coax the slack side back to life.

During the day, Luzia and the men walked behind him, following his loping step. He kept his eyes cast downward, wary of snakes. He guided them through that maze of thorns and trees, seeming to recognize each rock formation, each black-trunked pau-preto, each hillside, each gulley. In the scrub, even small accomplishments—finding a fresh-water spring hidden between two boulders, or spotting an umbuzeiro tree with shade and thick, tuberous roots that they could dig up and suck in order to trick their thirst—became miracles. The Hawk always found them. His consistency made his findings seem more than lucky. They were larger, more significant, like gifts from a guiding hand.

Some nights, he insisted they light no fires and smoke no cigarettes. Other nights he woke everyone and made them all leave camp. Whatever his whims, the men obeyed. He was their quiet, brooding teacher, collecting leaves and carving away bark to instruct them on which were poisons and which were cures. He showed them how to make teas, pastes, and poultices to treat toothaches, ulcers, headaches, and cuts. He was their stern father, intolerant of carelessness. Just as he divined their route through the scrub, he seemed to divine how to please each man and how to shame him. Once, he'd cut off Ponta Fina's silk bandanna when the boy hadn't buried their food scraps deep enough and they'd looked back and seen vultures circling their abandoned campsite, giving away the cangaceiros' presence. The Hawk was their brother, mussing Ponta Fina's hair, patting Inteligente's shoulder, or clapping wildly after Sabiá sang one of his mournful ballads. And, above all, he was their stoop-shouldered priest, their counselor who treated them not as slaves or thugs, but as men.

Luzia disliked his strange whims. There was no logic in his calls for silence—he would simply cock his head toward some indecipherable sound and motion with his hands. "Stop breathing," he would order her in a low, stern whisper. "You have a heavy walk," he chided, making Luzia feel like an unruly child. "Don't drag your feet."

When he spoke to her, Luzia felt a terrible heat inside, as if she'd swallowed a cup of malagueta peppers. That nervous heat overtook her each time the Hawk watched her sew. It made her clumsy with her stitches and made her speech jumbled and stuttering. Luzia hated him for it. When he said prayers, she made herself focus on parts of him and not the whole, in order to thwart her nervousness. She stared at his wrist, so narrow and tapered compared to his thick hands. A blue vein ran upward, underneath the skin, disappearing into his jacket sleeve. She stared at his ears—curved and brown, like tamboril tree seeds. She stared at each of his square, white-rimmed nails.

"If our enemies find us," the Hawk said, continuing his prayer, "they will have eyes but will not see us. They will have ears, but will not hear us. They will have mouths, but they will not speak to us. Beloved Redeemer, arm us with the weapons of São Jorge. Protect us with the sword of Abraham. Feed us with the milk of our Virgin Mother. Hide us in the ark of Noah. Close our bodies with the keys of São Pedro, where no one may hurt us, kill us, or take the blood from our veins. Amen."

Luzia had attended mass all of her life and had never heard Padre Otto say such prayers. But the priest had never knelt before them as the Hawk did. The priest had never used such a deep, sad tone, praying with such fervor that his voice cracked. When this happened, the Hawk seemed fragile, confused. It proved he was a man, like any other, and this was a comfort.

"Amen," the cangaceiros muttered. They unclasped their hands. They lifted their heads. One by one, they leaned forward and spat upon the objects before them.

It always shocked her—the way they cleared their throats and pursed their lips, the quick, startling trajectory of their spit. The men glanced uncomfortably at Luzia. Perhaps her face registered her disapproval. The objects before them were inert and blameless in Luzia's eyes, which gave the spitting an unnecessary, calculated violence. Afterward, the men wiped their objects clean and stuffed them quickly back into their bornais without meeting her eye.

Luzia also carried a pair of canvas bornais. Days after leaving Taquaritinga, the men had emptied her old valise. They'd taken the case and filled it with their camp's refuse—used coffee grounds, maxixe stems, an empty brilliantine tin—and buried it. Then the cangaceiros inspected the items Emília had packed for Luzia, shaking their heads at the old dress, the embroidery thread, the pincushion, the torn knickers. They'd laughed at her penknife until the Hawk made them return it. Luzia was surprised at first, but when he placed the knife back into her hands it seemed small and pathetic, and she knew he hadn't returned it out of kindness. He wanted to show his men and Luzia how powerless she was. Even armed, she posed no threat. Some of the cangaceiros did not agree. They didn't see Luzia as a physical danger, but as a deeper one.

"Women are rotten luck," she'd heard Half-Moon mutter once as they set up camp. Several of the men concurred before Baiano hushed them.

The men tolerated Luzia's presence but didn't like it. She wore their uniform, she carried bornais, and she drank the bitter xiquexique, as they had during their initiations, but she was not one of them. Often, Luzia caught the men staring, studying her as she studied them during prayers. But on their faces were not looks of curiosity or friendliness. There was only concern and expectation, as if the men were waiting for her to reveal her purpose. Luzia didn't understand these looks until the boy cangaceiro explained them.

Outside of the Hawk, only Ponta Fina spoke to her. And since her burnt throat prohibited her from asking questions or disagreeing with the boy, Luzia could do nothing but listen and nod. Because of his age, the men either teased Ponta or shouted orders at him. They rarely tolerated his conversation. In Luzia he found a willing listener and pupil. He showed her how to skin the sweet-faced mocó rats, or scrape scales from the teús. Sometimes he spoke of the other men, venting his frustrations. Once, he speculated about her presence.

"The captain saw you in his prayers," the boy whispered. "He said we had to take you with us. For luck. For some kind of purpose you'll serve. Everyone's guessing how you'll help. There're bets, you know." The boy smiled, revealing his brown-edged teeth. "Some say you won't help at all, but they won't tell that to the captain. My bet is it's got something to do with your name—like the saint. Baiano says maybe you'll give us vision. Show us a new path."

Luzia nodded. That night, her monthly blood came. Luzia had to put the old dress that Emília had packed to a different use. With her penknife, she quickly shredded the dress's fabric. She kept the feathers from the rolinha doves the men caught, and at night, sewed clumps of them between the dress's shreds. Then she took her feather creations and walked away from camp, into the scrub. The men did not question or follow her. They'd seen her ripping her dress apart and seemed to sense that what led her into the scrub was some mysterious, feminine duty that they wanted no knowledge of.

Wary of scorpions and snakes, Luzia quickly crouched and put a feather roll between her legs. Later, when a roll became heavy with blood, Luzia returned to the scrub and buried it. *Blessed are you among women,* she prayed as she dug. *And blessed is the fruit of your womb.* Luzia prayed to the Virgin because she understood what it was like to be doubted by some men and made into a talisman by others. When the boy had told her the Hawk's reasons, Luzia was confused and disappointed. During her first days with the group, she'd felt both fear and pride in the belief that he'd taken her as a prize, that he saw something of value in her. In the end, she was nothing but a charm—like his medallions, his prayer papers, his crystal rock—her worth measured by something as capricious and unfaithful as luck.

4

/ / / / / / / /

One day, they made camp earlier than ususal. A stray goat had wandered near their path. Chico Coffin had heard the animal's brass chocalho clanging around its neck and set off into the scrub. He appeared minutes later, tugging the bleating goat by its horns. The cangaceiros stopped walking to celebrate his find.

As the men set up their toldas and Canjica built a fire, Luzia sat on a rock, her back to the sun. They'd picked a spot between a gulley and a cluster of giant boulders. One of the boulders had cracked along its center. Urtiga grew in the crooked fissure. Hummingbirds made their nests within the plant's branches, unfazed by its stinging nettles. The birds chased each other, zooming between gaps in the rocks. Sometimes they hovered in midair near Luzia, their wings blurred and their emerald bodies still, like jewels suspended before her.

Luzia straightened her shoulders. She'd shucked off her belongings but she slouched, as if their weight was still upon her. She took her bornal in her lap and tugged a needle and embroidery thread through its thick cloth. She was grateful for her sister's erratic packing. The bornal's strap was one palm wide and seven long and she had already covered it with embroidery. Along the edges she'd sewn a curling scroll stitch. Inside she'd scattered São Jorge's cross and added several cross-stitched fleur-de-lis, as if the ratty bag was one of Dona Conceição's fancy tablecloths. Sewing soothed her. The stitches were reliable and familiar. Each had its own method—the placement of the needle, the order of its threading—which never changed.

A few meters away, the goat bleated. Inteligente—the man with the most brute force—clapped its skull with the butt of his rifle. Stunned, the animal fell silent. Little Ear straddled it. He cradled its limp head in his arms and, with one quick jab, punctured its neck. A dark puddle formed at Little Ear's feet. Luzia looked away. She concentrated on her embroidery until Ponta Fina called her aside.

"Come on," the boy said, his hands fidgeting with his knife holsters. "We've got to treat it."

He did not look at her when he spoke; he kept his eyes at his feet, or on some faraway point in the distance. Luzia put away her embroidery and followed Ponta to the gulley. There, Inteligente hung the goat upside down from a thick-limbed umbuzeiro. Her dry udders hung limply against her belly. The white fur on her head and neck were stained pink. Ponta removed one of his knives. He cut circles around the goat's ankles. He sliced slowly along its sides. Then he slipped the blade into his incisions, moving between meat and skin as if peeling a fruit. When he finished, a pink, muscled body hung from the tree.

"Have you guessed why the call me Ponta Fina?" He smiled, flashing his knife.

Luzia shrugged. The goat's teeth were clenched, as if it was cold without its skin. She placed one of Canjica's large tin bowls beneath the animal.

"My father was a butcher," Ponta continued. "The greatest butcher on this side of the Rio São Francisco." He regarded the blade in his hand, tracing its curved edge with his fingertip. "This is a lambedeira. It's for skinning and slicing."

Luzia nodded. Ponta slid the knife down the goat's belly. With both hands, he pressed his weight on the animal's ribs and eased them open carefully, so their tips would not cut him. A rush of heat erupted from the animal, like a foul breath. Ponta stepped back. Intestines shifted and curled like pale snakes, then splattered into the bowl below.

Ponta wiped his hands. One by one, he removed the other knives from their holsters. He showed her the facão, with its thick, flat blade for cutting scrub and opening pathways. He showed her the short, sharp knife he used to scale river fish and bleed animals. He showed her the pajeuzeira, a long, straight knife with a rounded tip that looked harmless compared to the rest. It was a medicine man's knife, he said, made to cut bark and roots. The final knife was the long, silver blade all of the cangaceiros stuffed prominently into the front of their belts. It was not a knife, but a punhal—a long, shining steel rod with no flat edge.

"Mine's only fifty centimeters." Ponta sighed. "The captain's is seventy!" He balanced it across the palms of his hands. "Want to hold it?"

Luzia nodded. Ponta kept his fingers around the silver handle and laid the rod across her open palms. It was heavy and cold.

"It goes clean through," he whispered, as if imparting a secret. "It's more a bullet than a knife."

Half-Moon appeared. In the fading light of dusk, his injured eye took on a blue tinge. Ponta Fina quickly put away the punhal.

"Hurry up and treat that goat," Half-Moon said. "We're hungry."

They would make buchada: boiling the intestines and organs, mincing them, and then stuffing them inside the stomach bag with spices to cook again. Ponta untied the goat and moved it to a flat rock where he sliced it apart. Luzia carried the heavy bowl to the gulley. Winter rains made the gulley deep and wide. Tree limbs moved within its brown waters. Luzia squatted at its edge. She washed the innards piece by piece, turning the intestines inside out with a small stick, as if threading a long needle. She scrubbed the honeycombed stomach, the rubbery white gullet.

Farther downstream, the Hawk appeared. Half of the men accompanied him. They moved several meters apart from one another and knelt at the edge of the water. They removed their hats and jackets. They pulled their tunics over their heads. The Hawk scrubbed his hands clean, then splashed water on his face. His torso was squat and lean. He poured a handful of water over his head. With each movement, Luzia could see the workings of his muscles beneath his brown skin. It was as if the scrub's unyielding heat had simmered away any excess from him. The Hawk looked up. Luzia quickly scooped the innards into their tin bowl and left the gulley.

It was inconsiderate of him, she fumed, and the rest of them, to bathe and forget that she was nearby, cleaning their dinner. As if she didn't merit modesty. As if she was not a woman.

At camp, the rest of the men sat around the cook fire. With a set of metal tongs, Canjica gingerly removed two fist-size rocks from the flames. He dropped them into a coffeepot filled with water. The rocks sizzled.

"I can't wait to dance some forró," Sweet Talker said, extending his arms and shuffling his feet back and forth.

"You want to do more than dance," Baiano said, smiling. "I saw a little boy who looked like you in that last town we visited."

"There're little boys who look like him all over Pernambuco!" Little Ear said.

The men laughed. Inteligente looked at them, confused. Canjica shook his head. He touched the coffeepot, then quickly pulled his hand away. The rocks had already heated the water. He wrapped a cloth around its handle.

When Luzia emerged from the shadows, the men stopped laughing. The bowl in her hands was heavy. She handed it to Canjica. Little Ear stepped toward them. His hair was pulled back and the fire was behind him, making the edges of his ears glow pink. He inspected the tin bowl, swishing the contents with his fingers.

"These aren't clean," he said, staring at Luzia. "Wash them again."

"We can boil away what's left," Canjica said, taking the bowl. Little Ear stopped him.

"It's a sloppy job," he said. "Wash them again."

Luzia met his eyes. The men were bathing in the gulley; she could not go back. She put her hand to her throat and shook her head.

Little Ear squatted and grabbed a handful of sand. He held it over the bowl of innards and opened his fingers. With a plop, the sand fell. Behind him, one of the men chuckled.

"See here," he said. "It's dirty. We don't eat dirty food." He placed the bowl on the ground beside his feet. "Pick it up and wash them again."

Luzia's breath was short and quick. She bent down. Beside them, cooling on a circle of rocks, was the coffeepot. Instead of reaching for the tin bowl at Little Ear's feet, her good arm grabbed the pot and flung it forward. Hot water splattered her hand, stinging her skin.

"Shit!" Little Ear cried. He staggered backward, batting the front of his trousers. "Shit!"

There was silence, then muffled laughter.

"She burned his *pinto*!" Branco cried.

"Doesn't matter," Sweet Talker said, "he never used it!"

The men held their stomachs with laughter. Little Ear stared at the circle of cangaceiros, then at Luzia. He slid the punhal from behind his belt. Baiano held his arm. Luzia picked up the tin bowl and hurried into the scrub.

5

/ / / / / / / /

She did not go to the gulley. Not directly. She crouched in the scrub, her hands shaking, her breath shallow. She saw the Hawk and his men move back toward camp, the tops of their tunics wet and clinging to their chests. Luzia held her breath until they passed. When she reached the gully it loomed before her, its waters dark and churning. She could not swim. Perhaps the men secretly wanted her to cross it, to leave them. Luzia set down the tin bowl, suddenly angry. She would not lope away like a dog. She would return with their silly buchada and would sit beside them, invisible and irritating, like a thorn beneath their skin.

Her throat burned. Luzia chided herself. She'd dreamed of water, craved it. Yet when she had a river before her she did not drink. She took one handful, then another. She could not stop herself. Water ran down her chin, soaking her jacket. It soothed her throat, but as soon as she swallowed, it became raw and dry again.

Behind her, there was rustling. Luzia smelled the waxy, perfumed scent of brilliantine. She heard footsteps behind her. She kept drinking.

"It's time to take you off the xique-xique," he said, squatting beside her. "I'd rather have you argue with my men than injure them."

Luzia wiped her chin. She would not look at him.

"The men," he continued slowly, "some of them aren't happy you're with us. Every day we say the corpo fechado prayer to seal our bodies, and here I am, bringing you along, opening us up like watermelons so any bullet will go through." He rubbed his face roughly, then looked at Luzia. "Most women carry sadness. Bad luck. It's not your fault. It's just your nature."

Luzia coughed. The water she'd gulped rose up into her throat, but different now, more acidic. She'd had too much.

He cleared his throat. "That morning, on the ridge, I thought the bird thief would be a boy. Some poor kid. When I make a guess, I'm usually right. But there you were: hair braided, shoes on your feet. A family girl. You surprised me. Not much surprises me these days." He sighed and shook his head. "I can't tell my men what kind of luck you'll bring us," he said, "because I don't know myself."

If she had a voice, Luzia would have told him he didn't know anything at all. She was no paper saint, no necklace of red string.

"Look there," the Hawk said. He stood suddenly and pointed into the scrub.

It was a mandacaru cactus, its trunk as brown and thick as a tree's except for the finger-length spines emerging from it. Above them, its limbs were green and tube shaped. A few smooth bulbs emerged from its surface.

"Sit still," the Hawk said.

The sky darkened. Sapo-boi frogs moaned in the distance, their faraway calls resembling the bleating of cows. Above them, on the cactus, a bulb broke open. A white petal pushed out. Luzia's neck felt stiff but she didn't move, afraid of startling the flower back into its bulb. More petals unfolded, each thick and white.

Slowly, Luzia turned her eyes to him. The line of scarred flesh on his face was as white as that mandacaru flower. Luzia stared at it as if it, too, would open and reveal itself. She eyed his wet hair, his shaved face. The men in Taquaritinga, the rowdy ones people called "cabra valente," all wore beards. They swore and drank and shot their pistols into the air. She'd believed a cangaceiro would be worse.

But she could not imagine him yelling, and with a certainty that startled her, she knew that if he shot, it would not be into the air.

"They open once," the Hawk said. "Before a big rain. Tomorrow it will be gone."

He faced her. Luzia quickly looked up at the bloom. She could not bring herself to rise and leave. There was something growing within her, something unwanted and insistent, like the onion grass that invaded Aunt Sofia's garden in thick, green clumps. It was attractive but could choke out every other plant if left unchecked. The only solution was to pluck it from the root and burn it in the fire, if anything else was to survive.

6

The mandacaru flower had predicted correctly. That night, rain filled the makeshift moats around their toldas. It splattered onto their blankets. The oilcloth tarps above them bulged with water. The ropes that tied the cloth to the scrub trees grew taut. Chico Coffin was the sentry. He hunched near the covered fire pit and watched the simmering buchada pot. His head slowly slumped to his chest.

The other men were quiet, bunched beneath their toldas. They'd dined on goat's meat and there would be buchada for breakfast. Luzia hoped that their full bellies and the promise of more food had lulled them to sleep. Some might be awake, she thought, and restless. But the rain would protect her; the rain would muffle her movements. It fell loudly, slapping their tarps and hitting the ground in thousands of soft thuds. There was also the racket of frogs, croaking and hooting in the scrub. A celebration, Luzia thought. And in the distance, beneath the rain and the animals, she heard the low rumble of the gulley.

Luzia sat up. Quickly, she pulled her bornal over her head and straightened it across her chest. In one swift motion, she rose from her tolda and stepped into the rain.

In her first few days away from Taquaritinga, she'd prayed for large and weighty things—for rescue, for a miracle. Later, she prayed for water in her canteen instead of cactus juice. She prayed for a hat, a good needle, more embroidery thread. And, mechanically, she prayed for escape. It seemed unnatural not to. She should want to flee, to slip away as quickly and stealthily as a scrub fox. But what would she do if she escaped? Where could she go? People in Taquaritinga would assume the worst. They would say she was worse than ruined—she would be tainted. No one wanted a tainted woman sewing their clothes or measuring their dead. A tainted woman had only one vocation. But that night, after watching the mandacaru flower bloom, Luzia realized that the longer she stayed, the more dependent she became upon the Hawk's belief in her. With each passing day, Luzia felt a strange gratitude growing toward him. The Hawk's faith in her purpose kept Luzia safe, even respected. But, if she did not prove useful, how long would his faith last? And if she unwittingly brought bad luck, would there be any faith at all?

She resisted the urge to run. The rain blurred her vision and soaked her clothes, making her movements awkward and uncertain. She had to go slowly, she told herself, recalling Half-Moon's milky eye. The scrub was dense and dark. She wove her way through it, using her locked elbow to push away branches. Rain clouds dulled the moon's light. Still, she knew where to walk, following the sound of water until she reached the gully. There was a village beyond it. The cangaceiros had spoken of getting supplies there. Luzia believed that if she crossed the gulley, she could find it. She could hide there. She'd learned enough about survival in the scrub to withstand a few days alone. But if there was no village, she could die of exposure. Or she could drown in that gulley; she did not know how to swim. Luzia shivered and shook her head. It was not a river, she reasoned. It could not be deep. She closed her eyes and pictured it in the summer: nothing but a dry ditch. Soon it would be summer again. The nights would be silent and dry. There would be no more noises to hide her escape. No rain to cover her tracks. No gulley to block the cangaceiros from coming after her.

Luzia waded inside. Water crept into her sandals. It pushed against her legs. Luzia pushed back, taking long, hard strides. The current made the water feel thick, as if she was wading through syrup. She ballooned out farther than she'd intended. Halfway across, the water reached her chest. Something scraped her foot—a tree branch, perhaps, pulled downstream. It caught her sandal. Luzia tried to shake herself free. The weight of the current buckled her knees. Water rushed into her ears, her nose. It had a metallic taste, like clay. Luzia choked it out. She tugged her foot again, harder this time. The branch tore away from her sandal but the current still carried her. Luzia moved her feet to steady herself but she could not find the bottom. Was it deeper than she remembered? Or had the current tricked her, flipping her upside down? Luzia's chest burned. She craned her neck, kicked and tossed her body. Her bent arm flapped like a useless wing. When she broke through the gully's surface, she took a breath and swallowed water. Above her was rain. Everywhere, there was water. She could not escape it.

When she had fallen from the mango tree, Luzia had experienced a silence so deep and enveloping it seemed a liquid thing, filling her from the inside out, tamping her ears, her nose, her eyes, her every pore shut. In the gulley, she felt that silence again. She felt the current tugging her under, felt the uselessness of movement. When she was still, the water offered no resistance. It covered her, cloaked her, pulled her inside itself.

Something wrapped around her, pressing beneath her armpits, then tightening across her chest. It lifted her. Rain pelted her face. The roar of water made her dizzy. Luzia took a long, desperate swallow of air.

"Pull!" a voice cried beside her, so loud it hurt her ear. "Pull!"

Luzia saw the outline of Inteligente's thick frame on the bank. His arm was hooked to Baiano's, who stood knee deep in the water. Baiano's other arm was hooked to a third cangaceiro, who was hooked to a fourth, then a fifth, and then the sixth, who held her.

Luzia twisted her body. The arm about her chest tightened, like a clamp around her lungs. His face was centimeters from hers. The good side clenched with effort, the scarred side impassive.

The current tugged them down. The men pulled them toward shore. Luzia's eyes stung. Her limbs felt weak. Inteligente, the anchor that held them all, might feel his strength buckle under the pull of the water. If so, Luzia would be returned to the silence, with the Hawk at her side. Or the current might give them up, releasing them to the men who would drag them back onto that dark shore. Luzia closed her eyes and waited to see which would win.

7

After the rains, the caatinga bloomed. Orange flowers, their petals as thin and dry as paper, emerged from the quipá's prickly rounds. The malva bushes grew as tall as men. Bromeliads released red blooms. Bees swarmed the scrub. When Luzia closed her eyes, their buzzing reminded her of rushing water.

After they'd pulled her from the gully, the men regarded her with a quiet respect. They called her Miss Luzia instead of avoiding her name altogether. Ponta Fina gave her honey for her throat, building fires beneath beehives and, when the smoke drove the bees away, tugging the round, potlike combs from the hive walls. Little Ear stayed quiet and wary, but never retaliated for his burn. Luzia wondered if the men's newfound respect came from her fight with Little Ear, or because she had walked into the gully alone at night, like some kind of witch. Most likely, it came from the fact that the Hawk had deemed her worthy enough to save. He would not speak to her. After the gully, he kept his distance, no longer treating her feet or giving her extra food. She was off the xique-xique juice and her voice had returned, gravelly and hoarse.

Slowly, the scrub changed. The rains ended, but thunder still rolled across the sky in loud, angry rumbles. They walked past tenant farms with blossoming cotton fields and later, when the blossoms fell, the buds broke open with white fibers. The caatinga looked like it was covered in a vast, white sheet.

The tenant farmhouses were clay-and-stick huts inhabited by farmers or vaqueiros. Sometimes the homes were empty, but there were signs of life: lit embers in the cookstove, a skinny dog tied to a tree. The residents had seen the cangaceiros coming and hid in the scrub. If their food supplies were low, the Hawk instructed his men to take what they needed and leave. The cangaceiros tugged hocks of smoked meat off hooks over the cook fire. They grabbed blocks of rapadura and fistfuls of manioc flour and fava beans. Sometimes the absent tenants had small plantings of corn and melons beside their houses. The men ripped the ears and fruits from their stalks. They left no payment. Luzia felt terrible taking the food, but like the cangaceiros, she ate it all the same.

Some tenants stayed in their homes. The women wore stained head scarves and crossed their arms over their bulging bellies. They staggered about, rounding up their many children, who ran naked around their yards. The children had swollen stomachs and sticklike arms. A clear, sticky substance ran from their noses and onto their upper lips, which they wiped clean with their tongues. The fathers were the last to appear. They came from the fields, or from inside the huts. Some were dark skinned and tight lipped. Others had a yellow pallor, their eyes bloodshot from drink. All were hunched from years of planting and reaping.

Luzia was forced to hide nearby, in the scrub along with Ponta Fina, so she would not be seen. Still, she liked watching the women. It seemed like years since she'd heard a woman's voice. Once, a woman did see her, but she'd simply stared at Luzia's legs, more startled to see a woman wearing trousers than anything else.

The cangaceiros were kinder to those who stayed. They did not invade their homes or pilfer their crops. Instead, they asked if they had food to sell. They always did. The Hawk paid well, offering thirty mil-réis for a block of cheese that would have cost no more than three. He paid for their loyalty, their discretion. Many of the tenant farmers allowed the cangaceiros to stay the night on their land.

They instructed them as to where the nearest town was located, or informed the Hawk if the Military Police or a colonel's capangas had passed through in recent days. Some farmers refused payment; they asked instead for the Hawk's blessing and his protection.

In all of their wanderings, Luzia had not seen a church. One of the tenant families admitted to traveling three days in order to attend Christmas services. Luzia did not like how they knelt, quiet and reverent, before the Hawk. They worshipped him, she thought, because they didn't know better.

They closed their eyes. The Hawk placed his hand on each of their heads. Luzia shuddered. He'd touched her dozens of times—massaging her feet, bolstering her up, forcing her to eat—but in the way one would touch a sick animal, deftly and efficiently, in case it bit. When he blessed these farmers, he did it lovingly. He placed his calloused fingertips on their foreheads, their chins, and on each of their hollow cheeks. Luzia touched her own cheek, then quickly took her hand away.

One morning they neared the outskirts of a farm whose cotton had already been cleared. The cangaceiros hung back, hiding in the scrub. The farm's wooden gate hung crookedly, leaning out toward the road as if straining against its hinges. A thick rope tied the gate closed. Beyond it was a brick farmhouse with rounded, clay roof tiles.

The Hawk and his men cocked their rifles, holding them level with their thighs. The jolt from their Winchesters could dislocate a shoulder, Ponta had explained to her, so they made sure to shoot from the hip. They did this before entering any house—sitting for hours in the scrub and surveying the area, counting the inhabitants, analyzing the tracks going to and from the property before making contact. "It's better to be patient, and live," the Hawk always reminded his men, "than to be avexado and die." When their observations were complete, Half-Moon placed two fingers in his mouth and let out a high-pitched whistle.

An old man appeared in the doorway and whistled back. He had gray hair and took small, dragging steps, as if his bones ached. Luzia tried to focus on his face but it was blurred. She rubbed her eyes; Aunt Sofia had warned her about embroidering in the dark. When he untied the gate, Luzia was surprised to see that the man was younger than she had imagined—a father instead of a grandfather. Two deep wrinkles ran from his nostrils down the sides of his mouth, like a wooden doll she'd had as a child, whose jaws opened and shut when she pulled a lever attached to its back.

When he saw the Hawk, the man smiled and walked toward him, his steps faster than they had been before. The two men grabbed each other's shoulders.

"Your gate's crooked," the Hawk said.

"Had a lot of rain, praise God," the man said. There was a raised mound on his forehead, its center scabbed with blood. He messed his hair forward, cringing when his hand met the wound.

"You should get your boys to fix it," the Hawk replied.

"They're gone. Left six months back. Found work as vaqueiros, in Exu."

"Tomás, too?"

"No. He's out." The man pointed his chin toward the horizon, to a line of tall, tightly interlaced fences. "Herding the goats."

"And Lia?" the Hawk asked. "I remember when she used to run and open this gate for us. Now she makes her father do it?"

"She's grown shy. Not a girl anymore," the man replied, staring at the rope in his hands. He looked questioningly at Luzia. "Got some new faces?"

The Hawk nodded. The man stepped toward Luzia.

"You're a big one," he said, stretching out his hand. "Francisco Louriano. They call me Seu Chico."

"We've come to return your accordion," the Hawk interrupted. He pointed to the older wooden instrument tied to Half-Moon's back. "We don't get an invitation inside?"

"It's not as you remember it," Seu Chico sighed, then led them to the house.

The brick facade was cracked and dented, worn away in some places by the rains. There were several holes along the front wall, each small and perfectly round, the width of Luzia's thumb. Near the back were a series of goat fences, their sticks tall and tightly interlaced. The pens were empty. Luzia heard the distant clang of chocalhos. She looked again at the house. A young girl stared out from one of the windows. Her face was thin and tan. Dark crescents shaded the skin beneath her eyes. They focused on Luzia with a startled intensity, like an animal prepared either to attack or to run, depending on the threat. Without warning, she ducked inside and disappeared.

Before entering, the Hawk kicked his alpercatas clean. The other men did the same. Baiano, Sweet Talker, Ponta Fina, and Safety Pin did not enter. They stood guard along the sides of the house instead. Luzia was the last to duck through the door.

There were several stools with ripped leather seat covers. A few had been hastily sewn back together. On the rest, the leather dangled in slashed pieces. There was a brown stain smeared across the wall. Several wooden caritós were snugly built into the room's corners. One held a singed portrait of São Jorge. The others held fragments of clay saints: a shrouded head, an arm with birds at its fingertips, a pair of chipped feet. Each broken piece had a candle beside it. There was an odor Luzia could not define—on the surface it smelled of smoke from the cookstove, but underneath was something sharp and heady, like the scent that came from the cauldrons Dona Chaves's husband used to cure animal hides back in Taquaritinga.

"Who was here?" the Hawk asked.

Seu Chico bowed his head. A clicking sound erupted from his throat. He covered his eyes.

"Sit down, friend," the Hawk said, dragging a stool toward Seu Chico.

The man waved his hands as if shooing away a bug. He walked down a dark corridor and brought out a chair, a real chair, with a wooden back. He put the chair before the Hawk.

"You sit first," Seu Chico said. "Please."

The curtain that shrouded the kitchen door moved open. The girl peeked out from behind the fabric. She was no older than

Ponta Fina. A shaft of sunlight fell through a gap in the roof tiles, making her hair glow.

"It happened fifteen days back," Seu Chico said. "A group of Colonel Machado's men—his capangas—came here from Fidalga. I have to sell my cotton to him. Except . . ." Seu Chico coughed. He threaded his crooked fingers. "What he pays isn't just. Part of my harvest I sold to a man from Campina. The colonel found out. Those colonels, they think a man's back is just a place to wipe their knives clean."

"How many were here?" the Hawk asked.

"Six."

"What time?"

"Near dusk. Tomás was out, bringing home the goats. It was only me and Lia here."

Seu Chico looked nervously toward the kitchen. The curtain was closed, the girl gone. He growled out mucus, then spat. When it hit the floor he raised his eyebrows, alarmed. He quickly rubbed it into the dirt with the tip of his sandal.

"They took my old papo-amarelo," he continued. "My father gave me that rifle. They burned the beds. Broke our saints. Shat in the water tank. It took me and Tomás a week to clean it out. Praise God we had rain this winter. If they'd done that in the summer, we would've died of thirst."

"And Lia?" the Hawk asked, his voice a whisper.

The man touched the wound on his head.

"One hit me with the butt of his rifle. Knocked me out cold. I still feel like I drank too much branquinha. When I came to, I thought they'd left. I looked for Lia, couldn't find her. Then I heard them. Heard those capangas laughing in the back bedroom. They held the door shut. I heard Lia in there, with them. She was calling for me and I couldn't get in. I hit it as hard as I could, that door, but it wouldn't move." Seu Chico stared at the Hawk for a long time. "Lia's in back," he finally said. "Won't come out. Not with men here. She can't be in a room with her own father now. I wish they'd killed us both." Seu Chico put his head in his hands. The cangaceiros were quiet. The Hawk's left brow furrowed. The corner of his mouth twitched. His scarred side stayed placid, expressionless except for his watery eye, which he gently dabbed with his handkerchief.

8

The town of Fidalga was half a day's walk from Seu Chico's farm and it belonged to Colonel Floriano Machado. He'd named the town in honor of his deceased mother, a Portuguese, and in the town's square he'd placed a stone bust of the woman, her jaw set in a stern underbite, her eyes staring steadily to the east, as if looking toward her country. Luzia studied the bust each time she and Ponta Fina went to Fidalga.

Before their trips, Ponta tied his hair back and removed all of his knife holsters but one. He wore trousers and a sackcloth shirt that belonged to one of Seu Chico's sons. Luzia wore a dress. It was baggy and short. Seu Chico had kept all of his deceased wife's frocks, but the woman was small and squat compared to Luzia, who had to sew another layer of cloth around the hem of the borrowed dress so that it would cover her calves. When she wore it for the first time, Luzia missed her trousers. The dress felt too airy, too vulnerable.

"You will be our eyes," the Hawk said before her first trip into town with Ponta.

Ponta Fina hadn't yet grown the telltale cangaceiro calluses on his shoulders, but his hair was long and his back was hunched. The townspeople would mistrust a strange, long-haired boy, but they would not suspect a woman. Not a brother and sister. They visited Fidalga three times, posing as orphan travelers in need of supplies. Ponta always held her arm tightly. The first time she walked on Fidalga's narrow dirt paths, Luzia felt the townspeople's eyes on her. They stared at her bent arm, her baggy dress, her calloused feet. On their second visit, she and Ponta purchased dried beef and blocks of rapadura. By the third visit, she and Ponta had become familiar faces, and their humble looks and prompt payment loosened merchants' lips.

Colonel Machado's property extended as far as the horizon on all sides. Even on horseback, a man could not cross all of his land in one day. Fidalga's first houses had been built by tenant farmers. Later, the colonel built a small chapel and allowed stores, bars, a dance hall, a Saturday fair. Like other colonels, Machado's contract was simple: people did not pay a single tostão to live on his land, but in return they owed him their obedience, and a sizable percentage of whatever they harvested or sold. If Colonel Machado did not like a house's color, he ordered it repainted. If he did not like the looks of someone, he asked them to leave. And if they refused or broke his contract in any way, they no longer dealt with the colonel himself, but with his hired men, his capangas.

After each visit, Luzia and Ponta took a convoluted route back to Seu Chico's farm. When they arrived, they sat with the Hawk and described Fidalga: the location of its grain shop, its makeshift prison, and the colonel's powder blue mansion at the far edge of town. Like the colonel's house, his capangas were easy to locate. During their second visit, Luzia saw a group of men sitting on wooden stools outside the town's largest shop. They wore short-brimmed, round vaqueiro hats whose leather was warped from sweat and rain. There were six of them.

"As big as a horse," the oldest capanga, a broad-chested man in his forties, said and nodded at Luzia.

"As good looking, too!" another snickered. He was no older than Ponta Fina.

During this visit they also learned that Colonel Machado had traveled to Pará to buy cattle and would be gone for another two months.

"No matter," the Hawk said. "We don't need his permission."

After that, the Hawk put an end to their trips. He took several rolls of mil-réis notes from his bornal—enough to buy a dozen pedal-operated Singers—and left with four of his men. They headed toward the São Francisco River, to visit a rancher friend he called "a man of character."

Baiano took charge of the group. The remaining men camped in the scrub beside Seu Chico's house, hidden from sight. They rationed their coffee and rapadura. Once a week, Seu Chico butchered a goat and each Saturday he and his son, Tomás, made a trip into Fidalga for manioc flour and sun-dried beef. They could buy only small quantities so as not to attract suspicion. Luzia and Lia made cheese from the goats' milk and dug macaxeira root from the ground, but it was not enough to feed all of the men. Luzia felt a constant, dull ache in her stomach. The cangaceiros did not complain. They were accustomed to living with little food, but they grew restless with inactivity. Each night, Luzia heard their arguments over games of dominoes.

She slept inside the house, on the floor beside Lia. She often thought of Emília and their shared bed, but Lia was nothing like her sister. She was more like one of Seu Chico's goats: thin necked, with a large oval face and bulging eyes. Like the goats, Lia was sweet natured and skittish, jumping at any odd noise, ducking in the storage pantry whenever Ponta Fina or Baiano came near the house. Despite their delicate appearance, Seu Chico's goats were hardy and resourceful creatures. Determined to survive in the scrub, they consumed the toughest plants, peeling away bark with their teeth and uncovering the soft, pulpy centers of trees. Luzia saw this same determination in Lia. Each morning, the girl held palma cactus in her bare hands, chopping it into cubes and dumping the sticky chunks into the goats' feeding bins. She grabbed newborn kids by their back legs and squirted mercurochrome into their bloody bellybuttons so efficiently and mercilessly that the kids didn't have time to squirm or be frightened.

Some nights, Lia cried out in her sleep. The first time this happened, Luzia tried to comfort her. The girl slapped her away and then curled into a ball, trembling in the early morning air. Luzia had heard people in Fidalga gossiping about Lia. It was a shame, they said, that she had been ruined; Lia would have made a good wife.

But after the capangas' visit, she could never marry. She would have to take care of her father, and when Seu Chico died, she would be at the mercy of Colonel Machado.

Luzia could have escaped a dozen times. She could have lifted herself from their makeshift bed and walked out of the front gate without the men noticing. The cangaceiros were listless and, out of respect to Seu Chico and Lia, they rarely came near the house. But each time Luzia contemplated leaving, she felt Lia's wide, startled eyes on her. They rarely spoke, but each afternoon they sat in the shade and shucked beans from their shells. Each evening they sewed together, and Lia peered over Luzia's shoulder to copy her stitches. There was something else holding her as well, an anticipation Luzia would not acknowledge until she caught herself listening for clapping at the front gate, or for a whistle, or for the Hawk's deep voice signaling his return. Once, she heard the men hooting outside and nearly tripped over the milk basin as she ran to the window. It was only a celebration for catching three fat mocó rats. Luzia silently wiped up the splattered goat's milk and cursed herself for such foolishness. Still, each evening she leaned against the goat pens with Ponta Fina and questioned the boy.

"You'd be surprised who our friends are," Ponta said, smiling. He answered her questions coyly, which annoyed Luzia.

"He took money with him," Luzia said. "What does he mean to buy?"

"Just because he took it doesn't mean he'll use it. Our protection is worth more than money."

"Protection?"

"The captain's a man of his word." Ponta sighed, irritated by her ignorance. "No one wants to be at the end of his knife."

He spoke slowly, as if the speed of his words would help her understanding. There were ranchers, colonels, even police captains who traded with the Hawk, burying munitions or food or other gifts at predetermined locations where the cangaceiros would eventually dig them up. In exchange, the Hawk paid them with money or with the promise of protection from rival colonels and their capangas. In the case of the police, there were some captains who paid them to stage fights. Their feats appeared in the papers but no one was actually harmed.

"We've got buried treasure all over the state," Ponta said. His voice cracked. A stiff layer of fuzz now covered his face.

Behind the corral fence, the goats bleated and settled in for the night. Two billy goats reared up on their hindquarters and rammed each other. Their horns clacked together.

"When will he be back?" Luzia asked.

"Why?" Ponta smiled. "Do you miss him?"

"You shouldn't talk to a girl that way. It's disrespectful. Didn't anyone teach you that?"

"No," Ponta said quietly. He stared at his feet.

"What about your father," Luzia said, softening her voice. "Didn't he teach you?"

"He's dead," Ponta muttered. "Killed." Ponta kicked the bottom edge of the corral fence. "Another butcher, a no-good son of a bitch, told everyone my father weighed his meat wrong; said he tricked the scale. But he didn't. I was there. You can't let a man say those kinds of things. Papai did what he had to do, to protect his name. He just didn't win." Ponta looked at Luzia, then kicked the fence harder. "You ever seen somebody stabbed?"

Luzia nodded. She'd never witnessed the act itself, but she'd seen the results. Once, on her way to school with Emília, a boy had run up to them. "Seu Zé the carpenter's dying," he shouted. "Come see!" When they turned the corner, they saw Seu Zé's body, covered with a sheet, slumped on the ground.

"Don't feel sorry for me," Ponta Fina said. "After he killed Papai, I killed him right back. I stole his knives and left. The captain didn't want me at first. Said I was too small. He said, 'This is a dead end. Once you're in, you can't go back.' But I didn't want to go back. I showed him those knives. I told him what I'd done. He let me join. He said a man who doesn't revenge himself has no morals. I liked that. He called me a man straight away."

"So all your knives belonged to—"

"The cabra who killed Papai," Ponta interrupted. "And this"—he unbuttoned his jacket and showed her a wooden crucifix on a leather cord—"this belonged to Papai."

Behind the fence, the billy goats' horns had stuck together. The two animals pulled back wildly, trying to pry apart. Ponta ran into the corral.

"We've got to separate these two!" he shouted.

But Luzia was already in the corral. She knew that goats, like men, were stubborn creatures. If left alone, they would stay locked together and starve. Or they would pull until their horns were pried from their heads and one, or both, bled to death. Either way, Luzia knew, there could be no winner.

9

The goats were the first to sense the Hawk's return. In reaction to a stranger's presence, the animals walked in circles and let out low-pitched, warbling cries that woke Lia and Luzia. The Hawk and his four men—Chico Coffin, Sweet Talker, Jurema, and Vanity—arrived with a mule. The animal's legs and belly were badly lacerated from the thorny scrub. Several cloth-covered bundles were fastened to its back.

That night, the Hawk instructed Seu Chico to prepare a feast. The old man and his son Tomás killed three goats before dawn. Lia and Luzia spent the morning cleaning out the insides for buchadas, stoking the cook fire, and preparing a vat of beans. Lia was resourceful in the kitchen but Luzia was not. No matter how hard she tried, she ended up making the fire too hot, or forgetting to stir the beans, or cooking the buchada until it was rubbery and tough.

At lunchtime, Luzia stayed with Lia. They watched from the kitchen window as the men took their places beneath the mottled shade of Seu Chico's juazeiro trees. Seu Chico had brought out a table, stools, and his straight-backed chair. Those who did not have seats sat cross-legged on the ground. There weren't enough bowls or wooden utensils for all of the men; the newest members would wait until the older members finished their meals.

Before they began, the Hawk called Luzia outside. He produced his crystal rock. One by one, the men knelt. Luzia followed. Seu Chico's son Tomás bowed his head before the Hawk. Inside his leather vaqueiro jacket, the boy had pinned a lock of Lia's hair.

"You are small and quick," the Hawk said. Tomás smiled. "Your name will be Beija-flor."

"I seal myself," Tomás repeated after the corpo fechado prayer.

The men clapped. Afterward, a few took their places and began to eat. The rest polished the long, thin barrels of their new rifles. Some of the men also received square, blunt-nosed pistols. The old mule had carried ammunition and weapons, and the cangaceiros were giddy and loud as they examined their new equipment. Those with new guns bragged about their weapons, while those who would not part with their old weapons defended theirs. Luzia lingered near the juazeiro trees. The weapons were made of dull, dark metal, like the Singer sewing machine. Like the machine, she noticed, the guns had many clicking parts. And like her embroidery stitches, each weapon had a distinct quality, and advantages and disadvantages one had to consider before its use.

The men debated. The new German parabellum pistols which, loaded with cartridges in their butts, would be easier to reload than their old Colt "little horse" revolvers with their circular chamber of loose bullets. Some did not like pistols. They preferred to stick with their revolvers because, they said, pistol cartridges would be hard to acquire outside the capital. Then there were the rifles: the old ten-shots had less rounds, but shorter barrels. They wouldn't heat up in their hands. The newer, twelve-shot rifles had long iron barrels. They had more rounds, but after sixty shots, the men speculated, the barrel would be as hot as fire.

"You'll burn your hands off," Sweet Talker warned. He saw Luzia watching and winked at her. "She'll decide. Which do you think is better? A ten- or a twelve-shot?"

The other men chuckled. The Hawk wiped his mouth and waited for her reply.

"She's going to give us a lesson?" Little Ear asked, shaking his head.

"It shouldn't matter," Luzia said, speaking slowly. "Bad seamstresses—"

"A sewing lesson!" Half-Moon interrupted.

Luzia raised her voice above the laughter. She regretted responding. She hated their smug faces, their self-satisfied chuckling.

"Bad seamstresses always talk about their machines. Or their needles. Good ones just sew. Seems to me it's the same with shooting. Ten or twelve, that's talk for people who can't aim."

The Hawk let out a long, deep laugh. Slowly, the other men followed suit, chuckling and congratulating Luzia for her cleverness. Except Little Ear. He took a bite of his food, then spit out a clump of beans.

"These are burnt!" he said, wiping his mouth with his jacket sleeve. He paused and stared at Luzia. "Bring me some salt . . . Victrola."

She hadn't heard that name in weeks. She'd believed it was forgotten, buried in the scrub, like her old leather valise. Before she could reply, the Hawk spoke. His voice was low and coaxing. He fixed his eyes on hers.

"Please," he said. "Bring the salt. Bring the whole tin."

Little Ear smiled triumphantly. Luzia walked quickly toward the kitchen, relieved to escape the men. Little Ear's words had startled her, but the Hawk's request had stung. He was the group's guide, its ground, its reason for being. The men took their cues from him, and in an instant he'd made her their servant, their errand girl. A person meant to be mocked and ordered about.

Luzia entered the kitchen, startling Lia. She grabbed the salt tin and kept her face down, looking at her feet. They'd grown thick and yellow, like hooves. Aunt Sofia had always said that people were born with a fixed amount of tears. Some were given more than others. Luzia believed that she'd been given few, and that over the last few weeks, she'd used up the tiny amount of tears allotted for her life. But now Luzia's eyes stung. Her cheeks burned. She walked outside, careful to keep her face down, and set the salt tin roughly on the table. Then she walked away.

"Wait," the Hawk said. "Stay."

Luzia kept walking. She would not wait upon him. She would not hold out her hands like a servant and take the salt tin back.

"Luzia," he called sternly. She stopped.

"Give me your bowl," the Hawk said to Little Ear. The cangaceiro smiled and obeyed. The Hawk took the salt tin in both hands. He turned it over. A large, white mound fell onto Little Ear's bowl, covering his beans and manioc flour.

"You asked for salt," the Hawk said. "Now you'll eat it. And next time you'll remember your manners."

10

After the meal, the men napped peacefully in the scrub. Little Ear, his lips white and chapped, sat beneath a juazeiro and drank cup after cup of water. Slowly, the goats returned from the pasture. Luzia helped Lia milk the mothers, whose udders had grown bloated and sore. Afterward, while Lia fed the animals, Luzia poured the milk through a cheesecloth and into an iron pot. She balanced the bucket in her bent arm and tried to pour with the other. The pail was heavy, its handle slippery with milk. There was movement in the doorway, but Luzia could not look away from her task. She smelled a mixture of sweat and brilliantine paste.

"Need help?"

"No." Her bent arm wobbled. Milk splattered onto the floor.

The Hawk stepped beside her, anchoring the bucket in his hands. It was hot beside the cookstove. The milk slowly drained. The cheesecloth clogged with hairs, gnats, and specks of blood. When they'd finished, Luzia pulled the cloth away and lifted the iron milk pot onto the stove.

"Lia's taken with you," the Hawk said. "She'll be sad to see you go."

"She's sad for her brother," Luzia replied. "She's sad to lose her home."

After lunch, she'd caught Lia crying in the pantry. Tomás would go with the cangaceiros the next day, to extract his revenge in Fidalga. Lia and Seu Chico would have to sell their goats and leave. They would move to Exu, where her other brothers worked.

"They wouldn't be safe here," the Hawk said. "Their family was shamed. Her brother will take away that shame."

"That shame isn't his," Luzia said, suddenly angry. "It's hers. Lia should be able to do with it as she pleases. She wants to stay here. They have a home and animals. They have a calm life. A quiet life."

"You're a brejo girl," the Hawk chuckled. "You would think that."

"What does that have to do with anything?"

"You grew up on a mountain. And when you look down from a mountain, like the one in Taquaritinga, everything below it is faraway and pretty as a picture—even when it's brown and dying. When you live down here, in the caatinga, it's different. You see the world for what it really is. We're different kinds of people, brejo people and caatinga people."

Luzia stoked the fire with more kindling. Emília used to categorize people in that way: northerners versus southerners, city people versus inlanders. Luzia didn't see the value in it.

"You're a caatinga man then?" she asked.

"That's right."

"That's why you're partial to it. People are always partial to what they know."

"Not some people. Some people want to run away from what they know." The Hawk smiled. "You know," he continued, his hand resting dangerously near the stove's lit cinders, "your cooking is awful."

Luzia stared at his rust-colored skin, his white scar, his meaty, lopsided lips. "Why did you eat it then?" she asked. "You weren't obliged to."

She grabbed a thatched fan from beside the stove and flicked it up and down with her good arm. He was the most frustrating person she had ever encountered—as moody as a long-eared Zebu cow that followed you one minute and kicked you the next. The cook fire rose and smoked. Luzia coughed and fanned faster.

The Hawk gripped her wrist tightly. Luzia could no longer flick her fan. She looked at him.

"I want them to show you respect. To be loyal," he said.

"They're not dogs," she said. "You can't force them."

"No," he said smiling. "But I can make them eat whatever you cook."

His fingers relaxed around her wrist, but he did not remove his hand. It was warm, the skin rough. Luzia moved away.

11

They left Seu Chico's in the middle of the night, before the orange-winged leather jackets emerged from their dangling treetop nests. Before the goats crowded at the corral's gate and bleated to be released to pasture. Lia stood at the kitchen window with a candle in her hands. The night was cool and moonless. When Luzia looked back, she saw the girl against the dark backdrop of the farmhouse, her face glowing and expressionless, like a saint's statue.

Luzia hadn't slept that night, nervous about the raid. The men were animated and focused. They'd coached Tomás, now called Beija-flor, on how to point and shoot. Hours later, when they arrived at the outskirts of Fidalga, the group split.

"Don't waste bullets," the Hawk whispered to the men before they parted. "Keep your eyes sharp, your guns aimed. When we're done, you'll have time to yourselves. Respect families. Respect decent people. If a girl wants to fool with you," he said, glancing at Sweet Talker, "make sure she's not too young. And don't pay too much for raparigas."

His instructions startled her. Luzia had expected a mention of bullets and guns. But *rapariga* was an ugly word. Since leaving Taquaritinga, Luzia felt a strange kinship with those women. She'd never met any, but she imagined that beneath the rouge and lip grease, they were simple girls. The Hawk's mention of them made her question the intentions of the Fidalga raid. The cangaceiros' excitement took on a different light. Luzia had overheard the men in the evenings, after they'd made camp, bragging about girls offering themselves. Only monkeys or perverts took them by force; the Hawk's cangaceiros prided themselves on this distinction. Luzia wondered if the raid was truly meant to avenge Lia, or to put on a show for Fildalga's young women. *Men have needs,* Aunt Sofia used to warn her and Emília. *Urges,* she'd called them. And that was why men should be avoided at all costs, Aunt Sofia declared, because they were like billy goats: fierce, unpredictable creatures that would not calm until those urges were met. Before Luzia could fully register the Hawk's instructions, Ponta Fina took her arm.

"Come on," he said sullenly.

He'd been ordered to watch her. Baiano led half of the cangaceiros to the east while the Hawk led the other half to the west. She and Ponta quietly slipped into Fidalga, ducking into a dark shop doorway that faced the town's square. Luzia hunched so that her head would not hit the thick frame. The shop doors were barred shut. Across the square, a lantern flickered in a window. Luzia smelled the beginnings of a cook fire. Dark lines of smoke emerged from the town's thatched roofs. Most of the houses were made of clay and sat slumped and crooked around the square, as if resting against one another. In the distance, Luzia heard several loud pops. They sounded in rapid succession, like São João firecrackers. In the window across the square, the lantern quickly went out.

Shadows appeared along Fidalga's main road. One by one, the cangaceiros emerged, pushing Colonel Machado's capangas before them. Baiano, Branco, and Caju brought in the first set of men. Two wore rumpled nightclothes; the third had been shot in the shoulder. Blood ran down his shirtfront and streaked his trousers. Little Ear, Sweet Talker, and Half-Moon herded two more of the colonel's hired men into the square. They wore stained leather vests and their eyes were half closed. Safety Pin, Vanity, and Tatu brought in the last and youngest capanga. His long underwear was crookedly buttoned. Two women with rouged faces and red lips came pleading behind him. A procession of the other capangas' women—mothers, daughters, wives—huddled at the edges of the square, their shawls thrown hastily across their nightgowns, their hair unevenly stacked upon their heads.

The sun rose. Fidalga's clay houses glowed orange. In the scrub, Luzia heard birds calling cheerfully to one another, unaware of the events in town. The Hawk and two more cangaceiros appeared, flanking a young man Luzia did not recognize. He wore a linen dressing robe over pin-striped pajamas. His face was as white as the wax of a candle.

"That's Colonel Machado's son," Ponta Fina whispered.

The Hawk ordered the six capangas and his well-dressed captive to kneel beside the stone bust of Dona Fidalga.

"Good morning," he shouted, addressing the town's shuttered houses and closed doors and not the kneeling men. His good eye squinted in the morning sunlight. The eye on his scarred side stayed open. He shaded it with his handkerchief.

"I am Captain Antônio Teixeira," he announced. "We have business with these men. No one else."

He ordered his captives to stand. Baiano prodded each man with the butt of his Winchester. Tomás stood before them. He aimed his new pistol with both hands. Luzia saw a tremor in his wrists.

"Strip," the Hawk ordered.

Slowly, the capangas removed their nightshirts, their leather vests, their long underwear. The pale young man shook off his robe and slowly stepped out of his pajamas. The injured man hunched slightly, holding his shoulder. His soaked shirt fell to the ground with a slap. His chest was smeared with pink. Dry rivulets ran down his stomach and traced the insides of his thighs. Colonel Machado's pale son cupped his hands over himself, but the rest of the men stood proudly, their heads up and legs wide, as if waiting for inspection.

Luzia was not shocked by the men's nakedness—she had seen all kinds of bodies when she'd measured the dead—but these men were alive, their faces shining with sweat, their limbs loose, not rigid. They reminded her of the onion beetles that invaded Aunt Sofia's house each summer; when trapped, the bugs spun helplessly on their backs, exposing skinny legs and pale underbellies.

Beside her, Ponta Fina giggled. Around the square, all window shutters remained closed. She'd heard that Colonel Machado did not allow his tenants to carry firearms. Still, the cangaceiros took precautions: Chico Coffin and Sabiá squatted behind feed barrels and aimed their new pistols. Jacaré crouched beneath a warty-trunked angico. Jurema and Coral, their Winchesters cocked and aimed, hid in doorways.

Another group walked along the road. Luzia squinted to see Inteligente, his shadow long and slender across the ground, herding three more men toward the square. Canjica followed them. Unlike the capangas, these new captives had been allowed to change out of their nightclothes. They wore rumpled slacks and coarse canvas tunics. One of the men cradled a wooden accordion. Another carried a cowbell. The third held a triangle.

"We're going to have a quadrilha," the Hawk shouted, then turned to the naked capangas. "I hope you like quadrilhas."

Across the square, a shutter opened. Another followed.

The Hawk greeted the musicians, patting their backs. The men held tightly to their instruments. They kept their eyes focused on their feet. The Hawk smiled so widely that even the scarred side of his mouth lifted slightly. The slack side of his face looked pleased, as if he had just shared a sly joke, while the active side stretched wildly, its teeth bared, its eye wide.

"Play," he ordered.

The first musician nervously shook his cowbell. The accordion player followed the bell's rhythm, tugging apart the handles of his instrument and pushing them back together quickly. The accordion released a series of shallow, frenzied gasps. The triangle player hurried to catch up.

"Slow it down," the Hawk instructed, then faced the naked captives. "Round and round."

Luzia had never liked quadrilhas. Ever since she was a girl, she'd hated the burden of choosing a partner and following the announcer's shouted commands. She could never perform the twirls and turns as fast as the announcer called them out.

"Round and round!" the Hawk yelled.

The naked men bowed their heads. They shuffled slowly in a circle around the statue of Dona Fidalga. The stone bust seemed to watch them, her under bite stern and disapproving. With their free hands, the cangaceiros slapped their thighs in time to the music.

"Compliment your partner," the Hawk said.

The capangas bowed stiffly to one another.

"Alavantu!" the Hawk yelled.

The men fumbled for each other's hands. The colonel's son hesitated, reluctant to uncup himself. Sweet Talker flicked him with his silver-studded riding crop. The hit left a red welt across the man's pale thighs. He shuddered, then quickly took hold of a capanga's hand. The naked men lifted their arms up and down halfheartedly. The Hawk nodded to Baiano.

"Balancê," Baiano drawled.

The men released hands and stumbled into one another, picking partners. They held each other gingerly, staring at the ground or at the sky. The colonel's son was left without a partner. He shuffled back and forth, alone.

One by one the other cangaceiros called out moves, telling the men to twirl, curtsy, and bow. Giggles came from an open window. Some townspeople watched from their doorways. Others had lost their initial fear and stood in the street, clapping.

The morning sun had invaded the doorway where Luzia stood, warming her face. Yet she felt a shiver within herself, like drinking a cup of water and feeling it—thrilling, cold—course through her and settle in her stomach. There was a chilling satisfaction in the knowledge that those men were being bossed, prodded, and shamed. Just as they had shamed Lia.

"One thumb in your mouth," Little Ear yelled. "The other up your ass!"

The naked men did as they were told.

"Switch thumbs!" Half-Moon called out. The cangaceiros pealed with laughter.

Luzia's stomach cramped. She closed her eyes.

"Stop," the Hawk said. "Stop playing."

The men quieted. The accordion wheezed to a halt. Luzia opened her eyes. His face had changed; his smile was gone. His cheeks were flushed red except for his scar, which remained white and jagged, like a bone protruding from his skin. He unsheathed his punhal.

"Kneel," he said.

The blade was as long as a rifle's barrel. Sunlight reflected off its squared sides. The Hawk stood behind the first kneeling capanga. He guided Tomás behind the second.

"Do you know your mother's name?" the Hawk asked the man on the ground before him. Luzia recognized him—it was the older, dark-haired capanga who had compared her to a horse. His hair was wet from sweat. His eyes were fierce.

"Maria Aparecida da Silva," the man called out.

"Do your know your father's name?" the Hawk asked.

"To hell with you."

The Hawk bent his elbows. He lifted his punhal. The knife was like a long needle. Luzia recalled Ponta Fina's knife lessons—if placed in the correct spot, the punhal could pierce straight into the body, skewering heart, lungs, stomach. There was an indentation at the base of the capanga's neck, a natural dip between collarbone and shoulder. The Hawk pressed the tip of his punhal to it.

"Who do you work for?" he asked.

"I work for Colonel Machado," the capanga replied. "A real man, not like you, cangaceiro vagabundo!"

The Hawk smiled. He kept his arms rigid, his knife perfectly still. "Do you know why you're being judged?" he asked.

"Only God will judge me!" the capanga shouted.

The Hawk straightened his arms. The blade moved into the shoulder's indentation, then disappeared. A fine, dark spray shot upward. It spattered the Hawk's cuffs. He let out a long breath, then leaned forward, as if whispering into the capanga's ear. The man's eyes opened wide. He wobbled, then slumped forward. Gently, the Hawk eased out his punhal and handed it to Tomás.

The process was repeated with the next man, except Seu Chico's son asked his questions nervously. The Hawk stood beside him, coaxing him to slow down. The boy felt for the dip between collarbone and shoulder, then steadied the punhal. An instant before leaning forward, Tomás shuddered. The punhal lost its placement. Partway down, it stuck. The capanga moaned. Tomás tugged out the knife. Ponta Fina ran from the doorway.

Ponta handed Seu Chico's son a thick-bladed facão; the same knife he used to sever the heads of goats and scrubland lizards with one clean hack. Tomás, his face shining with sweat, took the new knife and aimed for the neck. Luzia covered her eyes. The clay door frame felt cool against her face. She slumped against it. There was a thud—like the hollow, splitting sound of a pumpkin chopped open—then silence. Luzia heard coughing and the splatter of liquid. She lifted her hands from her face. Colonel Machado's son had vomited. Tomás had missed again and the capanga before him was still alive, wobbling on his knees. The man's eyes were glazed over and his mouth bobbed open. A string of saliva fell from it. There was a gash on his back where Tomás's poorly aimed swing had struck. A lung, pink and shining, swelled through the wound. The Hawk looked annoyed.

"Never shut your eyes when you aim," he said to Tomás. "It makes it worse."

He took his punhal and leaned over the injured man. In the Hawk's hands, the knife moved in easily, cleanly. The capanga fell forward. As they moved on to the next man, the Hawk's face remained placid. He tapped his cartridge belt with his fingers. He told Tomás to go quickly, to be efficient.

The gossips in Taquaritinga had said that the Hawk craved blood, that he loved it. But Luzia had butchered goats and chickens and teú lizards; she knew how easy it became to snap a neck, to sever a tendon, to slice open a belly. How tedious. Blood was a mess, an afterthought. It appeared after everything important had already occurred. She recalled the Hawk's face during the quadrilha and the questioning—its intoxicated giddiness, its manic smile. He took pleasure in their shame and in his showmanship. Everyone did—even Luzia herself. Hadn't she felt a cool thrill when he'd ordered them to strip, to bow, to kneel? Hadn't her breath caught when he'd produced his punhal and gently, easily slipped it into their necks?

Luzia's stomach knotted. The second man's lung had deflated, disappearing back inside the gash. The other men slumped on the ground like flour sacks. Luzia's saliva became thick and warm. She ducked from the doorway and ran.

12

Behind the square was a dirt road lined with more clay houses. Chickens calmly pecked at the ground, oblivious to the proceedings in the square. Luzia stumbled; her body seemed to move without her mind's guidance. The chickens scattered.

She knocked on a nearby door. Inside, she heard shuffling and low voices but no one answered. She hit the door with the heel of her hand and then ran to the next, then the next. At the end of the row of houses, she saw the back doors to Fidalga's chapel. It was a small entrance blocked by a set of wrought-iron gates. Luzia squeezed her hands though the curling iron. She shook the gates. A small man peeked from behind the chapel door. He wore brown robes and had a shaved, circular friar's haircut.

"Who are you?" the monk asked. His eyes moved across her face, her bornal, her water gourds, and finally settled on her trousers. "You're with those men."

"Please," Luzia whispered, afraid of yelling. "Hide me."

"You're their harlot," the monk replied. "You'll ransack the chapel."

Luzia shook the gate with all of her force. The hinges creaked. The monk's eyes widened. He fumbled with the chapel door and slammed it shut.

Luzia leaned against the gate. Her body felt too heavy for her legs.

The slumped men in the square had reminded her of the Judas doll. Each Easter, the women in Taquaritinga sewed a cloth doll the size of a man and stuffed him with capim grass. Dona Conceição donated a torn pair of trousers and an old shirt. Some men made him a braided palha hat. They hung the finished doll in the town square. On Easter morning, all of the children gathered sticks and rocks. They hit that Judas doll until he slouched and fell from his rope harness. Once on the ground, they hit him more. They spat and kicked. The adults laughed. When she was a child, Luzia loved hitting that doll. She pressed between the mob of children. She used her good arm and hit the doll until her muscles ached. The snap of sticks against the doll's cloth skin used to thrill her. The sharp smell of its shredded-grass insides used to make her giddy. Now the thought of them made her ill.

Luzia pressed her forehead to the chapel gates. The morning air had grown hot and dry. The heat had muted the scrub birds and awakened the cicadas. Their high-pitched buzzing rang in her ears. Beneath the sound of the cicadas she heard gravel crunch along the road, and a series of quick, shallow breaths. Luzia felt a tug on her arm. Ponta Fina stood beside her, winded.

"Where have you been?" he asked.

Before she could respond, he tugged at her locked elbow, trying to lift her from the ground. Luzia resisted. She pried free of his grip and stood. She walked quickly, not knowing where she would go, but wanting to move away from him, from the square, from that town.

"Wait!" Ponta called. He jogged alongside her, unable to match her strides. He unsheathed one of his knives. It was the blunt-ended pajeuzeira. Luzia stopped.

"If you go, he'll say it was my fault," Ponta said. His voice cracked. "He'll blame me."

His jaw line was squared but his cheeks were still round and fat, like a boy's. There was a smear on his left cheek, near his nose. It was dark—the color of cinnamon, or of the chicken-blood sauce Aunt Sofia used to pour across their cornmeal. The smear was dry and cracking. Luzia took a handkerchief from her bornal. She pressed it to the lip of her water gourd and wiped his face clean.

13
///////

They did not harm Colonel Machado's son. Instead, the pale young man spent the long, cloudless day tied to his grandmother's stone bust. The capangas' bodies were removed from the square and piled on Colonel Machado's porch. They lay face-to-face, their teeth clenched in strange smiles. Crusted lines ran from the two dark holes where their eyes had been, as if they had cried bloody tears.

Tomás sifted through the capangas' clothing and belongings. He took a pistol, a leather hat, a crucifix, and a handkerchief. Everything else was burned. The Hawk knocked on Fidalga's chapel doors until the trembling friar opened them and invited everyone—cangaceiros and townspeople—inside. Afterward, Ponta Fina went door to door, requesting the townspeople's presence at a celebration in the square. Like most of the cangaceiros' requests, it was an order rather than an invitation. The only ones not expected to attend were the capangas' women, who'd placed black head scarves over their hair and congregated near the colonel's house, to mourn their dead. They knelt outside the colonel's gates and prayed for their men's souls. They were not allowed to bury the bodies, as they would be a gift for Colonel Machado when he returned from Pará. Without burial, the souls would not rest; they would wander aimlessly. The Hawk tied white rags to each of the body's legs so that the souls would not follow him, or his men.

That night, the air was cool but the fire warmed them. Baiano and Inteligente had butchered Colonel Machado's best sows and Canjica had built a massive fire over which he skewered the meat. Local women grilled cobs of corn. A group of men smoked thick palha cigarettes. The three musicians from that morning sat near the fire and played the cangaceiros' requests. Coins shone at their feet. Beyond the whine of the accordion, Luzia heard the fierce growls of feral dogs in the distance, feasting at Colonel Machado's. Beneath it all she occasionally heard prayers, loud and steady, coming from the same direction. *Ave Maria, full of grace, our Lord is with thee.* Then the cowbell shook loudly and the triangle clanged, drowning them out again.

Luzia sat on a low stool, removed from the fire and the festivities. Vanity had brought her a cob of grilled corn, but she could not eat it. Everything tasted sour. A strong smell of perfume wafted through the smoke. The possibility of dancing with local girls had prompted the cangaceiros to buy a crate of Dirce perfume and pour bottle after bottle over their heads. Several of the cangaceiros guided girls around the fire. They kept a respectful distance from their timid partners. Baiano danced calmly, moving a beat slower than the music. Jacaré kept his head lifted and smiled, showing off his white teeth. Sweet Talker was the best dancer—his feet and hips swiveling loosely, as if they were oiled. Caju moved his partner about stiffly. And Ponta Fina stared at his sandals, worried about stepping on his partner's feet. Half of the group, with the Hawk's blessing, had opted not to attend the party. Instead, they'd followed the rouged women they'd seen that morning to their place of business.

Luzia heard high-pitched laughter. Near her, a group of children huddled on the ground and constructed fire balloons. Before the festivities, the Hawk had purchased a ream of colored paper and a kilo of unrefined manioc goma. The children made a paste with the starch and dipped their fingers into the thick white mixture. With it, they attached the paper to a skeleton of sticks. One of them glued a paper mustache to the statue of Dona Fidalga.

Colonel Machado's son had been untied from the statue and locked in his father's stables so he would not ruin the festivities. Behind her, Luzia overheard a cluster of local girls affirming how pleasant it was to have a party without the colonel's permission, without his capangas skulking about and spoiling everyone's fun. The same group of girls had given the Hawk gifts of bread and manioc pancakes. They had washed their hair and put on their best dresses. They lingered near him, clasping his hand and asking for his blessing. Back in Taquaritinga there had been dozens of girls like those— misled to believe that cangaceiros were brave, romantic souls. Dazzled by the men's silk bandannas, their collections of gold rings.

Luzia smoothed out her trousers. She fidgeted with her braid. No one spoke to her. A group of women had come up to her shyly, offering buttered manioc pancakes and corn pudding. After they'd given their gifts they backed away, staring at her trousers and whispering to one another. Luzia wished for one of her old dresses: the white cotton one with yellow piping, or the light green one that Emília said complemented her eyes. Across the dance circle, the Hawk moved slowly through the crowd. It was the first time he'd risen from his seat beside the fire. The local girls twittered with excitement. Luzia kicked at the ground. All of that excitement for a foul-smelling, long-haired cangaceiro! He was no priest. He was no colonel. That night, he simply had the power of a colonel. That was what made him alluring to those girls, nothing else. Eventually, Colonel Machado would return. No one at the party seemed to realize that. Colonel Machado would return and he, too, would want revenge. Revenge, after all, was every caatinga man's right. When he returned, Fidalga's men and women would be forced to fawn over him just as they had over the Hawk, in order to save their skins.

When Luzia looked up, she saw that the Hawk was headed toward her. When he reached her, he stretched out his hand.

"I don't dance," she said.

"I'm not asking you to," he replied, his hand still extended. "I want you to come with me."

His smile was different from the strange, overly zealous one he'd had that morning—it was relaxed, his features softened by the fire-light. Luzia paused. Her palms felt slick. "I'm fine here."

"Are you scared?" He laughed.

Her fear was ridiculous; his laughter confirmed it. Luzia looked down at her trousers, her crooked arm, her calloused feet. There were dozens of fine-looking girls around the fire. There were the rouged women down the road. To think that he would show an interest in her was silly. Luzia rose from her seat. She would rather take a risk than endure his mockery.

She did not take his hand. Still, he clasped hers tightly and guided her away from the fire, toward the chapel. He pushed open the chapel's arched wooden door and motioned for her to enter. Luzia hesitated.

"I want to show you something," he said. "It won't take long."

On the floor, before the rows of pews, were sacks of beans, tablets of rapadura, and a pile of new blankets. They stepped over the cangaceiros' new supplies and moved toward the back of the chapel, to a basin of blessed water. Beneath the basin sat a sewing machine. It was thin necked and black. Like Aunt Sofia's old machine, it had a silver hand crank, but it was not rusted or old. It shone. Around the machine sat several spools of thread.

"It's for you," he said. "To decorate bornais. Hats, too. There's a thick needle inside the drawer. It can sew straight through leather."

Luzia knelt. She turned the handle. It felt cool beneath her fingers. She ran her hands along the machine's curved needle foot and across its etched silver face. It had come from Colonel Machado's house, no doubt.

"I can't carry this," she said.

"Inteligente will carry it."

"I can't let him do that. It's too heavy."

"It's nothing for him. It weighs as much as an accordion. He'll want to do it. I've seen him, and the rest, admiring your sewing."

He knelt beside her. Luzia kept her eyes on the machine. She spoke softly, as if addressing the Singer.

"Why do you ask for their parents' names?" she asked.

He sighed and wove his thick fingers together. "There's so much land here and so few people. I don't want to hurt someone related to one of our friends. Our allies."

"If they're known, they're spared?"

"Sometimes yes. Sometimes no."

Luzia recalled the sightless capangas stacked on the colonel's porch. She recalled Aunt Sofia's nursery rhyme. "Why do people call you the Hawk?"

He reached out and patted the sewing machine tentatively, as if trying to tame a creature.

"My mother sewed," he said. "She always wanted a machine like this. When I was a boy, we planted sweet melons, and she taught me how to put a tile underneath them so their undersides wouldn't rot. I like melons. And corn. We planted that, too, my mother and I. She was strong, like an ox. I wanted a plot of land for us. Our own land. I wanted to raise goats. But that wasn't the life I was born for. Sometimes God makes you put down your enxada and take up a gun. Doesn't matter if that's not what you wanted. That's the path God chose. Sometimes we have to disobey ourselves to obey God. That's the hardest thing a man can do."

He took his hand from the Singer and stood. He stared up at the chapel ceiling. Luzia stared, too. There were only wooden beams and tiles.

"There are blessings to this life," he said, his voice louder than before. "There's no colonel telling us how to live. There's no colonel ordering us to raise his cattle and goats, promising us a few in payment, and then branding all the newborns in his name. There's no colonel to blame us when the crops don't come up because it didn't rain. There's no tax collector saying we can't sell our pigs or our goats because we haven't paid some fee that will end up in his pocket. There're no monkeys coming in from the capital, tearing up our houses and shaming our sisters or our mothers. We're at God's mercy. No one else's."

Outside the chapel there was a shout, then clapping. The Hawk shook his head, startled from his speech, and walked toward the chapel doors.

"They're letting the fire balloons go," he said. "Come see."

There were three balloons, each large and lantern shaped. One wobbled in the sky. The other two sat in the dirt. A few men stuck their arms into the balloons, lighting their small kerosene tins. Once lit, the men stretched their arms wide and held the balloons high, waiting for a gust of wind. When it came, the entire town craned their necks, watching as the balloons slowly rose, one following the other. Luzia squinted at the sky.

Next to her, the Hawk unbuttoned a leather case attached to his cartridge belt. Inside were his brass binoculars. He offered them to Luzia.

The cangaceiros carried many items that had nothing to do with their daily survival. That night, Luzia finally understood their significance. She'd seen Tomás pin the lock of Lia's hair inside his jacket. She knew then that beneath each of the men's jackets, protected from the scrub's sun and heat, were items that had belonged to their loved ones. In Fidalga, Luzia watched Tomás ransack the capangas' possessions. And during mass that afternoon, she saw Tomás carefully place the items he'd stolen from the capangas on the floor before him. He spat on each one. Next to Tomás, Ponta Fina spat on the knives he'd taken from his victim. Sweet Talker spat on his riding crop. Chico Coffin spat on his bag of gold teeth. The cangaceiros carried the relics of the dead. The dead who had, in life, wronged the cangaceiros or someone they'd loved.

The binoculars were heavy and cold in her palms. Their handle was discolored.

"Who did these belong to?" Luzia asked.

The Hawk stared at her. The eye on his scarred side, the one that barely blinked, was rheumy and red.

"I can't recall," he replied. "But I liked the looks of them."

Luzia nodded. She pressed the binoculars to her eyes. The stars seemed centimeters away. The paper balloons looked close enough to touch. She followed their bright path through the sky. They did not have the grace or the swiftness of birds. They bobbed awkwardly, dependent on the wind. Despite this they rose higher and higher, and for an instant, Luzia believed that they would disappear into the heavens. Then, one by one, they burst into flames and fell toward land.

Chapter 5

EMÍLIA

Recife
December 1928–March 1929

1

/////////

he Great Western Railroad of Brazil equipped its first-class cars with electric lamps and rotating ceiling fans. Hidden behind frosted sconces, the electric bulbs emitted the same weak glow as candles or gas flames. They disappointed Emília, but the fan did not. Its blades moved as if touched by an invisible hand. Emília could not take her eyes from them. Degas noticed her fascination and went into a lengthy lesson on electricity. Emília nodded. She tried to listen, but Degas' words were overshadowed by the hum of the fan above them, the click of domino pieces placed on the car's game table by the two old gentlemen in the front row, the whistling breaths of slumped travelers, and the sound of the train itself. It had the same clattering rhythm as the pedal-operated Singer, but its pedaler never tired. The train pushed forward, resolute and inexhaustible, through the scrub.

"You must be fatigued," Degas murmured.

It was Emília's duty to pat his hand and tell him to go on, to reassure him that his electricity talk was interesting, but she would have her whole life to listen to her husband and only this night on the train.

"Yes," Emília said. "I think I'll sleep."

Degas nodded, then faced forward and closed his eyes.

Earlier, the waiters had served juice and round, flaky empadas filled with shredded chicken and olives. Degas had looked at them dubiously and ordered a coffee, but Emília took empada after empada from the waiter's tray. It was, after all, her wedding night. She'd had no reception, no sugar-coated cake. There wasn't time; Degas' law school classes had already begun. After their ceremony, he and Emília had ridden to Caruaru and caught the night train into Recife. Dona Conceição had counseled against their leaving so quickly. The wedding night was sacred. Spending it on a train instead of in a bedroom would only confirm people's suspicions that Degas had already sampled his bride. The colonel offered his guest room to the newlyweds but Degas declined. Emília didn't mind one bit—she didn't want Dona Conceição and all of her curious maids inspecting their sheets the next morning. Their courtship and marriage had been out of the ordinary; their wedding night would be no different.

Degas had promised her a reception in Recife, where people would appreciate a tiered cake and fine food. It would have been wasted in Taquaritinga, he explained, and Emília halfheartedly agreed. She would have liked to have a grand party, to show those gossips and pé-rapados that she was no longer Emília dos Santos, the ruined seamstress, but Dona Emília Coelho.

Emília pulled the window lever. Cool air whistled through the open sliver. The moon was out. It's light fell on the scrub, giving the leafless trees a white glow. Emília undid the clasp on her new traveling bag and took out her and Luzia's Communion portrait. During the wedding ceremony, she'd placed the portrait—disguised under an embroidered towel—in the front pew, and afterward, during their horseback ride down the mountain and their carriage trip to Caruaru, she'd held the portrait close. Degas didn't ask what was beneath the embroidered towel. He treated it as a lucky trinket, a whim that brought Emília comfort but was none of his concern. His discretion, or disinterest, was a relief.

Outside, beneath the arbor of that leafless scrub forest, was darkness. The tree trunks disappeared into shadow. There was no ground.

It was as if a great ream of dark cloth had been rolled out before them, and they floated upon it. With each shudder of the train, Emília felt giddy and fearful. It was the feeling she'd had long ago, when she and Luzia had run toward that mango tree in their church dresses.

"Recife," Emília whispered. Stripped to its syllables, the city's name sounded even lovelier. *Hehhh,* as if letting out a long breath. *Ciii,* like the hiss of water and waves. And *fe,* the final, soft syllable that alone meant *faith.*

2

When they stepped out of the train, the sun was bright. It made Emília's eyes water. Sweat beaded on her upper lip. Her hair curled wildly; the closer to the coast they traveled the frizzier it became until, upon arriving in Recife's Central Station, it was a wiry muff that sprang from beneath the small-brimmed cloche Degas had purchased for her. Above them, perched on the domed roof, were four brass hawks, their wings open and luminous in the afternoon sun. Emília felt a tug on the skirt of her new traveling suit. She looked down and saw an urchin. One of his eyes was clouded with pus.

"Tia!" the boy cried. "Spare a coin?"

"Scat!" Degas ordered. The beggar child ran.

Degas gripped Emília's arm and steered her away. He tended to do this: to hold her hand too tightly, to pull her wrist too forcefully. Back in Caruaru, before they'd seated themselves, Degas had tugged off her travel jacket without regard to the clasps, which caught on her blouse and nearly ripped the cuff. Emília believed it was awkwardness, a childlike impatience that she could remedy, given time. She hugged her traveling bag and let Degas lead her to their carriage.

She'd clipped many photographs of Recife—images of manicured gardens; wrought-iron bridges; paved streets with trolley tracks that extended, long and curving, like metal ribbons laid upon the ground. Emília had not considered what might lay in the margins of those photographs, beyond the boundaries of their frames. Gutters were filled with rotting vegetables and shards of green glass. Barefoot women balanced baskets of red cashew fruits on their heads. Trolley cars screeched along their metal rails. There were the shouts of peddlers, the yelps of street dogs, the wild calls of birds. The Capibaribe River extended wide and brown beside them. Emília had never seen so much water. Wooden shanties slumped precariously along its sides. She feared they would collapse at any moment. Humidity from the winter rains still hung in the air. The sun hit piles of horse dung scattered along the streets. Emília wiped her brow. When she closed her eyes, she felt as if she were inside a great, reeking mouth. She quickly opened them.

Months later, when she and her mother-in-law, Dona Dulce, took their first strolls around Derby Square, Emília finally encountered the gardens and smartly dressed women she'd seen in the photographs. Dona Dulce pointed each woman out, whispering her married name, her maiden name, and if she belonged to one of the Old families or the New. Sometimes they crossed paths with these women and were forced to stop and chat. Emília had not mastered the art of conversation. She could not keep track of all the words Dona Dulce had forbidden her to use. She was not allowed to talk about her family background. She was not allowed to make any references to sewing. She could not gesticulate like a country person, could not touch her hair or tug the fingertips of her gloves. Emília found safety in silence. It made her agreeable, charming, imperceptible. Out of politeness, the women spoke to her and inevitably asked her first impressions of Recife. Emília could not tell them she'd felt deceived. She could not describe her panic, her nausea. *Courtesy,* Dona Dulce often told her during their endless etiquette lessons, *demands that you never be disagreeable.* So when the women asked, Emília skipped her arrival altogether and began with the Coelho house.

She'd cried in relief when she saw it. The two-story house was painted white, with curling ceramic accents along its seams and around its windows. Its arched shutters and doorways were butter yellow and perched on top of each roof peak were large ceramic pinha fruits, their scaly rinds glazed and shining in the afternoon sun.

"It looks like a wedding cake!" Emília cried.

Degas laughed. He left her with a maid, who escorted Emília through the house's wide, tiled hallways. The maid—a girl Emília's age, perhaps younger—walked quickly. Emília could not peek inside the house's many doorways. She could not run her hand along the main staircase's brass banister. The girl led her through the central courtyard. There was a fern-lined fountain where a miniature horse with the tail of a fish spat water from its mouth. Emília wanted to touch its green scales.

On the other side of the courtyard, the maid opened a set of glass-paneled doors. She motioned Emília inside.

"Your hat," the maid said, holding out her hand. She was square jawed and thin. She wore a starched white cap with a lace band that tied across her forehead, making the girl look elegant and almost regal, like an actress Emília had once seen in *Fon Fon*.

"No," Emília said, holding her cloche to her head. She could not remove it and reveal her frizzing hair.

The maid shrugged, then attempted to take her bag. Emília pulled back.

"I'm fine."

"Wait then," the girl said, "Dona Dulce will be here soon."

After the maid left, Emília inspected the room. Nailed into its upper corners were four plaster cherubs, their cheeks puffed and round, their chubby arms outstretched. In alcoves along the walls, dozens of wooden Madonnas fixed their sad stares upon the room's wicker-backed settees and mahogany chairs. In the far corner, a portable fan whirred. It was large and silver, with a metal grille in front of its blades. Inside the grille sat a block of ice. Emília stood before the fan. Cool air swept her face. She had heard of ice but had never seen it. It was translucent and shining, like a precious stone.

"I detest that contraption." A woman's voice rose over the din of the fan. "But my husband insists on it."

She was the color of uncooked bread. Her wheat-colored hair, pulled back into a large, tight bun, blended with her pale skin, making her look like one of the porcelain Madonnas along the walls—long faced and flawless. The only difference was her eyes, narrow and amber colored, like a pair of cat's-eye marbles embedded in her doughy face. They showed none of the Madonna's mercy. Emília stepped away from the fan.

"It drips on my floor," the woman said, pointing to a silver bowl beneath the ice. "I'm not partial to electricity," she continued. "But all of the New families have it, so we must as well."

She wore a long, dark gown with pearl buttons. Each time she shook her head, the dress's crepe collar made a scratching noise against her neck. The woman stared, as if waiting for a response.

"Dona Conceição's house wasn't electrified," Emília blurted out.

The woman seemed pleased by this. "You were her seamstress?" Emília nodded.

"Poor woman. Her son is a wisp of a man. I think he's tubercular. Dr. Duarte has warned Degas a dozen times about visiting him. I've also heard that the colonel is a horror. They say he can't read or write." The woman smiled at Emília. "You can read and write, can't you, dear?"

"Yes."

"Good."

Dona Dulce walked toward Emília, taking short, controlled steps. The heels of her shoes barely clicked against the tiles.

"That is an original Franz Post," she said, pointing to the painting behind the fan. "Do you know his work?"

The painting's gilded frame overwhelmed the canvas. There was a town and a church, much like Taquaritinga. Black figures walked along the road, balancing baskets on their heads. The sun was setting and yellow brushstrokes fell upon the church steeple, making it golden, dazzling. In the corner there was darkness, a jungle. Animals—an alligator, a brightly colored bird, an armadillo—stared at the town. Whether they were invading or retreating, Emília could not tell, but she envied those animals, hidden in the dark, detached from life instead of in the very middle of it.

"It's all right, dear," Dona Dulce said, saving Emília from answering. "I didn't expect you to know his work. He was Dutch. Quite famous."

"I like it very much," Emília said. Her head itched beneath the woolen cloche.

The young maid returned carrying a tray with a steaming silver pot. There were four lizardlike feet on the pot's bottom. Its handle had hundreds of silver scales molded into a dragon's tail. Its spout was the head—eyes open, mouth wide.

"This heat is oppressive," Dona Dulce announced, then turned to Emília. "Wouldn't you like to remove your hat?"

"No, thank you," Emília replied. "My hair, it's all esculhambado."

The maid glanced up from pouring coffee. Dona Dulce's close-lipped smile remained frozen but her eyes widened, her brow twitched. She took Emília's arm.

"Let me show you our courtyard," she said.

Sunlight reflected off the fountain's tiles. Emília's eyes watered. Dona Dulce drew her close, keeping her arm tight around Emília's.

"Don't ever use that word," she whispered, "it's low."

"Low?"

"It's something country people use," Dona Dulce said, frowning. "You know which one I am referring to. I will not repeat it. Erase it from your vocabulary. Instead, use the word *disheveled*. And when you compliment someone's things, such as my painting, you should say, 'This is lovely.' No one is interested in your likes or dislikes. That is vulgar."

Emília's eyes had finally adjusted to the courtyard sunlight. There were small ferns growing from the cracks between the fountain tiles. She touched them with the toe of her shoe. Flowers grew along the courtyard's edges but they were not like Aunt Sofia's dahlias. The Coelhos' plants were thick, rubbery, impenetrable. Birds-of-paradise grew in clumps, their orange shoots tapering to a sharp point. Red and pink "ice cream" flowers grew in bicolored cones near the glass doorways. Emília could see into the Coelhos' dining room, their study, their upstairs bedrooms, their dining hall. Each room stared into the other. From the inside, it was not like a wedding cake at all, but like a series of glass jars.

"Chin up!" Dona Dulce ordered.

Startled, Emília obeyed.

"You must grow a thick skin," Dona Dulce said. "You must be able to tolerate criticism more severe than mine. I told Degas to think clearly. To consider what his decision would mean for you, and for the rest of us."

"What does it mean?" Emília asked.

Dona Dulce stared. She examined Emília's face with the same intensity she'd had when admiring her Franz Post painting, but there was no admiration in her expression now. Dona Dulce looked as though she'd encountered a strange insect and was weighing her options—determining whether the creature before her was a harmless nuisance or a real danger. Before speaking, Dona Dulce surveyed the courtyard.

"It means that you are a Coelho now," she said. "I can't know your intentions here. I'm not a clairvoyant. It's futile, and unseemly, for me to imagine what preoccupies your mind. I do know that this is a vast improvement over your last situation. I'm sure you also knew this when you married my son. What you might not know is the responsibility that comes with your good fortune. You'll have to live up to your new name. And Degas, his father, and I will have to make sure you do. This is our responsibility now. Because whatever you do or say from this moment on is a reflection on all of us. Do you understand?"

Emília nodded. She took off her hat and smoothed down her hair. A dark object scuttled near her feet. She gasped.

"Oh, those are my husband's turtles," Dona Dulce said loudly, eyeing the maid who had come into the courtyard. Dona Dulce smiled, took Emília's arm, and led her away from the animals. "Don't touch them, dear. They're liable to bite off a finger."

3

///////

At first glance, Emília believed that the Coelho house, with its wide stone staircase and musty carpet-lined hall, was the master house of a once glorious engenho. She had seen countless watercolor pictures in Padre Otto's history books of the plantations with their majestic master houses surrounded by fields of sugarcane. During dinner, Dr. Duarte Coelho dispelled Emília's notions. The Coelho house was only ten years old, a modern wonder wrapped in an antiquated shell. Dr. Duarte had thought of everything. Their water came from a well in the backyard where he had installed a cata-vento, which used the force of the wind to pull water into their pipes. In the kitchen there were a series of gas cylinders that heated the water before it mysteriously wound its way up to the bathroom. There were electric fans and lamps, a phonograph, a dumbwaiter, a radio, an icebox. All powered by wires that ran to wooden posts along the street.

"I paid good money to have those posts installed," Dr. Duarte said.

Dona Dulce cleared her throat.

"Those are my property," he continued, pressing a thick finger against the tablecloth. "I bought the wood, hired the men. I met with Tramways and gave them an incentive to extend their electrical lines here. Next thing you know, other families were moving to Madalena. New families. No riffraff."

He was a thick, squat man with bags beneath his eyes and a soft waddle of skin below his square chin. He reminded Emília of an old bull, sedate yet still menacing.

Dr. Duarte declared that the Coelhos were one of the first families with enough foresight to move to the young neighborhood of Madalena. Recife was bursting out of its original territories. Only the Old families still insisted on living on the tiny Milk Island, or in the neighborhoods of São José and Boa Vista. The New families were building modern homes on the mainland, across the Capunga Bridge, away from the hubbub of the islands, the commerce of the port, and all of the unfortunate elements that came with it: the cabarets, the houses of disrepute, the artists and vagabonds who frequented the Casino Imperial. Dr. Duarte stared at Degas. Emília's husband did not meet his father's eyes, concentrating instead on his half-empty plate.

Degas looked like a diluted version of his father. Everything about Duarte Coelho—his barrel chest; his beaked nose; his dark eyes and thick, white brows—seemed more condensed, more intense. But Dr. Duarte never raised his voice or clasped his silverware as tightly as his son did. Emília wondered if time had tamed him.

"You have to agree that the world is changing," her father-in-law said, interrupting Emília's thoughts. He tapped his dinner plate with his fork. "We must change with it."

"Of course," Dona Dulce said, staring at Emília. "We must all suffer change."

Before they entered the dining room, Dona Dulce had warned Emília that her husband liked to share his opinions. She needn't participate in Dr. Duarte's discussions, Dona Dulce said, because a lady never talked about anything substantial during meals. Although it frightened her, Emília was grateful for her father-in-law's conversation. It allowed her to concentrate on something other than the strange food on her plate, the rows of mysterious utensils beside it, and Dona Dulce's unwavering stare.

4

In Taquaritinga, people with means had outhouses. The Coelhos had a lavatory. Upstairs, near the bedrooms, was a room covered in square upon square of pink tile. In the center was a massive white tub with feet that resembled a panther's thick paws. Steam rose from the tub's surface. In the corner, attached to the floor, was a porcelain bowl with a water box and a pull-cord flush. Emília tugged the cord. The machine gurgled, then roared with water. Emília recoiled. She nearly dropped her traveling bag. She'd kept the purse—with her Communion portrait hidden inside it—near her feet during dinner and took it upstairs afterward, when Dona Dulce insisted she have a bath. Emília waited for the water in the toilet bowl to settle. She pulled the cord again.

"Miss Emília?" a woman called. She opened the lavatory door. It was Raimunda, an older maid with a creased brow and sagging cheeks. She was thin and birdlike, but lacked the grace of a bird. She seemed more like one of Dona Chaves's chickens, interested in survival and not flight. A bit of her hair—kinky and brown—peeked out from her white lace cap. She looked toward the tub and frowned.

"It'll get cold if you don't get in there," she said.

"I know," Emília replied. Like the other maid, Raimunda addressed her as *you* and not *senhora*. It was as if they had instantly assessed Emília's status and determined she was not worth the trouble.

"I was admiring the room," Emília continued.

"You should be used to it," Raimunda said. She placed the tips of her fingers in the water.

"This is the first time I've seen it. I used the downstairs washroom when I arrived."

The maid pulled her hand from the bathwater.

"You're not to use that room," she said. "That's for the help."

Emília felt a surge of heat in her chest. Before dinner, the young maid had directed her to the washroom beside the kitchen. Inside were two clay chamber pots. Flies had circled their knee-high lids.

"Well, go along," Raimunda said, turning her back. "I won't look."

Emília placed her purse on the floor. She unbuttoned her blouse. She'd sewn it herself, using the beige linen she'd purchased with her savings. Degas had offered to buy her clothes before their wedding but Emília had accepted only a hat and a travel bag from him. Only a woman of the life received clothing from a man who wasn't her husband. She stepped out of her skirt. It was badly wrinkled. The hem was brown with dust. Dona Conceição had told her to wear an old dress on the trip, to keep her new suit and blouse fresh for her arrival in Recife. Emília hadn't listened. She'd wanted to leave town looking glorious.

She eased herself into the tub. The water stung her skin. Raimunda turned around and stood beside her. The maid pushed her palm against Emília's scalp.

"Dunk," she said. "Go ahead, you won't drown."

Emília closed her eyes and went under. She imagined the fruits in Aunt Sofia's jams, plopped into boiling sugar water until their skin fell away and all that was left was the meat underneath. When she came back up, Raimunda lathered her back and arms with a loofah. She scrubbed hard. Emília slid back and forth in the slick tub. She pressed her hands to its sides to keep from going under.

"Maria shouldn't have taken you to that washroom," Raimunda said. "She shouldn't be greeting people. She's too young for that. Dona Dulce uses her because she's pretty, not because she does a good job. Dona Dulce's very particular about appearances."

Raimunda put shampoo into her hands and tugged it through Emília's hair. Emília squeezed her eyes shut. She wanted to know more about Dona Dulce but was afraid to ask.

"You're lucky you're pretty," the maid said. "Got nice teeth. It'll make things easier."

"What things?" Emília asked.

"Living here." Raimunda scrubbed her scalp harder.

"Why?"

"Dunk," Raimunda ordered, pushing down her head before Emília could speak. The water had grown lukewarm and foggy. Emília came up quickly, rubbing her eyes.

"I don't think living here will be hard at all," she said. "It's a beautiful house. So big. So modern."

"That's Dr. Duarte's doing," Raimunda said. "If Dona Dulce had her way, we'd be living like the Old families."

"What does that mean? Everyone talks about Old and New. I don't understand."

"You will, soon enough. It's not too different from the family fights in the interior. You are from the interior, aren't you?"

"Yes."

"Your daddy a colonel?"

"No."

"A rancher?"

"No."

Raimunda paused, then pointed her finger to the murky water. "Wash down there," she said and turned her back. Emília fumbled with the soap.

"Are you from the interior?" Emília asked. She pushed herself out of the tub, holding fast to the sides.

"Yes," Raimunda replied. She knelt and toweled off Emília's feet.

"Why did you come to Recife?"

Raimunda moved the towel faster along Emília's torso. "You shouldn't ask me questions."

"Why not?"

"Because you shouldn't."

"But you asked me questions."

"And if you had any sense, you wouldn't have answered."

"I don't understand," Emília said. She felt cold. She wanted to grab the towel and dry herself. "I thought you were being friendly."

"It's not my place to be friendly. And it's not yours to allow me to be." Raimunda worked the towel roughly through her hair, then stopped. They stood face-to-face. Raimunda looked both sympathetic and exasperated. It was the same way Aunt Sofia had stared into their bare pantry, stocked only with sour manioc flour and wilted greens, and been forced to figure out how to make them useful. Raimunda opened a tin of perfumed talcum powder.

"It's not my place to give advice," she said. "I'm not your momma." She sprinkled the powder across Emília's chest and under her arms. "But when you're surrounded by frogs, you'd better learn to jump."

5

///////

Emília's bridal bed was sturdy and old. According to Dona Dulce, the bed had been in her family since the first Dutch army had taken Recife from the Portuguese, three centuries before. One of Dona Dulce's Dutch ancestors, a van der Ley, had been so enamored of the Indian cashew that he had the bell-shaped fruits carved into his headboard. Since then, every van der Ley bride had spent her bridal night in that bed. Though she was now a Coelho, Emília would be no different.

The bed's massive frame was a far cry from the four crooked posts that supported her capim grass mattress in Taquaritinga. And the sheets! It would have taken Luzia months to produce the rows of blue and white flowers that crisscrossed the coverlet and lined the edges of the pillowcases. It seemed wrong to muss those sheets, to lay her head on those perfectly square pillows. Emília stood beside the bed. The night air felt wet and soupy. The perfumed talcum powder under her arms had clumped with sweat.

Down the hall, a scratchy female voice blared from the Coelhos' phonograph.

Estou com pressa, it said, first in Portuguese, and then in a strange, clipped gibberish.

"I am in a hurry," Degas repeated, his voice drifting down the hall and into their room.

After dinner, Degas had gathered a stack of English language records and shut himself up in his childhood bedroom. "I must get back to my studies," he'd said, then quickly kissed Emília's forehead.

Bom dia, senhora. Good morning, ma'am. The record's voice chimed.

"Good mor-ning, maaaam," she heard Degas repeat.

Emília inspected her nightgown. She'd sewn it herself, trimming the capped sleeves with lace, cutting and hemming the vertical slit in a perfect line just below the belly. This nightgown, along with a dozen others, had originally been made for Dona Conceição's nieces and placed in their hope chests. On Emília's wedding day, Dona

Conceição had pressed a soft bundle into her hands and whispered, "For your bridal night." Emília didn't unfold the gift or admire it. She already knew what it was. She and Luzia had embroidered each of the nightdresses, sewing small, red crosses above the slits. They hadn't stopped giggling as they sewed. Aunt Sofia had hushed them both. "When the time comes, that cross will be a comfort for those girls," their aunt shouted. "They will lie back and think of God."

Com licença, senhor, the record said. "Excuse me, sir," Degas repeated.

Emília knelt on the Coelhos' wooden floor. She clasped her hands the way Aunt Sofia had taught her, and called upon the Virgin for mercy and guidance. But the Virgin, Emília thought, had had her first relations with God. The Holy Mother did not have to wait, nervous and sweating, for her husband to finish his English lessons and lie with her. The Holy Mother did not have to wear a slit-front nightgown. And later, when she lay with Joseph, she already knew what to do. She had already had relations with God, so relations with a man must have been simple after that. Emília stood. She could not concentrate on prayers.

É urgente. "It's urgent."

Emília opened the large wooden wardrobe beside her bed. It was bare except for two dresses from Taquaritinga, her empty travel bag, and a few undergarments. Carefully, Emília slid the Communion portrait from its hiding place beneath her slips. She unwrapped the portrait and stared at her younger sister. Luzia's eyes were wide. Her locked arm was uncovered. The lace that had draped it had slipped off; the camera captured it in midfall. It hovered over the floor, white and fluttering, like a bird. Emília looked back at her bridal bed. What would Luzia do in her place? Wait? Pray? Neither, Emília told herself. Luzia would not have married Degas.

Across the hall, the phonograph clicked off. Emília felt a flutter in her chest. She carefully tucked the portrait away and ran to bed. The mattress was hard. The sheets were stiff with starch. Emília spread her hair carefully over her pillow and lay very still. When he entered the room, Degas did not turn on the light. He quickly took off his robe and slipped into bed beside her. Emília shut her eyes. She thought of all of those van der Ley women, pallid and unflinching, like Dona Dulce. She thought of the old gossips in Taquaritinga. They had called her ambitious, loose, even demented. But no one had ever called her fearful. Emília navigated her hand beneath the sheet. She clasped Degas' fingers.

"Emília?" he said, startled.

"Yes?" she replied.

"We've had a long day," Degas said, releasing his hand from her grip. "It's best we sleep."

Emília felt her anxiety draining from her, replaced by annoyance—she'd readied herself for this night, prepared herself to perform her duty, only to have Degas shirk his. Of course he was tired, she thought, after staying up late to listen to records. "Why are you studying English," Emília asked. "If you already know it?"

Degas shifted. "I have no one to practice with here. I want to stay sharp, to keep my pronunciation accurate. If I go back to Britain, I don't want to be rusty."

Emília turned toward him. *I*, he'd said, not *we*. "Go back?"

"For a trip." Degas sighed, as if he'd detected irritation in her voice. "I know you must feel overwhelmed, Emília. It will take time for you to adjust. It took me years when I came back from Britain. Can you imagine, coming back to this dreadful heat? And barely any electricity, my mother still using chamber pots, my father shouting about cranial measurements, and those damned Madonnas everywhere."

"I don't mind the Madonnas."

"Yes," Degas said. "Perhaps you'll like it here."

"You don't?" Emília asked.

Degas faced the ceiling. He spoke slowly, as if praying. "Each time I return here, I have to relearn the rules, that's all. No one likes doing that."

"What kind of rules?" Emília asked, concerned. She'd had to follow so many silly rules in Aunt Sofia's house; Emília had hoped that in the city things would be less rigid.

"The kind no one speaks of," Degas replied. "It's difficult to explain."

"Then how can you follow them?"

"I don't think this is something you should worry about now."

That "now" hung in the air between them like a mosquito, buzzing in Emília's ears. *Now* she wouldn't have to worry about Recife's unspoken rules, but later she would? Emília recalled Dona Dulce's courtyard speech.

"Your mother doesn't like me," she whispered.

Degas sighed. "She dislikes the situation. You must understand: Mamãe is tied to tradition. She wanted a lavish wedding for me. It will take time for her to understand all of this. And even if she didn't like you, she'd never show it. She'd never treat you poorly, Emília. Mamãe prides herself on keeping her composure. It's a change, to have another lady in the house with her. She's always been the dona here. And that's fine, isn't it? You wouldn't want the responsibility of running a house, would you? Let her be the dona. You be my wife. Then she'll see you were a good choice."

Degas shifted closer. Emília stiffened. Her heart pounded. She was his wife and would have to perform the main duty that came with that title. She closed her eyes, ready.

Degas squeezed her fingers. "Good night, Emília," he said, and turned away.

6

A week after Emília's arrival, the cata-vento stopped its slow rotation. The hot, windless days forced Dr. Duarte to turn off the fountains. The sound of gurgling water was replaced by the buzz of a diesel motor pumping water though the house's iron pipes. The half horse, half fish in the center courtyard lost his slick shine. The hallway rugs gave off a stale odor, as if all of the residue that had accidentally collected in their woven fibers—dirty footsteps, spilled drinks, overturned breakfast trays—was evaporating simultaneously in the summer heat. The courtyard ferns wilted. Only the thick, waxy flowers remained. The rows of manicured pitanga trees, which hid the ancient-looking servants' quarters, turned white with blooms. A colony of bees hovered around the trees. Degas transferred their Chrysler Imperial automobile from its usual showplace in front of the house to the shade of the side yard. Even Dr. Duarte's turtles avoided the heat, chewing their lettuce leaves in the few covered areas of the courtyard.

Only in the mornings, before the sun became too hot to bear, did the Coelho house seem alive. At dawn the ice wagon clambered through the front gates. Emília stood at her bedroom window and watched gloved men heave the great, steaming slabs of ice into a wheelbarrow and cart them into the kitchen. She spied the milk carriage as well, and watched the Coelhos' maids as they carried the frothy liquid in zinc buckets to the back of the house.

In the side yard, Dr. Duarte performed his morning ritual of toe touches, leg lifts, and body twists. The first time Emília witnessed this, she thought he'd gone mad.

"My calisthenics," he'd yelled cheerfully when he caught her staring. "Daily exercise oxygenates the brain!"

After his exercises, Dr. Duarte walked outside the gate and inspected the concrete wall surrounding the Coelho house for graffiti, taking note of the placement and size of the drawings. Once, over breakfast, Dr. Duarte spoke excitedly about how he'd caught a boy urinating on the wall. Instead of chastising the child, he'd called the boy over and measured his scalp.

"And what did I find?" Dr. Duarte asked. He sipped his viscous concoction of lemon water, raw egg, and malagueta peppers before informing them. "Asymmetrical ears!"

Her father-in-law rarely spoke of his import business or his money lending. He considered himself a man of science. In the afternoons, after he visited his warehouses and met with his political group at the British Club, Dr. Duarte locked himself in his study and pored over his scientific journals. He received parcels from Italy and the United

States every few weeks. Once, the maid opened one of these parcels and Emília caught a glimpse of the journals inside. On the cover was a drawing of a man's skull sectioned into many parts.

Emília did not completely understand her father-in-law's ideas, but she nodded and often let her breakfast grow cold so that she could give Dr. Duarte her full attention. He did not slow his pace or use simple words when he spoke to her, as Dona Dulce did. And since returning to the Federal University, Degas barely spoke to her at all. He had become rushed and distracted, leaving each morning after breakfast and returning late for dinner. Degas explained that he spent his afternoons in the legal library and his evenings discussing cases with Felipe and other fellow students in São José. Dr. Duarte tolerated Degas' long days, as long as it was intellectual stimulation he was after.

"Remember," Dr. Duarte often warned before Degas excused himself from breakfast, "drunkenness inflames the passions. It obscures mental and moral facilities."

Dona Dulce spent her days coordinating her staff. There were Raimunda and the young maid who'd escorted Emília that first day. There was a heavyset woman who did the wash, and an elderly cook with thick, swollen ankles. A woman whose skin was as dark and flaccid as a prune's was responsible for ironing clothing; Seu Tomás was the groundskeeper and carriage driver; and a houseboy ran errands, split wood, and dragged the chamber pots to their mysterious dumping ground each day.

During the long, stifling summer days, the only sound in the Coelho house came from the kitchen. The hallway leading to the back of the house was dark and steamy. It smelled of smoke and garlic, of wet chicken feathers and ripe fruit. Emília often stood in that hallway and closed her eyes just to take in the scents, which reminded her of Aunt Sofia's kitchen. This was the only similarity between them, however. The Coelho kitchen was large and tiled, and filled with modern contraptions. But despite Dr. Duarte's insistence on modernity, the kitchen was Dona Dulce's domain. The gas stove was used only to heat water. Each morning, the cook built a fire beneath the brick-lined cookstove in order to make their meals. Instead of using the electric iron, the prune-skinned servant pressed their clothes with a heavy coal-filled one. Behind the kitchen was a massive tank where the washerwoman, her arms tanned and muscled, scrubbed their clothes. And in the backyard was a small chicken pen and an ancient chopping block, stained black from years of gutting and cleaning.

The swampy grounds of Madalena were prone to mosquitoes, lizards, rain, mold, rot, and rust. Each day, Dona Dulce fought these tendencies. She glided through the Coelho house sniffing the draperies and sheets, her amber eyes scanning for spiders, dust, scuffs, and any other unwelcome elements. Without raising her voice or wrinkling her brow, she guided the servants through their myriad regular tasks and assigned them new ones.

"Maids are like children," Dona Dulce told Emília. "They may have good intentions, but their intentions don't matter. They must be disciplined to do things as you like them and no other way."

In the afternoons, she tied her scallop-edged apron around her waist and headed for the kitchen. She had been raised on an engenho, the daughter and granddaughter of cane producers, and she believed in the necessity of sugar. Inside the Coelho pantry were barrels and barrels of it, their lids sealed in wax and covered in cloth. Even in Taquaritinga's stores, Emília had never seen so much. Dona Dulce scooped kilo upon kilo into her copper jam pots. Then, with the same ease and efficiency she used when slicing open her correspondence with her silver mail opener, Dona Dulce cut out the insides of guavas. She squeezed the pits from jackfruits. She halved limes and mashed bananas. Then she watched the cook mix the caramelized sugar and fruits, but never went near the steaming pots because, Dona Dulce proclaimed, a lady did not stir.

Emília tried to show interest in Dona Dulce's household management and jam making. Her mother-in-law believed that respectability began inside the home, but Emília wanted to be outside. She had done enough cooking and cleaning in Taquaritinga. In Recife, she wanted to see the city, to attend luncheons, to stroll through the parks. Dona Dulce insisted that respectable young women did not wander the streets of Recife alone, without a destination. Respectable women had social agendas. Until Emília had an agenda of her own, she had to stay put.

Tired of the kitchen, Emília tried to occupy her time by embroidering in the shaded section of the courtyard. Inevitably she threw down her sewing hoop. The maids dragged the dusty hallway rugs into the courtyard and beat them until Emília's eyes watered and she began to sneeze. When she tried to find solace in her bedroom, they decided to air out the mattress and fluff the pillows. And if she roamed the hallways, the maids were always a step behind, waxing the floors and rubbing the mirrors with ammonia.

The Coelho house fascinated her with its wide corridors and cluttered rooms. There were massive tables whose feet were carved to resemble bird's talons gripping wooden balls. There were chairs with cracked leather stretched across their backs, held in place by discolored metal studs. There were glass cases that held ancient crystal bowls and scratched chalices. It frustrated Emília to think that Dona Dulce filled her home with such old, creaking things when she had the means to buy new ones. What disconcerted Emília most was the spotlessness of the place. Emília dropped bits of thread on the floors. She hugged a pillow and placed it crookedly back in its chair. She pressed her fingers to the glass cases. She took one of the leather-bound books from its shelf and slipped it in a new location. But when she returned the next day, the book was back where it belonged. The pillows were straightened. The floors were swept. The glass was wiped clean.

Emília took walks in the garden, under the shade of the pitanga trees. Seu Tomás, the groundskeeper, always lurked nearby. He had strict orders to keep her within his sight, as if she were a wayward child waiting for an opportunity to slip through the main gate. Emília endured this humiliation, and others. At the dining table, her napkins were sloppily folded. Her coffee spoon was often smudged.

Her bath towels were never fully dry. The pleats of her dresses were crookedly ironed.

Though she noticed every detail in the Coelho house, Dona Dulce didn't notice the maids' sloppiness with regard to Emília. Or she pretended not to. Emília's mother-in-law didn't chastise her servants for specific errors, but she insisted that they "treat Degas' wife with respect and obey her as if she was your dona!" The more Dona Dulce demanded they obey Emília, the sloppier the maids became. Had her mother-in-law been overtly mean to her, the maids might have felt sympathy for Emília; they might have considered her an ally. But the more Dona Dulce put Emília above them, the more the maids hated her. After having worked in the colonel's house, Emília knew the kinds of petty jealousies a dona could create among her staff and sometimes even her family. She suspected Dona Dulce knew, too. Each time Emília went into the servants' area, the maids grew silent. Only Raimunda addressed her, asking if there was anything she needed. Emília made things up—a cup of water, more embroidery thread, a slice of cake. Once, after she left, she heard them laughing. "Matuta," one of them giggled. "Probably never tasted cake in her life!"

Degas had told her that the maids lived in shacks in the flood-prone Afogados and Mustardinha, but they were born Recifians and that fact alone made them hold themselves above her. In the countryside, Emília would have been considered an excellent wife. She knew how to pound manioc root into farinha, how to grind corn until it became fubá, how to plant beans, how to sew a lady's dress and a gentleman's shirt. These talents were suddenly handicaps in Recife. Emília had no family name. She was not a colonel's daughter or a wealthy rancher's relation. She was no one, and the poorly folded napkins, the dirty spoons and humid towels were the maids' reminders of this.

In Taquaritinga, Degas had promised her fine dresses, a wedding party, a ride in his motorcar. The only promise that had materialized was a wedding announcement, days after they'd arrived in Recife. News of their union was featured in the society pages of the *Diário de Pernambuco* newspaper, without a photograph.

Mr. Degas van der Ley Feijó Coelho traveled inland and wed Miss Emília dos Santos, resident of Toritama, in an intimate ceremony. A honeymoon voyage was delayed due to the groom's legal studies at the Federal University of Pernambuco.

They had erred in her hometown. Emília was upset, but Degas assured her that those kinds of mistakes often occurred. Their wedding party would be scheduled when the weather cooled, he said. The dresses, the driving, the dinners and luncheons would come with time. He was very busy with his studies, Degas said. Surely she must understand.

Emília nodded. The tragic men of her childhood fantasies were gone. The deaf, dumb, handsome figures from the pages of *Fon Fon* had been replaced by a real man. And from him, Emília had not expected love or romance. She'd only expected his attention, his guidance. She'd hoped her husband would serve as a teacher, escorting her through Recife society and eventually showing her the world. But as soon as they'd arrived in the city, Degas became closed and hard to grasp. He had no more stories to tell her, no more compliments to give. Each day he treated her politely, pulling out her chair at breakfast and kissing her cheek before leaving. Emília was suspicious of his courtesy, seeing it as a gentlemanly way of tolerating her. Each night, after Emília had gotten into bed, Degas crept into their room and took his pajamas from the closet. Then he promptly returned to his childhood bedroom.

In *Fon Fon*'s photo spreads of elegant houses and apartments, the master bedrooms often had two twin beds—one for the husband and one for the wife. In the colonel's house, Dona Conceição couldn't tolerate her husband's snoring, so they slept in separate bedrooms connected by a door. Emília could accept this; she liked having a bed to herself. But she worried about her wifely duty. Every other day the Coelho maids changed Emília's bedsheets. No one inspected them. Dona Dulce and Dr. Duarte didn't look for the reddish-brown blot that would prove Emília's purity. Emília convinced herself that city people didn't practice the same barbaric post-wedding rituals as country people. Perhaps Degas' behavior was normal, she thought. Perhaps gentlemen took their time.

"All men are billy goats," Aunt Sofia had warned her once, when she'd caught Emília fawning over an actor in *Fon Fon*. "They all have urges. Rich ones are the worst; they're sneaks!" But what did Aunt Sofia know about gentlemen? Degas had no urges. Except for his quick hellos and good-byes, he hadn't touched Emília. She took longer baths, spritzed herself with perfume, and discarded her dowdy, slit-front nightgown for an embroidered gown and robe the Coelhos had given her. Degas did not seem to notice these improvements. Her husband, like everything else in Emília's new surroundings, was foreign to her. The city and the Coelho house had different smells, different sounds, different bugs and birds, different plants, different rules. Why then, did she expect her husband to act like the farmers she'd grown up with? Overwhelmed by so many changes, Emília locked herself in her bedroom for a few minutes each day. She lay on her bed, took deep breaths, and shut her eyes. Perhaps *she* was different, and everything around her normal. Perhaps it wasn't Degas who was deficient or odd, but her. If he hadn't touched her, there must be a reason—was Degas revolted by her country ways? Did he, like the Coelho housemaids, silently condemn his choice of a wife?

During their quick courtship, Emília had let herself think of only the benefits of their union. She'd thought only of spaces filled with furniture and gas ovens and comfortable rugs. She hadn't thought of the empty spaces: the bed with its wide white expanse of sheets; the dining table, with its long, creased tablecloth and its place settings separating one diner from the next. And the narrow upstairs hallway where, each night, Degas left Emília standing as he walked into his childhood bedroom and shut the door.

7

There were many wild birds on the Coelho property. They called to each other in the pitanga trees. They hopped about the courtyard. Above their cries and twitters rose the sharp, unchanging song of Dr. Duarte's corrupião. It had been a gift from one of the men in his political group, and it arrived at the Coelho house knowing nothing except the tune that accompanied the first strophe of the national anthem. The bird varied only its pace. When the maids entered the study, the song was fast and panicked. After it received a fresh helping of pumpkin seeds and water, its song was slow and lazy. In the evenings, when Dr. Duarte tried to teach it the second strophe, the bird held stubbornly to the old tune.

One afternoon, as Emília embroidered in the Coelhos' courtyard, the bird's song was choppy and frenzied. The glass door to Dr. Duarte's study was open. The corrupião had been left in the sun. It hopped frantically from one end of its cage to the other. It dipped its orange wings into its empty water bowl. Emília put down her embroidery. She stepped into the study and dragged the bird's pedestal into the shade.

A hot beam of sunlight ran across Dr. Duarte's massive wooden desk. Beside it, on a pedestal similar to the corrupião's, sat a porcelain bust. The head was divided into large, labeled sections: *Hope. Logic. Amativeness. Wit. Benevolence. Destructiveness.*

The room's walls were lined with shelves. Books sat on most of them. On others were skulls ranging in size from tiny to large. In the back, caught in the sunlight's farthest reach, were glass jars with bulbous lids. Emília shielded her eyes with her hand. They resembled Dona Dulce's jam jars, except they were larger. And instead of containing dark, sweet preserves they were filled with amber and yellow liquids that glowed brightly in the sun. Emília closed the study's glass doors and pulled down their shades. She walked toward the back shelves.

There were objects floating in the jars. They were filmy and dull, as if the liquid surrounding them had leached their color. In one jar, there floated a tongue, curled and muscular. In another, a pale gray heart. Emília could not recognize the other jars' contents. There were two bean-shaped organs, a large yellow mass that looked fibrous and thick, and a flaccid brown organ that leaned against its glass confines. Above these was the largest jar, alone on a shelf. The glass was labeled *Mermaid Girl*.

Her eyes were closed. Her head was bowed, her body curled. A layer of hair—downy and fine—covered the fetus's small head. The infant looked as if she were in a deep, peaceful sleep and could wake at any moment. Emília wished the corrupião would stop its incessant singing. Two smooth stumps tapered from the girl's tiny torso, making it look as if she was hiding her arms behind her back. Her legs were fused together, like a fin. Emília touched the jar. Strands of the girl's hair waved back and forth in the amber fluid.

The study's hallway door opened. Emília moved away from the shelf. Dr. Duarte entered. He started at the sight of her.

"I'm sorry," Emília said, "I came in to move the corrupião out of the sun and to close the shades."

Dr. Duarte grunted. He placed his briefcase on the desk, then stood beside Emília. He smelled of cigar smoke and cologne and something else—a mixture of overripe fruit and salt air; the smell of warehouses along the port, the smell of the city.

"Spying on my collection?" he said.

"Oh no!" Emília replied. Her heart beat fast. She wanted to leave, but Dr. Duarte blocked her path. He examined her face.

"I obtained these things after the subjects passed on," he laughed. "No need to look at me like that, I'm not the lobisomem!"

"Of course not," Emília whispered. A blush burned her cheeks. For an instant, when she'd first seen the jars' contents, Emília had thought of the tale of the lobisomem. It was an awful story that the kids in Padre Otto's school used to tell—the tale of a wealthy old man cursed by one of his servants and forced to kidnap children and eat their organs so he would not turn into a werewolf.

"She is an anomaly," Dr. Duarte said, pointing to the jar nearest Emília.

"A what?"

"An abnormality. There are only one in a hundred thousand fetuses with fused legs and hands. Her mother was a criminal, perhaps an alcoholic. She inherited this, poor dear."

He turned the jar around. The girl's shoulder bumped against the glass. Her hair waved.

"She died at birth," Dr. Duarte said. "It's best. She would have become a criminaloid like her mother."

"Because she has no legs?" Emília said. She placed her hand on the jar, hoping to steady it. "That isn't her fault."

"That is the problem!" Dr. Duarte shouted, clapping his hands together. Emília jumped.

"Most medical criminologists," Dr. Duarte continued, "even pioneers like Lombroso, believed that obvious deformities—a tail or several nipples or a receding chin—identified a criminal. That's because they had no way to measure exactly how these things affected human behavior."

He stared at her, waiting for a response.

"My aunt Sofia didn't trust men with scanty beards," Emília finally said.

Dr. Duarte tilted his head back and released a loud laugh.

"Your aunt is in the same camp as our esteemed Lombroso!" He smiled. His face was flushed, his eyes bright. "You cannot simply look at someone and see their criminal potential. That is archaic mumbo jumbo. Some poor unfortunate may have a terrible, flattened nose, but no other criminal characteristics. Now, don't misunderstand me, I wholeheartedly agree with Mr. Lombroso—he is, after all, the founder of the Modern School! Criminals differ from the rest of us. They are knowable, measurable, and predictable. Only the truth is not in our eyes, but in mathematics. It is all a question of scale."

Emília nodded. He spoke clearly and forcefully, but when his words reached her ears they seemed jumbled and obscure. She thought of her measuring tape, of stretching it across shoulders and around waists. Aunt Sofia had always told them that a seamstress must be silent and sensible because she was privy to great secrets. With her measuring tape, Emília had noticed the curve of a suddenly swollen belly. She had held the tape gently around bruised arms. She had watched as new brides' gangly, loose frames began to thicken and slump with time. Was this what Dr. Duarte meant—that what was measurable was knowable?

"Measurement allows us to see what is unseen," Dr. Duarte continued. "The brain's formation gives us a chance to distinguish between incurable criminals and deviants."

"Deviants?" Emília asked.

"Petty thieves. Perverts," Dr. Duarte said, bunching his thick fingers. "They are weak-minded individuals. They feel remorse after exhibiting degenerate behavior, but they're selfish. They don't want to give up private pleasures for the betterment of society. They can be salvaged, though, with discipline and sometimes with harsher measures: restraint, confinement, hormonal injections. Forgive me," Dr. Duarte said suddenly. He ran his fingers through his thinning hair. "This is not a discussion for ladies."

"I enjoy it," Emília said, happy to be having a discussion with anyone at all. Dr. Duarte smiled but it was without the gleam and energy he had had before. Behind them, the corrupião sang.

"How are you liking it here, so far?" Dr. Duarte asked.

"Oh," Emília stammered. "It is . . . what I'd wanted."

"Good."

She stared again at the Mermaid Girl. Powdery detritus floated at the bottom of the glass. How long had she been in that jar? Would she stay that way forever, silent and curled, or would she slowly slough away, turning into a heap of powder? Emília wanted to ask Dr. Duarte but the question seemed silly.

"You have to agree," he said, "that a wife is a motivating force for a man. Degas is finally concentrating on his studies. Dona Dulce wanted him to marry a Recife girl. She says that Cupid has short wings for a reason." Dr. Duarte chuckled. "I must admit, I was taken aback when I received Degas' telegrams about your . . . your association with each other. I thought it was another one of his tales at first. I wanted him to do the honorable thing, of course. And after some thought, I grew to like the idea." Dr. Duarte reddened. "I certainly didn't like him tarnishing an honest girl's honor! What I mean to say is: it was a relief to know he'd found a wife. A good, hardy country girl is just what he needs."

"Tarnishing?" Emília repeated

"It's an expression," Dr. Duarte said, waving his hand in the air impatiently. "Regardless of the circumstances, it was time. Fair or not, when a man gets older it's a strike against him to be a bachelor. You have to agree, Emília, that Degas might have misbehaved with you, but he righted that wrong when he gave you his name."

Her father-in-law liked to start his sentences with such phrases— *You have to agree* or *It is obvious that*—giving his listeners little choice. Emília lowered her head. Her ears tingled, her breath was short. It was one thing for people in Taquaritinga to believe she'd been ruined, but quite another for her in-laws to think such things. She'd never asked Degas about the telegrams he'd sent to Recife. She'd assumed he'd represented her fairly.

"Nothing to be ashamed of, my dear!" Dr. Duarte said. "These things happen. Even Dona Dulce will grow to understand that. Mothers always worry needlessly over their sons. When my father sent me to Europe to study medicine, my mother cried for three months. There was no money in having an education back then, but the Old families sent their boys off, so my father said his boy would be no different. My mother, pour soul, worried herself sick. She believed too much culture could rot a man. As if culture was like sugar and men like teeth!" Dr. Duarte quieted. "I understand better now, what she meant."

There was a light knocking on the courtyard door. Dona Dulce stepped inside.

"I heard the bird," she said, looking at Dr. Duarte, then at Emília. "He seemed to be agitated, but I couldn't step away from the kitchen."

"Emília took care of it," Dr. Duarte said.

"Good." Dona Dulce smiled. Her teeth were small and her gums wide, like Degas'. "I hope you weren't frightened by Dr. Duarte's knickknacks. Between science and politics, I'd rather have science in my house. It's the least unsavory."

Dr. Duarte released a puff of air through his nose.

"Come," Dona Dulce chirped, holding out her pale hand to Emília. "Don't let him pester you with his conversation. He is always looking for a willing ear."

8

That night, Emília could not sleep. She lay uncomfortably between the starched sheets of her bridal bed. That afternoon, in Dr. Duarte's study, she'd learned why no attention had been paid to those sheets. The entire household thought Degas had ruined Emília before the wedding, that she was a loose woman. Perhaps this was why Dona Dulce disliked her.

Down the hall, Degas' English record blared. *Onde posso achar o bonde?* "Where can I find the trolley?"

Emília got up. She put on her linen robe and walked to Degas' childhood bedroom. Gently, Emília knocked on the door. When her husband didn't answer, she let herself in. The room was smoky and cluttered. A Victrola phonograph stood in the corner. Unlike the ones in Taquaritinga, it did not have a brass horn. Instead, Degas' model was housed in a tall wooden cabinet. Above the Victrola were shelves cluttered with relics of her husband's childhood: a wooden puppet, it strings badly tangled; a cluster of tin animals; a train set. There were legal books scattered about, and at the base of the twin bed, a steamer trunk. The brass latches were dull with age. Along the leather lid were stickers covered with the emblems of countries. Degas sat in an armchair beside the room's only window, which faced the Coelho courtyard. He smoked. Between puffs, he repeated the record's strange phrases. When he saw Emília, Degas stopped in midsentence.

"Is everything all right?" he asked, clicking off the Victrola.

"No," Emília said. "I can't sleep."

Degas turned toward the window. "Neither can I."

Emília closed the collar of her robe. She stared at her bare feet, her fat toes. She regretted interrupting Degas' lessons, but her father-in-law's words still stung her.

Degas turned from the window. "Would you like a smoke?"

"No," Emília replied, though she was curious to try a cigarette. "Dona Dulce says ladies don't smoke."

Degas clicked his tongue. "Half the ladies in Recife smoke. Mother knows that. It's all right to have a vice, Emília." Degas removed a tightly rolled cigarette from its silver case. "Just don't get caught. It's not the vice, but the discovery that's dangerous here."

"In this house, you mean?" Emília asked.

Degas shrugged. "This city," he replied. "Anywhere, really." His eyelids sagged, making him appear more tired than he proclaimed himself to be.

Emília took the cigarette. It felt delicate and weightless between her fingers. She recalled the long-necked actresses in her old magazines, how they posed with their cigarettes, and felt a rush of excitement. When Degas flicked his lighter, Emília found it hard to stay perfectly still. She took a long first puff. The smoke burned her throat. It made her nose tingle. Emília let out a violent cough. Degas moved closer.

"I don't want to corrupt you," he said and tried to take the cigarette from her hand.

Emília stepped back, moving out of his reach. "I'm not a child," she coughed, her throat still scratchy. She bristled at Degas' protectiveness, believing he'd given her the cigarette just to have the fun of taking it away. Emília took another puff, forcing herself to swallow the smoke.

"I spoke to your father today," she said. "In his study. He told me about the telegrams you sent. The ones about me."

Degas' eyes widened. He shoved his silver lighter into his pocket. "It was the only way, Emília. My parents wouldn't have consented otherwise."

"Now I know why the maids whisper about me," Emília said. Her mouth tasted both sweet and smoky. The cigarette in her hand was partway gone; a gray clot of ashes stuck to its lit end. Quickly, Emília took another puff.

"That's nonsense," Degas replied, lowering his voice. "They don't know a thing. My mother is discreet. She'd never let the real reason get out."

"But it's not real."

Degas bit the side of his cheek. "Sometimes we must tell people what is necessary and not what is true."

Because of the cigarette, Emília felt light-headed. She leaned against the Victrola's wooden cabinet.

"It's my name that's ruined. Not yours," she said softly. "You made yourself look honorable, marrying me even though . . ." Emília's ears rang. She held tighter to the record player. "You never took liberties with me, Degas. I wouldn't have let you. I want you to tell your parents. I want them to know. It won't make a difference for you, now that we're married. But it will for me."

Degas blinked. He leaned against the other side of the wooden record player. Gently, his fingers stroked its brass label. On it was the image of a dog, its ear cocked toward a record horn. Above it, the word *Victrola* was printed in large, curling letters.

"I heard this was your sister's name," Degas said. "Such a strange name."

Emília felt queasy; she'd smoked too much. The cigarette was hot in her hands, its lit tip almost reaching her fingers. "It was a nickname," she replied.

"That's terrible luck, what happened to her," Degas continued, ignoring Emília. "Just terrible. You'd think because she was crippled, those cangaceiros would have let her be."

"I didn't think you knew about her," Emília said.

Degas smiled faintly. "It's sweet you would think that. It proves how pure you are, how uncontaminated by gossip. Felipe told me, but everyone spoke of it. Even the colonel's maids. Never in front of you, of course."

Degas moved around the Victrola. He placed his hands on Emília's shoulders.

"Everyone believes that silence is a consideration," he said softly. "But really, it's a persecution. When someone's the object of gossip, they're really the object of silence. You know what that's like. So do I. That's why I was drawn to you, Emília. I wanted to help you out of that undignified situation."

"God rest her soul," Emília choked out, staring at the Victrola.

"Don't be upset," Degas said. He wrapped his arms tightly around her. "I won't tell anyone what happened to her. Father is perverse about such things. He calls himself an authority on criminals. Really, he doesn't know what he's talking about; he just adds a dash of mathematics to his conclusions so they sound more expert." Degas loosened his grip. When he spoke again, he lowered his voice. "We have to be discreet about your family troubles, Emília. What hurts your reputation hurts mine, and vice versa. It's like the story I told my parents: true or not, it wouldn't do you or me any good to spread such things about. That's what's noble about marriage—we are bound to shield each other from talk."

Emília nodded absently. Part of her felt strangely grateful to Degas, while the other part wanted to return to her bedroom and lock the door.

"You don't look well," Degas said gently. "Get to bed." He took the cigarette stub from her hand. "It's easy to overdo it, Emília. You don't know your limits yet, but you'll learn."

9

The next day, Dona Dulce found Emília in the courtyard.

"You've had enough rest," Dona Dulce said, untying her starched apron. "Now, we must work."

She led Emília into a vast, mirrored space on the house's lower level. The room was hot and dark. Reception chairs were stacked along its walls. Dona Dulce locked the hallway door behind them. She left the courtyard door's curtains closed.

"It's no good keeping you cooped up in the house," Dona Dulce said. "People will think we're hiding you and come up with all kinds of reasons as to why."

A long, thin stick leaned against the room's mirrored wall. Dona Dulce took it in her hands.

"Walk," she said.

The room's mirrors made it seem as if there were rows and rows of wheaten-haired Dona Dulces, all stern and commanding, their amber eyes set on Emília.

"Walk," Dona Dulce repeated.

Emília stepped away from her mother-in-law. Dona Dulce watched her in the mirrors.

"Don't be stiff," she called out.

Emília quickened her pace.

"No!" Dona Dulce shouted. "Don't stride as if you were a horse. And do not swing your arms. You aren't swatting flies! Go slowly. Don't rush—that indicates nervousness."

Suddenly, Dona Dulce glided beside her. She poked Emília's stomach hard with the stick.

"Tuck it in," she said firmly. "This was the way the nuns taught me. It's not easy, but it must be done. Be thankful I am willing to teach you or else you'd never be able to leave the house. It will be easier to mold your habits since you haven't been previously taught. In this regard, I'd rather have you than some of these obstinate young women in this city, who think they can do away with manners altogether. Tuck it in!"

Dona Dulce poked Emília's shoulders, her rear, her chest. It seemed that when she tucked one in, the others naturally popped out. Still, Dona Dulce repeated her phrase over and over, as if singing a hymn. Next, she produced a broomstick from beside the covered chairs. She placed it behind Emília's neck and roped her arms over it. Emília's chest jutted forward.

"Our posture reveals our nature," Dona Dulce said. "The sloucher is lazy—she hasn't the self-discipline to hold herself up. Now walk."

They spent many afternoons in that hot, mirrored room. Each time they left it, Emília's dresses were damp, her hair matted to her forehead, her feet and neck sore. Even Dona Dulce had a hint of red flushing her pale cheeks. In the evenings, Emília watched street peddlers from her upstairs window. She watched how the men carried their entire stock—feather dusters and aluminum pails, brooms, bottles, and clay jugs—swinging from the pole across their shoulders, as precisely balanced as a scale. After Emília mastered her posture, Dona Dulce uncovered a chair and made her repeat the ritual of taking a seat and straightening her skirt. Emília rose and sat until her knees pained her. All the while, Dona Dulce kept her stick at hand and imparted other, subtler lessons to Emília: never sit beside a man who is not your husband; never reveal discomfort or dislike; never perform introductions unless you are the hostess; never shake hands.

With each rule, Dona Dulce's voice grew lower, her jabs with the stick harder. She seemed irritated at having to say such things aloud, as if speaking them lessened their value. If Emília asked for explanations, Dona Dulce replied sharply.

"The chatterer reveals every corner of her shallow mind," she said. "Better to keep your mouth closed until you are asked a question."

Rules were rules, Dona Dulce explained. Had Emília been born into that world, had she been properly groomed and molded, such things wouldn't need saying; they wouldn't be simplified by words or made to sound like the cheap guidelines found in fashion magazines. They would have soaked in, through years of observation and routine, until there was no other way of being.

As summer wore on, there were more and more rules to memorize. After each lesson, Emília felt exhausted and shaken. There were so many mistakes she could make, so many vulgarities she could unknowingly commit. Still, Emília was determined to refine herself. If she learned the rules of her new world, if she embodied them, Emília believed that the stain on her character would be wiped away. Dona Dulce would respect her. Degas would treat her as a wife, and not as a poor country girl he'd rescued. He would take her to luncheons, to the cinema, and perhaps even on a honeymoon in Rio de Janeiro as he'd promised. And on that honeymoon, he might touch her as a husband should touch a wife. Emília sat taller, walked straighter. During meals she didn't fuss with the dining implements. She kept her hands away from her face. She dabbed at the corners of her mouth with her napkin instead of smearing it across her lips. She continued to have a horrible time identifying silverware, which Dona Dulce liked to set in elaborate rows beside and above their plates. During moments of doubt, Emília imagined Dona Dulce behind her, holding her hands like a puppet's and saying, "Take your time. Do not shovel. Attack your food with vigor, but with as little ferocity as possible. And for all that's holy, do not push away your plate when you are done."

If she looked across the table and saw Dona Dulce's wheaten eyebrows rise in reproach, Emília didn't get upset or stop eating. Instead, she stared hard at the crisp line in the middle of the linen tablecloth and recalled what Dona Dulce had told her when she'd begun her lessons—that there was no mystery to all of this, that the road to refinement was as straight and unwavering as the crease that ran down the center of that cloth.

10

////////

As a reward for her progress, Dona Dulce took Emília to buy fabric and meet with a dressmaker on Rua da Imperatriz. Emília hadn't been able to sleep the night before, recalling the fashions she had seen in *Fon Fon*: tubular dresses with calf-length skirts and delicately ruffled collars. She deeply regretted leaving her magazines in Taquaritinga; Dona Dulce did not subscribe to *Fon Fon*.

The dressmaker's atelier had a showroom and a fitting area for clients. Stacked against the room's walls were tightly rolled bolts of fabrics. There were printed silks, shining taffetas, translucent crepes. Emília believed she would faint with excitement. Finally, she would be the one on the pedestal instead of the one holding the measuring tape. She would stand before the mirror and give orders to tuck this or hem that. Her excitement quickly faded. Dona Dulce placed no value on cloche hats, smart dresses, or heeled shoes with delicate clasps. She chose "classic" linens, all drab and neutral colored, and instructed the stylist to cut dresses similar to the simplest ones in the shop window: discreetly collared, low waisted, with straight skirts that revealed ankle but covered any hint of calf.

The dressmaker nodded approvingly and lamented to Dona Dulce about the new styles coming out of Rio de Janeiro. As Emília stood on the fitting platform, she listened to what they praised and what they criticized. She'd believed that all city ladies wore the newest, most daring fashions. She saw now that there was a distinction between what was new and what was acceptable. If a lady took the flapper style to the extreme—wearing short skirts and athletic-inspired dresses—she was rumored to be morally liberal, or worse: a suffragette. But ladies who dressed too traditionally, in full skirts with corseted waists, were also mocked for being outdated. As she stood beside those many-colored bolts of fabric, Emília realized that a refined woman was the opposite of the Coelho house: she had the lacquer of modernity on the outside, but an antiquated core.

In the dressing stall, as Emília changed back into her linen travel suit, she heard the familiar clatter of sewing machines. When she left the stall, Emília did not return to the front of the store; she followed the clatter instead. At the end of the narrow hallway, the sound grew louder. There was a wooden door; Emília peeked inside. A waft of stale air made her recoil. The room was dimly lit and hot. Three rows of pedal-operated Singers cluttered the small workspace. Young women hunched over the machines, feverishly pumping the pedals and moving cloth through the needles. Some of the girls wore head scarves, which stuck to their foreheads, wet with perspiration. One girl looked up at Emília, then went quickly back to work.

"You've gone through the wrong door," Dona Dulce said loudly, her voice carrying over the machines' racket. She stood behind Emília.

"Are those dressmakers, too?" Emília asked.

"No, dear," Dona Dulce replied, steering Emília away. "Those are the seamstresses. A dressmaker designs. Seamstresses just string things together. I thought you knew that."

Emília fumbled with her gloves. She'd forgotten to put them back on and was conscious now of the old sewing calluses on her fingertips. They'd softened since she'd left Taquaritinga; in the Coelho house all Emília did was embroider, listen to music, take walks around the garden, and practice her etiquette with Dona Dulce. But those calluses—those markers of her old life—remained on her hands. Dona Dulce led Emília up the hall. They stopped at the back of the shop's showroom, where the dressmaker kept bolts of fustão, all waffled and honeycombed in shades of pinks and blues.

"Isn't this fine?" Dona Dulce asked, fingering a bolt. "We'll be needing this soon, I expect. Since I wasn't allowed to plan a wedding, at least you'll let me plan a baptism."

Emília nodded absently. She could not shake the image of that oppressive sewing room. If she had come to the city alone, as she'd once planned, she might have been trapped in such a place.

"Ceremony is important, Emília," Dona Dulce continued. "Country people are not always hindered, so to speak, by the same conventions we keep in the city. It's a shame you had to spend your nuptial night on the train—that's what I always tell my staff." Dulce stared at Emília, her amber eyes searching her face. "Do you remember what I taught you about maids? They have large mouths. They can't help it. It's in their nature. They have nothing to talk about in their lives so they must talk about ours. They have a verifiable network around the city. If, for example, a newly wedded groom takes to sleeping in his childhood bedroom, each time a maid makes the beds, she will speculate as to why he's not visiting his wife in her room. Sometimes she will tell her mistress. And if you aren't careful, she will tell others. Soon, all of Recife will know."

Emília's throat tightened. She had always believed that there were a dozen pairs of eyes watching her in the Coelho house. She tried to move away from the waffled fabrics, but Dulce held her. Her mother-in-law straightened her back, becoming stiff and business-like, as if dealing with a member of her staff.

"You should treat your husband like a guest," she said. "A good hostess learns to predict her guests' expectations, and to meet them."

"But Degas has no expectations," Emília said, her voice cracking. "I can't please him."

Dulce once again smoothed the pink, waffled fustão between her fingertips. "No man knows what he prefers. Especially Degas. He's easily swayed by poor influences, like that Felipe. But you are his wife now; you must influence him. It's a wife's job to train her husband to have tastes—so that she can practice the flattery of fulfilling them. A wife becomes indispensable that way. She becomes more than just a momentary lapse in judgment."

The dressmaker interrupted their talk, calling them back to the measuring stand. Dona Dulce smiled widely at the woman, flashing each of her small, immaculate teeth.

11

/ / / / / / / / /

Three weeks after visiting the atelier, Emília received her collection of beige, brown, and gray linen dresses. Dona Dulce had also supervised the purchase of two pairs—one brown, one black—of tasteful, low-heeled lace-up slippers. She'd ordered Emília a black silk parasol and a broad-brimmed hat with interchangeable grosgrain bands to match her dresses. Emília contemplated leaving the hideous hat in the courtyard, at the mercy of the turtles. She contemplated angering the prune-skinned maid so that the woman might be careless with the embers that flew from her iron when she pressed the dresses. But Emília could not bring herself to do this—the dresses' linen was expensive, the hat's straw finely woven, and the shoes' leather the softest she had ever owned. If she could not have stylish things, at least she had fine ones.

That day, instead of leading Emília to the mirrored room for her afternoon lesson, Dona Dulce instructed her to put on a new dress and pin back her hair.

"We must put your lessons into practice," Dona Dulce said.

The afternoon heat had subsided by the time they arrived in Derby Square. A sea breeze cooled the air. The trolley cars did not clang their bells. The few street peddlers who circled the park had already sold the bulk of their vegetables or brooms, and they were quiet. The trolleys' black wires crisscrossed the skyline, resembling the cat's cradles Emília and Luzia had woven between their fingers. Homes, larger and more beautiful than the Coelho house, circled the park. At its farthest end sat the immense, white-domed headquarters of the Military Police. Emília and Dulce began their promenade along the park's winding path.

Other women, some young, some old, all well dressed, walked side by side along the pathways or sat demurely on the wrought-iron benches. When Dulce and Emília passed, the women smiled or gave a polite nod. Then, as if there was an unspoken agreement between them all, they were silent until they had left each other's range of vision. Only afterward did they tilt their heads together and whisper.

Dona Dulce also followed this code, pulling Emília close and quietly explaining who they had just passed and if they were Old or New. The women from the Old families were thin lipped and tasteful. Their dresses had intricately beaded collars with round, pearl brooches at the throats. Their hats were short-brimmed cloches with a single thick feather tucked into the bands. When they saw Dulce and Emília, they nodded but rarely smiled. The New women did not have the same imperturbable elegance as the Old. They wore shorter dresses with more jewels and many-feathered hats. Some even wore flesh-colored silk stockings, giving their calves a nude appearance. They, too, eyed Emília and Dulce, but often smiled and stopped to chat, speaking loudly and letting out long, high laughs.

"Welcome!" Teresa Raposo, the dark-haired matriarch of a New family, said. She'd tried to pry Emília away, but Dulce had held fast to her arm. Thwarted, Dona Raposo lowered her voice and winked. "This city needs new blood."

"Disgusting," Dona Dulce muttered once they had left Teresa Raposo. "Like a horde of vampires. As if the old blood wasn't good enough!"

Emília remained silent. Her feet hurt from her new shoes. Her head pounded from the worry of making a mistake: slouching or rushing or fidgeting when she wasn't supposed to. Dona Dulce walked quickly toward their carriage. She'd had enough for the day. She was still tall, rigid, commanding, but she had looked old-fashioned and tense beside the New women, and nervous and reverent in the face of the Old. When they reentered the Coelhos' gates, Dona Dulce let out a long sigh, of relief or fatigue Emília could not be sure.

They went to Derby Square once a week after that, to perform their "footing," as Dona Dulce called it. Slowly, through Dona Dulce's hissed rules, Dr. Duarte's stories, and Emília's own observations, the city and its divisions began to take shape. Any person of importance was either Old or New. The rest—dark skinned or light, educated or dumb, street sweeper or scholar—were part of a nebulous horde without money or family title. Newspaper reporters, seamstresses, basket vendors, trolley conductors, even the children of ranchers and colonels fell into this group. Either they were nameless, or poor, or both, and they would live and pray and suffer as the nameless and the poor always had—invisibly.

Many of the Old families had lost their fortunes, or at least substantial chunks of them, but not their prestige. Their ancestors were the Portuguese and Dutch who had cleared away trees in the Zona da Mata and planted sugarcane or pau-brasil trees grown for their red dye and fine violin wood. They were the Feijós, the Sampaios, the Cavalcantis, the Carvalhos, the Coimbras, the Furtados, the van der Leys. They owned vast plantations and sent their children to Recife, then Europe for their educations. But the price of sugar fell, the need for dye subsided, and the families preferred to live in the capital and not on their farms. Still, they had their elegance, their political influence, and most important, their good names.

The New families weren't new at all, not in Emília's mind. Most had been in Recife for centuries since the Dutch had invaded and allowed all kinds of groups—Jews and Gypsies and Indian traders— to do their business freely, turning the city into what the Portuguese called a Sodom and Gomorrah. The New families could not trace their lines as neatly as the Old, so their pasts had the possible taint of trading boats and fishmongers and moneylenders. The New families were not interested in land, but in business. They were the Raposos—a dark-haired clan whose women had the subtle sheen of mustaches on their upper lips and whose men were squat and prone to brawling. They owned the hugely successful Macaxeira textile mill. The Lobos owned the *Diário de Pernambuco* newspaper. Their men were quick-witted and charming, their women energetic. All shared the large, curved Lobo nose. The Albuquerques owned the Poseidon Fish Company, and were a short, bronze-skinned clan known for their quiet and patience. And the Lundgrens, who owned the Torre and Tacaruna textile mills, were tall, long-faced people often teased for their dull humor but praised for their handsome daughters.

As weeks passed, Emília was allowed to take more walks in Derby Square and to accompany the Coelhos to Sunday mass. They attended a newly built church in Madalena, with white walls and cushioned pews. The Old families worshipped in the city center's ancient cathedral, which had a longer mass and vaulted ceilings. There were many unspoken differences between the clans. They preferred different newspapers, backed different politicians, lived in different neighborhoods. Men—New and Old—often did business together. Dr. Duarte imported machines for one of the Feijós' molasses mills. The Lundgrens' factory made burlap bags for the Coimbras' sugar harvest. Dr. Duarte sometimes lunched with an Old family man at his club, and Emília often saw Old and New men standing in the shade of Derby Square, smoking cigars and patting each other's backs. But those same men would never invite each other for lunch or coffee at their homes. Their wives would not allow it.

The Recife women, it seemed, had longer memories and harder hearts. There were two prestigious women's clubs in the city: the Princess Isabel Society and the Ladies' Auxiliary of Recife. The Princess Isabels were all descendents of the Old families, and they believed that by helping the church—funding new chapels in the countryside and performing time-consuming restoration projects in the city—they helped society. The Ladies' Auxiliary, a New family creation, performed food drives, knitting marathons, and benefit dinners in order to aid the poor directly. The Old family women proclaimed the Auxiliary vulgar, while the New family women called the Isabels useless. They generally kept their distance, except in Derby Square. Once a haunt of the Old families, the New had slowly tried to claim it. Neither would part with their afternoon footings in the square, so Old and New walked side by side along the Derby's pebbled paths, and Emília walked among them. She felt nervous and awkward. She didn't know when to smile and when to simply nod. It upset her when the women from the Old families began to ignore her. Some even chuckled when she and Dulce passed.

"That is a good sign," Dona Dulce said when they returned to the Coelho house. Her voice was strained and tired. Each outing seemed to exhaust her. "If one group loathes you, the other will surely take you up."

That evening, the young housemaid interrupted dinner. She held a tray with a single envelope upon it.

"Come along," Dulce snapped, motioning for the maid.

"It's for Senhora Emília," the girl replied.

The envelope was thick and the color of freshly whipped butter. On the front, written in blue ink was her name, and on the back, a seal embossed with:

Baroness Margarida Carvalho Pinto Lapa

"She is a baroness by marriage, not by blood," Dona Dulce said.

The baroness had been Margarida Carvalho, a cattle rancher's daughter, Dona Dulce continued. She'd been a spinster until the elderly Geraldo Pinto Lapa, one of Brazil's last remaining barons, met her and took her to Recife. Shortly after their only daughter was born, the baron died, leaving Margarida to dictate her own allegiances. She'd married into a respectable Old family, but her presence had made it a New.

"She's the only female partner in the International Club," Degas said, smiling. "It's an important visit."

"That daughter of hers is a horror," Dona Dulce interjected. "A suffragette." She frowned and inspected the invitation. "I will have to accompany you."

12

~~~~~~~~~

The baroness resembled one of the courtyard turtles. Her chin jutted square and firm above her wrinkled neck, which moved slowly from side to side. She tilted her eyes, as dark and bulging as two jabuticaba berries, back and forth between Dona Dulce and Emília. They sat in deep wicker chairs on her porch, which overlooked Derby Square and the palatial headquarters of the Military Police. A trolley slid down the street, screeching along its rails and forcing the women to pause in their conversation until the car passed. Emília stared at the baroness's jasmine trees, shaped into perfect squares. Pink and white quartz stones were set in a round pattern, slicing the front garden into a pie that alternated between flowers and stones. Dona Dulce sat, smiling and rigid, beside Emília. She spoke of her Carnaval preparations and lamented how late the holiday would fall that year—in the first week of March instead of in the month of February. The baroness swayed in her wicker rocker. She wore a string of pearls, each as large as one of Emília's front teeth. Her gray hair lifted and flattened in the breeze.

"Does this girl speak?" the Baroness interrupted. "Or is she a mute?"

"She's shy," Dona Dulce replied.

"Do you like sweets?" the baroness asked, tapping Emília's arm. She had large, knobby-knuckled hands. Her fingers were crooked and stiff, like pink claws.

"Yes, senhora," Emília responded.

"Good. I'm suspicious of people who dislike sweets."

The baroness rang her serving bell. A maid appeared and deposited a tray of grapes dipped in condensed milk and rolled in sugar. She placed the grapes before Emília.

"So, you've married Degas," the baroness said. "He was a quiet child. He played with my Lindalva, remember, Dulce?" The old woman chuckled. "He adored her dolls."

Dona Dulce smiled widely. "The two of you share something in common," she said. "Emília is from the countryside as well."

"I know," Baroness Margarida replied. She picked through the sugared grapes. "The marriage announcement in the paper was so small I could barely read it. It said you're from Toritama? I'm not familiar with that town."

"I'm from Taquaritinga do Norte," Emília said. "It was a misprint."

"Taquaritinga!" the baroness said, forgetting the grapes. "We're both mountain girls, then. I was raised in Garanhuns. I adore the interior. I make a trip each year during the wet months on account of my arthritis."

The baroness held up her crooked hands.

"My daddy was a cattle rancher," the old woman continued. "Paulo Carvalho—ever heard of him?"

Emília shook her head. The baroness frowned.

"Well, no matter. The Carvalhos are extinct now. Except for myself and my Lindalva. Thank God for the old baron! Everyone thought he was a banana tree that had already given its fruit," she winked, "but he proved us all wrong."

Emília smiled. Dona Dulce's cheeks reddened.

A girl stepped out of the side door. Her dress was the color of an egg yolk. Its skirt revealed her calves and a pair of smart white shoes. Her black hair was cut even shorter than Emília's and held by a white scarf wrapped around her head, in the style of a bohemian or a film artist. Emília looked down at her gray gown. She felt ridiculous.

"Ah, Lindalva!" The baroness smiled. "Speak of the devil."

Lindalva leaned behind her mother's chair. Her face was smooth and round, like the convex side of one of Dona Dulce's silver soup spoons. There was a large gap between her front teeth.

"Hello!" she breathed, as if she had just run onto the porch.

"Lindalva was the one who spotted you puttering around Derby Square," the baroness said, motioning to the park. "Spying to see which side would pick you up." She winked at Dona Dulce, then tilted her eyes to Emília. "Do you like my garden?"

"It's lovely," Emília replied, quickly recalling Dona Dulce's first lesson.

"I built the wall around it low so that, from our porch, we can see Derby Square. It's quite pleasant. We can see who comes and goes. But, the price we pay for our curiosity is that all of those Old family gossips can peek over my wall and into my garden. If they peek today, they will see that you are having tea here, with us." She smiled. Her jabuticaba-berry eyes shone. "You will find, my dear, that Recife is a city of noble families with low walls."

"I'd like to show her the house," Lindalva said, extending her plump, short-fingered hand to Emília. "Come along. Mother will keep Dulce company."

They walked hand in hand into the house. It was larger then the Coelho house, but simpler. The baroness had less furniture and many large windows. They entered a bright room with a black-and-white-checkered floor. Lindalva guided Emília onto a cushioned love seat and sat closely beside her. She scanned Emília's gray dress, as if seeing it for the first time.

"Are you in mourning?" Lindalva asked, her brow wrinkling in concern.

"No," Emília replied, then sputtered, "yes."

"Which is it?"

"My aunt and my sister, they passed away last June, but then I was married and—"

"Did Dulce pick that out for you?" Lindalva interrupted.

"Yes," Emília sighed, relieved.

"Well, I hope you don't mind my saying so," Lindalva said, leaning closer to Emília, "but it's completely boring. You're a lovely girl. You should emphasize your figure. There's a shop in Rio de Janeiro that makes *spectacular* mourning dresses. Premade, of course. Everyone in the South is buying prêt-à-porter these days. I'll give you their address. I just got back from there. I graduated from the Federal University, in Portuguese literature. Would you like to see a photograph of my graduation?"

Emília nodded absently. Lindalva had the energy of a hummingbird, staying still just long enough for Emília to grasp what she was saying before she darted on to something else entirely. Emília had no desire to see the photograph but she couldn't be disagreeable. Lindalva rushed across the room, her yellow skirt fluttering behind her. She returned with a velvet case. Inside was a large photograph. A group of young women in white ball gowns sat in two orderly rows.

"There were so few girls in my class. Before he passed away my father insisted I go to school. Mother studied at the Catholic University here in Recife after they married, did you know that? It was quite radical at the time." Lindalva smiled and handed Emília the plate. "Pick me out."

Emília stared at the spoon-faced girl before her, then back at the photograph. There were so many girls. How would she choose? She quickly scanned their gray-and-white faces, and finally pointed to the girl with the gown she thought was the prettiest—a flounced dress covered in ribbons and tulle.

"Good lord no!" Lindalva chuckled. "I'm not dark skinned now and I certainly wasn't then! Try again."

Emília's head ached. She wanted to go back to the porch, to sit quietly and listen to Dona Dulce ramble on about Carnaval. She absently pointed to another girl.

"No." Lindalva smiled. "Here I am."

She pointed to a girl in the back row, wearing a large hat with a single white feather protruding from its front brim. Emília recognized the round face, the gap-toothed smile. Lindalva quickly shut the photograph's velvet box.

"I promised my mother I'd return to Recife. I'm very fond of the city, but the people here are completely dull. Especially the women. Things are so rigid. It's not at all modern. You *must* visit São Paulo. There, a woman can walk alone on the street. She can drive a motorcar without being sneered at. I saw you in the park and begged Mother to invite you. I thought you would be so different from these ninnies. I mean, you've held a job! A seamstress!" She clasped Emília's hand. "I'm a firm believer in women not living parasitically.

"I'm sure Dulce and Dr. Duarte are happy about you. They've been absolutely salivating to marry Degas off." Lindalva's face reddened and she gripped Emília's hand tighter. "How on earth did you come to know Degas Coelho?"

"I came to know him," Emília repeated, as if Lindalva's words were like the lessons on Degas' language records, "in Taquaritinga. During his winter vacation."

"What convinced you to marry him?"

"His shoes," Emília said absently, recalling Degas' polished, two-toned wingtips. The instant she'd said it, Emília regretted admitting such a thing aloud. She sounded like the ninnies Lindalva had disparaged earlier. She wanted to say that Degas was new and different. That his presence made her forget the dull monotony that her life had become; that during their walks he'd called her innocent and pure, while everyone else in town thought just the opposite. In the end, he didn't have to convince her. He'd simply claimed her, and she'd let him.

Lindalva let out a laugh. "I've heard worse reasons for marrying," she said brightly. "Mother says we women would be better off if we forgot about love. She thinks that an ugly, liberal husband is the best kind."

"Well, I don't," Emília said. "I think love is important. It's essential."

She was startled by the firmness of her own voice, and angry, suddenly, at the spoon-faced girl. Angry, too, at Dona Dulce for her constant prodding and correcting. Angry at Degas for his cool kisses on her forehead, and for his silence each night when he turned his back to her and slipped into his childhood bedroom.

"I've upset you," Lindalva said. "I'm sorry."

"No," Emília replied, patting her face. "I'm not upset."

"I don't want you to think of me as a horrible gossip. I'm speaking candidly because that's how I would like to be spoken to. You'll see that it's a rare thing here." Lindalva took a breath and pressed her hand to Emília's knee. "What are your plans?"

"My plans?"

"Yes. Your goals. The Coelhos can't coop you up indoors forever. Especially you—a working woman! I'm sure you're used to having an exterior life."

"I don't have plans," Emília replied.

Lindalva sucked air through the gap in her teeth. "If you don't make one for yourself, Dulce will make it for you."

Emília picked at the fingertips of her gloves. She recalled their trip to the dressmaker, their conversation beside the reams of pink and blue fustão.

"Dulce always has plans," Lindalva continued. "If she didn't, she wouldn't bother taking you about. It's known that she can't abide my mother. Dulce's from one of those ancient families that was all title and no money. After she married Dr. Duarte, the Old families didn't want her. And she thinks she is above all of the New families." Lindalva paused. She stared at Emília. "People are saying that you're an orphan; that you're from a country family that died off, one by one, from consumption, and that you had to sustain yourself by sewing. They say that Degas rescued you. Is that true?"

"Who would say that?" Emília asked.

"Who do you think?" Lindalva asked, titling her head toward the porch. She shrugged. "The New families love tragic tales. Especially when the tragedy is far from their own lives."

"But they could easily find out it wasn't true," Emília said. She thought of Colonel Pereira's son, Felipe. She'd found out, through Dona Dulce's warnings to Degas, that Felipe attended law school and lived in a boardinghouse in Bairro Recife, where ladies and gentlemen did not wander. In the capital, Felipe was transformed into a lowly student, not Old or New, but a part of that other, nameless group. Still, he was from Taquaritinga and he knew her origins.

"Listen very carefully to me," Lindalva said, once again taking Emília's hands between her own. "If you dig deep enough into any of these so-called-noble families, Old or New, the search will end up in the jungle or in the kitchen. No one here will question you too deeply, as long as you know that questioning can go both ways."

Emília shifted. Her dress was tight beneath the armpits. She wanted to loosen her hand from Lindalva's grip and leave. To her great relief, a maid entered and informed them that coffee had been served. They returned to the porch and sat with the Baroness and Dona Dulce. Emília concentrated on her coffee cup, uncomfortable with Lindalva's constant chatter, and the friendly, collusive smiles she directed toward Emília each time Dona Dulce spoke. When they left, the Baroness Margarida pressed Emília's hand between her red, clawlike fingers.

"I'll see you again, after Carnaval," the baroness announced. "There will be no need to interrupt your day, Dulce. I'll send my car to pick her up."

Emília's head ached. Lindalva beamed.

13

Two weeks before Carnaval, clouds blew in from the Atlantic. The cata-vento twirled. Rain fell for five straight days, causing mud slides that carried houses down the hills of Casa Amarela. Recife's gutters overflowed into the swelling Capibaribe. Seamstresses arrived at the Coelho house under the cover of sturdy umbrellas, clutching sagging reams of tulle and sewing bags filled with sequins and iridescent feathers. For their first Carnaval as husband and wife, Degas and Emília would have coordinating costumes—they would be Amazonian Indians for two nights and a ruffle-collared Pierrot clown and his masked mate, the Columbina, for two more. Degas' costumes had already been made, but Emília's were more elaborate and required the Carnaval seamstresses to make a house visit.

The Coelho house was empty. Dr. Duarte and Dona Dulce had gone to their traditional Carnaval luncheon at the British Club, while Degas enjoyed "the Course" along Concórdia Street. The young set from Recife's best families, Old and New, gathered in their automobiles and drove up and down the two-lane avenue. They threw confetti and long strands of paper serpentines. They held ether-soaked handkerchiefs to their faces and with the remaining contents of their glass flasks, they doused each other and the spectators along the street. Masses gathered along the roadway hoping to get a spray of ether and a glimpse of the gentlemen and young ladies ruining each other's costumes. Emília had wanted to witness it for herself. She'd begged Degas to take her, but he said it wouldn't be fitting for her first social outing. The Course could get ugly. Rival families were known to throw terrible things at each other's cars: molasses, flour, rotten fruit, even urine.

"He's too old to take part in those games," Raimunda muttered before the Carnaval seamstresses arrived. The front bell clanged, signaling their appearance.

"These women would gossip about their own mothers," Raimunda warned. Emília nodded.

Dona Dulce had also warned her about the seamstresses. The mother-and-daughter team made only costumes, not real clothes. Their talents with sequins, feathers, crystals, and multicolored fabrics made them highly coveted during Carnaval, but shunned the rest of the year. Because of their popularity during the months of January and February, the seamstresses worked for dozens of families—Old and New—and were allowed into their vast homes. The women had sharp eyes and even sharper tongues, and they left each house with stories to tell at the next one. Emília's fitting was held in the Coelhos' sitting room. This way, the seamstresses could say that they'd been treated respectfully, but they couldn't spy on the kind of private information found in a bedroom. Raimunda placed a low stool in the middle of the sitting room, and Emília stood upon it, wearing her best silk slip. The Carnaval seamstresses stared at her.

The mother had a wide smile and short hair, cut in a style that seemed at odds with her thick body and old-fashioned flowered dress. The daughter was thin and boyish. Both women had skin that was dark and oily, like well-roasted coffee beans. The women draped their gaudy creations across Emília's body; they'd made her a long skirt of feathers, a shiny gold top, and an Indian headdress. Emília slipped the costume over her head. Mosquitoes swirled around her legs. The mother seamstress also circled her, tucking and folding the costume, making final adjustments. Raimunda stood nearby, pouring Emília glasses of water and warning the seamstresses to be careful with their pins.

"Such a nice figure!" the older seamstress said, patting Emília's thigh. "Thin girls are no good."

Emília didn't nod or show any sign of agreement, afraid the woman would tell other clients that Mrs. Degas Coelho had maligned thin women. The mother shrugged her shoulders. The daughter laid a mound of iridescent feathers on the sitting room table and began to enlarge the Amazonian headdress.

"Indians and clowns are classic," the mother said approvingly. "No one else picked them this year. You'll be one of a kind. Did you choose the themes?"

"No," Emília replied. "My husband did."

The mother smiled widely. "Is it your first Carnaval?"

"This is Dona Emília's first year in Recife," Raimunda interrupted. "You didn't make a costume for her last year, did you?"

The seamstress fixed her eyes on Raimunda. The maid crossed her arms and stared back.

After their first meeting in the Coelhos' bathroom, Raimunda had become a constant, quiet presence in Emília's life. Emília appreciated her silence. Everyone—Dona Dulce, Degas, Dr. Duarte, Miss Lindalva—had advice for her. Everyone spoke in riddles that Emília was tired of decoding. Raimunda did not. The maid dressed her, combed her hair, fixed her snared stockings, and clipped her nails with a solemn, dutiful efficiency. She did not ask for conversation and Emília did not offer it. After Dona Dulce's revelation at the fabric store, Emília felt as if even the jaboti turtles and long-faced Madonnas could be Dona Dulce's informants. Emília was thankful for Raimunda's protection from the Carnaval seamstresses, but she couldn't allow it. A maid was expected to defend her employers only when they weren't present. A dona was required to speak for herself; she couldn't have a maid do it for her.

"I'm only nineteen," Emília said, trying to re-create Dona Dulce's voice, a mix of boredom and sternness. "In the interior, a young lady doesn't play Carnaval."

In fact, in Taquaritinga no one celebrated Carnaval; they only observed Lent. "You have all of the sacrifice and none of the fun," Degas had said once, during his stay at the colonel's. Emília hoped that the seamstresses had never traveled outside Recife, so they wouldn't know any better. The mother nodded and stared at Emília keenly, making a new assessment of her; it was widely known that wealthy residents of the interior sent their girls to convent schools, not to become nuns, but to be protected by high fences and strict rules. Emília bowed her head piously.

"Yes, Dona Emília," the mother said. "Young girls shouldn't be exposed to Carnaval. But the International Club is different. It's not like the streets. There'll be so many fine costumes . . ."

Emília nodded. The woman described the elaborate costumes she'd made for the Coimbras, the Feijós, the Tavareses, and others. Emília recognized the seamstress's friendly tone, her enthusiastic banter in order to make a customer comfortable. Emília had done the same thing to her clients, not long ago.

"One man wanted a cangaceiro costume," the daughter interrupted, looking up from her headdress work.

"I wouldn't do it," the mother quickly said. "There's nothing elegant about them. No sequins. No feathers. *I* don't make costumes out of sackcloth." The mother studied Emília's face and, noticing her interest, continued. "Did you hear about the latest attack?"

Emília shook her head.

"One of my clients has a colonel staying in her house," the mother said, putting down her pincushion. "Colonel Machado-something-or-other. He's in town to ask the governor for troops. He's spitting mad. Some cangaceiros nearly killed his son. They attacked his town, killed seven men. Horrible."

"Which ones?" Emília asked. "Which cangaceiros?"

The seamstress waved her hand. A pin fell. "One's named after some bird—the Parakeet. The Rooster—"

"The Hawk?" Emília breathed.

"Yes. That's it." The mother looked questioningly at Emília.

"They're common birds," Emília replied, examining her finger-nails. Her heart pounded; she hoped the seamstress couldn't see its rise and fall through her slip.

"What else did he say," Emília asked, "this colonel?"

In the back of the sitting room, Raimunda cleared her throat. Emília knew she shouldn't be curious about such morbid things. The Carnaval seamstress, however, ignored Raimunda and was eager to oblige.

"Oh, I heard it was a terrible attack," she said. "Just terrible. They had a party afterward and danced over the bodies. There was a friar, poor dear, who saw the whole thing. He was so shaken, he said one of the bandits was a woman. It's an easy mistake—they all have long hair. But he insisted. Can you imagine?" The mother lowered her voice. "What kind of woman does that? What kind of family would let her? It's shameful."

Emília nodded. Her mouth felt dry.

"She must be as ugly as a cão!" the daughter laughed.

"Don't insult a poor mutt," the mother replied, giggling. "Comparing him to her." When she realized Emília wasn't laughing, she stopped. "Terrible fate for a girl," she clucked. "If she's real."

The room felt too stuffy. Emília's slip clung to her stomach. The feathered skirt had dozens of nibs that scratched the backs of her thighs. A mosquito buzzed near her ear but Emília didn't swat it away, afraid of losing her balance on top of the stool. Raimunda stepped forward.

"You look pale," she said.

"I need a rest," Emília replied, stepping from the stool.

Before the seamstresses could complain, they heard the front gate creak open. Degas had returned. Raimunda stopped the fitting. Emília pulled off the costume and left the room, allowing Raimunda to take charge and order the seamstresses to put the final touches on her Indian headdress.

In the front hall, Emília saw her husband. Degas had worn his Pierrot costume to the Course; it was ruined. The rain had not dampened the Course's usual rowdiness. Degas' hair was stiff with molasses, his costume coated in a clumpy, yellow batter. His eyes were glazed and heavy lidded. He laughed when he saw Emília standing in her slip, then stumbled up the main stairs. In the hallway, Degas pushed open Emília's bedroom door and fell into her bed.

Emília followed him. Degas' laugh had been a mean-spirited snort. Derisive. Ugly. And now he was splayed across her clean sheets, his sticky hair staining her pillows. Emília wished the ants that regularly invaded Dona Dulce's kitchen would find him. There would be no one to wash the sheets, to turn down the bed. Half of the Coelhos' staff had been given a holiday. Raimunda and the iron-ing woman would be busy caring for Emília's costume, Dona Dulce's gown, and Dr. Duarte's tuxedo. The Coelhos had reserved a table at the International Club ball that evening.

Emília tugged a set of sheets from their shelf in the linen closet. Let Degas sleep in his filth when they returned from the Carnaval party, she thought. She would make her own bed.

Emília removed the sheets from Degas' childhood mattress; she refused to sleep on anything he'd touched. She pounded the pillows and tucked in clean sheets with quick, violent motions. Her finger hit the baseboard. Her nail snapped in half. Blood bloomed along the broken edge. Emília put her finger in her mouth and sat beside the half-made bed.

She stared at the English records stacked beside the Victrola. She stared at the machine itself. At its fat, crooked arm. At its sharp-tipped needle.

As a child, she had always been the dutiful one, unlike Luzia, who had made it clear through her quiet stubbornness that even if she obeyed, it was because she chose to. Emília missed her sister. She'd missed Luzia's quiet strength, the way she covered her mouth when she laughed, the way she hooked her crooked arm through Emília's wherever they walked. Every day Emília waited for word: an article in the paper mentioning the cangaceiros, a letter from Dona Conceição saying that Luzia had returned. None came.

Her finger continued to bleed, tasting salty and metallic in her mouth. The broken nail scraped against her tongue. Emília wanted to ask the Carnaval seamstresses more questions. She wanted to find out which family was housing the offended colonel and to pay him a visit. As soon as the idea entered her mind, Emília had to let it go. Expressing an interest in criminals would expose her to malicious talk—a lady didn't ask about such things. A lady couldn't care about cangaceiros. Emília recalled the seamstress's questions: What kind of woman would stay with such men? What kind of family would let her? A shameful one, the seamstress had concluded.

Emília bit off her ripped nail. She braced for the pain of it, but when it came, it didn't distract her from her anger. Her stomach burned, as if she'd drunk one of Dr. Duarte's raw-egg-and-pepper concoctions. Emília was angry with those seamstresses for their speculations, their judgments. She was angry with Luzia for putting herself in a position to be judged by such gossips. But had she? Was there really a woman in that cangaceiro group? If so, was she Luzia? Emília felt like a child again—compelled to defend her sister, to take Victrola's side and to be isolated and ridiculed for doing so. When they were children, Luzia held her hand or brushed Emília's hair in thanks for her loyalty. Now Luzia was lost. She was like a ghost—neither alive nor dead, but floating in Emília's memory, disrupting her new life. She couldn't mourn Luzia, but she couldn't save her either.

Emília had hoped that Recife would be a large, bustling metropolis. Large enough to make her forget about the things she had lost. Large enough to envelop and transform her. But, as Dr. Duarte often said, it was all a question of scale. The Coelhos' world was confined to the Old and New, to private clubs and Derby Square and their gated house. Emília often felt as if she were locked within a vast, well-kept reception room. With all of its luxury, she felt cramped, closed in, unable to breathe. Sometimes, when she sat at the Coelhos' breakfast table or lay in bed, she felt the urge to shout or to whistle for help.

Years before, on the day of her father's funeral mass, when she and Luzia knelt side by side before the front pew and their father's body lay wrapped like a cocoon in its white hammock, Emília had felt a similar urge. She'd curled her chin deep into her chest and placed two fingers in her mouth. The church was so quiet she could hear the hiss of kerosene lanterns, the rubbing of chapped hands, the smacking of lips as people sucked their Communion wafers. Emília breathed in, then out, releasing a whistle that made her tongue vibrate against her cheeks. There were gasps and murmers. "Horrible child!" a woman behind her hissed. Luzia smiled.

Even when Aunt Sofia dragged Emília outside and whipped her right there, in front of the congregation, she barely felt the spanking. All she could think of was that whistle—so shrill and loud it broke through the sounds around her and rose past the pews, past Padre Otto's altar, past the cross, and up, into the darkest corners of the painted church ceiling, to a place no one could reach. And she thought of Luzia's smile. How proud she had felt to receive it. How they had looked at each other, as if some secret had passed between them. As if they had caught a glimpse of something grand and mysterious within each other, something that they could keep, and if one forgot its presence the other would always be there to remind her.

14

Silver and gold streamers draped the International Club's chandeliers. On the stage, a band dressed in white tuxedos played a fast-paced samba. Emília straightened her feather headdress. It was bulky and awkward. The feathers' bony nibs scratched her forehead. Degas held her hand. They'd settled on the Indian costumes, since his clown jumper was ruined. Before they left, Degas jammed a long glass ether vial and two handkerchiefs behind his feathered waist belt.

Dr. Duarte's table was in a prestigious spot beside the dance floor. Degas pulled Emília past their seats. He introduced her to other Indians and to Portuguese explorers, monks, pharaohs, and Greeks. She saw one of the Raposo women wearing an enormous hoop skirt and a white wig. Perched on top of the wig was a small gilded cage that held a finch. The bird fluttered back and forth nervously. A tall Lundgren girl had dressed as an Egyptian princess and wore a tiny, jeweled skullcap. Emília envied her. Her own headdress constantly shifted, snagging her hair and forcing her to support it with her hand. Felipe, the colonel's son, stood in a crowd at the back of the room. He was dressed as a Gypsy, a scarf knotted on his head. He looked skinnier and more freckled than she remembered. He nodded to them. Degas nodded back. The ballroom was divided. The coveted front ends, nearest the band, belonged to the Old and New families, seated on different sides of the dance floor. The back of the room had no tables or chairs. It was, Emília discovered, the space meant for those who had invitations but not places at the family tables. Degas steered them back to his father's table. He ordered glass after glass of sugarcane liquor mixed with mashed limes. Emília was curious to taste the drinks, but she didn't take a sip. Dona Dulce stood near the base of the stage beside Dr. Duarte, watching Emília from afar.

"Comport yourself," Dona Dulce had commanded before they'd left the house. So Emília sat quietly, one hand on her headdress, the other around a glass of guaraná soda, and watched the dance floor. When the Old families rose to dance, the New sat. The two groups eyed each other, the gentlemen laughing boisterously, the ladies whispering behind cupped palms.

Emília did not know how to samba or waltz or frevo. She only knew how to dance the quadrilha and forro. She'd memorized Dulce's teachings about dances: never interlace your fingers, never touch faces, always use your elbow as a break to avoid coming too close to your partner.

The trumpets suddenly blared. The tambourine player's arms shook at a frantic pace. The band charged into a frevo. The guests cheered. Both sides of the room stood. People let go of their partners. They jumped left and right, balancing on their heels, as if they would tip over backward, then quickly coming upright and repeating the frantic motion. The club staff handed out small golden umbrellas and the guests popped them open, swinging the umbrellas up and down to the music's frenetic pace. Degas smiled. He gripped Emília's arm and led her to the dance floor.

An umbrella popped open beside her. Emília's headdress slouched forward, covering her eyes. She lost her balance and fell on Degas.

"You must relax!" he shouted. He took the glass vial from his pocket and broke open the top. He poured the ether into his handkerchief and threw the empty vial onto a nearby waiter's tray. Then he held the handkerchief firmly over Emília's nose and mouth.

Her nostrils felt cold. Her throat tingled. Her head felt strangely light; she saw the headdress fall, then disappear beneath dozens of stomping feet. Confetti stuck to her eyelashes. She felt as if her chest would burst. The ceiling swirled and heightened. The music played faster, then faster still, until it became tinny and strange, like one long ringing in her ears. Emília heard laughter. The sound of it startled her. She turned around and around to see where it had come from. Umbrellas popped open and shut in a golden blur. The laughter grew louder. Emília realized it was her own. She could not stop. When she tried, she laughed more. It became frantic, frightening. She saw the white-wigged Raposo woman beside her. The finch's body bumped against the golden bars of its cage. Its wings did not open. Emília's laughter faded. Her heartbeat quickened. Emília searched for Degas, but could not find him. She pushed her way through the crowd.

She did not know how long she stood at the edge of the dance floor with her eyes closed. She did not know how long it took for her head to stop spinning. When she opened her eyes, the frevo was over. Her headdress was gone. Her scalp hurt. She was on the Old families' side of the floor. When she realized this, Emília quickly doubled back, avoiding the dance floor. She moved across the dark, table-free area. There, she saw Degas.

He stood with a group dressed as Gypsies and sailors. Their costumes were not as elaborate as the Old and New families'; the sailor men and women wore white hats; the Gypsies wore makeshift scarves. In the midst of such simple costumes, Degas—in his iridescent feathered headdress and chest plate—looked like a peacock. He stood behind Felipe, whose head scarf had come undone. Degas hesitated, then held the scarf's ends. Beneath his feathered chest plate, Degas' arms were bare. His hands looked small and clumsy, but they knotted the scarf gently around Felipe's head. A lock of Felipe's hair had escaped and fell over his ear. With the tips of his fingers, Degas tucked it away. His hand lingered on Felipe's neck. The young man craned his freckled face back, toward Degas.

A notion as swift and chilling as ether swept through Emília's mind. Then it faded.

15

Dona Dulce sat, rigid and alone, sipping a glass of punch at the Coelho table. Emília did not want to sit beside her. Cigarette smoke clouded the ballroom and made her eyes burn. The music was too loud. She went outside for air. A line of automobiles and carriages sat at the front entrance. Two dark-haired Raposo girls made their way to their family's motorcar. One of them recognized Emília from Derby Square.

"You don't look well," she said, her thick eyebrows knitting together. "We live in Torre. It's right near Madalena. We'll give you a lift."

With the nerve and resourcefulness befitting a Raposo woman, the girl took Emília's arm, guided her to the car, and tapped loudly on the window to wake the driver. When Emília protested, the girl would not hear a word of it. The driver was coming back, she said, to pick up the rest of the clan. He would inform the Coelhos that she had left early. Emília was truly tired of the party. She was grateful for the girl's kindness. This changed as soon as they pulled away from the International Club.

Every well-bred girl over fifteen was a prospective bride and they liked to debate the qualities of a good suitor. After a brief discussion of the party, the Raposo girls settled upon comparing young men.

"I saw that Lobo boy," one sister said. "He's positively bent on you."

The other Raposo made a sour face. "You think I want that safado? He's got no future. No ambition. He'll live off his father for the rest of his life. If we married, he'd have me living in his parents' house! A girl should have her own servants. Her own house. Don't you agree, Emília?"

The sisters giggled. Emília shrugged. For the rest of the ride, she feigned sleep. At the Coelho gate, the sisters gave Emília terse good-byes.

The Coelho house was dark, the night air muggy. In the distance there was the low rumble of street music, a steady drumming that switched to the fast beats of a frevo. A crowd cheered. Emília felt a sudden, terrible loneliness. She considered taking her Communion portrait from the closet and admiring it, but she didn't have the strength to walk up those winding stairs. She let herself into Dr. Duarte's study instead. There, curled up and sleeping, was the Mermaid Girl. Emília lifted the jar from its shelf. She held it in her lap. The glass felt cold at first, but slowly warmed to the temperature of her skin.

Emília didn't understand all of Dr. Duarte's ideas, but she liked the simplicity of measurement. Men were mysterious creatures. Even gentlemen, with their trimmed beards and perfumed elegance, could not always be trusted. How nice then, to be able to measure a man. And through these measurements, to determine who was kind and who was cruel. Who was capable of providing happiness and who was not.

Emília quickly put the Mermaid Girl back on her shelf. The child was not living, she reminded herself. And people were not like dresses. They could not be measured, marked, cut to size. The Raposo girls' conversation, with its veiled jabs, plagued Emília. A good husband had ambition, while a bad one was dependent upon his father. No woman wanted that. Women wanted their own houses, their own servants. They wanted to be donas, not daughters-in-law.

Emília had always considered Degas a worthy groom. After arriving in Recife, she believed herself to be deficient, countrified, and in need of refining. She'd believed that her husband's disinterest stemmed from her deficiencies. Now she knew better.

Emília appreciated the luxuries of her new life with Degas. Without him, she might have been one of those poor Recife seamstresses, trapped in a hot room and hunched over a machine for hours on end. But beyond Degas' ability to provide dresses, or houses, or servants, Emília had hoped that an educated husband would bring her contentment. That together, they could make their married life resemble a fine cloth, with any irregular threads tucked away so deftly that they were unseen, making the fabric look smooth and lovely. But as Emília stood in that dark study, among foreign books and jars filled with pale remains, she recalled the chill of ether at the Carnaval party, recalled her husband's hands gently tying a Gypsy scarf, and she felt a fearful certainty: she'd chosen poorly. And everyone around her—Dona Dulce, the Coelho maids, even those Raposo girls—seemed to suspect what Emília finally knew: that Degas was unable to weave together those many invisible threads that formed a woman's happiness.

16

When the Coelhos returned, Emília was asleep on Degas' childhood bed. She heard the faraway rumble of an engine. She woke with the click of the bedroom door. In the doorway stood the shadow of a man, dark and wide. Iridescent feathers shimmered around his waist and neck. Large white circles patterned the feathers, like a dozen pairs of eyes. Emília sat up.

"We looked everywhere for you," Degas said. "Why did you leave?"

"I was tired," Emília replied. "My eyes stung."

"You should have told me."

"The Raposos' driver told you, didn't he?"

"Yes. Mother is furious."

"Why?" Emília asked, suddenly angry herself.

"A wife doesn't leave without her husband."

Emília lay back down. The feathers of her costume poked through its shining fabric, pricking her skin.

"And with the Raposos, of all people," Degas continued. "Everyone in Recife will be talking tomorrow."

"Let them talk," Emília snapped. "They'll be talking about me. That didn't bother you before."

She heard Degas' heavy breaths, the buzz of a mosquito, the deep pounding of maracatu drums in the distance. Degas reached for the bed, as if his eyes had not yet adjusted to the darkness. He slumped beside her, nearly sitting on her legs. He sat on her skirt instead, pinning her down. A yeasty, sour smell—a mix of alcohol and sweat—came from him.

"What do you know of me?" he asked. His voice was urgent, his eyes liquid and dark.

Emília felt a rush of annoyance. She could ask the same question. Degas never wanted to know how she spent her days. He never inquired after her feelings. Emília was simply something useful and attractive—like his Victrola or his wingtipped shoes—occupying a peripheral space in his world.

"You've never kissed me," she said.

"I've kissed you dozens of times."

"No," Emília said. "Not the way you should kiss a wife."

Degas rubbed his face with his hands. He choked out a sigh.

"No, I suppose I haven't," he said, staring at Emília. He smoothed her sweaty hair with his palm. "I haven't lived up to my part of the bargain."

"Bargain," Emília repeated numbly. That's what she used to do at the Saturday market, but she never liked it. Emília hated it, in fact. She always paid too much and received too little. Emília crumpled the edge of the starched sheet in her hand.

"Your mother wants a grandchild," she said, her voice trembling and thick. "She blames me."

"I'm sorry," Degas whispered. "It isn't just."

He stood and held out his hand.

"Come along," he said.

He spoke so gently that Emília stood. Degas held her arms above her head. He lifted off her wrinkled costume. Beneath it, she wore a slip and cotton shorts. Still, Emília felt strangely cold. She crossed her arms over her bosom.

"Lie down," Degas whispered.

The sheets felt rough against her back. His hands were cold. They moved hesitantly at first, then grew forceful, grasping and pulling as if he were molding her beneath his thin fingers. Soon, her shorts were gone. The slip was bunched around her bosom. Degas was very heavy. Emília's chest could barely rise or fall. Her breath grew short. Her head ached. She closed her eyes and recalled the flour mill in Taquaritinga: its moist heat, its sharp smell of manioc, its sweating men and women hunched over the pale tubers that were scraped, pressed, squeezed, and pounded until they became something else entirely.

Chapter 6

LUZIA

Caatinga scrubland, interior of Pernambuco
São Francisco River Valley, Bahia
December 1928–November 1929

1

⟋⟋⟋⟋⟋⟋⟋⟋

Beneath the needle of her Singer appeared the pink starbursts of macambira plants. Across the front flaps of bornais and along the cracked brims of the men's hats, she sewed green appliquéd circles resembling the monk's–head cactus. She sewed swirling orange shapes mimicking the imburana trees' peeling bark. Luzia forgot the silly butterflies and roses of Dona Conceição's tablecloths and towels. The scrub became her palette.

In that tangled mass of gray brush, any hint of color was startling. Luzia collected the husks of dead beetles that clung, golden and translucent, to tree branches. She admired yellow juá berries before mashing them into a foamy pulp to wash her hair. And when she heard the periquito-da-caatinga parrots' sharp twitters—which broke through the stifling afternoon silence, like glass shattering above them—she searched the sky until she caught sight of their green wings. She could not see the birds, only their blurred outline, like a smear of color in the sky. Luzia strained to see faraway trees or ridges. She squinted to make things crisp instead of hazy and indistinct. Slowly, she began to ignore everything in the distance. She could see well enough—she could read the newspapers that the Hawk gave her and could clearly distinguish her stitches when she sewed. She didn't need to see what was far off, only what was before her.

The cangaceiros appreciated her sewing. When the group invaded a town, the men looked for cloth and thread. They searched dusty stockrooms. They raided ladies' sewing closets. Then they presented their findings to Luzia. The only items she would not accept were measuring tapes. She used only her own tape—the one Emília had packed for her—because she'd made it herself and was certain of its accuracy. "Never trust a strange tape," Luzia told the men, echoing Aunt Sofia's advice.

Only the very wealthy—colonels, merchants, politicians—had richly embroidered and appliquéd treasures. Now the cangaceiros did as well. And like everything they valued, they wanted more. They asked Luzia to adorn their cartridge belts, to make covers for their water gourds and canteens, to sew their initials onto their leather vaqueiro gloves. Even Little Ear and Half-Moon quietly handed her their possessions to decorate. So the cangaceiros, at first suspicious of Luzia's presence, grew to believe that the Hawk's prediction had partially come true: Luzia had not yet brought them good luck or bad, but she had proven useful.

Each evening she guided a faded bornal under her machine's needle. Ponta Fina proudly turned the hand crank. The rest of the men watched. Luzia embroidered the more delicate stitches by hand but used the Singer to attach the appliqué fabrics—meticulously cut into tiny triangles, diamonds, crescents, and circles—onto bags and canteen covers. The machine had transformed sewing into an acceptable skill, a useful trade. Men did not fuss with lace or embroidery hoops but they could operate machines. Between the clatter, the cangaceiros asked Luzia questions and admired her work. Some tried their hand at sewing, but they were an impatient bunch. They tugged the practice cloth too fast through the machine's needle. They allowed the bobbin thread to clump into thick knots. They wanted their talent to come all at once. Luzia shook her head.

"You must pay attention to each stitch," she said, gathering her embroidery hoops and making the men sew by hand.

Each stitch was a design in itself. Each had its starting point, its ending point, its length, its tension. A skilled tailor (she didn't dare

call the men "seamstresses") could read stitches like letters in an alphabet, Luzia said, and when she was met with the men's blank
stares, she corrected herself. A skilled tailor was like a good vaqueiro:
he could decipher between stitches as he deciphered each cow in his
herd. This took memorization, and the men had terrible memories.
They renamed the stitches to help themselves remember. The back-
stitch became Baiano because it was consistent, straightforward, and
used whenever you wanted the cleanest line. The caterpillar stitch
was Vanity, because when you twirled the thread around the embroidery needle, the stitch looked elegant and complicated, but the
result was always less than expected—just a few odd-shaped nubs
along the cloth. Inteligente and Canjica were satin stitch and its outline. Satin was a thick filler stitch. It could be cumbersome and
crooked without its outline to guide it and hem it in. Little Ear, to
Ponta Fina's delight, was the thorn stitch: a simple line of thread held
down by pairs of sharply crossed stitches. Every new stitch that Luzia
introduced had a man to go with it.

"And the captain?" Ponta asked. "What would he be?"

"I don't know," Luzia said, focusing her attention back on the
Singer. "I haven't discovered such a stitch."

This was a lie. His was the first stitch she'd thought of when
they'd started their memorization game. He was the shadow stitch.
It did not resemble a stitch at all, but a block of color that showed
through a fabric's weave. It was made on the reverse side of a thin,
almost transparent cloth—a fine linen or a light crepe. From the
front, it was impossible to know how the effect was made or what
stitch was used. Admirers knew that there was something behind the
cloth but did not know what. The effect was lovely and disconcert-
ing. The shadow stitch was deceiving—it was either the sign of a
great seamstress or a way for a poor one to hide her mistakes. Whenever Luzia saw the stitch, she hated turning the cloth over. On the
back of the cloth, the stitches could be well wrought and tight, or a
messy clump of knots.

Luzia could not reveal this to the men, though they prodded her,
teasing when she became flustered and impatient. They meant no

harm; the cangaceiros taunted one another relentlessly and the fact that Luzia was included in their jokes solidified her place in the group. Some—Little Ear, Half-Moon, and Caju—were still wary of her, but the others became playful and relaxed. They treated Luzia as if she were a tomboy cousin they'd known since childhood—placing frogs between her blankets, teaching her how to play dominoes, and trying, unsuccessfully, to shock her with their conversations. After weeks in the scrub without a visit to a village or town, the men became bawdy and restless. They spoke of past conquests and envisioned new ones.

Luzia sewed quietly, pretending not to listen. The men recalled the salty, perfumed taste of women's sweat. How, when dancing forró, they liked a girl's hot breath on their necks. How, when a girl was nervous, her mouth was dry at the beginning of a kiss. And how, an instant afterward, it became wet and warm again. Luzia listened, mesmerized by the cangaceiros' knowledge. They spoke of smells, of bodies, of hair and softness. They showed the same intense, technical appreciation as when they spoke of their guns, but there was more wonder in their voices. More reverence.

Luzia often glanced at the Hawk during these discussions. He never took part in them; most nights he didn't even pay attention, choosing instead to make the next day's plans with Baiano. But sometimes the Hawk sat back and listened, smiling at the men's observations as if he agreed. Luzia sewed faster then, sticking the needle roughly through her hooped fabric. She was a woman, too, she assured herself. But would a man ever speak of her hair, her breath, her kiss? She did not resemble the perfumed and solicitous creatures the cangaceiros courted in towns—girls trembling in fear and curiosity, some offering warm macaxeira cakes on platters, some dancing and turning their faces coquettishly when the men tried to kiss them during a song. They danced stiffly at first, but by the middle of the night, the men and their partners moved close together, their hips swiveling in time with one another, their feet shuffling so quickly on the dirt floor that Ponta Fina had to splash water across it so that dust would not rise and sting their eyes. By the end of the night, the dancing couples often disappeared together. Luzia made camp with Ponta Fina and any other cangaceiros who'd already had their fun. The Hawk never danced, but a few times he'd disappeared as well and Luzia spent an uncomfortable night on her blankets, unable to sleep. She was angry that he'd found a woman for the night, but also strangely reassured; he was not a celibate or a saint but a man with weaknesses and needs, like the other cangaceiros.

Luzia had learned to control her clumsiness and slow her speech when she spoke to the Hawk. She still felt a terrible heat rise in her stomach and flush her cheeks if he came too close. She'd tried to uproot it, then to contain it. She tried to be an invisible part of the group and not think of the future or the past. There was no time for daydreams. The Hawk had charmed his men, but Luzia resolved that he would not charm her. He was moody, impatient, often vain. Still, it was hard not to be affected by his confidence. In the scrub, nothing was certain—not the rain, not their dinners, not their lives. But the Hawk never wavered, never backtracked, never lost his faith. He was skilled with a knife and often helped Ponta Fina skin their dinners. He was a patient teacher. He was an excellent marksman. It seemed that there was nothing he couldn't do, so when he took people aside and asked for their help or advice, he made them feel unique and necessary. He did this to Luzia. She tried to ignore it, but to have his full attention, to have his eyes focused on her as if she were the only person in the scrub, thrilled her.

"Read to me," he often asked, handing her a battered copy of a newspaper he had managed to buy from a merchant or coax from a traveling repentista singer. Newspapers were hard to find; few people outside the capital and the larger towns in the backlands knew how to read. The Hawk always said it hurt his eyes to read the articles' small print. Luzia didn't know if this was the truth or if he was a poor reader. Each day he read his collection of prayers aloud, but perhaps he was like Aunt Sofia—clever enough to feign reading through repetition and memorization.

The *Caruaru Weekly,* a thin rag printed in the countryside, featured article after article about the attack on Fidalga and Colonel

Machado's response. Upon returning to Fidalga to find his capangas dead and his son humiliated, Colonel Machado had traveled to the capital. He used all of his influence to petition the governor for troops. Elections were scheduled for January 1930, but campaigning had already begun. Brigade 1761, led by a young captain Higino Ribeiro arrived in Caruaru by train with much fanfare. They had new green uniforms with a yellow stripe down the sides. The local colonel distributed flowers to be thrown at the troops when they descended from the train. From there, it would take the troops weeks to walk through the scrub and investigate the Hawk's whereabouts.

"What about the *real* paper?" the Hawk asked after Luzia had read through the *Weekly*. The *Diário de Pernambuco* was the thick daily printed in the capital. In it there was only a small blurb about the troop deployment, on page eleven, sandwiched between the obituaries and an ad for hair tonic. The front pages of the *Diário* were filled with news on the upcoming presidential elections. A short, beak-nosed Southerner named Celestino Gomes dominated the front pages.

"Gomes!" the Hawk growled. "Who's this Gomes? What's he done to get the front page every blasted day?"

Luzia read the articles aloud slowly, emphasizing each word. Gomes would run for president under his new party, the Liberal Alliance. To everyone's surprise, his running mate would be a Northerner. A man named José Bandeira. Before she was finished, the Hawk had lit a cigarette and walked away.

Luzia continued reading. She liked the gaudy images of cinema ads with short-haired women draped in the arms of gallant men. She liked the reports of runaway trolley cars and missing horses. All of it reminded her of Emília and her sister's love for such things. She thought of Emília often. She tried to recall the smell of Emília's lavender soap, the feel of Emília's strong hands. Luzia wondered if she'd escaped with Professor Célio. If so, Luzia prayed he wouldn't mistreat her sister. She worried about what Emília would endure to fulfill her dreams of having a fine house and a tiled kitchen.

One evening, Luzia's worries increased. The last paper the men had bought, a *Diário de Pernambuco* purchased from a mule driver, was months old and reeked of manure. In the Society Section was a wedding announcement. *Miss Emília dos Santos,* the paper's small print said. *Miss Emília dos Santos.* Luzia read it over and over again. Dos Santos was a common name. So was Emília. And Toritama was not Taquaritinga. Still, Luzia ripped the announcement from the page and stuffed it in her bornal.

Their group moved inland—not to escape the troops, the Hawk insisted, but to follow the rains. The state of Pernambuco was long and thin. The wet season began on the coast as early as May and slowly moved westward, reaching the end of the state in January. That year, the rains dwindled the farther inland they moved, as if the clouds were exhausted by their travels. The small, waxy leaves that emerged from the caatinga trees had no time to thrive. Gullies narrowed into thin trickles of water. Vines shriveled and Luzia believed they were dead. She was wrong. The scrub, the Hawk told her, liked to play tricks on people's eyes. On the outside, the plants were gray and lifeless. But when the Hawk twisted a twig off an angico tree, Luzia saw that beneath the gray bark, the tree was green. Alive. Enclosed in a veil of thorns and a thick, impenetrable skin.

Luzia envied those hardy caatinga plants. When she walked, even in the early mornings, Luzia felt as if she were trapped in a cookstove. Sweat evaporated from her body before cooling it. Her leather shin guards, her hat, and the strap of her water gourd hardened and cracked in the sun. Each day at noon, the men stopped walking and searched for shade. The heat made everyone slow and quiet. When they left their shaded spot in the late afternoon, once the sun had cooled, Ponta Fina made a makeshift broom from scrub brush and dragged it behind him to erase their footprints. If they came upon a farm's stone fence, they balanced on top of its rock ledge and walked in a line so that they wouldn't leave tracks. Since the evenings were cooler, their group walked well into the night. Luzia could not sew. There was no light, no time, and the Hawk said that the machine's clatter was too loud. But despite all of their precautions, the men could be spotted from kilometers away. In the gray scrub, their embroidered and appliquéd treasures—covered in reds and greens, pinks and yellows—made them stand out like brilliantly plumed birds. Luzia suggested they tear out the stitching but the Hawk would not have it.

"If those troops are lucky enough to find us," he said, "they'll see that we're no vagabundos."

Luzia recalled the photograph of Captain Higino and felt uneasy. The newspaper picture had been blurry and badly printed, but the young man stood out. His uniform was simple, his boots polished. He was short but was not dwarfed by the train or the surging crowd. He kept his hands comfortably at his sides instead of placing them rigidly on his belt, like the older officials beside him did. He seemed at ease. Smiling even, as if he was in for a great adventure. Luzia consoled her fears with Ponta Fina's stories. Perhaps this Captain Higino was like the others—eager for a show but not a fight. And how would a battalion of ill-equipped city boys withstand the scrub?

Luzia did not know how many weeks they'd walked when, suddenly, Ponta Fina let out a high-pitched howl. When she and the cangaceiros climbed the ridge where the boy stood, she saw a great blur of green in the distance and beside it, a wide expanse of water. The mirages she saw in the scrub gleamed like metal plates, but this river had no shine, no glimmer. It was the color of coffee and milk. It was the São Francisco. The Old Chico, as Aunt Sofia used to call it, and it flowed through the scrubland hills, making them green and bright, dividing the state of Pernambuco from the state of Bahia with its wide, brown waters.

"We've arrived," the Hawk said, taking a deep breath.

Luzia breathed, too. She could smell it. It had the scent of moss, of wet earth. The air softened in her nostrils. She heard birds in the distance. Houses clustered near the river's banks. Two clouds of black smoke rose from dark mounds stacked before a massive, whitewashed building. Captain Higino and his troops were forgotten.

2

The river town of São Tomé had no clay-and-stick shacks. All of its houses were made of brick and covered in a thick layer of white-washed cement. There was a telegraph office, a schoolhouse, and beside the two smoking piles of cottonseed was the second largest gin in Pernambuco. All of it belonged to Colonel Clóvis Lucena.

The old colonel spent his days on his ranch, dressed in a pair of blue pajamas. A peixeira, its blade sheathed in a leather case, was tucked into the pajamas' drawstring waist. It was rumored that, years ago, a capanga had tried to strangle him with his own necktie. After that, the colonel refused to wear suits. Luzia had heard this story back in Taquaritinga but was never certain of its truth.

When he greeted them, Colonel Clóvis smiled. Like a goat, he had only a top row of teeth. The bottom was gums. His only son, Marcos Lucena, stood beside him. Marcos was middle-aged and re-sembled a cururu toad: his legs short, his stance wide, his eyes heavy lidded and sleepy, but watchful.

Like any good host, Colonel Clóvis strove to make his guests happy. Upon their arrival, he ordered one of his best cows killed. He had several cabritos skinned and roasted. Despite his cook's protests, Colonel Clóvis gave Canjica full reign of the kitchen. The colonel's house had a wide veranda shaded by rows of blooming ipê trees. Yel-low petals covered the roof and ground like a golden blanket. Next to the house was the largest goat corral Luzia had ever seen. In one of its many pens, kids bayed and jumped wildly, butting heads and nudging each other's thin legs.

"You're still an ugly son of a bitch," the old colonel said, smiling at the Hawk. He jutted out his chin at Luzia. "Got yourself a wife?"

"A charm," the Hawk replied. "For luck."

The colonel laughed and turned to Luzia. "My wife, God rest her soul, was a large woman. Strongest woman who ever lived. My Marcos wants to marry a little chicken from Salvador." The old man kicked his son's shoe roughly. "She won't survive out here."

"When we marry," Marcos muttered, "she won't live here." He focused his sleepy gaze on the Hawk. "Come to collect?"

The Hawk smiled. His good eye glittered.

"No!" the Colonel quickly intervened. "I know why you've come. I heard about the mess you made up in Fidalga! It's about time you started feuding with Floriano Machado—that sack of shit. Sends his cotton all the way to Campina Grande instead of selling it to me. He's always been jealous of my gin . . . of our gin." Colonel Clóvis smiled, then tapped Luzia. "That Machado is a cabra-de-peia. You know what that means, girl? He's an old goat with no character. No word. He don't respect the old ways . . . has to cry to the governor to get troops instead of settling things himself."

"According to the *Weekly*," Marcos interrupted, "they want to haul you and your group to Recife. The governor needs good press."

The colonel released a puff of air from his nostrils. "That little bastard Higino won't set foot on my land! I'd like to see the governor force me. I gave him more votes in the last election than any other colonel. I raised voters from the dead! He's having trouble with the new party. He can't afford to make me mad."

"New party?" the Hawk asked, creasing his brow into a confused look.

"How long you been in the scrub, boy?" the colonel shouted. "Down in Minas. Celestino Gomes is running for president and he got a local boy from Paraíba to run with him, to lock in the North. They're promising a national roadway, and to give women the vote. I don't like it. But as long as they stay out of my business, I'll stay out of theirs. Of course, their party's sniffing around us. Promising us this and that if we switch sides. I haven't decided yet."

"Can't trust Southerners," the Hawk said.

Colonel Clóvis nodded thoughtfully. He smoothed a hand across the few strands of hair above his ears. The sunspots on his bald skull were brown and plump, like ticks.

"Some say if Gomes wins, we'll all be shitting gold," Clóvis continued. "Others say it'll be gloom and doom—the death of the colonels." He sighed, then smiled at Luzia. "A colonel's power is like capim grass, girl. The more you cut it, the more it grows. It's like a cangaceiro."

He'd befriended many great cangaceiros in his long life. Cabeleira, Chico Flores, Casimiro, Zé do Mato. He'd known them all. Every generation, Clóvis reminisced, had its great cangaceiros. Ever since his great-grandfather's time—when there were no politicians, no god-awful fences, no telegraph lines—cangaceiros and colonels had their alliances and their feuds.

"They're like the sagüi monkey and the angico trees," Clóvis said. "One can't live without the other."

"The trees could live fine," Marcos mumbled.

His father glared at him. The Hawk smiled.

"Enough of this loose talk," the colonel said, waving his wrinkled hand. "Let's have a drink."

They moved toward the porch. A row of intricately carved rockers sat empty. Luzia fell back. She wanted to find Ponta Fina and Inteligente; they had her sewing machine. Upon their arrival, the men had scattered. Some searched the house and grounds, making sure they were safe. Others built camp and helped Canjica prepare their dinner feast. Luzia stared past the maze of goat corrals, looking for a sign of the men. She felt a firm tug on her bent arm. Colonel Clóvis stood beside her.

"Don't be a matuta and run off," he said. "Sit with us." With incredible strength, Clóvis tugged again at Luzia's locked arm, bringing her closer. Luzia leaned toward him.

"See that?" he whispered, pointing to the corral of kids. "Those are my cabritos. Purebreds. The sweetest meat you ever tasted. Their mothers are loose." Colonel Clóvis winked. "Out to pasture, I mean. I don't use shepherds. No need for them. I'll tell you my trick: if I want to trap the mother, I hold on to her cabrito."

Luzia leaned back. The old man's breath was pungent, a mixture of rotted teeth and chewing tobacco. She stared at the porch. The Hawk had doubled back toward them. The colonel's grip tightened.

"What's your grace?" he asked.

"Luzia."

"Ahhh," the colonel sighed, as if she'd said something remarkable. "Tomorrow's the thirteenth of December. Your saint's day."

Luzia hadn't kept track of dates. She would be eighteen and would have to fulfill her promise to Saint Expedito. Her long hair was a burden in the scrub. Even in a braid, it snagged in the trees. She could rarely wash it and had to comb it with her fingers. Still, Luzia couldn't imagine cutting it. Beneath the trousers, the blankets, the bornais, and the leather hat, she was a woman, not a cangaceiro. Saint Expedito would have to wait.

"What kind of luck do you give?" the colonel asked, interrupting her thoughts. "The good kind? Or the bad?"

"None at all," Luzia replied, tugging free of his hand.

The colonel flashed his few, ancient teeth.

3

That night, in honor of Saint Luzia, the cangaceiros made a bonfire in the colonel's yard. Farmhands and their families crouched near the fire but did not dance or sing. They watched the cangaceiros and shot worried glances at Colonel Clóvis, who swayed in a rocker on his porch. The hands' wives brought out a wide tin basin, stained black with soot. They filled it with cashew pods and placed the basin over the fire. Flames rose alongside the basin, then dipped inside it. The seedpods burst open. Oil leaked from their shells and dripped into the fire. A few women stirred the flaming cashews with long sticks, keeping their faces turned from the venomous smoke.

Luzia sat far from the fire, but her eyes watered. She turned from the smoke and faced the porch. There, the Hawk sat with Marcos and Colonel Clóvis. They swayed back and forth in rockers. The colonel's sandaled feet barely touched the floor. Marcos's wide body spilled out of his chair. Uncomfortable with the rocker's movement, the Hawk sat at the edge of the chair with his feet planted. The rocker's back end lifted high off the floor; Luzia worried it would topple over. The Hawk was a wary guest. When a maid served a bottle of amber liquid, he removed a silver spoon from his bornal and placed it in his tumbler. The spoon was well polished; it shone in his hands. Previously, Luzia had seen him dip the utensil into bags of manioc flour in the colonel's pantry and any other food he thought suspect. If the spoon tarnished, something poisonous had been added. The colonel's whiskey proved safe, but even after the Hawk dried the spoon and replaced it in his bornal, he waited for his host to take the first sip.

That afternoon, at the colonel's insistence, Luzia had sat on the porch beside the men, but she had not drunk. She'd only listened. They'd spoken of the price of uncleaned cotton, how much the gin had processed, how long it would take the cleaned bales to arrive in Recife, and how much the textile mills would pay. The harvest had overproduced, the colonel said, and the mills would surely pay less. The Hawk complimented the colonel's negotiating skills. He said that their gin would surely turn a profit. Colonel Clóvis shuffled his jaw from side to side, as if rearranging it in his mouth. Marcos rocked faster in his chair. Luzia stared at the Hawk. He held his glass tumbler with both hands, like a child. He did not resemble a land-owner, but that afternoon he had spoken like one. *Their gin,* he'd said to the colonel. And Luzia realized that the Hawk and his canga-ceiros hadn't gone to Clóvis for protection, but for profit.

From the beginning, she'd known that the cangaceiros were not isolated creatures of the caatinga. They depended on the scrub's residents—rich and poor—for clothing, weapons, lodging, and pro-tection. This web of connections was fragile: built upon the Hawk's reputation as a fair man and easily broken if that fairness wavered. Other bandits might be needlessly brutal, but the Hawk and his can-gaceiros could not afford to be. Their acts were never random. If the men sliced off a merchant's ear, it was for rudeness; if they removed a man's tongue, it was for talking to soldiers or defaming the canga-ceiros; and if they used their punhais, it was for larger offenses against them or their friends. Most important, a woman's honor was her family's treasure, the Hawk often said. He and his men respected families. They relied on them. "Only birds shit where they eat," he said. "And we are not birds. We are cangaceiros."

That day, on the colonel's porch, Luzia realized that they were businessmen as well. This gave her a strange feeling of reassurance. Businessmen had plans. They had futures. Cangaceiros did not. She recalled Ponta Fina's account of entering the group; how the Hawk had warned him that it was a dead end. The hopes she'd heard the men express were fleeting ones: dancing, eating a fine meal, loving a woman. Beyond that, they hoped to die in a fair fight. But if the Hawk owned something, if he was a partner in the cotton gin, it meant he had influence and a yearly income. Steady earnings meant that he could plan ahead, could save, could buy land for himself and his men. And with land came respectability. With land came the hope of something beyond survival and certain death.

Near the fire, the cashews were ready. With quick precision the women placed their stirring sticks on either side of the tin basin and hoisted it from the fire. Then they flipped the basin over. The blackened cashews fell onto the dirt. Children surrounded the smoking pile and cooled it with sand. Near her, Sabiá sang without the accompaniment of an accordion. His song was quick, its rhythm choppy. He took deep breaths between each verse.

> "Bodies are my garden
> My pistol is my hoe
> My bullets are like rain
> I am a son of the sertão."

Beside the fire, the cangaceiros danced. They stood in two rows, their rifles in their hands, their faces locked in stern expressions. In time to Sabiá's song, they advanced three steps with their right feet, then stepped quickly forward with their left. They'd loosened their alpercatas so that the soles dragged in the dirt. The leather made a *sha, sha, sha* sound against the sand. Their rifles were their partners and they held them rigidly, as they'd held the timid girls in Fidalga.

The men were not allowed to drink, although the colonel had offered them sugarcane liquor. Still, the unending supply of meat and river water made the cangaceiros giddy. Suddenly, the Hawk left the porch. Luzia believed he would chastise the men for dancing. Instead, he joined them. He led the first row, stomping and shuffling in time with the others. His movements were sharper, more controlled. There was grace in his exactitude, a strange fluidity in his stiff-jointed rhythms.

> "My rifle's the best lawyer.
> My bullets are police.
> My punhal's the fairest judge,
> And death is my release."

Luzia watched him. She hoped that when he stopped dancing, he would stand near her. She wanted to thank him. Earlier, when she and Ponta Fina had gone to retrieve her sewing machine from the colonel's back porch, the Hawk had left her a gift. They'd made camp far from Colonel Clóvis's house, leaving the sewing machine on the porch so it wouldn't bake in the sun. When Luzia and Ponta went to retrieve it, there was a small bundle on the Singer's base. It was tied with twine. When Luzia pulled apart the brown butcher paper, silk poured into her hands. It was slippery, like oil. Luzia gasped and scooped it up before it hit the ground. The silk was the color of finely grated corn meal. There was two meters of it. In Taquaritinga she would have thought such a gift silly and useless. But it had been a long time since she'd felt something so soft. For months she'd only felt coarse leather, scratchy woolen blankets, the thorns and burrs of the scrub, and her own calloused skin. Ponta Fina asked to touch the silk. "It must be from the captain," he'd said. For her birthday, Luzia assumed. Her saint's day. She'd wanted to thank the Hawk all evening but could not find the words.

Sabiá's song ended. The men stopped dancing.

"It's nearly midnight," the Hawk announced. "Time to say the prayer."

The farmhands and cangaceiros congregated around a large, flat rock a few meters from the fire. Canjica held a tin of salt and a wooden spoon. He handed the items to Luzia, then guided her toward the rock. The Hawk knelt before her. The others followed. He removed a crumpled paper from his jacket pocket. He looked at Luzia, then bent his head.

"My Santa Luzia," he said slowly, pronouncing each syllable. "Give me sight. You, who did not lose your faith even after they drained your blood. You, who did not lose your vision even after they cut out your eyes. Defend me against blindness. Conserve the light of my eyes. Give me the strength to keep them always open, so that I may see the good from the wicked, the true from the false. You, who were given four eyes instead of two, look into the heavens and tell us what the months will bring."

Canjica scooped out a spoonful of salt from the tin in Luzia's hands. He placed it on the rock.

"January!" the farmhands and cangaceiros yelled.

Canjica placed another spoonful of salt beside the first.

"February!"

Another spoonful.

"March!"

Another scoop was April, another May, and finally June.

It was a prophecy. Luzia had heard of vaqueiros and farmers performing this trick. The mounds would be left out until morning. For each mound that the night's dew dissolved, there would be a month with rain. If the mounds were intact, there would be drought. Something had to be given to the saint in return for her willingness to predict the future. Luzia knew nothing about prophecy, but she knew about saints. For any request, they needed proof of faith. For any blessing, they always wanted something in return.

The Hawk untied a long leather pouch from his belt. He held it beside the salt mounds, then opened its wide mouth and turned it over. A pile of marble-size orbs fell out. Some were shriveled and raisinlike. Others were warped like bent coins. Some had kept their roundness but were slightly deflated. These had the curdled color of Half-Moon's bad eye.

Luzia quickly left the center of the prayer circle. She recalled the hollow-eyed capangas from Fidalga, piled on Colonel Machado's porch. She recalled her aunt Sofia's rhyme. *The hawk, caracará, looks for children who aren't wise . . .*

Luzia waited for a reaction: a pain in her stomach, a trembling in her fingers. She had none. Over the past months, her fear, her disgust, her pity had evaporated beneath the scrub's unyielding sun. Just as the skin on her feet and hands had blistered, darkened, grown calloused and thick, something within her had hardened as well. They often found the bodies of baby goats in the scrub. They found the carcasses of cattle and the dried and leathery bodies of frogs. All of them were blinded, their eyes carried away by lines of saúva ants, or snatched up by hungry birds. It was inevitable. In the scrub, one predator was no better or worse than another.

Outside the circle, Luzia knelt. She stared at the dark sky. A scattering of stars lay above the horizon, like spilled salt. Each night she prayed to those heavens. Each day they floated above her, blue and unreachable, home to an unrelenting sun. She looked at the Hawk's broad shoulders, at his bowed head. When he prayed, he looked not at the sky but at the ground. Luzia straightened her good arm. She pressed her hand to the earth. She was surprised by how cool it felt, how firm.

There was shuffling beside her. Luzia saw the colonel's leather alpercatas and within them, his withered toes. He leaned on a wooden cane.

"I'm no saint, but I'll tell you it won't rain this year," he said. "When my goats sneeze, it means rain. They haven't sneezed yet."

A knife handle protruded crookedly from the waistband of his pajamas. Luzia looked toward the porch. Marcos was gone. Colonel Clóvis shook his head.

"That boy," he said, jutting his cane toward the Hawk, "takes everything at face value. Thank God there's no saint who likes hearts. Or bowels." He chuckled, then looked down at Luzia. "I saw that machine on my porch. You been decorating those boys? They're starting to look like my wife's kitchen towels. They like luxury but go too far with it. Is that what you did before you ran off with him? Sew?"

Luzia rose and wiped her hands on her trousers. "I didn't run off."

"He do that to your arm?"

"No."

The colonel pondered this for a moment, shuffling his jaw. "Maybe that's why he's fond of you. You're crippled, like him." He edged closer. "You ever heard of Colonel Bartolomeu? The one he's famous for killing?"

"Yes," Luzia replied. It had been big news, an eighteen-year-old boy killing a colonel and getting away.

"That was his daddy." Clóvis smiled. "Or so people say. His mother was some poor unfortunate. A young chicken who got herself disgraced. Told people that the colonel had taken advantage of her, that he was the boy's father. No one listened, but she kept insisting. She wanted money. That's what all these tenant women want. Bartolomeu got tired of it and sent his capangas. They shut her up and did that service to the boy." Colonel Clóvis traced a line down the side of his own, withered face. "Isn't that how the story goes?"

"I suppose," Luzia said.

"He hasn't told you?"

"I never asked."

Colonel Clóvis wobbled his cane back and forth. "You must have done something real nice to make him break his promise."

"What promise?"

The colonel inspected her face. His jowls were pendulous and fatty, as if all the mass from his face had sunk into them. He shrugged and looked away.

"He's probably made so many promises it's hard to keep track. I'd be kissing the saints' asses, too, if I were him."

"What promise?" Luzia insisted. The colonel smiled.

"I finally got your attention, uh? Very first time he came here to collect, he said he'd gotten a sign from one of his saints. Said he'd never let a woman in his group. Said women were for marrying. Or for fun."

"Not me," Luzia declared.

"Don't worry about propriety with me, girl. I understand your lot." Clóvis looked at the Hawk and shook his head. "We all have to make our bargains. We all have to cut deals."

He tapped his cane several times, as if calling something out of the earth.

"How'd you like that silk I left you? Fine stuff, uh?" Colonel Clóvis asked, pressing against Luzia. "There's more in my room if you want it. Women like gifts." He rapped her legs with his cane. "Even when they dress like a man."

Before them, the crowd of farmhands and cangaceiros lined up in front of the rock where the salt mounds sat. One by one they touched the rock and asked for the saint's blessing. Luzia excused herself and found a place beside them.

4

Santa Luzia's predictions were dire. The next morning, only three of the salt mounds were partially dissolved by dew. The rest were intact. For days rain was all the cangaceiros talked about. Luzia did not care. She was preoccupied with the yellow silk. She'd tucked it back into its butcher-paper wrapping and hidden it at the bottom of her bornal but she still felt its presence. She recalled its slipperiness against her hands. She was ashamed by having accepted a gift from the colonel and more ashamed by her joy in thinking it was from the Hawk. Yet she could not return it. Colonel Clóvis was an old goat but he was still their host. Finally, Luzia sneaked into the colonel's kitchen and left it in his pantry, hoping the cook or a maid would find it and keep it for herself.

Everything in the colonel's house—the pantry, the lace curtains, the stack of laundered bed linens—had a charred scent. The more cotton the gin processed, the more smoke settled over São Tomé. The black piles Luzia had seen burning outside the gin were cottonseeds. Over the months, their smoke turned the whitewashed town a sooty gray. It made the kids in Clóvis's corral pant and hack out dry coughs. Each afternoon, mother goats wandered back from pasture with their coats covered in a fine black dust. Brass chocalhos bobbed below their necks, clanging as they ran. Kids crowded the front gate. They bayed wildly as the mass of mother goats stormed their group, sniffing kids and butting them aside until they found their own. The kids looked identical—speckled black and brown with dangling ears and sturdy frames. Luzia marveled at the mothers' ability to pick their young from the pack.

While his son, Marcos, loped about, rarely speaking and often taking long rides on his prize mare, Colonel Clóvis seemed to enjoy the cangaceiros' presence. He encouraged them to stay on. Once the cotton was cleaned, baled, and transported, he and Marcos would go to Salvador to bargain for the price. When they returned, they assured the Hawk that he would receive a percentage. Each evening, when the last of the goats returned from pasture, the cangaceiros took turns going into town. There, they sang and played lively music. They bought a ream of silk to make new neck scarves. They watched workers load bales of cotton onto barges headed for Salvador. And they visited the businesses of experienced women, which the cangaceiros later bragged about in camp. Even Colonel Clóvis joined them on those trips. "Men have needs," the old man said once, cornering Luzia near the goat corral. "Can't stifle them."

Luzia grew annoyed with the cangaceiros' flamboyant behavior. Soon, even the most hopeless troops would find them. The Hawk didn't seem concerned. He encouraged the men's trips into town. When a group left, he waited anxiously for their return, pacing back and forth as if his legs missed their daily walks in the scrub. When the men returned, half of them took the long way into camp, avoiding the colonel's front gate. They carried heavy strings of ammunition, enough to give each man at least five hundred bullets. When they could find one, they brought a newspaper.

Luzia read the papers aloud. There were no articles about the troops. Only once was there a brief mention of a telegram sent by Captain Higino, assuring readers that he was on the cangaceiros' trail. Outside that, the search had been forgotten in favor of the election. The Hawk bored easily with such news, but Luzia slogged through the articles in hopes of finding a mention of Emília. She read about the new party colors: green for Gomes and blue for the current leader. She studied Gomes's manifesto, which called for a minimum wage, women's suffrage, and the relinquishing of power from the São Paulo coffee barons and the colonels. In his reprinted speeches, Gomes called for modernization: new industries, better ports, and most important, a national roadway. A roadway would link the nation to its capital, as arteries linked a body to its heart, giving life to Brazil's forgotten limbs. His words were poetic and forceful, and they distracted Luzia from the Society Section where, one afternoon, she nearly skipped over a blurb about Carnaval. However, something drew her to a photograph of a brightly lit ballroom at the International Club. She did not recognize any of the costumed revelers but beneath the photograph was a recap of the night's festivities. Embedded in this chatty summary were the words:

> Sadly, on her first appearance at the club, the mysterious Mrs. Emília Coelho left early. Her husband, Mr. Degas Coelho, cited exhaustion for his new bride's escape. It's no surprise that a country girl has difficulty acclimating to our cosmopolitan hours! Mr. Degas Coelho, however, had no trouble at all; he remained and enjoyed the festivities with his law school chum Mr. Felipe Pereira.

Luzia tore out the blurb.

"Anything important?" the Hawk asked, startling her. He'd been spying.

"No," Luzia said. "Just an announcement."

"What kind?"

"About a party," Luzia replied. She should have said it was an obituary or a cinema ad; only silly girls clipped party announcements. Luzia folded the newspaper roughly. She hated his spying. Each day on the colonel's property made him more paranoid. He refused to eat anything unless he saw Canjica prepare it. He walked incessantly. He spoke in hushed tones to Baiano. He had circles beneath his eyes from lack of sleep. Each day Luzia wondered why they stayed at the colonel's if the Hawk did not trust him.

"Take a walk with me," he said. "Put the paper away."

Luzia stood. She shoved the Society Section into her bornal. If he questioned her about keeping it, she would lie. He'd met Emília in Taquaritinga, but Luzia wasn't sure he recalled her sister's name. If he did remember it, Luzia didn't want the Hawk to know that Emília had married a wealthy city man. She felt the need to protect her sister—from what, Luzia wasn't sure. There was no proof that the woman mentioned in the papers was *her* Emília. But Felipe Pereira—the colonel's son from Taquaritinga—had also appeared in the article. Luzia sensed this wasn't a coincidence; Mrs. Emília Coelho had to be her sister.

During their walk, the Hawk didn't bring up the newspaper article. He did not speak at all. They took a long route, past the goat corral. The released goats had scavenged the area, chewing away any stray leaves or vines and leaving it bare. In the distance stood a flowering ipê. The tree's blooms glowed yellow. The Hawk stopped ten meters before the trunk. He unbuttoned the clasp of his shoulder holster and removed a revolver. With a flick of his finger he opened the circular chamber and inspected it. He slipped two small bullets from his cartridge belt and pressed them into the chamber's empty holes. There were six shots. Luzia stepped back. The Hawk clicked the chamber shut and pointed the revolver toward the ground. He handed it butt first to Luzia.

"It's no good to own a gun you can't use," he said.

"I don't own a gun."

"You do now," he said and stepped beside her. He held her good arm and placed the revolver in its hand. His fingers were warm. He lifted her arm. The gun was heavier than she'd expected. Luzia's wrist bent. The Hawk clamped his hand around it.

"Keep your munheca stiff, like wood," he said, then prodded her locked arm. "Use the crooked one to prop up the good one, to keep it steady. With practice you'll get strong enough to shoot one-handed."

She felt his breath on her neck. Luzia's hand sweated. The butt felt slick in her grip.

"If you shoot, hold your breath," he said. "Don't forget or the bullets won't go where you want them to."

She nodded. He clicked back the safety.

"Look at that tree trunk," he whispered. "Shoot."

The gray trunk and its yellow flowers were blurs. Luzia closed her eyes. He smelled of brilliantine paste and cloves. And sweat. His hand loosened around her wrist.

"Shoot," he repeated, louder this time. He moved closer, his chest pressing against her back.

Luzia squeezed the trigger. There was a loud pop. A jolt moved through her hand and up her arm. She'd moved without meaning to.

"You took a breath," the Hawk said sternly. "Don't waste bullets with simple mistakes. Bullets are precious. Now shoot again."

Luzia clicked down the safety. With her locked arm, she gripped her good arm harder. Still, the revolver's recoil made her hand move upward. The Hawk sighed.

"You have to befriend your gun," he said. "You have to know it like you know yourself. How far it will shoot. How much it moves your arm. Your gun will save you, but only if you know it." He moved away from her, keeping to her side. "That will come with time. Right now," he said, smiling, "we have to work on your aim."

Luzia pointed the revolver toward the ground. The Hawk fumbled with his belt, unhooking the leather slingshot he used to kill rolinhas and other scrub birds. He squatted and picked up pebbles.

"Why are you teaching me this?" she asked.

He shrugged and sorted pebbles, picking the roundest ones. "It's useful to know. Especially now."

"Why now?

"Troops will be here soon."

"When?" Luzia asked, her voice louder than she wanted it to be. "How do you know?"

The Hawk sighed. He dropped the pebbles on the ground. "Back on our first night, the night of Santa Luzia, Marcos left. He went into town and sent a telegram to the capital. 'Cows in the pasture,' that's what he sent. Trying to be clever."

"How do you know?"

"Baiano talked to the telegraph clerk. Those goddamn machines are a pestilence. The clerk's just a boy; he told us everything. Even if it weren't for that, I would've guessed. Clóvis keeps telling us to stay. Usually he can't wait to be rid of me. He pays me before the cotton even goes downriver. Now he says he doesn't have the money. That we should wait all these months."

Luzia's mouth felt dry. The revolver dangled heavily from her hand. "You're waiting until he pays you?" she asked. "You're risking the men for money?"

The Hawk looked up. The brow of his good eye furrowed. His slack eye was glassy, making it look large and childlike. Luzia saw a flash of sadness, of hurt, dart across the Hawk's face. Then he took a breath and closed his eyes. When they reopened, he seemed ancient and tired, as if he had never been a child at all.

"Money's useful," he said. "It's what Clóvis loves. I'll take as much of it as I can. If he loved his cattle or his goats as much, then I'd take those instead. He made a deal. I'm sure of that. I'm just not sure who with—Machado or the politicians. Either way, it doesn't matter. We'll stay and we'll surprise them. I want them to see that I know. That I knew all along."

"But you only have twenty men," Luzia said.

"We know how to fight here. They'll come through the front gate. As far as they know, this ranch has one entrance. And a place with one entrance is the same as a grave. I'm telling you because if they find you . . ." He paused and looked down. When he faced her again, he spoke forcefully. "They can't find you. You know what they do to women. So you'll have to shoot. Or you can leave now."

Luzia's hand tightened around the revolver's butt. She took a long breath but could not keep from trembling. He wanted attention. He wanted to make the front page of the *Diário de Pernambuco*. She had left her family. She had ruined her feet, her hands, her reputation. For what? To escape, yes. To see the world. To be anything but Victrola. This was what she'd told herself all of those months, during endless walks and chilly nights. But she realized now that she'd gone for the silliest reason of all: because of him. To be near him. She had never forgotten about her height or her crooked arm; had never allowed herself romantic ambitions. She didn't expect his love or even his interest. She'd simply wanted to watch him. To hear him call her name—her given name—and make it sound powerful and lovely. Now he told her that she could leave. That she held no value as a charm or as a woman.

"I will leave," she said.

The Hawk stood. "Where will you go?"

"Home."

"That wouldn't be good. No man will marry you."

"I don't want to marry."

"How will you live?"

"I'll sew."

"No one wants a cangaceira sewing their clothes."

"I'm not a cangaceira."

He jutted his chin toward the revolver in her hands. "You could kill me," he said. "Give me to the troops."

Luzia shook her head.

"Why not?" he asked, stepping toward her.

Her voice caught in her throat. She closed her eyes, furious with her body for betraying her.

"Why not?" he asked again, his voice a whisper.

"If you die, it will be God's doing. Not mine," Luzia said. "I may not be able to marry or be a seamstress. But you won't damn me. I won't let you."

The Hawk moved back. He stared at her as he'd stared at the saint's salt mounds, at his slips of prayer paper, at the makeshift crosses mounted on the walls of scrubland chapels—not with fear or desire, but with reverence.

Luzia handed him the revolver and ran.

5

Three years later, when she'd become a better shot than the Hawk himself, when President Celestino Gomes had started building his Trans-Nordestino Highway through the scrubland, when the drought was in its fourth long month, and when her legs ached and her feet swelled from carrying her third and final child, Luzia often wondered what would have happened if she'd left when he'd given her the chance. If she had run for the river instead of back to camp. If she had taken a barge and found her way to Recife, to the residence of the new bride, Miss Emília dos Santos Coelho. Luzia contemplated heading for the São Francisco, but she had no money for barge fare. She had no dress and no desire to wear one, either. She wanted to prove to him that she was not afraid. She would not leave simply because he had warned her. And she was curious. Luzia wanted to see if he was right, if the troops would come, and if they came, how he would beat them.

Two days after Luzia's shooting lesson, one of the colonel's vaqueiros finally warned them of Captain Higino's arrival. Colonel Clóvis and Marcos had left the day before on their cotton sales trip. The vaqueiro was herding cattle when he saw the brigade— the bright yellow lines still visible down the sides of their ripped uniforms. They were a forlorn bunch, with gaunt faces and slow, staggering walks. Their leader, he said, was a small man and the only one who moved quickly.

In the hours before the troops arrived, the Hawk and the other cangaceiros collected dried oricuri palm fronds. They arched the brown fronds in half, so that they resembled the half-moon shape of their hats. Then they placed the arched fronds in trees and stuffed them into termite mounds. He spread his men out, placing some inside the colonel's fenced property and others outside, beyond the colonel's front gate. The cangaceiros stationed before the gate would move in slowly, surrounding the soldiers in what the Hawk called a "retroguarda." They would force Higino's troops into the colonel's fenced yard, penning them in. The cangaceiros within the colonel's yard would stay at its periphery, ready to slide beneath the fence and into the scrub. The Hawk told his men to shoot barricaded behind rocks or trees, with their bellies to the ground. Then he ripped the brass-belled leather collars off twenty-two goats and handed them to his men. He gave one to Luzia.

"When I say so," the Hawk said, "put this on. Until then, stuff a cloth into the bell so it stays quiet."

It was dusk when the troops appeared on the road, marching as the Hawk had predicted, toward the front gate. The soldiers moved in several straight lines and kept their rifles pointed. The ranch house was quiet. Inside, the Hawk had left the lanterns lit. He and Luzia crouched at the far edge of the colonel's yard, near the entrance to the goat corral. The Hawk held tightly to her bent arm.

The setting sun made shadows fall across the scrub. From far away, the arched oricuri palms looked like motionless cangaceiros, dozens of them, scattered in the scrub. A startled soldier fired into the trees. The shot cracked. In the corral beside Luzia, goats bleated wildly. Quickly, the Hawk opened the corral door.

With the second and third shots from the soldiers, the frightened goats moved in a great, confused wave from their confinement. The animals pushed and bucked. Their brass bells clanged like a large, deranged band. There were more shots. Beside her, Luzia heard a high-pitched buzzing. It whisked past her and entered the corral post with a thump. The Hawk pushed her onto her stomach. Dust—dry and gritty—entered Luzia's mouth. The Hawk fastened a goat collar around his neck and ordered Luzia to do the same.

The other cangaceiros crouched and moved along the fence line beside the jumbled mass of goats. They, too, had put on the clanging collars, and in that shadowed dusk with the sound of so many bells, it was hard to tell man from animal.

The handful of cangaceiros outside the gates advanced, shooting at the soldiers from all angles and herding them inside the yard. The Hawk's men were an invisible enemy. Bullets came from everywhere, from nowhere. In the darkening evening, it was easy to confuse the oricuri palm decoys with real men. The troops divided frantically. Soldiers stumbled against one another. Some fell. Survivors from the first round of shots aimed their ancient rifles at goats, at trees.

"Fuck you cangaceiros!" a soldier yelled.

"Fuck your mother, monkey!" Ponta Fina, laughing, yelled back.

The Hawk released Luzia's arm. He aimed and cocked his Winchester. The rifle clicked, then discharged. After the blast, Luzia's ears felt as if they were filled with water. The men's yells seemed far away. Another rifle fired, then another. Luzia's revolver hung, heavy and useless, from the holster the Hawk had given her. She had not practiced her shooting, and in the midst of those clanging bells, that smoke, those horrible blasts, Luzia could only focus on crouching near the Hawk.

As night fell, a green glow came from their guns each time they shot, illuminating the men's faces. They lodged themselves behind corral posts, boulders, ipê trunks. They quickly uncocked their rifles and slipped more shells inside. Near her, Baiano cursed the hot barrel of his gun. He undid his trousers and crouched over the rifle. The gun's barrel sizzled. The smell of urine wafted through the dust and smoke. Baiano redid his trousers and took up the cooled Winchester.

Luzia did not know how long they shot and crawled. Her knees were chafed raw. Her leg muscles burned and shook each time she moved. The ringing in her ears was deafening. Finally, the Hawk let out a shrill whistle. He'd planned it this way, knowing that they could not eliminate all of the troops. The cangaceiros would slowly retreat, separating into pairs, crossing the river, and eventually meeting at the Marimbondo church. The place was an abandoned chapel on the Bahia side of the river. Red wasps had built their nests in the chapel's eaves, behind its altar, and beneath its broken pews; the church had become one huge hive. People rarely went near it, making the scrub surrounding the chapel a perfect hiding place.

Like the frantic goats, the cangaceiros shimmied beneath the lowest rung of the colonel's fence. The Hawk ripped off his belled collar and grabbed Luzia's. It was hard to see him in the dark, with so much smoke. She felt his fingers against her neck, tugging at the leather collar. When he finally pried it free, Luzia heard a familiar buzzing. A goat fell beside her. The Hawk froze. He took up his rifle. The buzzing whirred near them again, but when it stopped it thumped softly, like a fist against a pillow. The Hawk took a sharp breath. He staggered and gripped Luzia's hand.

6

A brittle net of branches crisscrossed their path. Dried vines coiled dark and snakelike around the trees. As they moved through the scrub, the Hawk leaned against Luzia. A sheen of sweat glistened on his face. His breath was quick and jagged. They moved slowly. The sky became the color of tin. Birds let out short, hesitant chirps, as if making certain they still had voices. When the sun rose, they were quiet again.

Luzia found shade under a spindly juazeiro. Earlier, the Hawk had slipped off his bornal bags and tied his jacket tightly around his injured calf. Blood had soaked through the canvas. It trickled into his alpercata, staining the sandal's leather and coating his foot. Luzia knelt beside him. She unbuttoned her jacket. She was embarrassed by the shirt she wore beneath it—she'd cut the bottom half from her old nightgown but still used the top. It was yellowed and fraying. Luzia did not let herself dwell on it; there was no time for vanity. She untied the stiff, blood-soaked jacket from his leg and replaced it with her own. The Hawk shuddered when she tied the sleeves tight.

"Here," he said, sliding his short peixeira from its sheath. "Use this. Bury the bloody jacket."

Luzia took the knife and began to dig. The Hawk coughed. His upper lip glistened with sweat. She wanted to run her thumb across it but stopped herself.

"The river's not far," he said. "About two hundred meters. We need to get across. We'll be safe in Bahia."

Luzia heard the São Francisco. She smelled it. They'd walked parallel to the river all night but had not gone near it, cautious of the remaining troops. They would move downstream until the Hawk deemed it safe to cross. When she finished burying the jacket, they split a chunk of dried meat. With shaking hands, the Hawk taught her how to carve open a monk's-head and eat its soft insides. Luzia wanted to clean his wound; she still had mercurochrome in her bornal from her first months in the scrub. The Hawk shook his head and insisted they keep moving.

He leaned on her throughout the day. Sometimes his skin burned. Other times, when she placed her hand against his neck, it was clammy and moist, like a frog's. By late afternoon he could not kneel but he still prayed, propping himself against a smooth-trunked tree and grabbing hold of his saints' medallions. When he was finished he slumped to the ground. Luzia pressed her water gourd to his mouth; fever made him thirsty. He drank and closed his eyes. His lips moved in prayer or perhaps delirium. Luzia could not tell which. He swallowed hard and spoke.

"When I was a boy, before they gave me this," he said, pointing to his scar, "I threw a rock at a beehive. It was a stupid thing to do. They were Italians, not uruçus, so they had stingers. I heard buzzing. I felt wings in my ears, my nose. Everywhere. Then it burned. Burned so bad. I slapped my arms, my neck. I felt them crunch under my hands, like it wasn't my skin anymore. It was some other skin. A skin of bees. People poured water on me. Carried me home. My mother promised my soul to every saint there was. The water, the neighbors, the prayer—I don't recall any of that. I only heard buzzing. That god-awful buzzing. I hear it now."

His voice grew fainter with each word. Afraid, Luzia leaned close to him. His rheumy eye was crusted and tearing. Luzia wiped it with a handkerchief. When his eyes suddenly fluttered open, she backed away. He grabbed hold of her hand.

"Do you know why I took you?" he asked.

His grip was not as firm as it had been before, when the bullet hit him and he'd pulled her into the scrub. Now he held her fingers lightly and Luzia wondered if it was out of weakness or affection.

"For luck," Luzia mumbled.

The Hawk gave her a slow, lopsided smile. " 'God help me.' That's what I thought when I first saw you on that ridge. 'God help me.' "

He moved his eyes away from Luzia's, staring instead at her hand in his. "Before I climbed that mountain to Taquaritinga, I'd been feeling this . . . this thing inside me. A dark thing. Bitter. Like I'd eaten a pile of cashew fruits. I was tired, that's all. Seemed everyone I came across wanted something from me. But not you. You looked at me on that ridge and didn't want a thing. Not mercy. Not money. Not protection.

"*God help me*, I thought. Then I didn't want to look at you anymore. I sent you away and I put my knife into those monkeys and capangas. I went to that damn colonel's house and ate and drank. Played accordion. Nothing helped. I felt worse than before. Agitated, like the bees were on me again. Chasing me. Stinging me. Making my skin burn. I couldn't sleep all that night. I had a colonel's feather bed and I couldn't sleep. I stood on that porch, looked over the town. Nothing seemed the way it should be. Even those goddamn bougainvilleas. I'd seen those flowers a hundred times in my life, but they were different that night. I couldn't explain it. All I could think was: where is she? Where's that seamstress? She's somewhere, sleeping, and I don't know where. I don't know if it's in a hammock or on a bed. If she's alone. If she's got a pillow under her head. I didn't know any of it. And it put me in a foul humor, not knowing. I wanted to know. I had to know. And not just that night, but all nights. So I took you."

Luzia let go of his hand. It was the most she'd ever heard him speak and she was ashamed by how eagerly she'd listened. "You didn't take me," she said roughly. "I left on my own."

The Hawk puffed air through his nose. He swallowed hard and closed his eyes. "I've had prettier women want to come with me," he said, "Lord knows I have."

Luzia wanted to shake him awake. He always did this: gave her a gleam of hope, brought her to the edge of belief, and then disappointed her.

She unwrapped her jacket from his leg. The wound had stopped bleeding but his calf was so swollen that his pants leg clung to it like a second skin. Luzia looked through his bornais and found the golden shaving set. She removed his beard scissors and carefully cut along the pant's seam. She loosened the trouser leg with water and then peeled it back. A brown and yellow crust covered the wound. Red, veinlike rays diffused around his calf. A sharp smell emerged. It reminded Luzia of rust mixed with a heady sweetness, like the smell of a meat market in the afternoon, when all of the prime cuts were sold and only the discolored, fly-ridden scraps remained. Luzia searched his bornal. She found salt and malagueta peppers left over from their time at Clóvis's, when he didn't trust anyone's seasoning but his own. Luzia recalled Lia and how the girl had made a paste of ashes, malagueta, and salt to heal a newborn goat's freshly cut umbilical cord. They did not have ashes but Luzia mashed the peppers and salt. The malaguetas made her eyes water. When the paste was ready, she poured mercurochrome onto the wound. The Hawk jolted awake. He gasped. Luzia held down his leg. The left side of his face twitched uncontrollably. The medicine loosened the wound's crust and Luzia picked it off. The hole was as wide and round as a spool of thread. It had swollen pink edges. One palm down from the wound, beneath the striped red skin of his calf, was a massive lump. Luzia poured mercurochrome into the hole. The Hawk cursed and shuddered. She tamped the wound with the salt and pepper paste and wrapped it with a sewing rag. The Hawk slumped back, exhausted.

Inside his bornal, along with his gold shaving kit, she found his binoculars, his prayer papers, and a dozen rolls of mil-réis notes. There was enough to buy ten pedal-operated Singers, enough to buy a motorcar, a fine meal, a doctor's care. But those bills were worthless in the scrub. All of his gold rings, all of his saints' medallions and shaving sets could not rescue them. Luzia placed a water gourd beside him. She combed her hair with her fingers and rebraided it. Her hands were stained pink from the mercurochrome but she had no way of cleaning them. She snapped the long, shining revolver back into her shoulder holster, took a roll of mil-réis from his bag, and made her way toward the river.

7

There were several large properties along the São Francisco; wealthy ranchers prized the land near the river because water was always available. Luzia didn't want to set foot on those ranches, however, afraid they were harboring troops. Fishermen's shacks also dotted the riverbanks; outside one shack was a donkey. The animal chewed palma cactus beneath a tin-roofed corral. There were two boats beside the clay shack: a long canoe and a flat-bottomed raft, both grounded on the shore. Near the raft, a heavyset woman slapped laundry on river rocks. She stood ankle deep in water and scrubbed forcefully.

Luzia watched from the scrub as the cangaceiros used to do,

looking for any sign of soldiers. She saw none. She inspected her pink hands, her bloodstained shirt, her trousers. For an instant, Luzia worried about what the washerwoman would think of her. She shook her head; she had no time for shyness or shame. Soon, the sun would set, making it hard to find her way. Luzia tugged her leather shoulder holster under her armpit, trying to conceal the revolver. She moved forward. The woman looked up from her washing. When she saw Luzia, the wet shirt she'd been scrubbing fell from her hand, plopping into the water. She froze. Her expression was a mixture of fright and astonishment, as if a spotted panther had stepped from the scrub. The woman opened her mouth. Luzia stepped closer and raised her hands.

"Please," she said. "I need help." She kept her shoulders back and her voice steady. "My . . . husband, he's hurt. I can't move him by myself."

The woman shouted a man's name. Her voice was shrill and loud. The man who emerged from the clay-and-stick house was a typical backlands type—short and thickly built, with tan skin and dark hair. The washerwoman moved from the water and stood beside him. Luzia repeated her request. He stared at her for a long while, his expression stern.

"Have mercy," Luzia said, unable to keep her voice from cracking.

The fisherman nodded. "Let me get my mule," he replied.

He tied a rope bridle around the animal's snout and followed Luzia into the scrub. When they reached the Hawk, he was still slumped against the tree trunk. His skin was pasty and yellowed, the color of a spoiled egg. The fisherman scanned the body, the bandaged leg.

"He's alive," Luzia said. "Just hurt. We need to get across the river."

The fisherman looked up to the sky, as if seeking guidance. He sighed. "You'll have to help me load him."

Together, they heaved the Hawk onto the mule. His eyes opened only once, when Luzia accidentally bumped his calf. They placed him stomach side down over the mule's bare back. The animal was short legged; the Hawk's feet nearly brushed the ground. The fisherman led the animal slowly while Luzia walked beside it, gripping the Hawk's arm. His body slipped back and forth across the animal's back. Once, they stopped to rearrange him. At the shore, they carried him onto the flat-bottomed raft and wrapped him in a blanket. Luzia could not see the other side of the river—everything was blurred. The fisherman steered them across, dipping a long pole into and out of the water.

The setting sun was bright and the river shone beneath it, like Colonel Clóvis's yellow silk. The raft bobbed and shook, making Luzia queasy. Water sprayed her trousers. The shore on the Bahia side was rocky and uneven. As soon as they'd grounded the boat, the fisherman whistled. A young man emerged from a lone shack. Luzia forced herself to stand as tall as she could. She kept her stance wide, like a man's, and did not lower her eyes when the young man approached.

"He needs treatment," she said, pointing to the wrapped body on the raft.

"There's a ranch near here," the young man replied quietly, keeping his eyes down. "It's got a doctor, a real one. I can show you."

They placed the Hawk on top of the young man's mare. Then the old fisherman stepped back onto his raft. Luzia stopped him. She took the roll of mil-réis notes from her bornal and offered it to him. The fisherman shook his head.

"I helped because I'm a man of God. I don't want trouble." He pointed to the roll of bills. "A man who takes stolen money is no better than a thief himself."

Then he turned and pushed his boat onto the river.

8

Luzia expected an animal doctor or a curandeiro living in a shack filled with dried herbs and bark scrapings. When the young man led her to the gate of a large white ranch house, Luzia grew suspicious. She would not move past the gate.

"Have him come out here," she said, grabbing the mare's reins. "I won't go in until I see him."

She stood beside the gate's pillars, wondering nervously if the mare could take both her weight and the Hawk's. He lay belly side down, like a corpse, on the horse's back. A middle-aged man emerged from the house with a kerosene lantern in his hand. He did not look like a colonel or a soldier. He was very thin, with hunched shoulders and a curving neck, as if his head weighed more than his body could carry. His hair was wet and lank over his ears. He wore a pressed shirt and brass-rimmed spectacles that shone like jewelry on his face. The lenses magnified his eyes, making them look round and bulging, like a newborn bird's. He held the lantern high and addressed Luzia.

"You've interrupted my supper," he said.

Luzia pointed to the mare behind her. "He's shot."

"I'm sorry. I do not treat animals," the man replied.

"He's no animal," Luzia said, angry with the doctor's impatience. She took the lantern from his hand and shone it over the horse. When the doctor saw the blanket-covered body, he opened the gate and motioned her inside.

They placed the Hawk on a long wooden table in the doctor's kitchen. An elderly maid set a cauldron of water on the cookstove. When it boiled, the doctor dropped a set of metal instruments in it. The doctor filled another basin, rolled up his sleeves, and washed his hands. Like his head, they were exceptionally pale and large. When he finished, he unwrapped the Hawk's injured leg. The old bandage stuck to the wound. The doctor slowly loosened it, then pulled firmly to yank it off. The Hawk flinched. He opened his eyes and tried to sit. The doctor pushed him down.

"Your leg is infected," he said, hunching near the Hawk's face. "I'm going to clean it and take out whatever is lodged inside."

The Hawk stared around the room. When he caught sight of Luzia, he relaxed. The doctor uncorked a bottle of sugarcane liquor and propped up the Hawk's head.

"Drink this," he ordered.

The left side of the Hawk's mouth fell in a frown. "You drink first," he said, his voice raspy and weak.

The doctor moved the bottle closer to the Hawk's mouth. "There's no advantage in poisoning you. I could do nothing and you'd die just the same. Now drink."

The Hawk stared at the man, then at Luzia. He gulped the cane liquor until it dribbled down the edges of his mouth. Then he coughed and lay back.

"I'm going to turn you over," the doctor said. "We'll have to tie down your legs and arms."

He motioned to Luzia and the two of them rolled the Hawk onto his stomach. The elderly maid quickly knotted kitchen towels together and handed them to the doctor, who tied the Hawk's ankles and wrists firmly to the legs of the table.

"You," the doctor said, addressing Luzia for the first time since they'd entered the kitchen, "hold down his shoulders and his head. I can't have him bucking."

The maid collected ten lanterns from the rest of the house and placed them in the kitchen. They hissed and sputtered. The room glowed with light. Luzia leaned over the Hawk's head. His face was turned sideways, scarred side down. His eyes were open. On account of her locked arm, Luzia leaned forward and placed her forearms firmly on his shoulder blades. The Hawk took shallow, ragged breaths. Each time he exhaled, Luzia smelled cane liquor.

The doctor poured iodine on his hands, then cleaned the Hawk's leg. When he took up his instruments, Luzia looked down. She stared at the Hawk's stained tunic, at his matted hair. Around them, the lanterns quickly heated the kitchen. Luzia felt as if she was back in the scrub at midday. Sweat stung her eyes. The smell of kerosene made her dizzy. Beneath her, the Hawk's body stiffened. His torso reared up. His arms pulled at their cloth ties.

"Distract him!" the doctor snapped. His face was flushed, his eyes huge. His shirt stuck to his chest.

Luzia leaned in farther, pressing more weight on his back. She bowed her head, her mouth nearly touching his hair. She did not know what to say or how to speak to him. She could only think of his pain, and how, to a small degree, she understood it.

"When I was a girl," she began, "I fell from a tree . . ."

The doctor resumed his probing. The Hawk stiffened again. Luzia raised her voice. She told him about the mango tree, about the silence after her fall, about the encanadeira's butter balm and the sour smell it left on her. She told him about Emília, about the saints' closet in Aunt Sofia's kitchen, about the promise she'd made to Saint Expedito and the dents she'd left in the dirt floor. The Hawk's body relaxed.

There was the sound of metal clinking against a porcelain bowl. Then there was the pop of a cork, the hiss of carbolic acid cauterizing the wound, and the smell of burnt hair. The doctor sighed. Beneath her, the Hawk shuddered and went limp.

9

Dr. Eronildes Epifano was from the capital city of Salvador, on the coast of Bahia. He'd been trained in medicine at the Federal University but he'd abandoned his practice and bought a vast plot of land along the São Francisco River.

"He was heartsick," Eronildes' maid whispered. She smoked a corncob pipe and shifted it from side to side between her dark gums. Dr. Eronildes had had a fiancée in Salvador, the elderly maid continued, but the girl caught dengue fever and he could not cure her. After she died he left the city, disgusted with life. He still kept a large portrait of the girl on his mantel. Luzia had seen it when they'd entered the house. The girl was long necked and exceptionally pale.

"White!" the old maid laughed. "Like a tapuru!"

Luzia shuddered. She wasn't fond of insects, especially those translucent white worms that burrowed into guava fruits. The maid handed Luzia a perfumed cake of soap and a washcloth. There was a metal washtub in the center of Dr. Eronildes' guest room. The maid had filled it with steaming water. The room was spare, with only a sturdy wooden bed and a dressing stand with a mirror. That night, after the Hawk's operation, they'd moved him to a small room beside the kitchen. He slept on a vaqueiro cot, made of cowhide stretched across four wooden poles. Luzia had slept on the ground beside him. She hadn't realized how tired she was until she lay down. Every muscle seemed to pulse beneath her skin. She'd slept past sunrise, when the maid shook her and told her she had to bathe. Dr. Eronildes insisted on it.

Luzia had no parasites. The cangaceiros had a remedy for lice: a paste made of crushed pinha seeds and pequi oil that they slathered on their heads and exposed to the sun. Still, Luzia did not object to Eronildes' orders; it had been months since she'd had a real bath. In the scrub, she'd become accustomed to washing quickly and stealthily, rolling up her pants legs as far as they would go and splashing water on herself, then squatting, untying her trousers, and doing the same. When it came to her upper body she kept her tunic on and maneuvered beneath it, whisking water onto her underarms, her chest, her back. When water was scarce, she had not bathed at all.

Eronildes' elderly maid did not leave the guest room. She sat on a small stool with her back to the tub and talked while Luzia bathed. The maid was eager to speak to another woman, even if it was a cangaceira in trousers. Occasionally, the old woman peeked over her shoulder. When Luzia spied her, the maid quickly turned around. Luzia wasn't angry about the old woman's curiosity. She, too, was curious about herself. On the wall before her, the dressing table's mirror hung large and round. Luzia saw herself in its glass. The mirror revealed that she looked like a poorly made rag doll—her hands and feet and face one color, the rest of her another. A red rash ran along the insides of her thighs, where her trousers chafed her. Her hair was tangled and light at the tips. Her cheeks and nose were freckled in the places where the skin had burned and peeled. Her eyes looked greener now that her face had darkened. Her breasts were small, the nipples the same tan color as her hands. There were calluses on her shoulders, small ones, from the bornais and the water gourds. Her hip bones jutted from beneath her skin, reminding her of the mother goats she'd seen, their hides stretched thinly over their hips from the weight of their udders. Below her darkened neckline, her collarbones formed a deep V.

When Luzia finished, the maid handed her a flowered bundle.

"It's a dress," the old woman said. "It's not right for a woman to wear trousers. It's not the Lord's intention."

Luzia's trousers were dirty and stained with blood. The dress was big around the waist and short at the hem, but it would have to do. Afterward, Luzia and the maid carried a basin of hot water to the Hawk's bedside. The maid propped him up. He moaned but did not wake. Blood crusted his hands. A smear of dirt ran down his neck. The maid tried to remove his soiled tunic but she could not hold him up alone.

"No time for shyness, girl," the old woman snapped, her pipe still bobbing in her mouth. "Help me."

Luzia pulled off his tunic. His skin was hot with fever. The maid took a sharp peixeira and cut off what remained of his stained trousers. Beneath them, he wore small canvas shorts. The maid handed Luzia a bundle of rags and a cake of soap.

"You have to tend to him," she said. "I have my own work to do."

The old woman scooped up his soiled clothes and left. Luzia stared at the doorway, then at the steaming basin. The water would grow cold if she didn't start soon. He would catch a chill. She took a deep breath. She would wash him as she had measured the dead in Taquaritinga: quickly and efficiently, looking at pieces and not the whole. She began with his saints' medallions, untangling the red strings and gold chains. The Hawk stirred but did not wake. Luzia moved a wet cloth around his eyes, down the mashed bridge of his nose, around his white scar, along his tanned neck.

Luzia held tightly to the washrag. She did not let it slip from her fingers. There were parts of him that were dark: his hands, his fat fingers, his ankles and feet. The skin was thick and ridged, like the peel of an orange. There were other parts that had not been exposed to the sun and thorns of the scrub. The small of his back, the insides of his legs, the undersides of his arms were all pale and soft, like the skin of a child. His nipples were small and round, with a purplish tinge, as if two berries had been placed on his chest. There were hairs, some golden and downy, others black and thick, like thread. Around his waist, at the place where his cartridge belt usually sat, the skin was darker and calloused. The belt had rubbed the skin raw, making a ring around him. There were other scars, too. Some were shining and round, like coins. Others were star shaped and ragged edged, like macambira plants. And many were tiny and misshapen— insect bites that had been scratched too many times. Or perhaps they were the bee stings he'd received as a child.

Luzia pushed aside the washrag. She pressed her fingertip to one of those round bites.

Once, long ago, she'd flipped though Emília's *Fon Fon* magazines. She'd read the silly prayers, the recipes and magic tricks. All were designed to win a man's heart. The heart, they said, was the instrument of love. Luzia did not believe any of it. She'd seen plenty of hearts; she'd held them in her hands. A cow's was as big as a newborn baby's head. A chicken's was tear shaped and rubbery, the size of a cajá fruit. A goat's was in between, like a miniature mango. No matter what their size, they were all thick and muscular. They were built for work, for efficiency, not love.

When she was a girl, Aunt Sofia had taught her how to gut chickens. Her aunt had always warned Luzia about a small organ, the size of a fingernail, attached to the kidneys. It was green and slick. Aunt Sofia did not know what it was called or why it existed. If you left it in the animal or if you punctured it, the meat was ruined. It soured everything. Luzia had always wondered if such an organ existed in men and women. Now, she knew it must. That organ—frail, glistening, dangerous—was the opposite of a heart. It, Luzia believed, was the instrument of love.

"He has an amazing wound."

Dr. Eronildes stood in the doorway. Luzia yanked her finger from the Hawk's leg and took up the washcloth. The doctor stepped closer. He wore perfume, but not the strong scent of the cangacieros' Fleur d'Amour. Eronildes smelled soapy and crisp, like a starched shirt.

"Do you know how he acquired it?" the doctor asked, pushing his spectacles up the bridge of his nose.

"He was shot," Luzia replied. "You saw the bullet."

His interruption had flustered her and she accidentally addressed him as "you," and not as "senhor" or even "doctor."

"I don't mean his leg," Eronildes continued, unfazed. "I mean his face. The scar." Eronildes leaned closer. The Hawk shifted in his feverish sleep. "It goes near his ear. I think they partially severed the facial nerve, but not entirely. That's why he still has limited movement in his right brow and mouth. If they'd severed it completely, he wouldn't speak normally."

Luzia wrung out the washcloth. The water in the washbasin was brown. She would have to heat more—she hadn't even washed the Hawk's hair. Dr. Eronildes stepped back from the bed. He wore knee-high leather boots, like a colonel.

"He's a famous man, this Hawk. I subscribe to *A Tarde*, the Bahian daily, and the *Diário de Pernambuco*. The riverboat delivers them. They had a blurb on him recently. Now my farmhands tell me there was a skirmish over in São Tomé, on Colonel Clóvis's land. It seems that there are troops looking for him. And you, too?"

Luzia nodded. Dr. Eronildes fidgeted with a loose thread on his trouser pocket.

"Don't worry," he said. "You're in Bahia now. I don't want Pernambucan troops snooping around here. Our governors aren't friendly, you know. Ours is a fan of Gomes."

He looked away from Luzia and placed a pale hand on the Hawk's throat, then his forehead.

"He has a fever. He's fortunate though—the bullet didn't go clean through. Those shots make a small entrance but they tear up everything when they exit. He could have lost his leg. We'll have to keep it clean. I'll tell my maid, Honorata, to feed him quixabeira tea every hour, to flush out the infection." Eronildes looked at Luzia. His large eyes settled briefly on her wet hair, her new dress. He cleared his throat. "I'll also tell Honorata to set another place for lunch. I rarely have visitors. I'd appreciate the company."

Before Luzia could object, the doctor strode out, his boots clicking upon the wooden floor.

10

For lunch, the old servant cooked a freshly caught surubim, its fins sharp and its body striped like a wildcat. Luzia had never eaten fresh fish, only dried cod on Easter. She wasn't accustomed to plates, either. At Aunt Sofia's house they'd eaten their beans and cornmeal in bowls. A plate was too flat, too slick. Everything placed on it was hard to scoop. Luzia had forgotten to bring the Hawk's silver spoon and stared warily at the steaming white mass on her plate. Even the toasted manioc flour and brown beans looked sinister. Dr. Eronildes stared at her, waiting for his guest to take a bite before he began. Luzia took up her fork. She stabbed at the fish, but it was slimy with butter and would not stick to the prongs. Eating with a gentleman was exasperating. She'd never been at a gentleman's table and wondered why Dr. Eronildes had invited her. It was clear she was no lady. She should be in the kitchen with the maid, or sitting beside the Hawk's bed waiting for him to wake. Luzia heard Emília's voice, clear and haughty, in her mind: the doctor was gracious and cultured and Luzia should appreciate his gesture. Luzia shifted her feet, as if kicking her sister's presence away. Perhaps it was gracious, but she would rather be in the smoky kitchen than trapped behind that long, linen-covered table.

"You don't like surubim?" Dr. Eronildes asked.

"I want a bowl," Luzia said. She pursed her lips. Her months with the cangaceiros had ruined her manners. She'd forgotten to add "please" or "thank you," and by the time she'd remembered, it was too late; Dr. Eronildes had already told the maid to exchange Luzia's place setting.

"I hope you don't mind my noting," he said, "but you have amazingly healthy teeth for a woman of the *campo*. How do you keep them from spoiling?"

"It's juá," Luzia replied. "I chew juá bark."

Dr. Eronildes' eyes widened. He took a miniature pencil and a small, leather-bound notebook from his vest pocket and began to scribble.

"Juá! Wonderful!" he exclaimed. "I'll have to find the plant's scientific name." He looked up from his writing. "I'm trying to evaluate the medicinal properties of caatinga flora, you see. My mother insists that there is nothing worthwhile here, but where she sees desert, I see commerce."

Luzia nodded. The cangaceiros had taught her about juá. She thought of Ponta Fina, Baiano, Intéligente, and Canjica. Had they been hurt? Had they found the meeting place? If so, they would wait for the Hawk, but not forever.

"How long before he can walk again?" Luzia asked.

Eronildes blinked. His eyes were magnified by his lenses, his lashes dark and thick. "Oh!" he sighed. "You mean our patient. He was lucky. The bullet went through muscle but no bone. It hit him in the meatiest part of his calf. Still, it should be several weeks before he's up and about, no sooner."

"I'll have to get word to his men," Luzia said.

"You'll have to do that after he recovers," Eronildes said, straightening his glasses.

"They won't wait that long," Luzia replied. "They'll come looking for him."

"I can't allow that," Eronildes said. "I would rather not have his gang here."

"You saved him. They won't hurt you."

"I'm not frightened," Eronildes said. He stabbed the miniature pencil back into his notebook and slapped it shut. "For the past three years, I've been neighbors with a colonel who's vowed to castrate me, brand me, send me back to Salvador in a coffin. I'm not afraid of a colonel and I'm certainly not afraid of a few cangaceiros!"

He pursed his lips and his breath escaped loudly through his nose. His skin became flushed and blotchy, as if he'd touched an urtiga bush. He stuffed two large forkfuls of fish into his mouth.

"I'm sorry," Luzia said. "You've been very kind. I don't think you're afraid. If they came here, the men would behave. They'd be quiet. They just need to know he's recovering." Luzia paused and thought of the saints—how they appreciated a gift, a favor or a sacrifice in trade for their kindnesses. Perhaps men were no different. "They can help you," she said. "In your feud with that colonel. They can make it so he won't bother you again."

Eronildes put down his fork.

"I don't want that kind of help," he said. "When I came here, I resolved to set an example. My workers thought I was a twit because I didn't threaten them or beat them. Here, the only language is violence. You have to be a cabra macho. But I won't abide that. You see, Miss Luzia, the reason I'm having trouble with my neighbor the colonel is because, unlike him, I pay my laborers fairly. So after their initial hesitation and making fun, people preferred to work for me and not for him. I have some of his best vaqueiros now. I have his best farmhands. They sneaked away. He killed some after they'd come over to my side, of course. But that didn't stop others. What he and your cangaceiros don't understand is that commerce will be the great liberator. Commerce will take away his power better than a gun will. So I don't need your hooligans here, causing me trouble."

"They're not hooligans," Luzia said. "They'll come whether you like it or not."

"Let them come then!" Eronildes yelled. He slapped the dining table with his long, pale hand. Their water glasses shook and spilled over. "Let them drag him out of here for all I care!"

Eronildes grabbed his tumbler and gulped the amber liquid in it. Luzia stayed quiet. If Emília were there, her sister would have given her a good kick under the table. The doctor sighed and hunched into his chair. With a tremulous hand, he pushed back his glasses.

"Forgive my outburst," he said. "I don't like to lose my temper. I have nothing against your cangaceiros. I would almost respect them if they weren't just petty thieves."

"They steal for necessity," Luzia said, her hands bunched into fists, her face hot. She knew this was a lie but could not shake the possibility of the Hawk waking and listening from the little room near the kitchen. What would he say if she did not defend him?

Eronildes laughed. His teeth were long and stained, like pale kernels of corn.

"Necessity!" He chuckled. "Those gold rings I saw were a necessity? And those necklaces?" He shook his head. "What a waste. What a great waste. The rebellious men are thieves and the rest are led, like animals on a tether, by the colonels. The Northerner will never be a modern man until we educate the whole lot." Eronildes pointed toward the kitchen door. "That man in there, I'm betting he's a smart one. He has to be, to have made a life in the scrub for so long. If he had been properly educated, he wouldn't be in the predicament he's in now."

"He knows how to read," Luzia said.

"That doesn't make an educated man," Eronildes replied. "A man must think things through, not reach for a knife. He must see the consequences of his actions. He must forget superstition and belief. He must realize that we are not wards of divinity, but citizens of a state, a nation."

Luzia stared at her plate. Some of Eronildes' words confused her. Others angered her. She mashed the fish back and forth in her bowl. *Don't be a matuta,* Emília would chide, had she been present. *Nod your head. Be polite. Agree.* But Emília wasn't there and Luzia could not hold her tongue.

"I think people need schooling, too. A priest taught me to read, to write, to look at maps and do sums. I'm glad of it. But with schooling, people want to make something of themselves and there's nothing here to be but a maid or a vaqueiro or a cangaceiro. Who wants to be any of those things? With schooling, they'll want to go to the capital."

"Not many," Eronildes contested. "Salvador is far away. So is Recife. And they're different worlds. There are no goats, no caatinga. The capitals are all coastline and clutter. People will want to stay with what they know."

"Not with schooling," she said. "They'll want to know more. They'll want to be doctors, like you."

Eronildes laughed. "I admire your vision," he said. "But I think you're taking my idea of education too far."

"Why?"

"People won't want that much. Most will want to read and to vote. Nothing more."

"That's like giving a bird a larger cage, just to stretch its wings," Luzia said.

Eronildes smiled. "That's good. Where did you learn that saying?"

"From my aunt Sofia."

"Well, I learned a saying from my father: Those born as parakeets will never be parrots."

Luzia stared at her food. It was cold and she was not hungry. She wanted Emília beside her. Her sister always knew how to comport herself. Emília always said the right things, and was wise enough not to insist on unpleasant conversation.

Dr. Eronildes arranged his utensils in a neat diagonal on his plate. He placed his napkin on the table.

"You're quite direct," he said. "I appreciate that. You know, if we rebroke that arm of yours and set it again, it might work properly. The elbow is a tricky joint, but it is not impossible."

Luzia slid her bent arm off the table.

"It's fine," she said. "I'm used to it."

11

The month of May brought a series of fleeting rainstorms. Each day, Dr. Eronildes' elderly maid prayed to São Pedro. Farmhands made bets about when the rains would fall and how long they would last. Along the São Francisco, fishermen frantically planted their roçados of beans, pumpkin, and manioc. The rains arrived, but they disappeared quickly. The crops were weak. Still, people thanked their saints by making fires and setting up altars because a little food was better than none at all. Even Dr. Eronildes expressed gratitude for the weak rains, though he did not pray. The only time he was silent and worshipful was in the evenings, when he sat before the pale girl's portrait in his front room. Slowly, when the Hawk was well enough to move about, he sat beside Eronildes and took sips of the White Horse whiskey the doctor had shipped from Salvador. In the beginning, the doctor quizzed his patient on medicinal plants. The Hawk rattled off a series of remedies and Dr. Eronildes feverishly wrote them down, his pale bride temporarily forgotten.

Their conversations quickly strayed beyond barks and teas. Luzia sewed nearby and grew distracted, constantly pricking her finger with the embroidery needle Eronildes had given her. She worried that the men would argue, that the Hawk would lose his temper and that Dr. Eronildes would stop offering his care. But the man who lost his temper most was the doctor, while the Hawk smiled and sipped his drink. He looked at Eronildes with amused admiration, as one would look on a puppy or a younger sibling—something harmless and sweet yet intent on having its way. Eronildes bristled at this treatment but tolerated it because he, in return, respected the Hawk. Luzia could not determine if Eronildes' admiration was for the Hawk himself or simply for his resilient body and its ability to withstand the doctor's daily prodding and cleanings. He called him "Antônio," not "Hawk" or "Captain," or even "sir." To Luzia's surprise, the Hawk did not correct him. Eronildes was not a colonel or a rancher or a vaqueiro; he was another creature altogether, immune from the caatinga's rules.

"You're like a priest," the Hawk said, making Dr. Eronildes frown. The doctor's displeasure drove the Hawk on. "You both save lives."

"No, Antônio," Eronildes replied. "Priests don't save. They feed fears. I'm wary of men who serve invisible masters. I serve bodies. I serve what is real, what is tangible. What is proven."

"Nothing's proven," the Hawk replied, moving a mandacaru thorn between his teeth. "Except death."

Luzia looked up from her sewing. Eronildes, pale and hunched, puffed impatiently on a cigarette. Beside him, the Hawk picked his teeth. His short, sturdy leg was propped on a wooden stool. His face was still tan, despite his time away from the caatinga sun. Between them, looking down from her portrait, Eronildes' bride looked languid and bored, as if she was tired of their arguing.

Their evenings became more animated after Dr. Eronildes received his newspapers. Once a month he traveled downriver to pick up his supplies shipped from Salvador. Since they could not be delivered daily, his newspapers accumulated and arrived in large bundles tied with string, their pages wet and torn, with some sections pilfered by curious riverboat captains. Still, it took Dr. Eronildes days to read through all of the papers. The Hawk sat beside him and read what the doctor had discarded. Or pretended to. Later, in the quiet of his room, he asked Luzia to look through the papers again, to catch anything he'd missed. Luzia liked sitting beside him, alone in that dim room without Eronildes' interruptions. She was glad the Hawk was awake and alert, but she secretly missed the time when he was feverish and sleepy and she could stare at him in peace. After the Hawk recovered, Eronildes rarely let them be alone, pressing them with questions.

Luzia appreciated the doctor, but for all of his generosity and goodwill, she could not like him. She grew tired of his constant scribbling and note taking, as if her actions and observations were subjects of an experiment she knew nothing about. On the eve of São João, when Eronildes distributed corn to his workers and allowed them to build bonfires and play an accordion, Luzia sat with the Hawk and the doctor on his porch and watched the festivities from afar. Luzia squinted. She could see only the glow of the fire and the shadows of the men and women dancing. When she looked away, she caught Eronildes observing her instead of the bonfire. The next day, when the Hawk was resting, Dr. Eronildes invited her into his study. There were stacks of books, a magnifying glass, and a large black writing board fastened to the wall. The board was dull with chalk dust. Across it, Eronildes had written letters, ranging from large to small. Then he told Luzia to stand at the far end of the room and read them aloud. She crossed her arms.

"I know my letters," she said, unwilling to move.

"Then prove it," he said, smiling.

Luzia stalked to the other end of the room and called out the large top letters but the bottom ones were blurs.

"It's all right," Eronildes assured her. "Without my spectacles, I couldn't read any of these."

Luzia nodded and watched him scribble notes in his book. The Hawk called Eronildes "a gentle soul," and despite their disagreements he respected the doctor, preferring a man who had opinions to one who had none. Luzia agreed: Eronildes was a good man. Plainly good. He invited them to his table, he never raised his voice, never treated her like a servant. But receiving his goodness felt like being under a very bright light—the warmth was comforting at first but it soon became stifling, glaring, with everything exposed and stark. Luzia preferred the Hawk's presence. She liked entering his little room beside the kitchen, where it was dark and cool. It took time for her eyes to adjust, and even when they did, even when she could see the outlines of his vaqueiro's cot, his misshapen hat hanging on a peg in the wall, his chest rising and falling, there were still shadows. But looking up from his bed, he, too, would not be able to see her entirely. He would see only her outline, and would have to imagine the rest.

In the early mornings, when the sun was still cool, they took walks along the riverbank to exercise his leg. Eronildes discouraged the walks at first, saying that dust and sand would dirty the Hawk's wound and reinfect it. It was better to rest, Eronildes insisted, to stay in bed. The Hawk would not have it.

"I'm not afraid of dying standing up, in the scrub," he said, "but God help me, I won't die in a bed."

Reluctantly, Eronildes outfitted him with a pair of wooden crutches. The Hawk swung his body forward between them. Sometimes he tried to put weight on his leg, then drew back in pain. Luzia stayed close beside him, steadying him whenever his stride became too long and he lost his balance. The Hawk brushed her away. He looked at Luzia harshly when she interfered, as if he would have preferred to fall.

Once they'd walked far enough away from Eronildes' house, they practiced shooting. They started each lesson using his slingshot, aiming at lizards, rolinha doves, butterflies, and beetles. If she squinted hard enough, Luzia could hit her target. At the end of her practice, the Hawk handed her the revolver. Luzia admired the gun. She liked inspecting the chamber and clicking back the safety and knowing that any of those small and seemingly meaningless parts could paralyze the entire machine. She grew to love the loud crack of a shot and, afterward, the force of its jolt. Luzia liked the way it moved her, but the Hawk did not.

"Get this in your head," he said. "Taking a shot without meaning to kill can kill all the same. So you'd better aim right."

His words frightened her but his voice didn't. It was stern but never angry. And each time he arranged the revolver in her hands, he was gentle, wrapping her fingers around the butt as if preparing her for prayer. At the end of each lesson, when they walked back to Eronildes' house, Luzia let him walk ahead of her, swinging determinedly between his crutches. She watched him balance and hop. He stopped before a tree. It was gray and leafless, like all of the scrub trees that didn't border the river. He twisted off a twig, and when he saw the green marrow inside, he nodded, reassured.

When they returned, Eronildes was waiting. He held a newspaper in his hand. He'd recently picked up his new batch and had spent his days reading. The Hawk lifted his crutches onto the porch, then swung his body up. Eronildes handed him the newspaper.

"I think they've written about you," Eronildes said. "Nothing good, of course."

The Hawk snatched for the paper. He nearly lost his balance. Luzia steadied him and read over his shoulder. It was an outdated edition, over a month old.

Diário de Pernambuco / *Recife* / *June 23, 1929*
Troublesome Cangaceiro Evades Troops

In the backlands, perversity reigns.

Captain Higino Ribeiro, one of the few survivors of a cangaceiro ambush near São Tomé this past April, has finally returned to Recife. Despite his loss, the captain asserts that he will not be deterred. "The Vulture is a bandit of the worst class," Captain Higino declared, "and I am committed to catching him."

"The Vulture," as he is popularly called in the backlands, invaded the ranch of Colonel Clóvis Lucena in December. Mr. Marcos Lucena reported that the cangaceiros dominated the ranch for four months before aid arrived. Wanted for previous atrocities committed in Fidalga, including the slaying of seven innocent men and the terrorization of the town's residents, "the Vulture" sought asylum in São Tomé. There, his audacity and ferocity did not diminish. He used perverse tactics to lure and trap Pernambucan troops. Reports indicate that the cangaceiros were colorfully adorned and were accompanied by a female consort.

The conditions that create the development of brigandage of this caliber are easily summed up: they are 1) poor administration by our leaders and 2) the possession of convenient hiding places. It is hard to stomach, but these malefactors are celebrated among the residents of distant farms, far from civilized lands. As Pernambucans, we cannot give prestige or protection to groups of popular bandits, men without scruples or faith.

Our leaders lead a weak campaign against banditry. Will only elections change the current state? When will the martyrdom of our fine, uniformed boys end? Why, this reporter asks, must we continue to lose them in those ungrateful backlands?

12

The Hawk stopped their morning walks. He did not debate with Eronildes in the evenings. At night, as Luzia lay in the guest bedroom, she heard the thumps of crutches against the wood floor and then a slow, dragging jump, as if a three-legged beast was pacing back and forth in the little room beside the kitchen.

When the Hawk finally spoke, he told Eronildes that he'd spent enough time convalescing. He was going to meet his men. Dr. Eronildes insisted that the leg had not healed and if the Hawk left, all of his work would have been in vain. When the Hawk persisted, Eronildes sat on the porch alone and smoked several cigarettes before returning to the room beside the kitchen.

"Tell your men to come here," Eronildes said, his voice low. "But tell them to comport themselves."

"They aren't animals," the Hawk replied. "You are a friend and we treat friends with respect. The sooner they arrive, the sooner you'll be free of me." He looked at Luzia, then back toward the doctor. "Of us."

The Hawk asked for a notecard and a fountain pen. With slow, awkward strokes, he scrawled his signature, *Captain Antônio*, on the card and wrapped it in his green neck scarf. Luzia sewed the bundle into the lining of a plain bornal belonging to Eronildes' vaqueiro. The man put the bag over his shoulder and set out for the Marimbondo church.

Weeks later, nine men returned with the vaqueiro: Baiano, Canjica, Inteligente, Little Ear, Sweet Talker, Half-Moon, Caju, Sabiá, and Ponta Fina. The rest had died or deserted. The remaining cangaceiros were gaunt. Their clothes were stained and frayed. Ponta Fina wore his arm in a sling. Raised red bumps dotted the men's faces, necks, and hands. They'd made camp away from the Marimbondo chapel, but the wasps had found them. The men circled the Hawk. One by one, he inspected their cuts, scrapes, sprains, and wasp bites, like a proud father. Then he clasped each of them in a hug. Eronildes stood on his porch. When the Hawk pointed to him, the doctor tucked his large, white hands into his vest pockets.

"This is Dr. Eronildes," the Hawk said. "He is our greatest ally and friend. I owe him my life."

Luzia had been happy until that point. Who had gotten them across the river? Who had found Dr. Eronildes? She looked down at her oversize and ragged dress. She wanted her trousers back. The old maid had washed and hidden them. As soon as the men made camp, Luzia decided that she would find them again.

The men were fed well. They scraped their bowls clean. They sucked on their wooden spoons. The elderly maid wove through the group, doling out more beans. The Hawk limped from man to man, crouching beside them and speaking hurriedly to each one. The men's presence had reinvigorated him, making him more limber on his crutches. The men nodded and smiled at him, their mouths full. Occasionally they glanced at Luzia, then looked back at their food. They'd made camp near the house, stringing up all of Dr. Eronildes' available caroá rope hammocks. The Hawk helped Canjica build a fire and then called them to prayer. Luzia knelt beside Ponta Fina, who looked at her nervously, then down at his palms. Afterward, she spoke to him.

"What happened to your arm?" Luzia asked.

Ponta shrugged. "Shot."

"Is the bullet still inside?"

"No," Ponta mumbled. "It went clean through."

"Your bornal's gone," she said. "We'll have to make a new one." She missed her sewing machine and thought, angrily, that the maids at Colonel Clóvis's house had probably left it in the scrub to rust.

"I don't want a new one," Ponta said. "Not from you."

Luzia stepped back. She felt as if she'd been stung.

Ponta screwed his face into a stern grimace. "The captain got shot," he said. "We lost half our group. That never happened before you came along. Women don't belong in the cangaço." He paused and stared intently at his hands, as if reading his next lines. "They're bad luck."

Luzia's throat felt dry. She clamped her arms across her chest, steadying herself. If she cried, he'd think she believed him. He'd think he was right—that she was like the stones people picked up when they were sick or troubled. They spoke to those stones, told them about their ailments and fears, then kissed them and chucked them far away, believing that the stone would take on the burden of their misfortune and that they would be cured.

"It was your captain's choice to attack the troops, not mine," she said sternly, taking the tone Aunt Sofia had used when she was a child. "Real men take responsibility for themselves. They don't blame luck. Or women."

With rest, food, and Dr. Eronildes' treatments of teas and proper hygiene, the men slowly recovered. Luzia made herself quietly indispensable, mending their torn clothes, serving their dinners, chiding them for forgetting to change their bandages. The Hawk still slept in the kitchen room, but he spent less time in the house. There were no more shooting lessons. No more late-night discussions. Eronildes frequently went to Luzia with his notepad and his questions.

He asked her about the men's morning prayers. Did she believe in that crystal rock? Did she believe that saying the corpo fechado would seal her body from harm? Luzia did not know how to answer such questions. She was not ignorant—the crystal rock was a rock; the saints in her old closet were made of wood and clay; the bloody-toed Jesus above Padre Otto's altar was gesso and wire. She did not kneel to those things. Her faith was not in wood or clay or wire. Since the Hawk was occupied with his men, each afternoon Luzia walked beside the river alone. She watched fishermen stretch their canvas sails on the shore to dry. She saw boys balance on the backs of narrow boats and steer them downriver with long, crooked poles. She saw the whitewashed altars of saints set beside the water. She saw the snarling faces of wooden carrancas carved onto mastheads to scare away river demons. It was a way of life she had never imagined existed. The fishermen had their superstitions, their demons, their preferred saints. And beneath the brown waters of the Old Chico was another world. A place inhabited by striped surubim fish and other creatures beyond her imagination. It was a world she could not inhabit or explain, but she knew it existed.

When she came back from her walk, she saw Dr. Eronildes on his mare, returning from a trip downriver. His vaqueiro rode beside him on a pack mule. In its cargo baskets the animal carried several parcels, two tins of kerosene, and a stack of newspapers. Eronildes' elderly maid stepped off the porch and greeted him. The doctor climbed awkwardly off his horse. He waved to Luzia.

"I have something for you!" he shouted.

Eronildes walked briskly toward her. He patted his vest pocket and produced a small black case.

"A gift," he said.

Luzia took the case hesitantly. It was hard leather, with a snap clasp. She flicked open the lid. Inside, the lining was soft. Velvet. Tucked into its dark recesses, like a seed in its pod, was a pair of brass-rimmed spectacles.

"I had them shipped from Salvador," Eronildes said excitedly. "We did an eye exam not long ago, remember? It wasn't completely accurate, but I think it will do. You're nearsighted, like me. These will correct your vision."

The spectacles were nearly weightless in her hands. Luzia was afraid to unfold them. She fumbled with their thin arms. Eronildes helped her wrap the rounded ends around her ears. The metal felt cold. It tickled the bridge of her nose. Behind Dr. Eronildes, Luzia saw each crack in the whitewashed walls of his house. She saw the crooked grain of the porch's wooden beams, each oval leaf of the juazeiro tree beside his window, and the Hawk, standing beside the house's white wall. He'd come to see about the newspapers, but he'd stopped short. He propped a thick-fingered hand upon the house's wall and watched them. Luzia slipped off the spectacles.

"It's overwhelming at first," Eronildes said, "but you'll grow accustomed to it."

"Thank you," Luzia replied. The Hawk was still there but blurred now, a shadow.

"Luzia," Eronildes said. He paused and wove his white fingers together. "The men, the cangaceiros, are plotting to leave soon. Once they all recuperate."

She nodded. Eronildes looked at her intently.

"My father taught me another useful saying," he continued. " 'If you live by the gun, you'll die by the gun.' Have you heard that one?"

"Yes."

"When the men leave, you're welcome to stay. You have a place here. I hope you know this."

"Yes," she said. Luzia fidgeted with the spectacles, slipping them back into the case. "Thank you."

Her room was dim. The days were shorter; the sun had already dipped below the river's hills. Luzia did not light a candle. She stood before the mirror and opened the leather case. Aunt Sofia had instructed her to never look in a mirror after dark. If she did, her aunt warned, she would see her own death. But it wasn't dark yet. Luzia hooked the spectacles behind her ears. The lenses were much thinner than those in Eronildes' glasses. The brass frames were perfectly round, like hollowed-out coins. They shone around Luzia's eyes.

Perhaps she would stay, she thought. Perhaps she would telegraph Emília. Perhaps she would go to the capital and become a famous dressmaker.

Behind her, the guest room door opened. In the mirror she saw the Hawk. Luzia saw each sun-baked crease on the good side of his face, each strand of hair pulled into a messy ponytail, each tangled saint's medallion. She turned and faced him.

"What are those?" he asked, his lips crimped tight.

"Spectacles," she replied.

The Hawk walked toward her. His hand snapped out. Luzia felt a flutter in her chest, as if a moth were trapped there. She braced for a hit but his fingers snatched at the spectacles. Luzia twisted out of his reach. She took the glasses off. Their hooked ends caught in her hair.

"What is the matter with you?" she yelled.

"I don't want him giving you jewelry."

"They're not jewelry," Luzia replied, the glasses clamped tightly in her hand. "They're a remedy. For my eyes. To correct my vision."

He held her hand firmly. The glasses dug into her palm.

"You don't need correcting," he said.

His eyes were glistening and dark. The unscarred side of his face furrowed, rising and falling as if unable to decide what expression to take. Finally Luzia touched it, so that it would be still.

She already knew him—each wrinkle, each muscle, each dark and shining scar—and this knowledge made her bold. Luzia stared at his crooked lips. They seemed strange and inaccessible to her but his scars did not. Before he could move away, she pressed her mouth to the mark on his neck, to the circular bites on his hand, to the long and crooked cut on his forearm. He tasted like salt and cloves. He pulled her braid aside and leaned into her neck. He did not kiss—he inhaled, moving toward her ear, breathing her in. His voice was low and urgent. Luzia could not hear his words, could not tell whether they were pleas or prayers.

The spectacles fell from her hand. Luzia closed her eyes and felt as if she were back in that gulley, wading into strange waters and suddenly stepping too deep. She was gripped, enfolded, pulled under. He was beside her on that hard guest room floor. Luzia felt a chilly wave of fear. She could not catch her breath. There was movement, then pain, then a great burst of heat within her, like the pouring of burnt sugar in her belly. She stiffened and grabbed him, breathing back his strange vows, ending them not with *amen* but with *Antônio*.

13

They married in November, in the shade of Eronildes' front porch. Luzia wore a clean blouse and skirt loaned to her by one of the farmhand's wives. She'd had to extend the hems, sewing a ruffle of rough cotton mescla around the skirt and shirt cuffs. She carried an orange-blossom bouquet, its stems tied with twine. She wore her spectacles.

Normally before a ceremony the groom and his relatives walked to the bride's home, where she said good-bye to her family and walked to the chapel beside her betrothed. There was no chapel on Eronildes' ranch and Luzia had neither home nor family, so she stood on Eronildes' back porch and waited with the elderly maid. The old woman had put away her pipe. She'd given Luzia no heartfelt warnings or advice. She'd simply braided Luzia's hair very tightly, told her to chew cloves for her breath, and pilfered some of the doctor's Royal Briar lotion and wiped it along Luzia's neck and arms. The perfumed lotion was potent, and as Luzia stood on the back porch and waited for Antônio, she smelled like Dr. Eronildes, like a starched sheet.

Antônio arrived accompanied by his men. His hair was slicked back with so much brilliantine that it shone like a silk cap. His alpercatas were polished with the hair paste, too. He must have used a whole tin, Luzia thought. The unscarred side of his face trembled— his mouth rose, his cheek followed, and the skin around his eye crinkled. They were small movements that would have been subtle on anyone else, but when coupled with the placid, immutable stare of his scarred side, they seemed exaggerated and involuntary. It was easier to turn away, to look at the calm side despite its ridged scar. But Luzia focused on his moving side; that was the side she knew she must watch.

When he stepped on the back porch and extended his hand, Luzia turned her back to him and knelt. Tradition dictated that she fall to her knees and kiss her parents' hands good-bye. But there was only the old maid. Luzia reached for her hand. It was thin boned and coarse, like a chicken foot.

Antônio led her to the front porch where Dr. Eronildes waited. There were no priests near his ranch and they could not call on one from the nearest river town. It would attract too much attention. At first, Eronildes had not wanted to officiate at the ceremony. He had no Bible, he said. He knew no prayers, but Antônio had insisted. He wanted a true wedding. He pointed to the framed medical diploma written in sharp-edged, calligraphic script and hanging in Eronildes' front parlor. The diploma made Eronildes an official, Antônio said. It made him nearly as good as a priest.

The ceremony was quick. When it came time for the ring, Luzia held out her hand but Antônio shook his head. He unbuttoned his jacket and untangled a gold chain from around his neck. It was a Santa Luzia medallion—a round charm with two gold eyes in its center. Antônio slipped it over Luzia's head.

The cangaceiros stood below the porch, in the sun. They wore serious, concentrated expressions on their faces. The same expressions they used when hiding in the scrub and watching a ranch or town from afar, taking note of its merits and its threats. Still, a wedding meant a party and this animated them. Canjica and the elderly maid had roasted three lambs and three chickens. They'd opened jars of caju jam and bottles of sugarcane liquor. The men ate and danced. When Luzia broke apart her bouquet and threw the orange blossoms into the air, they playfully pushed each other aside to grab them.

Only Dr. Eronildes kept away from the festivities. In the fading afternoon light, he sat on his porch and read through his last remaining newspapers. A bottle of whiskey sat half empty beside him.

"Are we going to toast?" Antônio asked him. "You promised us a toast."

Eronildes looked up. His glasses were smudged, his eyes red. He bunched a newspaper in his hand. "This isn't the occasion for a toast."

Antônio frowned. Eronildes quickly gulped down a tumbler of whiskey. Then he threw a newspaper at Luzia.

"Read it," he said, coughing. "The market crashed."

"It's caved in?" Luzia said, confused. For no reason at all she thought of Emília and was worried. "Which one? Where?"

"Not a building!" Eronildes said, holding his forehead. "The monetary market, in the United States. Sugar, cotton, coffee, it's all worthless now. We're doomed."

Luzia smoothed out the crumpled paper. It was weeks old, dated as the last days of October. The coffee barons of São Paulo and Minas stood in a line, looking tired and stern. Their crops had no value. In the United States they called the financial trouble "the Crash," but in Brazil it was called "the Crisis." The sugar farmers around Recife were burning cane, hoping it would bring up the price. The presidential election had been delayed until March of the next year. The candidates blamed each other's parties for the Crisis.

"God knows what's happened since," Eronildes said. "That paper's old. I'll have to telegram Salvador tomorrow to see if my mother is all right. Things must be a mess in the capitals." He took another gulp of whiskey. His fingers shook. "Electing Gomes is our only salvation now."

"Our salvation's not on this earth," Antônio replied.

"I mean commercially," Eronildes snapped, his words slurring. "Modernization's our only hope, whether we want it or not."

"What's new isn't always what's best," Antônio said.

Eronildes poured himself more whiskey. It dribbled on his trousers.

"You use rifles, don't you?" the doctor asked. "You can shoot men from meters away. That's a modern invention."

"A rifle's useful," Antônio replied. "I admit that. But any fool can shoot one. To kill a man with a punhal takes more skill. That's the problem with modern things—they encourage fools to think they're just as capable as men."

Eronildes let out a shrill laugh. A wilted orange blossom fell from his buttonhole.

"Well, *Mrs. Teixeira*," he said, emphasizing each syllable, "what do you think of all this? Who is the fool and who is the man?"

Luzia heard him but could not speak. She'd picked up the Society Section of another discarded paper. Under its heading was a photograph labeled "Ladies' Auxiliary of Recife Annual Parasol Contest, 1929." A row of smiling women held elaborately decorated parasols. The first-place winner had ribbons dangling from its edges and a design sewn into each paneled section: a rain cloud, a corncob, a sun, a dahlia. The woman holding this parasol wore a round hat with one striped feather emerging from its brim. Her hair was chin length and curled. Her lips were dark. Her eyes were closed. Still, Luzia knew her.

Chapter 7

EMÍLIA

Recife
September 1929–December 1930

1

⟋⟋⟋⟋⟋⟋⟋⟋

*T*he annual parasol contest of the Ladies' Auxiliary of Recife occurred in the last week of September. Late enough not to be overshadowed by the rowdy Independence Day parades in the beginning of the month, but early enough to avoid October's stifling heat. That year, the competition was held on Boa Viagem Beach.

Degas drove to the ceremony. Emília sat in the Chrysler Imperial's backseat beside Dona Dulce, who gripped the leather armrest between them. Degas preferred speed to caution. He veered around donkey carts and bumped over curbs. In the passenger seat, Dr. Duarte shifted uneasily. "No need for recklessness," he muttered. With each swerve and jostle, Dr. Duarte's face reddened and he held fast to the sides of his seat. Several times, he threatened to hire a chauffeur. Degas smiled. Automobiles were a still a novelty in Recife and operating a car was considered a luxurious skill, like reading and painting. There were few capable drivers in Recife, and Degas considered himself one of them. Dr. Duarte grunted. Emília was the only one who appreciated her husband's haste. She was eager to see the ocean.

Years before, the city government had built a bridge to the swampy region of Pina, making Boa Viagem Beach accessible by automobile and carriage. Soon, the trolley line was installed, and later, the main avenida was paved. By the time Emília became familiar with Recife, Boa Viagem Beach had a reputation as a popular summer vacation spot. The palm-frond fishing huts that lined the beach were slowly being replaced by brick-and-mortar mansions.

The baroness had invited Emília to participate in the parasol contest. She'd said it was a silly competition—each contestant received a simple cloth parasol and had three weeks to decorate it—but the results were worth the tedious work. The winner was awarded a seat on the Ladies' Auxiliary. Emília spent a day decorating her parasol, covering it with things inspired by Aunt Sofia's garden: yellow silk corncobs, red crepe dahlias, blue beaded strands of rain. Emília kept the design colorful but simple; she did not want to seem too eager. She sensed that the Auxiliary judges had made their decision long before the contest. The prior year they had accepted Lindalva, though she'd simply pinned pages of poetry to her parasol on the way to the competition. Her mother was, after all, the baroness. If you did not have a family member on the Auxiliary, you had to be accepted through your merits. You had to belong to a New family. You had to have a skill like sewing, painting, music, or, in Lindalva's case, oratory. And, most important, you had to be interesting, because the Auxiliary women hated boring meetings. "But you cannot be too interesting," the baroness warned. "Then you become vulgar."

In the nine months since her first, disorienting Carnaval in Recife, Emília had met every member of the Ladies' Auxiliary. One by one they'd appeared at the baroness's home on the same days that Emília made her visits to Lindalva. They drank coffee together on the baroness's porch, where the Auxiliary women calmly inspected Emília.

"Oh," they'd said, pressing embroidered handkerchiefs to their brows and patting away any unsightly beads of sweat. "This must be very different from the backlands."

They rarely said *countryside* or *interior*. They preferred *backlands,* a word that made Emília think of the musty recesses of a hard-to-reach drawer or cabinet. A dark space filled with forgotten things, opened only in moments of need or nostalgia and then quickly shut.

Over time, the Auxiliary women extended Emília invitations to teas, luncheons, and dinner dances at the International Club. At each of these events, the women regarded her with fascination and a touch of wariness and pity, like a wild animal one traps as a pet but never particularly trusts. Emília realized that her friendship with the baroness had given her social clout, but the possible seediness of her origins made her alluring to the Auxiliary women. They'd proclaimed her interesting.

As a seamstress for the colonel and Dona Conceição, Emília had learned how to be a successful servant: watching her mistress closely, understanding her changing moods, deciphering her wants, and being both immediately available and invisible, depending on the situation. Emília used these skills with the Recife women. She laughed at the proper times. Was energetic but not overly eager. Learned when to listen sympathetically and when to turn her head and pretend to give the women privacy. But Emília could not be too accommodating; the Recife women had spent their lives commanding hired help. If Emília took the demeanor of a servant, she would be treated like one. So she had to temper her compliant nature with strong opinions.

Emília took books from the Coelhos' library shelves and forced herself to read them. The novels, poems, and geography books were hard to understand at first but she'd slogged through. She'd looked up large words in Degas' tattered dictionary. She'd read countless newspapers and studied Dr. Duarte's international news magazines and the manifestos in Lindalva's feminist bulletins. Through her readings, Emília learned that the distinction between what was vulgar and what was acceptable fluctuated as much as women's hemlines. What was improper one month became avant-garde the next, and before long, was positively fashionable.

Recife, like other Brazilian capitals, was modernizing. Ladies were stepping out of their gated homes and into dark cinemas to watch silent films. They were exchanging the manicured gardens of Derby Square for Rua Nova, to perform their "footings" where there were teahouses and jazz bands. In Rio, photographs of the beach showed women wearing sleeveless bathing suits with dangerously low necklines. And thanks to the presidential campaign and the upcoming elections, even suffrage became acceptable. Lindalva convinced the Auxiliary to undertake a campaign to give literate women the vote. Voting, they argued, was a moral duty like any other: bearing children, keeping house, and raising the young leaders of tomorrow. The suffragettes did not add the right to divorce or to own property to their demands, separating such liberties from their campaign as strictly as Dona Dulce separated food in her pantry—moving black beans and ham hocks into the servants' section even though she'd once admitted to Emília that, on cool and rainy evenings, she often craved those fatty foods. Like most donas, she never gave in to her cravings. They were unseemly, Dona Dulce said, and seeing a wife consume such things would be too much for any husband to stomach.

Dona Dulce was not a suffragette. She looked at the news articles with disgust and a tremor of fear. Not only nameless typists, schoolteachers, and telephone operators, but also fine family girls were falling into what Dona Dulce called the "vortex of modern life." She believed Emília was a casualty of this, too. Emília pretended to disregard her mother-in-law, but she secretly used Dona Dulce as a warning post, so she wouldn't go too far with her opinions and ambitions. Emília, like the women in the Auxiliary, had to keep the delicate balance between being current and being respectable.

At Boa Viagem Beach, members of the Ladies' Auxiliary milled about, greeting the contestants, who showed off their parasols. Dug into the densely packed sand near the road were rows of wooden chairs where judges and guests sat. Emília stayed on the outskirts of the crowd, near a coconut palm. She did not mingle. Her parasol remained unopened, forgotten in her hands.

The ocean lay before her, vast and dark, the color of a bruise. It was not green, as she'd once imagined. Like all things in Recife, it was not what Emília had envisioned. It alarmed her, all of that water. Near the shore, giant, foamy waves receded and advanced. Emília closed her eyes. The breakers sounded like cloth ripping.

"Emília!" a woman's voice, breathless and urgent, yelled.

Emília opened her eyes. Lindalva hurried toward her.

Her friend's formerly ruffled, bohemian style was replaced with a green pleated skirt and matching cardigan. A "twin set," Emília called it when she'd first spotted the style on a British tennis star in one of Dr. Duarte's news magazines. Emília had admired the tennis player's tidy skirts and practical tops. Inspired, she'd holed up in her bedroom, sat behind her newly purchased Singer, and sewed herself a twin set. When Lindalva saw the outfit, she insisted on having one. Emília instructed the baroness's seamstress on the design, teaching the girl how to make pleats. Several ladies from the Auxiliary approached Emília and inquired if they, too, could share the pattern with their dressmakers. Before long, every influential woman in Recife had a twin set. At social functions, these women stopped referring to Emília's origins or asking her about the backlands. Instead, they grilled her about fashions. During these conversations, the women's demeanor changed—they nodded, smiled, became deferential—and Emília realized that admiration came not only from social status or fine manners but also from ideas; her talent could erase her past.

Lindalva kissed Emília's cheek. In one swift movement she took the parasol from Emília's hands and popped it open. Lindalva inspected her work.

"A country theme! Oh, the judges will eat this up," she said. "Once this silly business is done, you'll have a seat on the Auxiliary and we can concentrate on more important matters. I've found a girl. Very spirited. Says she knows how to sew. You'll have to see if she's any good, of course. And then we'll need a location. It can't be Mother's house—everyone will see us coming and going with cloth and seamstresses. We must have our own location—"

"Yes," Emília interrupted, taking Lindalva's hand. Emília had gotten used to reining in her friend's constant chatter. "I want the seamstresses to have a nice place to work—a room with windows and fresh air. And we can't have them at the machines from morning until night. I want the Auxiliary women to volunteer to run a class. To teach them to read."

"That's brilliant!" Lindalva smiled widely, revealing the gap in her teeth. "It will give us more voters!"

She squeezed Emília's hand and guided her toward the crowd.

During the winter months, when rain had fallen in heavy sideways sheets, making the trolleys' cables crackle on their electric lines, Emília and Lindalva had sat on the baroness's porch and read suffrage magazines. They'd giggled uncontrollably when Lindalva taught Emília the tango—a dance the newspapers called "lascivious"—pressing their cheeks together, extending their arms and marching back and forth across the baroness's sitting room. And after Emília created her successful twin sets, she and Lindalva plotted to open their own atelier. They would copy the newest, most daring fashions from Europe and introduce them to Recife, making clothing that even Rio and São Paulo women would covet. Emília would be the creative force, while Lindalva would handle the finances. As a married woman, Emília was considered a ward of her husband, like a child or a demented relative. Any business they created would have to be in Lindalva's name; that way, they wouldn't need Degas' permission and were not required to give him a share of the profits if they succeeded. If they failed, however, Lindalva would bear the brunt of the burden.

Emília appreciated her friend's generosity. Still, she was wary of Lindalva. She recalled Dona Dulce's warning: Recife women made alliances, not friendships. In Lindalva's presence, Emília was afraid of saying too much, of slipping into her old habits or speaking with her country accent. Emília never mentioned Luzia. She didn't like to talk about her past, though Lindalva begged to hear about "the life of a working woman." Emília felt envious of Lindalva's good fortune; her friend never had to worry about making social errors. Lindalva was not married and didn't have to be. She could buy her own clothes, organize suffrage rallies, make fun of Recife society while still being accepted by it. Worse was that Lindalva believed such freedom was available to any woman, if she only wanted it badly enough.

At the parasol contest, Lindalva steered Emília toward the Auxiliary judges, who admired her work. Nearby, Dr. Duarte socialized with Auxiliary husbands. Degas smoked and looked at his pocket watch. Dona Dulce surveyed the crowd. She wore a tan dress and hat. She had packed away her blue and green dresses when the election campaign began, opting for neutral colors. Politics was vulgar, Dona Dulce said, and she wanted to steer clear of it. The city had divided into two camps: Green and Blue. Each day photographs of opposition candidate Celestino Gomes—his military uniform rumpled, his tall boots taking up most of his squat frame—appeared arm in arm with his running mate, José Bandeira.

The Old families were not partial to Gomes. They feared he was a populist with his calls for a minimum wage, women's suffrage, and a secret ballot. Most New family leaders, including Dr. Duarte, believed Gomes and his Green Party would modernize Brazil. Recife women, Old and New, did not delve into politics, but they fiercely supported their husbands' choices. During her walks through Derby Square, Emília saw that the Old family matriarchs wore sapphire and aquamarine jewelry. They wore blue dresses and had milliners pin iridescent blue feathers to their hats. On Boa Viagem Beach however, the dominant color was green. The members of the Ladies' Auxiliary preferred emeralds. Their husbands, even Dr. Duarte, wore neckties in mint, leaf, and sage.

Emília, too, wore green. Her new cloche had a single, olive-hued feather cocked in its band. The hat was a gift from Degas. He'd given her many presents in the months after Carnaval: reams of fabric for her new outfits, beaded shawls, a pair of reptile-skin shoes whose leather was so soft it felt like cloth in Emília's hands. He gave her a large, velvet-lined jewelry box and promised to fill it with products sold by Mr. Sato, the Japanese jeweler who appeared at the Coelhos' door once a month and carefully spread his selection of broaches, rings, and pendants on Dona Dulce's table. Degas presented his gifts before meals, with everyone present. During these awkward exchanges, Dr. Duarte beamed by his son's side and Dona Dulce wore her tight, smiling mask. Emília knew what was expected of her.

They wanted a child. All of them—Degas, Dr. Duarte, Dona Dulce—questioned her each morning, asking how she felt and watching to see if she ate her breakfast. Each month when Emília asked to go to the pharmacy for feminine supplies, she saw Dona Dulce's back stiffen and her dough-colored lips tighten. Dr. Duarte attributed Emília's infertility to a uterine disorder. He began to serve her spoonfuls of cod liver oil with each meal. "We will fortify your fragile organs!" Dr. Duarte declared as Emília held her nose and gulped down the pungent yellow oil.

They even called a medical doctor, one of Dr. Duarte's colleagues, to examine her. The man pressed upon her stomach as Emília lay paralyzed beneath the bedsheet. He declared her healthy and said that perhaps the humid Recife climate didn't agree with her. He prescribed vitamin pills, which Emília placed under her tongue each morning and later spat out. She filched mil-réis bills from Degas' trouser pockets and gave them to Raimunda, who secretly purchased caju roxo bark at the market. With the bark, Emília made tea and drank it daily. It was an old trick Aunt Sofia had prescribed for some of her married and desperate clients who didn't want to bear any more children. Emília had watched those farm girls—her former classmates—grow pale and drained from pregnancies. She saw their breasts become shrunken and oblong, like old papayas. And she recalled her own mother, who'd died because the midwife's large, capable hands were trained only to save infants. Even Recife women, with their meticulous diets and attentive doctors, died in childbirth at a rate that frightened and disgusted Emília. It wasn't simply the possibility of death that deterred her; she would gladly have taken the risk if a child was something she wanted. But it wasn't. Back in Taquaritinga, Emília had always envisioned herself as a dona, never a mother. She'd believed that the desire to have a child would come to her eventually, like a sudden craving for different food. But after a year in Recife, she realized that a child would bind her inside the Coelho house just as she was learning how to slip away from it.

Degas still spent his mornings at the Federal University Law School, his afternoons studying with Felipe, and his evenings cloistered in his childhood bedroom listening to English-language records. Once a week he came to Emília's bedroom. She wore her slit-front nightgown and when Degas was finished, he returned to his room across the hall. He no longer promised wedding parties or honeymoons, and Emília appreciated this. In public, she and Degas were straightforward and courteous to each other. Each Sunday, they attended the International Club's dinner dances and during orchestra breaks, when couples came to their table to compliment Emília's drape-backed gowns with uneven scarf hems, Degas edged his chair closer to hers. Irritated, Emília scooted her chair away. There were times when she felt jolts of anger and loathing toward Degas. Other times she felt pity, and if Degas sensed this he scowled and snapped at her.

"Don't wear so much perfume. You smell like a flophouse."

"How would you know?" Emília hissed back, saddened by the way she and Degas interacted. They were like two roosters forced to occupy the same yard: both proud, both bound to peck at each other to maintain their dignity.

All of her life, Emília had been warned by Aunt Sofia that men were brutes. A woman must suffer through her husband's desires until she became accustomed to them, until they became as natural as washing a shirt or cleaning out a chicken. This seemed plausible to Emília, even tolerable. If one person got pleasure and the other a noble sense of sacrifice, then at least both gained something. But if there was no desire there could be no sacrifice, no righteous surrender. If both husband and wife saw desire as a duty, then there was only dread. There was only a forced, fumbling awkwardness and, afterward, loathing. Settling in their bellies like silt. Accumulating until it became heavy. Until one couldn't bear the sight of the other. In the cinema, scenes faded to black after couples kissed. Degas said that they never went beyond that for propriety's sake, but Emília believed they'd done it on purpose. They'd gotten it right. Beyond that first, frightening kiss there was nothing worth showing.

After weeks of the Coelhos' silent pressure for a child, Emília decided to press back. She hated visiting the dressmaker with Dona Dulce. She was ashamed of her dull outfits. Emília wanted to sew her own clothes. Dona Dulce had taught her the art of asking without seeming to ask, and Emília followed her mother-in-law's teachings. She told Degas and Dr. Duarte of her homesickness. How she missed the clatter of her old sewing machine, the feel of cloth beneath her fingertips. How she and her sister liked to sew baby bibs and baptism dresses. Finally, Degas understood. He had a pedal-operated Singer delivered to the Coelhos' house. Dona Dulce did not approve of Emília's pleated creations. She said they were too athletic. But Dr. Duarte declared them modern and charming, and Degas appreciated the attention they brought. Soon they would be in the Society Section, he said brightly.

He was right. At the parasol contest, before the judges revealed the winner, a *Diário de Pernambuco* photographer guided the contestants onto the beach. He made them stand in a line, their parasols open, in front of a new statue of Our Lady of Boa Viagem. Emília's feet sank into the beach sand. It felt alive, as if it were moving beneath her. It entered her shoes and made her toes feel gritty within her stockings. She did not like it.

Fishermen had erected a simple Virgin statue years before to bless their voyages. The old statue sat beneath a palm-frond hut, several paces from the new one. The new Virgin was made of plaster and set upon stone. There were starfish carved at her feet and her robe looked like water, foaming at the hem. She had blue eyes and tilted her head to one side, as if she was intrigued by something on the water. She did not look merciful or compassionate, but dull. Blank faced. Emília wanted to inspect the old statue—surely it looked wiser—but the other contestants crowded around her, blocking her path and bumping into her parasol.

Emília turned her head. At the waterline, a group of fishermen's wives had gathered. Waves lapped their wide, bare feet and sometimes surged up, wetting the hems of the women's faded skirts. They huddled together, tan arms crossed over simple blouses, and surveyed Emília and the other contestants. The fisherwomen's faces were creased into expressions of permanent worry. Emília smiled at them. The women looked at her sternly, suspicious of the strange gaggle that had invaded their beach.

"Face forward, ladies," the photographer instructed. "Face forward."

The contestants around Emília twittered and smiled. They did not look at their sandy shoes. They did not pick at their gloves. They lived without bearing the marks of life—no sweat stains or mussed hair or bitten nails. Emília wanted to say this aloud. She wanted someone to listen. Dona Dulce would scold her for such a comment. Lindalva would think it cute. Only Luzia would understand.

All winter there'd been articles about the brigade of troops sent to capture the Hawk. It was hard for Emília to read a newspaper in the Coelho house—Dr. Duarte got priority, and he frequently clipped articles related to criminals in order to bolster his criminology theories, and political articles to take to his British Club meetings. When he was finished with the paper, it had more holes than one of Dona Dulce's doilies. Emília's mother-in-law was another obstacle. "A lady doesn't read newspapers out in the open, for all to see," Dona Dulce insisted. Ladies couldn't appear to care about vulgar news. Dona Dulce was always the second person to read the newspaper, and she locked herself in the sitting room so no one could see her pore over the Society Section. Degas got his news at the Federal University Law School, so Emília was third in line for the paper, but by the time she was allowed to look at it, it was late in the day and most of the articles that interested her had been removed. Emília couldn't ask Dr. Duarte for the articles he'd clipped; a lady could not be interested in cangaceiros or their tawdry crimes. So each time Emília visited the baroness's home, she pored through the week's newspapers. Lindalva saved the *Diários* for her friend, believing Emília was interested in politics. But she didn't care about Gomes or his "New Brazil." She was looking for Luzia.

News about the troops dwindled as the presidential campaign grew more hostile. Emília believed that Captain Higino and his soldiers were lost in the scrub until, one day, on the paper's second page, there was an article. "The Vulture," they'd erroneously dubbed the cangaceiro who'd taken Luzia. They said he'd ambushed government troops on Colonel Clóvis Lucena's ranch and then escaped to Bahia. Emília clipped the article and locked it inside her jewelry box, along with her Communion portrait. Alone in her room, she read the article over and over again. The reporter stated that among the escaped cangaceiros was a female consort. *Consort;* it sounded seedy. Was this woman Luzia? Was she held against her will? The thought frightened Emília but she could not bring herself to believe it. Luzia's will was strong, stronger than any Emília had encountered. If she had not died or escaped, then Luzia had stayed of her own accord. This possibility frightened Emília even more.

To drive such thoughts from her head, Emília closed her eyes. Even when she heard the pop of the photographer's flash, she did not open them. She felt her feet sinking into the sand.

How she would like to have Luzia with her on that sandy stage, their arms linked. All of her life, Emília had been compared to Luzia, defined by her. Back in Taquaritinga, Luzia's awkwardness brought out Emília's poise. Luzia's temper highlighted Emília's mildness, her sharp tongue Emília's quiet. In Recife Luzia wasn't present, but every day Emília recalled her, resurrected her—the smart, strong sister. Although Emília felt herself to be neither of those things, she took comfort in knowing that Luzia was. They shared the same blood; perhaps some of Luzia's strengths were mingled with her own, so that Emília could cultivate her sister's strength within herself. But ever since Emília had read the newspaper article about the cangaceiros and their "consort," she'd felt Luzia's presence slipping away. Emília's memories of her sister seemed tarnished. Who had Luzia become? And who was Emília, next to such a woman?

She'd decided to place herself beside another image. The women in Lindalva's feminist magazines were educated and modern. Lindalva was fond of the *idea* of modernity, but Emília liked its look, its sheen. She appreciated the smart hats, the bold dresses, the triumphant image of herself driving a motorcar, or striding into a voting center with a neatly folded ballot in her hand. Most of all, Emília pictured a many-windowed atelier with a dozen pedal-operated Singers humming to her command.

If Emília took on the sheen of modernity, if she wore the right dresses, expressed the right opinions, acted industriously and creatively, she would win Recife's admiration. She had let go of her girlish dreams of owning a home and becoming a dona. She'd accepted the fact that Degas would never be a kind teacher or a loving husband. And if she could not be loved, then she resolved to be admired.

"The winner is . . . Mrs. Degas Coelho," a woman called out. There was a wave of polite applause and then laughter. "Mrs. Degas Coelho," the voice called again.

Emília opened her eyes.

2

One month after the contest, the Crisis occurred and Emília's business plans were stalled. It was a Thursday, the day Dona Dulce set aside to wash linens and air mattresses. The Coelhos' maids were frantic, stripping sheets from beds and carrying the white bundles downstairs, lifting mattresses and dragging them to the Coelhos' covered laundry area to be beaten and spritzed with lavender water. From her bedroom, Emília heard the great thwacks of rattan sticks hitting mattress cushions. She heard the washerwoman's shouts. She took advantage of the commotion and sneaked into the kitchen, where she brewed her special tea and drank until her belly sloshed with liquid. As she took her last gulp, Dona Dulce entered the kitchen. She stared coolly at Emília, then made her way to the laundry area, where she told the maids to stop working.

"Keep quiet," Dona Dulce ordered. "Dr. Duarte is in a nervous mood."

Lunch was muted and rushed. Dona Dulce allowed Dr. Duarte to shovel in his food and go to the parlor, to listen to the radio. Degas accompanied his father, leaving Emília alone with Dona Dulce and their dessert—a papaya pudding with blood red crème de cassis swirled on top. Agitated, her mother-in-law also left the table and followed the radio's static into the parlor. The forgotten helpings of pudding turned warm and runny in their glass bowls. Emília realized that something important and terrible had happened.

The scratchy, faraway radio voices announced that the stock market in the United States had crashed. Dr. Duarte and Degas sat beside the radio all afternoon and into the night. Emília did not understand financial markets. How could things as useful as sugar, coffee, and rubber be valuable one day and worthless the next?

On Friday, the announcers were reluctantly optimistic. All weekend, the Coelhos waited for news. On Monday, papers and radio broadcasts said that markets around the world were crashing in response to the news from New York. They dubbed the day "Black Monday," and the next was "Black Tuesday," and afterward the days did not need such labels because all seemed bleak. Recife went into a panic. Businesses shut their doors. The cook complained that the markets had no vendors. Meat became scarce. News announcers said that, in the United States, the crash had led to a depression that would be felt around the world. In Brazil, the economic slump was called "the Crisis," and in Recife, the Old familes were the first to feel it.

Slowly, sugar-mill owners began to appear at the Coelho house wearing dark mourning suits and carrying sheaves of paper beneath their arms. They were promptly escorted into Dr. Duarte's office. Some brought their wives with them, as if they were paying a social visit, although Emília had never seen an Old family woman set foot in the Coelho house. Dona Dulce and Emília sat with these black-cloaked women. Emília recognized some from her walks in Derby Square. Most were cordial and smiling. They sipped their coffee and chatted as if they'd been meaning to visit for ages but had never gotten around to it. Despite their cordiality, Emília noticed the careless way the women handled Dona Dulce's china. They placed their saucers noisily back on the serving tray and clinked their spoons sharply against the cups' thin lips, as if hoping to accidentally break them.

Beneath the women's politeness was anger. Emília learned that the papers their husbands carried into Dr. Duarte's office were deeds: titles to houses along Rosa e Silva Street, claims to beach property in Boa Viagem and empty warehouses near the port. They gave Dr. Duarte all they owned in Recife so as not to default on their loans and lose their imported machines, and in turn, their plantations.

Because of his loans, Dr. Duarte knew each Recife family's "podres," as he called them. Emília thought it was telling that he did not say "secrets," but "rots," as if the families' troubles were like a foul scent, detected by all but unable to be rooted out. Only Dr. Duarte knew the source and the extent of the decay. He had the power to boast, to spread a family's failings around the city, but he didn't. Dr. Duarte had a reputation for discretion; when he took over a property, no one knew if it had been foreclosed or simply sold to him. Because of this, the Old family couples who entered the Coelho house tempered their repulsion with a cool respect. And the Old family men who belonged to the ruling Blue Party allowed Dr. Duarte to support Gomes and his Green Party without political retribution.

Several textile-mill owners also visited Dr. Duarte. These men were cheerful and sweating beneath their wool fedoras and starched three-piece suits. Their mills weren't booming, but they were healthy. From her bedroom window, Emília could see the long columns of smoke rising from the brick stacks of the Torre Thread and Cloth Company, and from its rivals in Macaxeira and Tacaruna. On her trips to the fabric store, Emília saw lines of migrants snaking outside the factory doors. People who had lost their jobs cutting sugarcane flocked by the hundreds to Recife, hoping for a job in the mills. Dr. Duarte announced that he would use his import-export company to bring in machines for the mill owners and to send out cloth.

After the Crash, the presidential campaign continued. In late November, Blue Party leaders called for staying the course and keeping with tradition. They assured citizens that the Crisis would pass. The Green Party did not offer such reassurance; it called for modernization, for a "New Brazil" that was less dependent on farming and more on industry. Pernambuco's governor and Recife's mayor—both Blue Party men—cracked down on Green Party supporters. They ordered police to break up rallies, invade pro-Gomes newspapers, and keep close watch on the British Club, where Dr. Duarte's political group met. Despite this intimidation, more and more people pasted pictures of Celestino Gomes over their doors, in store windows, and in market stalls, next to the portraits of protecting saints.

In the city of Recife, Gomes supporters were mostly New families and the middle class. Elsewhere in Brazil, Gomes's fans were an incongruent alliance: military men who wanted one of their own in office; disillusioned Catholics who did not like the Blue government's separation of church and state; social reformers who wanted limits on factory abuses and child labor; and a hodgepodge of suffragettes, merchants, and intellectuals. These seemingly disparate groups had one thing in common—for years they'd been ignored by the São Paulo oligarchies that controlled the Blue party. During his campaign, Gomes courted them all. And although his messages were sometimes contradictory, his charm and enthusiasm were contagious, so each group of Gomes supporters believed he was "their man," and was willing to gamble that, if elected, Gomes would serve them first.

Because of the Blue government's restrictions in Recife, most Gomes supporters could not broadcast their allegiances.

"Even dogs on the street support Gomes," Lindalva often whispered over lunch. "But they can't talk about it. No one can."

Street dogs, with their patchy-haired bodies and protruding ribs, were the lowest caste in Recife's streets. They were ignored, shooed away, kicked. But during the last stages of Gomes's presidential campaign, people began to respect the dogs. One by one, they appeared with green Gomes bandannas tied around their necks or to the tips of their tails. As they sniffed for scraps around the outdoor markets, fought in alleyways, or lolled sleepy-eyed in the sun within the city's gated parks, the dogs became living advertisements for the opposition.

Emília saw one for the first time in January 1930—three months after the stock-market crash—outside a fabric store on Imperatriz Street. She and Lindalva were making their way to the baroness's car. A clerk followed them, carrying a bolt of dark crepe georgette wrapped tightly in parchment paper. Tucked within the package were two slide fasteners.

"It's the newest trend, a replacement for buttons," the salesman had said, and with a flourish he'd pulled the fastener up and down.

Emília watched in amazement as the teeth gathered in on themselves like a line of tiny, metal stitches. She was eager to return to the Coelho house and admire the slide fasteners in private. The Crisis had hindered her and Lindalva's plans for an atelier. The baroness and her daughter, like the Coelhos, were secure financially, but many others weren't. Women did not want new dresses, and if they did, the styles they bought were demure, dark toned, and simply cut. Fashions had taken on the world's somber mood; Emília had to re-think her designs.

Outside the fabric shop, in her rush to Lindalva's car, Emília didn't see the street dog on the ground before her. She stepped on its tail. The animal yelped and then growled. The store clerk cocked his foot to kick it but stopped short—there was a green bandanna around its skinny neck. The dog skulked away. Lindalva, Emília, and the store clerk hurried to the car.

After that, Emília began to see the Gomes dogs everywhere. They lay on the dirt path just beyond the Coelhos' gate, contorting themselves in strange positions in order to gnaw away at the green cloths tied to their legs and tails. At the house's back gate, Dr. Duarte placed bowls of milk and scraps of food for the mutts. On Rua Nova, where each Saturday she and Degas strolled arm in arm beside other New family couples, the mutts swerved between their feet. They raced across city streets, expertly dodging the trolley cars departing from Alfonso Pena Park. They begged for food before the golden doors of the Leite Restaurant, where Emília and Lindalva often lunched with the Baroness Margarida. And on the rare occasions when Degas took her to the cinema in São José, Emília saw the dogs crossing the covered metal bridge leading to the Bairro Recife. It was a neighborhood of casinos and flophouses, a neighborhood that respectable women never entered. Even men were known to cross themselves before crossing that bridge. But the street dogs didn't care about propriety. They strutted back and forth across the iron bridge, the green cloths tied to their tails flapping like flags.

Unlike the street dogs, few people acknowledged their support of Gomes. But many listened to him. Each evening when they finished dinner, Emília and the Coelhos sat in the parlor and listened to Celestino Gomes's speeches. In the doorway, the maids jumbled together in pairs, taking turns in their work so that they, too, could listen.

"This republic is unequal!" Gomes yelled, his voice crackling from the radio speaker. "São Paulo coffee barons run the country, leaving crumbs for the rest of the states! Corrupt colonels run the interior. Where is government? The chief executive needs to fight for Brazil! Citizens—my friends, my compatriots—this will be a long journey to victory. And during this journey, I will need you. I will need you as much as you will need me."

Emília wondered how such a powerful voice could come from such a small man. During his first speeches, Emília was riveted by Gomes's proclamations. He wanted to fight crime, embrace science, promote morality, build consumers' cooperatives, create pension plans, and enforce protections for working women and children. All of these ideas sounded exciting and just to Emília, but after a few weeks of listening to his radio speeches, Emília began to take her embroidery hoop into the parlor and work while Gomes spoke. His voice was always excited but his words never changed. There were no details, no new specifics. There were only exclamations and yelling and his final, trademark phrase, "Fight for a New Brazil!"

After each radio address, Dr. Duarte stood and applauded.

"That's how a man makes a speech, Degas," he said, kicking his son's shoe. "Listen and take note."

Degas pursed his mouth as if he'd eaten something sour. That night, he didn't listen to his English records. He went directly to

Emília's room and settled into bed beside her. She believed Degas had come for his weekly ritual of trying to conceive a child, and Emília lay stiffly, waiting for him to touch her hand, as if asking for permission, and then to reluctantly climb on top of her. He did neither of those things. Degas kept to his side, and spoke.

"I'd rather be in the dentist's chair than listen to any more of that man's blustering," Degas said, yanking up the bedsheet.

"You father means well—" Emília began.

"Not *him*," Degas hissed. "Thankfully I can get away from *him*. But every time I leave the house I hear Gomes. The fellows at the legal college turn on the common room's radio to listen to his blasted speeches! And if it isn't the radio, it's people whispering about the speeches, or the papers printing his quotes."

Degas lay back, resting his head on their embroidered pillows. Emília stared at the shadow of her husband's rounded stomach, then at his lovely profile: the curved nose, the thick eyelashes. She had admired him long ago on Taquaritinga's mountainside, and she felt astonishment and dread at the thought that she knew as little about his opinions now as she had then.

"You mean . . . ," Emília began, lowering her voice to a whisper. "You're a Blue man?"

Degas puffed air from his nose. "I can't be. Not in this house. You're fortunate you don't have to vote."

"I want to vote," Emília replied. "Just because you don't appreciate your good fortune doesn't mean others wouldn't."

"I forgot. You're a suffragette," Degas chuckled. "Please, Emília, you're much too pretty to be one of those 'Miss Almas.' I'd hate to see you wearing glasses and sensible shoes, preaching for liberty."

Degas' voice had the easy, teasing tone he used to rile Emília. Despite herself, she fell into his trap.

"There are no 'Miss Almas'!" Emília said. "None of the women in the Auxiliary looks like the ones in those nasty cartoons. And every woman in the Ladies' Auxiliary is for suffrage. Every one."

"I know, I know." Degas sighed. "But do you really think Gomes will give you the vote?"

"He says he will."

"That's awfully naive logic."

"You used to praise me for that."

Degas shifted beneath the bedsheet. His feet brushed Emília's leg. They were cold and rough.

"I know a fraud when I hear one," Degas said. "He's making promises to everyone. At some point he'll have to break them. Compromise is inevitable. We're all obliged to do it. Don't think Gomes is any different. He'll disappoint you."

"Why me?" Emília asked. "Why not the military men? Why not the scientists, or your father?"

Degas turned toward her. Emília felt his breath, hot and smelling of baking soda, on her cheek.

"Sometimes I wonder if it's innocence in you, or stubbornness," he said. "Sometimes I think you see everything around you quite clearly, you're just too hardheaded to admit it."

"Admit what?" Emília asked. She felt pressure in her temples, the beginnings of a headache. Her body was tired but her mind was not, and she sensed the same agitated fatigue she'd experienced as a child, before the onset of a fever.

Degas sighed. Emília turned her head but his voice filled her ear. It was a hesitant whisper, reminding Emília of Luzia and their secrets before bed.

"I envy those criminals my father studies," he said.

"Why?" Emília whispered.

"There's no cure for them. They are what they are."

"But they're doomed," she said, recalling Dr. Duarte's breakfast lectures. "There's no betterment for them. No escape. That's awful, Degas."

"Not as awful as having a choice. Thinking you could reverse things, make yourself better, if only you weren't so weak. So corruptible."

Degas coughed. His breath was phlegmy and clipped, as if it had snagged in his throat. Emília shut her eyes. She would have preferred his awkward fumbling on top of her to these strange confidences.

Earlier in their marriage she might have comforted him. During her first days in Recife, Emília had believed that married couples confided in each other before bed, sharing stories and exposing their deepest feelings. Impelled by this belief, she might have wheedled Degas into revealing more, explaining himself. Now she didn't want to hear him. Emília felt the same chilling sensation she'd experienced during their first Carnaval, watching Degas with Felipe. The men studied together, went on drives, attended school, though Felipe never appeared at the Coelho house. Gentlemen were different from farmers, Emília told herself. City men had close friendships; these were signs of refinement, of a worldliness she couldn't yet comprehend. But she sensed something different with Degas, some depth of feeling that frightened him, and her.

"Good night," Emília said, turning her back to him. Degas did not answer.

3

As elections approached, the Blue Party tried to discredit Gomes by condemning the suffragettes. Blue Party newspaper reporters printed articles about the "dangerous emancipation" being offered to young women. They printed cartoons of frazzled husbands left with a brood of crying children while their wives—always elephantine and never stylish, Emília noticed—left the house with briefcases and trolley fare in hand. A short-lived women's radio program called *Five Minutes of Feminism* was bookended by cheery samba songs proclaiming:

> She'll take all she wants.
> She'll do anything she can,
> But, dear fellows, she'll never be a man!

Each evening, Dr. Duarte tapped his feet to such songs while Degas shot Emília knowing looks.

"I hate those songs," Emília finally said, unable to tolerate Degas' smugness.

Dr. Duarte looked at her, startled. Dona Dulce nodded.

"Samba is terrible," she said. "I've always thought so."

Dr. Duarte's brow wrinkled. He stared at the radio as if contemplating the machine for the first time. After a moment, he clicked it off.

"It's all Blue Party propaganda," he said gruffly. "They want us to remain stationary. But we will rise! We will rise!"

He poked his thick finger in the air excitedly. When no one responded, he clicked on the radio and listened intently to *Five Minutes of Feminism*.

Dr. Duarte, like most Green Party men, believed that suffrage was an inevitable step toward modernity. He and many women in the Ladies' Auxiliary were convinced that voting would not interfere with a woman's duties to her family. Brazilian feminists were not, after all, like those radical British women who martyred themselves and bombed buildings, Lindalva often said, and Emília always detected wistfulness in her voice.

In retaliation for the Blue Party's attacks, Recife's Green journalists printed salacious crime stories, charging that the Blue government had lost hold of the country's moral authority. In Pernambuco, papers wrote about the Hawk's group. The cangaceiro leader had surprised reporters and government officials by telegramming Recife. His message made the *Diário de Pernambuco*'s front page:

> Correcting a mistake in your paper. STOP.
> Vultures take what is already dead. STOP.
> Hawks are different. STOP.
> They hunt, kill, then eat. STOP.
> I am alive and well. STOP.
> When more troops come, make sure they pack water. STOP.
> I don't want them to die of thirst. STOP.
> Signed,
> Captain Antônio Teixeira
> *vulgo,* The Hawk

Since their ambush on government troops, there had been a brief lull in the cangaceiros' activities, followed by more violence. The Hawk's group kidnapped a colonel's daughter and later released her for a hefty ransom. They robbed a train in the town of Aparecida, Great Western of Brazil's westernmost station. The train's cargo cars were filled with corn and manioc flour destined for sale on the coast. The cangaceiros shot the conductor in the thigh and distributed the food among the locals.

When the first of such articles appeared in the *Diário de Pernambuco,* Degas read it aloud during breakfast.

"Please," Dona Dulce said, waving her pale hand in Degas' direction, "I won't have gore at the table."

"I'll skip over the gore then," Degas said, "for your sake, and Emília's."

Beside her, Degas opened the *Diário* to the article's second page. Emília smelled the newsprint's ink. She sensed Degas' stare, as if he was daring her to look at the paper. Emília recalled their conversation in his bedroom, when she'd smoked her first and last cigarette. Felipe and the colonel's maids had told Degas all about her kidnapped sister with the crooked arm. He knew the Hawk had taken Luzia.

Emília kept her head bowed and her eyes upon the runny egg on her plate. She stabbed its yolk, then ran her knife in quick diagonals across it.

"Read on, son," Dr. Duarte said.

After Degas read the first cangaceiro article, Emília was determined not to be surprised again. She woke each day at dawn and took the newspaper before anyone else did.

Emília smuggled the papers into the mirrored reception room, where maids rarely entered. There, in the room's dim light, she read. Slowly, the newspapers' favorite topic shifted from the Hawk to his companion. A woman, they said. A woman who dressed like a man. According to interviews with locals, the cangaceiros called her the Seamstress. At first, people doubted her existence and the reports printed no specifics about the cangaceira's looks, which frustrated Emília. Finally, a Recife reporter caught sight of the Hawk's group while traveling in the backlands. The cangaceiros fleeced him of his money and smashed his typewriter, but he managed to return to Recife alive and write a series of articles about his adventures.

"The Seamstress" Revealed: A Profile
by Joaquim Cardoso

Who is this Seamstress? One could say she is just a woman, but she wears men's trousers and brass-rimmed spectacles of considerable value. One hint of womanliness can be found on her belongings: her bags and canteens are decorated in gaudy colors. In this respect, she is like many women in the backland's small, dingy towns: trying to look presentable but failing. She is unusually tall and has a deformed arm. Despite these unique attributes, in every other sense she is like any farmer's wife. She has big feet, dirty nails, a meaty mouth, and flaccid breasts. She is a vulgar woman, and the backlands are filled with such women.

What sets the Seamstress apart is that she is *not* a farmer's wife. She has wed a bandit—a dark-skinned, ugly, foul-smelling man. She has a troubling and furtive gaze. She puts her own life at risk, protects the weakest of the band, and with silent repulsion she allows her husband's sanguine atrocities. She is insensitive and yet sentimental, frigid and yet fierce—in short, she is a woman. And what man would be capable of penetrating the mysteries of such a contradictory soul?

Emília read the article until its words became blurs. Luzia was alive. There was no doubt now. But her relief was quickly replaced by anger. Who was this reporter, to say such things? Luzia's gaze was not furtive. Her sister was not vulgar. Then came fear: What if Luzia had changed? Hadn't Emília herself become someone different during her time in Recife? Sadness pressed on her, like a rock set upon her chest. It was as if something precious had been stolen from her and then returned, but in an unrecognizable form. Who was this woman? This Seamstress? Beneath everything, Emília felt something strange. Cold. The way she used to feel when she looked at a lovely piece of lace and could not own it. The way she sometimes felt about the *Fon Fon* models, with their perfect hair and smart dresses. She had always envied Luzia's freedom, her strength. She envied it still.

Emília wanted to clip the article and place it with her Communion portrait, but she could not. She had to carefully refold the paper, as she did each day, and return it to the mailbox beside the Coelhos' iron gate. At breakfast, Degas read the article hesitantly, as if its contents troubled him. Impatient, Dr. Duarte snatched the paper from his son's hands and finished it himself. Then he asked a maid for a pair of scissors and clipped the article at the table, despite Dona Dulce's objections.

The clipping sat on his desk, in his study. Emília was forced to see it each afternoon. She'd become her father-in-law's personal secretary. After his political meetings at the British Club, Dr. Duarte had many ideas and plans. Emília's father-in-law kept whatever Green Party strategies he knew a secret, but Dr. Duarte believed that after the election his criminology theories would be accepted and enforced. He had to be able to explain his science succinctly and effectively to Green Party leaders. Dr. Duarte could not keep all of his ideas in his head, but he could not write them down fast enough either. When he did, he couldn't understand his own penmanship. He didn't want to hire "some silly girl" who would gossip about his plans. The party would not approve. Dr. Duarte needed someone discreet, trustworthy, and immediately available. Emília was the obvious choice. As Dr. Duarte spoke, she wrote, though she didn't always spell his words correctly.

There were Dr. Ernst Kretschmer's three body types: Asthenic, or bony and narrow; Athletic, or muscular; and Pyknic, or rotund and fatty. The Asthenics were often schizophrenics, eccentrics, and criminals. The Athletics were generally normal. The Pyknics were philosophers, idlers, depressives. There was the inherent difference between a criminaloid (one who commits crimes or practices perversions because of his weak nature, which can be cured) and the true criminal, the *homo delinquins* (one who perpetuates crimes from childhood, showing no remorse and having no possibility of a cure). The true criminal was similar to primitive races and to children, both of whom were hedonistic, curious, and cruel.

"Among savage peoples," Dr. Duarte said as he paced his office, "the female appears to be less sensitive. That is, more cruel than the male and more inclined to vindictiveness. But no one knows if that's true in today's criminal. There are so few female offenders."

He looked down at his desk and brushed the newspaper clipping gently with the tips of his fingers.

"How I would like to measure her," he sighed. His voice was soft, affectionate.

"What would you see?" Emília asked.

Dr. Duarte looked up, startled by her voice.

"What would you see . . . in her?" Emília repeated.

"I don't know. But I have my theories." Dr. Duarte pursed his lips and looked at Emília, then opened a desk drawer and removed a wooden box. Inside, set within a velvet casing, was a set of silver pincers. They were large and curved. Their ends were flat. Dr. Duarte removed them from the box. They had handles like scissors.

"Allow me to show you?" he said.

Emília put down her notepad. "Oh, no! No, Dr. Duarte. It was just a silly question."

"Please," he said. "It's my pleasure to explain. And it will help with your note taking if you know what I'm referring to." He walked around the desk, calipers in hand. "No need to be frightened, my dear!" Dr. Duarte chuckled. "Now sit up straight. I may muss your hair."

He placed one of the caliper's flat ends between her eyes and stretched the other to the back of her skull. The metal felt cold.

"Root of nose to the back of skull is the maximum anterior posterior diameter," Dr. Duarte said. He took her notepad and pen. He scribbled a measurement on it and hid it from her view. Then, Dr. Duarte moved the calipers to either side of her head, pressing her temples. "The transverse diameter."

Emília closed her eyes. His suit smelled strongly of limes. It was the citrus cologne he spritzed on before each meeting at the British Club. She heard him mark another measurement.

He reset the calipers to the top of her scalp and at the base of her neck. "Transverse or bi-auricular curve," he said, then scribbled.

She felt his fingers—strong and stubby—hold the base of her skull straight. He was measuring with his hands now. Emília swallowed hard. She opened her eyes.

"There," Dr. Duarte said. "Finished. Now we do a bit of math. I have to add all five elements to get your cranial capacity, then apply a formula to get what we call the cephalic index."

Emília nodded. Dr. Duarte sat at his desk and hunched over the notepad. Emília turned in her chair. The Mermaid Girl was still placed on the back shelf, calm and sleeping.

"Ahem," Dr. Duarte coughed. "Emília?"

She turned back.

"You, my dear, are a brachycephalic."

"A what?"

Dr. Duarte laughed. "You have a perfectly lovely cranium, well within the normal index for women."

Emília sighed. Dr. Duarte smiled.

"Were you worried?" he asked, sitting back in his chair and weaving his nubby fingers together. "Criminal women are egotistical and malicious. They are liars. You, Emília, are none of those things."

Emília nodded and excused herself.

In her room, she slid the Communion portrait from its hiding place in her jewelry box. Emília wanted to pray, but for what? In thanks for her normalcy? For her lovely skull? She'd been nervous in Dr. Duarte's office. Even a bit frightened. When he'd revealed her results, she was both relieved and disappointed—she was normal, knowable. And Luzia was not. Luzia was immeasurable. She was as murky and unpredictable as the Capibaribe that dissected the city with its brown waters. Calm one moment, turbulent and frightening the next.

But to what extent, Emília thought, did their physical attributes dictate their fates? Aunt Sofia and Padre Otto believed that the body was a shell for the soul. It was the soul—that intangible spiritual essence—that shaped a person. But even souls had their limitations; Padre Otto said that Jesus saw into people's souls and knew every sin humans would commit before they'd even committed them. Instead of preventing those sins, he'd died for them. He'd given his life for their forgiveness, because the sins were inevitable.

Dr. Duarte attended mass and took Communion, but he believed that people's skulls—not their souls—dictated their futures. Skulls were shaped to accommodate brains, which were shaped by heritage. The Mermaid Girl's mother had been a drinker and a criminaloid, so her daughter, had she lived, would have inherited the same traits. Emília's father had been a drunk, but neither she nor Luzia could stand the smell of cane liquor. Dr. Duarte did not know her family history, yet he'd proclaimed her normal—not deceptive or malicious or selfish. And he was wrong; Emília knew that she carried all of those flaws. She'd lied, telling the Coelhos that her sister was dead. Some days, after bearing one of Dona Dulce's scathing remarks, Emília had sneaked into the kitchen, licked a spoon, and inserted it into all of her mother-in-law's precious jars of jam, maliciously hoping to sour them. And the other night, instead of comforting her husband after his strange confession, she'd turned from him, too concerned with her own fears to care about his.

Degas had confessed that he preferred a prescribed, predetermined life; it was comforting for him to believe his actions were inevitable, his brain inflexible.

Emília couldn't imagine entire lives being dictated by such coarse and vulnerable things as bodies or such elusive things as souls. She couldn't convince herself that her fate, or Degas', or Luzia's had been doomed from the beginning. Emília was accustomed to choice. Every seamstress was. Even the dullest, roughest muslin could be dyed, cut, and shaped into a fine dress if the right choices were made. Similar choices could turn the loveliest silk into a dimpled, snagged catastrophe. But individual fabrics, like people, had unique limitations and benefits. Some were tissue thin, lovely but fragile, undone by the smallest snag. Some were so closely woven that you could not see the fibers. Others were coarse, thick, and scratchy. There was no changing the character of a cloth. It could be cut, ripped, sewn into dresses or trousers or table settings, but no matter the form it took, a cloth always remained the same. Its true nature was fixed. Any good seamstress knew this.

Emília stared at the girls in her Communion portrait. She traced the line of Luzia's bent arm, traced the subtle curves of her own child's body that was turning into a woman's, and she wondered what in their characters was fixed and what had been a matter of choice. Emília recalled the pressure of Dr. Duarte's hands on her skull, the cold metal of his pincers. She recalled the words of the clipping on his desk: *And what man would be capable of penetrating the mysteries of such a contradictory soul?*

"No man," Emília whispered to the girls in her Communion portrait. "And certainly no pair of calipers."

Over the following weeks, Emília began to study trouser patterns. "Ladies' boating pants" was what the European fashion magazines called them. They were white and narrow waisted, with button flaps and wide legs. She could never sew a pair for herself; they were too risqué and the Auxiliary women would not approve. Still, she dreamed of the pants. Each afternoon, she stole change from Dr. Duarte's billfold and bought her own newspapers. She stopped at a newsstand on her way home from Lindalva's house. The stand's owner was her conspirator. He wrapped her *Diário de Pernambuco* in fashion magazines and winked as he handed it to her. She clipped the articles she wanted and locked them in her jewelry box. She read about Luzia's life as if her sister were a dark heroine in a romance. Emília felt excited to wake each day. Excited to see what Luzia would do next. Her sister was hundreds of kilometers away, but Emília felt as if Luzia was near her again. As if she was harboring a fugitive under the Coelhos' noses.

4

/ / / / / / / /

In March, Celestino Gomes lost his bid to become president. On election day, Dr. Duarte and other wealthy Green Party members wore emerald lapel pins and drove their Chryslers to downtown voting stations. When the state's votes were tallied, Gomes won Recife but lost the countryside. The colonels had united against him, giving all of the backlands' votes to the current president and Blue Party candidate. The same thing happened throughout the North, while in the South, Celestino Gomes won his home state of Minas Gerais but lost all of São Paulo and Rio de Janeiro, where the Blue Party was strongest.

Recife's mayor—a Blue Party man—called for a day of celebration. Dr. Duarte sulked in his study. Dona Dulce fretted over the consequences of her husband's politics; she made three vats of banana jam in one afternoon. Emília could not make her weekly visits to Lindalva because there were reports of clashes in the streets. Green Party crowds milled about, declaring the election a fraud, while Blue Party supporters celebrated. In the days after the election, dozens of street dogs were killed, their green bandannas stuffed into their mouths.

After the killings, student leaders planned a Green Party rally outside the mayor's palace. Emília and the Coelhos learned of the rally while listening to the parlor radio.

Dr. Duarte tapped his son's arm. "I'm too old for agitation," he said, "but you should join your peers."

Color rose in Degas' face. On election day, he'd reluctantly gone to the Green voting station with his father.

"It's useless agitation," Degas replied. "The elections are finished—"

"I agree," Dona Dulce interrupted. She'd come from the kitchen and still wore her white apron, its scalloped edges wilted from the stove's heat. There was an uncharacteristic flush to her cheeks. "Please, Duarte, no more political talk in the house. What's done is done."

Dr. Duarte wrapped his thick fingers together. He looked at Emília as if searching for an ally. She quickly returned her focus to her embroidery hoop. For once, Emília agreed with Dona Dulce and Degas. She was relieved that the elections were over and there would be no more Blue and Green nonsense.

"All right," Dr. Duarte said, smoothing his thick white hair. "I'll talk of science instead. You can't deny me that. Emília, refresh my old mind. Of Dr. Kretschmer's body types, the rotund ones—the men who are idlers and doubters—what are they called again?"

Emília looked up. Dona Dulce stared, her face rigid and expressionless, as if she'd dipped her skin in starch. Degas shifted in his chair. The stiff smoothness of his dress shirt wrinkled at the fold above his belly. On his face flickered the same worried look he'd given Emília each time he'd held her hand in public, as if pleading with her not to tug away.

"I don't recall," she replied.

She knew the word her father-in-law was looking for; it was *Pyknic*. When she'd first heard it, Emília had assumed the word was German, like the doctor who'd invented it, and it had reminded her of Padre Otto, although his bulk made him comforting and hearty, not lazy or weak natured.

"That's surprising, Emília," Dr. Duarte said. "You usually have such an exact memory."

"Gomes should accept his loss," Degas blurted out. "Isn't that what you like to say: 'Men honor their debts and accept their losses.'"

"Fair losses," Dr. Duarte replied. "Men should accept fair losses and fight unfair ones. I'd hope my son would understand the difference."

"I do," Degas said. "To you—to us—the results are unfair. But to the Blue Party they're more than fair, they're right."

"I didn't think you'd become a turncoat so quickly," Dr. Duarte said, smoothing his mustache.

Degas rose. His brow twitched, making it look as if he had something in his eye.

"Is your loyalty smashing a window?" he asked quietly. "Is it shouting in the street? That's easy enough. I'll go and do it."

"You will stay put," Dona Dulce interrupted. She focused her amber eyes on her husband. "Don't goad him, Duarte. We'll lose enough, now that your side hasn't won. I will not have our son identified with this insanity."

Dona Dulce rarely fought her husband. In the past months she'd been outvoted in her dislike of Emília's new wardrobe. She'd allowed the acquisition of a sewing machine despite her muttered complaints that her house was not a seamstress's office. She'd smiled patiently when Dr. Duarte wore his green ties and she'd endured all of Gomes's radio speeches. But that night, she had reached her limit.

Dr. Duarte nodded. "Thank your mother, Degas. She protects you. She always has."

Degas pushed past Dona Dulce and left the parlor.

After that evening, Degas spoke curtly to his mother. He avoided Dona Dulce's gaze and brushed her away if she tried to straighten his collar or fuss with his thin wisps of hair. Degas winced each time Dr. Duarte spoke of Gomes, but he did not argue with his father again. He dutifully attended his legal classes. Instead of spending his afternoons away from the Coelho house, Degas began to stay home and sit in his father's study. He accompanied Dr. Duarte on trips to visit the Coelho properties around the city and make sure the buildings hadn't been vandalized by Blue Party loyalists. Degas was too busy with his father to spend time with his law school friends, or with Emília. He refused to take Emília to the fabric store because of the street clashes between Green and Blue supporters. Denied sewing supplies, and unable to make visits to Lindalva's house, Emília was forced back into the Coelho courtyard, where she pretended to embroider. Secretly, she spied through the open study doors and observed her husband and father-in-law.

Dr. Duarte was still sore at Degas for not being a true Green Party loyalist. He needled his son with stories of Gomes patriots, and when Degas looked uncomfortable—his mouth set in a scowl, his body fidgeting, as if his chair was covered in bristles—Dr. Duarte changed tacks, complimenting Degas on his focus and his newfound

attention to the family properties. Hearing these things, Degas hesitantly perked up. He reminded Emília of a horse on a tether, stubbornly tugging against its captivity but never breaking the tie. It
tugged just to show it could, and when its owner returned with oats
and a reassuring pat, it was reluctantly content.

Emília felt sorry for her husband, but she didn't deserve to be
denied her sewing materials. In response, Emília barely spoke to
Degas. Dr. Duarte was also angry with his wife for her overprotec-
tiveness. And Dona Dulce was furious with all of them: with Dr.
Duarte for his crude politics, with Degas for his brusqueness, and
with Emília for bearing witness to her disappointments. Dona Dulce
took her anger out on the maids, who, in turn, overstarched the
laundry and singed Dr. Duarte's best shirts with the iron. Only the
courtyard turtles and the corrupião bore no grudges.

As winter arrived, a muggy heat pressed on the city. There were
two trolley car collisions, several knifings, and a riot at a local market when it was rumored that vendors were secretly selling donkey
meat. From her room in the Coelho house, Emília caught a whiff of
something decaying, like rotting fruit or poorly salted beef that had
not kept. Soon, the scent invaded the Coelho house. She believed it
was the city—its stale air, its stagnant swamp water—but the errand
boy discovered that it was a street dog, dumped over the Coelhos'
back gate, its coat pocked with sores, its teeth set in a frozen snarl, its
body bloated and ready to burst.

5

On May 22, 1930, at the same time that the Blue Party candidate
was inaugurated as president in Rio de Janeiro, the *Graf Zeppelin*
landed in Recife. The city papers buried the inauguration on page
three, giving priority to the German dirigible. For weeks, the *Graf
Zeppelin* had overshadowed politics. It would cross the Atlantic to
make its first landing in South America, and the privileged site was

not Rio de Janeiro but Recife. The North had trumped the South. After the elections, the city government built a landing tower in the flat marsh of Afogados. They named it Camp Jiquiá and equipped it with a fuel post, a pavilion for ceremonies, a chapel, and a radio tower. The *Graf Zeppelin*'s arrival was expected to draw a large crowd. In order to pay for Camp Jiquiá's construction, the city planned to charge admission. The mayor declared the landing an official holiday and even the Coelho maids took the afternoon off in the hopes of seeing the dirigible.

The *Graf Zeppelin* was 230 meters long; Emília had read its dimensions in the papers. It could reach 110 kilometers an hour and would cross the Atlantic Ocean in a record three days. The newspaper called it "the Silver Fish." Dr. Duarte called it a flying cow. When Emília asked what he meant, Dr. Duarte let out a sigh and smiled, as if relieved that someone other than Degas had taken notice of him.

"After the Dutch invaded," Dr. Duarte began, setting down his breakfast utensils, "there's a story that they wanted to build a bridge but had no money. Count de Nassau, the Dutch governor, built a platform and said that a cow was going to fly from it. People came in droves to watch and he charged admission! Nassau was a clever man, but devious. I would have liked to measure him." Dr. Duarte paused and stared at his plate, as if imagining this measuring session. After a minute, he shook his head and continued. "There was no flying cow of course. They took a cowhide and stuffed it, then dropped it from the platform. People were so busy looking at the cow that they forgot they'd been cheated by the Dutchman."

"They weren't cheated, dearest," Dona Dulce interrupted. "They got a bridge, after all."

"They had their pockets picked!" Dr. Duarte snapped.

"They gave their money freely," Dona Dulce continued, her voice soothing. "Don't you always say that only born fools are drawn toward foolishness?"

Dr. Duarte grunted and returned to his meal. After breakfast, Dona Dulce took Emília aside and told her not to encourage his outbursts. Dr. Duarte was still bitter about the election. Contrary to Dona Dulce's worries, he'd lost little influence. Many of the Old families and Blue Party leaders owed him money, which made them act favorably toward him. And despite the distraction of the *Graf Zeppelin,* the Green Party had not disappeared entirely. There were still harsh editorials in the *Diário de Pernambuco* about the continuing effects of the Crisis. There were still student opposition groups, which Degas, hoping to reconcile with his father, claimed to have joined. There were hushed references to a revolt. And Dr. Duarte still went to his meetings at the British Club, although he wore his Green Party pin hidden underneath his lapel. Emília wasn't sure if he hid it from public view or from Dona Dulce.

On the day of the *Graf Zeppelin*'s landing, Emília spotted the pin's gold nub protruding from Dr. Duarte's lapel. Anyone openly displaying green, the city government said, would be barred from the landing ceremony. They did not want agitators, especially on the ceremonial pavilion where the Coelhos, along with the mayor and other prominent families, had been invited to view the Graf's landing. The pavilion's borders were draped in blue fabric and in its center were rows of white wooden chairs. No one sat. There was a better chance of catching a breeze standing up, although when wind arrived it was warm and moist, like a pant. Handkerchiefs were out in abundance. Men wiped their foreheads and cheeks. Women waved silk fans before their faces. A small orchestra played at the narrow end of the pavilion. Sweat ran down the musicians' necks and darkened their collars. A waiter in a white jacket worn so thin it looked like gauze placed a cup of fruit juice in Emília's hands. The juice was sugary and lukewarm.

Emília felt the fabric of her dress clinging to her back. It was one of her creations—a belted, yellow-and-white gown that fell just below the knee.

"You look like an egg," Dona Dulce had said before they left the Coelho house.

"I look like Coco Chanel," Emília replied.

Her dress was not nearly as elegant as the Frenchwoman's she'd seen in magazines, but she didn't care. She no longer needed to heed Dona Dulce's old-fashioned warnings. Emília was a member of the Ladies' Auxiliary. She had social weight. She had her own agenda. The campaign for suffrage had ended with the March election but Emília's dream of her own atelier had not. In the months since the election, she'd resurrected her weekly visits to Lindalva. Emília slowly transformed her friend's disappointment into resolve. They could thumb their noses at the Blue leaders and run a business, Emília told her friend. They could single-handedly bring women's trousers into style. They could educate their seamstresses, making them literate workingwomen to join the ranks of typists, schoolteachers, and telephone operators. Emília had even hinted at her plans to Dr. Duarte. The elections had thwarted his dreams for a state-sponsored Criminology Institute and he no longer needed a secretary, but Emília still went to his study whenever Degas did not. She listened to Dr. Duarte's ideas and cautiously shared her own. When she spoke of her desire to outfit Recife women, she made sure to use the words Dr. Duarte liked best: modernity, advancement, innovation. She never used the term *business*; instead she said *hobby*. Dr. Duarte chuckled at her talk of dresses and hats and hemlines, but when Dona Dulce asserted that Emília could not wear her yellow-and-white dress to the *Graf Zeppelin* landing, Dr. Duarte shook his head.

"We must greet modernity with modern style," he said, settling the matter and smiling at Emília.

The *Graf Zeppelin* was scheduled to arrive at four PM. By five o'clock it had not appeared. Below the pavilion, the crowds grew agitated. Trolley cars had worked triple shifts in order to bring spectators to the event. City workers had cleared an area for mid-range ticket holders: students, journalists, merchants, and families that were not invited to the pavilion. In this area, planks had been placed over the muddy ground and long, wooden pathways with handrails were constructed to steer the middle-income crowds back and forth from their trolleys. Beyond this, in a fenced and muddy expanse bordered by a thousand police officers, stood "the masses," as Dona Dulce called them. They were loud and jubilant, singing and dancing despite the heat. Emília saw two little girls, barefoot and giggling, weave through the crowd. They wore green ribbons in their hair.

Beside Emília, Degas leaned slightly over the pavilion's rails. Below, in the middle-class platform, stood Felipe. He wore a tatty suit and a misshapen fedora. Back in Taquaritinga, Emília recalled, she used to think Felipe's clothes were the picture of elegance.

When he saw Degas, Felipe took off his hat and waved it, slowly at first and then more energetically. Degas turned his back, staring intently at the pavilion's band. Felipe stopped waving. He looked directly at Emília, who quickly turned away. According to Degas, Felipe had been expelled from the Federal University Law School because of his continued vocal support of the Green Party. Since then, they'd had no study sessions together. Degas' grades had fallen.

At six PM, the orchestra stopped playing. The mayor began his speech. Emília shaded her eyes and stared at the landing tower. It looked like a giant cup and saucer balanced on top of a red-and-white post. The mayor explained that the tower acted as a kind of hitching post, connecting to the end of the *Graf Zeppelin* and stabilizing it. Passengers and crew would exit at ground level from the cabin attached to the dirigible's belly. They would not stay in Recife long. The *Graf Zeppelin* would refuel and fly to Rio de Janeiro. The "captain," Claudio Chevalier, an aristocrat, pilot, and the mayor's guest of honor, had traveled all the way from Rio to participate in the landing. Once the *Graf Zeppelin* had refueled, Captain Chevalier would board the dirigible and assist with the flight.

The mayor's voice was strong, but it could not carry to the crowd below, who began to mill about. On the pavilion, people clapped politely for Chevalier. Emília watched the crowd below shade their eyes and stare at the sky, believing the *Graf Zeppelin* had arrived. Chevalier removed his black pilot's cap and waved.

He was a small man with dark crescents beneath his eyes and a tangle of brown hair. He reminded Emília of a sagüi. Such monkeys were common in Taquaritinga and, to Emília's surprise, in Recife as well, where they skipped along the Tramways power lines, stole fruit, and filled the air with their high-pitched squeaks. Like Chevalier, they had small, glistening eyes and muffs of fur protruding from their heads.

Beside her, Degas pulled out a handkerchief. He gently dabbed his face and neck. When the clapping subsided and the orchestra began to play, he stuffed the handkerchief back into his pocket and left. Emília straightened her hat and followed her husband.

Degas wove through the guests until he reached the front of the pavilion, where Chevalier stood. The pilot greeted a crowd of ladies. Degas edged near him. When the group of ladies fell away, Chevalier smiled and extended a hand. Degas' forehead shone with sweat. Without his usual charm, Degas sputtered an introduction, then wiped his palm on his suit trousers and gripped the pilot's hand. Her husband looked large and awkward compared to the sprightly Chevalier. Emília felt a pang of pity for him.

The pilot smiled and looked past Degas. He jutted his chin toward Emília.

"I have another lady fan," Chevalier said.

Degas turned around. Emília saw a flash of recognition on his face followed by annoyance.

"Oh, no," Degas muttered. "This is my wife."

Captain Chevalier took Emília's hand in his, pulling her forward, loosening her glove.

"I was told Northerners were unattractive," Chevalier said, his eyes remaining on Degas. "Now I know that's false."

His Rio accent was thick and exaggerated. He did not pronounce his *t*'s. Emília slipped her hand away. She tugged her glove straight.

"I was told that Southerners were tall," she said. "But now I know that's false."

Chevalier blinked. Degas wrinkled his brow. His mouth opened, but before he could speak, Chevalier did.

"She's a pistol," he said to Degas. "You have excellent taste."

Emília felt a prickling heat rise along the back of her neck. Chevalier spoke as if she were a well-chosen accessory—a pocket watch, a silk tie, a finely woven Panama hat—and nothing more. Emília stared at Degas. His starched collar was limp.

"You look flushed," Degas said, patting her back. "Find a waiter and get some punch, won't you? I don't want you fainting."

Emília nodded. She did not want to be near Degas or the pilot, though part of her wanted to stay, to intrude on their conversation. Emília headed for the pavilion's bar. There, she ordered a cup of sugarcane liquor topped with fruit juice. Before she took a sip, a hand gripped her shoulder and wrenched it back.

"Stand up straight! Don't sulk!"

The voice was low and nasal. When it tried to bark another order, it dissolved into giggles. Emília turned around. Lindalva pulled her close, kissing her cheeks. Her friend wore a huge straw hat, the brim lifted and held back with a pearl-studded pin. The hat's straw was bleached white and so finely woven that it was soft and malleable, like a manioc pancake. Lindalva lifted the cup from Emília's hand and took a sip. She pursed her lips.

"Your drink is spiked, Mrs. Coelho," Lindalva said.

Emília took the cup back. "I hate this Zeppelin."

"How do you know?" Lindalva laughed. "You haven't even met it."

"I don't need to."

"You sound like Mother," Lindalva said.

The baroness had left town before the *Graf Zeppelin*'s landing, preferring to spend the winter at her country house in Garanhuns.

"Well, this Zeppelin character is very rude," Lindalva said. "He's late for his own party."

Emília nodded and sipped her punch. Her gullet burned. Through the crowd she watched Degas. He hunched close to Chevalier and nodded intently as the pilot spoke. Chevalier smiled and gestured with his hands, adoring the attention. Degas offered him a cigarette and he accepted, leaning close as Degas lit it.

Lindalva took the punch from Emília and had another sip.

"That Captain Chevalier is a cad," she said. "Someone should introduce him to a hairbrush."

Below them, on the muddy ground, the crowd cheered.

"Oh," Lindalva sighed, taking Emília's hand. "Look."

In the distance was a glimmer, like a mirror in the setting sun. Emília squinted. The orchestra stopped. A hush fell upon the crowd. Slowly, the *Graf Zeppelin* hovered, moving toward the marsh. It was long and bullet-shaped, narrowing at the end with a finned tail. It floated toward them serenely, like a silver cloud. From far away it looked small and weightless, reminding Emília of the fire balloons she and Luzia had made. As it moved closer to Camp Jiquiá, Emília realized that it was massive.

"It's like a great whale," a woman beside her said.

"No," a man replied, "it's like a ship, sailing in the air."

"Viva Mr. Zé Pelin!" a voice from the crowd below called out. There was a wave of laughter. On the pavilion, ladies and gentlemen chuckled.

The sun had nearly set when the *Graf Zeppelin* loomed over them, shading the pavilion. Its engine buzzed. The white passenger box attached to its belly looked miniscule. As the *Graf Zeppelin* descended toward the landing tower, ropes were dropped. Uniformed officers shouted and ran along the landing strip, as if commanding a giant, clumsy animal. When it lurched into position, its nose connecting to the landing tower and its belly touching down, the crowd erupted.

There were cheers, whistles, and then the faraway pop of firecrackers. Emília looked away from the *Graf Zeppelin* and into the crowd. Fireworks and explosives of any kind had been strictly forbidden near the dirigible. In the crowd below, a green flag unfurled.

"Viva Gomes!" a man yelled. "Fight for a New Brazil!"

On the pavilion, there were gasps. Below, in the middle-class section, a group of students released green streamers. Emília saw Felipe in the crowd, hooking his arm back and throwing the green serpentinas to the masses, who cheered. The circle of police surged inward.

There were more loud pops, then screams. Penned within Camp Jiquiá, the crowd moved forward. The pavilion lurched. Emília felt the painted wooden planks shift beneath her feet, like the sand on Boa Viagem Beach.

"Come along," a man beside Emília said to his wife. "Let's leave before some disgrace occurs."

Around her, there were whispers and then prodding. Emília looked for Dr. Duarte, for Dona Dulce, for Degas. She could not see them within the jostling group, all headed for the pavilion's front, blue-bannered staircase. Lindalva's hat was knocked from her head. Emília saw the orchestra members move quickly down the pavilion's back stairs, holding their instruments above their heads as if wading through water. She took hold of Lindalva's hand and followed them.

6

The back stairs led to the trolleys. The cars sat in a line, their normal route signs covered in white banners scrawled with "Camp Jiquiá." Escapees from the middle-class section crowded the path. Trolley conductors blew their brass whistles and guided people aboard. Emília felt dizzy, her mouth too dry. She held firmly to Lindalva's hand and boarded a car.

Emília had been told never to ride a trolley. If there was an emergency, if she found herself with no recourse, Dona Dulce had advised her to ride only the first-class Cristaleira. The Cristaleira cars had electric fans, glass windows, and dress requirements: gloves for ladies, ties and jackets for gentlemen. Her mother-in-law said that there were brawls aboard second-class cars. There were perverts who peeked up women's skirts.

All of the Camp Jiquiá trolleys were second class, with metal rails and simple wooden seats. There was no room to sit. People pressed together until the car's center became packed and airless. Lindalva gripped Emília's arm. Men hung from the trolley's side rails, balancing their feet on its entrance step. Emília envied them: it would be cooler there than inside. The assistant conductor walked around the outside of the car. His navy uniform looked terribly hot. He blew his whistle to indicate that the car was full. No one listened. People pushed past him, nearly knocking off his leather ticket satchel, and climbed abroad. In the crush, Emília believed she saw Felipe—his freckled cheeks flushed, his hand clapped on top of his fedora so the hat would not fall off. Then he disappeared.

"Go!" one of the orchestra men yelled to the conductor. "Or we'll be crushed!"

The assistant hopped aboard the back rail of the car. The conductor rang the car's bell, and with a jolt, the trolley pushed forward.

The orchestra men stood in a huddle near Emília. They'd opened their suit jackets and unbuttoned their collars. Some still wore the blue satin sash the mayor had required of all pavilion workers. Beside Emília, a boy held a half-eaten cob of grilled corn. Another small child hugged its mother's leg. The woman stared suspiciously at Emília's cloche. Beyond those packed closest to her, Emília saw only rows of hands gripping the trolley's rails and the sweat-stained underarms of jackets and shirts. Emília wanted to take her hat off— her hair was dripping underneath it—but she had nowhere to put it. She held the trolley rail with one hand and her purse with the other. There was nothing in the bag but some hairpins, a handkerchief, and a one mil-réis note that she'd filched from Degas. It was practically worthless, but it gave her comfort. Emília hoped it would be enough to pay their fare.

She didn't know how much a trolley cost. Imagine! When she was in Taquaritinga, she'd dreamed of riding trolleys. It was, after all, the way most Recifans traveled. Compared to Dona Conceição's mules it was luxurious. Painted along the car's ceiling were colorful advertisements. *Take Nogueira's Vitamin Elixir! Use Dorly Soap! Make Your Hair Shine with Egg-Oil Hair Cream! Smoke Flores Cigarettes— They're Made in Recife!*

The trolley moved out of the lowlands and past rows of white-washed houses, carpenters' shops, juice stands, and open-air diners. In the hills were the mocambos: rows upon rows of crooked, palm-frond huts constructed by immigrants from the countryside. The sun had set completely and the sky turned a dark gray. Crickets sang. Inside the trolley, the passengers had calmed. They sighed and smiled at their escape. They shouted "Here!" at the conductor whenever he neared their stop. The assistant conductor hopped off and took their payment in his leather satchel. Lindalva kept her eyes closed and her hand locked around Emília's arm. Emília did not know how far the trolley would go or where it would stop, but she did not feel scared. She felt giddy. Wasn't this what she'd imagined Recife to be—this noisy crush, this ringing trolley bell, these smells, this chatter? Wasn't this the city she had dreamed of?

As people exited the trolley, the car became less cramped. Emília paid closer attention to Lindalva. Her friend smiled weakly and patted her face with a handkerchief.

"We're almost there," Emília assured her, but she didn't know where "there" was. She did not want to return to the Coelho house. She did not want to exit at Derby Square.

"Good heavens!" a woman chided from the back of the trolley. "Mind yourselves!"

There was a scuffle. Emília saw one of the orchestra men pushing a drunk in ratty clothes. There was shouting. Their faces were flushed and angry. They grappled. The remaining orchestra members cheered their friend. The drunk ripped off the orchestra member's blue sash. The assistant conductor blew his whistle. The other trolley riders moved away from the fight, crowding Emília and obscuring her view.

"Mother Mary!" a woman screamed.

"Stop the car!" a man shouted.

The conductor looked back. "We've got to wait for the next stop," he yelled. "It'll cause a collision to stop in the middle of the tracks."

There was another scream. The drunk jumped off the trolley car. In the dusk light, Emília saw something glimmer in his hands.

"Viva Gomes!" he shouted from the ground.

Another orchestra member jumped from the car, then another and another. They chased the drunk, their figures becoming shadows as the trolley moved forward. The remaining passengers backed away from the trolley's center, pinning themselves against its waist-high walls. The boy beside Emília dropped his corncob. Lindalva gasped and gripped Emília's arm tighter.

She will leave a bruise, Emília thought.

The corncob rolled to the center of the car. The fighting orchestra man knelt. He crossed his arms against his stomach, like a child with a bellyache. His remaining band mates looked on, their instruments in their limp hands. An inky stain spread across his shirt. He sucked in a long breath and wobbled backward. His arms loosened and then let go. There was a dark slash across his midsection. His insides unfurled from the cut like a flower blooming from his belly.

Emília heard the screech of the trolley car. She felt herself moving backward. She saw the cob of corn, stained now, rolling toward her. The dark, shining puddle beneath the slumped musician trickled toward her shoes. Lindalva fainted. She fell onto Emília, knocking the air from her lungs. Emília stumbled backward with Lindalva in her arms. She was ready to fall. Ready to hit the wet floor. She closed her eyes but did not feel the impact.

When the trolley came to a full stop, Emília opened her eyes. There was a hand upon her waist and another along her back, cradling her. Propping her up. The hands felt strong and, for an instant, Emília recalled her childhood heroes—those romantic and brooding men from the pages of *Fon Fon*. Quickly, she regained her balance and heaved up Lindalva. Then she turned to face her rescuer.

Emília did not see the broad forehead and massive frame of one of her romantic heroes. Instead, she saw a freckle-spotted face. Its brown eyes were lined with pale lashes. She recalled Luzia's old teasing: *Pig eyes! Pig eyes!* Emília recoiled.

"I'll help you," Felipe said, moving to Lindalva's other side.

His sandy hair was matted; during the cramped trolley ride he'd lost his fedora. Together, he and Emília carried Lindalva from the trolley. They were in a working-class neighborhood. Small, white-washed shop fronts with crookedly painted signs lined the street. On the corner was a diner. The owners and patrons had left their tables and stood in the restaurant's open doorways to watch the trolley. Emília and Felipe carried Lindalva inside and propped her in a chair.

"I'll see if I can get some vinegar," Felipe said. Emília nodded.

Outside, the trolley's electric lights had clicked on. The conductor shouted. He and the remaining orchestra members moved the dead man. Emília wanted to ask for a lit candle to place in his hands and guide his soul. She wanted to run into the neighborhood's dark alleys, away from Felipe, but she had Lindalva to consider. Emília took a newspaper from the dining table and fanned her friend's face. Felipe returned with the restaurant owner's wife, who waved a bottle of vinegar beneath Lindalva's nose. When she woke, she drank two cups of sugar water. Her face was pallid, her hands trembling.

Felipe handed Emília a cup of sugar water.

"You should have some," he said.

Under the restaurant's gas lamps, his freckles took on the color of cooked condensed milk, heated and stirred until it became caramel. Emília felt short of breath.

"No thank you," she said, pushing the cup away.

"Drink it," he said gently. "You may feel fine, but what we saw . . . it was a terrible shock."

She felt angry, suddenly, at his courtesy.

"I know what I need and don't need, thank you," Emília said, imitating the indifferent tone Dona Dulce used with her maids.

"Pardon me, Mrs. Coelho," Felipe said. He set down the cup of sugar water and glanced at Lindalva. She'd closed her eyes again and was taking deep breaths, guided by the restaurant owner's wife.

"Degas went down the front steps with that pilot. I saw him," Felipe said. "He left us both to the trolleys."

"I didn't look for him," Emília replied. "I left on my own."

Felipe lifted the cup of sugar water meant for Emília. He took a long sip. His lips—pink and thin, bordered unevenly by freckles—

pursed. Opening his jacket, Felipe rifled through the pockets and removed a small pencil and his *Graf Zeppelin* ticket stub. The middle-class tickets were meant to be mementos, printed on thick paper with a sketch of the dirigible and the date, May 22, 1930, stamped across their faces. Felipe bent over the restaurant's wooden table and wrote on the ticket stub. When he finished, he folded it into quarters and handed the fat square to Emília.

"Give this to him, would you?"

Emília glanced at Lindalva. Her friend kept her eyes closed and gulped another serving of sugar water offered by a waitress.

"Deliver it yourself," Emília said. "You're his friend."

"I'm not allowed near the legal college," Felipe replied, staring intently at the folded ticket. His pink mouth twitched. "Degas avoids me. Dona Dulce doesn't want me calling at your house."

Felipe leaned forward. Emília smelled sweat and cigarette smoke on his suit jacket. He clamped his hand over hers. Moving brusquely, he turned Emília's wrist over and fumbled with her fingers until she and Felipe were caught in an awkward handshake. He pushed the square of paper into her gloved palm.

Emília thought of Professor Célio, of their note exchanges, of how greedy she'd been for his replies, of how feverishly she'd waited to see him each month. She saw that same greed, that same awkward eagerness in Felipe and felt a stirring of sympathy for him. But when his grip loosened, Emília instinctively tugged away. She dropped the folded ticket onto the table.

"I won't," she said.

Felipe nodded stiffly. His brown eyes were wide, their pupils large, as if he'd caught a fever.

"You worked in my house," he said, his voice hushed. "Not that long ago. You were a giggler. But your sister wasn't. She couldn't afford to be silly, not with that crooked arm. It's a shame, what happened to her."

Emília felt a sharp pain in her breast. It was as if a needle had pricked her lungs, deflating them. She let out a long breath. Emília reached for the half-empty glass of sugar water and finished it.

"You don't have to remind me of our acquaintance," she said, putting down the cup and taking up the folded ticket stub. "You never spoke to me in Taquaritinga. Now you know what it's like to be avoided."

Emília glanced at Lindalva; her friend's eyes were still closed, her head down. Emília slipped the stub into her glove, poking it down past her wrist until it settled into her palm.

Outside, their trolley car was gone, moved before there was a collision on the tracks. Lindalva had left her purse inside the car. Emília did not have enough money for their fare to Derby Square. She could not telephone the Coelho house; there were no phone lines in the neighborhood.

"We'll need trolley fare," Emília said, startling Felipe from his thoughts. "Degas doesn't give me pocket money."

Felipe nodded. Once Lindalva felt stronger, they walked to the nearest trolley stop where Felipe paid for their tickets and cautiously waved good-bye. Emília and Lindalva rode to Derby Square in silence. Each time Emília closed her hand into a fist, the ticket's pointed edges pressed into her skin. Her sympathy was replaced by anger—at Felipe for making her a messenger, at her husband for his convenient escape, and at herself for her weakness, her shame.

In the months since the first articles had appeared about the Seamstress, Emília had convinced herself that only Degas knew the similarities between the cangaceira and Luzia, and that his suspicions could not be proven. Emília had made herself believe that Felipe—who'd never gone near his mother's sewing room and rarely returned to Taquaritinga after starting at the university—didn't remember Luzia. But he did. When he'd mentioned Luzia, Emília hadn't thought of claiming her sister or defending her. The comfort and pride she'd felt each time she read an article about the Seamstress were replaced by shame, by fear. Emília recalled her long lessons with Dona Dulce, her many walks in Derby Square in the hopes of gaining acceptance. She thought of her membership in the Ladies' Auxiliary and of the very real possibility of opening her own atelier—that many-windowed and spotless place she'd often dreamed of, with rows of well-fed seamstresses creating her designs. All of her work, all of her plans would be lost if people knew about Luzia. Emília could hear the Recife women's shocked voices: what kind of family allows a girl to be carted off by cangaceiros? Only poor unfortunates kept their daughters so weakly guarded; only people with no background, no money, and worse—no decency. No respectable woman bought dresses from a criminal's relative. No one, not even the baroness and Lindalva, would associate with a person of such low caliber. Dr. Duarte would want to measure Emília again, to study her as he studied the families of prisoners at the Downtown Detention Center. Dona Dulce would not want her in the Coelho house. Emília would be sent into the streets.

She shivered and leaned against the trolley's wooden rail. The planks' studs dug into her back. Next to her, Lindalva kept her eyes closed and her hands firmly around a napkin from the diner, given to her in place of a handkerchief. Emília wondered if her friend was still upset by the murder on the trolley, or if Lindalva was ignoring her. How much of Felipe's conversation had her friend heard? What did Lindalva suspect? Emília took a deep breath and stared into the city streets. The closer they got to Derby Square, the less dark the city became. Gas streetlamps created yellow circles of light. Modest, one-story shacks disappeared, replaced by taller, bulkier homes with decorative fences. Guard dogs howled behind their gates. Emília's eyes stung.

She had failed Luzia once before, when the cangaceiros took her. Emília had kept quiet, had not defended her sister, had not offered herself in Luzia's place. Now, though the circumstances were different, Emília felt she had done the same thing. The ticket stub in her glove was moist with sweat. Emília's heart beat heavily in her chest. It felt too large—cumbersome and bumbling, like the *Graf Zeppelin*. *I will have to learn how to tether it,* she thought. *I will have to rope it down.*

At the baroness's house, a maid phoned the Coelhos. Lindalva, still shocked by the murder, hugged Emília tightly and cried. "I can only think of that poor man on the trolley!" Lindalva said, sniffling. "I keep seeing his face. Everything's a blur after that. I hope I wasn't too much trouble for you?" Emília shook her head, relieved by Lindalva's forgetfulness.

Thirty minutes later, Degas arrived in the Chrysler Imperial. During their ride to Madalena, he recalled the chaos at the Zeppelin pavilion and explained how he and Captain Chevalier were guided immediately into the mayor's automobile. Emília did not think to ask about Dr. Duarte and Dona Dulce: if they'd left the pavilion, if they'd arrived home safely. Degas drove quickly, as always. Recife's roads were only recently equipped for cars; there were few stops. At the single traffic light at the intersection of Visconde de Albuquerque and Rua José Osório Emília pulled off her glove and handed Degas the folded square within it.

"Here," she said.

"What's this?"

"A note. From Felipe."

Degas stared at her. The traffic light, built into a post on the corner, projected a red glow onto his face.

"He was on the trolley," Emília said, her voice irritatingly shaky. "Take it."

Like Felipe, she pushed the square into Degas' hand.

"What does it say?" he asked.

"I don't know. I don't read other people's notes."

Degas was still. He held the ticket stub in one hand and gripped the steering wheel with the other. When the light changed, he did not accelerate. A breeze came through the car's windows, bringing with it the rank, mossy scent of the Capibaribe River, which they'd just crossed.

"He told me," Emília said, "that he's been having trouble finding you now that he's been expelled."

"It was stupid of him," Degas spat out. "He cares more about Gomes than anything else. Just like Father." He ran his hand along the ribbed steering wheel. "Father's promised me a stake in his business. If I finish at the university, if I don't make any mistakes, I'll have a share. I'll have responsibilities. He's going to let me manage his properties, Emília. I can't risk losing that."

Degas threw the note into her lap.

"Tear it up," he said. "I don't want it."

"He'll think I didn't deliver it."

"So?"

"He mentioned Taquaritinga," Emília said. "My sister. He remembers her."

Degas stared at the road ahead. The muscle at the base of his jaw twitched, as if he was clenching and unclenching his teeth. Without turning his head, Degas reached into Emília's lap and, fumbling with the skirt of her dress, took back the note.

"Don't tell Mother you took a trolley," he said. Then he shifted gears and pressed the gas pedal.

7

In June, winter rains washed away the city's dank smells. They flooded Camp Jiquiá. They forced construction of the Madalena trolley line to stop. They made the Capibaribe swell and surge onto the city's streets, carrying away summer's refuse. And they bred fat mosquitoes, made bold and awkward by their size. Emília killed them with one good slap.

The rains drove people indoors and seemed to dilute any political fervor. Arrests were made after the *Graf Zeppelin* riots, the instigators put into the Downtown Detention Center and forgotten. Even the newspapers calmed. They did not talk of revolution or political wrangling. Instead, they wrote about a meeting of sugar planters to discuss the precarious market; the first hydroplane, piloted by Mr. Chevalier, touching down in Recife's harbor; a shipment of oranges that England would not accept because they came bearing "tropical diseases"; and the invention of the alcohol motor. All faraway and unfamiliar things, Emília thought. All distractions.

Slowly, the downpours ebbed and became a fine mist, as if the old rains were being shaken through a sieve. On July twenty-sixth,

Degas came home early from classes. His face was flushed. He crumpled his hat in his hands. Dona Dulce ordered a maid to bring him water. Dr Duarte stepped out of his study to find out what was causing the commotion.

"Bandeira's been killed," Degas said. "Shot. Here. Downtown."

José Bandeira—Gomes's former vice-presidential candidate and Green Party hero—had been shot while eating pastries at the Gloria Bakery. Government radio reports claimed that the shooter was a jealous husband. They said that Bandeira had been fooling around with a cabaret singer and had died carrying a box from Krauze Jewelers in his pocket, a gift for his sweetheart. There were no photos of the woman, so Green Party newspapers and radio stations called her a hoax. When the killer was apprehended, he was identified as a political rival from Bandeira's native state of Paraíba. After that, many accused the Blue Party of slander and assassination. To prove his party's innocence, Recife's mayor placed the killer in the Downtown Detention Center.

There was a three-day funeral procession for José Bandeira. Throughout Recife and the entire North, windows were shrouded in black curtains. Candles were lit. Men wore black armbands. Military posts hung funeral wreaths from their gates in solidarity with Gomes, their fellow military man. The owner of the Pernambuco Tramways ordered new uniforms for his trolley conductors, trading their blue suits for green. Green rags were tied to lampposts and to the handrails of trolleys. The decorated street dogs returned.

In the months after Bandeira's death, as the wet season gave way to the dry, Recife's Blue Party government arrested two prominent Gomes supporters after they'd discovered stockpiles of dynamite in the men's Boa Vista homes. The British Club—Dr. Duarte's favorite haunt—was closed due to unpatriotic activities. Blue officials arrested a twelve-year-old gazetteer for the *Jornal da Tarde,* the official newspaper of Gomes's Liberal Alliance, claiming that the boy's daily shouting of headlines was a call to arms. City police raided pensões and luncheonettes in the São José neighborhood, looking for student activists. Degas read the arrest reports aloud at the breakfast table. One morning, he could not finish his recitation. As he held the newspaper, the color drained from Degas' cheeks.

"Well?" Dr. Duarte muttered. "Go on."

"Mr. Felipe Pereira," Degas mumbled. "Son of a colonel, taken into custody and placed in the Downtown Detention Center."

Dr. Duarte put down his fork. "He's that friend of yours, Degas?"

"Yes," Degas answered. He ruffled the paper.

"He's loyal to the party," Dr. Duarte said.

When Degas did not respond, Dr. Duarte heaved himself forward and tugged the newspaper from Degas' hands, revealing his son's face. Dr. Duarte stared. His white eyebrows sloped downward, making a crease in his forehead. His eyes did not mirror his brow's concern. His gaze had the same nervous intensity Emília had seen Dr. Duarte present before, in his study, each time he described a new theory or a potential candidate for measurement.

"I could use my influence," Dr. Duarte said. "Get him out."

Dona Dulce stirred her coffee. Her spoon grazed the bottom of the cup, producing a constant, dull scraping. Under the table, Emília felt the frantic tapping of Degas' leg. It brushed against hers.

"No," Degas answered.

Dona Dulce stopped her stirring. Degas' voice seemed to echo in Emília's mind. She recalled the crush of the trolley, the steady feel of Felipe's arm holding her up, and later, the desperate grip of his hand.

"His family housed you all of those months during the university strike," Emília blurted out. "He was our chaperone. Your friend."

Degas' leg tapped frantically. He did not face her. Instead, he stared at the newspaper article.

"That was the past. We've gone in different directions. He's loyal to the party, but too vocal about it. He puts us all in danger. Makes us all look bad."

"These days, one can't be too vocal," Dona Dulce said, staring at Emília. "Better to keep your mouth shut and be thought a fool than to open it and remove all doubt."

"Green members aren't fools," Dr. Duarte said. "But I agree, Degas. We're all soldiers in this struggle. We can't be casualties of our own egos. Some men are too involved in their own adventures to think of the collective good. The strongest men show restraint." Dr. Duarte patted his son's hand roughly. "I'm glad I won't have to waste my influence."

Degas nodded. He continued reading the list of arrests in a calm voice, but beneath the table Emília felt his leg tapping.

8

Days later, government officials questioned Dr. Duarte. His import-export business was investigated for tax fraud. His warehouses and rental properties were searched. Despite all of this, Dr. Duarte remained unruffled. He sat in his study and read his phrenology journals. He smiled and whistled the national anthem along with his corrupião. He listened to the radio religiously. Degas lingered near his father. Like one of the winter's large, awkward mosquitoes, Degas carefully circled Dr. Duarte, asking about the latest science journals, talking about their properties and the government's investigation, until he finally touched down upon the subject that concerned him most.

"Will there be a revolt?" Degas asked.

On the evening of October third, 1930, radio reports said that Celestino Gomes and a group of loyal military men had taken over the governor's office in the Southern state of Rio Grande do Sul. In the North, in their neighboring state of Paraíba, a pro-Gomes group took control of a military base.

"It's beginning," Dr. Duarte said.

Despite Dona Dulce's objections, Dr. Duarte ordered all of the maids and the errand boy to their homes in faraway Mustardinha. When they'd left, he put chains around the front and back gates. He unfurled a green flag and hung it outside the Coelhos' concrete fence. Then he took an ancient revolver from its shelf and huddled with it beside the radio. Before dawn on October fourth, reports said that a group from Recife's *Jornal da Tarde* office was caught smuggling guns in rolls of newspaper. Soon afterward, the Pernambuco Tramways shut down its offices. There was no electric or telephone service in the state capital. The Coelhos' radio went dead.

An hour later, dozens of leaflets flew over the Coelhos' wall. The Frattelli Vita soda company had printed flyers on their bottle labels and distributed them throughout the city. They called upon all loyal Gomes men. *Revolution!* the flyers said. *Fight for a New Brazil!*

Dr. Duarte brought a flyer inside the house. He'd spent the night beside the radio and his suit was wrinkled, his face unshaven. He placed the flyer and his revolver into Degas' hands.

"If I were thirty years younger, I would fight beside you," Dr. Duarte said, his eyes shining.

Degas read the flyer. He gripped the gun tightly. Dr. Duarte's enthusiasm made Emília believe that Degas would leave that instant, wearing only his striped pajamas. That was the way Taquaritinga boys reacted to fights. Growing up, Emília had watched dozens of fathers and sons leave their houses with such urgency in reaction to a family fight or territory feud, they'd left even their alpercata sandals behind. They took only their knives. In the Coelho house, things were different. Dr. Duarte escorted his son to the dining room and waited while Dona Dulce and Emília—left without maids or a cook—toasted bread, made manioc pancakes, and steamed cornmeal. Degas ate slowly. There was a hush over the breakfast table, and whatever Degas wanted—salt, jam, butter—was placed in his hands before he even reached for it. Afterward, Dr. Duarte escorted his son upstairs to help him shave his face. Dona Dulce found a satchel and packed a dozen hard-boiled eggs, several jars of pickled beets and banana jam, a loaf of bread, a set of handkerchiefs. Emília was ordered to iron a pair of Degas' trousers.

She hadn't pressed clothes since her last days in Taquaritinga. The iron felt heavy and awkward in her hands. Emília was careful with the trousers even though she believed ironing them was ridiculous; they were bound to get wrinkled and dirty. Who knew what kind of fighting was going on beyond the Coelho gate? The question frightened Emília. It made her feel sorry for Degas.

When she'd finished pressing the pants, she draped them over a hanger and went in search of her husband. He was not in the lavatory, or in his childhood bedroom, or in Emília's room. She felt frustrated by his disappearance. Emília couldn't go back to the kitchen; Dona Dulce would chastise her, declare her incapable. Emília resolved to search every room of the house.

She went to the courtyard and stared into the house's glass-paneled doors. In the parlor, she saw Dr. Duarte fidgeting with the radio dials, hoping to receive a signal. In his study, the doors were open but only the corrupião was inside. The mirrored reception room's shades were drawn. Emília was about to open its doors when she saw movement in the sitting room. A shadow. She stepped closer and looked through the door's glass pane. The room was exactly as it had been on her first day in the Coelho house, except the electric fan was off and Degas stood in the corner, before the largest wooden Madonna. He wore a dress shirt and pajama bottoms. He stared at the statue, his head tilted up like a supplicant.

When Emília opened the courtyard door, he quickly stepped away from the Madonna.

"Come to herd me outside?" Degas asked.

"No," Emília replied, holding up his trousers. "To give you these."

"Good," he said, tugging the pants from their hanger. "I was taking a last look around."

"It won't be the last," Emília said, unable to hide the hesitation in her voice.

"Part of me hopes it will be," Degas said. He draped the trousers over a chair.

"Is that what you were praying for?" Emília asked.

"No," Degas snapped. "I don't pray. I was studying her, that's all."

Emília looked up at the Virgin's wooden face. The statue's painted eyes looked wet and alive.

"Mother doesn't like her," Degas said. "She's scared of her."

Emília surveyed the sitting room and its collection of Madonnas. There were at least a dozen, large and small, wood and clay, set upon shelves and end tables beside other knickknacks.

"Then why would she collect so many?" Emília asked.

Degas shrugged. "Some were gifts. They're valuable. Mother can't exile her from the house; it's not proper. But she can't stand to look at her either. That's why they're all locked in here and not scattered about."

"How do you know?"

"Mother told me once. She said she'd rather have God's fury than her mercy."

Emília nodded. Padre Otto used to say that the Madonna's mercy was her power. That people feared the very kindness they requested because it bound them to the giver. Emília agreed; in Recife, any kindness became like one of Dr. Duarte's loans—it could never be repaid, only accepted and worried over.

"I understand that," Emília said. Degas looked surprised.

"Do you?" he asked.

"You took me away from Taquaritinga. Made me respectable. People remind me of your kindness often enough."

Degas sighed. "I did what I had to do, Emília, to keep your secret. Don't pester me for it."

"For what?"

"He's in that detention center because of his actions, not mine," Degas hissed.

"But you kept him there," she said. "You kept him locked up for your own reasons. Not for me."

Emília tried to speak with conviction, but she wasn't sure of Degas' motives. They frightened her. She recalled what he'd said nearly two years earlier, when they were newly married and he'd brought up Luzia: *We are bound to shield each other from talk.*

Degas rested his hand on the ironed trousers and studied them, checking Emília's work. She stepped forward and pulled the trousers from the chair's back. Degas looked up, startled.

"Your mother's waiting," Emília said. "Put these on."

"I've thought it through," Degas replied. "If we win, he'll be released. People will call him a patriot. Me, too, if I fight. Patriots, they're respected. They're given all sorts of medals and honors. If we win, Father will have sway. I'll ask him to give Felipe a post, somewhere nice. He'll forget everything—me, your sister—for that opportunity. People have short memories when they're given something better. You know that."

"What if you lose?" Emília asked.

Degas shrugged. "They'd prefer a dead hero to a live son. And you'll be a widow. That's better than a wife, isn't it?"

"Don't talk that way," Emília said. Her insides tingled, as if there were a dozen angry hens within her, pecking away. Without thinking, she gripped the trousers too tightly; her hands creased them. Emília laid the pants across the sofa and tried to smooth away the wrinkles.

"I'll have to do these over," Emília said. "I've spoiled them."

Degas took her hand. "They're fine. It was silly to iron them in the first place," he chuckled. "When I went back to Britain as a young man—after I'd passed my gymnasium exams and convinced Father to send me back there, to a college prep school—I didn't have to live in a dormitory like I had as a boy. I rented a room. But I didn't know how to wash or iron or darn my socks. I was a mess. People on the streets, they stared at my wrinkled suits. At the terrible ties Mother sent to me. At my Panamas. The boardinghouse owner saw that I was in need of advice. She said, 'Coelho' (she called all of her boarders by their last names), 'Coelho, make yourself invisible.' So that very day I took the allowance check from my father and purchased a tweed suit, a trench coat, a striped tie, and a bowler, just like every other man in the city. I sat in my classes and at the pubs. No one singled me out. No one expected anything of me. It was wonderful."

Degas faced Emília. His cheeks were flushed, his eyes glassy.

"It's not like here. Here there's no peace for me. Everyone looks and judges. You know it, because they've done it to you. They watch how I pick up my coffee cup, how I steer my car. Here, I'm expected to pull up my socks and marry. I'm expected to pick up a gun and fight in this damned revolution."

"Is that why you chose me?" Emília asked. "You thought I wouldn't expect anything of you?"

"Maybe," Degas said. "Actually, no. You did expect things of me, but everything you wanted was simple, defined. You seemed very practical. You had no notions of romance in your head. Everything you wanted, I could give to you. I should've known better."

"Better how?" Emília asked.

"People change. Women especially. You always want more than you've got."

"And you don't?" she asked.

"I do. Of course I do. But I'm not foolish enough to hope for it."

Degas moved toward her as if to kiss her cheek. Emília smelled his shaving musk and the stale smoke of cigarettes. When he reached her face, he did not kiss her but whispered instead.

"If I don't come back," he said, "I've told Father to give you a house of your own. Someplace nice. He's got dozens around the city. I owe you that much."

He folded the trousers over his arm and left.

8

After Degas disappeared beyond the Coelho gates to fight, Dona Dulce frantically searched the house. She separated out her best linens, her silver coffeepot, her porcelain, her Franz Post painting and carried them to the maids' quarters. The rooms were starkly furnished and dark.

"If they invade," Dona Dulce said, pushing her valuables beneath the maids' empty beds, "they'll burn the main house down. Not the servants' quarters."

Emília saw plumes of smoke rise beyond the Coelhos' gate. She heard the faraway popping of guns, like firecrackers. She heard the corrupião's constant singing of the national anthem. Without electric power, she and the Coelhos' went to bed early, though no one slept. Dr. Duarte opened the parlor's courtyard doors and fussed with the radio, futilely trying to get a signal. Dona Dulce swept the courtyard to make up for the maids' absence. Emília looked out her bedroom window. The sky glowed with faraway fires.

Emília worried for Degas, forced out into the city's stench and smoke. She worried for Lindalva and the baroness, trapped in Derby Square beside the city's Military Police Headquarters. And she worried for the city itself. What would become of it after the fighting? Would it be in ruins? She did not know Recife, not really. She did not know the beaches, the bustling markets, the narrow, peak-roofed buildings that lined Aurora Street. She'd only driven past them, shuttled from one destination to the next. She knew only the confines of the Coelho house, the International Club, the fabric store, and the baroness's mansion. Nothing more. And now the revolution would tear the city down before she even had a chance to know it.

As the night dragged on, Emília's thoughts became strange, her fears exaggerated. What if only the Coelho house survived? What if she was trapped there for good? *Life's too short!* It was one of Lindalva's favorite phrases. She used it as a rallying call, an excuse, a motivation. But during that first revolution night, Emília saw that Lindalva was wrong. Emília thought of the minutes, the hours, the days, the years, and the decades before her. If Degas did not return from the fighting, then Emília would become a widow, as he'd predicted, but it would not be a release. She would be forever dependent upon the Coelhos' goodwill. But if Degas did come back, their lives would continue exactly as before. Emília's chest tightened. How would she fill so much time?

In the weeks after the revolution of 1930, when electricity returned to the city and presses began printing again, Emília pored over newspapers to understand what had happened while she'd been trapped in the Coelho house. In the early hours of October fourth, seventeen members of the Green Party—professors, merchants, students, bakers, street sweepers, trolley conductors—invaded the city's largest munitions depot. It was not clear if the soldiers inside had helped them, or simply sat back while they took their weapons. Green Party men occupied Recife's tallest buildings and shot at Blue Party police. When they stood on the second floor and looked out the windows, they saw sandbags and troops placed at the March 6th Bridge, the Boa Vista Bridge, and the Princess Isabel Bridge. The governor and his staff were in the palace across the river and did not want the revolutionaries to invade. Telegraph clerks loyal to Gomes cut lines so that the Blue Party governor could not communicate with the South. Throughout Brazil, in key capital cities, Gomes staged his revolution.

In the end, Degas did return. He told Emília and his parents about the things he'd seen during the fighting: houses belonging to both Blue and Green Party members were looted; the offices of the *Jornal do Commércio*—the Blue Party's official newspaper—were burned down, its typeset machines thrown through the windows. The Cinema Arruda, owned by Gomes supporters, was set on fire by a Blue Party militia. Delivery cars were covered with guava paste tins and used as makeshift tanks by Green Party members.

During the three days and four nights of fighting, Emília did not know any of this. She tried to make herself useful in the Coelho house. While Dona Dulce frantically swept and dusted, trying to keep her house "livable," Emília had free rein in the kitchen. There was no ice delivery; most of the food in the icebox rotted. The milk clumped. The cheeses soured. The greens wilted. They did not know when the next gas delivery would be, so Emília used the wood-burning stove to cook any leftover meat. She opened Dona Dulce's jars of jam, pickled beets, and cucumbers. She cooked vats of the beans and manioc flour reserved for the maids. Thanks to the backyard well, the Coelho house had safe drinking water. There was no wind for the cata-vento to propel the pump, so Emília carried bucket after bucket from the yard to refill their water supply.

By October seventh, the city was tired of fighting. The governor and a few Blue Party loyalists escaped Recife by boat, vowing to come back with reinforcements. They never did. Gomes had already taken over five major states, including the nation's capital in Rio de Janeiro. Gomes's rival, the recent president elect of the Blue Party, was barricaded in the Presidential Palace with no way out. In Recife, Green forces led by Captain Higino Ribeiro had quickly set up a provisional government. Pernambuco Tramways was reopened. Electricity and radio returned. Trolleys would be working as soon as streets were cleared of debris. Captain Higino wanted normalcy. He asked patriots to return any weapons and prohibited the sale of alcohol. Newspapers printed that shops and markets would function normally. They encouraged patriots to get out of their houses and walk about. By living normal lives, they would be celebrating the revolution.

When Degas returned—his knees scraped, his fingers black with grime, his eyes nearly closed from fatigue—he slept for two days. On the third day, Dr. Duarte forced him from bed. He unlocked the front gate and made them go out, arm in arm, with green bands tied to their jackets and dress sleeves. Dona Dulce wore a black dress, as if in mourning. Degas moved gingerly, his body still sore from crouching behind sandbags. They walked down Real da Torre Street and over the bridge. Other families wandered the city alongside them, dazed and wary.

Pharmacy owners swept glass off the sidewalks. Peddlers sang happily, selling dozens of brooms and buckets. Buildings were pocked with bullet holes so numerous and close together they made the walls look like lace. The air smelled smoky and foul, like singed hair. Across the bridge, a large crowd gathered in a square. They'd ripped branches from trees and waved the leafy bouquets over their heads. They stood around a bronze bust of the escaped Blue Party governor and defaced it—covering him in a woman's dress and tying a pink ribbon around his metal hair.

"Any excuse for vulgarity and they'll be out on the streets," Dona Dulce sneered.

"This is my son!" Dr. Duarte said excitedly to anyone who passed. "He fought!"

People shook Degas' hand. Some hugged him. Degas shifted nervously at first, but soon became used to the attention.

Each day the papers printed lists of the dead. Any unknowns were buried in a mass grave on a farm outside Recife. The papers gave descriptions of unknowns, hoping to find their families. There were innocent casualties: a man in blue pajamas; a girl with a yellow ribbon around her wrist; a German immigrant found in a boarding-house. Emília studied these descriptions, never knowing what or who she was looking for. Surely Luzia would not be there, among the dead. Still, Emília pictured her sister as the girl with the yellow ribbon around her wrist. Why yellow? Why around her wrist and not in her hair?

Emília could not shake such questions from her thoughts, until she found two more obituaries embedded in the newspaper's last sections. Colonel Clóvis Lucena and his son Marcos had been killed on their ranch in the countryside. The father's body, found inside his ranch house, had a single gunshot wound to the head. The son's cause of death could not be determined—only his bones were found in the front yard. Though the cause of death was a mystery, the killers' identities were not: the obituary said that the colonel and his son were the cangaceiros' latest victims. The Hawk and the Seamstress had written a note to Marcos Lucena's new wife who lived on the coast, informing her of his death. The canga-ceiros had returned to the site of their ambush and had taken their revenge, as well as the deeds to the colonel's ranch and cotton gin. No one except Emília, it seemed, took note of this obituary. The petty rifts between colonels and cangaceiros didn't matter to Recifians—they were too busy mourning the revolution's many casualties.

The most casualties came from within the Downtown Deten-tion Center, where Green Party mobs had entered in the hopes of finding José Bandeira's killer. The building was too small to hold the masses that invaded it, and many prisoners, along with the rowdy trespassers, were trampled and killed. Listed among the identified dead was:

> A young Mr. Felipe Pereira, law student, survived by his father, Colonel Pereira, and his mother, Dona Conceição Pereira, from Taquaritinga do Norte, a small town in the interior of the state. His body was transported back to his birthplace.

Degas coughed loudly when Dr. Duarte read this. He excused himself from the breakfast table and locked himself in his childhood bedroom, where he played his English records for the rest of the day.

In the following weeks, Celestino Gomes took over the Presidential Palace. The gaúcho cowboys who had fought for him in the South rode their horses through the main avenida of Rio de Janeiro and hitched them to the city's obelisk. Newspaper photographs showed Gomes arriving in the palace wearing his trademark military uniform and tall boots. He smoked a cigar and then posed for a portrait with his generals and advisors, who squeezed close to him. He was the shortest man in the bunch. His belt was crooked, the buckle far to his left. For no reason at all, Emília clipped his picture, placing it beside her Communion portrait and the growing stack of articles about the Seamstress.

After the news of Felipe's death, Degas slept more. He wore his pajamas to lunch and dinner, spilled his coffee, locked himself in his childhood bedroom for hours on end. Dona Dulce attributed his lethargy to the "barbarities" he must have seen during the revolution. Dr. Duarte prescribed him an invigorating diet, with plenty of cabbage, greens, and malagueta pepper drinks. Degas barely touched his food.

Before the revolution, Dr. Duarte would have chided his son for such pickiness. Dona Dulce would have nagged him for his unkempt appearance. But neither his parents, nor the maids, nor the handful of Green Party loyalists who visited Degas during his convalescence commented on his behavior. They all looked at him with respect and concern. Though Degas finally had the attention he'd hoped for, he didn't seem to enjoy it. He brushed away his mother's hands upon his forehead. When Dr. Duarte or one of the Green Party men congratulated him, Degas looked as indifferent as one of the courtyard turtles.

The only time Degas agreed to dress and leave the house was to attend the Revolutionary Celebration Dinner at the Saint Isabel Theater. Dr. Duarte insisted upon it. Green Party fighters and financial backers from all of the Northeast states were invited. Dr. Duarte, it seemed, had given a substantial amount to the cause.

The Saint Isabel Theater was a massive building, painted pale pink with white trim around its arched doors and windows. Inside, the main room was circular. The theater's chairs had been removed and replaced by a series of long dining tables. These were covered in linen and set with green, leafy centerpieces. Only men—officers, fighters, donors—sat at the center tables. Around the periphery of the theater, near the doors where the coats were hung, were tables for wives and daughters. Emília was placed beside Dona Dulce, who fingered the table linen and clucked loudly. Across the room, at the other end of the women's tables, Emília spotted Lindalva and the baroness. Lindalva waved and smiled.

Above them, crammed around the theater's rows of circular white balconies, were the less prestigious guests. Flags were draped from the balconies in long, colorful rows. There were several copies of the state flag of Pernambuco, with its rainbow, sun, and red cross. There were many Brazilian flags, with their yellow diamond and the words *Order and Progress* prominently sewn across their starred blue globes. And there were green flags, dozens of them, hanging from the balconies and above the entrance doors. The largest hung above the theater's stage, where the most prestigious table sat above the rest. There, Captain Higino Ribeiro and visiting Green Party officials from the South made toasts and led the singing of the national anthem.

Emília picked at her food. The greens were wilted and bitter, the chicken rubbery. After each long-winded toast, the men at the center tables shouted, "Here, here!" and tapped their crystal goblets excitedly with their forks. Emília spotted Chevalier and his tangled head of hair at one of the tables. Degas sat a few chairs down from him, next to Dr. Duarte. Emília's husband looked pasty and skittish. He gulped glass after glass of wine.

Before dessert, Captain Higino was expected to deliver a message directly from Celestino Gomes. When the dinner plates were taken away, however, the captain continued to chat with his neighbors on the Saint Isabel stage. The women in the theater's periphery remained in their seats while, in the center of the theater, their husbands and sons and brothers mingled. The men left their chairs and shook hands, patted backs. Degas ignored his father's prodding and headed directly for Chevalier. Emília stood.

"Where are you off to?" Dona Dulce asked. A dark stain of wine ringed her lips.

"To say hello to Lindalva," Emília replied.

"Not now, dear," Dona Dulce ordered, shaking her head and smiling at the women on either side of them. "Emília's anxious to be the first at everything. If the men mingle, she must as well." Dona Dulce returned her gaze to Emília. "Sit down. Captain Higino's wife is the hostess. We must wait for her to stand before we do."

Emília looked down the row of women.

"I'd think you'd recognize her immediately," Dona Dulce continued. "With all the newspapers you read."

Emília sat. "I don't know what you mean."

"Seu Tomás tells me you've been buying papers from his friend who runs the corner newsstand. He says you hide them in your fashion magazines."

Emília's palms felt warm. She fidgeted with her gloves. "I don't hide them. I'm being discreet like you taught me. You said a lady shouldn't be seen reading the newspaper."

"You're a sharp pupil," Dona Dulce said, laughing. Her small teeth shone. Beside her, the other women smiled politely.

"I understand, dear," Dona Dulce continued. "You have to keep current to help Dr. Duarte. I have no patience for such things. I'm so glad you'll be helping him again, with his sciences and such. I would hate to hire one of those ghastly secretaries. Especially when we already have you." Dona Dulce turned to their table companions. "Women who can't be mothers must find another occupation."

"And men who can't be fathers," Emília answered, "find their own distractions."

Dona Dulce took another sip of wine. "Yes. Sadly, they do. Unlike you modern girls, they don't have as many diversions to keep them occupied. You have your fashions and your haircuts and your special teas. Emília drinks a special tea for her skin. That's how it stays so smooth and clear. It's one of your country remedies, isn't it?"

"Yes."

"You should tell us what it is." Dona Dulce smiled. "Don't be a miser with your beauty secrets. Raimunda wouldn't tell me. I had a talk with her—a frank talk. She says she buys some kind of bark at the market, but nothing like that is on my grocery list. She says you give her your own lists. I'm thrilled that you're taking responsibility, Emília. Taking charge of the staff, making grocery orders. I should let you have the run of things. It would be a fine vacation from my worries."

As she spoke, Dona Dulce's voice grew louder. The neighboring women looked away, examining their dessert plates.

"You'd find something new to worry over," Emília said. "You always do."

"That's the life of a good wife. When you have your own home, you'll understand."

"I don't expect that. Degas likes your home too much. And he can't be without his father."

Dona Dulce glanced down the long table of women. She took her napkin from her lap.

"I saw Dona Ribeiro rise in her chair," she said. "Emília, accompany me to the ladies' room. Excuse us."

The women around them nodded politely. When Emília stood, Dona Dulce clamped her arm under her own.

They moved out of the theater and into the lobby. Several waiters milled about. Electric lamps buzzed above them, their light reflected in the lobby's collection of gilded mirrors. Arranged in rows across the tile floor were circular sofas. They looked like massive red cakes covered in velvet and dimpled with buttons. From their centers rose similarly upholstered cylinders, meant to support theatergoers' tired backs. Dona Dulce steered past several couches, stopping before one that was far from the theater's doors, but nowhere near the ladies' room.

She let go of Emília's arm. Behind her mother-in-law, seated on a circular couch and partially concealed by its cylindrical backrest, sat a man. Dona Dulce did not notice him. Her lips trembled. She pinched them together. Emília felt small and frightened, as she had on her first day in the Coelho sitting room, but she did not look away from her mother-in-law. She would not let herself cower.

When Dona Dulce finally spoke, her breath was sour from wine.

"You may think that just because you've won a contest, you can speak to me in that tone. That you can prance about in your silly dresses. That you can make *insinuations* about my son. But don't get too bold. Those New family women in there, they laugh at you. When you aren't near them. They think it's quaint, the way you try to be a lady. They think it's entertaining. I know. I've heard them. And the maids tell me. You don't think maids listen to their mistress's talk? You don't think they tell each other? That word doesn't spread from house to house about Degas Coelho's country wife? Don't fool yourself. Let me say this in a way that you'll understand, being from the backlands: Do you know what happens when an ant grows wings? It gets a big head. It flies about like a bird. But it will always be an insect. And you will always be a seamstress."

Emília's legs wobbled. She locked her knees, willing herself to stand tall.

"Don't come back to my table," Dona Dulce said, straightening her skirt. "I'll tell them you feel ill."

When her mother-in-law had walked away, Emília slumped onto the couch behind her. A mirror hung on the opposite wall. It was large and wide, unlike the bit of glass she'd had in Taquaritinga. She could see herself fully instead of in fragments. She didn't look any different from the other women in the Ladies' Auxiliary—she was dark but not too dark, plump but not too plump, her hair curly but not kinky. The women in the Auxiliary copied her clothing. They sat next to her at sewing circles and invited her for coffee. But what did they do after Emília left their homes? Did they scald her used coffee cup with boiling water? She'd seen them do this to Mr. Sato's—the traveling jeweler's—used cup because, even though he was too refined to use the servants' dishware, he was considered suspect. Unclean.

Emília put her head in her gloved hands.

During her lessons, Dona Dulce had purposefully simplified things. Emília could memorize table settings, she could train herself to walk, to dab her mouth, to hold a coffee cup, to listen with just enough interest, to laugh with just enough mirth. But there were things she could never learn: codes that were hidden from her, motives that could never be explained. The road to respectability was not as straight as the crease in a tablecloth, as Dona Dulce had led her to believe. It was jagged and mysterious, like the metallic teeth of her slide fasteners, which came together so simply, but were just as easily snagged and undone.

"She got that saying wrong."

The voice was gentle. A man's. He sat on the couch across from her, no longer hidden by the backrest. He was thin necked and hunched, his body lost within his oversize suit. The pants bunched above tall rancher's boots, though he didn't look like a rancher. His hair was lank and brown. He wore it longer than was fashionable for Recife men, and partially slicked back, as though he'd made an attempt at formality. He looked no older than Degas, but his pale skin was dotted with sunspots. Unlike Felipe's freckles, this man's didn't seem to be a natural part of him, but a product of many sunburns.

Brass spectacles sat on the bridge of his ample nose. His eyes looked glassy, as if he'd participated in the men's many toasts and downed his wineglass each time.

"I beg your pardon," Emília said, wiping her face.

"You don't have to beg. I'll give it freely," he said, and smiled. "She got that saying wrong. My father liked sayings. He was a collector of them, if you can collect such things. 'When an ant grows wings, it disappears.' That's what the saying is. What it means is up to the listener. Some might take it to mean that even the smallest can rise above their circumstances. Move on to something else."

"Gentlemen don't listen to other people's conversations," Emília said. She balled her hands into fists so they wouldn't shake. She wanted to escape, to find the ladies' room and sit in peace.

"I'm not a gentleman; I work for my living. I'm trained as a doctor."

"You don't look like a doctor," Emília said, inspecting him again. She'd met plenty of Dr. Duarte's colleagues—including the medical man who'd felt her stomach beneath the sheet and prescribed her vitamins—and they were all grave, bearded men with aloof manners and metal thermometer boxes peeking out from their suit pockets instead of handkerchiefs.

"Thank you," the man replied. "I'm actually a rancher now, out in Bahia. But no one in Recife cares for my current profession. They're only impressed by my old one. So I use that, when introducing myself."

Emília nodded. She stared at her gloves, hoping he would leave her alone.

"I'm sorry I overheard," he said. "I didn't mean to. I had to escape the auditorium. It's too noisy. The whole city is."

"You get used to it."

"I won't. I traveled a long way for this celebration, but I can't wait to get back to the country."

"It's just as noisy there. But not because of trolleys or people. It's goats and frogs out there."

"You've been?"

Emília nodded. "I'm from there. I escaped. I thought you overheard that part."

The man reddened. He choked out a laugh. "It's hardly an escape."

"Not for you. You can go back and forth as you please. But without means or a profession, you're stuck there. I was lucky. I was a seamstress."

"And now?"

"A wife. A poor one, according to my mother-in law." Emília smiled. The man chuckled.

"I'm a poor rancher, if that's any consolation."

"I thought all ranchers were against Gomes."

"Not all." The man frowned. "The colonels, yes. But their loyalties will have to change. They'll have to support Gomes now. And I hope he'll finish them off. He'll change the countryside. The colonels don't want that."

"You do?" Emília asked.

"Yes. Of course. There aren't roads. Or schools. It's a miserable life out there. You know that better than I."

"But you said you liked it? You traded a city life for it."

The man straightened his spectacles. He shifted to the edge of his couch, his knees nearly touching Emília's, and lowered his voice.

"The countryside, the backlands, the caatinga, whatever you want to call it—it frightens me. It always has. Ever since I was a boy, back in Salvador, I was terrified by the stories people told. Terrified of the place, and everything that came out of it: the snakes, the bandits, the droughts, the people. City people, they turn their heads the other way. They want to look at the ocean, the palm trees. But I never wanted to turn away. A life in the city is fine, but it's an effortless life. Everything's been settled and paved. But in the caatinga, it's still new. It can still be molded. It can be made into something else. Something better. The colonels had their chance. Now it's Gomes's turn."

The man spoke with such conviction, such raw hopefulness that Emília felt moved by his beliefs and ashamed of her own. She'd abandoned the place he wanted to change. And where he saw a new land she saw an ancient one, as intractable in its beliefs as Aunt Sofia had been in hers. Yet Emília was touched that he argued for the countryside at all. He didn't ignore it like Recifians. He didn't keep its traditions like the colonels. Why couldn't the countryside have telegraphs, phones, schools, and roadways like the cities? What, Emília agreed, was wrong with bringing the countryside up to speed with the coast?

Before she could respond to the doctor, there was a wave of applause inside the theater.

"Higino's going to give Gomes's message," the doctor said, rising from his spot on the couch. "We should listen."

Emília nodded. She followed the doctor to the theater door, but did not accompany him inside. She did not want to hide in the back of the theater, exiled from her table by Dona Dulce. Instead, Emília climbed the stairway to the second level. There, she pressed through the middle-class crowd—many of whom stared at her green gown and silk gloves—and stood near a balcony. From above, she had a clear view of Captain Higino standing before his table and holding a yellow telegram in his hands. She saw the rows of men seated before him, saw the crowns of their heads with their bald spots and pomaded hair. She saw the New family women around the theater's edges, their heads obediently turned toward the stage but their eyes flitting along their own tables, examining each other.

At first, Dona Dulce's words had saddened Emília. Now she felt relieved by them. It was as if a pane of glass had been before her, rubbed as clear and spotless as the windows in the Coelho house, and Dona Dulce's speech had made a smudge. Like an insect flying into a window and leaving its remains, showing Emília that there was a barrier before her. Instead of feeling disappointed, Emília felt liberated. It was freeing to finally understand her place. To see that she'd allowed the smallest compliments to become victories and the slightest errors defeats. If she allowed herself to be so easily swayed, to believe a barrier did not exist between her and the Recife women, she would always fail. She would be trapped, always observing and imitating them through the glass instead of making them see her.

In his speech, Captain Higino expressed Gomes's goals for the region. In Recife, they would replace all gas lamps with electric lights. City workers would open roads into Recife's swampy periphery. They would fill the marshlands to create areas for "popular homes": real brick structures set to replace the palm-frond mocambos set precariously on hills and alongside rivers. Gomes called for a new sewage system. He called for vaccination drives to combat cholera, leprosy, and diphtheria. "The ideal man will wear only one tattoo: his vaccination scar," Captain Higino announced. Finally, Higino revealed Gomes's most ambitious plan of all: a roadway. The Trans-Nordestino would unite the Northern states and cut across the state of Pernambuco. It would open up the backlands. It would connect coast to countryside. East to west.

As he spoke, Emília felt chills. She pictured that roadway—wide, smooth, and flat, like a black ribbon. It would be a clean line, stitching the state together. Forcing people to look inward, toward the countryside instead of away from it. If such a road had been in place years before, she and Luzia might have made different choices. Their lives wouldn't have been so closed from opportunity. They wouldn't have had to make such desperate escapes.

"The roadway," Captain Higino read, "will be a uniting force, a civilizing force."

Emília looked down into the crowd of men. She tried to find the rancher-doctor but could not. Instead, she spotted Degas and Dr. Duarte. Her father-in-law stood. He clapped vehemently for the roadway. Emília felt a stirring in her stomach. Beneath her excitement she discovered a layer of dread, cold and heavy. She recalled the Mermaid Girl. Recalled the porcelain skull in Dr. Duarte's office, its cranium dissected by a series of black lines separating reason from amativeness, idealism from caution, benevolence from courage.

Chapter 8

LUZIA

Caatinga scrubland, Pernambuco
São Francisco River Valley, Bahia
January 1932–July 1932

1

//////////

The road into and out of the scrubland was not a road at all. It was a cattle trail: a wide dirt path used by vaqueiros to bring their herds to Recife for slaughter. The trail's route was dictated not by distance or efficiency, but by water. Twice a year, vaqueiros led their cattle near the Navio River, the Curupiti, the Riacho do Meio, the Ipojuca, the Capibaribe, and all of the springs and offshoots in between. This way their animals wouldn't die before reaching Recife, where they were fattened on farms just outside the city and periodically sent to meat markets. The rest of the year, the cattle on the trail were replaced by modest travelers: merchants with mule carts, young men walking to the coast in hopes of finding jobs, and, after Gomes's revolution, caravans of escaping Blue Party loyalists.

By late January 1932, the trail was empty. Only the Hawk's cangaceiros crouched along its edges, poorly hidden behind the scrub's short, leafless trees. They'd separated into four groups staggered along the trail. There were forty cangaceiros in all. So many new men had joined the group that Luzia had trouble recalling each of their nicknames. In the past, Antônio hadn't allowed men to join for the fun of it. He'd wanted warriors, not revelers. "Men who join for necessity or for revenge, they are men of fiber," he'd once explained to Luzia. "The others are perverse." But after losing most of his group in the ambush at Colonel Clovis's ranch, Antônio relaxed his criteria. He wanted to build an army. Some new members met Antônio's old requirements: they'd settled scores with colonels and could not live safely in their towns. Life had hardened these young men, so they understood that the cangaço was the only route left for them, and that the cangaceiros were the last family they would have. These men obediently shouldered the weight of their bornal bags and rifles. Other young men joined because they were tired of toiling on their fathers' farms and were excited by the prospect of roaming the Northeast and invading towns. They weren't perverse as much as impressionable. Wary of their overexcitement, Antônio gave them uniforms and half-moon hats but not guns. Discipline would come first, he told the new recruits, then firearms. He made Baiano, Little Ear, and Ponta Fina into "subcaptains." Each man was responsible for a group of recruits. Each subcaptain hid along the cattle trail with his men.

Luzia and Antônio crouched behind a boulder. In the noonday heat, there were no birdcalls, no buzzing insects. Breezes were heard before they were felt, rattling the branches of faraway trees, shaking dried leaves until a collective crackle moved across the scrub. Luzia closed her eyes in anticipation. Breezes gave a reprieve from the heat, but they also stirred up sand. The cangaceiros tied silk neckerchiefs over their noses and mouths to block out dust. Luzia did the same. Her bandanna was damp with sweat, making it difficult to breathe. She couldn't see the other cangaceiros but she heard their chorus of breath. She tried to match her inhales and exhales to theirs. Antônio had taught them this: to mask their presence by making their sounds uniform. That way, forty men's breathing blended together to sound like one large beast, or the respiration of the scrub itself.

They'd gotten word of travelers along the cattle trail. The well-stocked caravans of escaping Blue Party officials had dwindled in the months after the revolution. The cangaceiros were excited about robbing new, unexpected travelers.

"Stragglers," Antônio suspected.

"Maybe not," Luzia countered. Maybe these new travelers were escapees of the latest group Gomes disliked. The Blue Party escapees had come with families in tow. According to a saddle maker Little Ear had caught earlier in the week, the new travelers were all men. The saddle maker was returning from a job in Carpina and had passed a group of city men. They traveled with five pack mules. The escaping Blue Party officials had traveled in carriages whose wheels creaked under the weight of wooden trunks filled with linens, dish sets, dresses, and jewelry. Sometimes there were sewing machines. Antônio's group had blocked their paths and demanded gifts in order to pass. Most complied without incident, handing over leather purses filled with mil-réis and jewelry. Luzia let the men have those luxuries; she'd wanted only newspapers. Most escapees brought a pile of *Diário de Pernambuco*s to show their relatives and hosts in the countryside. Luzia took the papers and searched for news of Emília.

Now Luzia didn't want news; she wanted food. Five pack mules would be well stocked with bags of beans, good manioc flour, and possibly cornmeal. Surely they would have meat, Luzia thought. It would be dried of course, but better than what was available in the scrub. At the end of the dry season, the meat was so thoroughly salted to disguise rot that it had to be cut into bits because it was impossible to chew.

The memory of such beef created an odd swirling in Luzia's stomach. She was going to be sick. Luzia crouched lower in her hiding place. She pulled the bandanna from her face and took several breaths. Antônio pivoted toward her. Untroubled by dust, he wore no mouth cover.

"My Saint?" he whispered. This was his name for her now. Not Luzia. Not "the Seamstress," as the papers called her. Little Ear was responsible for that silly name. In one town, someone had asked about Luzia. "Who is that?" they'd said, and Little Ear, annoyed, replied, "She's our seamstress." The name stuck, but only outside the group.

"I'm thirsty," she replied. "That's all."

Antônio nodded. Quickly, he unfastened his metal canteen—a gift from a colonel—and handed it to her. Luzia drank. The water was warm and silty. Grains of sand gritted between her teeth. Luzia forced herself to swallow. She hoped it wouldn't come back up. Recently, she'd experienced similar moments of queasiness. A week before, she'd swooned at the scent of the men's Fleur d'Amour perfume poured over their greasy hair. The nausea was coupled with soreness in her chest and, each time she braided her hair, a tingling in her scalp. Luzia knew these pains were premonitions, like the ache in her locked elbow before a rain.

Recently, each time Antônio spotted a cloud on the horizon he asked Luzia if her bent arm hurt. She reluctantly said no. Back in December, none of the salt mounds laid out for Santa Luzia had dissolved overnight. Some of the cangaceiros blamed the salt itself, saying it was mixed with flour. Some blamed Canjica for not scooping it out properly; some found fault with Luzia, saying she hadn't blessed the bag of salt correctly; and some, like Little Ear, said it was because they hadn't given Santa Luzia a proper offering. They'd taken few eyes in the years after Gomes's revolution. Robbing the alarmed Blue Party officials had been easy, clean work. Most of the escapees had only old papo-amarelos with tight triggers and rusted barrels, if they carried weapons at all. And thanks to the revolution, the new president Gomes had called all troops to the coast to maintain his power in the capital cities. Like other politicians before him, Gomes believed that if he ruled Brazil's coastal capitals, he automatically harnessed the countryside connected to them. There were no monkeys in the caatinga to chase the cangaceiros. No colonel could amass an army large enough to defend itself against the Hawk's group. Little Ear urged Antônio to take advantage of this power. The new subcaptain wanted to invade more towns, to kill colonels, to take over their houses and brand their cattle in the Hawk's name. Antônio wouldn't allow it; before burning bridges with the colonels he wanted to see what President Gomes would do with his revolutionary troops. Gomes might prove himself to be different from previous presidents—after stabilizing the capitals, he might turn his attention to the countryside. Monkeys might return in larger numbers, looking to dominate the caatinga under the authority of the Green Party. If this happened, Antônio said, the cangaceiros and the colonels would need one another.

Peace with the colonels mellowed Antônio but bored Little Ear and the new recruits. The men wanted excitement, a chance to flaunt their newfound power as cangaceiros. Antônio couldn't deny them. He allowed Little Ear and his subgroup to take out their frustrations on Blue Party escapees. The cangaceiros kicked the escaping officials in their stomachs. They beat the backs of the men's legs with the wide sides of their knives. Antônio stopped the cangaceiros from doing worse. Each time he did, Luzia felt it was harder and harder for Antônio to get the men's attention. She recalled the mule breaker in Taquaritinga. He'd said that even obedient animals tested their masters, tugging reins or nipping hands, and if the leader did not stop these small rebellions he would have a larger one. Luzia began to watch Little Ear the same way she watched the cloudless sky: noticing each subtle shift, wary of what it might mean.

So far, Santa Luzia's predictions had proved to be true. December's rains hadn't fallen. By January, the month that usually marked the beginning of the wet season, the scrub was gray and brittle. Farmers living near the trail expressed worry; each time they fetched water, they saw the bottoms of their springs. Along the trail, travelers constructed makeshift altars to São Pedro. Antônio made his group stop and pray for rain at these altars. Each day they inspected the sky. Each day it was bright and blue.

Antônio liked to say that they had no master or colonel. Luzia disagreed. They lived under the scrub's yoke, and it was a temperamental overseer. During the wet months, when rain fell for thirty and sometimes forty days straight, the caatinga was kind. It gave them fresh corn and beans. It gave them flowers and honey. Scrub fruits grew, round and prickly, from trees and cacti. Calves were born and cow's milk became so cheap that the cangaceiros bought liters of it. They ate pumpkin mashed in milk and made cheese covered in rapadura shavings. Even with this bounty, everyone cured meat, dried beans, and ground corn, knowing their master would change. Each year during the dry months, the scrub became miserly and often cruel. It threw dust into their eyes, sunburned their skin, made them search for water. Just when they'd had enough, it presented them with a hidden spring or a healthy river. It gave them goats and docile armadillos with meaty underbellies. But it only gave if they paid close attention. Like good servants, caatinga residents learned to listen to their master, to anticipate its moods, to know that ants walking in long lines outside their holes meant rain, that a green-leafed gameleira tree growing from a rock's crevice meant a spring, that large mounds of termites meant dryness and thirst. If they learned to read this cruel master correctly during the dry months, they would live to greet a kinder master once the rains came.

That year, the scrub had remained hardhearted. "Not even Celestino Gomes can order it to rain!" Antônio liked to say, proud of the caatinga's stubbornness. It bothered Luzia when he spoke this way.

She capped the canteen and hooked it back to the strap slung across Antônio's shoulder. Farther down the trail, a mule bayed. Luzia heard the snap of a whip. Antônio took his brass binoculars from their case.

"Bird food?" Luzia whispered. That was what the newspapers had dubbed political escapees. The Hawk had attacked so many Blue caravans that the Green Party called him an ally; Gomes sent no soldiers to guard the trail.

"Men," Antônio replied. He signaled to Baiano, who crouched across the trail.

"City men?" Luzia asked.

Antônio nodded. "They've got long coats. And leather boots."

"But no families? No caravan?"

Antônio looked at her and smiled. "I've always wanted a pair of leather boots."

It was hard for him to blink the eye on the scarred side of his face. He had to make an effort, and even then the eye's lid shut lazily, if at all. Over the years, a cloudy film had formed, as if his eye was covered in milk. He insisted he was not losing his sight, but at night, after prayers, he knelt beside their blanket and whispered a series of pleas to Santa Luzia. Antônio kept other ailments hidden as well. During their walks, while he observed the scrubland, Luzia observed him. She saw each shallow breath, each pained step. His injured leg still bothered him. At night, he felt sharp pains on either side of his lower back. Each morning, he had trouble rising from his blanket.

Antônio handed Luzia the binoculars. She stared through them and saw a mule driver flick his animals' hindquarters with a whip. There were five mules. Two carried basic supplies: kerosene tins, a small barrel, lanterns, rope, a large burlap sack, a flank of sun-dried beef. The other three mules carried strange black tubes and a metal machine. The machine was long, with three legs and a bulky top covered in cloth. It reminded Luzia of the tripod and camera used to take her First Communion portrait years before.

Two men, perched on top of skinny horses, rode alongside the pack mules. One man was young and lean. He wore a driving coat, like a huge smock covering him. His face shone with sweat. His eyes were obscured by leather driving goggles. The other man was more sensible, Luzia thought. Less vain. He was middle-aged and portly, with short legs and a small head, like an armadillo. He'd balled up his driving coat and set it in his lap. He wore a cotton suit, stained yellow with dust, and cinched with a thick leather belt. The driving goggles hung limply around his neck. A straw fedora shaded his face.

Antônio tugged Luzia toward him.

"My Saint," he whispered. "Put a hole in that hat. Can you?"

It was a silly question. After three years of practice, Luzia could shoot a bullet into the coin-size mouth of an empty cachaça bottle, making it explode from the inside out. She could dent a brilliantine can from seven meters away. She could shatter knees, making a man as lame and useless as an injured horse. Or she could aim with a more conclusive purpose, setting her mark on head or throat or chest.

Luzia straightened her spectacles. Her eyelashes fluttered against the scratched lenses. She caught sight of the traveler's straw hat and aimed lower—at the hatband—knowing her hand would move upward. She held her breath.

As if hit by a swift wind, the hat flew off the portly man's head. The younger traveler's horse spooked at the sound of the shot. His rider tumbled to the ground. The man squirmed to avoid his horse's hooves, becoming tangled in his driving coat. The mule driver tugged his animals to a stop and fumbled in his leather pack. There wasn't time to retrieve his firearm. Antônio whistled. A contingent of cangaceiros surrounded the mule driver. They took away his small chumbo rifle. Antônio stepped out of the scrub. He ordered the mule driver to strip down to his underclothes and leave. The man obeyed, running into the gray trees. The mules bayed.

The young, goggled traveler finally stood. He put his hands between the folds of his driving coat and groped inside it.

"I hope you're reaching for a handkerchief," Antônio said.

Baiano stood behind the young man, pressing a Winchester into his back. The traveler froze. Antônio ordered him to remove his driving coat. Inside its pocket was a small snub-nosed pistol. Antônio took it, then whistled for the rest of the cangaceiros. They emerged from the scrub, tugging down their bandannas to expose their faces.

Life in the caatinga made the men's skin dark and leathery. It made their teeth fall out. Ponta Fina had grown a mustache. Baiano had shaved his head. Canjica had lost a finger playing with a child's hunting musket that had backfired in his hands. Chico Coffin's bald spot had grown but so had his remaining hair, making him look like a rebellious friar. Tufts of stiff, sun-bleached hairs sprouted from Little Ear's ears, making them look like round, thick, cactus pads. And Inteligente still had his childlike stare and his loping step, but his face was more creased and he couldn't shoulder as much weight. Because of this, the younger members took turns carrying the group's two portable Singers. They'd taken the machines from Blue Party caravans. Antônio had one Singer equipped with a saddle maker's needle to decorate leather. Ponta Fina, whose embroidery skills began to rival Luzia's, helped her teach the new recruits to sew. Ponta had grown into a quiet man—no longer the butt of the group's teasing but one of its founding members—and he conducted his sewing lessons in a serious and professional manner. Some recruits rejected sewing at first. After a few weeks, they discovered that life in the scrub was not as eventful as they'd imagined. During the dry season they spent long hours in the shade each afternoon waiting out the heat. Sewing relieved the cangaceiros' boredom. Before long, the new recruits—their throats raw from xique-xique juice— hoarsely asked to be included in Luzia and Ponta's lessons.

Luzia, like the rest of the men, left her hiding place. She didn't return her parabellum to its shoulder holster. Before she could reach Antônio, the older traveler slipped off his horse. His short legs made his descent cumbersome. He pried off his wedding ring and shook it at Antônio.

"Here," he said.

The good side of Antônio's mouth creased in a frown. "Why are you handing me that?"

"Take it. It's all we have."

"Did I ask for that?"

"No," the man replied.

"Then put it back or I'll shoot you."

The man jammed the ring onto his finger. Antônio shook his head.

"I'm disappointed," he said. "You're city boys. I know you weren't born in a goat corral. I know your mothers taught you manners. But before I can even introduce myself, you try to grab a pistol. And you! I haven't even made a threat, and you hand me your wedding band. What would your wife say to that?"

The older man stared at his boots. The young one lifted off his goggles. They left a red crease around his eyes, which were hazel and heavy lidded, like a teú lizard's. They gave him a lazy look, as if he was constantly unimpressed.

"My Saint," Antônio called. "Talk to them or I'll lose my patience."

Luzia took her place beside him. The city men stared up at her, their eyes wide. Antônio smiled.

"It's not well bred to stare at an honest woman," he said. "But I understand. You can't help it. Don't strain your necks."

Behind her, Luzia heard some cangaceiros chuckle. She gripped her parabellum tighter. In the beginning, she'd appreciated Antônio's fascination with her height. At first, Antônio whispered his compliments only to her, but as his eye clouded, as his shoulders hunched and his injured leg dragged, he began to praise her in front of others. The more his appearance weakened, the more concerned Antônio became with hers. He crowded her fingers with rings. He gave her silk handkerchiefs and a pair of leather gloves to keep her hands free of thorns. He presented her with a shoulder holster and a Lugar parabellum—a semiautomatic German pistol with eight shots, an easy trigger, and a furious recoil. He encouraged Luzia to pull back her shoulders and stand at her full height, to hold her locked arm proudly beside her and not to cradle it over her chest. With time Luzia's demeanor became as sure as her aim, but she was unsure if Antônio loved her appearance or the impression it made.

"What's your business here?" Luzia asked.

"We have no business," the older traveler said. "We're surveyors."

"You're what?" Antônio asked.

"Mapmakers," the young one snapped.

"You're headed the wrong way," Antônio said.

"No," the younger man replied. "We are headed inland."

"You'll starve to death. There's no rain."

The mapmakers looked at each other.

"I'm not fibbing," Antônio continued. "You won't get far. Horses need water. And food."

Antônio ordered the cangaceiros to empty the mules' cargo baskets. Pencils, pots of ink, white sheaves of paper, and a compass fell onto the dirt. Then there were the black tubes. The cangaceiros handled them gingerly, as if they were weapons. As they pried the mysterious tubes open, the portly man wrung his hands. The younger man scowled. Inside the tubes there were no treasures;

there were only papers. Luzia unrolled them on the ground. They were not newspapers, but large, penciled drawings with curving lines, tick marks, strange symbols, and city names. Maps. Above the drawings, Luzia read the name *National Roadway Institute*. Beneath them she saw a list of companies: Standard Oil, Pernambuco Tramways, Great Western of Brazil.

Antônio studied the unrolled maps at Luzia's feet. "Why do you want to draw this trail?"

"Not the trail," the older mapmaker whispered. "The trail is just a guide."

"For what?" Antônio asked, impatient.

"A roadway." Luzia answered, looking at another map. She saw a long black line starting at the coast and snaking into the scrubland. She traced it with her finger. It looked like a black river. The *Trans-Nordestino*.

"Yes. Exactly," the older mapmaker said, his lips twitching into a smile. "Madam is astute. We're just simple mapmakers. We work for private companies . . . and the government, of course," he added in response to his young coworker's scowl. "They're building the Trans-Nordestino. It's a road. They plan to run it from Recife all the way into the sertão."

Antônio laughed. He dabbed his milky eye with a handkerchief. "A roadway? Out here? For what?"

"For transport," the old mapmaker said. "To facilitate transport of cotton and cattle. And to have access."

"Access to what?" Antônio asked.

"To the land," the young man interrupted. "The North isn't just coastline. President Gomes says we can't run a country when it's unknown."

"It's known to the people who live here," Antônio said, stepping near the young mapmaker. "We don't need you running anything. We don't need your road. Gomes should stay out of our business."

Behind them, the cangaceiros laughed. One of them tried on an extra driving coat. Ponta Fina took the young man's goggles and cupped them to his eyes. Baiano looked through their surveyor's telescope. Little Ear kicked at the metal tripod, hoping to bend and break it. Canjica and Inteligente raided the food supplies, divvying them up between the cangaceiros' packs. Antônio pocketed their compass. Luzia crouched. She folded the largest map into a square and slipped it inside her bornal.

"That's ours!" the young mapmaker called out. The older one elbowed him, but he would not quiet. "Take anything else, but leave our work!"

Luzia wanted to hush him. If he wanted to save his maps, he should have pretended they were meaningless. Antônio calculated worth not by value but by affection. The more a person cared for something, the more he wanted to take it from them. Antônio lifted a tin of kerosene from one of the mule's baskets. He stood over the maps and poured the yellow liquid. The cangaceiros laughed. The older mapmaker cradled his head in his hands. Antônio lit a match and stepped away.

The maps burned quickly. Their heat made Luzia's face tingle. She covered her mouth from the smoke.

"They'll send more," the young mapmaker cried. He took shallow breaths. The tendons of his neck bulged with each inhalation.

"Of what?" Antônio asked.

"Of us. The road's already started. It's past Carpina. You think you can block it?"

"Why not?"

"You're a relic!" the young mapmaker yelled.

"A what?" Antônio asked.

The older man hushed his coworker. "He's a brash youth. He doesn't know what he's saying."

"I do," the young man interrupted. "Viva Gomes!"

Little Ear moved forward. He held the tripod's broken metal leg in his hands, ready to swing it at the surveyor.

"Step back," Antônio ordered, still staring at the young man.

The left side of Antônio's mouth moved up. The skin around his eyes crinkled. He bared his teeth.

When Antônio smiled in earnest, his eyes matched it. But when this false smile appeared, his eyes looked dull and dead, as if in a trance. Luzia had watched him with victims before. There were those who begged, sputtered, sometimes soiled themselves as they knelt before him. With these he was quick and businesslike, as if sparing them more embarrassment. In his eyes she saw sadness and reluctance, as if he was fulfilling obligations he did not fully understand or enjoy. When he showed mercy, he met their eyes and sighed, flicking his hand and telling them to get out of his sight, as if dealing with rebellious children. He encouraged his men to show mercy because it proved that they could dominate anything, even their own tempers. But when his false smile appeared, Luzia felt frightened. It was as if the slats of a shutter had opened, partially revealing something unsettling and unknown within him—an anger he could not dominate with the force of his will.

A familiar wave of nausea rose in the pit of Luzia's belly. She took a breath and held it back. Then she placed her hand on Antônio's arm.

"We could get more from them than their boots and jackets," she whispered. "We could put them up for ransom."

She felt his shoulders loosen. In the newspapers she'd taken from Blue Party escapees, Luzia had read of foreign investors. She'd studied photographs of Emília standing beside those speculators, those company executives. They might pay to have their surveyors back. They might pay for the map she'd slipped into her bornal.

Luzia calculated the money they could earn in exchange for those mapmakers. Not the petty sums they stole from Blue Party escapees or coerced from merchants. The money they carried was a fortune in the scrub, but it never totaled the impossible amount needed to buy land. If they ransomed those mapmakers, Luzia thought, maybe they could get enough to buy a large plot near the São Francisco River. Those cangaceiros who wanted to settle down could divide the land equally; they could build houses and plant crops. Buying was different from renting a plot from a rancher or toiling under a colonel in exchange for a home. Buying meant owning, and owning meant working your own hours, managing your own house, and selling the crops you harvested. These were luxuries reserved for men like Dr. Eronildes, or for colonels, or for the children of colonels. For an instant, Luzia let her hand rest on her stomach.

She replaced her parabellum in its holster and straightened her shoulders. She moved toward the surveyors. The men staggered backward.

"If this roadway's important, you must be, too," she said.

The men wouldn't meet her eyes. Instead, they stared at her crooked arm, at her canvas trousers. Luzia let them take a good look, knowing that they saw her richly embroidered bornal and not the tough beef and stale manioc inside it. They saw the two gold pendants around her neck, not the two babies she'd lost before her stomach had even swelled. They saw the shining pistol in her shoulder holster, not the numbness that now lived in her chest, as if her heart had become as thick and as calloused as her feet. They saw the Seamstress.

2

Her first child had craved mimo oranges. A few weeks after she and Antônio married on Dr. Eronildes' porch, Luzia's monthly blood disappeared. The yeasty smell of manioc flour made her retch. Her breasts became sore to the touch, her nipples hard and round, like the pits of pitomba fruits. One night, she dreamed of a mimo. She felt its peel under her fingernails. She took its soft, ear-shaped sections into her mouth. When she woke, she smelled the mimo on her hands, in the air, and around the edges of her coffee tin.

"I need an orange," she told Antônio. "A mimo."

He laughed. They'd have more luck finding a spotted panther. When Luzia insisted, he understood. A mother had to have the food she craved or else the child in her belly would die. That was what the women in Taquaritinga believed. One of Aunt Sofia's neighbors had almost lost her child because her husband delayed in bringing her the oxtail stew she'd craved. There was even the legend of the Cannibal Wife that Aunt Sofia often told them before bed, to frighten them. The pregnant Cannibal Wife sniffed her husband's arm, innocently at first, taking in its scent of sweat and dust. *Husband, I want a bite of your arm,* she said. The husband paused, unsure. Then he held it out. She took a bite. The husband screamed. Still, the wife was not satisfied. *Husband, I want another bite.* This time, he said no. When she gave birth, there were twins in her belly—one was alive, the other dead. The story's ending always made Luzia shiver. After Aunt Sofia blew out the candle, Luzia and Emília reached under the covers and tried to bite each other's arms until Aunt Sofia chided them. Secretly they hoped that there was some truth to the story, and each Saturday at the market Luzia and her sister stared at the vendors' forearms, hoping to find teeth marks. They never did.

Over the next few weeks Antônio asked merchants, colonels, and cotton vendors where he could find a mimo orange. He offered them jewelry, mil-réis notes, even his brass binoculars, but no one could deliver. Finally, at an outdoor fair near Triunfo, they found one. The vendor wrapped it neatly in newspaper and placed it in Antônio's hands. The skin was withered, the fruit sour. A week later, in the middle of the night, Luzia felt a terrible knotting in her belly. It felt as if she'd eaten a bunch of green bananas. She sat up. There was a warm stickiness between her legs.

On the ground around her, several meters in each direction, she saw the dark forms of cangaceiros sleeping. She heard Inteligente's snores. Cinders glowed in the cook fire. The sentries—Little Ear and a skinny young man called Thursday, after the day he joined the group—slumped near the weak fire. Hearing Luzia sit up, they instinctively turned toward her. Luzia closed her legs and looked away. She hated Little Ear and the boy for their attention. She suddenly disliked all of those sleeping men—even Antônio—who could do nothing to help her. She needed a woman. She needed Aunt Sofia, with her forceful voice and thick, stable body, to guide her. Luzia recalled stories of pregnant women in Taquaritinga. They'd bled before their time and lost the children in their bellies. Carefully, she stood. The cramping in her stomach released. More fluid expelled from her, wetting her trousers. She grabbed her bornal and moved quickly into the scrub. Antônio sat up but did not follow her.

Near their camp, hidden in the crevice of two large rocks, was a spring. Luzia saw the rocks' shadows. She headed toward them. The night was chilly and dark. Above her was a sharp sliver of moon, curved like a sickle. Another wave of cramps came upon her. Luzia crouched and held her belly.

At the spring, she carefully stepped out of her trousers and knickers. Her thighs were sticky. There was a sharp, metallic smell. She flattened her knickers on the dirt and stared at them. There was a dark stain. When she touched the wet spot, she felt slick, amorphous clumps. Her hand jerked back. *It's no different from your monthly blood,* she told herself but didn't believe it. Staring into the dark scrub, Luzia became nervous about Antônio or another man spying her. She wrapped her trousers over her naked haunches. Other women, Luzia thought bitterly, had rooms with doors. They could shut men out. They could rest in clean beds and wash themselves in tin basins. Luzia wanted to dunk herself in the spring but could not; it was a sin to contaminate drinking water. She took an extra bandanna from her bornal and soaked it. The spring water was cold. Luzia trembled as she wiped her legs.

In the following weeks, Antônio brewed curative teas for her. Canjica gave Luzia extra helpings of beans and manioc flour. Baiano tried to cheer her with shooting contests, but she refused. One night, Antônio led her away from camp. His hand felt hot in hers. The left side of his face moved frantically.

"My Saint," he said. "Our union must be blessed. If it's not blessed, our lives won't be."

Days later, when they reached the town of Venturosa, Antônio found a church. It was a simple, whitewashed chapel with a brick floor. The pews were a series of crooked wooden benches. Antônio placed a wad of mil-réis into the priest's hands.

"To build a proper confessional," Antônio explained. "In exchange for a service."

The old priest, pleased by the donation, became suddenly wary.

"We don't need a wedding," Antônio said. "Just your blessing. And a certificate."

The certificate was a lovely document, covered with wax seals and calligraphic letters. Some evenings, while the men played dominoes, Antônio unrolled the certificate and asked Luzia to read it.

> Antônio José Teixeira, 32 years, Catholic, captain, son of
> Verdejante, Pernambuco, Brasil, officially weds Luzia dos
> Santos, 19 years, Catholic, seamstress, daughter of Taquaritinga
> do Norte, Pernambuco, Brasil, on this sacred day, 28 April,
> the year of our Lord, 1930.

Antônio's superstition seemed to have merit: after receiving the certificate and the priest's blessing, their lives became easier. Really, it was Gomes and his revolution that brought them good fortune, though Antônio wouldn't admit it.

Monkeys weren't the only ones who disappeared from their posts in the caatinga after Gomes took over Brazil. Insignificant Blue Party officials who happened to be posted in the caatinga—a scattering of sheriffs, tax collectors, and a few odd judges—renounced their positions and either returned to the coast to court the Green Party, or hid in their country houses. In the scrub, order was left to the colonels and the cangaceiros. This wasn't a novelty for most caatinga residents. To them, the revolution was simply a faraway feud. People were relieved it wasn't happening on their properties. They were proud for not having such troubles themselves. And, as with all feuds, only women expressed concern.

"If there's a spark near a pile of burlap bags, the devil will blow on it," a farmer's wife whispered to Luzia. "The fire will spread."

Men didn't believe the caatinga would be affected by Gomes, or anyone else who took over Brazil. The countryside had always been ignored, and it would be no different this time. Antônio spoke with many tenant farmers, and most reacted to Gomes and his revolution with curiosity and amusement.

"That Blue Party got its tail caught," the farmers laughed. "That Gomes is president now." They always said *That Gomes* and never *Our president,* because Gomes was both a politician and a Southerner, making him doubly alien. Even the title *President* sounded remote, like some fancy brand of hair tonic.

In public, most colonels laughed at Gomes. Privately they built alliances among themselves and sought the Hawk's friendship and protection. Even the meanest colonels—the ones who hated cangaceiros the most—suddenly tried to reestablish ties with Antônio. The colonels disliked Gomes because of his promises of workers' rights and secret ballots. They didn't believe the new president would actually *give* caatinga residents these things, but simply bringing up such reforms gave Gomes power among the common people. Colonels had collaborated with previous governments, giving candidates the countryside's votes in exchange for autonomy. Gomes didn't want such bargains; he'd never reached out to the colonels and they'd gone against him in the elections before the revolution. Now they worried that their support of the Blue Party would come back to haunt them. Either Gomes would decide the countryside was too much trouble, as other presidents had, or he would try to change things. If the latter happened, the colonels were afraid their lands would be confiscated. They waited to see what Gomes would do. During this time, they also made plans for the worst; if faced with losing their lands and titles, the colonels would fight and they wanted the Hawk and his small army on their side. Colonels also armed their vaqueiros, tenant farmers, and goat herders.

"Every matuto has a rifle these days," Antônio often said, shaking his head. He didn't like most colonels and rarely agreed with them, but now he shared their concern. He didn't want Gomes's government or any government taking control of the countryside. He did not believe Gomes's promises of equality—plenty of other politicians had vowed the same things and never delivered. Antônio did not see Gomes as a president but as another type of colonel, bent on acquiring land and power.

With guns readily available and no soldiers in sight, the caatinga's population of thieves grew. A colonel asked Antônio to help him catch cattle robbers. A cotton farmer asked for the Hawk's help in settling a feud with his neighbor, who'd decided to fence his property. A merchant promised Antônio a percentage of his profits in exchange for the right to say that his business was under the Hawk's protection. That alone deterred thieves. The Hawk's group was well known and, as one merchant said, their word was as strong as iron.

"Iron rusts," Antônio corrected the man. "My word is gold."

After the revolution, several copycat cangaceiro groups sprang up and claimed to be the Hawk's. They kidnapped colonels' children and intimidated towns by using Antônio's fame. There were also crooked merchants who claimed to be under the Hawk's protection when they weren't. For weeks, Antônio insisted on traveling around the state to find and punish such liars. Little Ear encouraged these trips. Finally, in the mountain town of Garanhuns, Luzia found a papermaker and ordered six boxes of thick white calling cards embossed with the letter *H* on top. When they conducted business, Luzia handed merchants and ranchers the calling cards, complete with a written message in her impeccable handwriting, affirming that their protection was real. With the Hawk's card, a man could walk safely through the most dangerous stretches of the caatinga. For many, the cards became more valuable than currency.

Whenever Antônio punished his copycats—making them kneel before him and pressing his punhal into the bases of their necks—he left a calling card beside the slumped bodies. When he sliced off the ears of thieves, or dealt with rapists in the same way a farmer treated old roosters, neutering them with two strokes of a knife, Antônio left a card as proof of his presence. Luzia knew that such punishments were no worse than those inflicted by the colonels. She knew that Antônio hadn't taught his men cruelty, the scrub had. Their lives in the countryside had. From the time a boy could walk, he was taught to stab, to skin, to clean, and to gut. He was taught how to settle arguments. He was taught that in the caatinga, you did not take an eye for an eye. There were no such equivalents. There was only surpassing, outdoing. An eye for a life. A life for two. Two for four. The men became cangaceiros already knowing this. All Antônio had taught them was how to control their cruelty. How to make it useful. Antônio insisted that the people they targeted had been disrespectful, or had shamed a woman, or had cheated, lied, stolen, or committed any number of misdeeds that merited punishment. Luzia, like the cangaceiros, was swayed by the intoxicating certainty of Antônio's righteousness. It was dizzying and potent, like the smell of the caatinga in bloom.

Antônio insisted that he and his men were not for hire; they simply performed services for friends. In return, their friends gave them shelter and gifts, never payments. They did not need money—their bornais were already weighed down with rolls of mil-réis. More often than not, their gifts were guns and stocks of ammunition. During and after the revolution, when Gomes kept most munitions for his troops, shipments to the countryside became precarious. Antônio stockpiled whatever he could.

For her part, Luzia stockpiled newspapers acquired in their Blue Party robberies. After the revolution, the *Diário* stopped printing its Society Section. There were only photographs of Celestino Gomes in Rio de Janeiro's presidential palace, where he'd established his provisional government. And later, there were portraits of the "tenentes"—Green Party men appointed to temporarily govern each of the states until a new constitution was written. Captain Higino Ribeiro became the tenente of Pernambuco. For weeks, the paper's front page was stamped with his photograph.

Only later, after Carnaval of 1931, did Luzia find pictures of her sister. The *Diário de Pernambuco* printed photographs of ribbon cuttings, official dinners, and other festivities promoted by the new government. In one such picture, Emília stood in the crowd surrounding Dr. Otto Niemeyer, a foreign economist Gomes had invited to Brazil to create an economic improvement plan. In another photo, Emília was pictured at a dinner held for several pale men in business suits—representatives from foreign oil conglomerates, electric companies, and rubber firms. These men were the future, according to Gomes. He wanted large, noticeable projects to show that his government was working. At each groundbreaking ceremony or celebratory dinner, banners with Gomes's motto—*Urbanize, Modernize, Civilize!*—were draped behind the guests. Emília always stood in the crowd beneath these banners. Her hair was longer than Luzia remembered it, her face thinner. In one article, dated May 1931, a reporter quoted Emília. There had been a Women's Congress in Rio de Janeiro, where Gomes's delegates were drafting the country's new election code. In the document's initial version, suffrage was extended only to widows with property, and to wives with their husbands' permission. "We're troubled," Mrs. Degas Coelho said. "We hope this will be revised. Mr. Gomes made a promise, and when a man makes a promise to a lady, he must keep it."

Luzia smiled when she read this. Emília still believed in the powers of propriety and courtesy. Or she pretended to believe. When Luzia studied the photographs of her sister, Emília's face did not match the polite hopefulness of her words. The woman in the photos rarely smiled. She jutted her chin out. She pressed her lips together in what resembled an expression of defiance.

While Mrs. Degas Coelho attended Gomes's groundbreakings and inaugurations, Luzia and the cangaceiros attended their own dedication ceremonies. Antônio gave money to towns in order to repair their wells or renovate their chapels. He gave farmers new tools and their wives reams of cloth. He gave an elderly tailor a pouch filled with bills so that he and his sons could build their own shop.

The Hawk's group gained a reputation for both cruelty and generosity. More men wanted to join. New recruits stared at Antônio with reverence and fear. Luzia felt sorry for them. Soon, they would feel the effects of the bitter xique-xique juice. Soon, they would see that their captain was a fickle man. Despite their success after the revolution, Antônio became moody. His body weakened, his eye clouded, and his superstitions grew. On Friday, the sacred day, he didn't allow his men to sing or play dominoes or even speak. Luzia could not touch him on this day. Each night, Antônio's prayers became longer and the men shifted on their knees. Once, Little Ear and four new men complained about the length of the prayers. Antônio put his subcaptain on garbage duty for one month, giving Little Ear the lowly task of burying the group's refuse each time they left camp. After this, Antônio slept little. He lay beside Luzia and listened to the sentries' whispered conversations. Some nights he waited until the cangaceiros were asleep, then woke Luzia and moved the location of their blankets so no one knew exactly where they slept. Antônio's fear of poisoning also grew more acute, and he refused to eat if Luzia did not try the food first. If the new recruits questioned him or disappointed him, they were not allowed to pray for corpo fechado and seal off their bodies from harm. They were left unprotected and fearful. They were left without his approval or his love. To get it back, even Little Ear obeyed.

As a reward, Antônio made each man feel important. He counseled them and healed them. He gave long speeches about their freedom, their independence. Luzia sat on her blanket in the darkness and listened impatiently. His speeches frustrated her. Their life was not one of freedom but of escape: from their old lives, from past mistakes, from enemies, from colonels or monkeys or drought. And what good was freedom for its own sake? What good was that vast, open scrubland that caught at their clothes and cut their faces? What good was wandering simply to wander, with no cause, no goal, no future in sight?

Even the poorest, most disorganized shacks with dirt floors and dogs skulking in corners had order and permanence compared to Luzia's life in the scrub. In each of those shacks there was a sturdy wooden pillar for mashing dried corn into fubá and coffee beans into grounds. There were hooks above the stove for curing meat. There were chairs, cribs, and caroá rope hammocks—all things passed down from mother to daughter. All things Luzia could never carry through the scrub. "The Seamstress" possessed embroidered bags, jewelry, and a pistol, but she had no household.

At first, Luzia's envy was subtle. With time, it grew. A bilious feeling rose in the pit of her belly each time she entered a house, souring her mood for the rest of the day. She was ashamed of her jealousy and never spoke of it. She simply avoided houses. Antônio interpreted her dislike of closed spaces as a love for open ones, for the scrub itself. He approved.

"You have the finest house of any woman," he said, brushing loose hair behind her ears.

Her house was vast. Rivers, not walls, divided it. In the dry season, its roof was as blue as the glazed pottery sold near the banks of the São Francisco. During the wet months her roof became gray with bright streaks of lightning. Luzia's kitchen was well stocked with goats, armadillos, scrub rabbits, and rolinha doves. Her furniture was sturdy: small boulders made good chairs, evergreen juazeiro trees gave fine shade, and the rock formations that rose, round and massive like the humps of sleeping beasts, from the scrub's stunted arbor were first-rate armoires, storing ammunition and supplies in their crevices or buried at their bases.

Antônio whispered such things to Luzia when they were alone. In the mornings, before the sun rose, he woke her and led her away from camp. She followed him into that early morning darkness. She waited as he cleared a place for them on the ground. Sand often found its way onto their blanket, their hair, their skin. Ants, too. The morning air was cold. They shivered and held each other close. They could not be too loud, or the men would hear. They could

not move too freely in one direction or the other, or cacti and nettles would cut into their skin. Sometimes Luzia feared that there
were snakes or long-toothed caititu boars. She gripped Antônio
closer.

The pain of her first time was gone, replaced by urgency. Antônio often went fast—too fast—and soon his body took over, his
gaze grew remote. At first, Luzia was angry with him. He'd moved
to some faraway place and left her there, on that sandy blanket. Then
she felt him shudder. He looked at her, his eyes wide. *"Luzia!"* he
said, his voice urgent and pleading. Luzia felt a sudden, intoxicating
pride. This was the man people had called the devil. This was the
Hawk, docile under her hands. In that moment, she was in possession of him. And like any person who's managed to subdue a wild
thing, Luzia was thrilled and frightened.

She'd never admit her fear, but it was there, like the thin layer of
hair canvas concealed beneath the cloth of a gentleman's jacket. The
canvas was a rough, unseen element that gave the entire piece its
form. With his men, Antônio was a swaggering, moody captain.
When he entered towns and ranches, he was the unflinching Hawk.
With Luzia, he was Antônio—gentle, inquisitive, solicitous. It was
easy to feel affection for such a man. But some nights, when the
ground beneath her blanket was too rough, or the night air too cold,
or her locked arm ached and kept her awake, Luzia stared at Antônio's hunched back, at his calloused shoulders and long hair, and
wondered: if he wasn't also the Hawk, would she love him?

Her second child was different from the first. It did not crave
oranges. It did not make Luzia feel nauseous or tired. It was calm—a
child of the rainy months, when everything flourished. At night,
Luzia believed she could feel it moving in her belly, like a moth.
The nights were cold and wet. Luzia huddled beneath her blanket.
She covered herself in two jackets. She prayed to Our Lady of the
Good Birth. The child could not crave anything because Luzia
didn't give it a chance. She drank goat's milk each day. She sucked
on sweet blocks of rapadura. In mountain towns, she gulped down

the meaty, yellow insides of jackfruits. Whatever she could find, she ate. Despite Luzia's efforts, the child left her. At the first sign of cramping, they'd stopped at a ranch house. A farmer's wife gave Luzia her bed. She placed wet cloths on Luzia's forehead. Antônio paced outside the door. When Luzia finally rose, wearing her extra pair of trousers, Antônio was waiting.

"It's best," he said, shaking his head as if shooing away other thoughts. "Cangaceiros shouldn't have babies. They're dead weight."

Antônio had never hit her. He'd never yelled, or gripped her hand too tightly, or shoved her. In this respect, Luzia reminded herself, she was a lucky wife. Yet Luzia felt something harden inside her, like warm molasses poured into wooden blocks and set in the cold night to solidify into rapadura.

After losing her second child, she drank quixabeira-bark tea each day and swallowed one tiny chumbo pellet—the kind children poured into their BB guns to kill rolinha doves—each month to prevent another pregnancy. She began to join the men in their shooting games. Luzia picked through the pile of old papo-amarelos and muskets they'd stolen. Unlike the cangaceiros, she hated the chumbo muskets with their thick, blocklike barrels and their large metal pellets that scattered everywhere. The cangaceiros preferred Winchesters, but they also favored the chumbos. The guns' shots weren't clean but they rarely missed.

"You want deep holes," Baiano told her. "If you can't get deep, then the more the better. They let blood out and air in."

At first, Luzia had never aimed at a human target. During shooting contests, they practiced on trees, brilliantine cans, kerosene tins, and empty bottles. For these things, Luzia preferred the exactness of a pistol or a long-necked rifle. She copied the men's methods, snaking on her belly and balancing the gun against a rock to keep her shot steady. In the evenings, when it became too dark to embroider, Luzia joined the men in cleaning their weapons. Guns were precious. It angered Antônio to see rusted or dirty guns, made worthless by their owner's carelessness. "You clip a goat's hooves! You wash down a good horse! So why wouldn't you do the same for your gun?" Antônio often said. When the men cleaned their weapons, they did not speak. There were only the sounds of unlocking barrels, the clink of bullets, and the men's whispering to pass a rag or a can of brilliantine. They used sticks wrapped in soft cloths to get inside each of the chamber holes and the barrels. Baiano liked to apply a dab of brilliantine to grease his triggers

Before long, Luzia won every shooting contest. Antônio and the men—even Little Ear—praised her aim. They marveled at Luzia's shots but always congratulated the cangaceiro in second place. Luzia's wins weren't considered real because she'd never hit a man. A few months after the revolution, this changed. The cangaceiros returned to Colonel Clóvis Lucena's ranch to exact their revenge. There, Luzia took aim at her first human target. The colonel's son, Marcos, had married and left his new bride in the coastal city of Salvador; Luzia's perfect aim made the woman a widow.

After her first kill, shooting became easy for Luzia. When they raided a hostile colonel's house, or when they surprised a group of escaping Blue Party officials, Luzia and the other sharpshooters hid in doorways or behind tree trunks. At first, when she looked over the metal nib of her gun's barrel, Luzia expected her shots to make men whip around or flay their limbs. They didn't. Only the bad shots did that. If a bullet hit a joint, or a hip bone, or grazed the men's skin, they would jolt back and sometimes shudder or convulse. This was dangerous. As Baiano liked to say, even after a deadly shot a man could live for ten seconds, and ten seconds was long enough for him to shoot back. So Luzia wanted only good shots. She learned to aim for the head, the neck, and because the vital organs were higher in the body than she'd imagined, she aimed between the armpits and no lower. It became satisfying to hit her mark. This frightened her. It was confusing, how she was both willing and unwilling, proud and repentant, angry and afraid.

By early 1932, when they'd kidnapped the mapmakers, Luzia

was pregnant a third time. Shooting accurately became more important to her; she suddenly had two lives to defend instead of one. Each day she waited for the familiar cramping and release, but it never came. Despite the heat, the endless walking, and the thick, silted drinking water, the child held on. Its presence made Luzia understand the implications of something Antônio had once told her: the life of a cangaceiro was like a fire balloon, born to burn brightly and die quickly. This was why the men cherished their gold pendants, their rings, their embroidered bags and brass binoculars—because they secretly knew that those things would outlast them all. Unlike her possessions, Luzia's child was a living weight. She was determined it would outlast her.

8

Luzia preferred the older mapmaker. At midday, while the group crowded in scarce shade and waited for the sun to cool, Luzia unfolded the map she'd salvaged and spread it before the surveyor. He taught her how to read it. She'd seen only the large, colorful maps in Padre Otto's school; this one was different. It was drawn in black ink and neatly ruled, with plus and minus symbols for ground levels. Luzia asked the mapmaker to show her the locations of Taquaritinga, Recife, and the Old Chico. Some of the cangaceiros crowded around them, interested. The younger mapmaker scowled at the men's questions. Antônio also watched the lessons but never participated. He disliked maps. He distrusted anything that had to be written instead of kept in one's memory.

After kidnapping the mapmakers, they'd sent a telegram to the *Diário de Pernambuco* offices. They demanded a ransom of two hundred contos in exchange for the mapmakers. There were one thousand mil-réis in just one conto; Antônio insisted they start high. It would be like bargaining at the weekly market, he said. The Gomes government would try to whittle them down. Luzia hoped this wouldn't happen—even if they received the full amount, it would buy only a tiny property along the São Francisco River. Still, she thought, rightfully owning a small piece of land was better than having none at all.

Antônio had dictated the ransom request to a trembling telegram clerk, who'd wiped sweat from his fingers before tapping each word into the telegraph machine. In the message, Luzia and Antônio did not specify details of the ransom exchange. First they wanted a reply from the National Roadway Institute—yes or no to saving their mapmakers. In the telegram, they told the institute to print their answer in the *Diário*. And, in case Luzia and Antônio could not find the newspaper quickly enough in the scrub, they also required the roadway officials to send telegrams with their response to all major stations in the state. This way, Antônio said gleefully, no one would be able to pinpoint the cangaceiros' exact location, and, most important, the roadway institute would be forced to say yes. If they said no, in the newspaper and in widespread telegrams, everyone would know they hadn't tried to save their own men. The cangaceiros would shame Gomes's roadway institute into paying.

While Antônio thought only of the attention they'd receive for the kidnapping, Luzia thought of their next telegram. Each night she lay on her sandy blankets and composed the message in her head—if the roadway institute said yes to their demands, they would have to be ready with a meeting point. The Gomes government could easily send troops instead of funds, so the cangaceiros had to carefully coordinate an exchange. They could not trap themselves. Luzia thought of leaving the mapmakers in one location and receiving the money in another, to try to divert attention from the ransom. Perhaps one of their loyal helpers—a coiteiro—could be used to pick up the funds? Each time Luzia told her ideas to Antônio, he barely listened. He wanted to find newspapers. He wanted their names in print.

With the mapmakers in tow, the group had left the cattle trail and headed toward the São Francisco, a plentiful source of water. No one said the word *seca,* as if by ignoring it, the drought would not exist. Only the richest colonels could afford to take their herds of cattle to the highlands—towns like Taquaritinga, Garanhuns, and Triunfo—where there was more water. Smaller ranchers were forced to release their cattle into the scrub, hoping the animals would fend for themselves. In the dry heat, ticks multiplied. They infested the cows' ears and covered their noses like a bumpy brown skin. Vultures grew fat and numerous. Luzia saw saints' statues tied to the roofs of houses. The figurines were roped down, their faces toward the sun. Some were blindfolded. Some had hands missing or feet smashed off. People would return the limbs when it rained. It was only February 1932; residents would hold out hope until March 19. São José's day was an important marker: if it rained on or before the saint's day, crops could still be planted. If it didn't rain, there was no hope. Residents would have to dig into their food reserves—if they had them—and wait until next year. No one spoke of the possibility that, if a drought came, it would not rain the next year either. If their prayers for rain were answered, however, caatinga residents would untie the saints' statues, repair them, and worship them again. On one chapel's roof, Luzia saw the baby Jesus. His arms and legs were gone, leaving dark holes in his clay torso.

"They shouldn't do that," Luzia said.

"People don't know better," Antônio replied. "It's what they understand."

Luzia shook her head. "People understand threats. Saints don't."

"They were people once."

"Yes," Luzia said. "Maybe that's why they don't listen."

"They listen." Antônio stroked her cheek with the tips of his fingers. He did it quickly, so the men wouldn't see. "They just don't give us what we ask for. They have their reasons."

Antônio, like many residents, believed there was a reason behind the lack of rain. God and the saints had presented him with a message, a warning. Antônio believed the drought was an omen—it had begun after Gomes took power. The scrub and the people within it would now suffer under this man's watch. Antônio grew to distrust the president even more.

Food was scarce, but the cangaceiros never suffered. Mostly they caught the tiger-striped surubim from the São Francisco River. The smell of fish stayed on Luzia's hands, in her nose, on her clothing. She hated that bony fish with its flavorless white meat, but it was better than the sour manioc flour and tough jerked beef sold in towns. On good days, the men caught teú lizards or rolinha doves. The cangaceiros were used to walking long hours on little food. The mapmakers were not. Their feet became bloodied and tender. The men's beards grew unclipped and came to snarled points beneath their chins. They looked like wandering beatos, except they did not wear a tangle of rosaries or bear the burden of life-size wooden crosses.

Luzia could will her mind through the drought but her body demanded more. Her belly's skin tightened and her trousers became hard to button. Her hip bones felt oiled and slippery. Luzia stumbled. She bumped into the men as she walked. She felt as clumsy and awkward as a growing girl, her body changing in ways she did not understand. She felt tired. It wasn't the familiar fatigue of walking or living under the scrub's hot sun, but something deeper. The child was sapping her, feasting on her. Her stomach felt like the boil of a bichada, the parasites that burrowed under the hides of cattle and goats, then ate them from the inside out. One night, Ponta Fina brought her the heart of a rolinha dove. Luzia hadn't spoken of her condition, but Ponta had guessed. He knew the old legend: to predict a child's sex, the future mother punctures a chicken heart and holds it over a fire. If, after it's cooked, the heart is open, the child will be a girl. If it's closed, it will be a boy. They did not have a chicken heart but a rolinha's would do. Luzia put the tiny heart on the tip of her punhal. She held it over the cook fire. Ponta stood beside her. When she lifted the knife from the flames, the heart was dark and closed tight, like a fist.

By mid-February, they'd visited a dozen telegraph stations but no telegrams had arrived from the roadway institute. Dust rose from the ground in orange clouds, covering the cangaceiros' clothes, dulling the polish of their leather cartridge belts, and coating the insides of their mouths. Antônio's vision worsened. The eye on the scarred side of his face teared and itched. He could not blink out the sand and grit. Since water was too precious to waste, he cleaned his eye with a handkerchief. It was no use; the eye grew murky and dull, like a child's marble. Some nights, Antônio woke in a panic, worried that his other eye was clouding as well. He prayed to Santa Luzia. Finally, he decided to cross the São Francisco and see Dr. Eronildes.

The doctor, like others near the São Francisco, had the luxury of water. As long as food supplies held out, fishermen and tenant farmers could stay in their homes until it rained again. Despite the benefits of the Old Chico's waters, most ranchers like Eronildes had already left the region. The crash of 1929 and "the Crisis" that followed it had been the first blow to independent farmers; the drought debilitated them even more. Most had abandoned their farms, allowing neighboring colonels to take possession of the land. Dr. Eronildes wouldn't stomach this; despite the drought, he stayed.

The whitewash of his ranch house had faded to a dull, dirty yellow. The sun had bleached his front gate gray and made its wood splintered and warped. Eronildes opened the gate himself. The stresses of caatinga life had taken a physical toll on the doctor. Sunspots dotted the skin beneath Eronildes' eyes. His beard was poorly shaved. A rope belt had replaced the leather one he'd once worn. When he greeted Luzia, his hands shook. She smelled drink on his breath.

Without prompting, he examined each of the cangaceiros. He sterilized a small pair of pincers and squeezed thorns from red, painful bumps in the men's skin. He treated superficial wounds with a few, precious drops of hydrogen peroxide and iodine, and warned the men against using rusted knives. For most, he prescribed herbal remedies to soothe their coughs or the constipation brought on from their scanty diets. With his thin fingers, he inspected the men's teeth and gums. Some were loose and bloody and

Dr. Eronildes told the men to eat umbu, or any scrub fruits they could find. When he came to the mapmakers, Eronildes grew quiet. He cleaned their feet with the last of his hydrogen peroxide. Then he poured a diluted solution of carbolic acid over the broken skin, making the mapmakers wince. Dr. Eronildes told Ponta Fina to bandage the hostages' feet while he took Antônio and Luzia indoors. In his private study, Eronildes inspected Antônio's eyes.

"The left one is fine," Eronildes said. "The other eye can never be repaired. Only tolerated."

He opened a wooden cabinet and searched through its contents. After a while, he returned with a glass vial. It had a rubber top and an eyedropper.

"You will lose your sight in the right eye," Eronildes said. "But this will help with the dust. It's a solution to moisturize the eye."

Antônio examined the vial. Without asking Luzia to test it first, he opened the bottle and squirted several drops into his foggy eye. He clamped his eyes shut, then sat up. His cheek was wet.

"I'm very grateful to you," Antônio said. "You'll always have my protection."

Eronildes wiped his hands.

"I have something to show you," he said, then riffled through the stack of newspapers beside his desk. He pulled out a *Diário de Pernambuco* dated three weeks prior. "This was in my most recent shipment, my last one. The river's too low to carry barges now."

On the front page was an article about the mapmakers. Luzia read it aloud.

"A few perverse thieves will not deny the people their needs," Tenente Higino Ribeiro, the state's new leader, was quoted as saying. He assured readers that the government would send more surveyors. They would build the Trans-Nordestino. The article spoke of the duty the mapmakers had done for their country. How they had been fine, honorable men.

Gomes sent a letter from the presidential palace in Rio de Janeiro, stating that cangaceiros were small impediments on the path to a greater future: "There is no place for them in the New Brazil!" Dr. Duarte Coelho, the state's newly appointed special advisor on criminal matters, was also quoted. He funded a hefty reward for the cangaceiros' heads—25:000$00, or 25 contos for the Hawk and the Seamstress. City officials were trying to define the criminal mind, to make physical criteria they would use to weed out future offenders, to know which could be rehabilitated and which had to be destroyed.

"Like lame goats," Luzia said. "Like calves born blind or with only one teat." Such animals were doomed from the beginning, their destinies prescribed by their bodies and not their souls.

"We made the front page," Antônio said, ignoring her.

"You shouldn't joke," Dr. Eronildes replied. "That article might as well have been an obituary for those surveyors. They won't pay you for them. They don't care."

"They will care," Antônio said. "I'll make them."

"How?"

Antônio looked at Luzia. "We'll get a portrait made, with all of us. Prove they're alive."

"Don't do it," Eronildes said, his voice grave. "There's a price on your heads. Your protection is your anonymity. If you photograph yourselves, they'll know your faces. You'll never be free."

"We're already free," Antônio said. "But if we let that road in here, we won't be. That road will be like a fence; Gomes'll use it to herd us. To push us back and back into the caatinga until there's no caatinga left. And then he'll corner us for slaughter. We're men, Doctor, not cattle."

Eronildes sighed. He removed a bottle of White Horse whiskey and two glasses from his shelf. The doctor poured drinks. When Antônio declined, Eronildes quickly swallowed both servings.

"Things have changed," the doctor said, wiping his mouth.

Antônio nodded. "Whiskey's more common than water these days."

"That's not what I mean," Eronildes snapped. "Staying here, in

Bahia, won't remedy your troubles. Bahia, Pernambuco, Paraíba—all the states are united under Gomes now. One is no safer than the other. If you make an example of those surveyors, the law will have to make one of you."

"Gomes never complained when we stopped those Blue runaways," Antônio said. "But when we stop his men, we have a ransom on our heads." He looked down and fidgeted with his eyedropper. "There's something I've been meaning to ask you, Doctor. What's a *relic*?"

"A relic?" Eronildes replied, confused. "Something that's old. Useless. It's survived past its time."

Antônio nodded. His grip tightened on the eyedropper bottle; Luzia feared he'd break it.

"Why do you ask?" Eronildes said.

Antônio stared at the doctor. His eyes were still wet from the drops; Luzia wanted to reach out and wipe his face but didn't dare.

"I never bothered the capital. I never took my men past Limoeiro. I left the coast alone. Never intruded on their business. They should show the same respect for me, for my place."

"It's not about manners, Antônio," Eronildes said softly. "The scrub isn't yours."

The good side of Antônio's brow crinkled.

"Times change," Eronildes continued. "We must change with them."

"Or become relics?"

"Yes."

Antônio cleared his throat as if to spit. Instead, he spoke. "You're a son of the city, Doctor. I'm a son of the caatinga. And I'm a loyal son."

"Loyal to what? To the old ways?" Eronildes shook his head. "You want people to live under the same yoke."

"And you want them to take on new ones."

"The roadway's not a yoke, Antônio."

"People here will be against it. They'll take my side. They'll help me because I help them. They're loyal."

"No," Eronildes replied. "People are fickle. They'll make a hero out of the first man they can find until another, better one comes along. There's no loyalty here, Antônio. There's only need. People need food. They need money and security. Whoever gives them more, that's who they'll call a hero. The reward for your head will erase any loyalty."

"You're one of them then?" Antônio asked. "A Gomes man?"

Eronildes raised his sunspotted hands, as if to show he had no weapon. "What else is there to be? Tell me."

Antônio nodded. He placed the newspaper article under his arm and stalked out of the room, forgetting Luzia. When she moved to follow him, Eronildes skirted around his desk. He caught her locked elbow. Embarrassed, he quickly let go.

"I can order new lenses for your spectacles," Eronildes sputtered. "Yours are scratched."

"They work fine," Luzia said. "Thank you."

"You . . . Antônio won't come back here again, will he? This is the last time."

Luzia nodded. Antônio was suspicious of those he deemed "Gomes men," even if they had once been his friends. The doctor wrung his hands.

"I'm asking this as a doctor," Eronildes whispered. "And as a friend. How far along are you?"

Luzia looked up, startled.

"It's your face," Eronildes said. "The dark crescents under your eyes. And your trousers," he said, nodding toward Luzia's waist, "they barely button."

Luzia felt her face reddening. Men—even doctors—did not talk to women about such things. Only midwives dealt with feminine problems, but Luzia had no midwife. She had no guidance.

"It's been three moons," she said. "Since I . . ." Her words caught. She could not complete her sentence.

"You must rest," Eronildes said. "You must eat properly. You'll lose it if you don't."

"No. Not this one. This one is staying."

"Will you leave the group?"

Luzia shook her head, surprised that he would even consider it.

"How will you raise this child?" Eronildes said, indignant. *This child,* he said, as if it wasn't hers.

"I'll raise it properly."

"Where?"

She faltered, then spoke quietly. "Somewhere near the river. We're going to buy a plot of land with our ransom."

Eronildes snorted. "You're just as stubborn as him. They won't pay. Even if they did, it wouldn't help. The land is dead. No one's cotton crop—not even mine, here by the river—has flowered! And if it doesn't rain this year, you won't even have manioc growing. You'll starve."

"Where should I go then?" Luzia said, keeping her voice level. "A city? The capital? I'd starve there, too. No one wants to hire a cripple. Especially one with my belly."

"You could stay here."

"As your maid?" Luzia coughed. She didn't let the doctor answer. "Antônio wouldn't let me stay."

"If he loved you he would."

Luzia had never heard a man say the word *love* aloud. Emília used to say it, in whispers before bed. But men, especially caatinga men, didn't speak of such things. Luzia turned her face from the doctor's gaze.

"I hear you're a good shot," Eronildes said.

"Yes," Luzia replied, her voice too loud. "I am."

"Who taught you to shoot?"

"Antônio."

"Why?"

"To defend myself," Luzia replied, confused. She felt a twinge of shame for her shooting ability and was angry at Eronildes for making her feel this way. "He taught me because it would help me."

"Or was it to help himself?" the doctor continued. "So you'd be useful to him, now that his vision's failing?"

Luzia's heart thumped wildly. It was silly of him, to say such things to her. Didn't he see the parabellum in her shoulder holster? Didn't Eronildes know what she was capable of? Luzia's fingertips brushed the handle of her gun.

"Are you thinking of shooting me now?" Eronildes asked, his expression sad. "That would be easier, wouldn't it? Rather than listening to me. You see, when you call upon violence as a solution once, you will be tempted to do it again and again. Until one day, Luzia, you will not be able to decide for yourself whether to use it or not. It will come automatically, and you will not be able to contain it. How will you raise another human being, when you can't control yourself? What will you teach this child of yours?"

Luzia's chest felt tight, her breath short. "You've never had to shoot," she said. "You don't know anything about it."

Eronildes nodded. "That's true. But I know medicine. I know what it means to carry a child. And you know that there's no rain coming. You know that husband of yours will attack the roadway. He'll give you no peace. The country's changing, Luzia. The backlands will be a part of it whether he likes it or not. If that child is lucky, it will die the day it's born."

"Is that a curse?" Luzia asked.

"I don't believe in curses," Eronildes said. "If your child dies, don't blame a curse. Blame yourself."

Luzia left the study. She walked quickly through the dim corridors of Eronildes' house until she reached the kitchen door. Outside, she disappeared into the scrub where the cangaceiros had made camp.

4

Luzia still recalled her first kill and how it had changed her. One year and two months before kidnapping the mapmakers, while Gomes was organizing his new government on the coast, Antônio also decided to organize—gathering his new recruits and returning to Colonel Clóvis's ranch. Little had changed in São Tomé since their first, disastrous visit. Colonel Clóvis still wore pajamas with a peixeira knife tucked into his waistband. Marcos was no different, except for the gold wedding band that dug into his meaty finger. He'd married but kept his wife in the coastal city of Salvador, protected from the scrubland's sun and dust, and its cangaceiros. When Antônio's group took over the ranch, quickly overpowering the colonel's capangas, Marcos tried to escape out the back gate. Baiano caught him. Colonel Clóvis, on the other hand, sat placidly in his porch chair.

"I knew you'd come around," he said, jutting his whiskery chin at Antônio. "I can't abide waiting. Go ahead. Do what you mean to."

The colonel stood, handing Antônio his peixeira knife. Antônio nodded and took the old man inside the ranch house. From the porch, Luzia heard a single gunshot. When Antônio returned, he faced Marcos. The colonel's son stood between Baiano and Little Ear. The front of his dress shirt was damp with sweat. Its fabric clung to his chest.

"It was all Papai's idea," Marcos said hoarsely. "Papai made a deal with Colonel Machado—the one whose son you nearly killed. He would trade his entire cotton harvest if Papai would give you up. It was business." Marcos looked to Luzia, as if for sympathy. She stared back, her mouth rigid. Marcos wiped his forehead with the back of his hand. "It shouldn't matter now. Gomes is in. Troops are gone. You're alive."

"I lost half my men," Antônio replied. "Got shot in my leg. You know what it's like, crawling around the scrub with a shot leg?"

Marcos shook his head. He stared at his shoes.

"That day the troops came, you disappeared," Antônio continued. "I'm going let you do that again."

Marcos's eyes opened wide. "But the cotton," he said. "There's not much of it, but I have to start harvesting—"

"That's my concern now," Antônio interrupted.

"And if I stay?"

The porch was quiet except for Marcos's strained breathing—a whistle of air flowing in and out of his nose.

"You'd better saddle a horse," Antônio said. "Be quick or I'll change my mind."

Marcos nodded. Baiano guided him to the stables. When Little Ear protested that they were being too lenient, Antônio made him leave the porch.

"He'll come out at a gallop," Antônio whispered to Luzia. He reached beneath her armpit and gently snapped open her shoulder holster. He eased out the parabellum and placed it in her hands. "Hit him in the leg," he said. "Make him fall."

Antônio's voice was low and soft. It was the same tone he used when he asked her to read their wedding certificate aloud, or to make a compress for his bad eye. It made his orders seem like requests.

Luzia heard the beat of hooves. The parabellum felt very heavy in her hand. She recalled standing before an immense bolt of Portuguese silk, just after she'd injured her arm. *Cut straight and cut fast,* Aunt Sofia had said. *The first cut's always the hardest. After that, it gets easier.*

"My Saint," Antônio whispered.

Luzia brought up her good arm. She steadied it with her bent one. Marcos—large and toad like—bumped on top of his horse. Dust clouded the entrance path. Soon, he would be out of range. Luzia held her breath.

The cangaceiros complimented her. It was a hard shot: a moving target, with all of that dust. Her eyes were sharper than they'd imagined. Ponta Fina offered to clean her parabellum. Little Ear called it a lucky shot. Marcos spent the day dragging about the front yard, bumping against fence posts and the pillars of the house, trying to find the front gate. Antônio had tied a stiff canvas cloth over his eyes. At night, Marcos wept and moaned. Luzia couldn't sleep with the sound of it. The next day, Marcos was quiet. Antônio unsheathed his punhal and went into the yard. Black-necked vultures congregated on the fence and in the ipê trees' branches. Luzia stuffed cotton in her ears, but she could still hear the flapping of their wings. Her actions had brought those birds there.

She also avoided the colonel's kitchen. Over the cookstove's fire, where smoke was used to cure meat, Canjica had carefully hooked another offering to Santa Luzia. They were not round but lumpy, like balls of dough with several stringy pieces connected to their ends. After a few days in the smoke, they deflated and shriveled. Antônio placed them in his leather pouch.

At Antônio's request, Luzia penned a letter to Marcos's widow in Salvador, informing her that her husband, Marcos Lucena, and his father, Clóvis, had died. Antônio sent his deepest condolences. They assured the widow that the farm would be looked after. Out of fairness, she would receive a yearly share of the gin's profits. There was no need to visit or make inquiries. *The interior is no place for a lady,* Luzia added before sealing the letter. *If the senhora is wise, you will keep that in mind.*

Luzia hoped they would stay in São Tomé where they could work the land and live normally. After a month, Antônio grew restless. He argued that the property wasn't rightfully theirs and in order to protect their claim to it, he would need more men and more money. They left São Tomé and returned to the scrub. But Luzia couldn't leave behind the memory of that dusty yard, the slippery feel of the parabellum in her hands, or the loud thump Marcos made when he fell from his horse. She'd expected to feel guilt or remorse from these memories, but instead she felt anger. At what, she wasn't sure. It was as if her first kill had pulled a latch within her, opening the door to emotions that had been shut away. Luzia's girlhood rage returned.

In the months that followed, when the cangaceiros robbed Blue

Party loyalists on the cattle trail, Luzia stole only newspapers from the men. From the women, she took much more. The escapees often traveled with wives and daughters who looked at Luzia with a mixture of fear and disgust. They stared at her trousers and her bent arm. To them, she was the lowly Seamstress. Luzia yanked pendants from the women's necks, tugging until the chains broke off, until her palms hurt. She pulled the city women's hair taut and hacked it off, cutting so close she sometimes nicked the women's pale scalps. She could act on her rage now, unhindered by Aunt Sofia's rules or Emília's soothing voice. Now, Luzia could aim and shoot. She could hurt anyone before they hurt her.

After her argument with Dr. Eronildes, Luzia began to understand the consequences of this logic. She'd learned to be as cruel as the men. In the scrub, women were only taught to live alongside cruelty, to endure it, sometimes to prize it. As a woman, Luzia saw what Antônio and the other cangaceiros could not—cruelty could not be contained. It could not be used and then discarded, like an alpercata sandal. Once it was there, it stayed. It grew within her and the men, becoming numbness. Indifference. Eronildes was right. But Luzia had something else growing inside her, competing for space. The child in her belly could save her. It had prompted her to crave stability, to want a plot of land. That desire had given her the idea of kidnapping those mapmakers and asking for a ransom. If it could do this to her, Luzia thought, perhaps the child would change Antônio, too, prompting him to stop being a cangaceiro and become a father.

5

In their camp near Eronildes' house, Antônio showed the newspaper to his men. The mapmakers' kidnapping had made the front page. Gomes's government was scared of them. So scared, Antônio said, they'd offered a reward for their heads. The cangaceiros couldn't read, so they took their captain's word. Only Baiano knew his alphabet, but he couldn't hold the newspaper long enough. The men passed it about, cheering and laughing. They were famous, Antônio said. It merited a celebration. The men made a bonfire and cooked a steer Eronildes had given them. The animal was skinny and its meat was tough, but it had been weeks since anyone had eaten fresh beef. After dinner, some of the cangaceiros danced. Others, led by Little Ear, walked to a nearby village, hoping to find women-of-the-life. With those who stayed, Antônio tried to be jovial. He sang and took turns playing dominoes. When he tired, he moved away from the fire and sat beside Luzia.

Antônio removed his hat. Beneath it, the hair near his scalp had an oily sheen. At ear level, where the hat no longer protected it, his hair gradually lightened and changed texture, becoming dry and tangled until its honey blond ends brushed his shoulders.

"It's late, My Saint. You should rest. We're getting an early start tomorrow."

"To where?"

"Another town. Somewhere with a photographer." Antônio nodded to the mapmakers. They slumped beneath a nearby tree, their feet bound. Antônio had given the hostages meat; grease shone around their mouths.

"We'll send proof," he said.

"That they're alive?" Luzia asked.

Antônio wiped his clouded eye. "Proof of the capital's mistake."

Her husband had the habit of addressing the capital as if it were a living thing. *We'll teach the capital a lesson,* he often said. Or, *This will get the capital's attention.* It was easier for Antônio to say *the capital,* than to name Tenente Higino Ribeiro or even Gomes. It bothered Luzia. He'd begun to say it often, and adamantly, as if he were speaking of one man and not an entire city.

"The doctor asked about my health," Luzia said. She took a deep breath; if Antônio thought it improper, her revelation could kill Eronildes.

"What kinds of things did he ask?"

"He's worried for me. For our boy." Luzia coughed. It was the first time they'd spoken of the child.

"Are you worried?" Antônio asked.

Luzia couldn't nod. Worry would be a betrayal to Antônio, a way of saying that he couldn't care for her like a good husband should. Luzia hunched. She bent into him, resting her head on his shoulder. Antônio didn't like such displays. Near the fire, the map-makers and the cangaceiros were watching them. Luzia pressed her nose to Antônio's jacket. She took in his scent of dust, sweat, and Fleur d'Amour.

"My Saint," Antônio whispered, nudging her to face him. He rolled up his jacket sleeve, revealing his bare arm. It was paler than his hand but still brown. Luzia stared at its soft underside, at the shadows of its roping veins in the firelight. Antônio smiled.

"Take it," he said. "It's yours."

"You think I want that tough meat?"

"No," he replied, his smile gone. He continued to hold out his arm. "But if you did, I'd let you take as many bites as you needed. I'd let you eat me alive."

"I don't like that kind of talk," Luzia said. When they were newly married, she'd told him the story of the Cannibal Wife. Now, with a drought coming, the story wasn't amusing.

"It's the only kind of talk I know," Antônio replied, his voice low.

Luzia stared at his arm. If she brought it to her mouth, he would not flinch. He would not cry out. He would give. He would let her consume him, bit by bit, if that was what she needed.

The next day, as they prepared to leave Eronildes' ranch, Antônio thanked the doctor but did not shake his hand. Eronildes quietly reminded him to put the drops in his eyes. Minutes later, while the cangaceiros cleaned their camp and checked their bags, Eronildes took Luzia aside. He placed folded cloth in her hands. It was a sturdy, blue bramante.

"You'll need to sew yourself some trousers to accommodate your belly," Eronildes said. He placed his hands between the cloth's folds and removed a corked vial. Inside the brown glass was powder.

"It's cyanide," he whispered. "Please, only open it if you mean to use it. It's very strong. It's better than starving, or getting caught by soldiers. Especially soldiers. That's no way for a lady to die."

He pressed the vial into her palm.

"I'll die the way God intends," Luzia said. Still, she took the vial and slipped it into her bornal. Then she stared at the doctor. Eronildes' eyes were large and wide behind his thick lenses. Luzia thought of Antônio's binoculars—when she looked through them, everything became tangible and easy to reach, even when it wasn't. Perhaps that was the way Eronildes saw things. *Leave*, he'd urged her, thinking it was a simple act. Eronildes believed that leaving Antônio meant she loved her child. And if she didn't leave, the opposite was true.

"Love what is before you. Make no distinctions," Padre Otto had often said. But it was impossible *not* to make distinctions. The child in her belly was a phantom. He was unformed, unknown. He was fragile, and Luzia could not trust fragility. She could only trust strength. Antônio was flesh and bone. He was real, alive beside her. At that moment, he was the easier of the two to love.

People are weak, Luzia thought. *We fall back on what is easy. What is known.* One day, when he was old enough to understand, she would tell her boy this.

6

She'd never liked photographs. Never liked the way people looked in them—bodies stiff, faces frozen, eyes dark within their sockets like two soulless holes. Paintings, at least, were made by men's hands. And songs, like the ones the traveling repentistas sang while strumming their small violas, told stories. Photographs came from within a black box, products of a mysterious and godless creation.

They told no stories. You didn't know what had happened before the photograph was shot or what would happen after. You could only guess, and Luzia hated guessing. She preferred precision. A centimeter was the difference between trousers that were comfortable or ill fitting. Between embroidery that was even or lopsided. Between a shot that hit heart or lung, muscle or bone.

After a few weeks of walking near the São Francisco, they found a decent-size town equipped with a chapel, a struggling market, and a photographer. Luzia hesitated at the idea of a portrait.

"They'll know your face," she said. "They'll know mine."

"That's what I want," Antônio replied.

Forty cangaceiros lined up in three rows. The new recruits knelt on one knee, their alpercatas polished, the brims of their hats newly broken and tacked upward in the required half-moon. The second row of men crouched, their rifles at their sides for support. The third row stood. These were the group's senior members: Baiano, Canjica, Inteligente, Little Ear, Sweet Talker, Half-Moon, Caju, Sabiá, Ponta Fina. Rings gleamed on their dark fingers. They tightened the silk scarves around their necks and twisted their bornais forward to show off Luzia's embroidery. They were covered in her designs, Antônio most of all. They wore their punhais tucked at an angle into the waists of their pants, so that the knives' handles appeared above their cartridge belts. On the ground, just in front of the kneeling cangaceiros, were the mapmakers. They sat cross-legged in the dirt, their hands bound behind their backs. The bandages Eronildes had placed on their feet were stained and ragged.

Luzia stood in the center of the third row, beside Antônio. Like the men, she did not smile. She'd chewed juá bark obsessively, but her teeth had still suffered. After leaving Eronildes' ranch, one of her top teeth had begun to ache. When she'd sucked on the tooth, a rotten taste, like sour milk, emerged. It began to taint her breath. During their travels, they'd found a vaqueiro who owned tooth pliers. He'd made Luzia drink a cup of sugarcane liquor and then, while Antônio held her arms, the man tugged out her rotten tooth. Now another tooth ached. On account of the child, she'd traded her hat for a bottle of pure molasses. She hated the sweetness of it, but each day she spooned the syrup into her mouth. She'd been craving dirt again, and had even put a dusty chunk of the clay soil along the river into her mouth, only to spit it out. It was dangerous—earth had invisible worms that could take over her belly and eat the food meant for her child. Eating molasses ruined her teeth, but it lessened her cravings. It gave her the energy to rise from her blanket each morning and walk alongside Antônio.

The photographer Antônio had hired was skittish and wide-eyed, like the rock-dwelling mocós the cangaceiros hunted. He was nothing like the impatient, snooty man who had photographed Luzia and Emília on their First Communion. Luzia remembered the shame she'd felt when he'd covered her crooked arm with a doily from his prop bin. When the flash popped, Luzia had moved just to spite him. Emília never forgave her for ruining their photograph.

Antônio's photographer didn't dare hide Luzia's bent arm. If she shifted or blinked, he would snap another shot without protest. This time, Luzia didn't have to wear gloves or a starched Communion gown. Instead, she wore a canvas dress of her own design. She was only four months along, but her trousers were already too tight. After leaving Dr. Eronildes' ranch, Luzia had taken the fabric he'd given her and sewn a dress. It was sensible and smocklike, to hide her belly in the coming months. She'd made plenty of pockets along its skirt front so she wouldn't miss her trousers. She'd saved a satin ribbon taken from a Blue Party woman. Luzia used it as piping along the dress's seams. She embroidered white and red dots along the cuffs and in a V shape across her chest. Despite the heat, Luzia also wore thick stockings and leather shin guards.

Before her, the photographer hid beneath his camera's curtain. Dust and sun had turned the black cloth gray. People huddled behind him. The town's residents fanned their faces. Even in the late afternoon, the sun didn't weaken. It was March nineteenth—Saint José's Day—and there was no rain. The day wasn't over, though. People prayed to Saint Pedro in the hopes of convincing him to send water. Several pious women knelt around Antônio's photographer, hoping to continue their prayers and, at the same time, get a glimpse of the Hawk and the Seamstress.

"Chove-chuva, chove-chuva, chove-chuva," the women chanted. "Have compassion on us, dear Mother Mary. On our laments and our pains. On our pride and our stubbornness. We will all die of thirst because we are sinners. But we ask you, Holy Mother of land and of sea, to give us water. Give us this grace, so that we may love you more."

The photographer raised his flashbulb. The afternoon sun was so bright that they could not face it. Antônio didn't want squinting in his portrait. The photographer positioned them at an angle so that their eyes could be open. He assured Antônio that their faces would be clearly visible; the camera flash would expel any shadows. When the pictures were developed, the photographer promised to personally take them to Recife. Antônio gave him money for a train ticket and told the man that he could sell the photos for whatever sum he pleased and keep all the profits, as long as they were published in the papers.

The photographer began to count backward. Luzia smoothed her dress. She straightened her spectacles. Beside her, Antônio shifted. For the photograph he'd squeezed his feet into a pair of the mapmakers' high-topped leather boots. He'd slit open the sides but they were still too tight. He had to move back and forth to keep his feet from tingling. It took several seconds for the camera shutter to click. Luzia's eyes watered. She could sense the cangaceiros' anxiousness and her own. It burned in her chest, like a breath held too long. Suddenly, there was a pop. The flashbulbs exploded, leaving the smell of smoke and a grave silence, an instant of not knowing when or if to move.

The photographer emerged from beneath his gray veil. The cangaceiros cheered. Before they disbanded, they huddled around Luzia and extended their hands.

"Bless me, Mãe," each man said.

"You're blessed," she replied.

The men asked for Luzia's blessing each time they surveyed a town, or raided a disloyal colonel's house, or separated along the cattle trail in wait of travelers. The group's oldest members clasped her fingers and called her "Mãe," as if Luzia were a replacement for the mothers they'd left behind long ago. Little Ear and Half-Moon, still wary of her presence, took her blessings halfheartedly and only for the Hawk's sake. The group's newest members lowered their eyes and whispered like embarrassed suitors, "Bless me, Mãe." In the past weeks, the men had become more fervent in their reverence. After she'd traded her hat for the molasses, Antônio gave Luzia a long linen shawl that she wore over her head to protect her from the sun. The shawl, coupled with her growing belly, had affected the men. They kissed the cloth's dirty edges, placed small offerings of food at Luzia's feet, and argued over who would carry her sewing machine. Early on, Antônio had convinced his men that Luzia's presence protected them from harm, but even he was surprised by the strength of their reverence. He was proud, too. Luzia appreciated the men's respect, but she was also wary of it. She recalled the mangled saints' statues tied to people's roofs in punishment for their poor service. Reverence was always conditional. Luzia sensed that the cangaceiros' worship hinged on luck; they would love her until that luck ran out.

While the men received their blessings, the photographer set up a faded canvas backdrop. Before it, he placed a stool and two iron neck rods. The rods stood upright, like hat stands except adjustable in height and with metal semicircles attached to their tops.

"I don't want those," Antônio yelled. "They're for corpses."

Startled, the photographer quickly dismantled the neck braces. Antônio looked down at the mapmakers.

"You boys keep still. I want the capital to see you're alive and well."

The older man nodded. He'd lost much of the plumpness in his face, making his skin slack and his cheeks hollow. The younger one stared stubbornly forward, ignoring Antônio.

"Take that stool away, too," Antônio directed.

The photographer scratched his sunburned scalp. "Pardon me, Captain, but shouldn't the dona sit?"

"No. She'll stand. Won't you, My Saint?"

Luzia nodded. Quickly, she remembered his bad eye and faced him. "Yes," she said. "Of course,"

The photographer took away the stool. The mapmakers sat before the canvas backdrop, and Antônio stood behind them. Luzia took her place beside her husband. Antônio turned his good eye to face her. He straightened her spectacles, then reached behind her neck and brought her braid forward. It was thick and heavy. Its end touched her hip bone. Luzia had broken her childhood promise to Saint Expedito; on her eighteenth birthday she hadn't cut her hair and left it on the saint's altar as Aunt Sofia had instructed. Promise or no promise, Antônio wouldn't hear of cutting her hair short like the capital's women. He held Luzia's braid to his mouth and kissed it. Once again, the photographer crouched beneath his gray veil and lifted his flashbulb. Luzia's back ached. She wished Antônio had let them use the iron rods to brace their necks and hold their bodies straight.

As if divining her thoughts, Antônio said, "Stand tall, my Saint."

The flashbulbs popped in a neat row, leaving behind a cloud of smoke. For minutes afterward, Luzia could still see the white circles of light. Even when she closed her eyes, they floated in the darkness behind her lids, as if trapped there.

Instead of dismantling his tripod and backdrop, the photographer slid another plate into his camera. Behind him, Baiano, Sweet Talker, and Ponta Fina spoke to the praying women, gently escorting them away from the photo site and into the town's chapel. Above them, the sun was an orange orb, like the yolk of an egg. The mapmakers shifted, hot beneath their frayed driving coats. Luzia watched the photographer recalibrate his camera.

"There's no color in your face," Antônio said, holding her locked elbow. "Didn't you eat?"

"I'm tired of farinha," she replied. "It's all stale."

It wasn't the manioc's sour taste that sickened her but its texture, clumped and chewy. Her stomach turned each time the men dusted it onto their beans.

"I'll try to get you cornmeal," Antônio said, taking her arm and leading her out of the sun. "You should have some rapadura. To give you energy."

"Don't waste food," Luzia replied. "I'm fine. It's the flashbulbs, that's all. They hurt my eyes."

"It'll be worth it," he assured her. "Now they'll see us. They'll publish us for the capital! They'll see we're no vagabundos."

"Yes." Luzia nodded. "We'll get our ransom."

Antônio's unscarred side twitched. He wiped his rheumy eye. "Go sit in the chapel, my Saint. Join the women in their novenas."

Luzia shook her head. "He's going to take another picture. I saw him replace the plate."

"I don't want you here for that picture."

"Why not?" she asked, suddenly angry. Hadn't the ransom been her idea? Hadn't she written the telegram?

"You shouldn't see blood," Antônio replied.

Luzia stiffened. An expecting woman could not see death. She could not cross running water. She could not touch the scales of a lizard, or play with cats or dogs for fear that her child would resemble the animals. She could not set objects on her stomach because they would leave a mark on the baby's face. Wearing a key around her neck would cause a harelip. Seeing an eclipse would paint the child's skin, making him mottled or black. Luzia had heard all of those decrees. She believed none of them.

"What blood?" Luzia insisted.

"Those mapmakers," Antônio said. "Today's their last day."

Luzia felt a familiar tightness in her chest; it was the dread she experienced each time she took a shot, afraid she'd miss her mark and afraid she wouldn't.

"We haven't gotten our ransom," she said.

Antônio clicked his tongue, chiding her. "You think they'll pay? The doctor was right. The capital will replace them. We have to send a message. If not, they'll think they own us." He rested his hands on her shoulders. "I never expected money. I did this to show Gomes that I could, that we could. They want heads, and they'll get them."

Luzia looked toward the mapmakers. The younger one stared back intently, trying to comprehend their argument. The older one wiped his brow. During their map lessons he'd been serious and soft-spoken. He'd explained the trajectory of the proposed roadway without making Luzia feel uneducated or silly. In return for his kindness, Luzia had told him about the ransom request. She'd told him to be respectful and patient; that way, he'd survive.

"They haven't done anything wrong," she said. "The old one never insulted you."

"Measuring the trail insults me."

"Why?"

Antônio shook his head. "Men like Eronildes, they think we can invite the devil to our table. They think he'll eat what he's given and then thank us kindly. I know he won't. First Gomes wants a road, next he'll want two, then three. Then he'll want the land around the roads, then the land around that. I won't let him get that far. I won't let that devil past my gate."

"You don't have a gate," Luzia said numbly. "There's nothing that's ours."

Antônio closed his eyes. The foggy eye took longer to shut; it stared at her accusingly for seconds after the good eye had disappeared behind its lid.

"We've got names," Antônio said. "We've got the stories people tell. With these portraits, we'll have faces. We'll make an impression. That's worth more than a house or a gate."

"We should let them go," Luzia said.

Antônio opened his eyes. He gripped her shoulders tightly. His thumbs dug into the space above her collarbone.

"You think those mapmakers would respect you if you didn't have a gun? If you weren't the Seamstress?"

Luzia shook her head. Mucus thickened in her throat.

"My Saint," he said, loosening his grip on her. "This life isn't a set of clothes. You can't put it on one day and take it off the next. Even if we had land, people wouldn't call us ranchers. We'd still be cangaceiros. Worse—we'd be cangaceiros who ran away. Gomes would still want our heads. There'd always be some colonel wanting to fight us because he couldn't step on our necks, and some other colonel wanting to claim us as friends, inviting us to eat at his table and then hating us for being there. There's no escape for us."

"I'm not worried about us," Luzia said.

Antônio pressed his hand to her belly. "He'll be born. You have my word."

"And after?"

"Do you recall what Colonel Clóvis said about his goats? If he wanted to trap the mother, he kept her cabrito."

Luzia felt dizzy. She leaned slightly forward, pushing into Antônio's hand. He held her steady.

"People, they take advantage of weakness," Antônio continued. "We can't keep him. We'll trust him to a friend—that priest, the one in Taquaritinga you always talk about."

"I'll be big soon," Luzia argued. "I won't be able to keep up. Or to fight."

"You will," Antônio said, hooking a hand around her neck. He tugged her gently downward until they were eye to eye. "For me you will. I need your vision, my Saint. I need your aim."

His fingers stroked her neck. Luzia stared at the glazed center of his poor eye. It was tinged with blue and glinted in the sunlight, like a round pool of water. What did he see from it? How did the world look through such a cloudy lens? Was it filled with shadows? Were all sharp edges made dull, so he did not know what was dangerous and what was not, so that everything became a mystery and a threat? Luzia felt sympathy for him, even though she'd heard Antônio coax his men this way before. He used his flaws to make others feel vital.

He inspired loyalty by confiding his limitations, and fear by overcoming them. Luzia was angry at her susceptibility and at Antônio's perceptiveness. He was right: in the scrub, even animals exploited frailty. Fondness itself was a weakness; Antônio had taught her that, too. Because of this, their child would always be at risk. It would be better off somewhere else, far away from Luzia and the life she'd chosen. That's what made her most angry—it had been her choice. She'd left behind Victrola, and instead of freeing herself, she'd traded that name for a new one. She'd made the choice to become the Seamstress without understanding all she'd be forced to give up. Things she hadn't valued before—a house, a tame family life—were now barred from her reach. Luzia loosened her neck from Antônio's grip.

"They'll build that road," she said.

Antônio blinked. "You think they'll beat me?"

The wrong answer would hurt him. Luzia knew this, but could not stop herself.

"Yes," she said.

Antônio walked away. He called Little Ear to join him in front of the camera. He ordered the photographer to prepare to shoot, to hold up the flashbulbs. Antônio took hold of the surveyors' collars and pulled the men up from their cross-legged position. He told them to kneel, to bend their heads and pray. Little Ear unsheathed a machete. Antônio borrowed Ponta Fina's. Luzia turned away but could not shut her ears. The blades whistled on their way down. When they struck she heard heavy thuds, like two full water gourds falling to the dirt. The flashbulbs popped and smoked.

7

/ / / / / / /

Diário de Pernambuco / May 1, 1932
Despite More Surveyors' Deaths,
Trans-Nordestino Lives On
By Joaquim Cardoso

The situation in the backlands remains a grave one. Three
additional surveyors from the National Roadway Institute
have been killed by cangaceiros led by the notorious "Hawk."
A fourth surveyor, João Almeida, was kept alive in order
to report the killings. Shaken and fatigued, the brave
Senhor Almeida arrived at a loosely populated povoado
and related the devastating story of his comrades' deaths.
Captured on the notoriously unsafe cattle trail, the surveyors were stripped of their supplies and decapitated. Senhor
Almeida was spared and ordered to deliver a note to our
esteemed president. The audacious message (printed below)
was written on an embossed calling card.

Sir,

It's a shame. Men lose their heads these days. Keep yours on the
coast. I'll keep mine in the caatinga. Respectfully,

Governor Antônio Teixeira vulgo, the Hawk

Three weeks ago, this newspaper printed photographs of
Osvaldo Cunha and Henrique Andrade, the first government
surveyors executed by cangaceiros. The group photograph
(reprinted below) shows the surveyors alive, kneeling before
their captors. The other photograph—deemed unfit to print
by this newspaper's standards of taste and decency, particularly with regard to our lady readers—shows "the Hawk" and
a mestiço counterpart standing behind the surveyors, holding
the victims' severed heads.

The photographs, though deplorable, illustrate the ridicu-
lousness of the cangaceiros. The bandits are so grossly
ornamented they appear dressed for a Carnaval ball. Their
"Hawk" leader resembles a simple matuto. Dr. Duarte
Coelho analyzed the facial physiology of "the Seamstress,"

the Hawk's consort, and determined her to be "plainly a dangerous and irredeemable criminal type." The escaped surveyor, João Almeida, told officials that during his encounter with the cangaceiros, he saw that the Seamstress appeared to be expecting a child. The cangaceira's insistence on fighting even while pregnant proves that, to these criminal types, not even motherhood is sacred.

Tenente Higino Ribeiro has vowed to end the lawlessness in our farmlands. He cannot do this, however, without troops. Due to the recent rebellion in São Paulo, our esteemed President Gomes is forced to keep the bulk of federal troops in that unpatriotic metropolis. São Paulo's opposition to the revolution comes at a great cost to the rest of Brazil! The São Paulo rebellion is a dramatic illustration of how radical groups can damage our nation's stability. Prominent newspapers in both Rio de Janeiro and Minas Gerais published the Hawk's gruesome photographs accompanied by derisive articles. Southerners may mock our cangaceiros but, in truth, The Hawk's "dark-skinned army" is no different from the Communist scourge in the South, or São Paulo's supporters of the old republic. None can be ignored.

Despite a lack of troops, Tenente Higino has established a plan to break the cangaceiro network. His proposal is two-pronged: first, find all "coiteiros"—allies and family members of cangaceiros—and encourage them to be patriots. Second, provide cash incentives for the cangaceiros' capture, dead or alive. Dr. Duarte Coelho has increased his already generous reward: any patriotic citizens who bring him the Seamstress's skull paired with that of her child will receive 50:000$00 (50 contos). As the craniums will be used for scientific study, proof of identity must be presented in order to receive the reward.

The slain surveyors' bodies will be transported to Recife. Victims of sinister and needless violence, the surveyors died for a noble cause. The Trans-Nordestino, part of the National Roadway Project set to unite the country over the next fifteen years, will be a great artery connecting the Northeast not only to the rest of Brazil but also to prosperity. Oxcarts and donkey caravans are archaic when compared to the automobile. The São Francisco River—also known as

"Old Chico"—is an unreliable conduit for our agricultural goods. How can our textile mills produce fine cloth when the river level is too low for barges to transport cotton? How can the Northeast compete with our neighbors in the South when our growth depends on an ornery "Old Chico"?

The Trans-Nordestino is our best solution. Due to extremely dry conditions in the backlands and continued threats to surveyors, the National Roadway Institute is considering a radical solution to surveying the region: aerial mapping. The honorary "Captain," Carlos Chevalier, has offered to pilot his aeroplane over the region, accompanied by a cartographer and a photographer.

Currently, the roadway institute is making generous offers to landowners along the road's projected route. Landowners are encouraged to act as patriots. Their livelihoods will not be adversely affected. Plots beside the future roadway will be more valuable than any cotton crop or cattle pasture. Roadway travelers will need inns and rest stops, and petroleum companies will pay generously to set up posts. But financial rewards are not the only incentives. As President Gomes says, "Patriots will not only help build a roadway. They will build a nation."

8

On Palm Sunday, there were no leafy greens for caatinga residents to collect and present to their priests. Good Friday's procession of the Senhor Morto was more solemn than usual, without flowers or fruits to decorate the wooden Christ's deathbed. There were, however, plenty of dried grasses and dead leaves to fill Judas dolls. On Easter morning across the caatinga, adults grabbed sticks and joined children in beating the traitor figure. In such dry times, resurrection was hard to imagine but judgment was not. Residents condemned the Old Chico for growing shallow and making its tributaries—the Moxotó and Mandantes—turn into narrow trickles. People condemned their shriveled crops. Mothers berated themselves for nibbling the last pieces of dried beef they'd saved for their children. Vaqueiros cursed the thick thorns of the mandacaru cactus that, even after being seared in fire pits, clung to the plant's charred pulp and cut the mouths of hungry goats and cattle. The vaqueiros cursed the flies that feasted on the animals' bloody mouths. They cursed themselves for envying those flies.

Antônio experienced the same impotent rage as other residents but did not blame nature for his troubles. He blamed Celestino Gomes.

"He'll dig a road but not wells!" Antônio said each night after prayers. "He'll send mapmakers but not food! Spend good money on roadways but none on dams!"

For the first time, Antônio had a cause. He'd found a purpose. Before, his mission was simply to live as he pleased, without a colonel to boss him. He and the colonels had lived within a complicated web of favors and protections. The roadway, however, was uncomplicated. It would split the scrub into messy sections, like a sliced jackfruit. Antônio owed it no loyalty or respect. When Gomes declared that everything in the Trans-Nordestino's path would have to yield, Antônio resolved that he would not.

Most cangaceiros agreed. Antônio was their leader, their captain, and if he proclaimed a snake venomous or a plant dangerous, the men believed him. The threat of the Trans-Nordestino was no different. But the roadway was not real, not yet. Its construction sites were still far away, near the coast, so there were no engineers or construction crews or oxen teams for the cangaceiros to attack. The Trans-Nordestino's threat was in the future, and the cangaceiros had been conditioned to think of only the present. A few of the men—Little Ear in particular—wanted a tangible enemy, one they could fight immediately. The surveyor decapitations had satisfied Little Ear, but they didn't last long. After the Hawk's group had caught and executed six government surveyors, no more appeared on the cattle trail.

By June 1932, the only people on the trail were the drought's first escapees—women and children balancing large bundles on their heads—leaving for the coast before conditions got worse. People jeered at them, calling the escapees "quitters," and "traitors." No one spoke to the colonels this way. The land barons were also wary of the impending drought, and many collected their families and left the caatinga by passenger train. The colonels fled to vacation homes in Campina Grande, or Recife, or in the capital city of Paraíba, recently renamed "José Bandeira" after its fallen hero and Gomes's old running mate. It was easy for the colonels to mistrust the new president because he was a stranger. With most of them taking refuge on the coast, however, it would be convenient for Gomes to meet them. Luzia worried that the longer the colonels stayed away from the caatinga, the more Gomes would court them.

The National Roadway Institute began to offer vast sums in exchange for properties on and around the Trans-Nordestino's route. Like most of the land in the caatinga, those properties belonged to the colonels. Luzia didn't like the fact that they stood to profit from the roadway. Antônio also suspected the colonels' betrayal. So did Little Ear.

"We should've killed them when we had the chance," Little Ear said. "Taken over their land."

Antônio stared. Shadows from the firelight darkened his face, making the furrows of concern or disapproval—Luzia could not tell which—that gathered across the good side of his brow look deeper, more exaggerated. His scarred side hung slack. Since Antônio's right eye had clouded over, the injured side of his face no longer looked calm, it looked expressionless, like the dead-eyed stares of the suru-bim fish the cangaceiros hooked in the river.

"Then what?" Ponta Fina hissed. "If we'd killed them off, who'd get us bullets? You?"

The subcaptains and Luzia sat slightly removed from camp. They spoke softly so the other cangaceiros wouldn't hear their plans or arguments. Antônio allowed debate among his subcaptains, as long as they spoke respectfully and returned to camp as a united front. He'd given his subcaptains red handkerchiefs to knot around their necks, to distinguish their status. As captain, Antônio wore a green one. Luzia had only a ratty blue bandanna, like the other cangaceiros, but as their mãe she was allowed into the captains' meetings. Little Ear never looked at her when she spoke. Each time Little Ear offered his opinion, Luzia saw the shiny brown skin of Baiano's chin crinkle. When Baiano spoke—his voice quiet and unhurried—Little Ear tapped his foot. Ponta Fina complained about this. He and Little Ear often bickered.

"We shouldn't depend on colonels for bullets," Little Ear said. "We should find another way. That doctor could get guns for us."

"No," Antônio said.

"We can burn their houses," Little Ear persisted. "Show the colonels we don't want them back here. We can punish their vaqueiros, their maids. The ones who take care of things for them. It will teach people to be loyal to us, and not to the colonels."

"It's not the people's fault," Antônio said, shaking his head. "Their masters left them, scared of a drought. If the drought comes, we can help them. Get them food. Teach them to scavenge. They'll be grateful to us. They'll owe us, not the colonels or Gomes. That's how we'll earn their loyalty. And we'll need it, when the roadway comes."

Recently, Antônio had confided to Luzia that he saw the drought as an opportunity. It would be his chance to truly earn the trust of struggling tenant farmers, merchants, vaqueiros, and goat herders. He resolved to nourish them through the dry months in the hopes that they would take his side in an even bigger fight: the one against the Trans-Nordestino.

"The roadway," Little Ear said impatiently. "It's not real. They won't build. If there's a drought, they won't waste their time."

"They will build," Antônio said, raising his voice. "You think they'll come here when it's wet? Build in the mud? What farmer makes a house during the rains? Gomes wants the dry times. It'll make things easier for them. And they'll bring monkeys along."

"Monkeys," Little Ear repeated. He nodded toward Luzia. "Will we be allowed to fight them?"

Ponta Fina bowed his head. Baiano sighed. They all harbored the same worries, the same doubts. Even Luzia. Would they be able to fight with her present, or would she hold them back, make them vulnerable? She'd seen her face printed in the newspaper. Her portrait had been magnified to show only her head. Above the modified photograph was the word "Wanted" and the offer of 50:000$00. Below were the words: "Mother and Child."

Luzia shifted her place on the ground. The little food she'd eaten settled in her chest and burned there. The child pressed against her organs, jostling her insides. She was in her seventh month. Beneath her shawl, Luzia's belly was round but not soft. It was taut and hard, like a water gourd. Her ankles were shapeless and swollen, as thick as ouricuri palm trunks. She'd had to cut open her alpercata sandals to fit her feet. In her bornal was a collection of materials she'd need for the birth: a thick needle, a small pair of sewing scissors wiped free of rust, a mixture of crushed malagueta peppers and salt to place in the umbilical wound, and several scraps of clean cloth. Luzia had even decided on a name. She'd made a new promise to her childhood protector, Expedito, the patron saint of impossible causes. She'd broken her first promise to him; she would not break her second.

"My belly doesn't affect my aim," Luzia said. "And it'll be gone soon."

Gone. It sounded as if her belly were a nuisance, a temporary ailment, like a blister or a bee sting. To Little Ear and some of the cangaceiros, it was. To others, Luzia's massive belly was proof of her good luck, her strength. What other woman could carry a child through the scrubland? What other woman could survive such long walks and such dry times, and still look so plump, her stomach so round and full? Only the Virgin Mother herself.

"The child will be a giant, praise God," Baiano often said. Others agreed. Each day, Antônio gave Luzia half of his share of food in addition to her own. Ponta Fina divided his food with her as well. Of all the cangaceiros, Luzia felt the least hunger. To make up for this, she helped the men find dried gullies and streams. When they lacked energy, Luzia burrowed in the hot sand until water bubbled up. She dug around the bases of umbuzeiro trees and pried out round, tuberous roots as big as an infant's head. The water stored inside these roots was cloudy, resinous, and always warm. The work exhausted her, but Luzia had to make herself useful, to prove she was not a burden.

Gone. She could not say *born* because she didn't want to think of the birth. As a young man, Antônio had birthed plenty of cattle and goats. So had Ponta Fina. They would help Luzia if the child came earlier than expected. The next day, their group would stop at a colonel's abandoned house to pick up supplies, and then they would make their way to Taquaritinga. There, Luzia would find a midwife to perform the birth. After that, her boy really would be gone— delivered into the arms of Padre Otto.

Little Ear looked at Luzia. His lips were pinched together. Slowly, they relaxed and parted. He let out a breath, as if he'd had a realization.

"That's another reason we should go after any colonels' people," he said. "We should frighten them. They can't be trusted. They'll try to take her head, for the reward."

"You're like a dog," Ponta Fina said. "Sniffing after blood."

Little Ear stood. Ponta Fina followed. Antônio got between them, his arms outstretched, a hand on each man's shoulder. He faced Little Ear.

"We won't frighten anyone," Antônio said, his voice stern. "We won't go after anyone unless they go after us first. Save your energy. When the roadway comes, there'll be plenty of monkeys for us to fight. Right now, we have to win loyalty. We have to keep calm."

Little Ear shrugged off Antônio's hand. "I don't want calm."

"It doesn't matter what you want," Antônio said. He grabbed Little Ear's red neckerchief. "Take this off."

Little Ear's eyes widened. His mouth opened but he did not protest. He untied the neckerchief's knot and slipped the sweaty cloth from around his neck. Antônio took it from him.

"Control your temper," he said.

Little Ear nodded, bowing his head and extending his hands, ready to receive the red cloth back. Antônio ignored him. He handed the neckerchief to Luzia.

"Put it on, my Saint."

Luzia hesitated. The red scarf in Antônio's hands was stained with Little Ear's sweat. She could not wash it, could not waste water for something so trivial. Little Ear pressed his lips together tightly, as if afraid of the words that might escape from them. He didn't want her to be a subcaptain, to take his place. Luzia didn't want those things either. She wanted rest, not responsibility. In many ways, Little Ear was right: she was a burden, the colonels and their employees couldn't be trusted, the roadway was a dangerous obsession.

"Luzia," Antônio said, sternly this time. "Wear it."

In the dying firelight, she could see the outline of iris and pupil through the film of his dull eye. He knew something she didn't. That's how she'd felt these past months. His sleeplessness, his suspicions, his aches and pains were all things he tried to hide from her. They were signs of the distance that had grown between them. Luzia believed it was her pregnancy that had made Antônio remote. Now she saw that it was something else, something she couldn't decipher. It seemed Antônio had been waiting for this chance—for Little Ear to commit the smallest infraction so that Luzia could inherit his red scarf. She wouldn't have taken it otherwise. She wouldn't have chosen the role for herself. If a serious drought came, the cangaceiros would have to break into small groups in order to survive. Antônio expected his subcaptains to be leaders, to understand the caatinga, to be able to live without him. As he pressed the red scarf into her hands, Luzia understood that he expected the same things of her.

9
_/ / / / / / / /_

The next day they raided a colonel's abandoned house. Antônio, Luzia, and the cangaceiros often stopped at sympathetic colonels' ranches only to find the main houses closed. Vaqueiros, maids, and tenant farmers were ordered to remain and protect the ranches. They stayed for fear of losing their jobs. The men and women put up no resistance when Antônio opened the colonels' abandoned houses. He and the cangaceiros searched for food, newspapers, weapons, ammunition, anything useful.

Flanked by Ponta Fina and Baiano, Antônio spoke to the property's remaining farmhand. Little Ear and Luzia stood close by. The farmhand was stooped and toothless, but his hair was black. He wore a bowl-shaped vaqueiro cap pulled far forward on his head so the short brim shaded his eyes. The hat's leather chinstraps hung loosely below the man's lean face. His wife stood beside him, her hair hidden beneath a faded head scarf. Her chin was as round and brown as a sapoti fruit and jutted sharply beneath her mouth. Next to her was their daughter. The girl was young—no more than fifteen—and pretty. She propped a bare foot against her shin, balancing on one sinewy leg like the white-winged garças that followed cattle during the rainy seasons. Her dress hit midcalf, its fabric a jacquard—expensive and thick, with a pattern woven into the cloth. It had grown whiskery with wear. The dress's modern cut and style made Luzia believe that it had once belonged to a colonel's wife or daughter, and the farm girl had stolen it in their absence. The girl glanced at Ponta Fina, then bowed her head coquettishly.

Antônio spoke respectfully to the farmhand, and the man allowed the cangaceiros to camp nearby and to search the colonel's house. Antônio assured the family that his group wouldn't take all of their food reserves, just some. While the other men made camp and searched the ranch for ammunition and supplies, Ponta Fina volunteered to separate food from the colonel's pantry. When he and Luzia stepped into the kitchen, the farm girl blushed and covered her mouth. Luzia left the room.

The house's furniture was covered in white sheets, its beds stripped, its mosquito nets untied from the roof beams and neatly folded. Everything inside was carefully preserved, which didn't suggest a hasty exit. It was as if the colonel and his family had not escaped the drought, but had gone on a vacation and were determined to come back. Luzia made her way to the colonel's bedroom; she hoped to find a blanket for her boy. Something soft, something she could embroider in the weeks to come. When people spoke of giving birth, they said it was to *dar à luz*—to give the child to the light. Luzia's boy would leave the comforting darkness of her belly and be exposed to the bright immensity of the world. When this happened, Luzia wanted him to be wrapped in something soft.

There were no linens in the colonel's house. The master bed was stripped bare. Beside it, stacked next to a mound of fashion journals, was a mound of *Diário de Pernambuco*s. Luzia sifted through them. There were dozens of pictures of Gomes, articles on Green Party reforms, and photos of countless Recife society women. Luzia nearly gave up her search, then spotted an article on the opening of Recife's Criminology Institute. Buried inside the newspaper's local section were several photographs; Luzia focused on only one. The caption read:

> *Mrs. Degas Coelho tries her hand at science in Dr. Duarte Coelho's new Criminology Institute.*

Emília cradled a glass jar. Inside, floating in cloudy liquid, was an infant. The child's eyes were closed. Its face was perfectly formed but its body was stumpy and misshapen, like a clay saint left unfinished by its sculptor. A group of dark-suited men circled Emília, laughing. She seemed unaware of their presence. She stared at the child in the jar. She did not smile. Her face resembled a Madonna's, frozen in an expression of affectionate sadness.

The newspaper fluttered to Luzia's feet. She leaned against the wooden bed frame. Emília's pose with the jarred child unsettled her; perhaps this was her sister's aim. Luzia sensed a warning in Emília's photograph, but wasn't sure if she should trust her senses. She was becoming worse than Aunt Sofia, seeing dark omens everywhere.

Luzia heard a giggle. Forgetting the newspaper, she moved toward the sound. The kitchen was empty. Ponta Fina and the farm girl had disappeared. The pantry's slatted door was closed, and behind it, Luzia heard whispers, fumbling, and then more muffled laughter. She moved toward the pantry door, prepared to interrupt them; Antônio wouldn't like that behavior. Before her hand touched the wood, Luzia stopped. The girl seemed willing. Ponta Fina rarely accompanied the other cangaceiros when they visited women-of-the-life. He'd had so few pleasures in his short life, Luzia thought. Let him have this one.

That evening, the cangaceiros prepared a feast. Baiano and Inteligente caught several preá as wide as their hands; the rock-dwelling animals were meaty even after removing their fur. On the fire, Canjica prepared a small vat of beans. Next to him, piled carefully on a rock, was a stack of rapadura squares. A gray cloud of flies hovered above the sweating molasses blocks. Periodically Canjica waved his tan, four-fingered hand, and sliced the insect cloud apart. Antônio sat with the farmhand and his wife. He presented the couple with a wad of mil-réis in exchange for food and supplies. The farmhand massaged the money in his hands. He would save it, he said, and if the drought worsened, he would use the funds to escape to the coast.

Luzia sat apart from the group. Antônio had uncovered a wooden chair in the colonel's house and brought it outside for her to sit on. Luzia's belly had become so big, it was hard for her to lower herself to the ground without help. It felt good to sit upright, in a chair instead of on a blanket. In her lap she held the yellowed sheet that had covered her chair. The fabric was coarse, but could be made into a pretty blanket with the right embroidery. Luzia took out a needle and thread and began to work. Before she'd finished one flower, she heard footsteps and whispers near her. Luzia looked up from her sewing to see the farm girl, brown skinned and pretty, and Ponta Fina. They stood side by side, watching Luzia. Ponta Fina walked toward her. The girl stayed behind, fidgeting with the skirt of her stolen dress.

"Mãe?" Ponta Fina said as he approached her, his hat in his hands. Sweat beaded his forehead.

"Are you sick?" Luzia asked.

Ponta Fina shook his head.

"What is it then?"

He looked down. Luzia stared at him. She'd learned this tactic from Antônio: never say too much. People will inevitably speak and reveal themselves.

"I want to marry," Ponta said. "Like you and the captain."

Luzia laughed. "You've barely met her."

"I'm fond of her," Ponta replied.

"Bring her here then."

"She's scared. She won't come."

"She'll have to. If she wants to marry you, she can't be scared."

Ponta nodded. He walked back to the girl and coaxed her over. When she stood before Luzia, she kept her head down and curtsied. Her legs were dotted with scars, some jagged, some round.

"Let me talk to her," Luzia said, waving Ponta away. "What's your grace?"

"Maria de Lourdes," the girl muttered. "But everyone calls me Baby."

"Do you sew?" Luzia asked.

"Yes, ma'am."

"And, do you cook? Can you skin an animal?"

"Yes, ma'am. I'm not frightened by blood."

"And your relations?" Luzia asked, nodding to the hunched farmhand and his wife. "They know about this?"

"No, ma'am. They're not relations. My mãe died when I was born. Don't know my pai. The colonel who lived here gave me to them, to his hands, since they don't have children. All I do is work."

Luzia nodded. "If you join, there's no undoing it,' she said, repeating what Antônio had once told her. "It's not a suit of clothes. You can't put it on and take it off when you please."

"Can't be worse than working for them," Baby whispered. "It's hell here."

"The cangaço will be worse than hell," Luzia said.

Baby bit her lip, then nodded. "I'll die here. They won't feed me right, when the drought comes. And I like Ponta. He's handsome enough."

Luzia looked at the girl. Her face was soft and round, like a child's, but her hands and feet were calloused. Hard. She thought of her own stubbornness when she'd left Taquaritinga, afraid of being trapped behind a sewing machine. That fate didn't sound so terrible now. But if she hadn't left Taquaritinga, she and Emília might have ended up like Baby: forever indebted to a colonel.

"You'll have to swallow a chumbo pellet every month," Luzia said. "You can't get pregnant; it's for your own good. And there can't be foolishness. Once you're with Ponta, you're bound to him and only him. And you'll have to learn to shoot. Hear me?"

"Yes, ma'am."

Luzia had hoped to discourage the girl, to scare her, but was surprised by Baby's resolve. She called Ponta Fina back.

"I'm not the one to ask," Luzia said. "Go talk to your captain."

Ponta nodded. He took the girl's hand and walked hesitantly toward Antônio. Luzia wanted to watch them, to see Antônio's reaction. Instead, she turned her back and continued to embroider. She hoped to hear Antônio chastise Ponta, to convince the boy that including a woman like Baby in their group was a bad idea. Luzia tugged the thread roughly through her blanket's cloth. She was a woman, and she hadn't caused trouble. But Baby was pretty, and the group of cangaceiros was larger now, and included many young men.

Luzia heard someone behind her. She turned, believing she would see a disappointed Ponta Fina coming back to her for consolation. It was Antônio instead. Gingerly, as if his bones ached, he knelt on the ground beside her.

"Are you trying to marry off my men?" he asked. His voice sounded tired, but the left side of his mouth rose in a slight smile.

Luzia put down her embroidery. "I didn't encourage it."

Antônio nodded. "But I should let her in. That's what you think."

"No," Luzia replied, suddenly angry. "Did Ponta say that?"

Antônio shook his head. "I thought you would see her side of things."

"Just because we're both women doesn't mean I approve."

Antônio rubbed the slack side of his face. "They're following my example. Our example."

"So?"

"So, I'm saying yes."

"It's a bad idea," Luzia said.

"I know," Antônio replied. He stared at her, his left side smiling. Luzia pressed her hand to his face. Slowly, Antônio took off his hat and rested his head in her lap, his ear against her belly. Luzia closed her eyes. For a brief moment they were like any other young couple, stealing a moment of affection.

Voices came from the cangaceiros' camp. They rose to yells. Antônio sighed. Luzia did not want to open her eyes, but Antônio suddenly shifted away from her. His knees popped as he stood. Little Ear marched toward them. Behind him, Ponta Fina, Baby, Baiano, and a cluster of cangaceiros followed.

"He wants to marry," Little Ear said, pointing to Ponta Fina.

"I know," Antônio replied. He'd forgotten to put his hat back on. His hair was matted and parted at an odd angle, revealing a light patch of scalp along the side of his head. Luzia wanted to hide the vulnerable spot, to comb his hair with her fingernails.

"He can't marry," Little Ear said. "Unless he turns in his knives. Leaves the group."

A group had formed around them and a few cangaceiros nodded in agreement with Little Ear. Antônio's good eye narrowed. The active side of his mouth turned down. Bringing up such matters in front of the group was forbidden; Antônio would only let his men complain about each other in private, and only to him, in order to prevent infighting. He stepped closer to Little Ear.

"I don't allow deserters," he said.

Little Ear nodded. "I know."

"Seems like you know a lot these days," Antônio replied.

Luzia clasped the arms of her chair. She spread her knees wide, putting her weight into her legs. She tilted her pelvis up, heaving herself out of the chair. The entire group watched and Luzia hated her body for making her look so undignified. Little Ear shook his head.

"Women are trouble," he said, turning back to Antônio. "You said it yourself, we need to be an army, not a family."

"This isn't your concern," Antônio replied.

Little Ear jabbed his finger to his chest. "It is my concern. I'm part of this group. We can't let in every *rapariga* we see."

There were grumblings in the group. Some men shook their heads. Ponta Fina stepped forward, his *peixeira* sharp and gleaming in his hand. Baiano hooked an arm around Ponta and held the boy back.

"Apologize," Antônio said.

Little Ear looked back and forth between Ponta Fina and his captain. "What?"

"Apologize. You've insulted his woman. An honest woman. There are no *raparigas* here."

"I won't."

Antônio stepped closer to him. Little Ear held up his hands as if surrendering, then lowered them to his belt. Like the other men, he'd become accustomed to taking off his holsters and leaving his pistols and rifle on his blankets each evening. He carried only his knives. Little Ear removed the *punhal* wedged between his waistband and his cartridge belt. His face looked haggard and sad. He dropped the long, square-sided dagger onto the dirt.

"I'm leaving," he said.

Antônio made no move to pick up the *punhal*. "I told you. I don't allow deserters."

Little Ear's chin trembled. He crimped his lips to stop it. There was a tacit understanding between the cangaceiros and Antônio. By joining the group and sealing their bodies with the prayer of corpo fechado, every man assented to it. Luzia did as well. Antônio's love, his protection, his leadership came in exchange for obedience, for belief. The minute a man's belief wavered, that love was retracted. Little Ear had disobeyed his captain and he'd done it in front of the group. If Antônio didn't stick to the terms of his agreement, if he didn't punish those who disobeyed, he would lose respect and this would doom him.

Luzia felt a quiver in her belly. She saw movement beneath the tight canvas of her dress, then felt a jab to her lower ribs. Her boy delivered a swift kick, as if telling her to act, to move. Luzia stepped forward. She placed a hand on Antônio's arm.

"Let him leave," she said.

Little Ear snorted. "A woman's mercy."

Antônio stiffened. He snatched his arm away from Luzia. "Don't touch me," he said.

She pulled back. Antônio's hand was raised and balled into a fist, the knuckles white. Luzia placed her arms over her belly. She couldn't think clearly, couldn't recall what she'd meant to say to Antônio or to Little Ear. She could only recall the smoke-filled church in Taquaritinga and Padre Otto standing before her, delivering his yearly Easter sermon. The story didn't involve the Virgin Mother but that other Mary—the Magdalene—who had remained at the tomb of Christ long after all the other disciples had left and given up. Her reward was His appearance. But when she reached for him, He recoiled. "Do not hold on to me," He ordered. Even as a child, Luzia had disliked Him for this. He was no longer a man but a God, and this deification made him capable of pushing away the one who'd loved him best. Luzia had always preferred the man to the deity.

"Kneel," Antônio said.

Little Ear shook his head. "I'm one of your best men."

"I know," Antônio replied. "You've disobeyed. Now kneel."

Little Ear assented. He took off his hat and threw it beside his discarded punhal. Antônio moved beside him. Little Ear's eyes were cast downward but they didn't look at the ground. They stared at his jacket front, at his cartridge belt. Always watch a man's eyes; Antônio had taught Luzia this. He said to look carefully at men's eyes because they revealed their intentions. Men always stared where they would move next. Pregnant women were expected to look away from violence, but Luzia could not: she watched Little Ear. As Antônio unsheathed his punhal, Little Ear's hand moved. It was his right hand, hidden from Antônio's view because of his bad eye. Tucked into Little Ear's belt was another knife, a small one with a sharp tip, used to bleed animals. All of the cangaceiros carried similar knives. No one thought to take it away from him.

Luzia reached for her parabellum. It was in her shoulder holster, which rested snugly near the armpit of her bent arm. Her good arm reached over her enlarged breasts and her belly. She fumbled with the holster snap. On the ground before her, Little Ear reared up. His arm swung out in a large, graceful arc. In his hand, the knife blade glimmered, reflecting the firelight. Antônio dropped his punhal. Luzia finally tugged open her shoulder holster and, with her good arm, raised her parabellum. She could not aim correctly; Antônio had gripped Little Ear and the men grunted and fumbled in a strange embrace. Antônio's good eye was wide and it moved in all directions. He resembled a cow in the slaughter pen, looking for the knife.

Luzia found her target. She pulled the trigger. The shot was like a bottle being uncorked: startling because no one knew where it would land. The cangaceiros froze. Baby screamed and all eyes fell on the girl. For an instant, Antônio looked away from the knife's point. Little Ear struck. Then the small knife fell beside his feet.

"Shit!" Little Ear cried. His voice seemed to wake the men. Baiano moved forward, tugging Little Ear up by the arm. Already, the chest of Little Ear's jacket was dark, the stain growing. Luzia had hit him in the shoulder. Ponta Fina moved in with his thick-bladed machete, but Luzia stopped him. They heard a cough.

Antônio stood motionless, his back to Luzia and the men, his hands at his neck. Luzia touched Antônio's shoulder and he hunched toward her, his hands still clamped on his neck. His face was burgundy, as if he was angry. He coughed again. Blood spurted between his fingers.

As he fell, Luzia called his name. Her voice seemed far away. The parabellum slipped from her hand. She could smell something burning and realized it was the charred flesh of the preás, left on the cook fire. Luzia's belly made her cumbersome. She dropped beside Antônio, her knees hitting the ground hard. Her hands seemed to move without her guidance, frantically untying Antônio's wet neckerchief, then pressing her fingers against his face. The scarred side was calm, as always. The unscarred side looked perplexed. A wet, raspy noise erupted from the jagged tear in his throat, near his Adam's apple, where Little Ear's knife had punctured. Blood bubbled up, surprising Luzia with its intensity. She pressed her hands to the gash. It was warm! So warm! Like the thick water that sprang from dead riverbeds when she'd dug in them. Luzia pressed harder. The flies that had surrounded the stacks of rapadura had been startled away with the fighting, but suddenly, they were back. They landed on Antônio's neck and in the puddle beneath him.

Ponta Fina knelt beside Luzia. Cangaceiros crowded around them. Luzia's ears rang. They needed tasks, she thought. The cangaceiros needed to stay occupied.

"Bring me a hammock!" she yelled. "A clean hammock."

The men rushed about, hearing her urgency, believing that their captain would live if they only hurried. Several entered the colonel's abandoned house. Luzia heard them overturning things inside. She ordered Canjica and Caju to run and find a curandeiro or a midwife. Anyone who dealt with medicine, she told them. If they could not find someone, Luzia resolved to treat Antônio. She would place salt and ashes and malagueta peppers in the wound to stop its bleeding. She would sew it closed. Then they would carry Antônio to Dr. Eronildes. It was a long walk, but they would have to make it. She knew from her experience in slaughtering goats and other scrub animals that the neck concealed a vital tangle of tubes and blood vessels. Antônio would have to be treated quickly.

Antônio's hand twitched. His fingers brushed her leg, as if caressing it. Luzia tried to lean closer but her belly prohibited it.

"Stay here," she commanded him, her hands slippery against his wound. "Stay awake."

When the men returned with a hammock, Luzia tied a cloth around Antônio's neck. Baiano wrapped his captain carefully inside the hammock and with Inteligente's help, hoisted Antônio up. Dazed, they waited for Luzia's orders.

"Get inside," she said. "We have to clean him properly. Don't bounce too much."

They placed the hammock, stained and dripping, in the foyer of the colonel's house. Shriveled beans were scattered along the wood floor, remnants of the cangaceiros' raid on the pantry. The blood on Luzia's hands was already drying. It made her fingers hard to bend. When they shook, Luzia clenched them into fists. She could not let the men see her tremors.

She asked for Baiano's help and heaved herself down again, beside Antônio. Luzia recalled her father in Padre Otto's church, wrapped in a white funeral hammock. She was afraid to open the one that held Antônio, but the cangaceiros huddled around her, expectant. Quickly, Luzia parted the hammock's cloth.

Antônio's eyes were open. His crooked lips parted. Both sides of his face were calm. Luzia felt as if she'd swallowed a cactus needle. It ripped her from throat to stomach in one burning line.

The men moved closer. Luzia felt their eyes on her. She'd taken off her shawl earlier in the evening, and without it she was exposed—her poorly braided hair; her dress too tight around the belly; her thick legs; her swollen chest. The men saw everything.

Luzia placed her palms on the floor. She squatted, steadying herself on her feet. Then she took a breath and heaved herself up. Her knees creaked with the effort. Standing, Luzia saw Ponta Fina. Baby huddled near him. They'd caused this trouble, Luzia thought. So had Little Ear. In the commotion she'd forgotten about him. They'd left him outside, wounded. She had to punish him, but the thought made her dizzy. Luzia closed her eyes, steadying herself. She would manage the men around her before she dealt with Little Ear. She opened her eyes and focused on Ponta Fina.

"Give me your lambedeira," Luzia said.

He obeyed, handing her his sharpest knife, the one he used to cut meat from bone. With her locked arm, Luzia held the knife behind her neck. With her good arm, she grasped the bottom of her braid. It was tied with stiff twine. The top of her braid, near the base of her scalp, was very thick. Luzia sliced hard.

When she faced the men, she stood tall. She kept her hands steady. She looked into each cangaceiro's eyes, making sure not to miss one man. With her good arm, she raised the severed braid high, like a snake in her hands.

She didn't have time to be afraid. That's what Luzia later realized when she recalled that moment. She could have cried, mourned, whimpered as a wife was supposed to, but the men would have sniffed out her weakness and hated her for it. She would have been useless to them—no longer their blessed mãe, but a mere woman. Pregnant, at that. Seeing her with her hair shorn, her hands stained, her face stiff, had frightened them. Luzia saw it. In that instant, they feared her. They believed in her.

After cutting her braid, she felt faint. She'd gotten up too fast. The lambedeira knife fell from her hand. Luzia leaned on Baiano, who helped her to her knees. The men believed she was going to pray and they dutifully followed. Luzia uttered all of the prayers she knew—a stream of Ave Marias and Our Fathers—until she felt as if she was speaking in tongues.

All the while she watched Antônio. She waited for him to wink, to rise, to laugh at his terrible joke.

"We will light no fires," Luzia said, interrupting her prayers. "We will put no candles in his hand. His soul stays here. With us. I am your mãe and your captain now."

The men bowed their heads.

When they finally went outside, Little Ear was gone. Baiano offered to put together a search party, but Luzia wouldn't allow it.

"Let him bleed," she said. "He won't survive out there."

Luzia knew that some of the cangaceiros would think she was being too merciful to Little Ear. Others would think she was too cruel, letting him die of exposure instead of ending his life quickly. A captain did not have to explain his decisions to his men, so Luzia didn't either. She couldn't. Her reasons for letting Little Ear go had nothing to do with mercy or punishment—they had to do with the cangaceiros themselves. If Luzia ordered a search party, she couldn't go with the men. She was too clumsy to be stealthy and too shaken to lead them through the scrub. Luzia didn't want to admit this. She also didn't want the men separating from her. The search party could find Little Ear and help him, possibly join him. The men had also been shaken by Antônio's death, and their allegiance was fragile. The only way to control them was to keep them all in her sight.

Luzia spent the night awake, listening for whispers and watching for any sign of dissent. Baby planted herself next to Luzia. A few times, the girl's head nodded with sleep. When this happened, Baby jerked upright and let out a low cough to prove she was awake.

Custom called for three days of mourning while the soul roamed around its body. Custom called for relatives to clean the corpse before it stiffened. During the bath, you had to speak to the dead, saying, *Bend your arm!* or *Lift your leg!* You could not say the dead man's name, because that meant you were calling the spirit back. In the colonel's house, Luzia cleaned Antônio and dressed him, all the while addressing him by his first name. *Antônio!* she said loudly, so his spirit would hear. She made the men call him *Captain* in their prayers, as they'd always done. She kept his gold rings on each of his fingers, even though the dead were not allowed to bring gold to the afterlife. She would not kiss the bottom of his foot, which would prevent him from wandering. She wanted him to wander. She did not clean the dirt from the soles of his alpercatas, as was the custom, because the soul—so attracted toward earth—would miss the land under his feet and come back. She would not close his eyes. "Close your eyes and face God," she was supposed to say when they buried him. Instead Luzia said, "Antônio, look at me."

She was forcing his spirit to live a life here on earth. Hadn't he told her once that they were all damned? That despite his prayers, he would not go to God but to another, darker place. Wouldn't he rather be here, with her?

"If anyone asks if the Hawk is dead, he isn't," Luzia said to the men before they left the abandoned ranch.

Her plan worked; the cangaceiros were afraid of their captain's spirit. Each time there was a shake in the trees or a wind, the men shivered. Even Baiano seemed frightened. Each night, when they made camp, Luzia left a small meal for Antônio in the bushes. She poured a sip of water onto the ground. She was tempting him forward. It was a great risk—souls were like people, but worse. They could turn angry and bitter at their loved ones. They could haunt them forever. But Luzia wanted to be haunted. She would rather feel Antônio's wrath than his loss.

10

A good widow wore black. She draped her house with dark curtains. She wore two rings on her left hand and kept a portrait of her dead husband with fresh flowers underneath it. Some widows locked all of their husband possessions in a drawer, taking them out occasionally and reminiscing. It was another marriage—a morbid one—with memories as the mate. For Luzia, all of these traditions were impossible. There were no wedding rings, no flowers, and no portraits except for her newspaper clippings.

The scrub had been their house. Every tree, every hill, every lizard and rock reminded her of Antônio. The scrub was his world, not hers. She had never loved it as he had. It eluded her, frightened her, angered her. And now he had left her there, alone, with his army of men who followed her across rocky plains and up steep hills. They weren't going to Taquaritinga; Luzia had decided she didn't want Padre Otto looking after her child. She didn't want him raised in a place where people could identify his mother as Victrola. The cangaceiros walked toward the São Francisco River. After Antônio's body was safely buried, Luzia had unfolded the old surveyor's map. She'd asked Baiano: "Do you know how to get to Dr. Eronildes' ranch?" He'd nodded.

Luzia wrapped a cloth around her belly so that the child would not come out early. She'd taken Antônio's hat, his punhal, his crystal rock. In the evenings, she held the rock and conducted prayers. She sealed their bodies shut.

At night, she could not sleep. She listened for the men's snores. She watched Baby sleep curled on the blanket beside her. The stubborn girl would not leave Luzia's side, determined to make up for her loss. On nights when the moon was out, Luzia looked out over the dry scrubland. In the moonlight, the leafless trees looked like a white forest. That land was theirs, all theirs, Antônio had often said. It was God's land. Immense. Unbounded. He'd said this joyfully, but when Luzia looked at the scrub, she couldn't understand Antônio's happiness. The scrub was too large. Too empty. It frightened her with its immensity.

Many nights, she thought of the newspaper photograph of Emília cradling that jarred, malformed infant. Emília held it like she used to hold her dolls—carefully, lovingly. Her sister was always kind to her rag dolls. Not like Luzia, who broke them, cut them apart, pulled out their stuffing. Emília was gentle yet stern. She knew how to care for things without spoiling them. Beneath her sister's loveliness lay a strong will.

When she did sleep, Luzia dreamed of a man who wasn't Antônio, but who had his mashed nose, his small teeth, his fleshy lips, his eyes. Eyes so dark she could not see the pupils, dark like the seeds of the Maria Preta tree.

In the mornings, her bladder ached. Her back pinched, as if a punhal were stabbing her while she walked. She moved slowly. The men walked ahead, at her orders. Baiano and Ponta Fina stayed beside her. As the hills that bordered the Old Chico became clearer and larger, Luzia felt as if she were being driven toward an end she did not know. As soon as she had reached it, as soon as God deemed it over, the smallest grain of sand or the tiniest glistening umbuzeiro leaf could stop her. Until then, nothing would.

Chapter 9

EMÍLIA

Rio Branco Relief Camp
January–February 1933

1

January 2, 1933

Mrs. Degas Coelho
722 Rua Real da Torre
Bairro Madalena, Recife, PE

Dear Senhora Coelho,
    Happy New Year. You will not remember me by name but I hope the conversation we shared in the Saint Isabel Theater isn't completely forgotten. I had the pleasure of making your acquaintance in the lobby during the Green Party's celebration. We spoke briefly but did not exchange names. Thankfully, I have a keen memory for faces.
    I never read the Diário's Society Section until recently, when someone showed me your photograph. I was surprised to discover that the lady in the Society Section was the same one I'd met in Recife. It reminded me of a saying my ranch hands live by: Always ask a stranger's name because he may be a lost brother. I have lived in the Northeast all of my life and am still astonished that, despite the vastness of the land, our spheres of acquaintance are as small and as intricately woven as a bit of renda lace.
    I've read of your charity work with the flagelados who have escaped to Recife during these dry times. I admire your efforts. It is far easier to condemn your neighbors than to help them.

Like you, I have decided to assist the flagelados. If you recall, I am a medical man. I've given up ranching to supervise a modest hospital in the Rio Branco internment camp. There are many ills here. Many of my colleagues say that backlanders are a hardy race, able to withstand any misery. I say this is a foolish belief. As you know, Mrs. Coelho, and as my own medical training has shown me, backlanders are as mortal and as flawed as the rest of us. Backlanders are, however, more closely tied to the land, which has abandoned them during this drought. They are like motherless children.

I came to Rio Branco to save those orphaned by the drought. I'm not a religious man, but recently I've prayed. I've asked for a kind and loving hand to lift at least one child from misery and change its destiny.

We've finally come to the meaning of my letter, Mrs. Coelho. I thank you for your patience. I am a man of science, not words, so I will be frank. I need your assistance. Clothing, food, water, and medicines are greatly appreciated in the Rio Branco camp but, as you may already know, such charitable shipments from the capitals are easily diverted by corrupt merchants or stolen by cangaceiros. Donated supplies would be safer if accompanied by a delegation. Such a delegation would receive great attention in the press, giving the camp's residents the publicity they desperately need. The flagelados are starving people and not, as some journalists have dubbed them, freeloaders. This delegation cannot be composed of only government representatives or reporters, neither of which will inspire the camp's residents. You, Mrs. Coelho, bring favorable attention to every cause you support. You and your Ladies' Auxiliary can bring hope and warmth to our desolate home.

I am asking you to travel to a place most people wish to escape. I assure you, I do not ask this lightly. I've chosen my words carefully because I do not know you well. I have heard, however, that you are a woman with a fine heart and a strong will. I hope that my request isn't impossible and that if it is, I pray Santo Expedito will intervene and make it possible.

Atenciosamente,
Sr. Eronildes Epifano, M.D.

2

The first-class cabin's table trays were strewn with empty glasses. They shuddered and clinked against one another, moved by the train's vibrations. A waiter, the back of his serving coat darkened with sweat, tried to remove the glasses without waking passengers. Government men slept with their heads back and legs splayed. Their foreheads shone with sweat. Reporters and photographers accompanying the delegation had returned to their press car, so the government men had removed their suit jackets and loosened their ties. A collection of fedoras and straw panamas was scattered on table trays and empty seats. Degas' hat sat on his lap like a prized pet. He was awake. So was Emília.

The car's thermometer read 38 degrees Celsius. Flowers set in a hanging wall vase were limp, their petals scattered on the floor. Above Emília, ceiling fans groaned. Their blades whirled but could not force out the heat. It was dry and oppressive; it made Emília's cheeks prickle. The car's windows were open, its curtains pulled back. The sun shone so intensely it hurt Emília's eyes to look out the window. Minutes passed before her vision adjusted to the brightness. The view was always the same. Scrub plants were gray and brittle, as if they'd been scorched in an oven. Camouflaged among the trees Emília saw abandoned clay houses, their facades cracked and their doors left open. Except for the train and the clink of glasses—like ghostly echoes of the morning's toasts—there was no sound. Not even insects buzzed. It was enough to drive a person mad.

Perhaps this was why the government men had chosen to sleep. They'd been animated when the train left Recife's Central Station. There was a celebratory toast. Emília and Degas had held up their glasses, posing alongside Dr. Duarte and the group of government representatives while the delegation's official photographer snapped their picture. Afterward, there were several lengthy toasts in honor of President Gomes, Tenente Higino, and Dr. Duarte. The men's glasses were filled and refilled with cane liquor and lime juice. Degas stood on the group's outskirts, bending to listen to their toasts. He shoved his drink into their circle in order to clink glasses. Emília, along with the handful of women in the delegation, sat at the opposite end of the car. She wasn't included in the extended toasts. She drank only water.

When the toasts had waned, journalists packed the car and conducted interviews. The reporters worked for newspapers in Recife as well as some based in the states of Paraíba, Bahia, and Alagoas. All had been approved by Gomes's Department of Information and Propaganda, or DIP. The government men were Recife representatives for all of President Gomes's provisional ministries: Industry, Labor, Education, Transportation, and Health. All of the officials were eager to be quoted, but their talk of weather patterns, vaccinations, workers' identification cards, and food distribution were dull statistics memorized from DIP handouts, which the reporters already had. Only Dr. Duarte spoke candidly. Reporters and officials gathered around him as he held court from his cushioned train seat.

"This delegation is, first and foremost, a charitable endeavor," Dr. Duarte said as the train eased past sugarcane fields. "But it won't take away from our government's generosity and goodwill to say that this is also a scientific endeavor. Measuring the sertanejos—as the men and women of the caatinga are called—is an invaluable opportunity. We must gauge differences, if there are any, between our peoples. Not to isolate them! The Brasilidade movement we are so proud of is about our country's diverse groups coming together to form a nation! Within all groups, there are well-meaning citizens. There are also criminals—Communists, degenerates, thieves, sexual deviants—who have to be defined. Depending on their degree of criminality, they must be either contained, controlled, or cured. This is the only way to purify Brazil and heal its social ailments."

While his father spoke, Degas sat apart from the group. He seemed uninterested in his father's speech and focused instead on smoothing dents from his fedora. As the sun strengthened and the day warmed, the men's cheeks flushed. They fanned their faces with their hats. Their early morning drinks combined with the heat to make them woozy and tired. The reporters and photographers returned to their press car. As the train pushed past the cane fields of the Zona da Mata and entered into the drought-stricken scrub, the government men slowly fell asleep.

On the women's side of the car, five nuns from the Nossa Senhora das Dores Convent sat primly in dark brown suits. A young nun fingered her rosary. An older one occasionally glanced at Emília and gave her a tight-lipped smile. No one from the Ladies' Auxiliary had joined the delegation. Lindalva and the baroness were in Europe. The other Auxiliary members gave grave excuses, most dealing with a child's or a husband's illness. It seemed that a flu epidemic had struck Recife's elite and left everyone else alone. Only the nuns had accepted Emília's call to service. Oddly enough, an Old family woman named Mrs. Coimbra had also joined the delegation. She'd appeared at the Coelho house and informed Emília that she would represent the Princess Isabel Society.

Mrs. Coimbra sat across from Emília. She was a big-boned, square-bodied woman who was rumored to be in her sixties, though her hair was the color of coal. She wore a dark blue dress cut in a blocklike fashion with no waistline, just a decorative sash tied loosely at the hips. Such flapper-style dresses had been popular when Emília first arrived in Recife four years earlier, but now they were unfashionable. In Recife, the "nipped waistline" had become de rigueur, thanks, in part, to Emília and Lindalva's dress business.

Emília wore one of their designs—a flowered dress belted at the natural waist and accentuated with a cape-style collar. Because of the heat, she'd removed her linen bolero jacket, but only after the reporters and photographers had left the car. Her straw hat had a wider brim than her old cloches and was pinned in place, cocked jauntily to one side of her head. The pins tugged at Emília's hair. The hatband made her forehead sweat. Emília unpinned the hat and flung it on the seat beside her. It was too hot to be jaunty. Mrs. Coimbra nodded, praising Emília's good sense.

On the few occasions when Mrs. Coimbra spoke, she was polite yet brisk, the way most Old family women addressed Emília. Each time Mrs. Coimbra took this tone, Emília smiled and focused on the ugliness of the woman's dress. Such thoughts were vain and petty; Emília knew this. She also knew that Recife women—Old and New alike—judged her by things inconsequential to her character: her hint of a country accent, her inability or unwillingness to have children, her husband and his unmentionable predilection. Ever since the dinner at the Saint Isabel Theater, Emília sensed that Recife women believed she was below them in every way—except for stylishness. Realizing this had made Emília bold.

She dressed as she pleased, wearing bolero jackets, mermaid skirts inspired by Claudette Colbert, and, during the summer on Boa Viagem Beach, a broadcloth shirt tucked into a pair of checkered trousers. The more confident Emília became, the more the Recife women complimented her. As long as Emília didn't commit any flagrant violations—having a love affair, riding the trolley late at night, fraternizing with criminals or blacks—most Recife women admired her fashions and wanted to purchase them.

Emília took her inspiration from fashion magazines printed in France, Germany, Italy, and the United States. Dr. Duarte helped her order the magazines; they arrived in the same shipments as her father-in-law's phrenology journals. She changed some styles, replacing heavy fabrics with lighter ones in order to suit Recife's climate. Once she'd made an accurate pattern and discovered the perfect cloth to complement it, she presented the design to Lindalva. If they both liked the garment, they took it to their atelier.

Dr. Duarte had given Emília and Lindalva the use of one of his many properties. Emília insisted on paying rent. The atelier had a prime location on Rua Nova, the fashionable street connected to the steel-framed Boa Vista Bridge. People crossed the bridge to go shopping. Rua Nova was home to several fine shops: Casa Massilon sold school uniforms and military attire; Primavera was a Portuguese-owned department store for household goods; the Vitória pharmacy sold medications and housed doctors' offices above it; Parlophon sold Philco radios, Odeon records, iceboxes, and other modern luxuries.

Nestled between Recife's best shops was the atelier, E & L Designs. There was no outdoor sign; public advertisement indicated a need for profit, which was gauche. Emília and Lindalva were respectable women and the atelier was their hobby, not their business. From the outside, the atelier looked like an austere home, with white curtains and a brass buzzer beside the front door. When patrons rang, a serving girl answered and escorted them inside. Sometimes Emília or Lindalva was present, sometimes not. When they were in the atelier, they didn't act as salespeople but sat and chatted like fellow shoppers. No one handled money; payments were mailed or delivered later. There was no bargaining or bill collecting because no Recife woman, New or Old, wanted to be dubbed a cheapskate or a thief.

Emília and Lindalva offered a limited number of prêt-à-porter outfits. There were no long fittings or custom-made gowns. There was no exact pattern for all women, so Emília employed a seamstress to tailor the premade outfits after they'd been purchased, bringing up a hem for a shorter woman or nipping a dress's waist for a skinnier one. Emília manufactured only five items of each style. This compelled Recife women to buy the garments immediately. Emília's designs were inevitably imitated, but styles changed so quickly that, by the time another seamstress had learned to make the garments, they were already obsolete; Emília and Lindalva already had new creations in their shop.

When they first opened the atelier, they'd hired seven seamstresses. By then, President Gomes had required a minimum wage, mandatory employee bathrooms, and an eight-hour workday. Each laborer was issued a "Worker's Identification Card," which employers had to sign. The card admitted workers into Gomes's national union. All other unions were disbanded and strikes were outlawed. Gomes decreed that in order to receive the rights he'd bestowed, workers had to be loyal to the provisional government. Emília followed Gomes's laws and went beyond them: the atelier's sewing room had windows, several fans, and a radio for the seamstresses to listen to during their lunch hour. And Emília didn't complain when the seamstresses nailed an official photograph of Gomes, with the inscription "Father of the Poor" printed above his smiling face, on the sewing room's wall.

The Great Western train also displayed Gomes's photograph. He stared at Emília from above the cabin door. In this portrait he was not a smiling father but a stern-faced president in a tuxedo and sash. Emília rubbed her eyes. They stung from dust. A fine, brown layer of it filmed the train's windows. The men's empty drinking glasses had been collected and the car was silent except for the train's rumbling. A waiter poked his head into the cabin and counted passengers; soon he would serve lunch. Emília was hungry but didn't look forward to their meal. Since the drought had worsened, she felt guilty each time she ate.

The countryside had always experienced dry spells, so the drought wasn't reported in Recife newspapers until beef became scarce and expensive. Soon afterward, refugees appeared in the city. They shuffled along Recife's roads, walking as if it pained them to lift their feet. They'd traveled hundreds of kilometers hoping to find water, food, and work in Recife. The refugees wore tattered clothes. Their bodies were so thin and their faces so dirty that it was sometimes impossible to tell men from women. Babies hung limply in their mothers' arms. Children's faces were as haggard and wrinkled as old men's. Their heads looked enormous on their bony frames, and their stomachs swelled like balloons of skin, filled with air and nothing else. The refugees' suffering inspired newspapers to label them "flagelados."

Each time Emília went to the atelier she saw flagelados so disoriented by hunger that they walked the city's streets without regard for trolleys or automobiles. Emília stared at the refugees, worried that she might recognize a neighbor or a friend from Taquaritinga. Once, a woman came to the Chrysler's open window. She wore a dirty dress, the fabric nearly transparent with wear. The skin of her face was tanned and tightly stretched across her cheekbones, as if it had been baked on. She grabbed Emília's forearm. The woman's hand was dry, her grip strong. When Emília looked into her eyes, she saw that the woman was young, like herself. Degas hastily forced the car into gear and sped away, ignoring the stoplight. After they'd left the flagelada woman behind, Emília hid her face in her hands. Degas, always uneasy with crying, said he would return to the Coelho house so that Emília could wash her arm. She shook her head. No washing would erase the woman's grip; Emília still felt it upon her. Without Degas, without her rash marriage, she would have been a starving woman, a flagelada.

At the next Ladies' Auxiliary meeting, Emília announced that she would start a clothing drive. Following Emília's example, Auxiliary women donated fabric, thread, and their seamstresses' time. In the flagelados' tent cities built along Recife's outskirts, the Ladies' Auxiliary appeared with clothing, diapers, and blankets. Not to be outdone, Old family members of the Princess Isabel Society held garden parties and luncheons in order to raise money for doctors to treat the flagelados.

When Emília distributed food and supplies to the refugees, she did not wear gloves like the other women in the Auxiliary. She accepted the flagelados' handshakes and hugs. She held the skeletal, almost weightless babies in her bare hands. She had the urge to kiss these children, to hug them. She sought affection wherever she could find it. At the Coelho house she pressed her fingers through the bars of the corrupião's cage in order to pet its feathers. She slipped the jaboti turtles extra lettuce each day with the hope that they'd allow her to stroke their scaly faces. At the atelier, Emília cupped the seamstresses' hands in her own as she taught them how to refine their stitching. She patted the girls' backs and praised them whenever they held newly purchased measuring tapes against rulers in order to check for possible errors. "Never trust a strange tape," Emília said. And each time she left the atelier and hugged Lindalva good-bye, Emília lingered in the embrace.

Husbands were supposed to satisfy women's cravings for affection, but Degas was not a typical husband. After the revolution, Degas stopped his weekly visits to Emília's bedroom. Like other revolutionary fighters, he'd been congratulated and awarded a medal, but the credibility he expected to receive after fighting never came. Dr. Duarte was busy with his job as advisor to the tenente, and he allowed Degas to manage the Coelho properties. Degas collected rents and resolved maintenance issues, proving himself a capable manager. Despite this, Dr. Duarte didn't allow his son to buy or sell properties, or to take over the moneylending and import-export businesses. Degas wedged himself into business meetings and later, political ones. Dr. Duarte couldn't openly rebuff his only son, so he tolerated Degas' presence. Emília did not know whether Degas craved his father's approval or simply wanted to annoy Dr. Duarte, or both. Either way, he refused to be ignored. Degas purchased a membership to the British Club. When Dr. Duarte and his business associates strolled in Derby Square, Degas strode to catch up with them. At dinner parties, he squeezed himself into the men's circles of conversation. He offered his opinions even though he was never asked for them, and despite the fact that no one listened.

Only Captain Carlos Chevalier paid Degas attention. Emília saw them chatting amicably at Green Party events. Dr. Duarte called the pilot a braggart. Chevalier's offer to map the roadway had been made only to newspapers; the pilot never actually contacted Tenente Higino. Other Recife men also kept their distance from Chevalier, which brought the pilot closer to Degas.

When Emília was a child in Taquaritinga, two boys were caught in an abandoned farmhouse. Caught at *what* Emília hadn't known, though she'd pressed her aunt for details. "The devil's in the details!" Aunt Sofia had snapped. One of the boys was later killed by his father. The other ran off, disappearing into the caatinga. Recife was more civilized than the countryside, but Emília still feared for Degas. She understood the desperate desire to be loved, and couldn't condemn Degas for having it. There had been nights when, alone in her massive bridal bed, Emília had caressed her arms, her legs, her stomach, and below, craving a loving touch even if it was her own. Afterward she'd felt ashamed and confused. She imagined that, in some small way, this was how Degas felt.

What had begun as a trickle became a flood. By Christmas 1932, flagelados poured into Recife, increasing the city's population by 52 percent. Newspapers warned that flagelados were stifling Tenente

Higino's projects. He'd created a Recife Planning Commission that stressed verticalization of buildings, paved roads, and city parks. The commission had passed an anti-Mocambo law, which said that the construction of shanties within the city was prohibited. The flagelados ignored this law. In Recife's outskirts—along its rivers and within its bogs—they constructed neighborhoods of wood and tin. Tenente Higino appealed to President Gomes. Within weeks, 48,765 flagelados left on Lloyd passenger ships to the Amazon, where they would tap rubber.

"Don't go in the spirit of making your fortunes," Gomes said. "But to serve your country!"

Hunger made men angry and rebellious; Gomes understood this. He did not want another rebellion like the recent one in São Paulo, which had lasted two months and had cost seventy thousand government troops. To stop the influx of refugees into capital cities, he ordered seven relief camps built throughout the countryside. The camps were strategically placed in the scrub's more populous cities, where there were usually rivers and train routes. In Recife, train cars were filled with rolls of barbed wire, food, and medical supplies. The DIP advertised the camps as safe havens where refugees could wait out the drought.

Emília received Dr. Epifano's letter in late January. People were already planning their costumes for Carnaval. A group of Auxiliary husbands was plotting to dress as flagelados, darkening their faces with brown shoe polish and covering themselves in rags. Their wives wanted to imitate the Seamstress. The Recife women competed to make cangaceira costumes with the most embroidery, rhinestones, and false jewelry. Emília resolved not to attend any Carnaval parties.

She'd clipped the Seamstress's photograph. It had appeared in the newspaper, after the first surveyors were killed. Luzia stood in the center of the crowd of men, her shoulders squared, her neck long. The Hawk looked stooped and small next to her. Her thick braid was slung over her shoulder and fell nearly to her waist—she'd broken her childhood promise to Saint Expedito. Her face was dark.

She wore spectacles, and behind them, Emília could not see her eyes. The glare in the glasses made the woman look otherworldly. She was regal. Powerful. Like the queen of some forgotten tribe.

After the sixth surveyor's funeral, journalists speculated that the Seamstress, not the Hawk, had ordered the decapitations. She was merciless, the papers said. She had no shame. Emília had heard this expression many times before. Back in Taquaritinga, when she wore heeled shoes, or rouged her face, or when she and Degas took un- chaperoned walks during their brief courtship, Emília heard people whisper about her: *That girl has no shame!* Shame was admirable in a woman. Even in Recife it was important for ladies to have shame, though they didn't call it that. They called it composure.

The doctor's letter was curious. Emília read it seven times. The stationery was bent and stained. In one section, the ink was smudged. Emília sensed desperation in the doctor's words. Also tenderness. She remembered the man from the lobby as considerate, intelligent, and slightly tipsy. The letter revealed different aspects of his person- ality. He was a strange person: what man knew of renda lace? And why did he proclaim *not* to be religious in one section, and later re- fute that by ending the letter with a plea to Santo Expedito? He'd written about her "fine heart" and "strong will." Emília wondered who'd told him this. Despite the letter's peculiarities, Emília be- lieved him. Something the doctor had said in the theater lobby had stayed with Emília all of those years: "A life in the city is fine, but it's an effortless life." After opening her atelier, Emília thought she would finally be content, but this hadn't happened. Her life still felt bare, her accomplishments small. After receiving the doctor's letter, Emília saw an opportunity to enlarge her life.

She'd become an expert at dropping ideas into Dr. Duarte's head and making him believe they were his own. A charitable delegation would give Tenente Higino and President Gomes positive publicity and generate loyalty among "the masses." For Dr. Duarte, the Rio Branco camp presented vast opportunities for cranial measurement. Within weeks, the government commissioned a Great Western train and filled its cargo cars with food, medicine, and hygiene kits containing soap, dental powder, and combs. Each kit also carried a photograph of President Gomes, the "Father of the Poor."

Before their departure, Emília and Mrs. Coimbra posed for photographs. The pictures would be printed in newspapers across the Northeast, as well as those as far away as Rio de Janeiro and São Paulo. Emília and Mrs. Coimbra were called "brave souls," willing to face danger for the sake of charity. There had been attacks throughout the caatinga. After decapitating the second set of government surveyors, the Hawk had disappeared from the papers. There were rumors that his group had fractured because of the drought. Upon arriving in Recife, some refugees claimed that the famous cangaceiro had been stabbed and killed by one of his own men. This rumor made headlines but was quickly refuted. The Hawk's group attacked several trains carrying supplies for Gomes's relief camps. The cangaceiros distributed the stolen food to the hungry and, afterward, some flagelados said they'd seen the Hawk doling out farinha and meat. Others said they hadn't seen him; there were too many cangaceiros to distinguish one man from the other. Most were certain that they'd seen the Seamstress—that tall, lone woman with a crooked arm—attacking the trains and commanding the men.

By Christmas 1932, Tenente Higino had dispatched newly trained troops to guard the relief camps. Any soldier who killed a cangaceiro received two stripes on his uniform. By then, the Hawk had multiplied into two men. There were rival cangaceiro groups claiming his leadership: one group had the Seamstress; the other, more violent group had a man who branded women's faces as punishment for short hair or indecent dress. Emília saw one of the victims pictured in the newspaper. The girl had an oozing scar on her cheek. The brand burned onto her had the initials "L.E." The girl testified that the man who'd held the iron to her face was short, with very large ears. Emília vaguely recalled the cangaceiro—he was the one who'd come to Aunt Sofia's house and ordered them to carry their sewing equipment to the colonel's. He was not the Hawk, at least not the one Emília remembered.

Stories circulated about the Seamstress. There were rumors that she'd been pregnant; several flagelados in Recife said they'd seen the Seamstress with a large belly. When Dr. Duarte heard this, he added several contos of his own money to the reward fund. The offspring of two infamous criminals would be a valuable specimen. If the rumor was true, if the Seamstress was expecting, Dr. Duarte wanted the child as much as he wanted its mother—dead or alive.

The most scandalous rumor about the Seamstress involved her army of cangaceiros; people said her group included women. People said she'd kidnapped young girls—victims of the drought—and forced them to marry her men.

Emília lifted her purse into her lap. Inside her bag, she'd stowed the Communion portrait. Worried that her seatmate, Mrs. Coimbra, would ask to see the photo, Emília didn't remove it from its hiding place. Instead, she opened the mouth of her purse wide and stared at the two girls in the photograph. *Just in case*—this was what she'd thought when she'd packed the Communion portrait. In case the train was stopped, in case the delegation was attacked. Emília felt a strong, secret thrill each time she looked out the train's window and believed she saw movement in the scrub's gray tangle of trees. She wondered if the cangaceiros could stop a moving train, or if they would wait until it reached the Rio Branco station under the cover of night. The train was filled with supplies, the delegation's trip widely advertised. Perhaps the Hawk's group would wait and attack the relief camp, even though there were soldiers protecting it. Emília felt fear and excitement at the possibility of an attack. Secretly, she hoped for one. Though she could never admit it, her primary reason for taking this trip was not charity or adventure, but the chance of meeting the Seamstress.

Emília brushed her fingertips across the faces of the girls in the Communion portrait. She traced the blurry angles of Luzia's bent arm.

At three AM, the train slid safely into Rio Branco's station. A small military band greeted the delegation by playing the national anthem. The relief camp's sergeant shook hands with government officials as they descended from the train. Soldiers served as porters, placing the growing collection of bags onto carriages led by perilously skinny donkeys. Under the station's gas lanterns, Emília saw the ripples of the animals' ribs beneath their skin. The delegation's photographers didn't snap shots of the arrival; everyone on the train was tired, their bodies stiff, their suits wrinkled, their faces oily. Dr. Duarte announced that photos were best left for the next day, when they made their grand entrance into the camp. The delegates would sleep in the homes of Rio Branco's last decent citizens—those merchants and property owners who'd stayed despite the drought. The wives of those remaining Rio Branco men greeted Emília, Mrs. Coimbra, and the nuns with hugs and bouquets of fabric flowers. There were no real flowers left in Rio Branco. As the band continued to play, the nuns held hands and said a prayer for their safe arrival. Dr. Duarte loudly greeted camp officials. Degas stayed close behind his father. Near her husband, Emília saw the doctor. His hair was poorly cut, his cheeks sunburned. He wore glasses and had a large, beaklike nose. Moving purposefully through the crowd, he stopped and quickly shook hands with each man he came across, then continued his route toward Emília.

When he reached her, the doctor stared intently at her face. The crowd around them pressed in close, making Emília and Eronildes bump against each other. The doctor blushed.

"Mrs. Coelho," he finally said, squeezing her hand tightly. "I feel as if I know you."

3
////////

The sun revealed what night had hidden from the Recife delegation. Barbed wire, nailed tautly across posts two meters tall, surrounded the Rio Branco Relief Camp. Beyond the wire fence was the caatinga. The gray forest extended until the horizon, interrupted only by a brown scattering of termite mounds and the thin line of train tracks. Rio Branco—with its whitewashed buildings, its train station, and the relief camp's rows of canvas tents—seemed like an insignificant addition to the caatinga's territory. The town was eerily quiet. There were no birdcalls, no goats bleating, no peddlers shouting. There were only the sounds of the delegation walking toward the camp's entrance. Reporters shouted questions. Government officials exchanged observations. The nuns muttered prayers. Within the camp, residents stirred. They exited their tents, blinking in the sunlight. Long lines of men and women extended from their separate toilet areas—pits filled with lye located in the camp's far end. When the wind shifted, Emília's eyes burned from the lye. She placed a handkerchief over her nose to blot out the stink.

The flagelados's heads were shaved. Some still had white traces of delousing powder on their stubbled hair and necks. Women wore head scarves to disguise their baldness. Round metal identification tags stamped with numbers were pinned to each person's shirt.

The delegation stopped beneath a banner that said, *"Welcome! Viva Gomes! Father of the Poor!"* Emília and the other delegates posed for photographs as the camp's residents looked on.

During the night, soldiers had unloaded the train's supplies and erected distribution tents. Emília's tent, where she and Mrs. Coimbra would dole out clothing, was set next to Dr. Epifano's medical tent. Dr. Duarte had a measurement tent where he would press his calipers to flagelados' skulls and record data. He invited Dr. Eronildes to witness his measurements and monopolized the doctor's attention. Dr. Duarte loudly complimented Eronildes' work with the refugees, his diligence, his drive. He nudged Degas to agree. Emília's husband nodded curtly at Eronildes.

Due to the heat, the distribution and medical tents were open on all four sides. Only Dr. Eronildes' private residential tent, erected next to his medical one, had its canvas flaps closed. Behind his private tent was a yard enclosed by barbed wire and shaded by the camp's only juazeiro tree. Inside the yard, a goat with a bulging udder nibbled at the tree's bark. A soldier guarded the animal.

By nine AM, the sun began to bake the camp. Even under a tent's protection, the heat was stifling. Sweat stained the armpits of Emília's fashionable dress. It beaded on her forehead and ran into her eyes. Emília removed her hat and tied a scarf over her head. She and Mrs. Coimbra distributed clothing while the nuns wrote down each flagelado's identification number, making sure no one received double. The refugees were awkward and gruff; there were no "pleases" or "thank yous." Under her breath, Mrs. Coimbra said they were ungrateful. Emília corrected her.

"They're starving," she whispered, folding a pair of children's knickers. "Manners aren't important."

Mrs. Coimbra's eyes widened, as if she hadn't considered this possibility. She nodded and served the next flagelado.

To ease people's embarrassment about receiving charity, Emília was efficient and respectful, as if the flagelados were paying customers. She tried hard not to stare, but there were moments when she couldn't help looking at a refugee's blistered mouth. Most residents had eye infections, their lids crusted with pus. The flagelados' underfed children, with their bowed legs and enlarged stomachs, were the hardest to ignore. Emília spoke to them in a soft voice, handing them dolls. The newest children in the camp were often the skinniest and their eyes were glazed and blank. These children took the dolls reluctantly, disinterested in everything around them. The children who'd lived longer in the camp had been better fed, and they snatched the dolls from Emília's hands, clutching the toys against their bony, birdlike chests.

Throughout the morning, Emília felt the sensation of being watched. When she looked around, neither the nuns nor Mrs. Coimbra observed her. Only when she stared into the neighboring medical tent did she catch Dr. Eronildes staring back. When Emília sat down to take a break, she turned her stool toward the medical tent and watched the doctor work. Some patients were suspicious at first. They refused treatment and hid their children behind their legs. Dr. Eronildes calmly explained what he planned to do and how he planned to treat them. Before he touched a patient, he asked their permission. He gently tilted back their shaved heads and opened their infected eyes, squeezing in medicinal drops before the patient could flinch. He carefully spooned cod liver oil into their mouths, explaining that it would cure their night blindness, caused by hunger. There was a nurse—a flagelada herself—who helped him, taking over when he occasionally went into his private tent. Emília glimpsed an old woman in the tent. She bit a pipe between her lips and held something in her arms.

At noon, Degas arrived to announce lunch. The nuns had already left, escorted out of camp by a soldier. While another soldier dispersed the line in front of the clothing tent, Emília and Mrs. Coimbra closed the tent's canvas sides. Degas sat. He stared at the medical tent.

"They say that doctor's a coiteiro," Degas said.

"Who says?" Emília asked.

Degas shrugged. "Everyone. Why do you think Father's so complimentary to him? He wants information."

"If he'd harbored cangaceiros, he'd be investigated and charged," Emília said, keeping her voice low. "But he's here. He's a Gomes man."

"You can be both," Mrs. Coimbra said. "I've been to Salvador. He's from a fine family there. That's probably what's kept him out of trouble so far. And the fact that he's a medical man—"

"I've heard something else," Degas interrupted.

Mrs. Coimbra moved closer to his stool.

"This is a charity mission, Degas," Emília said. "Not a gossip column."

Degas ignored her. "He's got an infant in his tent. That's what the goat is for. A refugee tried to steal its milk and the doctor nearly had him shot."

Emília looked at the medical tent and next to it, the doctor's private quarters. She'd heard so many children cry that morning. She hadn't thought the cries came from Dr. Eronildes' residence.

"Goat's milk is good. It has nutrients," Mrs. Coimbra said, pulling off her soiled gloves and putting on a fresh white pair. "Is the child his?"

Degas shrugged and smiled. "I wonder what else the respectable doctor's hiding."

Emília stared at her husband. "We all have our demons."

Degas stood. "Shall we?" he said, holding out his arm to Mrs. Coimbra. She hesitated, then took it. He held his other arm toward Emília.

"Go ahead," she said, fidgeting with her head scarf. "I need to straighten up."

"Yes," Degas replied. "Let out your hair, or else the soldiers will confuse you with one of the refugee women."

After Degas left with Mrs. Coimbra, Emília spotted a soldier outside her tent. He would escort her from the camp. Emília quickly closed the tent flap. Inside, the soldier's shadow against the canvas was large and warped. The air grew stuffy, but Emília didn't want to leave the tent. Lunch would be a publicity event. Reporters would scribble in their notepads and photographers snap shots of the delegation. The lunch table would be crowded with government men complaining about the poor food. And all around them, beyond the porch, would be the caatinga, with its unsettling emptiness. How did Luzia survive in such a place? How did anyone?

A second shadow appeared along the tent flaps. The canvas curtain parted.

"Mrs. Coelho?" Dr. Eronildes said, peering inside. His dress shirt was wrinkled, his face shiny with sweat. He wiped a handkerchief across his brow.

"Would you like an escort?" he asked

"I already have one," Emília said, pointing to the soldier's shadow. "But I'd prefer your company."

Dr. Eronildes looked startled. Like a nervous suitor, he wiped the fronts of his trousers with his large hands. Emília saw his awkwardness and his constant staring as signs of attraction; the doctor had a crush on her. She felt suddenly proud of her ability to disconcert. In one easy movement, she put on her hat and stepped beside him.

They walked slowly through the camp. The noonday sun reflected off the canvas tents, making Emília and Eronildes squint. Flies tickled their arms and necks.

"We're late for the toast," Emília said. "The delegates always toast."

"That's why I stayed away," Eronildes replied. "I'm giving up drink."

Emília nodded. She recalled his flushed face and trembling hands during their talk at the Saint Isabel Theater.

"I'm responsible for something now," Dr. Eronildes continued. "I can't risk it. I have to keep my head clear."

The doctor looked at Emília, studying her reaction. No man—not even Professor Célio—had looked at her with such interest, such intensity. Emília tilted her hat farther over her face.

"I understand," she said. "People depend on you here. It's a terrible situation, this drought."

Eronildes stopped walking. "Are you afraid to be here?"

"No," Emília replied. "Should I be?"

Eronildes shook his head. "They won't attack. Not this camp."

"Why?" Emília asked, unable to hide her disappointment.

The doctor smiled. "Because I'm here."

"They . . ." Emília stopped and lowered her voice. "The cangaceiros respect you?"

"I helped them in the past. Does that bother you?"

"No." Emília felt suddenly dizzy. She looked around; there were soldiers nearby. Standing still would attract attention. Emília headed toward the camp's gates. Dr. Eronildes kept pace beside her.

"You shouldn't tell anyone else," she said. "Especially my father-in-law. He measures criminal types. He'll give you trouble."

"Do you believe in his measurements?"

No one had asked her that question before. Some in Recife called Dr. Duarte's work a fad. Others said it was an emerging science, gaining credibility in Germany, Italy, and the United States. All assumed that because Emília was Dr. Duarte's daughter-in-law she believed in his work.

"He measured me once," Emília said. "According to his data, I'm a normal specimen. I'm perfectly unextraordinary."

"You don't believe it?" Dr. Eronildes asked.

"No woman wants to believe that," Emília replied, smiling. She looked at him coquettishly from beneath her hat brim. Dr. Eronildes did not smile back.

"I think Dr. Duarte's right, about you at least," he said. "You aren't unique."

Emília felt as if she'd been pinched. She pushed up the brim of her hat, ready to insult the doctor, but when she faced him she couldn't be angry. He looked pained. His chin trembled. Emília had read him wrong—he didn't fancy her, but there was something else, something she didn't understand.

"I know a woman," he said, his voice trembling and low. "She doesn't look like you, not at first. But upon observation, you have the same mannerisms, the same way of moving, the same nose, the same shape of the face. When I look at you, I think you could be sisters."

Emília's mouth felt dry, her arm too heavy in his. She nodded and they walked on. It would look strange if she and the doctor arrived late for lunch.

During the meal, Emília didn't look at Eronildes or speak to him. Despite her efforts to ignore the doctor, she was extremely conscious of his movements, his voice, what he ate and did not eat, how he responded to Dr. Duarte's many medical questions.

Who is this man? Emília thought. He'd admitted to being a coiteiro, but which cangaceiros had he helped and why? And was Degas' other story true—did he harbor a child in his tent?

Over the course of lunch, Emília didn't answer the reporters' questions. She could barely lift her hands to swat flies from her mouth and her hair. Mrs. Coimbra stared at her. When the old woman spoke, Emília could barely hear. Mrs. Coimbra repeated her questions several times before concluding that Emília was suffering from heat exhaustion. She announced this to Degas and Dr. Duarte, who took turns analyzing Emília's pasty complexion.

"Pay a visit to our doctor!" Dr. Duarte said, grasping Eronildes' shoulder. "He'll cure you."

4

The doctor lowered three flaps of his medical tent in order to give Emília privacy. Decency, however, demanded that one flap stay open. A soldier stood near this opening, his back to the examination area. He'd been ordered to keep the line of sick flagelados at bay until Dona Emília Coelho had been treated. Eronildes' nurse remained in the tent as well. She placed a wet cloth across Emília's neck and poured her a glass of yellow, bitter-tasting water. At lunch, Emília hadn't contradicted Mrs. Coimbra's concerns about her health. Emília said she felt dizzy and had a slight headache, but made sure not to exaggerate her ailments—if she felt too ill, Degas would have to accompany her to Eronildes' tent.

She sat on a stool. The wet cloth on her neck cooled her. Its moisture seeped into the back of her dress, making the fabric stick to her skin. When she'd finished her water, Dr. Eronildes took the glass.

"May I?" he said, pointing to her forehead. Emília nodded.

He pressed his long, cool fingers to her brow.

"You're sweating, that's a good sign. Your skin isn't red or dry."

The nurse handed him a stethoscope.

"Please," he said, indicating the top buttons of Emília's dress. Emília undid two of them. The stethoscope's round, metal device felt cool on her chest. Dr. Eronildes listened.

"Your heart's beating fast," he said, removing the stethoscope's ear buds. "I think you need rest and—"

A cry came from the doctor's adjoining tent. It was shrill and urgent. Eronildes straightened. The nurse left their tent and entered the residential one. As she drew apart the flaps, Emília saw an old, pipe-smoking servant cooing to a bundle in her arms.

"I've taken on a child," Eronildes said.

"That's kind," Emília replied. "Did its mother die?"

"No. But I assume it's like death, giving up your only child."

Emília's head began truly to hurt. "Why would she do that? The mother?"

"She knew he wouldn't survive with her. It was too dangerous."

"It's not dangerous with you, in this camp?"

"He can't stay with me for long," Eronildes replied. "I promised to deliver him to his aunt."

The nurse returned. She nodded to indicate that the child was fine. Emília stared at the gap between the two tents, at the crooked line of the cloth flaps.

"How will you find her?" she asked.

Without asking permission, Dr. Eronildes gently pressed his fingertips to Emília's neck, feeling the glands beneath her jawbone. He leaned close.

"I already have," he whispered.

The child let out another cry. Emília stood. The damp cloth slid from her neck and flopped to the floor.

"Would you like to meet him?" Eronildes asked.

"Yes."

Dr. Eronildes strode to the tent flap and folded it open. Emília hesitated.

"He's already five months," Eronildes said. "I wasn't sure he'd survive, but he has. He's stubborn. Willful, like his mother."

Emília glanced back at the nurse, at the guarding soldier, at the tent's thin walls. She silently cursed them all. There were so many questions she wanted to ask, but couldn't.

"You knew her well?" she asked. "The mother?"

Eronildes dropped the door flap. He stared at his dusty rancher's boots. "Some people you can never know. Not truly. But I admired her, and pitied her."

Emília nodded. Quickly, she opened the flap and ducked inside.

It took several seconds for her eyes to adjust to the room's shade. A few paces in front of her, the boy wiggled in his nursemaid's arms. He was red faced and crying. Emília felt as if she was back on that Great Western train, moving forward yet not knowing why or how. Suddenly she was in front of the maid. The baby's whole body seemed flushed, his skin thin, like a film. On his eyelids and across his belly, Emília saw a webbing of veins, threadlike reds and thick blues. He balled his hands into fists. His lips trembled and then opened, releasing a cry so shrill and loud it startled her. The maid plopped him in Emília's arms. She removed the corncob pipe from her mouth and spoke over the boy's racket.

"Name's Expedito," she said. "That's how his mother wants it."

5

Mrs. Coimbra called him a child of the drought. The nuns called him an orphan. The delegation's reporters dubbed him "the foundling." Photographers used their last rolls of film to capture Emília cradling the infant on Rio Branco's platform. Mrs. Coimbra stood on one side of her, Dr. Duarte and Degas on the other. Behind them, shuddering like a horse ready to charge from its stable, was the Great Western train that would return them all to Recife.

The trip had been a success. Two days in the Rio Branco camp gave Dr. Duarte hundreds of cranial measurements to compare and analyze. The trip gave President Gomes a positive image in the minds of the camp's residents, who'd pinned photographs of the "Father of the Poor" on their tents. The nuns from Nossa Senhora das Dores had fulfilled their goal of serving the poor, and Mrs. Coimbra had done her duty for the Princess Isabel Society. The government delegates returned to Recife with a plan to restart the roadway project: put the relief camp's men to work. There were thousands of able-bodied husbands, fathers, and sons pouring into the camps and receiving free food and shelter. Once these men had recovered from starvation, why not put them to work? Tools could be included in the government's weekly shipments of tents, food, and barbed wire. Soldiers were already on hand to protect the camps. If native sertanejos worked the roadway, there was a chance the cangaceiros wouldn't attack—the Hawk and the Seamstress wouldn't have the audacity to kill their own people. Relief-camp workers could build the Trans-Nordestino from the inside out, working from the interior until they reached the coast. The government men were excited to present their plan to Tenente Higino.

Everyone in the delegation knew that Emília had pushed for the trip. Dr. Duarte, the nuns, Mrs. Coimbra, and the government men all had her to thank for their successes. Because of this, on their last morning in Rio Branco, when Emília left the relief camp's barbed-wire confines carrying a refugee child in her arms, no one had the nerve to dissuade her. She'd spoken to Dr. Duarte about the child beforehand. Her father-in-law had frowned and fondled his mustache, a habit of deep contemplation. Dr. Eronildes vouched for the child, attesting to its health. Finally, Dr. Duarte placed his hand on Emília's shoulder.

"I'll let you have him," he said, as if Expedito were an expensive and impractical whim, like a fur stole.

"We'll take care of the adoption papers in Recife," Dr. Duarte continued. "It will be an example to others, Emília. Modern nations—the United States, Great Britain, France—all have a spirit of charity. 'Fidelity, Equality, and Fraternity' as they say! Care for your brother! Brazilians should do the same. We Coelhos will be the first."

Before leaving the medical tent, Dr. Duarte invited Eronildes to Recife. National elections were coming up in May, Dr. Duarte announced. There would be many high-paying positions for bright, resourceful men like Eronildes. The doctor declined the invitation. He would stay in the Rio Branco camp until the drought subsided. Dr. Duarte smiled and slipped Eronildes his business card. Before they parted, Emília's father-in-law whispered something in the doctor's ear. Emília couldn't hear exactly what was said; she could only catch the word *trouble*. Dr. Eronildes reddened and shook Dr. Duarte's hand. When he said good-bye to Emília, Eronildes was reserved and formal.

"You've changed this boy's fate," he said. "Let me know of his progress."

Emília nodded. She had many questions for Eronildes, many messages to relay to Luzia, but she could do neither. Dr. Duarte waited impatiently by the medical tent's open flap.

"I was raised by my aunt," Emília said. "There's no replacement for a mother. My aunt knew this. She did her best."

Dr. Eronildes smiled. He pressed his long hand to Expedito's skull. The baby yawned and wiggled in Emília's arms.

Only Degas voiced concern about the hasty adoption. Before they left Rio Branco, he stared warily at the child. "Mother won't like it," he said.

Mrs. Coimbra, who'd taken a protective stance toward Emília, gave Degas a stern look.

"Your mother had a child," Mrs. Coimbra said. "She knows the joys of it. Nature's denied your wife those joys and she's found another way of having them. Your mother will understand."

Mrs. Coimbra, the nuns, Dr. Duarte, and everyone else in the delegation were convinced that Emília had found a natural solution to her barrenness. Emília let them voice the beliefs they'd always had: that her obsessions with fashions, the atelier, and suffrage were all empty endeavors used to cover up a larger, instinctual need. By adopting a child—even a refugee child—this need had finally been met. As Mrs. Coimbra whispered to Emília before they stepped on the train platform:

"The child's healthy and light skinned. No one can blame you for wanting him."

As the train left the Rio Branco station, Expedito let out shrill, accusing cries. He wiggled in Emília's arms, beat his tiny fists against his stomach. At her feet, Emília had a heavy leather bladder filled with goat's milk. She forced the bladder's nipple into Expedito's mouth. He quieted and drank, staring fixedly at Emília. His brown eyes were wet and shining with tears, their look so stern that Emília believed the boy was assessing her, wondering where his faithful nurse with the corncob pipe had gone and why he'd been abandoned yet again. Expedito sucked so determinedly on the bladder that Emília was afraid he'd drink up all his milk before the trip was finished. She pried it from his mouth. The boy's brow scrunched and he began to wail again. At the far end of the cabin, the government men stared. They'd laughed at Expedito's first cries; now they seemed irritated by them. Following Mrs. Coimbra's recommendation, Emília and the boy moved to an empty second-class car. The nuns and Mrs. Coimbra went with her.

There was no nanny to feed and burp the child, no maid to hustle him away when he soiled his cloth diapers. In camp, he hadn't worn diapers. There was no way to clean them—water was too precious to waste on boiling diaper cloth. So Eronildes' pipe-smoking maid had done what many caatinga mothers did: she'd watched the child closely, looking to see if he frowned, tensed, or squirmed. If he did this, the nursemaid rushed Expedito to a clay chamber pot and held him over it, doing this ten, fifteen, sometimes twenty times a day. There were no chamber pots on the train. Emília had a stack of coarse cotton strips. During the beginning of the trip, the nuns and Mrs. Coimbra helped Emília change Expedito. They squeezed into the train's small restroom and taught her how to wipe the baby, how to fold and pin a fresh diaper on him. They handed the soiled diapers to the train's waiter, who reluctantly disposed of the malodorous wads of cloth. Emília believed he threw them out the window.

By nightfall, the other women had moved back to their seats in the delegation car. They had the freedom to walk away from the child, to sleep, to eat leisurely dinners. Emília could do none of those things. She sat, frazzled. Her dress smelled of spilled goat's milk. Her bolero jacket was spotted with Expedito's spit-up. Her hat was crushed. In that empty train car, Emília understood the loneliness of motherhood.

Expedito slept in a bassinet woven from caroá fibers. Emília lifted him from it. The boy lay in her lap, his face soft with sleep. Sometimes he shook his tiny hands, as if batting away dreams. Each time he moved, Emília tensed. She worried he would wake and cry and she wouldn't know how to soothe him. He terrified her. But beneath her fears she felt a fierce affection. It grew within her, making her overlook her dirty dress, her cramped back, her loneliness. There was a satisfying liberation in forgetting herself and caring instead for this child.

Under the bassinet's blankets was a small canvas sack Dr. Eronildes had given her. "It's for the boy," he'd said. "His mother wanted him to have it." The sack contained a penknife. There was the image of a bee sloppily carved on its wooden handle. Earlier, Emília had removed the knife from its hiding spot. She'd fingered its dull blade.

At the end of the car, a door opened. Wind rushed between the train's compartments. Emília glanced at Expedito. His lips puckered, wrinkling his small chin, but he did not wake. Degas strolled down the car's aisle. He took the seat beside Emília.

"You and I, we're the only ones who don't sleep," he said, rubbing his eyes. "Why is that?"

Emília shook her head, careful not to disturb Expedito. "A guilty conscience keeps you awake. That's what my aunt Sofia used to say."

Degas cocked his head. "What are you guilty of?"

Emília stared out the train's window. The glass was dirty. There was no moon, making it too dark to observe the scrub. Emília studied her reflection instead. She hadn't taken care of her younger sister, hadn't protested when the cangaceiros took Luzia away. Afterward, she hadn't tried to rescue Luzia. And later, she'd tried to forget her sister, to deny their connection.

"Escaping," Emília finally said. "Forgetting."

"That doesn't make you guilty. That makes you smart," Degas said. He pointed a finger toward Expedito. "What will we name him?"

"He already has a name."

Degas pursed his thick lips. "I don't get a say in that, either? I should have known. Did you and Father come up with a name?"

"No. He already had one."

"What is it?"

"Expedito," Emília whispered. The child shifted in her arms.

"That's a matuto name if I ever heard one," Degas said. "His mother must have given him that."

"I don't know," Emília replied, wishing he'd leave. "It may have been the doctor's choice."

Degas shook his head. "He's a strange bird, that doctor. He gives out infants. He associates with cangaceiros. I understand why they'd associate with *him*—a doctor's a useful friend to have when you're a bandit. But I can't see why he risks associating with them. No one condemns him for it, either. Coiteiros are being taken into custody left and right, but not our Dr. Eronildes. His criminality makes him interesting. An asset. Did you see Father praising him? Inviting him to Recife?"

"Shhh!" Emília hushed. "Don't wake him!"

Degas stared at Expedito. He ran a fingertip along the boy's foot. "You used to wrinkle your nose at the mention of children. Even the Seamstress had a mother's instinct, but you didn't."

"That's nonsense," Emília whispered.

"It's not. She was pregnant," Degas continued. "That's what the papers said."

"She was starving, like those refugees. They all have big stomachs. It's worms."

Degas ignored her, moving his finger in circles along Expedito's bare foot. "I'd assume it's hard to give birth in the scrub. You'd need medical attention. A doctor—"

"That's why I don't want children of my own," Emília interrupted, determined to divert the conversation. "Births are awful. Mrs. Coimbra said it ruined her figure."

Degas smiled. "What happened to it, do you suppose?"

"To her figure?" Emília said. "She got thick in the waist."

"No," Degas replied. "To the child, the bandit child."

Emília faced him. "She killed it."

"What mother would do that?"

"A desperate one."

Degas clicked his tongue. "We've seen proof that that's not true. Those women in the relief camp were desperate. They were starving, but they kept their scrawny babies."

Degas reached over Emília's lap. He stroked Expedito's head, running a finger across each silky strand of the boy's hair.

"I think the Seamstress gave her child away. To a coiteiro, maybe.

To someone she deeply trusted." Degas cupped his hand over Expedito's head. "Father will want to measure him. Once he's fully formed."

Emília thought of the Mermaid Girl floating in her jar, trapped in a perpetual sleep. She pushed away Degas' hand.

"Let him be," she hissed.

"I can't," Degas said. He stared at Emília, his face scrunching as if he was in pain. "I'm his father now, even if it wasn't my choice, even if you asked Father first and not me. Everyone discounts me, even my own wife. But don't patronize me, Emília. I know what it is to conceal. I do it every waking hour."

Her hands felt clammy against Expedito's skin. The crooks of her elbows were moist with sweat. "I'm sorry," Emília said. "I should have asked you first. I was scared you would say no."

"And if I had?" Degas said. "You would've taken him regardless."

"Yes."

Degas sighed and sat back. He turned his head toward Emília.

"Tell me the truth," he asked. "What is so special about this child?"

"Nothing," Emília replied. "If you believe what your father believes, he isn't special at all. He's the opposite. That's why I want him."

Degas faced the ceiling. He pinched the bridge of his nose. When he stared down at Expedito again, his eyes shone. He abruptly stood.

"I'll talk to Mother when we arrive," Degas said. "I'll tell her I wanted him."

Emília watched Degas squeeze along the narrow aisle and disappear into the adjoining car. When he'd gone, she held Expedito close. The child woke. He cried but Emília didn't quiet him. She pressed her face against his, inhaling his milky-breathed sobs and letting her own escape.

Chapter 10

LUZIA

Caatinga scrubland, Pernambuco
September 1932–March 1933

1

- - - - - - - - -

*H*er boy was both obedient and stubborn. Obedient because, during the long walk to Dr. Eronildes' house, she'd asked her unborn son to stay inside her belly and he'd listened. He'd waited. Stubborn because even after she'd reached the doctor's house and installed herself in Eronildes' guest bedroom, the child wouldn't come out. Luzia's belly was so heavy that her organs felt pressed against the walls of her stomach and pushed up into her chest. Her back ached. She constantly had to urinate and could not sleep, could not find comfort lying down or standing up. Eronildes' ancient maid tried everything to coax the child out: tying a sweaty shirt around Luzia's neck, making her eat raw malagueta peppers, flapping a dusty rag under her nose to make her sneeze. Nothing worked.

When she'd first arrived at Eronildes' house, Luzia took the doctor's smooth hand and the maid's arthritic claw and made them both swear on the Bible. She'd made them swear to the Virgin, the mother of all mothers, that they wouldn't let her see or touch the child. If she did either of those things, Luzia would want to keep him.

Dr. Eronildes didn't preside over the birth; that was woman's work. The doctor and the cangaceiros were barred from Luzia's bedroom. They waited outside like a group of nervous fathers. Only Baby—Ponta Fina's wife—stayed with Luzia and the maid.

"It will come in its own time," the elderly woman said. "The more you want it, the more you will wait. It's like cooking milk: when you turn your back, it boils over."

The old woman was right. One afternoon, Luzia's body moved without her guidance or control. It reared and tensed. Her insides tightened, as if a horsewhip had wrapped itself around her. An invisible hand pulled and squeezed the whip, then released it. Baby placed a warm rag on Luzia's head. The elderly maid spit out her corncob pipe and pressed her hands to Luzia's thighs, opening them. She cracked open a clove of garlic and wiped it under Luzia's nose, then repeated the midwife's prayer.

"God save us. God save this saintly house. Where did God make his house?"

"Here!" Luzia replied, clasping her belly.

"And where is the blessed chalice?"

"Here!"

"Where is the scared host?"

"Here! Here!"

The maid boiled a pot of water infused with pepper and cumin seeds and placed the fragrant mixture by the bed. Then, she took a white onion, chopped it in half, and rubbed it on Luzia's thighs. Luzia kicked her away, already nauseous from the scent of garlic and her own sweat. With surprising strength, the old woman held down Luzia's legs.

"Our Lady of the Good Birth!" she cried. "Help us."

With each wave of pushing, the whip tightened. It burned. Luzia stared at the ceiling. She felt trapped in a dream, her body so focused on its task that her mind moved away, as if she were watching herself from afar. Her mind was useless. When he finally left her, that great wave of release should have been a relief, but Luzia felt that along with her child, she had pushed out any remaining feeling. All of the goodness, all of the love she had ever felt or would ever feel was in that boy.

She could not look at him. The guest room was dark, the curtains drawn so the child wouldn't be shocked or blinded when it was born. Quickly, the maid cut the cord, clamped it, and took the child away.

Luzia recalled the oath she'd made the old woman and Eronildes take. "I don't want my boy touching the handle of a punhal," Luzia had said when she'd first arrived. "I want him to be called Expedito." She'd shown Eronildes her collection of newspaper photos of Emília. Luzia made it clear that she wanted her boy delivered to her sister, on the coast, but she did not want to know how or when the doctor would do it.

That was before the birth. Before Luzia heard his cry. It was shrill, like the squawks of the green parrots that flew over the scrub. Her oaths and promises seemed silly then; Luzia took them all back. She wanted her boy. She shouted and her eyes searched the dark room but she could barely sit up. The old maid returned, her arms empty. Luzia tried to move from the bed. The maid stopped her, pushing Luzia onto her side and sitting on her hips.

"My Santa Margarida," the maid said, bouncing lightly on Luzia's hip. "Take these rotten meats out of her stomach."

Luzia spat. She cursed. She plotted all kinds of revenge against the maid—the scissors she'd used to cut the cord, where were they? Could she reach them? Seconds later, she felt the placenta pour out of her, warm and wet. The pillow beneath her cheek was damp with sweat. Luzia's eyelids felt heavy. She closed them.

When she woke, the room was light. The windows were open. The maid stared at her.

"Your boy's alive," she said. "The doctor left with him last night. God will look after him now."

Usually after a birth, the mother's house is filled with relatives, cooing over the baby. The proud father serves sugarcane liquor. The relatives bury the baby's umbilical cord at the door to the house so he won't travel far from home. But Luzia had no home, and now neither did her child. Just a few days old and Expedito was already a wanderer. Luzia's tongue felt dry and fat in her mouth. Her fingers pulsed, as if they'd filled with too much blood. Her ears rang. Outside the bedroom window, she heard Sabiá singing one of his ballads. The words were jumbled and indistinct, but the cangaceiro's voice was mournful. He sang about death. Luzia shivered. All of Sabiá's songs were death songs—she and Antônio had laughed about this in the past—but this ballad was different. Sabiá's voice grew softer and closer, until it was a whisper in her ear. When Luzia opened her eyes, no one was there. When she attempted to sit up in bed, she couldn't. Her body was too heavy to move. Later, she heard hushed conversations between Ponta Fina, Baiano, and Eronildes' maid. *Fever,* they said. *Blood.*

"Whose?" Luzia asked. "My boy's?"

Ponta Fina, Baiano, and the maid acted as if they didn't hear her. Luzia touched her lips—had she even spoken? When she closed her eyes, she saw her son in Emília's arms.

The elderly maid changed the soiled bedsheets. She set lavender seeds over the fire to freshen the room's smell. She forced spoonfuls of broth thickened with manioc flour into Luzia's mouth. When her fever broke, the maid brewed a bitter tea. She fed it to Luzia in order to dry up her milk. Luzia's breasts swelled and ached, like blisters ready to burst. They were mapped with blue veins, the nipples hard and rubbery. The old woman wrapped canvas tightly around Luzia's chest, binding it so she wouldn't leak. Beneath the bandages, Luzia felt the surge of milk. She felt its release. When this happened, she knew her boy was hungry. He was somewhere with Dr. Eronildes, crying for food and being fed goat's milk as a substitute for her own. Luzia knew because her body told her. It was as if an invisible thread hooked her to her boy. The thread could go taut or slack but it could never come undone, it could never reach the end of its spool because there was no end; it bound them forever.

2

New mothers were required to rest for three weeks during their resguardo period. They were not supposed to bathe or leave their beds. As children, Luzia and Emília had accompanied Aunt Sofia on congratulatory visits to new mothers. The women's rooms were dark and stuffy, like animals' dens. Bowls of lavender oil were placed under the mothers' beds but the perfume didn't mask the overpowering scent. The women smelled of sour milk, of sweat, of stale blood. Luzia knew she smelled just as bad as those new mothers she'd met during her childhood, because each time Ponta Fina came into her room, he wrinkled his nose.

Ponta Fina sat beside Luzia's bed and told her what went on outside her sickroom. Eronildes' maid had left the ranch. The old woman had joined the doctor because a man wasn't capable of looking after a newborn baby. Luzia didn't know where Dr. Eronildes was, or how he planned to deposit her son in the arms of her sister. Eronildes' route had to be kept secret—that was what they'd agreed upon before the birth—in order to prevent Luzia from going after him. She might want her child back, but she wouldn't know where to look for him.

"Food's scarce," Ponta Fina said, his eyes focused on the crucifix just above Luzia's bed. "The beans the doctor left are nearly gone. The Old Chico's low. We walked five meters in from the old banks and were only ankle deep. Word got to us that there're trains coming in from the capital. Gomes is sending supplies. He's building drought camps. Some of the men—Thursday, Sabiá, Canjica—are talking about leaving. They're wanting to stop the trains. Get some food. Me and Baiano, we told them to wait."

Luzia nodded. She'd been in bed for four days. If she stayed there much longer, the cangaceiros would see her as a normal woman—not their invincible captain or their vigorous mãe. She'd entered into an agreement with the men, just as Antônio had. She'd cut her hair and called herself captain. She'd frightened them into believing in her, making the men dependent on her leadership, just as they'd felt dependent on Antônio's. By doing this she'd promised to forgo her personal well-being for the group's. She'd promised to give the men direction. They, in turn, had promised to give her obedience.

Ponta Fina watched her intently, the way a farmer might watch an ailing cow—worried for the beast's welfare because he'd genuinely grown to care for it, but also because its well-being determined his own livelihood.

"Wait outside," Luzia said.

Once he'd left the room, Luzia flung away her sheets. She stepped out of bed and gingerly into her old trousers. Every movement threatened to tear open the wound her days in bed had repaired. Her legs felt wobbly, her stomach too slack, her hips oddly loose, like ropes that had been so badly stretched they'd never recover their original firmness. Luzia bound her breasts. She buttoned her jacket and snapped on her shoulder holster. She placed Antônio's hat on her head. These few actions tired Luzia and she was tempted to sit back on the bed. Ponta Fina prevented her from doing this; the cangaceiro paced just outside the bedroom door.

"Ponta!" Luzia yelled. The young man entered and stood at attention.

"Round up the men," she said. "We're leaving."

"But your resguardo?"

"I've birthed a boy, not an ox. Four days was plenty."

As soon as Ponta Fina left the ranch house, Luzia walked into the kitchen, rolled up her pregnancy dress, and threw it in the cook fire.

Outside, the men gathered on Eronildes' porch. Luzia held Antônio's crystal rock and led them in prayer. As she sealed their bodies and her own with the corpo fechado prayer, Luzia observed the kneeling cangaceiros. The men did not ask about her child. They did not inquire after her health. She understood how Antônio must have felt, surrounded by people yet always removed from them. Removed even from her—his own wife—who'd also considered him a guide, a decision maker. Now Luzia was Captain.

She stared at the gray scrubland. The drought would make the most mundane decisions important: where the cangaceiros walked and how far; what time they woke; what time they slept, if they slept at all, because night was the coolest time to walk through the scrub. Taking the wrong path or making the wrong choice would mean dehydration and death. Luzia's decisions would determine their survival. Ponta Fina and Baiano could advise her, but no matter how many opinions were shared, the men expected their captain to bear the burden of choice. The trade-off for leadership was loneliness.

Luzia stepped off the porch. The men followed. Before they entered the scrub, Luzia turned and faced them.

"We won't starve," she announced, mimicking Antônio's confidence. "If God wanted us dead, he would have done it a long time ago."

3

Along the old cattle trail were dozens of shallow graves dug for escapees who'd died of hunger. Some bodies were not buried and in the dry climate they did not decompose but lay openmouthed along the trail, their skins stiff as leather, their hair shining. Only the once soft and wet parts of them—their eyes, tongues, and stomachs—were missing, eaten by desperate animals.

Luzia's head ached. Dust coated her face like a brown mask. The dirt plugged her nose and ears until all of her senses seemed dulled. After dark, her vision waned and she could barely see. The cangaceiros also complained of such night blindness. Within weeks of leaving Eronildes' ranch, the cangaceiro group could travel only in daylight.

Water was the agent that coaxed out the scrub's smells and sounds. Without it, the place was silent. There was only the drone of flies, millions of them it seemed, covering the carcasses of animals and people. Luzia heard their buzzing from kilometers away. At first,

Luzia and the cangaceiros smelled the sweet, putrid scent of dead cattle, goats, and frogs. Soon, even that smell vanished. Dead things didn't have time to decay; they were eaten too quickly.

Luzia and her men found water in the inner folds of bromeliads and the cores of cacti. They pulled young stalks from the spiky caroá plant and sucked on their fleshy ends to trick their thirst. They did not have coffee, so Luzia recalled Antônio's teachings and looked for losna-da-serra, whose furry leaves did the work of seven pots of coffee. She found macambira plants, cut off their long, spiky spears until she held the medulla, and cooked it over the fire for several hours. After being set in the sun to dry, the yellowed orb was crushed to make coarse flour. The woody mucanã vine that wrapped around scrub trees was also a secret source of water. When Luzia cut the vine in the right place—with one quick slice on top and another on the bottom—there was juice. She and the cangaceiros had to hold the cut ends to their mouths quickly or else they'd lose the liquid.

Hunger numbed emotion. Luzia's connection to her son became vague, its pull subdued. She and the cangaceiros thought only of food but, because it hadn't rained during the planting season, there were no crops to reap, no provisions to buy or steal, and few animals to hunt. The cangaceiros' thoughts focused on Gomes's supply trains. Each night the men imagined what was inside the Great Western cargo cars: bags of beans turned into bubbling feijoadas complete with sausage and pigs' feet; cornmeal became steaming cuscuz topped with warm milk; flanks of beef were shredded and served on top of buttered macaxeira root. These dreams made the men determined to endure heat, hunger, and thirst, and to follow Luzia to the nearest Great Western station.

The farther they moved from the São Francisco River, the more homes the cangaceiros found abandoned. Sometimes entire towns were empty. Luzia and the cangaceiros searched houses and storerooms for food. One afternoon, inside a house she believed to be vacant, Luzia came across a woman.

The hem of her dress was shredded. Her arms were as thin as

branches, the bones of the elbows exaggerated knobs. Her cheeks were slack but her nose was wide and regal. At first, she didn't see the cangaceiros standing just outside the house's doorway. The woman's focus was on the ground.

"Get up!" she yelled. "Get up, damn you!"

A wall obscured Luzia's view; she couldn't see the object of the woman's fury. Luzia thought it was an animal—a pet dog perhaps. The woman took a breath, as if collecting her strength. She knelt and shook whatever was on the ground before her. Dust rose. Luzia stepped closer, craning her neck. She saw a tiny, sandaled foot peeking from behind the wall. Luzia entered the house. The men followed.

The child—Luzia could not tell if it was a boy or a girl—wore only stained shorts. Its head was too large for its body. Its mouth was open and its ribs protruded, making it resemble a plucked bird. Its eyes were closed, as if sleeping peacefully despite the woman's yelling. She wasn't scared or surprised to see the cangaceiros. She simply stared at the men and swayed, as if she might tip over. When Luzia uncapped a canteen, the woman's stare instantly changed. It was no longer dazed, but intent.

She would kill me for this brown water, Luzia thought, holding tight to her canteen. "Step aside," she said.

The woman scraped her dry tongue across her lips. "My girl," she croaked, pointing to the child. "My girl."

Luzia knelt. She slid her crooked arm beneath the child's neck. The girl's head was limp and very heavy, but fit perfectly into the bend of Luzia's locked arm. It seemed that this was what her arm had been made for, this was the purpose it was meant to serve: cradling, not shooting or sewing. Luzia felt something jerk inside her—that thread, that inexplicable connection, had been stifled but was not gone. She stared at the limp child. Shoving her canteen between her knees, Luzia used two fingers to open the child's mouth wide. The girl's lips were scaly, her tongue gray tinged. Luzia held the canteen to her mouth. The water inside was brown and sandy. Days before, Ponta Fina had found an old well and after he dug one meter deep into its sandy base, a viscous liquid had bubbled up.

The child did not swallow. Water pooled in her small mouth, then dribbled out, streaking her neck and bare chest. Luzia massaged her throat. She lifted the child's head higher and poured again.

"Drink!" she muttered.

Baiano stooped beside her. He removed his hat, then pressed two dark fingers to the child's neck. He shook his head. Luzia ignored him. She gave the child more water. Baiano put a hand on her shoulder. The whites of his eyes were yellowed, as if his dark irises were leaking their color.

"Don't waste it, Mãe," he said. "The mother's alive. She needs the water now."

The woman looked desperately between the canteen and her child, as if she had only enough energy to reach for one and didn't know which to choose. Her mouth twisted. Baiano moved behind her. He held her thin arms.

"Ready, Mãe," he said.

Luzia stood. If given the canteen, the woman would empty it. Luzia would have to feed her the water little by little. The woman took long, noisy gulps. When she tried to move her arms and clasp the canteen, Baiano held her back. Beneath the woman's worn, nearly transparent smock Luzia saw long and shriveled breasts—a mother's breasts, stretched by feedings.

"I gave her all the food I had," the woman said once she'd finished drinking. She addressed Luzia, but it was Baiano who nodded in response to her words, as if he and the woman were having a private talk.

"Grown people, we can tell ourselves we aren't hungry. We hear the voice inside, but don't speak to it," the woman said. "We can shut it out. Kids can't. They can't be tricked."

Luzia nodded. The woman's eyes were glassy, her focus far away.

"The more you give, the more they want," she continued. "I gave her our last bit of rapadura. I told her she had to hold it in her belly and remember it was there, like a present. A present her mamãe gave her. Three minutes later she was crying, saying she was hungry. God help me; I wanted to hit her."

The woman coughed and lowered her head.

"Feed her," Luzia ordered.

Baiano obeyed, opening his bornal and removing a sliver of dried beef. The meat had a green sheen but the woman eagerly accepted it. She chewed quickly and with her eyes closed. Luzia was suddenly ashamed to look at her; in the face of this refugee woman's grief, Luzia felt relieved. She wouldn't have to watch Expedito grow skinny, or endure his cries for food. Her boy had escaped the drought.

"What's your grace?" Luzia asked.

"Maria," the woman replied. "Maria das Dores."

Food made the woman more alert. Her eyes widened as she regarded the cangaceiros around her. Slowly, she edged away from Baiano and Luzia.

"Don't brand me," she said, clasping her hands. "Have mercy."

"Brand you?" Luzia said.

The woman nodded. "I know that's what you do. I met a girl with a brand on her face. The skin was burnt right through. She said a cangaceiro—a big-eared one—did that to her."

The woman scanned the group, looking for such a man.

"Big ears?" Luzia said. "What does he call himself?"

"The Hawk. They say he's got a bandaged arm. He has a small group, and he's been branding women. Only women. Especially the ones with short hair. He burns their faces, or stomachs, or chests. Like they're cattle."

"You saw him?" Luzia asked.

The woman shook her head. "I only saw the girl—the branded one. Her cheek was so swollen, she couldn't see out of her eye."

"Could you read the brand?"

"Can't read. But I remember the look of it." The woman knelt and then extended her hand. In the dirt before her, she drew shaky letters: *L E*

A warm spurt of bile rose in Luzia's throat. It burned like xique-xique juice. Little Ear was alive, and claiming to be the Hawk.

"We don't brand," Luzia said. "That cangaceiro's a fake."

"A traitor," Ponta Fina corrected her. Next to him, Baby shook her head.

The cangaceiros buried the child's body deep, so vultures wouldn't claim it. Ponta Fina made a cross out of two sticks and tied it together with his subcaptain's scarf. They'd passed dozens of similar graves during their walks. At each one, Luzia and the cangaceiros had stopped and made the sign of the cross. Luzia had done this out of habit and also superstition—she didn't want to anger the dead—but she'd never allowed herself to wonder about who filled those graves. After burying the little girl, Luzia was forced to think about all of the dead they'd passed. Who were those buried people? What were their names, their occupations? And if the drought worsened, would there be such unmarked graves for her men, for herself? Would they be so easily forgotten?

When they left the gravesite, Maria das Dores went with them. The men called her "Maria Magra" because of her thin frame, and they laughed at this nickname because they were all skinny; even Inteligente had lost his bulk.

"Take this," Luzia said and handed Maria Magra her canteen.

"She'll share mine," Baiano replied.

That night at camp, Luzia gave Baiano and Maria Magra the same lecture she'd given Ponta Fina and Baby. After prayers Luzia made both couples kneel before her. Antônio had taught her that ceremony was important—it made insubstantial things seem real. So Luzia took off her shawl and wrapped it around the couple's hands, binding them together. She made the men and women switch shoes. When they switched back, Luzia declared them married and Maria Magra became the third woman admitted into the cangaceiro group. Luzia sensed that she would not be the last.

4

///////

The Great Western cargo cars carried stacks of burlap bags, all stamped with red lettering that read STATE OF PERNAMBUCO. When the cangaceiros sliced open the bags, only manioc flour spilled into their hands. In another car there were blocks of rapadura and strips of dried meat as thin and tough as tanned hides. Gomes had sent food that could be consumed immediately, without water or heat. Luzia and the cangaceiros understood this logic, but Gomes's good sense made their dreams of elaborate meals seem silly and they hated him for this. When Baiano and Inteligente found stacks of flyers bearing Gomes's photograph and the title "Father of the Poor," the men took turns urinating on the president's likeness.

Trains were difficult to stop but not impossible. The first Great Western the cangaceiros ransacked had stopped of its own accord, to replace conductors and release passengers at the halfway point between Caruaru and Rio Branco. The station was called Belo Jardim and, when the train arrived, few people exited there; the drought compelled people to leave the scrub, not enter it. Luzia and her men staked out the station. Only five soldiers guarded the government shipment, but they were well armed. The men stepped off the train to smoke and relieve themselves. They walked to the side of the station, spread their legs, and unbuttoned their trousers. Luzia whistled. Her cangaceiros fired. Distracted, the monkeys were easy targets. Some didn't have time to turn around, and they slumped against the wet sections of the station wall. While Ponta Fina and Inteligente stripped the dead soldiers of their weapons, Luzia and the other cangaceiros entered the train.

Luzia didn't bother opening the safe or robbing the passenger cars: she could not eat mil-réis or drink gold jewelry. The real treasure was food, no matter how basic. The cangaceiros heaved supplies from the train. Word of the hijacking spread into the town of Belo Jardim and a crowd quickly formed.

The residents of Belo Jardim confirmed that Little Ear had

survived. They told Luzia that he'd been in their town a few weeks before, recruiting men by claiming to be the Hawk. Little Ear's cangaceiros were more brutal than Antônio or Luzia would have allowed. As punishment for wearing revealing dresses or for having short hair, Little Ear branded young women. He killed men for no good reason. Luzia knew that this would hurt her group—random violence made cangaceiros unpopular at a time when they most needed popular support. Little Ear's actions would throw people into the arms of Gomes, who'd begun to call himself "Father of the Poor."

Then I will be their mother, Luzia thought.

"Take only what we need," she ordered Ponta Fina as he unloaded the train. "We're giving the rest away."

After receiving the food, the men and women of Belo Jardim kissed the cangaceiros' hands. They praised the Seamstress. They offered the group shelter and protection. Luzia raised her hands to quiet the crowd.

"Remember," Luzia yelled, "the Hawk and the Seamstress did this for you. When you find us, you find protection. That other group is a fake—they claim to be cangaceiros, but they are vagabundos."

Weeks later, there were more trains, more grateful crowds. Luzia and her men piled dead cactus trunks, branches, and brush on train tracks. When she saw dark puffs of smoke rise from a train in the distance, Luzia lit the mound on fire. Conductors stopped their trains and got out to examine the obstruction, and this was when Luzia's cangaceiros moved in.

The trains carried newspapers as well as food. Soldiers and relief workers in Gomes's drought camps wanted to know what was happening on the coast. Gomes had approved the nation's new electoral code. It created a secret ballot and a federal agency called the Justiça Eleitoral to supervise elections. The code also gave literate women the right to vote. There were a few editorials and articles about this, but for the most part women's suffrage was overshadowed by the drought. Despite Gomes's relief camps, refugees still crowded the capital. Luzia read editorials advocating a mass relocation of back-lands residents. "The land is too poor," one article proclaimed, "and daily existence too precarious to allow Brazilian citizens to live in such a place."

There were calls to forcibly move the scrub's residents to the south, to work in São Paulo factories. Gomes agreed with the mi-gration of workers but did not condone abandoning the scrubland. Antônio had been right—Gomes would invade the caatinga and at-tempt to claim it.

"Brazil," Gomes said, "is a great body composed of many parts. Each is vital. None can be abandoned and allowed to become a ref-uge for criminals and anarchists!"

Luzia tried to concentrate on articles about the roadway and President Gomes's plans for Brazil, but her attention was always di-verted to the Society Section. The *Diário* printed extensive coverage of a charity trip, to the Rio Branco Relief Camp, organized by Mrs. Degas Coelho. The final photograph of the trip showed the delega-tion just before its triumphant return to Recife. They posed on the Rio Branco train platform. Mrs. Degas Coelho—the charity mis-sion's muse—stood in the center, surrounded by men and one el-derly woman. Emília held a baby in her arms.

"If we could all save one poor soul," a journalist wrote, "by giv-ing a child otherwise doomed to ignorance a chance at education and civilization, we would solve our social woes."

Within weeks, the Society Section reported that Mrs. Degas Coelho had started another trend, one that had nothing to do with fashion. Other wealthy Recife women wanted to rescue their own drought babies. There were unsavory stories of refugee women be-ing paid for their babies, while others had their infants snatched by servants who wanted to please their mistresses.

Luzia couldn't finish these articles. She thought of those Blue Party women she'd robbed years ago, when Antônio was still alive. She recalled their unnaturally white faces, dusted with powder. She recalled their shrill voices. They'd been at Luzia's mercy back then, on the cattle trail, and she'd been cruel to them. Now her boy was among such women, and he was at their mercy. He'd have Emília though, and Luzia comforted herself by thinking that her sister, her blood, wouldn't treat Expedito as a "foundling," but as a son. Even this thought made Luzia's chest ache and her hands curl into fists—she wanted her boy to be fervently loved, but she didn't want him to love Emília back with the same fervor, the way one would love a mother.

Luzia cut out and kept the newspaper photograph of the charity delegation. In the nights after a train robbery, after her hands and feet had been kissed by hundreds of starving men and women in thanks for her generosity, Luzia unfolded that photo and studied it. Emília's expression was triumphant—cocky, even. A blanket covered the child's face, so only his hands were visible. Luzia stared at those small, white fingers. They reached up, toward Emília. She was his savior. And Luzia was nothing, not even a memory.

5

Attacking a relief camp was a huge endeavor: the places were well guarded by troops and surrounded by barbed-wire fences. Government rations didn't go only to Gomes's relief camps, however. Before her child died, Maria Magra had been headed to a private camp run by a widow.

"The Widow Carvalho," Maria Magra told Luzia and Baiano. "She sold her land to the roadway. She's moving to Recife. People say she's still got water in her well. And she's got food; Gomes sent her rations. They said she's selling them off to make money for her trip. If I'd made it in time, I would've bought some. I would've fed my girl."

Maria Magra didn't know the camp's exact location, but Luzia and Baiano did. As the wife of the late Colonel Carvalho, the widow had inherited a ranch that extended as far as the cattle trail. Luzia, Antônio, and the cangaceiros had walked through her land many times but had never gone near her house; the widow had a poor reputation. Her husband had left her only land and no money, so she was forced to live frugally. Widow Carvalho was known as a tight-fisted manager with a bad temper. It was rumored she'd shot her late husband in the foot during an argument, but few believed the story. Any man—especially a colonel—would have killed his wife for such behavior, and the Widow Carvalho was still alive.

Her house was a massive, whitewashed structure—a blinding landmark in the gray scrub. A line of people snaked around the porch. Some held burlap bags, others dented tin cups. Men wore trousers held up with ropes, on account of the weight they'd lost. Women cradled babies and held the hands of skinny children. The men in line stared at their feet, as if ashamed to face those around them. The women, however, were above embarrassment; they looked directly at the house's porch. There, the Widow Carvalho collected coins in exchange for manioc flour, dried beef, and cooked beans.

Luzia's stomach cramped. In their hiding place in the scrub, the cangaceiros shifted and muttered, impatient. It was the scent of those beans that had prompted their trip to the widow's house. They'd smelled the food from kilometers away but hadn't believed it—cooked beans! At first, the men thought their noses had tricked them, that their food dreams had finally made them lose their senses. But it was no trick. There, on the widow's porch, alongside the burlap bags of dried food, sat a large, steaming vat of beans. How reckless, Luzia thought, to waste her last cups of well water on cooking.

From her hiding place in the scrub, Luzia watched the Widow Carvalho. She wore a long-sleeved black dress whose fabric had a dull shine, like a beetle's carapace. Around her waist was a brown leather belt with a purse attached. The widow dropped coins inside it. After she'd collected her fee, customers were herded to the porch where a trio of hunched, sweating women scooped food onto their plates. Above the porch was a large poster of President Celestino Gomes. He wore military garb. His chest was puffed out and he smiled sympathetically. Below his image were the words "Father of the Poor."

The widow's house didn't have the barbed-wire barrier of official relief camps, but it did have soldiers. Four armed men stood alongside the crowd, hustling people along in line. Luzia realized that the monkeys were not there as protection against cangaceiro attacks but to prevent riots among the widow's customers.

"There're two lines," Ponta Fina whispered. "Those who can pay and those who can't."

Luzia straightened her spectacles. Those who didn't give the Widow Carvalho money or some bit of jewelry were denied food and herded into a separate area. There, a soldier called out in a hoarse voice, "Roadway work! Roadway work!" and directed the refugee men to a nearby table. Seated behind it were two men wearing suits and bright white fedoras.

"Gomes's officials," Luzia whispered. Next to her, Baiano nodded.

One official made the refugee men dip their thumbs in ink and press them to a long sheet of paper. After they'd signed, the other official sprinkled the men's heads with delousing powder, handed them a bundle, and steered them back into the food line, where they were promptly served. If these newly acquired roadway workers had wives or children, they were also given food. Women without money, husbands, or fathers were left without food. Occasionally the Widow Carvalho moved off the porch and into this desperate group.

The widow's head emerged, white and vulnerable, from the black dress that encased her body like armor. She selected a girl from the destitute group and herded her to a separate section of the porch. There were a few other girls already huddled there. Luzia couldn't see their faces clearly enough to judge their ages, but there was one feature that distinguished them from the crowd of refugees: their lips were greased red. Compared to the drab palette of browns and grays in the dry scrubland, the women's mouths looked obscenely bright, like open wounds.

"What business is this?" Luzia asked. Ponta Fina grunted.

At Luzia's command, Baby and Maria Magra removed their gear and walked arm in arm into the widow's yard. The cangaceiras would pretend to be refugees and join the food line in order to observe the makeshift camp's workings. Baby and Maria Magra would make sure that there were no hidden soldiers and that the roadway officials weren't armed. Meanwhile, in the caatinga, Luzia assigned each of her cangaceiros a mark. During attacks, Antônio had given each man a specific task, a certain victim. Luzia marked the Widow Carvalho.

In the widow's yard, Maria Magra and Baby crossed themselves. This was the signal that it was safe to attack. Luzia whistled and Baiano led a small group of cangaceiros through the widow's front gate.

"Dirty monkeys!" they yelled. "Viva the Hawk and the Seamstress!"

Baiano fired a shot, hitting Gomes's poster. The monkeys behaved as Luzia expected them to: at the sight of Baiano and his group, the soldiers left their posts and charged the front gate. They were well trained but too eager. Luzia and the rest of the cangaceiros quickly surrounded the widow's yard, intent on performing one of Antônio's old tricks: the retroguarda. As soon as the monkeys raised their weapons, Luzia and Ponta Fina led the rest of the cangaceiros through the sides of the widow's yard, surrounding the soldiers. With a few quick shots, all four monkeys were down.

The two roadway officials also behaved as Luzia had predicted. As soon as the first shots were fired, the men squatted and clapped their hands over their heads, crushing their straw fedoras. The refugees, however, defied Luzia's expectations. During past attacks, caatinga men and women got out of the cangaceiros' way. They hid inside their houses or crouched quietly in the street, waiting for the attacks to be over. But the people in the widow's yard did not drop their tin plates and scurry away. Even after the first shots, they stayed in line. Seconds later they began pushing one another. They shoved lethargically at first, as if testing their strength. Before the cangaceiros could stop them, the mob advanced toward the porch. The Widow Carvalho swatted men and woman with a large wooden spoon. People ignored her and dunked their tins into the vat of beans. They clapped handfuls into their mouths. Brown juice ran down their faces. Others tore at the bags of farinha until white flour spilled out of them and onto the porch. Women scurried along the ground and scooped farinha into their skirts. The widow's helpers—the three hunched woman who'd distributed the food—did not step back from the chaos but began to help themselves to the widow's supplies.

"I was first! I was first!" an old man yelled, clawing his way up on the porch. A child, caught in the crush, wailed.

Luzia aimed her parabellum. She couldn't simply shoot into the air—the loud bursts of the cangaceiros' rifles hadn't startled the mob, so why would a pistol shot? She recalled her shooting lessons with Antônio, heard his voice in her ear: *If you take a shot, it can't be a useless one. Every bullet counts.* An able-bodied man stood over the vat of beans, scooping its last remnants into his mouth. Luzia aimed. She tried to shoot his arm, but because of the jostling crowd, she hit the man's chest instead. He bent forward. The people around him froze.

"Step back," Luzia yelled, her voice even and deep, like Antônio's once was. "Be calm. I'll give you food and let you keep your money. And your dignity."

The crowd stared at her, then at one another. Their faces were smeared with bean juice. Farinha was clumped between their fingers. Luzia kept her parabellum aimed. Slowly, the crowd dispersed. Canjica and Inteligente removed the dead refugee's body from the porch. Ponta Fina and Baiano bound the roadway officials' hands and feet. Luzia ordered the remaining cangaceiros to clean up the mess and organize any remaining food for distribution. When the Widow Carvalho tried to duck through her front door, Luzia grabbed her arm.

The widow's wide mouth puckered in a frown. Fine hairs darkened her upper lip. The woman's braid had come loose during the fray. With her free arm, the widow brushed gray hairs from her face.

"Where's the Hawk?" she asked.

Luzia tightened her grip around the old woman's arm. "Why?"

"I want to speak to him."

"He's busy. You're under my authority."

The widow cringed. "Then shoot me. Go ahead."

Luzia shook her head. Even with a pistol aimed at her, this woman gave orders. "I'm not a maid in your kitchen," she said. "I'll shoot you when I please."

"Fine," the widow replied. "But I don't deal with women."

Luzia laughed, startled by her own mirth. She was exhausted and hungry and afraid that once the laughter started, it would not stop. She wiped her mouth on the sleeve of her jacket, as if hoping to wipe away her smile.

"You won't be making any deals with me," Luzia replied. Then, unable to resist: "You don't trust your own kind?"

The widow sighed. "Women are mean. Especially to each other. I know because I am. You know, too."

Behind the Widow Carvalho, the group of red-lipped girls huddled together on the porch. They stared warily at the cangaceiros. The newest girl—the one the widow had chosen from the crowd before the attack—did not wear lip paint. Her mouth was dry and cracked. Two faded ribbons were tied around the ends of her braids, proof that although her hair was snarled and dusty, she'd cared for herself at some point. Or her mother had. The girl's eyes were dark brown, her lashes long. They resembled Emília's eyes, and Luzia knew that, had things been different, had she and her sister stayed in Taquaritinga, they could have become victims of this drought. Emília could have been that pigtailed girl who regarded Luzia with a frightened and angry stare, like a child who had just been hit.

"What about them?" Luzia asked.

The Widow Carvalho shrugged. "There will be a roadway construction site near here. They were going there."

"For what?"

"To work."

"What kind of work?" Luzia pressed.

The widow narrowed her eyes. "They won't be digging the road."

Luzia stared at the pigtailed girl. "What's your grace?"

"Doralinda," she mumbled. "But I'm called Dadá."

"Are you still a moça?"

The girl blushed. The Widow Carvalho laughed. "She's as pure as the drinking water. You can't find anything fresh around here anymore."

The widow eyed the cangaceiros in the yard and on the porch. She licked her lips and moved closer to Luzia.

"Each of your men can have a little time with them," the widow whispered. "I won't charge much. They'll have to stay outside, though. My house is not a harem."

Luzia let go of the woman's arm. She snatched the Widow Carvalho's money belt and coins fell onto the porch, clinking against the stone floor. When the widow moved to pick them up, Luzia held her arm.

"My husband left me nothing," the woman shrieked. "I need train fare to Recife."

"You sold your land to the roadway. Didn't Gomes pay you?"

"He gave me a promissory note. My money's in a bank in Recife. But I have to find my own way there. He sent soldiers and food, but I can't walk to the city."

"So you're selling them?" Luzia said, nodding toward the group of girls.

"We've made a trade. I give them food, they give me whatever the roadway men will pay them to go to the camps."

"They don't belong to you," Luzia said, "just because you're a colonel's wife."

"I know that. They go because they want to. I'm not pointing a gun at them."

The widow chuckled. Luzia pressed her parabellum into the old woman's neck, making her wince.

"They don't belong to you either," the Widow Carvalho hissed, her breath sour and warm. "We're no different—you and I. You'll give away this food and want something for your fine deed. I want their money. You want their allegiance. Which one of us is asking for more?"

"We're not alike," Luzia said, her mouth so close to the old widow's face she could kiss her. "You're a traitor, selling land to the roadway."

The widow shook her head. "I have every right to sell! It's my land. I can do as I please." She arched her neck, trying to face Luzia. "Why do you hate Gomes so much? He didn't cause this drought. He's sending supplies. Gomes's done more than the Blues ever did for your lot."

"My lot?" Luzia said. She pointed to the red-lipped girls. "My lot's being made to sell themselves because of that road. And those men out there are signing away their lives to work on the road for no wages. That's not fair treatment. Gomes will make us into slaves. He isn't helping us with this food. He's bribing us. I'll be the one to help my people, not him."

The widow's eyes sparkled. She spoke quietly, as if sharing a secret with Luzia. "You want to be the hero," she said. "Gomes is stealing your fire, is that it?"

The widow smiled slightly. She wasn't scared and Luzia wanted her to be. *Fear is good*, Antônio once said. *It means respect.* A burning pressure rose inside Luzia; she imagined it as being thick and dark, like beans cooked too long in their vat. Luzia felt the dark substance working inside her, burning away her stifled tears and turning them into something else, something dangerous but also useful.

The widow's dress had a double collar—one part high necked and tight, the other part opening at the collarbone into two wide flaps of embroidered black cloth. Luzia released the widow's arm and took hold of her collar. She folded over the cloth and inspected its underside. There were long, sloppy diagonals running from one design to the next; the seamstress had been too lazy to cut and knot her thread.

"This is shabby stitching," Luzia said.

The widow's expression changed from amusement to confusion. Luzia let go of her collar and faced the red-lipped girls. Some had tried to wipe away the lip grease and their chins were smeared with pink. Luzia looked above her; the poster of President Gomes—"Father of the Poor"—hung overhead, his face huge, his expression smiling and magnanimous. What must she look like, Luzia wondered, standing beneath such a large and handsome face? A starving, crippled woman? A terrible cangaceira? She stared at the crowd that surrounded the porch. Some looked at her with fear, others with doubt. The widow was right; Gomes wasn't completely evil. That's what made him dangerous. If Gomes became the people's hero, he would make the Seamstress and her cangaceiros into villains. He was already trying to do this in the papers, calling cangaceiros useless criminals. Dr. Eronildes had been right—people in the scrub had room in their hearts for only one hero. If she was to survive, Luzia would have to fight for that place.

"Look what Gomes's road will do!" she yelled. "It will make honest women into putas."

Some of the cangaceiros' eyes widened, shocked by her strong language. Some spit on the ground and cursed Gomes. Several of the refugees shook their heads, indignant. Luzia pointed to the Widow Carvalho.

"She's profiting off our misery," Luzia announced. "And Gomes is letting her—he trusted her with supplies! His soldiers sat here and let her sell our women. They turned a blind eye!"

Shouts rose from the crowd, cursing the widow. Luzia grabbed the woman and presented her to the angry mob.

"We aren't the same," she whispered into the widow's ear. "You keep their money. I'd rather have their good graces."

Luzia dug into the widow's leather money belt and found a tin of red lip grease. She opened it and dipped her finger inside. Then she swiped a red glob across the Widow Carvalho's thin mouth. The crowd laughed. Luzia raised her hand, quieting them. When they obeyed, her heart beat faster.

A mandacaru cactus grew in the center of the yard. The plant's crown had several green cylinders, like the fingers of a cupped hand. Its trunk was as brown and as thick as a tree's. Spines the size of sewing needles protruded from it.

"Now she'll know what it's like to be forced!" Luzia yelled to the crowd. "To hug and kiss what she doesn't want!"

The cangaceiros and refugees cheered. Luzia felt a strange rush—her face felt warm, as if the crowd were a fire and she was benefiting from its heat. Luzia dragged the widow off the porch and placed her in front of the mandacaru cactus.

"Hug it," Luzia said.

The widow clenched her arms to her sides. "I will not."

Luzia caught sight of the pigtailed girl on the porch and thought of Emília. What would her sister make of her actions? Luzia thought of her boy—would he be proud to have a mother who inflicted such cruel punishments? She felt the heat draining from her body. Her grip on the widow loosened, but the crowd pressed in around her.

"Hug it!" a woman cried.

"Make her hug it!" a boy called.

The crowd was impatient; Luzia could not lose face before them. If she was to beat Gomes, she would have to satisfy their sense of justice: a public crime called for a public punishment. Antônio had taught her this. In the days after his death, she'd asked him to haunt her. Now, she called on him again. Luzia put away her parabellum and removed Antônio's old punhal from her belt. She pressed it between the widow's hunched shoulder blades. The woman let out a dry yelp.

"Hug it tight," Luzia said.

The widow stared at the mandacaru cactus and slowly opened her arms. She turned her cheek and stepped forward. When she hugged the trunk she did so gingerly, her arms barely touching its spines. Luzia nodded at Baiano. On the other side of the trunk, the cangaceiro grabbed the widow's hands. He pulled her in tighter. The Widow Carvalho gasped and craned her neck backward, as if resisting an aggressive suitor's advances. Baiano tugged her again.

The mandacaru's spines punctured the widow's face. The woman shuddered. There were pinpricks of blood on her cheek. She tried to lift herself away from the needles but each time she moved, her chest pressed deeper into them. All the while, the widow stared at Luzia.

"You are an ignorant cripple," the old woman said.

Luzia recalled the teasing children and gossiping women of Taquaritinga. She recalled the name Victrola. She recalled her previous children, falling from her in pieces. She recalled the one who had lived—Expedito—only to be carried away. She thought of the hefty price on her head, of the many graves along the old cattle trail. She thought of Gomes and his roadway. It would slice the scrubland apart. Antônio had been right: the president would build despite the drought. He would make refugees into roadway workers, and women into whores. Luzia stared at those girls on the porch. They were skinny and pitiful looking, but their stares were angry, like her own. Those girls could learn to fight. They could learn to shoot. Luzia would train them and, together, they would attack the roadway and teach Gomes and the colonels and anyone else who doubted them a lesson: that the meek and the wretched of the earth could become strong.

Luzia extended her good arm and cupped the widow's head in her hand. The widow's skull felt warm. Luzia gave it a gentle push. The widow's neck stiffened. The mandacaru's thorns disappeared into the woman's face. Luzia pressed harder. A thorn pierced the widow's closed eyelid. A whimper, soft and childlike, escaped from her mouth. Luzia pressed again, then again, until the widow was quiet, until she gave no resistance. Around her, the crowd cheered.

Chapter 11

EMÍLIA

Recife
April 1933–November 1933

1

- - - - - - - -

Mrs. Haroldo Carvalho appeared on the covers of the *Diário de Pernambuco,* the *Recifian,* and even in the prestigious *Folha de São Paulo.* In all of her photographs, the Widow Carvalho angled her head to showcase the black patch over her left eye. The Seamstress had blinded her. The leather eye patch reflected the camera's flash, giving it a dull sheen. To Emília, this made the widow's patch resemble the large, dark lens of an insect, shielding not one eye but hundreds.

Emília had heard men—Dr. Duarte in particular—laugh over the incident; an old crone forced to embrace a cactus was amusing to city dwellers. Even though the widow was the subject of jokes, the Seamstress's attack was not. Cangaceiros had executed four soldiers and two roadway officials. They'd stolen government rations. They'd defiled a large poster of President Gomes. And, according to the Widow Carvalho, the Seamstress had slit a man's throat and drunk his blood, like a witch. In another newspaper interview, the widow said that the Seamstress had killed young children—babies especially—with a sharp knife. Worst of all, the cangaceira leader had taken several girls from the mob of flagelados and forced them to marry her men. Throughout Recife, people spoke of these new female bandits, holding them up as proof that the backlands was becoming lawless and depraved, a place where even women became criminals.

Newspapers clamored for interviews with the Widow Carvalho. There were dozens of flagelados who'd claimed they'd seen the Seamstress up close, but they were tenant farmers and pé-rapados, people so poor they couldn't afford shoes. The Widow Carvalho was a landowner, which made her credible. Shortly after the attack on her ranch, roadway officials visited, as scheduled, to gather new recruits from her food lines. Instead of workers, the roadway men found their recruiters and soliders massacred, and the widow tied to a cactus. They'd brought the old woman back to Recife to tell her story.

Government officials presented her with a check as payment for her land, and President Gomes sent the widow a handwritten note commending her patriotic spirit and thanking her for selling her ranch to the National Roadway Institute. All of these commendations appeared in Recife newspapers, making the widow a popular figure. Her story forced Tenente Higino to allocate more funds toward the recruitment and training of soldiers. Young flagelado men entering Recife in search of food and work found recruitment stations at the edges of the city, where they were given guns, uniforms, and the promise of a paycheck, and were immediately sent back into the scrubland to serve Brazil and President Gomes. After the Widow Carvalho's many interviews and the cangaceiros' continued attacks, people paid more attention to Dr. Duarte's theories. Emília's father-in-law appeared in the papers nearly as often as the widow herself, and his explanations about the criminal mind became widely accepted. Because of this newfound interest in his science, Dr. Duarte worked long hours in his Criminology Institute measuring craniums and attempting to find ways to catch his most coveted specimens: the Seamstress and the Hawk. Pernambucans were both outraged and enthralled by their state's famous bandit couple. And Recifians who, under different circumstances, would have considered the Widow Carvalho too coarse to keep their company, suddenly invited the old woman to lunches and afternoon coffees, wanting to hear her story firsthand in the hopes that this would bring them closer to the cangaceiros.

Members of the Ladies' Auxiliary rented out the famous Leite Restaurant and sponsored a luncheon for the Widow Carvalho. The old woman sat at the head of a long table at the restaurant's center. She wore a black dress and occasionally fingered her patch, drawing attention to her wounded eye. Waiters lingered near the table. Ladies' Auxiliary members craned their heads each time the widow spoke, but her conversation was limited.

"Pass the salt," she said. And later, "Don't you have any farinha?"

None of the widow's requests was followed by "please," or "thank you," and this bothered Emília. She sat at the middle of the table, beside the baroness and Lindalva, and barely touched her plate of codfish in cream. Emília, like the other Auxiliary women, was focused on the Widow Carvalho. The old woman sensed this and smiled as she ate. She had a small, thin-lipped mouth. *A mean mouth,* Emília thought, and watched the widow cut her meat; the old woman stabbed it so forcefully with her fork it seemed as if the steak was in danger of leaping off her plate. The old woman didn't put her napkin on her lap, and her elbows flapped wildly as she ate. Emília felt like Dona Dulce—privately chiding another's manners—and she disliked the Widow Carvalho for making her feel this way. All around her, the Auxiliary women complimented the widow and coaxed her to speak.

"They're wasting their breath," the baroness whispered. "I know her type. She'll wait until dessert to talk. Or she'll try to get another lunch out of us."

Lindalva shook her head. "If they spend another tostão on her, I'm resigning my membership."

Emília nodded. The Widow Carvalho's gory reports of her encounter with the Seamstress had displaced more important news. By April 1933, ninety thousand flagelados were housed in seven relief camps scattered throughout the Northeast. In Recife, the drought-baby adoption trend had declined as soon as the infants gained weight and lost their tragic preciousness. Recife society's grand dreams for the children's futures were forgotten. The drought babies were relegated to servants' quarters, where they would eventually be incorporated into the daily workings of large households as errand boys or maids. Lindalva was particularly frustrated because the Widow Carvalho's stories had overshadowed the upcoming election, the first in which females would be allowed to vote.

After his successful revolution, Celestino Gomes had taken the office of president by force and had appointed Green Party members to government posts across the country. Three years later, some people called his administration a dictatorship. In order to prove he was a democrat and a fair leader, Gomes called for national elections. They were scheduled for mid-May, yet only 15 percent of the women eligible to vote had registered. Lindalva wanted newspapers to publish exposés on the barriers to voter registration. Women had to take complicated literacy tests and deal with erratic registration hours; working women couldn't leave their jobs long enough to register, and wives couldn't leave their children and household duties either. Lindalva and Emília lobbied for the Ladies' Auxiliary to take a greater interest in these problems, but they were outvoted. Instead of sponsoring a campaign to promote fair registration, the Ladies' Auxiliary courted the Widow Carvalho.

Emília could never admit to Lindalva that her interest in suffrage was a selfish one: it made her appear less concerned with the Seamstress. Emília pretended to be unenthusiastic about meeting the Widow Carvalho. In truth, she barely slept the night before the luncheon. At the restaurant, Emília was aggravated by the woman's silence. Like the baroness, Emília also recognized the widow's type. Back in Taquaritinga, when she'd worked at Colonel Pereira's house, Emília had seen other colonels and their wives come and go as houseguests. The Widow Carvalho resembled the worst type of colonel's wife: eager to punish her husband and her servants; stingy with food and with praise; and outwardly pious yet always willing to gossip, to tell stories that served her purposes, even if they were lies.

Emília put down her utensils. Leaning into the table, she faced the widow.

"What did she look like?" Emília asked.

The Widow Carvalho responded with a mouth full of rice. "Who?"

"The Seamstress."

The table's occupants grew quiet. Near Emília, a waiter stopped filling water glasses. The Widow Carvalho took another forkful of food.

"Like a bandit," she said between bites. "Ugly as sin."

A twitter of laughter rose from the table. Emília stiffened.

"No one talks about the men's ugliness," she said. Her voice shook. Emília recalled Dona Dulce's many lessons on composure and how not to lose it. She took a sip of water and smiled.

"I've followed your interviews in the papers," Emília said. "You gave such detailed accounts. I wish I had your knack for observation. You saw so many things even though you were bound face-first to a cactus."

Lindalva chuckled. At the end of the table, the widow stopped eating. She studied Emília with her remaining eye. Emília smiled in response, but her palms were clammy. She and Luzia didn't look alike, but perhaps upon further inspection the widow—like Dr. Eronildes—had recognized some trait, some likeness Emília wasn't able to conceal. Emília's heart beat quickly. Why was she prodding this widow? Why was she taking such a risk? After a moment, the Widow Carvalho finally spoke.

"Have you ever seen a mandacaru, young lady?"

"Yes."

"Then you know how long and how sharp their thorns are. It doesn't matter what I saw or what I heard. What matters is, I survived. And the survivor has the right to tell whatever story she pleases."

"The papers love exaggerations," Emília replied. "They sell more because of them."

The Widow Carvalho sat back in her chair. "Do you support the cangaceiros?"

Emília balled her hands in her lap to stop them from shaking.

"No," she replied. "But I can't hold myself above them. None of us can say we don't agree with killing, because we killed for the revolution, didn't we?"

There was silence around the table. Some Ladies' Auxiliary members stared at their plates. Others looked at Emília, their mouths frozen in tight smiles but their eyes angry, like mothers too polite to openly condemn their children in public but warning them that punishment would come later. A few women looked pensive. One of these was the first to break the quiet.

"Men killed, not us," she said.

"But they were our husbands and sons," the baroness said. "And we stood by them."

A few women blushed. Whether they were afraid of the conversation or excited by it, Emília couldn't tell. At the head of the table, the Widow Carvalho took out a handkerchief and sniffled into it, bringing the group's attention back to her.

"The revolution was a noble cause," she said, patting her remaining eye and looking at Emília. "The cangaceiros kill for the fun of it. That's the difference. It's unforgivable what she did to me. She had no reason, and no remorse either."

Around the table, several Ladies' Auxiliary members nodded. The woman sitting nearest the Widow Carvalho patted her hand. Others complimented her bravery. Emília picked at her gloves. She felt an intense dislike for the widow, just as she'd disliked the girls who'd teased Luzia as a child, calling her "cripple" and "Victrola." Luzia used to attack those girls. She stomped their feet or slapped their faces, and Emília stood back and watched, mesmerized and afraid of her sister's rage. The teasing girls were hurt, but they'd deserved it, hadn't they? The sting of a slap went away. The bruise left by a punch faded with time. This schoolyard logic didn't seem to apply to the Seamstress's actions—the widow's punishment had done permanent damage. Emília had seen mandacarus up close; she'd touched their sharp spines. What kind of woman, Emília thought, would think up such a punishment? Worse, what kind would act it out? Whatever the Widow Carvalho had done wrong didn't merit the cruelty of the Seamstress's response. This knowledge made Emília keep quiet for the rest of the luncheon. Forced to endure the widow's stories, Emília drank glass after glass of coconut water so she would not speak out and embarrass herself. She left the lunch in a foul mood.

When Emília returned to the Coelho house, she went directly upstairs. She'd placed Expedito's crib in her room, beside her bed. Near the crib was a cot for the wet nurse she'd hired. The nurse was a large woman who, on her first day, immediately popped out her caramel-colored breast and fed the child in the house's foyer, in front of a horrified Dona Dulce. Emília had laughed out loud. Later, so as not to disturb her mother-in-law's sensibilities, Emília arranged a proper feeding schedule and found an embroidered cloth for the nurse to place over her chest.

She found the nurse in her room. Expedito suckled on the woman's breast, but his eyes slowly closed and his head lolled back. It was the end of his feeding and he was caught between his two greatest pleasures: sleep and food. Emília watched him. She was glad to have the wet nurse but felt sharp twinges of jealousy each time Expedito fell asleep in her arms. Emília took off her gloves and hat. She extended her hands and the wet nurse rose from her chair and handed over Expedito. When the nurse left the room, Emília pressed her face to the boy's head. His skull felt soft and malleable, like partially baked clay. Expedito's baby fat, which had been so hard for him to gain, was disappearing. At seven months, his chin and cheekbones were more defined. His neck had elongated. His arms slowly smoothed out, and the rolls of fat on his wrists—which looked as if strings had been tied around them—were disappearing. Emília worried about his ears, which were beginning to protrude. Each time she brushed Expedito's brown curls, Emília cupped her hand over his head, afraid of how it would grow, of the calculations Dr. Duarte might make.

Emília placed Expedito in his crib. She removed the tiny gold key she wore on a chain around her neck and used it to open her jewelry box. Next to the Communion portrait, stuffed beneath her pearl necklace and a ring, was Luzia's penknife. Emília inspected the knife. How would she explain its significance to Expedito?

One day, he would ask about his mother—his *real* mother. Those words made Emília angry. It was a petty, confusing anger she recalled from childhood. Luzia was the youngest and, because of this, she always got to eat chicken hearts at lunch, or sit on Aunt Sofia's lap. Luzia got horses whittled from corncobs. She got the ripest fruits. As the older, ignored sister, Emília didn't know which she wanted more: the adults' attention or her little sister's. She ended up cursing them both. When she thought of Expedito and the questions he'd eventually ask, Emília felt the same bitter mix of resentment and yearning she'd felt as a child.

Expedito had learned to say "ma-ma." Eventually, he'd want to call Emília "Mãe," and she would have to correct him. She would be "Tia Emília." She would tell him to pull up his socks, to write his alphabet and drink his cod-liver oil. Tia Emília would be a part of his daily reality, while his mother—his *real* mother—would be a part of his imagination, just as Emília's mother had been for her. Emília finally understood Aunt Sofia's burden: having to compete with an imagined mother who was always prettier, kinder, and smarter. Fantasy was always better than reality. One day, when he was old enough to keep a secret, Emília would have to tell Expedito exactly who his mother was. Even then, reality wouldn't beat out fantasy. His mother was brave, audacious, and strong. A cangaceira! What was Emília compared to this? No one called her brave.

Emília worried about Expedito's safety in the Coelho house. She sensed enemies in every room, both in the front of the house and in the back quarters. The washerwoman was loyal to Dona Dulce and sometimes did not boil Expedito's diapers, which led to rashes along his backside and thighs. The cook, bitter about having more work, sometimes hacked open old coconuts and mixed their foggy, sour contents with the rest of Expedito's coconut water. When Emília brought these things to Dona Dulce's attention, her mother-in-law expressed disbelief and reluctantly chastised the servants. Emília worried about what would happen when Expedito began to walk, to smudge and break things in Dona Dulce's pristine house. She wasn't sure what her mother-in-law was capable of; Dona Dulce often spoke of sending "that child," as she called Expedito, away to a religious academy "as soon as he learned to speak."

The day Expedito arrived, Dona Dulce had quickly declared her dislike. "I won't have another backlands beggar in my home!" she'd said. Dr. Duarte was forced to escort his family into the parlor and shut the doors.

"Emília will take care of him," Dr. Duarte had said. "Won't you?"

Emília nodded rigidly. She'd wanted to open the parlor's glass cabinets and break Dona Dulce's porcelain figurines, her ancient crystal, her precious knickknacks. Emília stayed still only because she needed her mother-in-law's acquiescence.

"I know you're a charitable woman, Mother," Degas chimed in. "We can help this boy. We'll be in the papers because of him. They've written such positive stories about me and Emília."

Dona Dulce stared helplessly at her son. Her pale lips slackened into a pout. "Fine," she said, shifting her gaze to Emília. "But he won't be a Coelho."

"Of course not, Dulce!" Dr. Duarte said. "We'll put another name on the documents."

Ever since then, Expedito had been considered a pet, a temporary distraction with no permanent claim on the Coelho legacy. Emília preferred it this way. She was responsible for Expedito's care, for his successes and his failures. On the adoption documents, she listed herself as his only guardian. She gave him her surname: dos Santos. Emília's maiden name had no distinctive roots or family legacy. It belonged to so many Northeasterners that it was untraceable.

Still, Emília worried that others would discover Expedito's origins. She avoided Dr. Duarte's study and his Criminology Institute. As Expedito grew, Emília feared her father-in-law's measuring eye. In Degas, Emília sensed greater dangers. He liked to watch Expedito crawl on the floor of Emília's bedroom. Sometimes Degas held out his hand to the boy and marveled at Expedito's strong grip. In these moments there was tenderness in Degas' voice, and his face softened into an awed, affectionate expression. Then, as if he didn't want to become too fond of the boy, Degas tugged away from Expedito and left the room.

Degas saw that Emília loved Expedito, and he used this to his advantage. During Expedito's first months in Recife, Degas made Emília accompany him to British Club luncheons and stand close to him during government-sponsored events. Emília didn't refuse Degas. She was careful not to obey him too eagerly though—that would indicate fear on her part, which would only confirm Degas' suspicions about Expedito. At any point Degas could tell Dr. Duarte or Dona Dulce that Emília's drought baby was really her nephew, and that her sister was a tall woman with a crooked arm, very much like the Seamstress.

Most often, Degas forced her to vouch for his whereabouts during the workweek. Emília often took Expedito and his nurse to the atelier. She continued to organize large donations of clothing for the flagelados. On the days when Emília worked, Degas appeared during the lunch hour. He told Emília to stay in the atelier instead of returning to the Coelho house to eat. Then he disappeared out the shop's side door. During dinner with Dr. Duarte and Dona Dulce, Degas made Emília say that they'd lunched together.

She'd followed Degas once, after he'd slipped through the shop door. Degas cocked his fedora low, shielding his face. He walked through the alleyways behind Rua Nova, crossing over the Maurício de Nassau Bridge and into the infamous Bairro Recife. Emília couldn't cross after him; only men and women "of the life" lived in the inns and gambling houses of that neighborhood. Whatever Degas' intentions were beyond that bridge, it was clever of him to escape into the Bairro Recife. If any gossips caught him there, they couldn't admit it for fear of incriminating themselves.

In her old *Fon Fons*, Emília had read about jealous wives becoming vindictive, but she knew that jealousy was often love gone awry. She and Degas had never been bound by love; they were bound by secrets. Emília believed they should not use each other's secrets as currency. She, more than anyone, knew what it meant to love a person she should not and to be made to feel ashamed of it. If Degas had simply asked her for help, Emília would have given it. But Degas never asked, he threatened. He knew who her sister was, and what it would mean to reveal that knowledge. Before, he'd threatened only Emília and she'd pitied him, knowing his manipulation was born of desperation. But now Degas threatened Expedito. This, Emília could not stomach. Each time she saw Degas at the breakfast table she felt the urge to kick his shins. She wanted to scratch his precious English-language records with her sewing needles, to spit in the tin of pomade he kept in the bathroom.

Emília understood that if she continued to live with Degas, she would be consumed by her anger and turn as bitter and sharptongued as Dona Dulce. In order to escape this fate, she envisioned a future beyond the Coelho house. Emília had always been a frugal saver. Sewing, with its measurements and pattern making, forced her to calculate numbers quickly in her head. Emília's ability with math translated to bookkeeping; she kept the ledgers for the atelier. Profits rose. At first, she and Lindalva had made only enough income to pay the rent and their seamstresses' salaries. By April 1933, Emília and Lindalva's smart suits and floral dresses were in great demand. The ink Emília used in their ledgers changed from red to green. She and Lindalva divided the profits evenly but, because of her marriage, Emília wasn't allowed to open a bank account without her husband's permission. Emília subverted this rule by filtering her earnings through Lindalva, who placed Emília's profits in a separate account for safekeeping. "Your escape fund," Lindalva called it. Emília never corrected her. And when Lindalva insisted on teaching her how to drive, Emília didn't object.

Like the Coelhos, the baroness also owned a Chrysler Imperial with large, owl-eyed headlamps and curved wheel fenders. Once a week, Emília left Expedito on the porch with the baroness and climbed into the automobile. She stepped onto the thick running board and into the driver's seat. Lindalva was a novice herself, but she instructed Emília from the passenger's side, telling her to press the clutch and brake before inserting the key. They would only go around the baroness's drive, but Emília's hands still sweated. The steering wheel felt slick. When the engine growled on, the car shook. Emília fussed with the gearshift, forcing it into first. She released the brake. Her feet barely touched the pedals—her toes strained to hold down the clutch. She pressed the accelerator. The car roared. Startled, Emília lifted her foot from the clutch. The Chrysler jerked forward. Its engine sputtered, then stalled. This happened six times before Emília learned to balance her right and left feet, removing one while slowly lowering the other. When she did this, the car floated forward.

"Oba!" Lindalva cheered.

Emília giggled. She turned the wheel to maneuver around the drive. Her foot remained planted on the accelerator and the car sped forward. Emília's heart beat wildly. It was too fast. At the next curve, she nearly nicked one of the baroness's manicured jasmine trees before she pressed her foot to the brake. The car screeched. Lindalva slid forward on the seat, clutching the dash. The Chrysler jerked and stalled again. Lindalva laughed.

"Excellent work, Mrs. Coelho," she said. Lindalva readjusted herself in the leather seat and faced Emília. "Are you going to the atelier tomorrow?"

"Yes," Emília said, wiping her hands on her dress. "We have another charity shipment to send out."

"Will you go with Degas?" Lindalva asked.

"Yes," Emília replied. "Why?"

Lindalva shifted on the seat. "I've heard talk."

"What kind of talk?"

"Oh, Emília! You of all people should know how people talk in this city. It's not the good kind."

"About Degas?" Emília asked.

"No," Lindalva continued. "About you."

"Me?"

"That you're covering for him. Encouraging him." Lindalva furrowed her plucked eyebrows. "Do you know where he goes in the afternoons?"

Emília nodded. "The Bairro Recife. I followed him once, but only to the bridge."

Lindalva sighed. She started to say something, then stopped and gripped Emília's hand. "When we met, I promised I'd speak frankly."

"So speak," Emília said.

"He meets that pilot—Chevalier. He isn't discreet about it. That's what people are saying, anyway. People have forked tongues, Emília. They talk about Degas, but they condemn you for not reining him in. It's not fair."

Emília nodded. Lindalva hugged her and they left the car. Later, as Emília rode the first-class trolley with Expedito in her lap, Lindalva's words lingered in her mind. Degas took great risks on his daily outings, yet Emília bore the brunt of the gossip. She felt a flicker of anger. She was used to being the subject of talk—she'd been gossiped about in both Taquaritinga and in Recife—but mostly as a result of her actions, not someone else's. Now it seemed Degas and the Seamstress could do whatever they pleased, while Emília was left to worry about the consequences.

The next day, when Degas told her to stay in the atelier during lunch, Emília refused. Degas didn't argue; they returned to the Coelho house where they ate alongside Dona Dulce and Dr. Duarte. During the meal, Degas brought up the Seamstress. When Dona Dulce chastised him, he changed his focus to Expedito.

"The boy's growing so quickly," he said, his gaze focused on Emília. "Father will be able to measure him soon."

Emília lost her grip on her fork. It hit a plate. The clatter reminded Emília of the hinged doors of Aunt Sofia's rat traps and how swiftly they fell once their counterweight was triggered. Her aunt refused to use poison, worried it would contaminate their food, so she used the metal traps instead and held the entire cage underwater, drowning the rats inside.

"Don't look forward to it," Emília finally said, staring at her plate. "I think you'll find he's a common boy."

"I agree," Dona Dulce said. "Common is the exact word."

Emília didn't argue with her mother-in-law. The next day, she allowed Degas to accompany her to the atelier and didn't object when he slipped out and left her to eat lunch alone, in her office. There, Emília stared at her ledgers and at the growing numbers in her bank account. She and Expedito would be gone before any measurements could be taken. They would abandon this life for another one. They would go to the South, or even abroad. Anyplace where there were no Coelhos and no cangaceiros.

2

At the end of April 1933, the Seamstress attacked two Trans-Nordestino work camps. According to newspaper reports, cangaceiros killed engineers and burned supplies and tools. They'd told the road workers—all men recruited from relief camps—either to go back to their families or join the group. Some men left with the cangaceiros; most walked back to the nearest relief camp. The workers who returned had stories about the Seamstress: she was a fine shot and she wore her hair short, like a man. From afar, the road workers couldn't tell her from the other cangaceiros, until she shouted orders. Her voice gave her away. Her height and crooked arm distinguished her from the other women in the Hawk's group. The workers confirmed that there were, in fact, several long-haired cangaceiras who fought alongside the men. According to the escaped workers, the armed women were the most violent of the bunch.

After the attack, President Gomes merged the National Mail Service and the General Telegraph Union into one government department. He required the state of Pernambuco to extend its telegraph lines. *Diário de Pernambuco* articles said that new telegraph offices would make communication along the roadway easier. Messages could be relayed to Recife in minutes. Troops could be dispersed to exact locations instead of relying on word-of-mouth reports. The new telegraph stations would connect from larger, already existing communication hubs like those in Caruaru, Rio Branco, and Garanhuns. When the new telegraph lines were installed, the Gomes government would send in recently trained telegraphers; after the Crisis, plenty of young men needed jobs. By early May, stacks of wooden posts, reams of wire, and boxes of porcelain-and-glass telegraph connectors left Recife for the interior. The supplies traveled by train and were then transferred to oxcarts in order to arrive in strategic towns throughout the backlands.

The Seamstress stopped many of these shipments. Train stations were burned. Government troops were attacked. The Hawk sent another note to the capital:

> The backlands needs dams and wells. Not machines. If I
> see another one of these telegrafs, I'll make one of your
> monkeys swallow it whole.

Emília didn't agree with the cangaceiros' fight against Gomes and the roadway, but she believed she understood their reasons. She recalled the day when her old boss, Colonel Pereira, brought his new motorcar to Taquaritinga. Some people—like Emília—had been thrilled by it. But most, including Aunt Sofia and Luzia, had stared suspiciously at the car. Later, their aunt proclaimed that the devil lay under the car's hood. Novelty was dangerous. Change was frightening, and caatinga residents didn't like being frightened. Instead of admitting their fear, they became angry. This, Emília thought, was what had happened to the Seamstress.

Coiteiros were taken into custody and questioned. During the drought, most colonels and ranchers had fled to cities like Campina Grande, Recife, and Salvador. All landowners were encouraged to pledge their loyalty to Gomes and his provisional government. To avoid the spectacle of being detained, several coiteiros appeared at the Coelho house to speak with Dr. Duarte. Most of these men wore tall rancher's boots and simple suits, the jackets cut from sturdy linen. One by one, Emília's father-in-law welcomed them into his study.

Emília wasn't allowed to sit in on these meetings. She couldn't eavesdrop from the courtyard either, because Dr. Duarte fastidiously closed all the doors to his study. The questioning of certain coiteiros was publicized but the ones who appeared at the Coelho house were strictly kept out of the newspaper; everyone knew that the Hawk and the Seamstress read the *Diário*. Once the drought ended, those colonels and ranchers who had met with Dr. Duarte would return to the countryside. Emília knew that, as former coiteiros, they would try to lure the cangaceiros back into friendship. They would try to trap them.

Ever since she'd adopted Expedito, Emília had taken the boy to as many social events as she could. Emília wore her most daring outfits: tight-fitting jackets; a dress with a revealing décolleté; a pair of boating pants. She wanted her photo in the Society Section. In each picture, she held Expedito in her arms or sat him on her lap. She would not pose for the photograph without him. Weeks before any of her charitable shipments went out, Emília mentioned it in the Society Section. She made sure the reporters included the train's name and destination in their blurbs about the shipments. When news of her clothing shipments appeared in the Society Section, the trains were never attacked. Emília sensed that the Seamstress was listening to her.

After the coiteiros began to meet with Dr. Duarte, Emília appeared at several social events. She found Society Section reporters and looped her arm around theirs. Emília kept mum on national topics but gave opinions on international ones, such as the boycott of Jewish businesses in Germany.

"I'd hate to live there!" Emília said, knowing that if she kept her voice high and her words bold, she'd surely get published. "Imagine a place where you can't tell friends from enemies! Where those who once supported you aren't allowed to anymore."

She hoped the Seamstress would heed her warnings. Emília had transformed herself into a city woman, but she still harbored a stubborn caatinga pride that made her hate trickery. Using coiteiros to trap the cangaceiros was a dishonest way to fight. At night, in her bed, Emília couldn't sleep, wondering if her warnings would cause more harm than good—wouldn't those turncoat coiteiros save innocent lives? The Seamstress was killing road workers and engineers. But the cangaceira had also given those men a choice: quit working or fight. If they chose to fight, wasn't this their folly and not the Seamstress's? Emília pushed her doubts aside and continued to appear in the papers.

Emília's quotes were published regularly because women's political opinions had become popular reading material. Each morning, Dr. Duarte chuckled as he read the *Diário*'s series: "What's on the Minds of Women Voters." Emília hated the stories they ran. "Can you imagine women's debates in choosing a candidate?" one journalist wrote. "Who is most handsome? Who wears his mustache better? When elections come, I would rather be locked up in Tamarineira Mental Hospital than be trapped in the voting booth!"

Emília was excited about voting until she read the list of candidates—all belonged to the Green Party. Elections were scheduled for May 15, 1933, and, although Gomes had promised a presidential election, Brazilians would only be allowed to choose representatives in the First National Assembly. These representatives would pick the next president—there would be no direct vote for that office. Since the Green Party dominated the ballots, elected representatives would surely pick Celestino Gomes. There were no other presidential candidates.

Before voting day, there were Green Party parades and rallies. Rows of uniformed schoolgirls—their hair tightly braided and tied with green ribbons—walked in neat lines, carrying banners scrawled with the words "Female Voters of Tomorrow!" Recife's department stores advertised sales for registered voters. The Justiça Eleitoral took over abandoned buildings and made them voting centers, complete with curtained areas for voters to fill out their secret ballots.

On election day, Emília wore a tapered mermaid skirt and a crisply ironed blouse. On her head, she wore the fez that Lindalva had brought back from Europe. The hat was made of waffled brown fabric; Dona Dulce shook her head when she saw it. Dr. Duarte had instructed the other Coelhos to look "snappy" on election day because there would be photographers at the main voting station, near the Saint Isabel Theater. Despite the election code's literacy requirements, President Gomes stressed the idea of a popular vote, so the Coelhos could not arrive at the voting station in their Chrysler Imperial. They, like other Green Party families, were encouraged to arrive on foot. Dr. Duarte instructed Degas to park the car in front of Emília's atelier. From there, the Coelhos would walk arm in arm to the voting station.

When they stepped from the car, Degas and Dr. Duarte lingered near the atelier's door. Dona Dulce crossed her arms and tapped a foot. Emília was also impatient to vote and go home; she didn't like leaving Expedito and his wet nurse alone with the Coelho maids.

The atelier was closed, the seamstresses given the day off. Dr. Duarte walked the perimeter of the building. Degas followed his father closely, pointing at the atelier and speaking in a low voice. Emília couldn't decipher his words. She stepped away from the car to better hear her husband. Before she'd moved a meter, Dona Dulce clamped her arm.

"Let them be," her mother-in-law said. "You take too much of his father's attention."

As Degas spoke, Dr. Duarte turned toward him. His eyes widened, as if Degas had surprised him. Dr. Duarte clapped his son on the back.

"Brilliant!" he proclaimed.

Degas blushed. Dr. Duarte held his son's shoulders.

"You see," he said, his voice loud and excited. "You've exercised discipline these past years, Degas, and it's paid off. It's strengthened your mind!"

Dr. Duarte shuffled toward Dona Dulce and Emília. "Come

along!" he said, waving Degas forward. "We'll go over details later. We can't be late to the polls."

Dr. Duarte took his wife's hand. Degas threaded his arm through Emília's.

"What's happened?" she asked.

Degas didn't meet her eye. He walked quickly, trying to catch up with his parents. The street was crowded. Vendors catered to the throngs of well-dressed voters. There were paper fans and green flags for sale. Drink stands sold sugarcane juice in order to give voters "energy at the polls!" In the distance, drums thumped ferociously and trumpets followed their fast-paced beat, playing the national anthem.

"I gave him an idea," Degas finally replied.

Emília tripped over a cobblestone. One of her shoes—high heels with peep toes that Dona Dulce deemed unhygienic—gave way. Her ankle bent unnaturally. Emília felt a sharp pain. She wobbled and Degas caught her. He circled an arm about her waist and Emília pressed into him, her chest against his. A passerby whistled, as if catching them in an illicit embrace. Degas quickly loosened his grip, making Emília step firmly on her injured foot. She winced. Ahead of them, Dr. Duarte and Dona Dulce disappeared into the crowd.

"Father will wrap it," Degas said, staring at her ankle. "After we've finished voting."

"Go ahead without me," Emília replied. "My vote won't matter. It's only for show."

"Now you don't want to vote!" Degas laughed. "That child's made you a different woman."

"It has nothing to do with him."

"Your priorities have changed," Degas said, his arm still around her waist. "I understand that."

Emília stared at her husband. His cheeks were flushed.

"What idea did you have, back at the atelier?" Emília asked.

Degas sighed. "I shared it with Father first," he said. "I knew you would understand that."

Emília took a deep breath. Her ankle throbbed.

"They're looking for a better means of shipping supplies into the countryside," Degas continued. "So they won't be attacked and stolen."

"What kinds of supplies?" Emília asked.

"Guns. Bullets. Things the cangaceiros shouldn't get their hands on."

"And?" Emília said.

"The Seamstress doesn't attack your charitable shipments," Degas replied. "You appear in the papers, announce the destination, and the items on that train always arrive safely."

"Those trains carry relief supplies," Emília said. "The cangaceiros know that. They respect charity."

"Exactly. That's what I told Father."

"Why?"

"We'll use it to our advantage," Degas said. "We'll wrap munitions in your charity clothes. They'll reach the camps and be distributed to troops. If soldiers have new weapons, the cangaceiros won't last."

Emília loosened her grip on his arm. She stood on her own. A shooting pain rose up her calf. Her ankle was thick, the skin swelling over the side of her shoe.

"I'm not sending any more shipments," she said. "Lindalva and I have decided. We've sent enough."

"If this idea works, Emília, I'll get the credit. Do you understand? People will believe I'm capable. They'll forget . . . everything else."

"You want to use me. Like always."

"No. I want your help."

"What if I don't?"

The crowd of voters pushed Emília and Degas, impatient with their stopping. Degas wrapped his arm about Emília's waist and lifted her roughly. She limped beside her husband, out of the crowd's way.

"Nothing is easy with you!" Degas hissed, letting Emília go. He closed his eyes and kneaded his face with his hands. "You . . . everyone . . . make me into a person I don't want to be. I like that boy. It would hurt me to tell Father who he is. I don't want to do that."

"Then don't," Emília said.

"I'm not a villain, Emília," Degas said. "She is. She's a criminal. She's killed many people. Don't forget that."

"I never do," Emília replied. "Don't punish Expedito for it."

"He'll be safer when she's caught," Degas said. "When he grows, if his cranium is malformed, who will protect him? The more Father respects me, the better chance that child has. Do you think Father or Mother will send a drought baby to a decent school? You know they won't. You know they expect him to be a gardener, or some sort of helper around the house. If this shipment plan works, Father will give me part of the business. We'll be able to afford our own house. I can have privacy. You can give that boy whatever he needs. We can leave him a legacy."

In the distance, the band stopped playing. Emília heard cheers; the polls were open. She experienced the same feelings she'd had years earlier, so many Carnavals ago, when Degas had placed the ether-soaked handkerchief over her nose and mouth—she was dizzy, confused, unsure of the words she'd heard. She only knew that she had to make a choice: doom her sister, or doom Expedito.

"His skull is normal," she said. "You can't prove a thing."

"No," Degas replied. "I can't. But Dr. Eronildes can. That doctor hasn't been detained because he's serving in the camps. Once the drought's over, Father will pressure him to talk. You know how persuasive Father is. If Dr. Eronildes is fragile, he'll buckle and we'll have to defend the child and ourselves. The more we pursue the Seamstress now, the less trouble we'll have later."

Degas turned his gaze toward the street. "This wouldn't have happened if you'd left the boy. You had no obligation to him. You were inviting trouble."

"And you? What are you inviting?" Emília said. "I know why you cross that bridge every day."

Degas looked at her, his eyes wide. He slumped against the shop's window.

"I'm sorry, Emília, but there's no choice now. Father's excited. You'll make another shipment whether you want to or not. We're all forced to do things we don't like."

They walked slowly toward the voting station. Emília's ankle throbbed, the blood pounding beneath its skin. Each time she wobbled, Degas tried to prop her up but she refused his help, pushing his hands away. The voting station was crowded with government officials, reporters, and most of Recife's female voters.

"Ladies first!" Tenente Higino announced. The crowd laughed and cheered. Emília limped toward the curtained voting booths. In the center of the room sat the steel urna where completed ballots were deposited. In the voting booths were a stack of ballots and a cup of pencils. Emília fingered a pencil's perfectly sharpened point. When she made dress patterns she liked her pencils this way; they made nice, even lines. If she made a mistake, she could always erase it. Ballots, she thought, shouldn't be in pencil; the government should provide stamps or ink pens. But in an election without competition, there would be nothing on the ballots worth erasing. Emília closed her booth's curtain. She hadn't followed Lindalva's example—Emília had registered to vote despite the election's limited candidates. Now she regretted it. She wished she'd stayed at the baroness's house in protest. She stared at the ballot and its candidates, all of them Gomes men. Emília checked random boxes, knowing her choice didn't matter.

3

In July 1933 the newly elected First National Assembly appointed Celestino Gomes to serve another term as president of the republic. For weeks after the appointment, troops in the Northeast complained about the endless drought and about their pursuit of the Hawk and the Seamstress.

"The cangaceiros have food and women," one soldier said to a *Diário* reporter. "Those girls—the cangaceiras—are so young, like little lambs! When we find their abandoned camps, I swear, I can smell the girls who were there. We soldiers have nothing but empty stomachs, torn clothes, and late salaries. We're like animals abandoned by fortune."

Dr. Duarte countered reports of the cangaceiros' dominance by insisting that the government could not abandon the backlands; this would only allow the cangaceiros to gain favor in residents' hearts. Roadway jobs, telegraph stations, new schools, and charitable efforts by private citizens—like Emília's clothing shipments—showed backlanders that the capital had not forgotten them during the drought.

Emília and her seamstresses continued to make clothes for the drought victims. Once a month, a team of movers hauled the crates of clothing to a government warehouse. Emília insisted on accompanying Degas and Dr. Duarte to this secret depot. There, she watched workers repack her charity shipments. Guns and ammunition were tucked between the tunics, trousers, skirts, and baby jumpers. There were new Winchester rifles, a German shipment of Mauser pistols, and several Brownings, all meant to replace the troops' ancient and clunky rifles.

Because the cargo bore Emília's name, it wasn't attacked. One week before the first gun shipment left Recife on a Great Western train, Emília appeared in the Society Section announcing her charity shipment's departure. Emília had stopped seeking reporters' attention but, during social events, Degas dragged the men to her. In her most unenthusiastic voice, Emília told reporters about her charity work. She did not smile in photographs and she'd stopped bringing Expedito to events, hoping his absence would create suspicion in the Seamstress's mind.

Expedito learned to walk with firm steps, pounding his tiny feet into the floor. He tried to pick up the jaboti turtles, grabbing the lips of their shells and heaving the animals into his arms. He liked to creep into the kitchen and hide in the pantry. At first, the Coelho maids screamed in fright when they found him there, in the darkness, his eyes wide and shining. Slowly, they got used to his presence. They grew to like it. When Dona Dulce wasn't looking, the maids slipped Expedito bites of cake or spoonfuls of jam. *Miss Emília's boy,* they called him at first, but soon Dr. Duarte gave him a nickname that stuck.

"Where did he get such seriousness?" Dr. Duarte laughed. "He looks like a colonel. I'm waiting for him to put a pipe in his mouth and denounce the government!"

After that, everyone called him Colonel, except for Dona Dulce; she had her own names for Expedito. She called him a "little barbarian," and a "terror." He left fingerprints on her varnished tables and glass cabinets. He secretly plucked the stuffing from her throw pillows and hid it in the courtyard.

He was quiet but not timid. When visitors coddled him or pinched his cheek, he stared sternly at them and walked away, to Emília. "How sweet," the uneasy visitor often said, "he's shy." But it wasn't shyness. Expedito never stood behind Emília. He never sought protection in her skirts. He stood beside her, clasping her fingers tightly in his small hand.

Dr. Duarte admired the boy's pluck, his quiet assertiveness. Each week, he took the Colonel to the Madalena Bird Fair and laughed as Expedito poked his fingers through the cages or fed banana slices directly into a parrot's beak. Emília worried constantly. She feared the fair's birds would peck Expedito's hands, or the jaboti turtles would snap at his fingers.

His eyes were dark brown with streaks of green in them. His jaw was square and set. He rarely smiled. Even when Dr. Duarte gave him a stuffed toy or a model plane, Expedito stayed serious. Only when Emília squealed at the touch of the jaboti turtles that he plopped in her lap, or when she tickled him before bed, did Expedito smile. Those smiles—so sweet and rare—were like gifts. Like secrets shared between them.

The first shipment of guns bore no results. After the second shipment, however, the Coelhos received a late-night phone call. Emília heard the distant ringing, but didn't wake until she heard Dr. Duarte in the hallway, pounding on Degas' bedroom door.

"Wake up!" her father-in-law called.

Expedito shifted in his crib. Emília quickly rose and opened her door. Dr. Duarte paced the hallway, his white hair tousled, his dress shirt untucked. When Degas finally opened his door, Dr. Duarte skittered toward it.

"Get dressed," he ordered breathlessly. "Drive me to the Criminology Institute."

"Why?" Degas asked.

Dr. Duarte waved his arms. "I don't trust my night vision, and I'm too anxious to heed road signs."

"What's so urgent?" Degas persisted.

"A specimen is what!" Dr. Duarte said. "There was a skirmish, a roadway attack. The troops won and brought one back for me."

"One what?"

"A cangaceira!" Dr. Duarte yelled.

Emília held the doorknob. Her knees wobbled and she felt like Expedito's wood-and-string dolls, whose legs gave out at the press of a button. Behind her, she heard the boy moving in his crib. From the hall she heard the faraway scream of a kettle.

"Your mother's making coffee," Dr. Duarte said. "Hurry along."

Degas stared across the dimly lit hall. He caught sight of Emília.

"A living specimen?" he asked, turning to his father.

Dr. Duarte shook his head. "I've begged those troop captains to hold a living one for me, but it's futile. You think they listen to my telegrams? They're half mad themselves with hunger and envy. They've sent a cranium. At least they had the sense to preserve it in a kerosene tin, otherwise it would be unrecognizable."

"Whose is it?" Degas asked, glancing again at Emília.

"I don't know!" Dr. Duarte said. "That's why I'm in a rush."

He followed Degas' gaze and looked over his shoulder, at Emília. Seeing her, Dr. Duarte smiled.

"I'm sorry to wake you," he said. "Business matters."

Emília held so tightly to the doorknob that her hand cramped. She knew she had to smile back, to accept her father-in-law's apology and insist she hadn't been disturbed, but Emília's face felt rigid, her mouth unable to open. Only her hands seemed to work; they slammed the bedroom door shut.

Emília heard the front gate creak open and the Chrysler's engine sputter. Her stomach knotted and cramped. She wanted a cup of water or chamomile tea, but she couldn't face Dona Dulce in the kitchen. She stayed in her room, staring at Expedito in his crib. For a few minutes the boy stared back, then he fell asleep again.

Hours later Emília heard the car return. She left her room and waited in the dark hallway. Degas padded up the stairs. When he saw Emília in her white nightgown, he jumped.

"Osh!" he cried. "You scared me."

Emília's mouth felt dry. If she spoke, she would ask only one question, and she was afraid of Degas' answer. Afraid, also, of what her hands might do to him in response. Degas shook his head.

"It wasn't her," he said

Emília closed her eyes. "How do you know?"

"The soldiers sent a note along. And the head was too small. None of the features matched the photograph."

"Who was it then?"

"I don't know. A girl. One of the wives."

Emília covered her face with her hands. She was relieved but also unsettled. She imagined the Mermaid Girl, forever trapped in a glass jar. The guns that had killed that young cangaceira were the same ones Emília had allowed into her charitable shipments. Degas tentatively patted her arm.

"They bring it upon themselves, Emília. It's not my fault. It's not yours."

Emília returned to her room. There, she lifted Expedito from his crib and into her bed. She examined his tiny, clenched fists; his long eyelashes; his soft feet.

There would be more gun shipments hidden in the folds of Emília's charity clothes, and afterward, more specimens brought back to the coast. Emília would have to stand in that dark hallway again and again, waiting for Degas to tell her if Dr. Duarte had received his prize specimen. Emília felt a pinch between her eyes. Her throat tightened. She hated that Seamstress! Why didn't the woman heed her warnings, give up, and disappear into the caatinga? Instead the Seamstress fought, making more headlines and making Emília's secret more serious. If she wasn't careful, or if Degas decided to open his mouth, Expedito himself could become a specimen. But if the Seamstress was caught, then the road could be finished, news reports would dwindle, and the cangaceiros would be forgotten. It would be better for all of them if the Seamstress died.

Emília covered her eyes. She tried to breathe through her mouth, to muffle the gurgles of her clogged nose. Despite her efforts to stay quiet, Expedito woke. He stared at her with the expression children use when they see an adult crying—a mix of confusion, worry, and reproach. In that moment, Emília saw Luzia staring at her from across their pedal-operated Singers, chastising her for passing notes to Professor Célio. She pressed her hand to Expedito's face.

The Seamstress was a criminal, but somewhere inside that woman was Luzia. And Luzia had sent Emília this boy, the greatest gift she'd ever received. Her sister had trusted Emília not only with Expedito's life but also with his memories. Emília would shape his idea of his real mother. And the way Emília remembered her was not as a cangaceira, but as Luzia: tall, long-haired, and proud. Awkwardly dancing alone in their childhood bedroom. Feeding the guinea hens in Aunt Sofia's yard. Praying in her saints' closet.

Emília couldn't prevent those armed charity shipments, but she could continue her subtle warnings. She would even offer clearer messages, if given the chance. If she didn't try to warn her sister, then she would be helping Dr. Duarte get his specimen. And when it came time to tell Expedito about his mother's death, how could Emília face him? How could she explain that she'd helped doom Luzia?

Chapter 12

LUZIA

Caatinga scrubland, Pernambuco
November 1933–August 1934

1

Necks were like the branches of caatinga trees: thin but tough. There were tendons, muscles, vertebrae, and other sinewy structures that made the cutting difficult. There were differences in men, too. Some necks were thicker than others. Luzia found herself evaluating men by their necks: which would be hard to slice, which would be easy. These thoughts came so naturally they scared her at first, and she had to focus on the fact that if Gomes's soldiers caught her they would take her head. In fact, they'd do worse—they'd disgrace her first. And they would be rewarded for their efforts; Gomes offered a hefty price for the Seamstress's skull. Tenente Higino also gave soldiers an incentive: any man who caught a cangaceiro or cangaceira could loot whatever was found on the bodies. Luzia found a letter of thanks printed in the *Diário*. It was from a soldier who'd recently shot one of her men.

"I've got plenty of gold necklaces and rings for my wife and daughters," the soldier wrote. "Praise God and Gomes! I found enough money in the thief's bornal to fix my mother's house!"

Because of this, Luzia enforced a new rule among her group: any soldiers who were caught, even dead ones, would have their heads removed and their possessions looted.

"Gomes can't boss us," Luzia told her cangaceiros after each raid. "We are our own masters."

At night, when she couldn't sleep, she recalled the bulandeiras of cotton. Before the drought, those mills worked at a breakneck pace, each operated by two strong mules. The animals were hitched to the mill wheel and they moved in great circles, pulling the wheel round and round. At the end of the day, the mules couldn't stop their circles. They were addled by the turning of the wheel, by the circular motion of the mill, and they bucked when workers tried to unhitch them. The mules became their own masters. Trapped by their own desperate need to keep going, they worked until they fell down dead.

Luzia understood those animals. Roadway raids led to newspaper articles, which led to a higher value on the cangaceiros' heads, which led to more monkeys sent into the scrub, which made the cangaceiros indignant and led to more raids. The Seamstress and her cangaceiros were caught in a great circle of their own making, and they would push themselves until death.

Each cangaceiro head that Gomes's soldiers removed supposedly belonged to either the Hawk or the Seamstress. Until the craniums arrived in Recife, bobbing in kerosene tins, and the skull scientists there declared the specimens belonged to other, unknown cangaceiros. Or until Luzia sent a telegram to the capital after an unsuccessful roadway attack or relief-camp raid and proved her existence. The telegrams were signed, "Captain Antônio Teixeira and Wife." Each time officials tried to confirm who had sent the messages, they could not. The telegraph stations had been burned; the telegraphers trapped inside.

In those telegraph stations and in the roadway camps and trains the cangaceiros looted, Luzia found newspapers. The latest *Diário* headline read:

Captured!
The Hawk Caught at Last!

Luzia found a photograph on the second page, with a warning above it advising ladies not to look. There was a wooden ammunition box and around it, a pile of half-moon hats and embroidered bornais. On top of the box, set in a neat row, were heads. Their hair was wild and long. Their faces looked fatter, the jowls loosened and spread without necks to hold them. Their mouths were open and their eyes closed, as if in a deep sleep. Only Little Ear's eyes were partially open, as if he'd blinked during the photograph. The craniums were taken to Recife, the paper said, to the Criminology Institute where they would be measured and studied. Little Ear had pretended to be the Hawk and he'd paid for his charade. Luzia cut out the photograph and slipped it into her bornal for later use. She would have to prove Gomes's skull scientists wrong; the Hawk was not dead and neither was the Seamstress.

At the roadway camp near Rio Branco, workers were separated into three crews: one to hack trees and cacti, one to pull out the trunks, and one to pound the earth flat. Oxen pulled carts over the flattened dirt, their hooves crushing rocks and making it even flatter. Each time she saw the land wiped bare, Luzia felt heaviness in her stomach. She felt as if those uprooted trees, those rocks, those hacked agave spears had all settled within her, weighing her down with their deaths. She understood Antônio's love for the scrubland: the birds, the sands, the rocks, the cacti, and the secret springs didn't look to the Seamstress for guidance or leadership. The caatinga asked nothing of Luzia. And Gomes with his roadway wanted to take this, her only comfort.

Near the construction site were rows of workers' tents. The arrangement resembled Gomes's relief camps except that there were no children or wives. Guarding the roadway camp was a pack of skinny dogs chained to scrub trees. The mutts sniffed the air. Luzia and her group crouched downwind, so the breeze wouldn't carry their scent to the dogs. Luzia watched the camp through Antônio's old binoculars. Near her, Ponta Fina peered through a German spyglass he'd taken from a roadway engineer months before. Behind them, the other cangaceiros waited.

Clouds of dust rose from the worksite. The roadway men were coated with this dirt, making their skin gray and dull, like stone. At dusk, a foreman stopped the roadwork with a whistle. Oxen were freed from their tethers and drank water from shallow bowls. Men moved slowly back to their tents. Instead of carrying shovels or hoes, some workers carried guns. Gomes's new monkeys weren't clueless city boys unaccustomed to the scrub's heat and vegetation. These new soldiers were former residents of the scrub who understood how to fight and how to hide in the caatinga. Instead of wearing the green uniforms that were so easily spotted in the dry scrub, the former flagelados dressed like road workers.

Luzia and her cangaceiros also wore more humble uniforms, but not by choice. During the drought, they'd traded their sewing machines for food. They didn't have the energy to carry such things and didn't have the time for embroidery. Their uniforms were stained and threadbare. The appliqués and fine stitching had faded. Their jewelry was dented and dull. The cangaceiros' gold saints' medallions were sacred, and could not be traded or sold. The rings, watches, and other jewelry they'd stolen over the years were considered worthless during the drought—people in the caatinga wanted useful things like knives, hats, shoes, and sewing machines. Only Gomes's soldiers coveted the cangaceiros' jewelry.

Their poor appearance didn't matter, Luzia told her men. Fine suits and polished sandals weren't what the cangaço was about. She often heard Antônio's voice—smooth and confident—in her ear and repeated all of the things he'd told her. The cangaço was about freedom. It was about dignity. The roadway was like a fence, like a giant corral that the city and Gomes would use to herd them. They were cangaceiros, not cattle.

These were the kinds of things Luzia told her group before a raid, though she knew such speeches weren't necessary; her men and women would attack without motivation or coaxing. They wanted to fight, and so did she.

As she looked at those road workers and poorly disguised soldiers, Luzia's fingers itched. Her ears rang. Her pulse quickened.

Before her first raids, she stoked her temper by thinking of Antônio's death and her son's absence. She thought of Gomes. She thought of city people, who claimed to be civilized and proper yet coveted the *Diário*'s gory reports. Cangaceiros who removed soldiers' heads were called brutes, but soldiers who cut off cangaceiros' heads were called patriots and scientists. Now, before a raid, Luzia didn't have to dig up anger. It already existed. Her dislike of Gomes, of the roadway, of soldiers, of the city, of the drought and all things outside her cangaceiros and her caatinga had grown as quickly and stealthily as a scrub cashew. The tree's crown and trunk were deceptively small, but its roots were thick and deep, thriving more underground than at the surface. Before she could control it, Luzia's dislike had penetrated as deeply as those cashew roots. It turned to hate. She tasted it in her mouth, like salt, making the sides of her tongue tingle. Luzia put down her binoculars.

"It's time," she whispered to Baby and Maria Magra.

The two women were her best cangaceiras. They'd put on simple dresses and taken off their holsters. Concealed under their clothes were peixeira knives, the blades tucked snugly into their armpits. Baby and Maria Magra knelt for Luzia's blessing. She pressed her fingers to their foreheads and made the sign of the cross.

"I seal you," Luzia said.

After this, the women rose and walked into the scrub. They hiked upwind of the roadway camp. The guard dogs barked. While Baby and Maria Magra's scent distracted the dogs, Luzia's group edged toward the camp.

With the two women's arrival, the roadway soldiers shouted. Baby and Maria Magra lifted their hands.

"We want work!" Baby shouted.

Two soldiers lumbered toward her, moving gingerly, as if their feet were burnt. This was why Luzia attacked at dusk: the road workers and soldiers were tired after a day of labor under the scrub's sun. Fatigue made the men's reflexes slow, their senses dull. Luzia, Ponta Fina, Baiano, and the rest of the cangaceiros—thirty in all— crouched and moved quietly toward the camp. Luzia could smell the oxen's fresh dung. She could hear the soldiers question her cangaceiras.

"What kind of work you looking for?"

Baby smiled, flashing her small brown teeth. "Whatever kind suits a woman."

Road workers peered from their tents. A few women already employed at the work camp moved toward the visitors and eyed their competition. The soldier began to reply to Baby but stopped. He stared into the scrub.

"Where'd you come from?" he said, raising his rifle. "You're not carrying water, or food."

Maria Magra undid the top button of her dress. Before the soldier could aim his gun, she reached under the dress collar and stepped forward. Baby followed suit. The soldiers had no time to shout or to run. In fact, it looked as if the women visitors had embraced the men. They stood, surprised and motionless, until one soldier grabbed his belly. Baby stepped back. A knife handle protruded from the man's midsection. She'd done as Luzia and Baiano had taught her, raking her knife through his belly in a *z* shape, ensuring death. Baby and Maria Magra grabbed the soldiers' weapons. Near them, a road worker shouted and more soldiers moved toward the women. Luzia aimed her rifle and fired.

Some women stood back during attacks, camouflaging themselves like scrub moths against the trees. Others learned to shoot and stab. These fought alongside Luzia and their husbands. The women attacked without showmanship or flourishes. They aimed for the head. They bit soldiers' hands to force them to release their pistols. The women attacked quietly and efficiently, with the same cool detachment they'd shown in their former lives when ringing the necks of chickens or slicing off the heads of goats, innately understanding that such tasks were grim but also necessary for their survival.

Luzia understood this brutality. She felt it in herself. Men could boast and joke during attacks because they faced only death—the soldiers wanted their heads and nothing else. With the cangaceiras it was different. If caught they faced disgrace, violation, and then, if they were lucky, death would come. The women fought with this in mind.

Road workers scattered. Startled by the loud popping of gunshots, oxen bucked and reared, breaking free from their tethers. The animals weren't used to running and they moved awkwardly. Some fell and, unable to lift their bulky bodies, crushed tents and the men hiding inside them. Worried for her own men, Luzia aimed for the animals' heads. When she shot, she thought of eating meat again, of oxtail and grilled flank. Her stomach growled.

"Witch! Snake!" a voice called behind her.

Luzia turned. She saw a man through the great clouds of dust and smoke. He was armed with a shovel and ready to strike. Instead, he stared.

Antônio had taught her that a man's reputation was his greatest weapon. A fine gun or the sharpest punhal was useless in the hands of a man of no repute. It was the opponents' fear, their awe, that saved you. It made their hands tremble, ruining their aim. It made their palms sweat, loosening their grips on their knives. It made them curious, wanting to catch a glimpse of the Seamstress before they attacked her. This gave Luzia time to shoot first.

2

If a raid was unsuccessful—if they were ambushed or chased off by monkeys—the cangaceiros felt ashamed and angry. Luzia didn't need to motivate them to attack another highway outpost or telegraph station; the men and women instinctively wanted revenge. But after a successful raid, once the exhilaration of fighting had worn off, the cangaceiros' bodies began to tell them that they were tired, hungry, injured.

Despite their fatigue, they had to pick the sites clean, lifting soldiers' bodies to remove guns and ammunition, searching through bags and barrels for food. There was no excitement in this, no righteousness. The cangaceiros were like vultures, dependent on the dead for their survival.

Luzia walked through the roadway camp, stepping over broken

tents and bodies. Her eyes watered from smoke. She blinked and adjusted her spectacles. Small fires glowed around the camp; blood would attract flies, vultures, all kinds of scrub pests and predators. The fires would deter them until the cangaceiros finished their work. The men and women moved quickly, stripping corpses of their hats and clothes. Inteligente tried on a soldier's alpercatas, tugging them onto his massive feet. Near him, old Canjica sliced open the dead oxen. The meat shone in the firelight. A dark pool accumulated beneath the animals. Canjica sweated as he butchered, removing oily hunks of fat and handing them to Sabiá, who distributed the lard among the wounded cangaceiros. They would use the fat to draw out any bullets lodged beneath the skin. Ponta Fina had already replenished his medical bag with the camp's supplies of iodine and mercurochrome, gauze and needles. There were no fatalities among Luzia's group, only a few wounded, but these had large and gaping bullet holes. One cangaceira had lost two fingers. The wounded would have to rest after leaving the roadway camp. Luzia and Ponta Fina would sew up the lesions and use Antônio's old remedies to prevent infection. They would search for bark and make poultices. If the wounds didn't heal this way, they would have to call upon Dr. Eronildes.

Luzia's foot caught. She looked down and saw an arm bent at an unnatural angle, the hand at its end closed in a fist. There was a body beside it. Luzia leaned down. Half of the face was coated with sand, which sparkled in the firelight. The other half was clean. His eyes were wide as if, even in death, he feared the Seamstress. His lips were open. There was no hair on his chin or his cheeks; he was twelve or thirteen years old at most. Luzia pressed her hand against his chin, closing his mouth. She thought of Expedito.

Luzia carried an envelope at the bottom of her bornal. Inside was a collection of photographs torn from the *Diário*: Emília with a bundle in her arms; Emília with a fat, dark-eyed infant on her hip; and later, Emília standing beside a boy dressed in tiny suits, like a little man. He gripped Emília's hand and frowned at the camera. Luzia allowed herself to look at the photos only once, the moment she found them, and never again. She put the pictures out of her mind. Sometimes though, when she reached into her bornal to retrieve a bit of food or Antônio's old binoculars, her fingers brushed against the envelope and Luzia felt a cramp in her stomach, like a cold hand gripping her insides.

Lately there had been no photos of him in the Society Section. Emília always appeared alone and stared smugly into the camera. She announced the departure of her charity shipments into the scrubland. Luzia understood her sister's message: Emília had done Luzia a great favor and she wanted protection in return. Luzia respected favors—her survival was based on them—and she followed Emília's wishes. She did not touch the charity shipments in the hopes that, in gratitude, Emília would photograph Expedito again. Luzia hadn't expected such mercenary behavior from her sister and she felt angry at Mrs. Degas Coelho for her stinginess. But Luzia was also thankful. Perhaps, she thought, it was better not knowing or seeing what her boy had become.

She didn't want to know about the dead boy before her either. She stopped herself from wondering about his name, his age, his likes and dislikes, and what had brought him to work on the roadway. He had no life before that life, the one he had chosen as a soldier. His choice had damned him. Luzia took his guns.

There were two: a black Browning pistol with a wide grip, and a long, shining Winchester armed with bullets Luzia had never seen before. Their tips were extremely thin and pointed, while their ends were thick and blunt.

"Those'll burst in a man. Tear away his insides," Baiano said. He stood near her, his expression pained, his arm in a sling. Ponta Fina was beside him.

"New guns," Luzia said. "All new guns. Bullets, too."

"Where're they getting them?" Ponta Fina said. "That's what we need to know."

"From Recife," Baiano said. "Maybe they get them as recruits. Leave the city with them in hand."

Luzia shook her head. "That's not in the papers. In the pictures the recruits leave clean—they've got uniforms and food, that's all.

Gomes won't give them guns in the beginning, so they won't be tempted to run off and join us. They give the guns to them here, when they're already stuck in the camps."

Ponta Fina sighed. "They're not on supply trains. We know that."

Luzia nodded. They'd attacked several supply trains and hadn't found weapons in any of them.

"It could be a colonel," Baiano said.

"How?" Ponta snapped. "We would've seen the distribution. We would've gotten word. They're getting these guns from the coast. They're not growing them on trees."

"If they are growing, I want that seed," Luzia said and smiled.

Ponta Fina shook his head. "Those charity trains give me an uneasiness."

"Do they?" Luzia said. "Why? You want new clothes?"

"Mãe," Ponta said, his voice urgent, "we've robbed everything: telegraph shipments, supply trains, colonels. Why not those charity loads? Just one, just to see what we find."

"We won't find anything."

"Are you sure?"

"Are you doubting me?"

Ponta and Baiano stared at her. During the drought, they were forced to let their beards grow because there was no water to shave with. The men scratched at their faces and necks, itching the bristly hairs that appeared. Soon, thick and tangled beards clumped with dust hid the men's faces. They looked wild and unkempt. Antônio wouldn't have approved but Luzia liked them this way; the men looked fearsome.

"I just don't like this," Ponta Fina said, pointing to the new guns. "Pardon, Mãe, but I don't feel right. Something about those charity trains doesn't feel right."

"Those shipments are for people we want on our side—our people," Luzia said. "If we stop them, we'll look like criminosos. Gomes wants that."

Ponta shook his head. "We stopped the food trains. No one

complained, seeing that we gave out the food onboard. We can do that with the clothes. We're not stopping the trains to steal, just to look."

"No," Luzia said. The heaviness in her stomach increased. "I have my reasons."

"Are they good ones?" Ponta said.

Luzia closed her eyes. "We don't always understand the things God does, or the saints, but we trust in them."

"We aren't God, Mãe," Ponta Fina whispered. "We can't see like He sees."

He was too polite to challenge her directly; he made her folly a collective one. Ponta's "we" really meant "you." *You aren't God. You can't see like he sees.* His words made her angry. There was a strategic purpose behind ignoring the charity shipments, but Luzia's reasons were also selfish. Did Ponta suspect this? Did he believe that she was putting them at risk to satisfy a personal favor, ensuring her son's safety by appeasing Emília? Luzia was ashamed by the thought.

"If you don't like my choices, leave," she said. "I don't need you."

Ponta Fina looked up, startled. He rubbed his bloodshot eyes.

"I go where you go," he said.

Luzia's chest burned. She felt the same irrepressible agitation she experienced before a raid, except the raid had passed. Their enemies were dead. There was no one left to fight.

Luzia removed the crystal rock from beneath her jacket. A paper was wrapped around the rock, a prayer she'd found in Antônio's bornal. She'd liked the prayer and used it after each successful raid, before the severing began. Luzia called her cangaceiros together and they knelt around her. The girls in the group watched her carefully. They listened to Luzia, obeyed her, and knelt before her during prayers, but unlike the men, the girls stared. They saw every tremble of her hand, every hesitation, every unsure step. They reminded Luzia of herself when she'd first joined, spying on the cangaceiros for any sign of weakness. Luzia could lead the men by awing them. The cangaceiros were intimidated by her height, her short hair, and the threat of Antônio's ghost. The women were different; sometimes Luzia regretted letting them join. The girls' wonder at her looks wore off after their first few days with the group. During that crucial time, Luzia had to become something else. She could not be seen as just another woman. If she could not awe the girls in her group, she had to frighten them. Slowly she became the Seamstress, neither woman nor man but something apart. Some scrubland predator: pitiless and unknowable.

After praying, the cangaceiros stood and spread out among the raided camp. Each man and woman found a dead soldier. They removed machetes from their sheaths. Luzia removed hers. She stared at the solider boy on the ground before her. He had no past and no future. He'd been relieved from life, whereas Luzia held on. She had a duty to her cangaceiros and to Antônio, even though she felt ancient at twenty-four. Her joints ached. Her vision was blurred. Her hair had thinned. She was as wasted and cynical as the old gossips in Taquaritinga, the ones who'd dubbed her Victrola. She'd been so eager to get away from that name, to escape becoming the useless cripple people believed her to be, that she'd allowed herself to become the Seamstress. But once, long ago, before the fall from that mango tree, she'd been Luzia. Who was that girl? What would she have become if people hadn't caged her inside Victrola? If she hadn't caged herself inside the Seamstress?

The Seamstress's only reward was revenge, and forgetfulness. Her machete sliced the air on its way down. The blade's sound was like a long, satisfied sigh. When it hit, the impact wasn't graceful or clean. But each time her machete cut, it was as if she was slicing away at that invisible thread that tethered her to Expedito—her only weakness and her last connection to a normal life.

3

///////

The thread, however, was sturdy. It wasn't easily severed; each time Luzia searched a newspaper in the hopes of finding her son's photograph, she felt its tug. In the Society Section she found only photos of Mrs. Degas Coelho, while the other sections were filled with articles about Celestino Gomes and his new government. In late November 1933, the newly elected First National Assembly convened to draft a constitution. There was intense debate. Southern states like São Paulo—home to vast coffee plantations and the Antarctica Brewing Company, which brought in more tax revenue than all Northern states combined—fought for states' rights. The North and Northeast disliked the South's dominance and favored Gomes's strong central government. Groups that Gomes had courted during the revolution also wanted their say: workers wanted labor rights, the Catholic Church lobbied for morality codes, the military for power.

The leader of Pernambuco—Tenente Higino Ribeiro—earned a new title. "Tenentes" were part of the provisional government, while "governors" were considered part of the old republic. State leaders needed a new designation. In December, the First National Assembly made Higino the official "interventor" of the state of Pernambuco. The Seamstress's title had also changed; the *Diário* reported that a North American newspaper had gotten wind of the cangaceiros' constant highway attacks. Papers throughout the Northeast translated the foreign headline:

Female Bandit Is the Terror of Brazil!

Luzia felt a surge of pride in the fact that people across the ocean were talking about the Seamstress, and that her status had changed: she wasn't simply the terror of the caatinga, but the terror of a nation. Her pride was short-lived however; Luzia knew that the real terror was the drought.

She and her cangaceiros were weak. Their gums bled. Their hair lost its pigment, turning a sickly orange and falling out in knotted clumps. Luzia's men and women began to look like terrified animals—a clear slime ran from their noses, their faces were gaunt, and their eyes bulged, the whites turned yellow. Soon, they wouldn't have the strength to fight. Soldiers and road workers also suffered, and newspapers deemed the scrub a "wasteland." Some editorials said the roadway should be stopped, that it was a useless and expensive endeavor.

Luzia felt a secret gratitude for the drought; it was better to die of starvation than to be killed by Gomes's soldiers. But before they starved, she would have to disband the group. If the drought continued and roadway construction stopped, she would tell her cangaceiros that it was easier to break apart, to separate into pairs and seek their fortunes in the South, or along the coast. Antônio would never have disbanded the group, but the thought gave Luzia a quiet comfort. Dr. Eronildes had told her that he could fix her locked arm. He could rebreak it. At the time, Luzia hadn't believed him. But the drought allowed her to hope. Maybe her fused bone, like a plant, could be trained to grow a different way. Maybe she could cast off her cangaceira's clothes, wash her face and hair, and put on a woman's dress. Emília was good at transformation; she could teach Luzia how it was done. They could travel to the South together. Luzia could show Expedito all of Antônio's cures. She'd teach him how to skin a goat, how to puncture an animal's throat without being afraid. She'd show him how to thread a needle, how to cut a pattern. She'd teach him when to measure, when to cut, and when to mend. If he shied away from her calloused hands or her too tight embrace, if he preferred his pretty aunt to his ungainly mother, Luzia could bear it.

Each day the cangaceiros prayed for rain and Luzia joined them. But in her secret prayers—the ones she said alone, at night—she asked for a sign. If the drought continued into February of the New Year, she would abandon the Seamstress for good. If it rained, it meant that she was destined to continue as a cangaceira, and that her battle with the roadway was not over.

Luzia looked to the scrub for an answer. When she'd first joined Antônio, she saw monotony in the caatinga's gray expanse. She'd been wrong; the scrub was always changing. The light, the wind, the positions of clouds constantly shifted. It was as if the caatinga was speaking to her, and Luzia listened. During the drought, it told her where it hid water and food. When more troops appeared, Luzia asked the scrub which routes were safe and which were sabotaged. The caatinga responded with a sudden gust of wind, or a wasp's nest blocking a certain path, telling her to beware. In January of the new year, the air changed. It was not the dry, sharp air that seemed to crackle with heat. Instead, it was heavy. Clouds blocked the sun, but this wasn't a novelty. So many clouds had hovered over them during the drought that Luzia and the cangaceiros had stopped seeing them as indicators of rain.

That night, after the group had made camp, a girl tugged at Luzia's bent arm. Her name was Fátima and she had nervous, darting eyes.

"Mãe," she said, "look."

The girl pointed to a mandacaru cactus. On its uppermost limb was a thick-petaled flower.

"It could be predicting dew," Luzia said. "A cold night after a hot day."

That night Luzia could not sleep. She lay on her blanket and listened for the sound of frogs coming up from their hiding places underground. Instead, she heard only panting and soft moans—several couples had moved away from camp to be together.

Each man was married to the girl he chose. They were not playing house, Luzia warned. They were entering into sacred unions, blessed by a priest when they could find one. The couples slept apart each Friday—the sacred day—and always before a highway attack, so they wouldn't sap each other's strength. There would be no swapping of husbands or wives. And there would be no babies. Any children born would be given to priests or to families leaving the caatinga. If the girls disobeyed, there would be no warnings or forgiveness. There was only one consequence for defiance; Luzia made sure the girls understood this.

"You have to choose," Luzia had said to each of them, "to be a cangaceira or a woman. You can't be both. And once you choose, you can't go back."

If a girl didn't flinch at this, Luzia let her in.

Most were victims of the drought. They'd lost their families or had been sold to houses of disrepute in exchange for food. Some girls begged to enter the group. Others were coaxed to join by the cangaceiros. Before long, each man had a companion.

She knew the girls' presence could unravel the group. She knew that the women brought the potential for rebellion and disaster, but Luzia let them in. Her reason was a selfish one: the girls would keep their men valiant. They would make the men want to fight, to prove themselves despite their hunger and doubts. The girls hadn't fallen for a group of scraggly, bleary-eyed boys but for cangaceiros with long rifles and half-moon-shaped hats and gold rings on their dusty fingers. They'd married bandits, not normal men, and they would remind their husbands of this each day. Luzia counted on it.

The girls addressed Luzia as "Mãe," never "Senhora." The only name that made her angry was Victrola, and no one called her that anymore. She made herself recall the name when she wanted to stir up rage before a roadway raid. As Victrola she'd been considered crippled and therefore ineffective. To be deemed harmless was the worst insult. It meant you could be easily dismissed. You could be brushed away like a housefly. The girls in the group understood this feeling. Before the drought, in their former lives as wives, daughters, and sisters they were the compromisers, the stoic recipients of life's and their husband's or father's or brother's punishments. They'd been told, time and again: *Agüenta, menina!* "Take it, girl!" They'd been forced to bow their heads and respond "Yes, senhor," to every man alive. So when they'd traded their head scarves for half-moon hats and canvas dresses, they harbored bitterness that no man could understand. But Luzia could, and she made the group's rules. There could be no hitting. Arguments between couples were settled with words, and if they couldn't be resolved this way Luzia intervened, ruling who was right and who was wrong. The women called their cangaceiro husbands by their nicknames and never "senhor." That name was reserved for God.

"Thank you, Senhor!" Luzia heard a girl cry as soon as the first drop fell.

It was late but most of the cangaceiros were still awake, sharing Luzia's anticipation. The wind had picked up. The air was cool. The first drop felt like a trick. Luzia looked up, wondering if an animal in the tree above her had relieved itself. There was another drop, then another. Luzia smelled wet dirt.

Baiano wept. Ponta Fina, Baby, Inteligente, and Maria Magra danced, hugged, whooped. The cangaceiros removed their weapons and rolled in the mud like children. Everyone's faces were wet from rain or tears; it didn't matter which. Luzia wanted to cry, but nothing came. It was as if the grit and sand of the drought had settled within her, heavy and numbing. God had answered. The scrub would flower and grow. People would take their faded and mutilated saints off rooftops and worship them again. And Luzia would stay where she was, as the Seamstress.

4

Food was still scarce after a few weeks of rains; crops and animals were slow to grow and reproduce. The scrub, however, quickly turned green and flowered. Towns across the caatinga followed the scrub's example and flourished. People bustled along dirt roads. They repaired houses. Some dug into their plots of land and planted corn and melon seeds. Villages that were once abandoned now buzzed with activity, and Luzia wondered where the residents had been hiding. They emerged from nowhere, like cicadas suddenly rising from their secret recesses and taking over.

Luzia led her cangaceiros along the Old Chico and into the river town where, years ago, she and Antônio had had their first photograph taken together. The town's church had received a new coating of whitewash, and it shone in the afternoon sun. Nearby, an entrepreneur had opened a cinema. It was an old cotton depository with high, wooden-framed ceilings. Electric wires ran from the cinema's rooftop to a nearby pole, then to another and another.

Luzia hoped that one of the town's merchants had ammunition. Her rolls of mil-réis were dwindling, as were Antônio's old ammunition stocks, buried throughout the scrub. During roadway raids the cangaceiros took soldiers' guns, but bullets for the new weapons were hard to find. "A gun without bullets is like a woman without a husband—worthless." That was what Antônio had said once, long before the roadway had cut across the scrub and soldiers appeared with modern guns. Gomes's monkeys had consistently better weapons. Because of this, raiding construction sites and train depots became difficult. During attacks, Luzia and her cangaceiros retreated more often than they pushed forward.

After the drought, every farmhouse seemed to be a trap. Luzia was more careful: she and her cangaceiros wouldn't enter homes whether they belonged to a colonel or to a simple vaqueiro. They observed a town for a full day before entering it. They had elaborate methods of communication with their coiteiros, requesting food and ammunition through a convoluted series of notes hidden in beehives and beneath piles of dried dung. Luzia appointed sub-captains, and when it became too dangerous to travel in a large group, they divided into smaller sets of ten, making it harder for troops to track them.

Any colonel or rancher who'd spent time on the coast was a potential traitor. After the rains, most returned to the scrubland but didn't ask for the Hawk's protection. Luzia understood that they trusted Gomes more than the Hawk. Even small farmers who'd once been her most loyal coiteiros now placed pictures of Gomes on their saints' altars. Dr. Eronildes had been right—people chose their heroes out of fear, not love.

Luzia hoped that the rains would put an end to Emília's charitable shipments, but Mrs. Degas Coelho refuted this. In an interview with the *Diário,* she made it clear that the recent rains didn't wipe away need.

"We will continue our shipments," Mrs. Degas Coelho said. "The necessity is still great. As is the danger."

Ponta Fina didn't push to attack the charity trains, but each time their group was forced to retreat during a roadway attack, he stared accusingly at Luzia. She'd instructed her cangaceiros to consider everyone a possible enemy, except for the woman behind the charity trains. As their captain, Luzia didn't have to give explanations, only orders. Even if she wanted to explain her reasons, she could not. She didn't want to think about what those charity shipments contained or where the soldiers' modern weapons came from. She could question a vaqueiro's loyalty and even a colonel's, but not Emília's.

Luzia went to the river town in the hopes of making her stolen weapons useful; perhaps a few monkeys had traded their new guns and ammunition—as they were prone to do—to relieve gambling debts.

Merchants inspected the new Brownings and Winchester rifles. They whistled and stroked the guns' barrels. They tried to cram other bullets into their chambers but none fit. Annoyed, Luzia asked for a new *Diário de Pernambuco.* The shopkeeper shook his head. The latest shipment had not come in.

"If you want news, you should watch the reels," a shop owner said nervously. "Over at the cinema. They're better than the paper. The picture's old—ten years at least. *The Lawyer's Daughter* it's called. But the reels are new. They come in from Salvador every three months."

Outside the old cotton depot hung a faded film poster. *The Lawyer's Daughter,* the poster read. It was a movie from 1928, but was considered new in the scrub. Attached to the bottom of the poster was a bright green sign with the words: "This film brought to you by DIP, the Department of Information and Propaganda and President Celestino Gomes."

Luzia bought thirty tickets.

The cinema was dim. Lanterns hung along the walls. Their smell of kerosene reminded Luzia of Dr. Eronildes' kitchen, long ago. She took a deep breath. On a raised table in the rear of the theater was a massive projector. Its round metal reels and protruding lens made it look like some strange weapon. Rows of wooden benches were lined up before a large white sheet stretched across the depository wall. Luzia and her cangaceiros crowded the room along with other patrons, who whispered and looked back warily. Luzia took a place in the rear of the theater, her back to the wall. She didn't want any surprises in the dark. Ponta Fina and Baby sat on a bench before her. Baiano and Maria Magra took their places beside Luzia. She heard some of the patrons whisper:

"Is that the Hawk?"

"He's a mulatto?"

Before the crowd could get a good look at the cangaceiros, a boy appeared and snuffed out the lanterns one by one. The darkness was soothing; it allowed Luzia to disappear. She was just another theater patron, not the Seamstress. She'd never seen a moving picture and felt strangely nervous. The theater's darkness, the crowd's hushed whispers, the wet sounds of stolen kisses should have distracted Luzia from her misgivings, but they didn't. Ponta Fina's doubts about the charity shipments had exposed her own, and these suspicions nagged at her, making her shift in her seat. Emília's last newspaper photograph was crumpled in Luzia's jacket pocket. She pressed her hand against it.

Beside the projector, a man flicked switches and checked the reels. When the machine clicked on, it sounded like her old Singer. There was a flicker of light and words appeared across the white sheet: "The Propaganda Ministry of Brazil," and below them a flag with the motto, "Order and Progress." It was a government newsreel. Luzia couldn't tell how old it was.

There was no sound, only the gentle ticking of the projector. The canvas sheet undulated with shadows and light. A scene appeared: gray ocean, blocks of square buildings, and the round hump of Sugar Loaf Mountain. Words appeared unevenly across the bottom of the screen:

Rio de Janeiro—After constitutional revision, delegates, guests, and family members join President Gomes in a visit to the newly inaugurated Christ the Redeemer statue.

The camera panned over a group of men and women, dwarfed before a giant stone Christ, his arms open, his head bowed. The camera's eye narrowed. Celestino Gomes appeared, laughing. He wore his military suit and tall boots. His movements were choppy and fast. He moved about the crowd, shaking hands with men and women. Among the mass of strangers' faces, Luzia recognized one. Emília wore a well-tailored dress. Her long hair was pinned back. Her lips were painted and dark, and they opened in a smile. A boy sat on her hip. He wore a sailor's hat, and as the crowd swarmed around Gomes, the cap was knocked from his head. He opened his mouth in a silent cry. His eyes—Antônio's eyes—stared accusingly into the camera. Before him, Celestino Gomes laughed. He patted the boy's head and moved on. The camera moved with him. Emília and the child disappeared.

Luzia stood.

Gomes appeared on the screen again, life size and smiling. He was made of light and shadow, like a ghost. Luzia made her way up the center aisle. Her shadow blocked the projection and the ghost was gone. Behind her, a man booed.

"Sit!" someone hissed.

Luzia turned around. The projector blinded her. She shaded her face with her good arm. In the dark room, the projector's light illuminated only her, revealing her lost teeth, her bent arm, her sunworn face.

"Shut it off," Luzia ordered.

The operator nodded but the projector kept ticking, the images swirling across Luzia's body. The young attendant lit a lantern. There were more hisses and boos. Luzia's eyes hurt from the projector's light. She closed them and saw Emília's awed smile. She saw Gomes's hand, reaching for her child.

"Shut it off!" Luzia yelled, her voice high-pitched with rage.

In the back, Baiano stood. His face was dark and stern. "Do what she says," he ordered.

The operator nodded, frantically pulling levers on the machine.

"If you don't like it, leave!" a voice in the darkened section of the theater shouted.

"Dirty cangaceiros!" another said.

Protected by darkness and by the lingering presence of Gomes's image, the patrons became braver. Luzia was disturbed by their anger.

"Communists!" a woman said.

"Ungrateful pigs," Ponta Fina shouted and stood. Soon, the other cangaceiros got to their feet.

"Monkey lovers!" Canjica spat out.

"Viva Gomes!" a young voice shouted.

Luzia's stomach burned as if she'd swallowed a hot cinder. She looked at the shadows of theater patrons. She'd saved people like these during the drought. She'd freed their daughters from prostitution camps. She'd hindered the roadway from tearing up their lands. This was the thanks she got? Like Emília, they'd picked Gomes over her. The theater patrons insulted her, knowing she would have to respond. She unhooked her holster and removed her parabellum pistol.

The projector kept running. Luzia aimed. She saw the eye of the lens, round and unfeeling, like that of a dead fish. She shot. In the dark pews, a woman screamed. There was the rustle of feet, the dragging of benches across the brick floor. People crowded the side and center aisles. On the front sheet there were no more images, just a crooked beam of light from the projector and Luzia's tall shadow. She aimed at the single lit lantern. It fell. Kerosene and flame spread across the floor, lapping at the foot of a bench. There was smoke and more gunshots. Luzia ordered her group outside.

In the crush she lost her hat. Her brass spectacles, the lenses scratched and frames bent, fell from her face. Luzia prodded and jabbed with her bent arm. Her skin felt hot and she wasn't sure if it was the fire or her anger that caused this. She recalled Dr. Eronildes' warning about her temper: "one day . . . you will not be able to contain it."

Once her group was outside, Luzia barred the depository's doors. Inside there were knocks and screams. Ponta Fina and Canjica stole tins of kerosene and poured them along the building's edges.

The theater burned like a great bonfire. Its flames rose fifteen meters in the air. The heat made Luzia's cheeks flush. It made her eyes water. It was hot enough to burn that horrible projector, to destroy that white sheet where she'd seen Gomes's ghost. Thick flakes of ash rained upon the cangaceiros. Orange cinders rose, floating from the theater and falling onto thatched houses, igniting roofs. Cinders landed on the cangaceiros' clothes, making the men and women swat themselves. An ember fell on Luzia's hand—the hand of her good arm—and burned, like a bullet entering her skin.

The cangaceiros ran into the scrub, retreating from the burning town. Luzia felt the blaze's heat upon her back. Faraway objects were blurs without her glasses, but Luzia could still see the fire's light: it faded and returned, like a memory.

Chapter 13

EMÍLIA

Recife, Pernambuco
November 1934–December 1934

1

/ / / / / / / /

*D*eath had a unique smell. The scent turned Emília's stomach. She didn't blame the dead—their natural odor of decay wasn't what disgusted her. The smells made by the living to cope with death were what bothered her. People burned thick sticks of incense to honor the dead and, at the same time, they squirted heavy amounts of creolina, bleach, and alcohol across floors and over furniture to wipe away any vestiges of the body's failure. Blood, urine, vomit, and spittle were all erased, their smells overpowered by the spicy and medicinal scents preferred by the living.

On Finados Day in Recife's most prestigious cemetery, Emília put a handkerchief over her nose to blot out the smell. Tombs of marble and granite shone with water and soap bubbles. Women from Old and New families gingerly held sponges and dabbed their ancestors' nameplates. Some cleaned the graves' statues, gently wiping angels' wings and faces. A group of well-dressed girls gossiped while they lit incense sticks and arranged large wreaths of flowers. Servant women—their hair wrapped under cloth, their faces intent—scrubbed the sepulchers with brooms. Their dead were far away, buried in unmarked graves along the cattle trail or in cemeteries at the edges of the city. They would honor their deceased later that day, after their mistresses let them go home. Until then, the servant women were forced to spend the holiday honoring strangers, as was Emília.

A wrought-iron fence—freshly painted black—demarcated the Coelho family tomb. In the stone structure were blank squares, empty spaces for Dr. Duarte, Dona Dulce, Degas, and his wife. Emília shuddered at the thought of spending eternity beside the Coelhos. She wiped the deceaseds' nameplates with a wet cloth. Near her, Dona Dulce scrubbed until the Coelho name shone. Raimunda swept the site. Expedito, on the ground beside Emília, enthusiastically pulled weeds from the tomb's edges. Dona Dulce glared at him. Small children stayed near their mothers, but older boys joined the men under the shade of the cemetery's largest tree. Dr. Duarte and Degas were there, chatting with other husbands and sons, waiting for the cleaning to end so that they could pay their respects.

Emília wiped her brow. Finados, she decided, was her least favorite holiday. She recalled how she and Luzia had whitewashed their parents' tombs in Taquaritinga. Their mother and father's graves had probably turned gray with dirt. Aunt Sofia's, too. All of Emília's dead had been left but not forgotten; she would light candles for them later, at the Coelho house. Emília would have liked to return to Taquaritinga. Not to show off, as she'd once dreamed of doing, but to take care of those graves she'd left behind. By doing this, she could show Expedito his true family. Unfortunately, it would be a long time before she could take him into the interior again—the countryside was too dangerous.

Despite Degas' covert weapons shipments, the Hawk and the Seamstress continued to successfully attack Trans-Nordestino construction sites. Cangaceiros began to steal soldiers' weapons, which was proof that they were running low on their own munitions. Still, the bandits managed to have a steady supply of bullets and guns. Dr. Duarte suspected that colonels and ranchers who'd returned to their farms after the drought had also returned to their roles as coiteiros. Most colonels disliked Gomes for dismantling their political machines in the countryside and making them powerless. They also disliked the Trans-Nordestino roadway cutting through their lands. Though they'd pledged their allegiance while in Recife, there was a chance that the colonels secretly supported the Hawk and the Seamstress in order to undermine Gomes. Emília often thought of Dr. Eronildes—the Rio Branco Relief Camp had closed after the rains and she hadn't heard from him since then. She assumed he'd gone back to his ranch but didn't know if he continued to help the Seamstress.

In the beginning of the year, rain had finally reached the backlands. Telegraphed reports had said that, as the first rains fell, relief-camp residents cried and screamed prayers of thanks to São Pedro. The rains were so heavy and the ground so dry that large, muddy gullies formed, uprooting trees and leveling abandoned houses. The mud became a problem and relief camps had to be closed without delay. Residents who wanted to return to farming were given a packet of seeds and sent away. Those who wanted to leave the Northeast were offered transportation south, where they worked in factories or in homes as domestics. Men who wished to work for President Gomes as soldiers or as roadway builders were herded into separate groups and given food and uniforms.

President Gomes sent a telegram from Rio and pressed Interventor Higino for a solution to the cangaceiro problem. Interventor Higino, in turn, pressed Dr. Duarte. The government had spent large amounts of money and resources to build the Criminology Institute on the basis of Dr. Duarte's assertion that his science could find practical solutions to crime. He'd promised to better understand the criminal mind and thus find ways to predict their behavior and catch offenders before more crimes could be committed. Now, Interventor Higino pressured Dr. Duarte to fulfill these promises. Emília's father-in-law became secretive. He kept his study locked. Instead of hiring a taxi, he made Degas drive him to all appointments. Each morning, Dr. Duarte and Degas drove to the port and returned to the Coelho house smelling of salt air and carrying packets of fresh fish for lunch. On the Finados holiday, Dr. Duarte sneaked away from the group of men under the cemetery tree and went to some unknown destination. Dona Dulce shook her head.

"He has no respect for the dead," she said and scrubbed the tomb's nameplates harder.

When Dr. Duarte returned, he bypassed the shade tree and walked straight to the Coelho tomb. There, he handed Expedito a gift. It was a medallion that looked like two z's interposed one over the other. To Emília, it resembled a smashed insect.

"It is German," Dr. Duarte had said, stooping to face Expedito. "A symbol of their new führer. It comes from across the ocean." He looked up at Emília. "Like our solution."

"To what?" she asked.

Dr. Duarte smiled. "Degas has brought the car around. We can't be late for the luncheon."

Beside Emília, Dona Dulce nodded. They would have to go back to the house and change clothes; they couldn't attend Interventor Higino's memorial luncheon smelling of bleach and sweat.

The Finados lunch was in honor of fallen soldiers, roadway workers, and victims of the Seamstress's notorious theater fire. Months before, newspapers had given extensive coverage to the theater disaster, where an entire town was burned and hundreds maimed on account of the Seamstress's foul temper. The fire had turned public opinion against the Seamstress and the Hawk: there were no more clever advertisements using the cangaceiros' images. One ad for vitamin pills had proclaimed, "The Hawk runs all day and all night. He takes Dr. Ross's life pills for vigor and stamina!" Another ad for a fabric store showed the only photograph of the Seamstress— the one taken alongside the first pair of kidnapped surveyors—and said, "The Seamstress has doubts about being arrested, but she never doubts that the Casa de Fazendas Bonitas will always be the cheapest!" After the theater disaster, these ads were pulled. Recifians found no humor in the cangaceiros. Even scrubland residents who'd once respected the cangaceiros now disliked them. The theater fire had killed many people's relatives, and vigilante groups went after the cangaceiros for revenge. President Gomes and Interventor

Higino latched on to this public outcry, calling the theater fire a "maiming of innocents," and dedicating a small memorial to the victims along Recife's Capibaribe River.

Emília had spent months feeling guilty because of the guns hidden in her charity shipments. After the theater fire she wondered if her guilt was misguided. Perhaps Degas was right—the Seamstress was a killer, and killers should be caught. Her previous targets had been linked to the Gomes government: soldiers, road workers, surveyors. Those killed in the fire were common citizens. Emília felt deeply disappointed and didn't understand why. To feel disappointment meant that she'd harbored expectations of the Seamstress, that she somehow believed the cangaceiros' fight was just and that they would act honorably. Rebellion was different from common criminality—this was the distinction Emília had made in her mind. The theater fire changed things. Suddenly, Celestino Gomes was seen as the man who would rid the countryside of violence. When Emília recalled her brief meeting with President Gomes in Rio, her disappointment quickly turned to dread. No matter her intentions— good or bad—the Seamstress had waged a war she could never win.

Emília had visited Rio de Janeiro back in July, after the new constitution was enacted. The newly elected First National Assembly had proclaimed Celestino Gomes president for a four-year term. In the assembly's constitution, all mines and major waterways became federal property, as did all banks and insurance companies. Gomes had substantial control, yet he wanted more. The assembly's constitution gave Gomes his workers' rights policies: an eight-hour workday, vacation time, and minimum wage. However, the constitution struck down his federalized union. Gomes felt frustrated by the document and he invited prominent Green Party members to Rio for a summit. The meeting was advertised as a "unity gathering," so Dr. Duarte and other invited officials brought their entire families. The trip was short. Emília didn't get to see much of Rio—her most extensive view was from above, at the Christ the Redeemer statue. There, she'd come face-to-face with President Gomes. He was a small man but the air around him seemed to crackle with energy.

When he looked at her, Emília sensed both magnetism and danger. She felt the inexplicable need to please him. Afterward, this annoyed her. She'd felt that way only once before, in the presence of the Hawk.

At the end of the Rio trip, when Emília heard that Gomes had united all of his Green Party invitees and taken them to the First National Assembly to protest the new constitution, she wasn't surprised. Gomes announced that the constitution was merely a guide, not a mandate, and he would either ignore the document or change it. No one went against his wishes.

The memorial luncheon was a smaller, more intimate gathering than the Green Party's celebration after the revolution. Black crepe hung from the International Club's walls. White flowers decorated the tables. Some male guests wore black armbands as tributes to the loved ones they'd lost that year. Women wore fashionable but modest dresses in muted colors. Emília scanned the room and saw several of her designs: gray mermaid skirts, jackets with padded shoulders, scarves tied at the neckline. She'd had a rush of orders for the Finados holiday and she'd drawn her inspiration from the leading ladies she'd seen in motion pictures at the Royal Theater: Jean Harlow, Claudette Colbert, Joan Crawford. They were moody, elegant, and tough. Their thinly plucked eyebrows were arched in constant surprise, or perhaps skepticism. Emília copied their shapely suits, their wet-waved hairstyles. Other Recife women followed.

Unlike the revolutionary celebration, men and women were not separated at the memorial luncheon. Families and friends sat together. Dr. Duarte had his own table, and the seating arrangements were similar to those at the Coelho house: Dona Dulce sat on Dr. Duarte's right; Degas sat beside his mother; Emília sat beside her husband. Guests were seated in order of importance, their rank determined by how close they sat to Dr. Duarte. Those deemed most important sat immediately to Dr. Duarte's left. Those less important sat farther away. At the memorial luncheon, Dr. Duarte placed a hand on the seat beside him.

"I'm reserving this for a special guest," he said.

"I'm not special, Duarte?" the baroness asked, resting her arthritic claw on his shoulder.

Dr. Duarte reddened. Dona Dulce straightened in her chair.

"Mother's teasing." Lindalva laughed. "We'll sit beside Emília."

"Of course," Dr. Duarte replied, smiling now. "It's better to have a full table."

To Dona Dulce's chagrin, the baroness and Lindalva took the places nearest Emília, closing off the table and leaving only three empty chairs. One belonged to Degas, who'd slipped off to the club's smoking room. When he returned, the pilot Carlos Chevalier joined him. The man's hair was bushy and wild because of the humidity. In his right hand was a silver-handled cane. Dr. Duarte raised his white eyebrows.

"What's wrong with your leg?" he asked, pointing at Chevalier's cane.

"Nothing," Chevalier said, shrugging his shoulders. "It's the fashion."

Dr. Duarte grunted. Degas directed Chevalier around the table, to the privileged spot beside his father.

"No," Dr. Duarte said. "Take a seat over there."

He pointed to the far end of the table—to the lone chair beside Lindalva. Degas pursed his lips. Chevalier smiled and walked around the group. As he moved past her, Emília smelled cigarette smoke and strong cologne. She wondered if Dr. Duarte had heard the same rumors about Degas and Chevalier that Lindalva had, or if her father-in-law simply disliked the pilot.

"Are you a captain in the army, Mr. Chevalier?" the baroness asked, her eyes glinting mischievously.

"No," he replied. "It's more of an honorary title. Like yours."

The baroness stared. "My title was earned, my boy. The baron had a fine soul, but he wasn't an easy husband."

"In that case, I earned my title, too," Chevalier replied. "I fly my own plane."

"An interesting hobby," Dona Dulce interjected. Her voice had the same wary tone she used when alerting Dr. Duarte to the fact that there was a salesman or a vagrant at the front gate. She exchanged a smile with the baroness. Emília was surprised to see the two women suddenly united.

Chevalier smiled. It was a wide grimace, as though he was mimicking the men in toothpaste ads.

"Flight is more than a hobby," he said. "It is my passion."

Degas fumbled with his napkin. Lindalva leaned forward in her chair.

"Are you part of the publishing Chevaliers, the ones who own papers in the South?"

"Yes."

"How is your family bearing the new constraints? Are they allowing the Propaganda Ministry's censorship?"

Chevalier laughed nervously. "I'm not involved in the newspaper business—"

"I wouldn't call it censorship, my dear," Dr. Duarte interrupted. "I would call it responsible monitoring. The revolution isn't guaranteed. We have to maintain a certain order. There are still Southern Communists led by Prestes. There are those São Paulo rebels funded by the old guard. We can't let such elements corrupt the people. Later we can relax our grip, but for now we must keep tight reins on the horse."

"My daddy was a horse breeder," the baroness said, wiping a piece of bread with butter. "Fine animals. Intelligent. The first thing Daddy taught me when I learned to ride was that the reins are an illusion—more for our comfort than theirs. You control a horse with your legs, and with kind authority. It is a relationship of equals. Or it should be."

Dr. Duarte wasn't listening. He stared across the room, transfixed. "My guest has arrived!" he said.

Emília turned in the direction of his gaze. Dr. Eronildes Epifano appeared in the dining room. His hair was still longer than a city man's, reaching his ears and haphazardly combed back, but it had thinned. His suit had been poorly pressed, leaving uneven folds in his jacket and crooked pleats in his pants. Around his right sleeve he wore a black band. When he came to their table, Emília saw dark, bruise-colored circles beneath his eyes. Broken capillaries, like bits of red thread trapped beneath his skin, were scattered across his nose and cheeks.

"Forgive me," Dr. Eronildes said, staring at Emília. Quickly, he turned his gaze to Dr. Duarte. "I'm late."

After shaking hands with Dr. Duarte, Eronildes wove around the table to introduce himself to Dona Dulce. As the guest drew close, Emília's mother-in-law scrunched up her nose. Emília attributed her mother-in-law's reaction to snobbery, but when Dr. Eronildes rounded the table and clasped her own hand, she realized she was wrong. Beneath the powdery scent of his shaving balm, Emília smelled something sweet and rank. It was as if his insides were fermenting beneath his skin. The scent reminded her of Recife's streets the morning after Carnaval, the gutters overflowing with spilled sugarcane liquor, fruit rinds, vomit, and other unsavory things expelled by revelers. Emília was confused by Eronildes' presence and repulsed by his smell. She quickly recalled Dona Dulce's lessons—above all, etiquette was about thoughtfulness. A lady never showed displeasure. Emília held tightly to Dr. Eronildes' hand and smiled.

For lunch there was broiled fish and sururu mussels. Coconut milk bubbled and frothed in massive silver tureens. Mussels bobbed in the broth. Waiters placed porcelain bowls of rice, manioc flour toasted to a golden brown, and individual plates of limes near each diner. Dr. Duarte scooped mounds of malagueta peppers onto his meal.

"Mr. Chevalier, do you eat peppers?" Dr. Duarte asked.

"My stomach is sensitive," the pilot replied.

"Nonsense!" Dr. Duarte snorted. He motioned for Chevalier's plate. Their guest obediently passed it to Dr. Duarte, who piled the small red peppers on it.

"You must learn to build resistance!" Dr. Duarte said. "The body is controlled by the mind. Isn't that right, Degas?"

"Yes, sir," Degas mumbled. He glanced at Chevalier, who took a bite of his food and quickly reached for his water glass. Chevalier took several long gulps and then wiped his eyes with a napkin. Lindalva giggled. Across from them, Dr. Eronildes smiled. Degas reddened.

"What brings you to Recife, Doctor?" Degas asked loudly. "Business?"

"Not exactly," Dr. Eronildes replied. He fingered his black armband. "My mother passed away in Salvador some weeks ago. I traveled there for the funeral. Now I have to settle some matters of her estate here in Recife."

"We're sorry for your loss," Emília said. Dr. Eronildes nodded.

"We're looking at properties after lunch," Dr. Duarte said. "For Eronildes' consultório."

A dry lump of manioc flour caught in Emília's throat. She coughed.

"Are you moving here?" she asked hoarsely.

"I'm considering it," Eronildes replied. "Salvador has too many memories."

"What about your ranch?" Emília said.

Dr. Eronildes stared at her, his eyes bloodshot. "It hasn't recovered from the drought. I planted everything new; it was a hefty investment. But the cotton's not producing like it used to. My cattle are young. They're too skinny to sell. It was my mother's wish—or requirement, really, in her will—that I return to the coast. She was worried for me. She wanted me to settle down, open a practice, marry."

"She's sensible," Dona Dulce interrupted.

Dr. Duarte nodded. "Farmers lose money. Doctors make it."

"That depends on the farmer," the baroness said.

"So, you have to make a choice now," Degas said. "You can't be two men anymore."

Eronildes held Degas' stare.

"I'll keep the ranch," the doctor finally said. "It won't be a working property, but I'll be able to visit. And I won't have to move anytime soon. My mother's wishes for her estate will take months for the lawyers to implement."

"You'll be returning to your ranch then?" Dr. Duarte asked. "For a long stint?"

Eronildes nodded. "I'm going back tonight."

"You won't leave without meeting Expedito," Dr. Duarte said. "He's a lad now: fat, hardy, full of pep!" He placed a pepper between his fingers and wagged it at Chevalier. "Less than three years old and the boy can eat a malagueta without flinching."

Chevalier stirred in his seat.

"No word from the boy's parents, I assume," Degas asked Eronildes.

"I'm his parent now," Emília interrupted.

"We'll go to the house after lunch," Dr. Duarte said, ignoring them. "So Eronildes can meet the boy."

"Sir," Degas said, "Mr. Chevalier and I would like to speak to you after lunch, in your study."

"We can speak here," Dr. Duarte said.

"It's business," Chevalier said, lowering his voice. "Government business."

"You should go to the interventor's office for that," Dr. Duarte replied. "I'm not a government worker. I'm only a scientist."

Chevalier looked at Degas.

"Papai," Degas said, forcing a laugh. "Don't be modest. We all know you're more important than you make yourself out to be."

"Modesty is a great virtue," Dr. Duarte said. "Almost as great as propriety."

"It has to do with the cangaceiros," Chevalier persisted. "Have you read the latest *Diário de Pernambuco*?"

Dr. Duarte stiffened. "Yes. Of course."

Emília watched Dr. Eronildes across the table. He stared at the pilot warily.

"So you've read my proposal in the editorial pages?" Chevalier said.

"About flying a plane over the scrub?" Lindalva said.

"Exactly!" The pilot smiled.

"There's popular support for it," Degas said. "I've heard people talking. It would be just like the war films!"

"Horrible stuff, those films," the baroness said.

"It will be much easier to weed out the cangaceiros by air," Chevalier continued. "Once I'm done, the police can find the bodies and bring them back to your lab for analysis."

"And how would you exterminate them?" Dr. Duarte asked.

Emília fumbled with her water glass. It knocked against her plate and spilled, darkening the tablecloth.

"Duarte!" Dona Dulce huffed. "We shouldn't talk about such things on Finados. Respect the dead."

The baroness waved her crooked hand. "The dead won't hear us," she said. "They've got bigger concerns."

"Have you ever flown in the backlands?" Dr. Duarte asked Chevalier.

"No," the pilot replied. "But I've flown over ocean and in fog. I know how to fly, sir."

"I'm not concerned about your flying," Dr. Duarte said. "I'm concerned about your landing."

"Oh, I can land, too," Chevalier said, smiling.

"Where?" Dr. Duarte asked, his cheeks flushed. "If I'm correct, when you fly in from Rio de Janeiro, you have to make several stops to refuel. Perhaps you don't realize this, but our state of Pernambuco is over eight hundred kilometers long. If you fly into the backlands, at some point you'll have to land. There are no airstrips. So, how would you propose to land?" Dr. Duarte tapped his fingers against the table.

"The government can easily build landing strips," Chevalier said. "Aren't you building a roadway?"

"Attempting to build a roadway. It has proved harder than we'd imagined."

"In Rio it would be a simple job," Chevalier said.

"We aren't in Rio," Dr. Duarte replied. "If you miss it, perhaps you should return there."

A sudden round of applause came from the front of the dining hall. Interventor Higino stood. He gave a brief speech about the sacrifices of the departed soldiers and road workers, and how all Brazilians should honor their brave spirits. When he eulogized the theater-fire victims, Emília glanced at Dr. Eronildes. He stared straight ahead, ignoring her. At the end of his speech there was another wave of clapping. Interventor Higino raised his hands, asking for quiet.

"I'd like to turn our attention to our city's most respected criminologist, Dr. Duarte Coelho."

Emília's father-in-law removed a batch of note cards from his pocket. He stood and smiled, then stared at the cards.

"The criminal," Dr. Duarte said in a deep, theatrical voice, "according to Dr. Caesar Lombroso, is an atavistic being—a relic of a vanished race. It is a race that kills and corrupts our fellow citizens, our loved ones. For this reason, we must do all we can to exterminate that race. Interventor Higino has asked me to use this sacred holiday to announce a plan that will, hopefully, allow our soldiers, our road workers, and our innocent citizens to remain alive, so that next Finados we will have fewer to mourn."

There was a smattering of applause.

"We are working with Germany," Dr. Duarte announced. "It's been kept out of the papers because the Hawk reads them. DIP's made editors promise not to print anything about it. But I suppose there's no harm in sharing our plan now. No one here has a loose tongue, I hope."

Guests laughed. Dr. Duarte continued.

"We've purchased several Bergmanns. 'Machine guns,' the Germans call them. They shoot five hundred rounds a minute. With them, ten men become ten thousand. The cangaceiros won't have time to think, or to shoot. They'll be gone before they touch their holsters."

Dr. Duarte winked at Emília.

"We'll ship the Bergmanns secretly," he said. "We won't let the cangaceiros get hold of such a weapon. We'll coax the cangaceiros into one spot, and then surprise them with our new firearm. Ladies and gentlemen, I have no doubt we will cure this scourge of criminality in our countryside. In the end, it is not the Bergmann gun that will do this, but our own resolve. As our great writer Euclides da Cunha said: the moral man does not destroy the criminal race by force of arms alone—he crushes it with civilization!"

The room thundered with applause. Emília felt an acidic mix of coconut milk and mussels rise into the back of her throat, burning it. She held her napkin over her mouth.

After Dr. Duarte sat, the lunch plates were swept away. Dessert was served.

"When will they arrive?" Emília asked. "These Bergmanns?"

Dr. Duarte hesitated, then whispered to his tablemates: "They're on a ship as we speak."

"Three months' time," Degas added. He placed a hand on Emília's forearm. Not knowing if this was meant to be a comfort or a warning, Emília moved her arm away. She felt pressure in her head and behind her eyes, as if her brain had swelled.

"I trust we'll all be discreet about this," Dr. Duarte said to his guests.

"Yes," Dr. Eronildes replied. He stared at Emília. "When I became a doctor, I took an oath. What I see or hear during treatment, and even outside treatment, that pertains to the lives of men, I will keep to myself."

"And women?" Emília asked. "What about their lives?"

"Yes," Lindalva chimed in, "our sex won't be pushed aside."

"I took the same oath," Dr. Duarte said, staring at Eronildes. His voice trembled. "Medical men are loyal men, especially to each other. That's part of the oath, too, if I recall correctly—'hold those who practice as equals and as brothers, and if they are in need of money, I will give them a share of mine.'" Dr. Duarte wiped his eyes with his napkin. He looked at his son. "It's a fine group to be a part of. A man is only worth the company he keeps."

"I agree," Degas said, his foot tapping wildly beneath the table. "I'm sure Dr. Eronildes agrees as well."

The table's occupants ate their desserts in silence. Emília gulped down her slice of cake, hardly tasting it. She wanted to hurry the meal along but, at the same time, she was reluctant to leave the dining room. As soon as the luncheon ended, they would return to the Coelho house and she'd have to introduce Expedito to Dr. Eronildes. Emília worried about the doctor's sudden appearance in Recife, his financial troubles, and Dr. Duarte's affinity for him. What worried her most were the Bergmanns. Dr. Duarte's words squeezed themselves into her thoughts, relentless and irritating, like flies trapped inside her head. *Ten men become ten thousand. They'll be gone before they touch their holsters.*

After dessert, Chevalier excused himself from the dining room. Degas also stood and announced that he would drive the pilot back to his hotel. Dr. Duarte raised his hand, ordering his son to wait.

"He's a grown man, Degas. I'm sure he'll find his way without you. You'll take us back to the house. Dr. Eronildes included."

Dr. Duarte smiled at his guest. When Degas began to protest, his father's good humor disappeared. Dr. Duarte's voice grew low and stern.

"Degas," he said, "you may have time to indulge playboys and media hogs, but I certainly do not. I don't want him in my company again."

Dr. Duarte stood and quickly escorted Dr. Eronildes from the table. Degas stared at his father's empty chair and then hurried after him.

2

At the Coelho house, Emília woke Expedito from his nap and carried the sleepy-eyed boy into the courtyard. The central fountain gurgled and spat water. The jabotis had crowded into the yard's only shady spot. Expedito collected wilted lettuce leaves scattered across the brick floor and fed the turtles. Emília knelt beside him. Soon the doors to Dr. Duarte's study opened and, inside, the corrupião burst into a startled song. Emília's father-in-law and Dr. Eronildes walked toward them.

"Ahhh!" Dr. Duarte said, extending his stubby hands. "There's the Colonel! That's what we call him around here."

Dr. Duarte patted Expedito's head. The boy stopped feeding the jabotis and turned his dark eyes toward the stranger. Dr. Eronildes' hands shook. He clamped one with the other.

"Are they jabotis?" Eronildes asked.

Expedito nodded.

"They live a human lifetime, you know," Eronildes said, "sometimes longer. They'll probably outlive us all."

Expedito watched the turtles, as if pondering the stranger's words.

"Except for Expedito," Emília said. "He'll live to see another set of turtles, God willing."

"Yes," Eronildes replied. "Of course he will. Thanks to you."

"And to you," Emília said. "We're both responsible for his life."

Dr. Eronildes nodded. His face was shiny and pallid, like a boiled round of inhame yam. He fidgeted with his jacket and wiggled his leg. Dr. Duarte placed a hand on his guest's back, as if to steady him.

"The Green Party's old-fashioned; it doesn't serve drinks at its events," Dr. Duarte said. "But I like a little *cana* now and again, to kill the parasites. I have some fine cachaça in my study, or White Horse if you prefer it."

Eronildes licked his lips. "White Horse," he said. "With ice."

Dr. Duarte nodded. "I'll tell the maid to crush some. It shouldn't take long. Emília and the Colonel will keep you company."

Emília watched her father-in-law walk away. She'd never seen Dr. Duarte move so quickly or pay such deference to a guest. He rarely shared his small stock of imported whiskey. Next to Emília, Dr. Eronildes sniffed the air. She smelled it, too—a burning odor, like rice left too long on the stove.

"Are bonfires customary here during Finados?" Eronildes asked.

"No," Emília replied.

Inside the house she heard Dr. Duarte shouting for ice. Eronildes edged closer.

"We should warn her," he said.

The burning smell had gotten stronger and she believed Eronildes was referring to it. "Dona Dulce's not cooking anything," Emília replied.

"No," he hissed. "About the Bergmanns."

Emília's mouth felt very dry, her tongue sandpapery. "Yes," she finally said. "You're going back to your farm. You do it."

"She won't believe me."

"Why not?"

"She's suspicious of anyone who comes to Recife, and rightly so. I'll need your backing."

"You have it. Tell her I heard about the Bergmanns, too."

"Why don't you tell her?"

"I can't talk about a gun in the society papers!" Emília said, irritated by his ignorance.

Dr. Eronildes shook his head. "No," he said. "Tell her in person."

The burning smell had grown stronger now—less grainy and more chemical. Near Emília's feet, Expedito stared intently at her and the doctor, as if he understood their conversation.

"How?" Emília asked.

Eronildes drew closer. His breath was warm and sour, tinged with stale liquor.

"I can set up a meeting at my ranch. Your husband said the Bergmanns would take three months to arrive. Maybe more if there are rough seas. And the ship may sit in port here, after it arrives, to be inspected."

Emília shook her head. "Dr. Duarte will get it out quickly. He has an export business. He knows all the customs agents."

"All right," Eronildes continued, "so we have ninety days at best. If you take a train south, to Maceió, it will take a full day.

Then you'd have to go to Propriá—near the São Francisco—and that would take at least two days because there are no train lines connecting them. I'm not sure how long a riverboat ride will last; that depends on the water level. Even if the boat ride takes two weeks, if you leave early enough, you'll reach my ranch before the Bergmanns reach Recife."

"You've thought this through."

Dr. Eronildes licked his lips. "Yes. All during lunch."

Emília felt ashamed by her panicked and illogical thoughts during the luncheon. She wanted to be as clearheaded as Eronildes, but even then, in the relative safety of the courtyard, she felt muddled and overwhelmed.

"I don't know," she said. "The Coelhos won't let me travel alone."

"Make up an excuse."

"How will she know I'm coming?" Emília asked, afraid to say her sister's name aloud.

"I'll tell her," Eronildes said.

"But you said she doesn't believe you."

Eronildes reddened. "She reads the papers. You can say something about your trip, to give her proof. And you should take the boy."

Emília stared at the courtyard doors, suddenly eager for Dr. Duarte to return, for their conversation to be cut short. Luzia would want Expedito back—what mother wouldn't want her child returned to her?

"No," Emília said. "It's too dangerous."

Beads of sweat dotted Dr. Eronildes' upper lip and his chest rose, as if he was taking a deep breath, but instead of inhaling he held his pale hand to his mouth.

"Are you all right?" Emília said, worried he was going to be sick.

Eronildes nodded. "It's unfortunate," he said. "You're right. We're human. We have to accept death as our destiny. Some are foolish enough to believe they can escape it by living calm lives. Others are foolish enough to tempt death; they think it won't touch them no matter how dangerously they behave. In reality, no one is immune. No one can be saved. Forgive me for asking you."

Eronildes spoke in a tone laced with disappointment, as if he was speaking to a selfish child. Emília wanted to get away, to leave the doctor stewing in that hot courtyard, but if she stormed off she would be acting exactly the way he made her feel—like a scared, infantile woman.

"I meant it's too dangerous for Expedito, not for me," Emília said.

"No, no," Eronildes replied, waving his hand. "A meeting's too risky for all of us. It's better to stay away. Sometimes we want to be upright, but in the end we have weaker natures than we'd hoped. I wish this weren't the case."

"Stop it," Emília said, annoyed by his sudden reluctance. "I'll do it, and so will you. There's no choice . . ."

Emília's voice cracked. She couldn't finish her sentence. Her thoughts were rapid and disjointed. They made her feel unbalanced. She reached behind her, searching for the fountain's tiled edge, and sat. Drops of water hit her neck and back. In the air, the burning smell intensified, reminding Emília of the days after the revolution. Dr. Eronildes wrung his hands and stared.

"I'll do whatever you decide," he said. "I'm sorry I've upset you."

Emília didn't respond. She wasn't upset; she was excited. Emília hadn't been strong enough to save her little sister when the cangaceiros took her away. She hadn't been strong enough to resist Degas when he'd insisted on using her charity shipments as a cover. Now she could be strong. Now she had the chance to save Luzia.

"Set up a meeting and I'll go," Emília whispered. "I'll warn her."

Before Eronildes could agree, Dr. Duarte returned to the courtyard empty-handed. Degas accompanied him.

"I just received a phone call," he said, his breath short. "Communists, anti-Gomes factions, are burning the port. We'll have to postpone our meeting."

"Of course," Dr. Eronildes said and followed Degas and Duarte into the house.

Emília remained seated. She ripped a fern from a crack in the fountain's tile. Near her, Expedito patted the jabotis' shells. He whispered to the turtles, drawing his face close to theirs as if he was informing them of the port fire. Maybe there would be another revolution, Emília thought. Maybe the port would be destroyed and the Bergmanns would never arrive. If that happened, there would be no threat to the cangaceiros, but then Emília would be denied her chance to save her sister. Which did she want more?

She stared at the place where Dr. Eronildes had stood just minutes before. She'd believed his presence at the Finados luncheon was an excuse to see her and arrange a meeting with Luzia, but he'd followed Dr. Duarte out of the courtyard so suddenly. He hadn't said good-bye. Emília sensed shame in his exit. His drinking had gotten worse; any man would be ashamed of such a dependence on liquor, Emília reasoned. But she'd sensed desperation in his voice, in the urgent way he'd whispered to her. He'd said that his mother's will was tied up and that his ranch wasn't profitable. His suit was threadbare and his rancher's boots were poorly polished, the leather cracking along the creases. Financial troubles would make any gentleman desperate, but Eronildes was a professional. He was a doctor, and he could turn to his profession in times of need. Emília closed her eyes. Doctoring was the only bond Dr. Duarte and Eronildes shared—nothing else joined them. Dr. Eronildes had acted honorably in the past, she told herself. He would continue to do so.

Expedito howled. Emília opened her eyes. A turtle had nipped the boy; he held one hand in the other. His face was red, his eyes welling. Expedito looked at Emília angrily, as if it had been her fault, as if she should have prevented it.

3

///////

The port attack was quickly subdued. It was a small flare-up compared to the 1932 rebellion in São Paulo, but it had occurred in Recife, and the Northeast was supposed to be a Gomes stronghold. The president sent in troops. Within two weeks, Gomes had drafted the National Security Law. His law closed courts and created the Supreme Security Tribunal to hear cases against persons suspected of threatening Brazil's national integrity. Habeas corpus was suspended. Anyone who contested Gomes or disturbed national order—from intellectuals to petty thieves—was jailed. Prisons became so crowded that naval ships were converted into floating jails in Rio de Janeiro's harbor. In Recife, Military Police circulated in neighborhoods, concentrating on downtown and in the Bairro Recife where there were liberals and students.

A local anthropologist and a friend of Lindalva's published a book that the *Diário de Pernambuco* deemed "pernicious, destructive, anarchist, and Communist." The book said that Brazilians were not only products of the Portuguese but also of African and native influences. They were not a monolithic culture, the anthropologist said, but a trinity. Dr. Duarte called the book pornographic. Gomes's government prohibited its sale and closed all African cultural centers and religious houses. The author went into exile in Europe.

Gomes enforced his National Security Law so quickly that people didn't have time to react or to protest. Dr. Duarte, like many others, believed that Communism was a larger threat than Gomes's new law. In the Coelho parlor, Emília sat between Degas and Dr. Duarte and listened to nightly radio reports. An Italian leader nicknamed Il Duce was preparing to invade Ethiopia. In Spain, there was talk of civil war. In São Paulo's port, two hundred German Jews had disembarked from a ship, fleeing their new führer. The entire world was in turmoil, and Brazil was no different. Many Brazilians believed that Gomes was like a strict father, trying to protect them from instability. Others decided to leave the country before things worsened. Several of Recife's scientists, writers, and professors discreetly took jobs abroad. Lindalva and the baroness closed their house on Derby Square and prepared for an extended trip to see a cousin in New York City. They packed trunks full of clothing and books. Lindalva closed her bank account and, during Emília's last lunch on the baroness's porch, she placed a large envelope in Emília's hands. Inside were thick stacks of bills.

"Your escape fund," Lindalva said. "Use it now. Come with us."

The baroness nodded. "I don't think a married woman should run from her responsibilities, but when a husband doesn't consider a couple's welfare, the wife must consider her own. The baron taught me that. The situation here will only get worse. Gomes has big eyes. He'll want more and more, and then he won't know what to do with it all."

"Tell the Coelhos that we'll be your chaperones," Lindalva said, smiling. "We'll keep you honest."

"I can't go," Emília replied.

"The shop can close," Lindalva pleaded. "The seamstresses will find work."

"It's not the shop," Emília said, unable to face her friend. She felt her throat closing.

Lindalva and the baroness swore that they would return to Brazil, but Emília knew that she was losing her only allies. She wanted to go with them, to begin a new life in a foreign city, but she could not. She'd promised to make another trip. Instead of leaving Brazil, Emília had vowed to travel deeper inside it. Because of the National Security Law, any threat against the state—even by country bandits—was credible. Dr. Duarte and Interventor Higino anxiously waited for the Bergmanns to arrive. They sent more troops into the countryside. It pained Emília to read the newspaper each day and wonder which cangaceiros had been caught and decapitated. She couldn't stand the strain. The only thing that gave her solace was Dr. Eronildes' proposition: Emília would travel into the countryside and warn her sister. Only then would she feel free.

After his visit, Dr. Eronildes had sent thank-you cards to each member of the Coelho family, expressing his gratitude for their company during the Finados holiday.

> *Senhora Emília,*
>
> *It was a pleasure seeing you and the boy again. I'm glad you are both in good health. You had mentioned that you wished to speak with a colleague of mine regarding Expedito's educational opportunities. Would you still like to have this meeting? I will be in Recife in two weeks' time. Please give me your response then, so that I may make the necessary arrangements. My colleague is difficult to get hold of, so time is of the essence.*
>
> *In the meantime, I have prayed to Santa Luzia, as you recommended. I hope she will answer our prayers. Like any saint, she needs proof of our good intentions.*
>
> Atenciosamente,
Sr. Eronildes Epifano, M.D.

With a little over two months left until the Bergmanns' arrival, Emília had to move forward with her plans. When Dr. Eronildes visited Recife, he would specify a meeting date. Then Emília would unlock her jewelry box and give Eronildes her sister's old penknife— the one with the bee carved on its handle—to pass along to the Seamstress. The knife would serve as proof that the meeting was real, that Emília would be present.

Emília told the Coelhos that she needed new fabrics to satisfy upcoming orders for New Year's and Carnaval balls. She said that she wanted to use different kinds of materials and that a shop in Maceió had a large selection. The charity shipments had made Dr. Duarte a fan of Emília's "sewing hobby." He had no objections to the trip. Dona Dulce was always happy to see Emília out of the house but didn't like the idea of a young wife traveling alone.

"I won't be alone," Emília said. "I'm taking Expedito. And Raimunda, of course, to mind him while I shop."

Dona Dulce had no complaints about this arrangement. Emília's mother-in-law was grateful to live without Expedito for a few days and hopeful that she could pump Raimunda for gossip about the trip once they'd returned. Only Degas resisted the trip—if Emília left, he'd have no one to cover for his whereabouts during lunchtimes. He could not cross into the Bairro Recife to meet Chevalier. Because of this, Degas asked questions about the textile shop: Where was it located? Why hadn't he heard of it? How could they offer anything better than Recife's many fabric stores? Emília had her answers planned out but none of them satisfied Degas. Finally, she discovered a response that would.

"When I come back," she said, "we'll have so much cloth, I'll have to go to the atelier seven days a week. You can drop by as often as you like. I'll need you to bring me breakfast, lunch, and dinner."

Dr. Duarte gave Emília a check for her train fare to and from Maceió; Emília decided that she would not use the return ticket. The riverboat ride to Eronildes' ranch would last much longer than the time she'd been allowed for her shopping trip. Emília sewed her escape fund into the linings of three bolero jackets. Once in Maceió, she would leave a note with the maid, Raimunda, saying she'd left Degas. There would be a scandal; she could never return to Recife. Degas might get angry and reveal the truth to Dr. Duarte about Luzia and Expedito. Emília wouldn't risk going back.

Emília wasn't sad to leave Recife. She and Degas had no future together, and she disliked the way the Coelhos talked about Expedito's prospects. They planned to steer him into a trade like carpentry or ironwork. If he stayed in Recife, Expedito would spend his life fixing the Coelhos' rented properties or lifting boxes in their warehouses. A "drought baby" couldn't attend the university. Emília had transformed her life once; she could do it again. But this time she didn't hope for romance or wealth or any of the childish expectations she'd once harbored. Emília hoped only for solace. She had enough money saved to travel south after leaving Dr. Eronildes' ranch. If Degas revealed their secret, Emília and Expedito could cross the southern border into Argentina. She could buy two second-class tickets on a steamer bound for New York, where Lindalva and the baroness had settled. Even in a foreign place, a good seamstress could always find work.

Emília began to arrange her bags weeks before her intended departure. She selected her wardrobe carefully—if she took too many clothes the Coelhos would be suspicious. Emília had to pack stylish dresses and hats, but her clothes couldn't be too smart or she would look odd on the riverboat trip. After she left Maceió, there would be no porters or butlers to wait on her, so her suitcase couldn't weigh more than she could carry. There were also Expedito's clothes to choose and worry over. Emília spent afternoons in her room, folding and unfolding garments.

One day, shortly before Dr. Eronildes was scheduled to arrive in Recife, Emília heard the front door slam. Downstairs, Dr. Duarte shouted at a servant; Emília couldn't make out his words. A maid scurried to the second floor and knocked on Emília's door.

"Dr. Duarte wants to see you," the girl said and lowered her voice. "He's cismado about something. Looks like he'll chew through leather—"

"Where's Expedito?" Emília interrupted, grabbing the maid's elbow.

Startled, the girl backed away. She replied that the boy was in the courtyard, playing with Raimunda. Emília let her go. The maid rubbed her arm and stalked downstairs. Emília leaned against the door frame. If Dr. Duarte had discovered the purpose of her trip, she was finished. She stared at the pile of clothes on her bed. Expedito was in the courtyard; if she had to, she could run and grab the boy. She could dash out of the Coelho house before they had a chance to stop her. Emília took a deep breath and walked downstairs.

Dr. Duarte's face was flushed. His lips were crimped together. He brusquely waved Emília inside his study and shut the door behind her. Inside, Degas waited. Emília's husband sat before Dr. Duarte's desk, his hat in his hands, his eyes darting between his father and his wife. Degas appeared as confused as Emília, making similar calculations as to what had caused Dr. Duarte's anger and how he could escape it. In the corner sat a rotating fan with a half-thawed block of ice upon its grille. Emília felt a burst of cold air upon her.

"Sit," Dr. Duarte commanded.

Emília obeyed. The fan turned its face away. The room suddenly felt stuffy and warm.

"I won't dillydally," Dr. Duarte said. "Degas has a habit of visiting you during lunch, Emília. At your atelier."

Her father-in-law's voice had none of the affectionate mocking he usually used when speaking to her. It was stern. Emília's heart beat fast. Degas looked at her.

"Yes," she said. "He visits."

"And what do you eat? Air?" Dr. Duarte said. "No one sees you at restaurants."

"They bring us food," Degas replied.

"Where are the receipts?" Dr. Duarte demanded. "Show me."

Degas stared at his lap. "I don't have them."

"Well then!" Dr. Duarte yelled, slapping his desk and startling Emília. "You eat imaginary food from imaginary restaurants brought to you by imaginary waiters!"

He stared at his son. Breath wheezed in and out of Dr. Duarte's nose.

"There are hundreds of Military Police patrolling the streets now," Dr. Duarte continued. "Did you think no one would see you? Did you think that the city is blind?"

Dr. Duarte stopped. Spittle had collected at the corners of his mouth. He wiped it away with the back of his hand and looked at Emília.

"I'm sure, Emília, that you were only showing loyalty to your husband. I'm sure you played no knowing part in his outings. Some unfortunate news has come to my attention, Degas. It seems that your friend Mr. Chevalier has been caught in . . . in . . ." Dr. Duarte wrung his thick fingers. "There are things I can't say in front of a lady. All I can tell you is that there is a street boy involved. A deviant. And Mr. Chevalier was quick to name you, Degas, as a dear friend."

"Me?" Degas said, reddening. "So I'm guilty by association!"

"There should be no association with those types!" Dr. Duarte spat out. He closed his eyes and took a deep breath.

"I've paid the police," he continued. "The street boy won't leave the station. Thanks to the National Security Law he'll be cleaning their lavatories for the rest of his life. I also posted bond for Mr. Chevalier. He'll go back to Rio tomorrow. By boat."

Dr. Duarte fell into his desk chair with a thump, as if his knees had given out.

"Son," he said weakly, "this is nothing that discipline and good-hearted effort won't cure. It isn't irreversible. It is a mental weakness. We will drain it from you. There is a clinic, just outside São Paulo—the Pinel Sanatorium. They specialize in this sort of thing. The Fonseca's boy went there, not too long ago. He came back cured."

Degas looked pale. Emília recalled Rubem Fonseca—once a short, sturdy soccer champion for the engineering school's team, he'd returned from his medical leave without any interest in the sport. At the International Club dances, Rubem Fonseca sat at a back table, smoking cigarette after cigarette, greeting tablemates with a dead stare and a weak handshake.

"I've spoken to the director," Dr. Duarte said. "They have a spot for you, Degas. I will accompany you. We'll leave this week and say it's a business trip. You'll stay as long as it takes; Dr. Loureiro said most cases take two months. I'll tell your mother you're traveling. Emília, you'll still go on your fabric trip. Things must continue as normally as possible—Dona Dulce can't suspect a thing. It will unhinge your mother, Degas. Don't go to her for help. Do you understand?"

Degas nodded. He'd crumpled his hat in his hands.

"Emília," Dr. Duarte said, "I know this is unpleasant information, but you must hear it. People will ask questions and you must give credible answers. You are your husband's moral guide. When he returns, he'll take you to dinners, to the theater, to the cinema. You won't budge from his side. That way, there can be no relapses."

Emília nodded. Dr. Duarte waved them away, claiming he had to purchase ship tickets and inform the Pinel Sanatorium of their arrival. Emília and Degas left the study and walked up the stairs as a pair, as if their penance had already begun.

Halfway up, Degas stumbled. Emília grabbed his arm, worried he'd faint and topple over the banister's edge. Degas closed his eyes.

Slowly, Emília guided him to sit. The tiled steps felt cool against the undersides of her legs. Degas leaned his forehead against the stairway rails, smudging the brass.

Emília felt a confusing mix of emotions. She was thankful Dr. Duarte's anger wasn't directed at her; he didn't suspect Emília's trip was a fake. She also felt vindicated because she'd been right about Chevalier—he was a cad—and Degas had finally been reprimanded for his deceit. But then she recalled the dead-eyed Fonseca boy and saw Degas before her, his face drained of color and his hands trembling. Emília didn't want him to be punished.

"I'm sorry," she said.

Degas gave her a crooked smile. "Do you think I'll be cured?"

"I don't know."

"But you hope for it," Degas spat out. "Everyone wants me to be a different man."

Emília shook her head. "I don't know you, Degas. How can I want someone different when I hardly understand you now?"

Degas covered his eyes with his hands.

"I wasn't really fond of Chevalier," he said. "It was convenient, that's all. It never felt undignified. I never had to linger on corners like a lout, waiting for some street boy. But I didn't like Chevalier, not truly. Not like Felipe . . ."

Degas' voice broke. He sucked at his lips, as if biting back words.

"I don't want to be cured!" he said through clenched teeth. "I don't want to be dead to these feelings. I've had moments of real joy, Emília. Do you understand?"

Degas took her hands in his, as if begging. Emília looked downstairs, in the shadows beyond the curved banister, and wondered if anyone was listening. She'd never felt physical love the way Degas expressed it. What she'd felt years ago for Professor Célio was a child's crush, nothing more. The only physical connections she'd had were with Luzia and Expedito, and these were a different kind of love. Emília pulled her hands away.

"No," Degas said quietly. "You wouldn't understand. I robbed you of that. I wish I could leave this place. I wish I were buried with Felipe."

"Don't say that," Emília replied.

"Do you know what they do in those sanatoriums? They use electricity. They inject hormones. They'll kill me in a different way. I'll come back, but I'll be dead."

Emília took his hand. "Don't go. You don't have to."

"What can I do? Run away?" Degas stared at her. "Running isn't as easy as you think, Emília."

"I know," she said, suddenly irritated by Degas' soft voice.

"Do you?" Degas asked. "Promise me you'll come back after Maceió."

"Why?"

"Promise."

"No."

Degas shifted. His knees bumped hers. "There's no textile shop, is there?"

Emília held the edge of the stair. She tried to prop herself up but Degas placed his arm across her legs.

"Stop it!" Emília said. "Stop being selfish! If I wanted to leave you, I'd have gone to New York with Lindalva. This has nothing to do with you, Degas. It's more important."

Degas' arm slumped into her lap. "How important?"

"What if you could have avoided this trouble?" Emília whispered. "What if someone had warned you ahead of time? You would've acted differently if you'd known."

"Maybe," Degas said. "But maybe I wanted to be caught. Maybe I wanted it to end." Degas edged closer to Emília. "The Bergmanns are coming," he whispered. "You can't stop it. Neither can she."

"I can warn her. At least she won't be blind to it."

Degas nodded. "How will you find her?"

"That's not your business," Emília replied, suspicious. "She'll come to me."

"It's that doctor," Degas said. "He's convinced you to go out there."

"No one has convinced me."

"Cancel the trip, Emília. Do it in the newspapers so she can read it. That way, he can't refute it."

"No," Emília said, sliding away from Degas. "Why?"

"He's using you," Degas said. He rubbed his hair roughly, as if trying to prod a memory from his head. "Remember in your old town, how Felipe kept birdcages on his porch? He explained to me once how he caught those birds. He used to put food in the cages, to lure them in, but they got wise to that trick. So he'd put another bird inside. He'd tie its legs to the perch. And an outside bird, a wild one, would see its brother in there and believe it was safe. It would hop inside. It wasn't the food that lured them, Emília. It was each other."

Emília slid as far away from Degas as she could. Her back pressed against the stairway wall, her head nearly hit the handrail bolted above her. Degas spoke of birds and cages because he thought she was too simple, too dense, to merit a real explanation. He thought she was easy to trick.

"Dr. Eronildes is a good man," Emília said. "He wouldn't put me or Expedito in danger. I need his help, not the other way around. I'm using him."

"Lucky for Dr. Eronildes then," Degas replied. "You're right, he wouldn't compromise you or the boy; he doesn't want you. He wants her. He will set a false date, and then send you a telegram at the last minute. He'll give some excuse to call off your trip. He will cancel with you, but not with her. She'll think she's going to meet you and instead she'll meet troops."

"What do you mean?" Emília said. "What have you heard?"

"Nothing . . . ," Degas sputtered. "He's a drunk, Emília, and he's desperate. That's why he's suddenly friendly with Father."

"He came here to visit me and Expedito; he used Dr. Duarte as an excuse. And he inherited plenty of money. He has no reason to be desperate."

Degas shook his head. "The government owns the banks, Emília. How will your doctor get his inheritance unless he cooperates, unless he gives them something in return? Everyone knows he's a coiteiro! Just like everyone knows my . . . situation . . . and pretends not to because of Father, but they hope, one day, to use it to their advantage. It's the same thing, Emília. If Eronildes moves to the coast, he'll need friends. He has no family anymore. His name means nothing here. If he doesn't cooperate, his name will be mud. You can't live in this place without a good name. You know that as well as I."

Emília stood. Her legs felt heavy and numb; she grabbed the handrail for support.

"Why are you telling me this?" she asked. "Why do you want to help me all of a sudden?"

Degas shrugged. "I don't care about Father's work anymore. In fact, I hope he never gets his precious heads. I hope he fails."

Emília gripped the handrail harder. She kicked Degas' thigh with the toe of her shoe, making him look up at her.

"You hope *I* fail," she said. "You want me to stay here and feel guilty, so I can suffer like you. You didn't save Felipe or warn him, and that's your fault. But I'm going to save—"

Emília's voice caught. She looked down the stairs; there were always maids lurking in the Coelhos' hallways and listening behind doors.

"You never liked the doctor because everyone else liked him," she continued. "People looked past his vice but they didn't look past yours, so you want to smear him. Dr. Eronildes has always been honorable with me, Degas. You haven't."

"So you don't believe me?" Degas asked.

"No."

Degas heaved himself up from his place on the stairs.

"You're right," he said. "He earned your trust. I didn't. Why should you listen to me? It was only a guess, anyhow."

He leaned in tentatively, as if he meant to kiss her cheek. Emília turned away.

"I'm sorry," Degas said and walked upstairs.

4

That night it rained. Swarms of oversize mosquitoes invaded the Coelho house. Dona Dulce combated them by lighting lemongrass candles, which made the house's corridors and rooms foggy with smoke. When she slipped into bed, Emília's sheets were damp and chilly. This kind of weather was odd for early December; Emília hooked a hammock across her room and lay inside it, swaying gently. She watched Expedito sleep. He kicked away the sheets of his tiny bed and lay uncovered beneath the mosquito netting. Emília was restless, her head overcrowded with doubts. Was Degas right about Eronildes? Would she be the lure that trapped the Seamstress? Emília decided to talk to Degas again, calmly, the next morning.

She woke to the sound of the Chrysler's engine and the groan of the front gate. Emília sat up. The sky was dark and the Coelho house was still; the servants hadn't started their chores. Outside, the rain continued. Despite the storm, a few birds tentatively announced daylight.

Degas wasn't at breakfast. He'd left a note saying he'd gone to collect some things from his downtown office in preparation for his upcoming trip. Dr. Duarte was bleary-eyed and grumpy when he read the note. The rains distracted Dona Dulce—they fell hard, splashing into the house and forcing the maids to close all of the courtyard doors. The rooms became stuffy and humid.

At lunchtime, Degas didn't arrive. Dr. Duarte called the Coelho office; one of the employees said that Degas hadn't been there.

"Shirking responsibility!" Dr. Duarte said as he sat down for lunch. He got hold of Dona Dulce's brass bell and ordered the maids to serve the meal.

"Something's happened," Dona Dulce said, shaking her head. "He never misses lunch without advising me."

Dr. Duarte snorted. "I've called the police. They'll keep an eye out for our car. I told them to cross the bridge to the Bairro Recife. He's probably there."

Dona Dulce reddened. They ate in silence.

That afternoon, when Expedito grew restless, Emília took him to the backyard. They ducked into the covered patio where the laundry dried. Rows of rope stretched along the patio ceiling. The lines sagged under the weight of soggy bedsheets, Degas' dress shirts, Dona Dulce's yellowed undergarments, Emília's embroidered slips.

Expedito hid. Emília counted to ten. She walked past the walls of sheets. She pulled them apart in search of the boy. With the humidity and rain, nothing had dried. A cold pillowcase slapped her shoulder. Emília gasped. There was the rumble of a car in the drive, and then the honk of a horn. *Degas,* she thought. Expedito giggled. She swooped down on his hiding spot, pulling aside a sheet. The boy squealed. He was warm in her arms and smelled of baby powder. Emília held him close.

Outside, there were quick footsteps.

"Miss Emília!" the maid Raimunda yelled. Her voice was strained. She pushed though the sheets and clothes. "Miss Emília!" she called again.

Expedito placed his tiny hand over Emília's mouth. She smiled and stayed quiet, but Raimunda soon found them. She looked frustrated and confused.

"You should go to the sitting room right away," Raimunda said. "They've found Mr. Degas."

Inside, Emília and the Coelhos met a green-uniformed police captain. He spoke in compact sentences.

Degas and the Coelhos' Chrysler had been found. Witnesses along the road said that the Chrysler Imperial had been moving fast. The rain was impossibly thick. It was just after breakfast time. The car looked as if it was going to squeeze between a trolley and a broom vendor, but it swerved just before the Capunga Bridge. It fell into the Capibaribe. The current was strong. The car bobbed at first. Degas stayed inside. Some said he'd hit his head and that his eyes were closed. Others said that they were open. A trolley operator threw in a rope but it didn't reach the car. The Chrysler lurched, then went under. No one swam in to save him; the river was too wild.

Dona Dulce slumped into her husband's arms. Dr. Duarte held his wife, his arms shaking with the effort. The policeman stood uncomfortably in the parlor, waiting for someone to excuse him. He looked pleadingly at Emília but she could not speak.

At the velório, there was a closed casket covered in flowers. So many flowers! Emília felt dizzy from their scent. Dr. Duarte had commissioned an oil portrait of Degas to sit above the casket. In it, his son was thinner, his jaw more defined, his eyes bright and confident. Emília stared at the strange man in the portrait. The police deemed Degas' death an accident but rumors still persisted. Some said that the car's turn was too sharp to be accidental, even for a reckless driver like Degas. Emília hadn't been allowed to see his body, but Dr. Duarte said it was bloated and unrecognizable. Degas' casket would have to be closed for the velório and later buried in the Coelhos' mausoleum.

Emília became the Widow Coelho; that's what the newspapers called her, and how mourners addressed her as they kissed her hand and shuffled inside the mirrored ballroom where, years before, Emília had learned how to walk and speak and act during lessons with Dona Dulce. Without Degas, Emília's place in the Coelho house was precarious. She would live the rest of her life as the Widow Coelho, dependent on Dr. Duarte's generosity and subject to Dona Dulce's watchful eye.

The room's mirrors were covered for the wake, draped in black cloth like every other pane of glass in the Coelho house. After the police officer's visit, Dona Dulce pulled her hair back into a painfully tight bun. She put so much starch on her mourning dresses that Emília could hear their skirts swishing through the house. She saw a red ring around Dona Dulce's neck where the stiff collar had chafed her skin. Emília's mother-in-law stopped checking each room in the Coelho house for dust and mildew. She stopped demanding extra effort from the maids. In the days after Degas' death, Dona Dulce had a glassy-eyed and unfocused stare, as if she was making secret trips to the liquor cabinet. Emília recalled her father back in Taquaritinga and how, after her mother died, he'd had the same stare as Dona Dulce—caused not by drunkenness but by irreparable grief.

During the velório, Expedito sat beside Emília and occasionally peeked under her mantilla. She didn't slap his hand away. She wanted Expedito to see her, to know that she was still there beneath the black lace. His peeking exposed her face, and Emília heard Dona Dulce hiss to one of the guests:

"Do you see? She is like a stone. Not even one tear!"

Emília couldn't cry. Each time she thought of Degas, she pictured him peaceful in the Chrysler's front seat as brown water rushed through the windows. Degas had finally escaped the Coelho house and all of its obligations. He'd returned to Felipe. But before leaving, Degas had placed a seed of doubt in Emília's mind and, in the days after his death, that seed opened and took root. Emília recalled their last conversation, on the stairs. She wasn't sure if Degas' warning was an attempt at redemption, or another self-serving lie.

The line of mourners moved slowly forward.

"I'm sorry for your loss," the men said. Some women whispered to Emília: "It's a shame there are no children to keep the family name. Children are a great comfort." Other women said: "It's a blessing there were no children to suffer through this." Emília nodded serenely after each comment, giving no hint of her emotions. Because the casket was closed there was no body to crowd around and inspect, so the guests observed Emília and the Coelhos instead. They also took the opportunity to study the rarely visited Coelho house. Mourners crowded the parlor, the sitting room, the ballroom, and the dining room with its buffet of cookies and large silver tureens of coffee. Only coffee was served in an effort to keep the mourners awake throughout the night.

Coffee made Emília jittery. She'd drunk too many cups of it and now, as the sky grew dark and the ballroom lights clicked on, Emília could not keep still. She shifted in her chair, smoothed her black dress, arranged her mantilla. Incense smoke seemed to coat her tongue, her throat. The room felt too small. Expedito was already upstairs, safely in bed, with Raimunda watching him. Children didn't have to stay up all night during a wake, but wives did. Emília sighed.

"Excuse me," she said to Dona Dulce, Dr. Duarte, and the other mourners who crowded around their chairs. Emília stood and quickly left the room. She needed air. The courtyard was filled with visitors, all dressed in black. They smoked, chatted, admired the fountain, and toyed with the jabotis. Emília bypassed the courtyard and moved toward the front door. She removed her mantilla, balling the small piece of black lace in her hand. She would leave the property—take a walk up and down Rua Real da Torre until the coffee had worn off. *A lady doesn't walk aimlessly.* She heard Dona Dulce's rule in her head. *A lady always has a destination, an agenda.*

I've got one, Emília thought.

Her bags were still packed, despite the fact that Dr. Duarte had canceled the check he'd written for Emília's train tickets to Maceió. For a full year after her husband's death, a widow was required to mourn at home. For the sake of propriety, Emília couldn't leave her house, she couldn't appear in the newspaper, she couldn't work at her atelier, and she certainly couldn't travel. Emília, however, had stopped caring about propriety. As soon as the mourners dissipated, as soon as Dona Dulce returned to her kitchen and stopped keenly observing Emília's expressions of grief, she would escape the Coelho house and go to the countryside. She didn't need Dr. Duarte's money—she had her escape fund. Even if she had to bribe the gardener and gatekeeper, even if she had to leave in the middle of the night, Emília would leave. She would not miss her meeting at Dr. Eronildes' ranch.

As if fate were confirming her intentions, Emília saw the doctor himself in the Coelhos' front hall, hunched over the guest book. Eronildes signed his name slowly. When he reached the "condolences" section, he pondered for a minute, then scribbled a message. His face was oily; his nose and forehead shone in the lamplight. He smiled at the Coelho maid who attended him, but when he saw Emília the smile disappeared.

"Thank you for coming," she said, motioning the maid away.

"I was already in Recife," Eronildes said. "I told you in my note that I'd planned to come. I didn't expect to find you here."

"Where else would I be?" Emília said.

"No, I meant in the hallway."

"I needed air."

Eronildes nodded. "I'm sorry for your loss. A terrible accident," he said. "You are in luto-fechado now. You can't leave the house for a year."

"Yes," Emília said. She looked around and then lowered her voice. "I'm not going to follow it."

"No?" Eronildes said, looking more relieved than surprised.

"The Bergmanns are on their way," Emília whispered. "When is the meeting?"

"I don't know."

Emília balled her mantilla tighter in her hands. "Why?"

"She wants proof. I came here to collect it. And to pay my respects, of course."

"Proof?"

"She won't commit to a date without proof. Something of yours."

Emília nodded.

"The more personal, the better—" Dr. Eronildes said.

"Excuse me," Emília interrupted.

Leaving the foyer, she climbed the front stairs two by two. In Emília's room, Raimunda dozed beside Expedito's bed. The boy lay with his face pressed against a pillow. Emília tiptoed inside. A floorboard creaked. Raimunda sat up.

"A velório's not the time to be soft footed," she hissed. "You'll scare someone to death." Remembering her duties, Raimunda smoothed her apron and began to get up. "What do you need?" she asked.

"Sit," Emília whispered. "I want my rosary, that's all."

Raimunda sat back and watched. In the dark, Emília could not judge the maid's expression. She knelt beside her bed and, hoping to hide her actions from Raimunda, turned her back. She eased the jewelry box from its hiding spot beneath the bed, took off the chain around her neck, and put the gold key into the box's lock. Quickly, Emília reached inside and removed the penknife. She felt its cool blade, its wooden handle with the bee carved into its side. Raimunda shifted in her chair. Emília cradled the knife close, locked the jewelry box again, and left the room.

Eronildes wasn't in the downstairs hallway. Emília searched the foyer but didn't find him; a maid had probably shuffled Eronildes into the black-curtained ballroom. Emília replaced her mantilla—wrinkled now, from being crumpled in her fist—over her hair and folded the penknife into her handkerchief. She would find a way to place it in Eronildes' hands, to slip it into his coat pocket.

The ballroom's air was thick with candle smoke. Mourners coughed. Emília stood behind them, cramped along the room's edges. Before she could say "Excuse me," and make her way back to her empty chair near Degas' portrait, she caught sight of Eronildes. He did not see her. In the front of the mourning line, the doctor bowed to Dona Dulce, who nodded politely. Next to her, Dr. Duarte rose from his chair. Instead of greeting Eronildes with a handshake, Emília's father-in-law clamped the doctor in a firm embrace. Eronildes did not stiffen in response to the hug. He did not politely pat Dr. Duarte's back and then try to release himself. Eronildes seemed dwarfed in Dr. Duarte's thick arms but he did not seem uncomfortable. Unable or unwilling to remove himself from the firm embrace, Eronildes slumped into it as if resigning himself.

Unseen in the back of the room, Emília shivered. Her insides seemed to cool and condense. Something within her fell into place, as certain as a lock sliding into its bolt. She'd felt this way twice before—once during her first Carnaval at the International Club, and later, the first time she'd held Expedito in her arms. Emília held the penknife tightly. She backed out of the ballroom and ran upstairs.

Raimunda was awake, as if she'd expected Emília's return.

"I don't want it after all," Emília whispered. "My rosary, I mean."

Raimunda didn't respond. Emília quickly opened the jewelry box and replaced the penknife, still wrapped in a handkerchief. She clicked the box shut and pushed it back under the bed with the toe of her shoe. Emília's pumps were black, like the rest of her outfit. Their patent leather made her feet shine. She was stylish even in mourning, Emília thought bitterly. Her hands shook. She had the urge to remove those shoes and chuck them out her window. Instead, she stared across the dark room at Expedito, asleep, and at Raimunda beside him.

"That doctor's here," Emília whispered. "Eronildes."

Raimunda nodded. "The drinker."

"Is that what you think of him?"

Raimunda clicked her tongue. "It's not my job to think anything of anyone."

"But if it were?"

"It's not. And it won't ever be. It's not my place to give an opinion. And it's not your place to care what I think."

Emília sighed. She sat on the bed and covered her face with her hands.

"I can tell you what I know about other's opinions," Raimunda said, her voice unusually soft. "I know that Mr. Degas, God rest his soul, didn't like that doctor. Dona Dulce says that Mr. Degas was misguided about some things, but that he was a good judge of character. Now, you were one of the people he judged—he picked you for his wife. So do you agree with Dona Dulce or not?"

Emília looked across the room. Her old sewing bag sat in the room's corner, and in it were needles, thread, ideas for patterns, and her measuring tape. She'd brought it from Taquaritinga—a hand-made strip of ribbon with each centimeter and meter mark carefully drawn on it.

Emília rose from the bed, riffled through her sewing supplies, and found the tape. She left the room without speaking to Raimunda. Emília needed an ink pen and she knew where to find one.

Degas' room hadn't been touched since his death. His bed was still unmade, his books scattered about the floor, his English records stacked precariously in a pile near the Victrola. Emília found a pen on Degas' desk. There, she spread out her measuring tape. She drew extra centimeters between the inky lines already on the tape. She scrambled the numbers, changing the 6 to an 8, the 11 to a 17.

"Measure right!" Aunt Sofia's voice echoed in Emília's mind. "Don't trust a strange tape. Trust your own eyes."

Emília rolled the measuring tape into a tight ball and hid it in her hands. Downstairs, as soon as she took her place beside the Coelhos, Dr. Eronildes moved to greet her.

"I'm very sorry for your loss," he said.

"Thank you," Emília replied.

Her palms were sweaty and Emília hoped the new ink marks had dried, that they hadn't bled onto her fingers. Eronildes gripped her hand and bent to kiss it. Emília pressed the tape into his palm.

"Proof," she whispered.

Eronildes stiffened. His lips were near her fingers. "I will confirm a date," he whispered back, then pressed his mouth to her hand.

One week later, Emília received a black-bordered envelope addressed to Mrs. Degas Coelho. There was no return address and the card inside had no condolences, only a date: *January 19.*

It would be after Christmas and New Year's, both of which would be muted holidays at the Coelho house.

"He will set a false date," Degas had said. "He will cancel with you, but not with her."

That didn't matter anymore. Emília could only hope that the measuring tape would communicate all that she could not. If Luzia read closely enough, she might see the wrong numbers and recall Aunt Sofia's old warning. Luzia might understand what Emília was trying to tell her—the meeting itself was a trick, a trap, just as Degas had predicted.

After the velório, Emília thought of Degas often. How frightened he must have been, with no candle to light his soul's path. But surely the route to heaven was not as murky and dark as the waters of the Capibaribe. Surely Degas could find a way. This thought—that even Degas could pull past the darker aspects of his nature in order to find the good—made Emília believe that she could as well. As soon as it was safe, she would run away. She would warn her sister without Dr. Eronildes' help. She would find Luzia and tell her about the Bergmanns. Until then, Emília hoped that the tape would relay her warning.

At night, in her dreams, Emília was a girl again. She and Luzia climbed that old mango tree. It was very tall—as tall as the *Graf Zeppelin*'s landing tower—and its fruits were heavy and yellow, shaped like teardrops. Luzia sat on the limb below Emília. She leaned back. She lost her balance. Emília reached for her. She fumbled for Luzia's hand but could not save her sister, not without letting go herself.

1

The soldier's body resembled a cross-stitch: his arms and legs were extended, his hands and feet firmly tied to tree trunks. Inteligente placed his massive brown hands at the sides of the soldier's head, holding it steady. The man writhed and squirmed for a long time, trying to break free. Luzia let him. Soon he was tired out and calm, as docile as a calf in the seconds before its branding, accepting of its fate. Baiano stuffed cotton into the man's nostrils, so he would have to keep his mouth open. Ponta Fina straddled the soldier. In his right hand Ponta held a pair of needle-nosed pliers stolen from a vaqueiro's satchel. The pliers were a useful tool, good for removing bullets, thorns, teeth.

Luzia squatted beside the soldier. His eyes followed her. His hands were red and swollen from the bindings. Luzia traced his fingers with her own, moving slowly across his palm, touching the deep lines across it.

"Speak," she said.

"I told you, I don't know anything," the soldier replied, his voice hoarse. "I left my squadron. I swear."

"I don't like swearing," Luzia said. Nearby, Baby and Maria Magra giggled.

"I promise!" the soldier sputtered.

Luzia nodded. A loyal bar owner had sent her a message that a monkey had deserted. The soldier had traded his gun for drinks. When Luzia's group arrived to question him, they found that the soldier had also given away his jacket and boots. The man was unkempt and incoherent. Until Luzia dragged him into the scrub, he'd planned to drink himself to death. The cangaceiros fed their prisoner only water, farinha, and meat, hoping to clear his head and loosen his tongue. After the theater fire, a wave of troops had entered the caatinga. Soldiers and residents alike tried to catch the cangaceiros. People across the scrubland condemned the Hawk and the Seamstress. Then, suddenly, the troops retreated. They abandoned their newly built posts and stopped trying to track down the Seamstress's group. Luzia sensed something unusual.

The deserter wouldn't tell her anything of value—only that Gomes had called his regiment back to the coast. But there was more to his story; Luzia felt it. The monkey wouldn't look at her when he spoke. He fidgeted, sighed, and wept. The cangaceiros kicked him. Ponta Fina held his punhal to the man's throat, but the soldier still wouldn't speak. When the cangaceiros gave him dried beef, the soldier took large bites. He had a complete set of teeth, all of them white and thick. Unlike many of Luzia's cangaceiros, who had to bite food gingerly or gum dried beef until it was soft enough to swallow, the soldier ate quickly and ferociously. One day, he begged for a piece of juá bark to rub across his teeth. At that moment, Luzia found his weakness. She, like Antônio, had become adept at discovering the things people valued most. She'd ordered the soldier strung up.

"You're a deserter," Luzia said, stroking the man's fingers. "Your promises aren't worth much. You left the army. Why keep their secrets now? Tell me, and I'll let you go. I'll take you back to that bar. I'll buy you a bottle of branquinha."

The soldier licked his lips. "I wasn't a captain. I don't know any plans."

"Why bring troops all the way out here, and then go back?"

"I don't know."

Beneath her hand, the soldier's finger twitched. Luzia stood. She nodded at Ponta Fina.

"Hold him tight!" Ponta said.

Inteligente clamped the soldier's head harder. Ponta took a leather strap and placed it in the man's mouth, tugging so that his jaw opened wide. Baiano knelt beside the soldier and held the strap with both hands, like reins.

"Start in the back," Luzia said.

Ponta nodded and bent forward. The pliers' metal prongs clicked against the man's molar. Saliva darkened the strap.

"If you move it'll crack, and hurt more," Ponta said.

Beneath him, the soldier stiffened. Ponta Fina grunted and tugged. There was a sucking sound. The man screamed.

His cry was both terrified and angry and Luzia wished she could quiet the soldier or clamp her hands over her ears. She heard that kind of scream each night, in her sleep. Ever since the theater fire, Luzia had dreamed of that dark cinema. In her dreams, the projector moved but didn't shed light on the canvas screen. Instead, the machine released a tinny rattle. The room became hot; not a stuffy heat but a searing one, like midday during the drought. Luzia's skin burned. Shadowy figures blocked her escape. She heard a bar scraping across the front door, locking it from the outside. In her dreams, Luzia was still inside, and around her were the cangaceiros—her men and women—their hats crooked, their eyes wide with surprise. *Mãe!* they screamed. *Mãe!* In their voices Luzia heard both sadness and accusation, as if she'd betrayed them. Each time she dreamed of the theater fire her stomach felt unsettled. It wasn't like the nausea she'd experienced when she was pregnant. Instead, it left a dry and coppery taste in her mouth, reminding her of the desperate days when, like an animal, she'd eaten dirt for sustenance.

The *Diário* called it a crime against innocents. They'd interviewed survivors. They'd called her heartless. In fact, it had been just the opposite: Luzia had felt too much in that theater. In the projector's light she was ashamed and confused. This made her angry. When she heard the patrons' insults, Luzia felt like the Cannibal Wife, a woman unable to control her gruesome cravings. Those theater patrons were innocents but they'd supported Gomes, which made them guilty. What did it mean, Luzia wondered, that she could redefine innocence and guilt so easily? If guilt was flexible, if it came and went at her whim, then the Seamstress was as capricious as a colonel. But the theater patrons had insulted the Seamstress and her cangaceiros, and that required punishment. If Luzia hadn't reacted, if she'd left the theater with her head down, the entire town would have believed that the Seamstress was weak and that the Hawk—whom everyone believed to be alive—hadn't come to her defense.

As soon as she'd dropped the thick wooden bar across the theater doors, sealing them shut, Luzia knew that her revenge was too harsh but she couldn't backtrack; she would look indecisive. Antônio had taught her that indecision led to a bad end. What he hadn't taught her, however, was that poor decisions often produced regrets, and regrets could not be cured. Antônio had shown her how to use the genipapo's bark to soothe sore muscles. He'd shown her how to boil jacurutu bark to cure ulcers and how to mash the marmeleiro's yellow flowers into a powerful expectorant. The cure for nervousness was eating the inside of a passion fruit, seeds and all. With all of these medicines, there was no plant or animal that eased remorse. There was no tea that flushed out guilt.

Ponta Fina fell backward onto the soldier's legs. He put down the pliers and cupped a bloody molar in his hands. Baiano and Inteligente craned their heads to look at the tooth's yellowed crown and forked roots. Underneath Ponta, the soldier twisted and bucked. Blood seeped from one side of his mouth, staining the leather strap. He gasped, choking.

"Lift his head," Luzia said. "Let him spit."

Inteligente obeyed. Baiano removed the strap from the soldier's mouth. The man coughed and a pink, viscous liquid dribbled down his chin.

"Tell me," Luzia said. "Where did your regiment go?"

"Near the São Francisco," he said, his voice nasal and stuffy. The cotton in his nose was wet and stained pink.

"Why?"

"I don't know."

Luzia closed her eyes. "Take another one," she said. "A front one."

Ponta nodded. Baiano moved to replace the strap.

The man coughed again, as if he were about to vomit. Instead, he made a high-pitched sound.

"What?" Luzia asked.

"A gun," he yelled. "I heard my captain talk about it. We were leaving for a ranch near the Old Chico and some of us were nervous and he told us not to worry because there was a gun. It would do all the work for us."

Luzia knelt to better hear him. "What kind of gun?"

"A fast gun. That's all he would say. He called it 'the better Seamstress.'"

"Why?" Luzia asked.

"Because it would outshoot you. That's what my captain said. Only a few of us would get to shoot it. There'd only be a few guns. We wouldn't need many. It shoots five hundred rounds without reloading."

"That's a lie," Baiano said.

The soldier shook his head, still propped in Inteligente's hands. "I swear . . . I promise. That's what he told us."

"Five hundred rounds," Ponta whispered.

Luzia felt inside her trouser pocket. The measuring tape was rolled into a messy ball; after receiving it, she'd unraveled the tape so many times that she'd stopped bothering to wind it back tightly. Luzia ran her finger across its frayed end.

"When will she get here?" Luzia said. "This better Seamstress?"

"She's . . . it's already here," the soldier said. "I mean, there . . . near the Old Chico. My captain said the guns would be ready when we got to the river."

Luzia nodded.

"What now, Mãe?" Ponta asked.

Luzia stared at the bound soldier. If she let him go as a reward for his honesty, he might become a useless drunk and brag about his encounter with the cangaceiros. Or he might feel guilty about his betrayal of his squadron. He might try to find them, to get a message to them about what he'd told the Seamstress. If this happened, it would be Luzia's fault. People would say she'd been too soft and that she'd put her group in danger. They would say it was just like a woman, to feel such useless compassion.

"Do it fast," Luzia said, glancing at the soldier. Ponta Fina nodded.

She walked away from the group and deeper into the scrub, rubbing the measuring tape between her fingers. Dr. Eronildes hadn't unwound it when he'd given it to her. She could tell by how tightly rolled the tape had been—Aunt Sofia had taught her and Emília to wind their tapes like that. Their aunt had also taught them never to trust tapes that weren't their own. People weren't careful, they made their tapes haphazardly and wrote the numbers incorrectly. Some seamstresses did this on purpose to guarantee business: they sold poorly made tapes so that their buyers would make inaccurate cuts, waste fabric, and finally call the seamstress in to fix their mistakes. Aunt Sofia herself had taught Luzia and Emília this lesson: when they were learning how to sew, she'd given them a bad tape. They'd trusted their aunt and, without inspecting the tape's numbers, Luzia and Emília had cut their cloth using the sabotaged measurements. Their creations came out lopsided and awful. "Trust your own eyes!" Aunt Sofia had chided. "Don't trust a strange tape, and don't trust its bearer."

2

Before Luzia had captured the soldier, Dr. Eronildes had delivered Emília's tape as proof of their upcoming meeting. Luzia had performed the exchange outside Eronildes' ranch; after the theater fire she wouldn't go into anyone's house, not even the doctor's. Eronildes arrived alone and on foot, afraid the scrub's thorns would blind his only horse. The doctor was pale, his hair drenched with sweat. The toes of his old boots were splattered with a chunky yellow substance.

"You were sick?" Luzia said upon meeting him. She was alone, having ordered the other cangaceiros to wait a few meters back.

Eronildes wiped his mouth. "I'm not used to exerting myself like this. In this heat."

Luzia offered him water. Eronildes declined. He handed her the tape.

"Your proof," he said.

Luzia's palms sweated. She unrolled a small section of tape. It was an old and sturdy ribbon, the same kind Aunt Sofia had given them to make their measuring tapes. The first numbers were evenly spaced and neatly drawn. The writing on the tape was Emília's. Before she could unwind it all the way, Eronildes spoke.

"I'll have to send an express letter to Recife, to confirm the date. She insists on meeting on January twelfth."

"So soon?" Luzia asked.

"The sooner the better."

"Her husband just passed," Luzia said. "She'll be in luto-fechado."

Eronildes' eyebrows rose and his eyes became wide.

"I saw the obituary," Luzia explained. "I found a new *Diário*."

"She's going to ignore her luto," Eronildes replied.

"How? She won't be allowed to travel."

"You share the common trait of resourcefulness," Eronildes said. "From what I understand, it's well known that Dona Emília didn't have much in common with her husband or his family. She suffers in their house. She's happy to escape it."

"Suffers?" Luzia said, staring at the tape in her hands. She recalled all of the newspaper images she'd collected: Emília wearing fine clothes, running her own business, and associating with Recife's high society. What she knew of her sister's life Luzia had gleaned from photographs, and she'd always assumed Emília's happiness. But Luzia knew better than most that images could lie, that they captured only an instant and never revealed the full truth. She felt a pang of sympathy for her sister—what had happened to Emília in

Recife? She also felt the need to discount her sister's plight. Emília had Expedito, a business, and a home; what did she truly know of suffering? As if hoping to discover the answer, Luzia turned her back to the doctor and unwound the tape completely.

"So, January twelfth then?" Eronildes said. "I have to head back. It is a long walk for me."

Emília's measurements were wrong. She'd written over the tape's cleanly drawn tick marks. She'd changed the numbers and made them incorrect on purpose. Emília's additions to the tape were hastily drawn—the ink smudged, the lines shaky—as if she'd felt fear or urgency when altering the measurements. Luzia felt dizzy. *Trust your own eyes! Don't trust the tape and don't trust its bearer.*

"How is he?" she asked.

"Who?"

"My boy."

"Fine. He's healthy."

"Safe?"

"Yes, safe."

Eronildes shifted. Luzia noticed a black band around his jacket sleeve.

"Who passed?" she asked.

"My mother."

"I'm sorry. Death's hard."

Eronildes snorted. "Is it?"

"Yes. Even for me."

"I have trouble believing you, Luzia."

"The theater was a mistake."

Eronildes shook his head. "People paid dearly for your mistake."

"So did I," Luzia said. "I lost many friends because of it."

Eronildes held his stomach. He turned his head and spat.

"Are you going to be sick again?" Luzia asked.

"No."

Luzia stared at the tape's uneven tick marks, its incorrect numbers. "A while back you talked about rebreaking my arm. Curing me. Would you still do that?"

"Why?"

"Would you?"

"It won't do any good. You will still be recognized."

"You used to encourage me to leave this life."

"That was a long time ago. It's too late now."

Luzia's hand tightened around the tape. "I live by the gun, so I'll die by the gun, is that right?"

Eronildes wiped his brow. "You made a decision, Luzia. You must live with your choice. We all must."

She nodded. "January twelfth, then?"

Eronildes looked relieved. "Yes."

"I won't go in your house."

"You won't have to," Eronildes replied and slowly made his way back to his ranch.

In the days after this meeting, Luzia studied the measuring tape. She recalled Antônio inserting his silver spoon into a suspect plate of food and watching as the spoon tarnished and turned black. They could not trust that food or the person who served it. Emília's tape, like Antônio's spoon, revealed a traitor.

At night, while the other cangaceiros slept, Luzia's heart beat fast. Her fingers felt cold. How many other coiteiros were ready to turn her in, to trick her? Luzia felt as though she were back in Padre Otto's schoolyard, surrounded by children who'd once been her friends but suddenly began to prod her crooked arm and call her Victrola. Padre Otto had witnessed this. As a girl, Luzia had watched the priest move toward the crowd and she'd believed that he would be the only one to redeem her. "Children," Padre Otto had yelled. "Leave Victrola alone." When she thought of Dr. Eronildes, Luzia felt the same stab of disappointment and anger she'd felt toward the priest. And now, in her scrub camp as well as in the schoolyard, she trusted only Emília.

Luzia worked the measuring tape between her fingers. Her sister had cared enough to warn her.

3

—————————

They buried the soldier whole. Luzia left his head on his neck out of respect for his honesty, but also because she did not want his death to be attributed to her group. She didn't want anyone to suspect that the Seamstress had captured a monkey and that he'd given her information. Luzia burned the soldier's green pants, leather hat, and canvas satchel. She waited until the items disintegrated completely so that curious farmers or vaqueiros couldn't sift through the ashes and find the remains. The blaze was hot. Luzia squatted before it. She opened her bornal and took out the pile of newspaper photographs at the bottom of her bag. Luzia felt a stab in her chest, near her heart, as if something had snagged there, like a hook on a line. It was painful to resist its pull. Quickly, before she could look at the photos, Luzia threw them into the fire. The images of Emília and Expedito blackened and curled. If she was killed, soldiers would take her bags; Luzia couldn't let them find the images and associate the Seamstress with the Widow Coelho.

Luzia kept only the measuring tape—proof of Emília's loyalty. She thought of her sister's warning. She recalled Dr. Eronildes' boots, covered in vomit and sand. And Luzia remembered fragments of the dead soldier's confession: *five hundred rounds, the "better seamstress," a ranch near the Old Chico.* Separately these memories seemed disparate and random but—like the paper pieces of a sewing pattern—when considered together they connected to form a recognizable entity.

"The meeting's a trap," Luzia said. "Eronildes wants to see me at the same time there are monkeys waiting by the Old Chico. Who do you think they're waiting for?"

Ponta Fina and Baiano joined her beside the fire. They fixed their eyes on Luzia.

"The new weapon's with him," she said. "Eronildes has got that 'better seamstress.'"

Baiano shook his head. Ponta Fina spat.

"Damn him," Ponta said. "He's worse than the rest."

"January twelfth," Luzia continued. "If .we hurry, we can make it."

"Mãe?" Baiano said.

Luzia recalled her first shooting lesson with Antônio, back on Colonel Clóvis's ranch—how heavy the revolver was, and how holding it had hurt her wrist. She recalled the argument she'd had with Antônio afterward.

"We'll surprise them," she said. "I want them to see that I know. That I knew all along."

"If we don't show, they'll see that," Ponta Fina said. "The doctor'll look like a fool."

Luzia shook her head. "I won't run."

"It's not running," Ponta replied. "We can go back later, when the doctor doesn't expect us. Why walk into a trap?"

Luzia stared at the fire. The photographs were gone, transformed into a dark pile beneath the flames.

"I want that gun," she said.

The men were quiet. Baiano wrapped his hands together, as if praying.

"Five hundred rounds," he said. "If that soldier wasn't fibbing, it's better than all our Winchesters put together. But it's a risk, going there."

"If we don't go, the risk is worse," Luzia said. "They'll use that gun on us some other time, and we won't know when or where. Now we know. Now we have the advantage."

"So we show up early?" Ponta asked.

Luzia shook her head. "We show up when we're supposed to and break into two groups. One will angle around, behind the monkeys. The other will go to the meeting spot. I'll go with that group. Gomes wants me; as long as I'm there, they'll think we don't know. I'll be the bait."

Baiano and Ponta Fina stared into the flames. Luzia examined their faces. She saw both worry and excitement there and wondered if her own expression revealed the same emotions. Luzia stuffed the measuring tape into her trouser pocket; there was no avoiding this fight. Pregnancy hadn't weakened her. The drought hadn't killed her. Gomes's many brigades of troops hadn't caught her. The Seamstress's head remained firmly upon her neck. Luzia couldn't let this new gun, this "better seamstress," change that.

4

On January twelfth, Luzia's group arrived on Eronildes' ranch. There were fifteen men and women with her, including Ponta Fina, Baby, Inteligente, Sabiá, and Canjica. The rest of the cangaceiros—the best shooters and attackers—went with Baiano into the hills around the river valley. They would find Gomes's troops and surprise them when Luzia gave the signal: a sharp whistle that resembled a hawk's call.

They camped in a dry gulley not far from the doctor's house. The sun slowly fell behind a ridge, filling the scrub with shadows. Luzia stared into the hills. Soldiers hid there, observing her and the cangaceiros. Baiano, in turn, observed the troops. They wouldn't attack until first light; Luzia felt certain of this. The monkeys couldn't risk having cangaceiros escape under the cover of night. And, most of all, they would want to clearly see the effects of their new weapon. The troops would want to witness the Seamstress's death. As soon as the sun rose, the soldiers would have a clear view. Until then, Luzia would put on a good show.

Three of Eronildes' ranch hands delivered baskets overflowing with manioc flour, beans, pumpkins, an entire hock of beef, and several bottles of wine. In one of the baskets was a note from Eronildes:

Meet in the morning. I will bring them to you.

Luzia put the note in her pocket, beside the measuring tape. She stared in the direction of Eronildes' house. The doctor underestimated a mother's instincts: Luzia's boy wasn't in that house. Neither was Emília. If they had been there, Luzia would've felt their presence the way she felt the presence of the São Francisco River a few hundred meters south—she could smell the river and hear the rush of its waters. Eronildes' house was closer than the Old Chico, yet Luzia couldn't smell smoke from a cook fire or hear pots clanging in Eronildes' kitchen. The house was empty.

Ponta Fina insisted on testing the food Eronildes had sent. He sniffed the meat and the pumpkin. He dipped Antônio's silver spoon into the dry goods and the wine. When everything came up clean, the group looked into the hills and cheered. Luzia ordered them to erect a spit and build a large fire under it. Beef fat dripped into the flames, making them hiss and crackle.

"Pour the wine!" Luzia shouted. Then, in a whisper: "Don't drink. We need to keep our wits."

The cangaceiros obeyed, taking long swigs from the bottles but pursing their lips before wine could enter their mouths. Above them was a new moon. When the fire's last ember died, the gulley became instantly dark, as if a shroud had been thrown over it. The cangaceiros pretended to sleep. Couples whispered nervously to one another. A few solitary men shifted upon their blankets. Luzia remained standing. Far away, in the hills beyond the gulley, she saw circles of orange light. They glowed and bobbed like insects.

Luzia recalled the theater fire: along with the dark flakes of ash that were produced by the blaze, there'd been cinders. The small points of light had risen quickly, escaping the fire's oppressive heat like souls escaping the confines of their earthly bodies. Luzia remembered the immense weight of the theater door's crossbar, and how her arms shook as she'd dropped it in place. Afterward the hinges had creaked and moaned but did not buckle. The fire inside grew hotter, the screams louder. Now, in that dark gulley, Luzia believed the cinders from the theater fire had never been extinguished. They'd followed her across the scrub, ready to consume her.

Luzia felt a chill across her neck, as if a cold hand had clamped it. She stepped back. Sand shifted beneath her feet. The land was so sensitive it responded to her most minute movements. They were small shifts, but important, like revising a target before taking aim. Like taking scissors to expensive cloth and deciding to cut outside the marked pattern. Instinct told the sand which way to shift, just as it told the shooter where to point, and the seamstress where to cut. Instinct told Luzia where a man would move before she shot him. It told her to sense changes in the air before a big rain. It told her how to sniff out the presence of water within the scrub. Now, instinct told Luzia what waited in those dark hills. It told her to run.

Luzia turned. Dark shapes covered the ground. Some cangaceiros still pretended to sleep but most of the men and women stared. Their eyes shone. They fixed their gazes upon Luzia like the saints in her girlhood closet, waiting for a prayer or a sacrifice. Ponta Fina and Baby were curled together on their blanket, facing her. Luzia contemplated kneeling beside Ponta and whispering to him, but what would she say? She couldn't correctly explain the sudden coldness in her belly, or why her hands had begun to shake. These sounded like symptoms of fear or regret—feelings Luzia could never admit to having.

"Sons of bitches," one of the cangaceiros whispered. "After we kill those filhos-da-puta, I'm going to steal their cigarettes."

There was muffled laughter.

Cigarettes? Luzia looked back at the hills. The orange circles of light were miniscule. Some disappeared while others remained, glowing amid the scrub's dark brush. They did not rise or ignite the trees around them, like cinders would. Luzia felt both relieved and angry—those monkeys were stupid enough to smoke! They were so confident in their hiding place that they believed the cangaceiros wouldn't notice. Luzia's chest burned. She wanted to scare those soldiers, to prove them wrong. Placing a hand upon her holster, she walked toward the gully's edge.

A loud rattling erupted from the hill. It was calculated and jarring, like the ticking of a frenzied clock. There were faraway shouts and the orange points of light disappeared. Luzia felt an invisible force push her backward. There was a searing pain in her good arm, as if it had caught fire from within.

"Mãe!" Ponta Fina yelled. The ticking noise grew louder. He pulled her to the ground.

Luzia's jacket sleeve was wet and heavy. When she tried to move her good arm, she felt a sickening jolt. Luzia angled her locked arm, placed its fingers in her mouth and whistled loudly. If he could not hear her signal, Baiano's group certainly heard the shots and would attack. Next to her, Ponta Fina aimed his rifle and shot at the dark hills. With her crooked arm, Luzia reached for her parabellum. The ticking sound continued. In the trees, gunpowder released a faint glow. Luzia shot haphazardly at these pockets of light. She sensed how well the monkeys knew her position by the height of their fire: the bullets came low, moving so close that their heat warmed her back. Luzia wanted to dig herself under the earth.

Around her the cangaceiros cursed and screamed. Some crawled for cover. Others rose and shot at the hills. Luzia heard the thuds of their bodies hitting the dirt. She spun onto her back and searched for a way to retreat, but the dry gulley in which they'd camped rose up and held the cangaceiros on all sides, like a grave. Bullets clinked against Canjica's metal pots and pans. Tree branches snapped and their limbs whirled off. Clumps of sand flew and disseminated, making Luzia's eyes sting. She blinked away the grit and saw Inteligente sprawled across the dirt, his massive body tangled in the blanket on which he'd pretended to sleep. Sabiá was slumped against a tree, his pistol still clenched in his hands. Other bodies, already dead, shivered under the unending waves of bullets. Baby—Ponta Fina's wife—inched forward on her belly, crawling toward him. The ticking grew louder. Baby rolled across the dirt, as if she were caught in a great gust of wind.

Seeing this, Ponta Fina stood. Luzia tried to drag him back down but her good arm hung limp and useless from her side. Ponta aimed and fired, then stopped. For an instant, his wide-cheeked and childlike face looked mesmerized by the faraway ticking. Then his body jolted and swayed, as if moving in a frightening dance.

Luzia aimed into the hills and held down the trigger of her gun. The parabellum clicked weakly. Its cartridge was empty and Luzia couldn't reload with only her bent arm. She heard whoops in the hills and then footsteps coming toward the gully. Luzia pressed herself into the dirt. Those soldiers would disgrace her. They would measure her. Her arm throbbed. Her heart drummed as quickly as the endless ticking of that gun. It was fast, too fast. She was dizzy. If she did not take a breath, her fear would explode into panic.

She felt for the measuring tape in her pocket. It was tangled and dirty, but its numbers had not faded. Luzia closed her eyes. Long ago, Emília had given her another warning: do not climb that old mango tree, do not lean too far back in its branches. Everyone believed the fall had been an accident, that Luzia had been startled by that angry neighbor. She'd never contradicted them. But Luzia knew—had always known—that she'd made a choice. She'd let go of the limb above her not out of fear but out of curiosity. She'd wanted to see if she could balance, if she could hold on. She'd wanted to test herself. Coming to the edge was frightening, but the moment she'd tipped over there were no more choices to make, no more limbs to grasp. There was only the fall.

Luzia rose. The measuring tape dropped from her hand. She pulled Antônio's punhal from her waist belt. The knife was heavy, its handle cold. Luzia advanced, climbing the gulley's edge, lifting her legs high so her feet wouldn't sink into the sand. Near her ear she felt a warm rush of air. It made a soft and high-pitched sound, like a whisper. She strained to hear it. A great force hit her shoulder, another hit her thigh. She heard another whisper, then another. Each bullet was a voice: Aunt Sofia correcting her sewing; the encanadeira wrapping her arm and telling her she would recover; Emília, sharing a secret in bed; the murmur of water covering Luzia's head when she'd tried to escape from the cangaceiros; Antônio's voice during their first shooting lessons, his breath hot on her ear. She heard Eronildes' elderly maid telling her to push. She heard her boy's first, hiccupping sobs. She heard colonels and their whispered bargains. She heard soldiers, informants, and Blue Party women. She heard voices she did not recognize, voices she'd never known. Voices she'd silenced.

Luzia's crooked arm whipped backward. With each whisper came a thump, like an extra heartbeat, and then a searing pain. Her entire body seemed to be burning from the inside out. She tried to move forward but each whisper pushed her back, and back, and back until she felt as if she was falling from a great height.

Luzia remembered the sensation from her childhood. As a girl she'd felt heavy, her body dragging her to the ground beneath the mango tree. Now Luzia felt light. Her locked arm felt loose. All of the burdens she carried—pistol, cartridge belt, knives, gold chains, binoculars, bullets—fell away. The sky above her was dark and boundless. She felt small in the face of it, and afraid. But she recalled those birds she'd released so long ago and how, after she'd opened their doors, they always hesitated at the edges of their cages. Then they flew.

EPILOGUE: EMÍLIA

Lloyd passenger ship: *Siqueira Campos*
Atlantic Ocean
June 23, 1935

In one of her many letters, Lindalva said that the English language had no masculine or feminine. Verbs were the same for men and for women. Objects, too, were neutral. "This is the beauty of English," Lindalva wrote, "its equality." After reading this letter, Emília paid attention to such things in her own language. Doors, beds, kitchens, and houses were all feminine. Cars, telephones, newspapers, and ships were masculine. The ocean—o mar—was also masculine, but the more she studied it from the ship's deck, the more Emília was sure it had been labeled the wrong sex. After two weeks aboard the *Siqueira Campos,* Emília saw how quickly the ocean changed: some days it was deep blue and so calm it seemed as though the ship's hull was slicing through glass; other days the sea was gray and rough, its waves slamming against the ship and tossing it from side to side. When this happened, Emília and Expedito stayed in their tiny cabin with its furniture bolted to the floor and vomited into designated "sick buckets."

"Mãe," Expedito whispered, his body heavy and hot in Emília's arms, "the ocean's mean today."

Emília nodded and wiped his brow. The buckets were collected by cheerful young porters and dumped into the ocean. "Feed the fishes!" one male passenger liked to yell each time the sick buckets were emptied. Some passengers didn't have time to reach their cabins and were sick over the side of the boat, with everyone watching. Many of these passengers—their faces pallid and their suits and dresses stained by their own vomit—cursed the ocean. Emília did not. When she leaned against the ship's rail and studied the water, she was both frightened and mesmerized. One passenger said that the moon controlled the tides, that it was responsible for the push and pull of the waves. Emília chose not to believe this. She preferred to think that the ocean's foul moods were caused by some secret suffering within its depths, by a loss people would never understand.

During the past five months, before she'd left Recife, there were times when Emília had wanted everyone around her to suffer, to feel as terrible as she was feeling. She'd yelled and broken anything within reach, scaring Expedito. The maids cursed her. Dona Dulce called her intolerable. The Coelhos' doctor called it nervousness and postdated grief over Degas. He'd prescribed sleeping medicine. In the weeks after Dr. Duarte received the criminal specimen he'd always wanted, Emília retreated to her room, unable to lift herself from bed. Sleep became her only comfort. When she looked back on those months—which hadn't felt like months at all, but like one oppressive and neverending day in her room with the curtains drawn so she couldn't tell morning from night—Emília recalled straining to hear the hushed conversations of doctors outside her door. She recalled Expedito sneaking into her bed and sleeping beside her, his body warm against her own. She recalled her eyes, swollen into slits, the lashes crusted and sticky. She'd stopped dabbing away her tears with a handkerchief, just as she'd stopped brushing her hair and changing into fresh nightdresses. She'd liked the smell of herself—stale, sweaty, slightly yeasty—and did not want to wash it away. She'd secretly hoped her dirty skin would harden and crack like dried clay. That it, and her bones, would break into a fine powder that could be blown from the room by the breeze of Dr. Duarte's electric fans.

Emília did not break apart; instead, she'd gotten out of bed, dressed, and bought two tickets on the *Siqueira Campos*. Days later she and Expedito were on their way to New York.

The boat was crowded. Emília and Expedito had a second-class cabin and were confined to one deck. Their accommodations were not as bad as third class, which was deep inside the boat, or as luxurious as first class, which had the use of the entire upper deck. Emília wasn't willing to splurge for first-class tickets; she had to keep her savings intact. She didn't want to rely completely on Lindalva and the baroness.

In her letters, Lindalva said New York City was an island. That it had more automobiles on the streets than any city in Brazil. That its buildings were so tall, they made São Paulo look like a provincial town. Emília imagined the city but knew it would be nothing like the pictures she created in her head. She'd learned not to have explicit expectations of places or of people—they always turned out differently than one imagined. She'd learned a few English phrases from Lindalva's letters and from Degas' records. The language was choppy and stern sounding. Whenever she tried to speak it, Emília had to force her tongue to move in different directions, and even then there were sounds she could not make: *ch, th,* and *r*'s were especially hard. Despite its difficulties, Emília was grateful to the strange language. It had saved her—or Degas' records had.

A few weeks before, Emília had believed she would never leave her bed. The electric fans—placed in each corner of her room in order to air it out—made so much noise that they drowned out the sounds of the Coelho house and the city. Everything sounded muddled and dull. One night, however, Emília heard a clear voice.

"A great seamstress must be brave," it said.

This was Aunt Sofia's rule, but the woman's voice didn't belong to Emília's aunt. It was a young voice, loud and forceful. Emília heaved herself from bed. It was the middle of the night but she searched for the voice, looking in her closet, under her bed, and up and down the dark hallway. Finally, she walked into Degas' old room. Everything there was intact. The Victrola sat in the corner with its crooked arm bent upward. Emília moved toward the wooden box. She hit it hard. Punched it right where the name "Victrola" was painted in gold lettering. Tears clouded Emília's vision. How could she mourn a person she didn't understand, a person who had done terrible things? Her knuckles ached. Behind all of the strange titles—Victrola, the Seamstress, the criminal, the specimen—there would always be one familiar name: Luzia. Emília hit the box again, harder this time. The needle fell. The machine began to play the record on its rotating base.

"How are you?" a woman's voice said, startling Emília.

"I am fine," another woman replied, then commanded in Portuguese: "Repeat!"

There was silence. "Repeat!" she ordered again.

"I am fine," Emília said.

"Repeat!"

"I am fine," she called out. "I am fine."

Emília listened to the record all night, playing it over and over. Before dawn, she went into the Coelhos' pink bathroom and took a bath. Emília combed her hair and put on a dress. Over it she wore a bolero jacket, made heavy by the money sewn into its lining. Emília opened the suitcase she'd packed months before for her trip into the countryside, a trip she'd waited too long to take. Because of her hesitation, the trip became unnecessary and Emília's warning about the Bergmanns useless. Emília rearranged the clothes inside the suitcase and stuffed her jewelry box and Communion portrait between them. Quietly, she and Expedito walked out of the Coelhos' front gate and into the city.

At Recife's port, she purchased two tickets on a boat headed to New York City. So she wouldn't lose her courage, Emília chose the first boat leaving that morning. At the telegraph station near the departure area, she sent Lindalva the ship's name and arrival date. As they left the harbor, Emília held tightly to Expedito's hand, afraid he would slip through the deck's rails. People at the port waved and signaled to their loved ones with handkerchiefs. The ship's passengers waved back. Expedito stared at Emília with a pleading look in his eyes. She nodded. The boy smiled and moved his arm back and forth, waving good-bye to strangers. Emília kept her hands at her side. She was happy to leave, happy to take Expedito to a place where no one would call him a "drought baby," or worse. In New York, they would have no past, no relatives, no connection to the countryside. There would be no talk of the Seamstress and her cangaceiros, or of the widths and circumferences of their heads.

Even if Emília had taken her trip to the countryside immediately after Degas' funeral, it would have come too late. Both Dr. Duarte and Dr. Eronildes had lied—the Bergmanns had arrived earlier than they'd announced. Just as Degas had warned, Eronildes had canceled with Emília, saying the meeting was too dangerous. At the time, she hadn't been worried. Emília had already sent the measuring tape via Eronildes and she'd trusted that Luzia would understand its message. She'd trusted that the Seamstress would not appear at any meeting Eronildes had set with her.

Soldiers gave interviews to the *Diário* after the ambush. Dr. Eronildes Epifano, they said, had telegrammed the capital and informed the government of the upcoming meeting with the Seamstress. A brigade secretly stationed itself on the doctor's land. The Bergmanns were waiting there, shipped by barge along the Old Chico. The soldiers had little time to practice shooting with the new weapons but it didn't matter; the gun would guarantee their success. Troops nicknamed the Bergmann "the better Seamstress" because when it fired there was no loud pop. Instead there was a continuous shudder, like that of a Singer sewing machine, and the bullets made dozens of perfect holes in everything—walls, trees, men—as if pricking them over and over with a needle.

The soldiers hid themselves in the hills above the cangaceiros' campground and planned to attack at sunrise, when there was enough light to see clearly. Until then they watched the cangaceiros eat, sing, and sleep. There were only fifteen men and women in the bandit group, which was a deep disappointment to the soldiers. Luckily, the Seamstress was among them. The government soldiers— some as young as fourteen—all saw her. In the *Diário*'s articles, troops described the infamous cangaceira as tall and crooked armed, with scraggly hair and a hunched back. Some laughed and said she was as skinny as a starving donkey. Others said she was green eyed and forbidding, like the scrub's extinct panthers. The troops were required to stay awake. They could not speak or move. When their captain wasn't looking, several soldiers lit cigarettes and smoked while they watched the cangaceiro encampment. In the dying embers of the camp's fire, they saw her. The Seamstress stood at the edge of camp and stared at the hills. Before they could extinguish their cigarettes, the Seamstress was walking toward them.

"It was the strangest thing," a soldier told the newspapers. "It was like she knew."

When the Seamstress took another step forward, one of the youngest soldiers accidentally squeezed the trigger of his new Bergmann. "I didn't realize it would go off so easily," he said in his interview. "But it was a blessing it did."

A "blessing," a "stroke of luck," a "sign that Gomes would prevail," that's how soldiers and government officials termed the unintentionally early attack. If they'd waited, the soldiers might have been overtaken by another group of cangaceiros hidden in the hills alongside them. The Seamstress had known about the ambush and had tried to trap the soldiers before they could trap her. There were dozens of reports speculating as to how she could have known. Many blamed Dr. Eronildes, saying he had been on her side all along. No one would know for certain though. Once troops had exterminated both groups of cangaceiros, they'd gone to Eronildes' ranch house and found him in his study. His back was arched, his eyes wide, his body stiff on the floor. An empty vial of strychnine sat on his desk.

At night, in their cabin aboard the *Siqueira Campos,* Emília opened her jewelry box. Expedito watched her. She showed him the penknife and then the Communion portrait.

"You see that girl," she said, pointing to Luzia's blurry image. "That's your Mãe."

Expedito pressed his finger to the glass, leaving a greasy print over Emília's childhood figure. "Who's that?" he asked.

"That's your other Mãe," she said. "You are lucky enough to have two."

"Where is she?" he asked, moving his finger back to Luzia.

The boat rocked beneath them. Emília's stomach knotted, the saliva in her mouth grew warm. She reached for the sick bucket. Expedito patted her back, mimicking her actions when he was sick.

Emília wiped her mouth. The smell of the bucket's contents rose and made her feel sicker.

"Stay in bed," she said to Expedito. "Be a good boy."

Emília lifted the bucket and opened the cabin door. Outside there was a strong breeze. It made her shiver. She hung the bucket near the door for the porters to pick up. Emília took a deep breath. Seasickness didn't bother her; she saw it as a release. It was as if she were ridding her body of the guilt that had lodged there, like an illness invisible to all but Emília. She looked in the circular cabin window and saw Expedito sitting obediently on the bed, his eyes fixed on the door. He would stay like that all night if necessary, waiting for her.

After the Bergmann ambush, the cangaceiros' heads were placed in kerosene tins and carried to Recife. On the way, the soldiers stopped for cheering crowds, taking the heads from their kerosene baths and setting them on church steps for photographs. Rocks were slipped under their chins to steady them. These photographs became important later, when the troops arrived in Recife. Amid the confusion of taking the heads in and out of their tins, they'd been exposed to air and began to puff and lose their shape. The troops had not labeled the kerosene tins. They did not know who was who, could not tell women from men. Upon their arrival in Recife, some heads were missing, particularly the one belonging to the Hawk. Dr. Duarte was furious. An expedition team slogged through the rains that inundated the countryside and returned to the ambush site to collect the bodies. Rains had filled the dry gulley where the cangaceiros had hidden. The bones had been carried into the São Francisco River and washed away.

There were rumors that the Hawk was still alive. People said that he'd escaped the ambush and had left the Northeast. Some said he'd bought a ranch in Minas. Some said he'd changed his looks and become an army captain, or an actor, or a simple family man. Disappearance was more interesting than death. Despite the soldiers' negligence, the cangaceiros' skulls were not spoiled by air and time. Bone retained its shape. Dr. Duarte's highly anticipated measurements of the cangaceiros' craniums appeared on the front page of the *Diário de Pernambuco*, and they would cast the first serious doubts on his science. In order to identify the Seamstress, Dr. Duarte looked for a specimen with short hair and green eyes. When he found one that fit these criteria, he labeled and measured her. The Seamstress's skull revealed that she was a brachycephalo. She was ordinary, like Emília. Like any other woman.

Emília moved toward the ship's railing. The moon was out and the ocean shone and rippled, like a snake's skin. She took another deep breath. On her exhale, a sob escaped and Emília clamped a hand over her mouth. Other passengers on deck stared. Emília leaned slightly over the rail, as if she was going to be sick. Perhaps she was; she had trouble telling the difference between grief and seasickness. Sometimes, she simply felt angry. Luzia had known the meeting was a trap, but she'd gone anyway. Was it bravery or pride that had driven her into that gulley? Emília recalled Degas and their last talk. "Maybe I wanted to be caught," he'd said. "Maybe I wanted it to end." Was it bravery or pride that had made Degas drive into the Capibaribe? Maybe it was neither, Emília thought as the ship swayed beneath her. Maybe it was an escape, a break from the trap he, and everyone around him, had confined him to. Emília was also escaping from a trap of her own making. She would move to an island. She would make another transformation. She stared over the guardrail and watched the black waves rise and fall, taking comfort in their steady rhythm.

In a few weeks, Lindalva would be waiting for her at a dock in New York. Her friend would be as buoyant and as energetic as she'd always been, but she would notice a change in Emília: a seriousness that Lindalva and the baroness would attribute to Degas' death and her subsequent escape from Brazil. Emília and Lindalva would open another shop together. This new atelier would be sandwiched between a deli and a shoe-repair shop, so every morning when Emília woke she would smell leather mixed with the sharp, pungent odor of cheese and beef. She and Expedito would live above the atelier, in a small room with a rust-stained sink and toilet in its corner. Each time Emília visited the baroness and Lindalva's apartment, they had copies of Brazilian newspapers and Lindalva read the articles aloud. Gomes flirted with Germany but never committed as its ally. Then German submarines shot and sank passenger ships near the ports of Recife and Salvador. Suddenly there were reports of rowdy, fair-haired Americans building an air base in Natal, and members of the U.S. Fourth Fleet crowding the bars and beaches of Recife. Brazil was at war. No one had the time or the energy to recall the canga-ceiros' deaths, and they fell away, forgotten. "Politicians change, like fashions," the baroness liked to say until her death after the war. She was right—eventually even Gomes went out of style. In 1952, when Expedito was just entering Columbia Medical School, old Celestino was called to resign. Instead, in showman fashion, he shot himself at his desk in the Presidential Palace. "I leave life to enter history," he scribbled on the notepad before him. After Gomes's demise, Lindalva returned to Brazil. In her letters, she said that radio stations played popular forró songs about the Hawk and the Seamstress. Clay figu-rines of the couple, dressed in half-moon hats and flowered uni-forms, began to appear in tourist markets. Scholars began to write articles about the Seamstress and the cangaceiro phenomenon. Emí-lia would be remarried by then. Chico Martins had emigrated from Minas Gerais and gone to Emília's dress shop to order a gift for the sweetheart he'd left behind. He wore his hair short and swept back, revealing a broad forehead. Chico's eyes were brown and shining, like two stones beneath clear pools. *Kind eyes,* Emília would think the first time she looked into them. He was a shy and earnest man, nothing at all like the heroes in her old *Fon Fon*s. She liked that about him. The next time he returned to the shop, Chico Martins said that he no longer wanted the dress—he wanted a dinner date. Emília accepted. Her daughters with Chico were two fine, sweet girls. Even as young women Sofia and Francisca retained the bold, guileless joy of their girlhood. Nothing, it seemed, could dampen their spirits. Emília and Expedito were the serious ones, the bores. The girls preferred to confide in Chico about their dreams and their romantic crushes. Emília was jealous but she understood. She could not deny that her love for Expedito was fuller and darker, like the first dahlia that bloomed on a stalk.

She could not see all of these eventualities from the deck of the *Siqueira Campos* but, as Emília leaned against the boat's railing, she sensed them. Beneath the water's dark and glistening surface were unfathomable depths and, just as she perceived the existence of this immeasurable space, Emília perceived the breadth of her new life. She quickly moved away from the rail.

Her tiny cabin was comforting and warm. Expedito hid beneath his covers and Emília pretended to look for him. When he giggled, she flung the blanket away and held Expedito in her lap. They sat this way for a long time, listening to the wind outside.

"I had a sister with a crooked arm," Emília whispered, not knowing if Expedito was asleep or awake. "People called her Victrola."

She closed her eyes and recalled Expedito's earlier question, about the blurry girl in the picture: *Where is she?* One day, Emília would have to answer this. Waves lapped against the ship's side. She imagined that dry gulley filling with rain and the bones within it floating into the São Francisco. In the river they hit rocks and bumped against the hulls of boats and broke into pieces. By the time they reached the coast, the bones had disintegrated into small, white bits. Children playing on Boa Viagem Beach picked up the particles and put them in their sand castles. Other pieces were scattered into the breeze. Some pieces stuck to the oily bodies of sunbathers. Some got caught in shoes and were swept into cars and carried into the finest houses in Recife. Some floated in the air and flew into the beaks of birds. And some were sucked into the ocean and would be kept in its blue depths for hundreds of years, only to land on another shore.

AUTHOR'S NOTE

This is a work of fiction inspired by historical events.

Writing this novel, I took creative liberties: changing the names of people and places, condensing events, simplifying politics by reducing the myriad actual political parties. All the characters in this book—including political figures—are fictional. Cangaceiros existed for centuries in northeastern Brazil. The Hawk, the Seamstress, and their group were inspired by several real cangaceiro groups throughout history. Details of the characters' daily lives, however, are as authentic as I could make them. I tried to accurately represent 1930s fashions and etiquette, caatinga flora and fauna, and the cangaceiros' rituals, natural cures, weapons, and clothing. Most major historical events and the details surrounding them are also real: the revolution of 1930; the drought of 1932 and the internment camps that were built as a result; women's suffrage in Brazil; the phrenology movement and the common practice of decapitating cangaceiros in order to study their heads.

History, family stories, and personal interviews provided fertile soil for my imagination. What sprouted and grew is, I hope, a story that is true in spirit.

ACKNOWLEDGMENTS

I would like to thank the following people, organizations, and places.

In the United States:

The Fulbright Program, the Michener-Copernicus Society of America, the Sacatar Foundation, and the Jentel Artist Residency Program for their generous support. Claire Wachtel and Dorian Karchmar, for your patience and guidance. Mika and Deanna, for reading countless versions of this book and offering wise counsel. James, for always listening. Danny, Melanie, and Maria Eliza for your encouragement. My teachers at Iowa, particularly Elizabeth McCracken and Sam Chang. The dressmakers at Dame Couture in Chicago, Illinois, for answering my sewing questions. Andréa Câmara, for being my second pair of eyes. Tatiana, for being my sister. Dedé, for encouraging me to splatter the matter, and Mamãe, for teaching me to clean it up.

In Brazil:

Moises and Mônica Andrade, Dona Ester, Múcio Souto and family, Jeanine, Jaqueline, Marcelo, Lucila, Tia Taciana, Rolim and Ivanilda, all of whom were my adoptive families in Recife. The Fundação Joaquim Nabuco, especially Rosí in the photo archive, who helped with my research. Rosa and Alan, my guides at Serra da Capivara Park in Piauí. Jairo, a fine historian who helped me during my trip to Sergipe and Alagoas. The community of Itaparica, Bahia. The town of Taquaritinga do Norte and within it, my dear Várzea da Onça, both of which inspired large sections of this book. Dr. Rosa Lapenda, who treated my leg. All those I interviewed during the research phase of this book, with particular thanks to: Dr. Gilberto, who gave me my first book on cangaceiros; Bezzera, taxi driver and storyteller; Dona Teresa, who answered my endless questions and taught me how to plant; Maria, who cooked all of my favorite foods and kept me healthy; Américo, who took me riding in the caatinga; Fernando Boiadeiro, a true *cabra macho,* and his wife, Tuta; Dona Aura, midwife; Mr. and Mrs. Manuel Barboza Camêlo. Thanks also to my grandfather Edgar de Pontes, a gentleman who took a risk and stopped his car beside an orange tree to talk to the pretty girl sitting beneath it, and thus put several stories—including my own—into motion. My grandmother Emília and her sisters, my great-aunts Luzia and Maria Augusta, whose perseverance and imaginations inspire me. The cangaceiros who lived and died the only way they knew how, and their victims, who were unfortunate casualties. All of my *antepassados,* known and unknown. And all the saints who looked after me during my travels and kept me company during my solitude.